INTRODUCTION

One day in March 1873 Tolstoy picked up a book which one of his children had left lying about and started reading aloud to his wife. 'The guests arrived at the country house,' began the fragmentary tale of Pushkin.

'That is the way to begin,' observed Tolstoy. 'Pushkin plunges his readers right into the middle of the action. Others would describe the guests, the rooms, but Pushkin at once gets down to business.'

And that evening in his study Tolstoy wrote the first pages of Anna Karenin, the subject of which had been in his mind since the inquest on a young woman who threw herself under a train near the station a few miles from Tolstoy's home.

Tolstoy was then forty-four, at the climax of his maturity, the artist and the moralist still in harmony. A few years earlier he had finished War and Peace and with Anna Karenin (the more perfect work) the psychological novel of the nineteenth century reaches its high-water mark.

In Anna Karenin, which has been acclaimed the world's greatest novel, we have a vast panorama of contemporary life in Russia and of humanity in general, yet continuity of action never flags and the principal characters are kept well in the foreground. Tolstoy points no moral: he leaves the shifting patterns of the kaleidoscope to bring home the meaning of the brooding words following the title. And we do not judge: we watch. For us there is but one solution – clemency and love. 'The evil existed before men,' says Dostoevsky. 'Caught into the whirlwind of life, men commit crimes and perish ineluctably.' Anna obeys the life-force, but must perish. No one may build his happiness on another's pain, and Anna sacrifices husband and son. For a brief space, when she lies in danger of death, the three main protagonists – Anna herself, her husband, and her lover – become simple and good. But, as she recovers, all three sense their impotence in the coming struggle in which 'they would be compelled to do the evil that the world considered the proper thing'. Her empty existence as the wife of Karenin has dulled her spiritual awareness and, with no true ideal to cling to, little by little her courageous mind is consumed by the madness of her passion. To her heart's shame, her life has no other object than to please her lover; jealousy tortures her; she refuses with terror for her vanity to bear children; at night she must take morphia to dull her sufferings – until bitter inward torment casts her to death beneath the wheels of the goods truck.

Side by side with Anna's tragedy develops another story, in many respects the history of Tolstoy and his wife. Here the parallels are innumerable: the love of Kitty and Levin is the transposition of Tolstoy's own domestic memories, just as the death of Levin's brother is the fateful evocation of the death of Tolstoy's brother. The scene of the birth of Kitty's baby is directly inspired by Tolstoy's emotional reaction to the birth of his own first-born. Tolstoy invests Levin with his own great physical strength, his love of the soil and the peasants, his swift changes of mood, his impulse to carry his ideas to extremes, the ability to 'destroy and recreate worlds' – and Tolstoy himself had an old Agatha Mihalovna, who managed his house at Yasnaya Polyana until he married! Then there is the close resemblance between Levin's proposal to Kitty and Tolstoy's to his wife, each pair tracing with a piece of chalk on a card-table the initial letters of the words they were too nervous to say. Like Levin, Tolstoy's rigid honesty impelled him to put his intimate diary into the hands of his beloved that she should know his past. (And Tolstoy's wife, like Kitty, was cruelly shocked and hurt.) Like Tolstoy, Levin attacks contemporary society, hypocrisy, fashionable liberalism, drawing-room religion – his campaign, too, is against the world 'which distorts all truthful feelings and inevitably crushes the generous enthusiasm of the mind'. This is the third element in the book.

Levin is racked by the conflict between reason and heart, the tromperie mutuelle of Pascal. In Levin's philosophic anxiety Tolstoy portrays the secret tragedy of a generation who felt themselves being edged out of life by their fear of death which made the whole of life meaningless.

'And Levin, a happy father and husband, in perfect health, was several times so near suicide that he had to hide a rope lest he be tempted to hang himself, and would not go out with a gun for fear of shooting himself.'

As Tolstoy wrote to Fet, 'Once a man has realized that death is the end of everything, then there is nothing worse than life either.' (One small but significant detail: of the 239 chapters in Anna Karenin only one has a title, and that title is – DEATH.) Salvation comes to Levin through the wisdom of an illiterate peasant who tells him that man must live, not for his needs, but for God and his own soul; whereupon Levin realizes that reason has taught him nothing – all that he knows has been given to him, revealed to him by the heart. The religious note which now sounds is an echo of the mental process taking place at this time in the mind of Tolstoy (who is soon to confess, 'I knew also that the standard of good and evil was not what people said or *did, not progress, but myself and my own heart*'). Levin's newly-found peace is not altogether convincing. It is a desired rather than an achieved state, and the relapse into doubt, one feels, is not far off. As with Tolstoy himself, the effacement of the intellect will not last long: both will demand the reward of happiness for their surrender of the world. They ask too much. 'Levin's mind,' says Dostoevsky, 'is over-restless. He will destroy his faith again ... he will tear himself on some mental nail of his own making.' One of Tolstoy's peasants remarked, as he stood at the graveside after his master had been committed to the ground, 'With too much book-learning, you often lose the way'. Like Tolstoy, Levin will not long be content but will try to change everything and arrange it for the better, after his own fashion.

Levin is a faithful reflection of Tolstoy himself. In the character of Levin, Tolstoy expresses his own convictions and views, sometimes even putting them into Levin's mouth by force. ('Lyovochka, you are Levin plus talent,' Countess Tolstoy used to say; 'and Levin is an unbearable fellow!')

Anna's husband, Karenin, is in some ways the antithesis of Levin. He is the town-dweller, the pompous bureaucrat, his mask of irony concealing intelligence in a narrow mind, generosity still-born through fear – a man, in the words of Romain Rolland, 'afraid to listen to his own heart, and rightly so afraid, since when he does surrender to it it ends by falling into a state of nonsensical mysticism'.

Then there is Stiva, Anna's brother, gay and irresponsible, his friendly smile endearing him to everyone he meets. And a host of other characters all observed with equal truth because Tolstoy's approach is analytical (and his response unfailing). He is concerned less, far less, with what his characters do. The why is all-important. Style suffers in the eager rush to render the psychological report which, like the life it records, is occasionally naïve, sometimes repetitive and always pulsing with vitality.

Anna Karenin appeared part by part in an important monthly magazine, until the final section, which was refused, since the views it expressed did not accord with the opinions of the editors. The whole was published separately in book form in 1878, a year after completion.

R. E.

TWO NOTES

1. Every Russian has three names: first name, patronymic (=father's Christian name plus a suffix meaning *son of*, *daughter of*), and family name. Although Russians never call each other by the family name but by Christian name and patronymic – thus, Oblonsky would be always Stepan Arkadyevich – for the sake of clarity I have used the surname wherever possible.

For the same reason I prefer the form *Anna Karenin*, since the feminine form (*Anna Karenina*) is not usual in English, where Countess Tolstoya appears as Countess Tolstoy, Madame Blavatskaya as Madame Blavatsky, and so on.

2. In pre-Revolution Russia only the innocent partner could apply for a divorce, which was difficult to obtain. The guilty party was not allowed to remarry and was deprived of the children.

R. E.

ANNA KARENIN

VENGEANCE IS MINE,
AND I WILL REPAY

PART ONE

I

ALL happy families are alike but an unhappy family is unhappy after its own fashion.

Everything had gone wrong in the Oblonsky household. The wife had found out about her husband's relationship with their former French governess and had announced that she could not go on living in the same house with him. This state of affairs had already continued for three days and was having a distressing effect on the couple themselves, on all the members of the family, and on the domestics. They all felt that there was no sense in their living together under the same roof and that any group of people who chanced to meet at a wayside inn would have more in common than they, the members of the Oblonsky family, and their servants. The wife did not leave her own rooms and the husband stayed away from home all day. The children strayed all over the house, not knowing what to do with themselves. The English governess had quarrelled with the housekeeper and had written a note asking a friend to find her a new place. The head-cook had gone out at dinner-time the day before. The under-cook and the coachman had given notice.

On the third morning after the quarrel Prince Stepan Arkadyevich Oblonsky – Stiva, as he was generally called by his friends – awoke at his usual time, which was about eight o'clock, not in his wife's bedroom but on a morocco-leather couch in his study. He turned his plump, pampered body over on the springs, as if he had a mind for a long sleep, and hugged the pillow, pressing his cheek to it; but with a start he sat up on the sofa and opened his eyes.

'Yes, now, how did it go?' he thought, recalling a dream. 'Now how did it go? Oh yes! Alabin was giving a dinner in Darmstadt. No, it wasn't Darmstadt but some American place. Yes, but the dream Darmstadt was in America. That's it – Alabin was giving a dinner on glass tables – and the tables were singing *Il mio tesoro*. No, not *Il mio tesoro,* something better; and there were some little decanters who were women,' he remembered.

Oblonsky's eyes began to sparkle merrily and he smiled as he continued with his thoughts. 'Yes, it was a nice dream – very nice indeed. There was a lot that was capital but not to be expressed in words or even thought about clearly now that I am awake.' Then, noticing the streak of light from one side of the heavy blinds, he cheerfully thrust his feet down to feel for the slippers which his wife had worked in gold morocco for his last birthday present. Next, without getting up, he stretched out his hand as he had done for the last nine years to where his dressing-gown usually hung in the bedroom. And then memory flashed on him how and why it was that he was sleeping not in his wife's room but in the study. The smile vanished from his face and he frowned.

'Oh dear, dear, dear!' he groaned, remembering what had happened. And he went over all the details of the scene with his wife, seeing the complete hopelessness of his position and, most tormenting thought of all, the fact that it was his own fault.

'No, she will never forgive me – she cannot forgive me! And the worst of it is that I am to blame for everything – I am to blame and yet I am not to blame. That is the whole tragedy,' he mused, and recalled despairingly the most painful aspects of the quarrel.

That first moment had been the worst, after he had returned from the theatre, happy and content, with a huge pear in his hand for his wife, and had not found her in the drawing-room. Nor, to his astonishment, was she in the study. At last he had discovered her in the bedroom, holding the wretched note that explained everything.

Dolly, whom he always thought of as busy, bustling, and rather foolish, now sat motionless, looking at him with an expression of horror, despair, and anger, the note in her hand.

'What is this? What does this mean?' she had demanded, pointing to the note.

As the scene came back to him, as often happens it was not so much the memory of the event that tormented him, as of the way he had replied to her.

It had been with him as it so often is when people are unexpectedly caught out in something disgraceful. He had been unable to assume an expression suitable to the situation in which he was placed by his wife's knowledge of his guilt. Instead of taking offence or denying the whole thing, instead of justifying himself or begging forgiveness or even remaining indifferent – any of which would have been better than what he actually did – in spite of himself ('by a reflex action of the brain,' now thought Oblonsky, who had a leaning towards physiology), in spite of himself he suddenly smiled his habitual, kind, and somewhat foolish smile.

This foolish smile he could not forgive himself. Seeing it, Dolly had shuddered as if with a physical pain and bursting with her usual vehemence into a stream of bitter words she had fled from the room. Since then she had refused to see her husband.

'It's all because of that silly smile,' thought Oblonsky.

'But what is to be done? What can I do?' he asked himself despairingly and found no answer.

2

OBLONSKY was a straightforward man in his dealings with himself. He could not deceive himself into believing that he repented of his conduct. He could not now feel sorry because he, a handsome, susceptible man of thirty-four, was not in love with his wife, who was the mother of five living and two dead children and only a year younger than himself. He only regretted that he had not managed to hide things from her better. Nevertheless, he felt the full gravity of his position and pitied his wife, his children, and himself. Perhaps he would have been more successful in hiding his wrongdoing from his wife had he suspected the effect that the discovery would have upon her. He had never clearly thought the matter out but had vaguely imagined that she had long since guessed his unfaithfulness and was turning a blind eye to it. She was a good mother but she was already faded and plain and no longer young, a simple, uninteresting woman; so it seemed to him that she really ought to be indulgent. But it proved to be quite the opposite.

'How terrible, how terrible!' Oblonsky repeated to himself but could think of no escape. 'And how well everything was going before this happened, how comfortable we were! She was contented and happy with the children, I did not interfere at all, I let her run them and the house in her own way. True, it was not nice that *she* should have been the governess we had in the house. Not at all nice! There is something banal and vulgar about making love to one's own governess. But what a governess! (He recalled Mademoiselle Roland's mischievous black eyes and her smile.) But all the same, so long as she lived in our house I did not permit myself any liberties. And the worst of it is that she is now ... Everything happens just to spite me! Oh dear, what am I to do?'

There was no answer, except life's usual answer to the most complex and insoluble questions. The answer is this: live from day to day; in other words, forget. But as he could not find forgetfulness in sleep, at least not until bed-time, nor return to the music sung by the little decanter-women, he must therefore lose himself in the dream of life.

'Well, we shall see,' Oblonsky said to himself; and getting up he put on his grey dressing-gown with the pale-blue silk lining, knotted the girdle and drawing a deep breath into his powerful lungs walked to the window with his usual spirited step, carrying his vigorous body lightly, raised the blind and rang loudly. The bell was answered immediately by his old friend and valet, Matvey, bearing clothes, boots, and a telegram. Behind Matvey came the barber with shaving things.

'Are there any papers from the court-house?' Oblonsky asked, taking the telegram and sitting down before the mirror.

'They are on the table,' replied Matvey, with a searching, sympathetic look at his master. Then, after a short pause, 'Someone came from the livery-stables,' he added with a sly smile.

Oblonsky made no reply but glanced at Matvey in the mirror. How perfectly they understood one another was apparent from the looks that they exchanged. Oblonsky's seemed to ask, 'Why do you say that? As if you didn't know!'

Matvey thrust his hands into his coat pockets and stood with legs apart, gazing at his master in silence, an almost imperceptible smile on his good-natured face.

'I told him to come back on Sunday and meanwhile not to bother you or himself for nothing,' he said, obviously repeating an answer prepared in advance.

Oblonsky could see that Matvey was in a humorous mood and wanted to draw attention to himself. He tore open the telegram and read it, guessing at the mis-spelled words usual in telegrams, and his face brightened.

'Matvey, my sister, Anna Arkadyevna, will be here to-morrow,' he said, staying for a moment the plump, shiny hand of the barber, who was combing a rosy parting between his long curly whiskers.

'Thanks be!' exclaimed Matvey, thereby showing that he understood the importance of this visit every bit as well as his master: Anna Arkadyevna, Oblonsky's beloved sister, might effect a reconciliation between husband and wife.

'By herself or with her husband?' inquired Matvey.

Oblonsky could not speak, as the barber was busy with his upper lip, so he raised one finger. Matvey nodded to him in the glass.

'By herself. Shall I have the upstairs room got ready?'

'Tell Daria Alexandrovna. Let her decide.'

'Daria Alexandrovna?' Matvey repeated doubtfully.

'Yes. And here, take the telegram to her and see what she says.'

'You want to sound her,' Matvey thought to himself, but all he said was 'Very well.'

Oblonsky had already completed his toilet and was about to dress when Matvey, stepping slowly in his squeaky boots, re-entered the room with the telegram in his hand. The barber had gone.

'Daria Alexandrovna told me to say that she is going away. "Let him do what he likes," she said.' And, with his hands in his pockets and his head on one side, Matvey stood staring at his master, a twinkle in his eye.

Oblonsky was silent for a moment. Then a kind, rather pathetic smile appeared on his handsome face.

'Well? What do you think, Matvey?' he said, shaking his head.

'It's nothing, sir. Things will right themselves,' replied Matvey.

'Right themselves?'

'That's it, sir.'

'You think so? Who is that?' Oblonsky asked, hearing the rustle of a woman's dress outside the door.

'It's me, sir,' said a firm, pleasant feminine voice, and Matriona Filimonovna, the children's nurse, thrust her stern, pock-marked face in at the door.

'Well, what is it, Matriosha?' asked Oblonsky, advancing towards her.

Although Oblonsky was entirely in the wrong as regards his wife, as he himself admitted, almost everyone in the house, even the nurse, Daria Alexandrovna's best friend, was on his side.

'Well, what is it?' he repeated despondently.

'You go down, sir, and confess you're in the wrong. The good Lord will do the rest. She is tormenting herself dreadfully and it's pitiful to see her. And the whole house is all upset. Besides, you must take pity on the children, sir. Tell her you're in the wrong, sir. It can't be helped. What else can you do?'

'But she would not see me …'

'Never mind, you will have done your part. The Lord is merciful; pray to Him, sir, pray to Him.'

'All right, then, you can go now,' said Oblonsky, suddenly blushing. 'Let me have my things,' he added, turning to Matvey and resolutely throwing off his dressing-gown.

Matvey blew some invisible speck off the shirt which he held ready gathered up like a horse's collar, and with evident satisfaction proceeded to envelop his master's carefully tended body.

3

WHEN he had finished dressing, Oblonsky sprayed himself with eau-de-Cologne, pulled down his cuffs, as usual distributed in different pockets cigarettes, pocket-book, matches, his watch with its double chain and seals, shook out his handkerchief, and, in spite of his unhappiness, feeling clean, fragrant, physically well, and cheerful, he went, with a slight spring in each step, into the dining-room, where his coffee was already waiting for him. Beside the coffee lay letters and papers from the court-house.

He read the letters. One was most unwelcome – it was from a merchant who was negotiating for the purchase of a forest on his wife's estate. This forest had to be sold; but now, until a reconciliation could be effected with his wife, it would be impossible to mention the matter. What was most unpleasant was that a financial consideration would now come into the impending reconciliation. The idea that self-interest might be his motive – that he could seek a reconciliation with his wife for the sake of selling the forest – upset him.

Having disposed of his letters, Oblonsky drew towards him the documents from the court-house, rapidly ran through two of them, made a few notes with a large pencil, then pushed them aside and started on his coffee. While he was drinking he unfolded the morning paper, which was still damp, and began to read.

Oblonsky subscribed to and read a liberal paper, not an extreme liberal paper but one that expressed the views held by most people.

And although he was not particularly interested in science, art, or politics, on all such subjects he adhered firmly to the views of the majority, as expressed by his paper, and changed them only when the majority changed theirs; or rather, he did not change them – they changed imperceptibly of their own accord.

Oblonsky never chose his tendencies and opinions any more than he chose the style of his hat or frock-coat. He always wore those which happened to be in fashion. Moving in a certain circle where a desire for some form of mental activity was part of maturity, he was obliged to hold views in the same way as he was obliged to wear a hat. If he had a reason for preferring Liberalism to the Conservatism of many in his set, it was not that he considered the liberal outlook more rational but because it corresponded better with his mode of life. The Liberal Party maintained that everything in Russia was bad; and in truth Oblonsky had many debts and decidedly too little money. The Liberal Party said that marriage was an obsolete institution which ought to be reformed; and indeed family life gave Oblonsky very little pleasure, forcing him to tell lies and dissemble, which was quite contrary to his nature. The Liberal Party said, or rather assumed, that religion was only a curb on the illiterate; and indeed Oblonsky could not stand through even the shortest church service without aching feet, or understand the point of all that dreadful, high-flown talk about the other world, when life in this world was really very pleasant. And then it sometimes amused Oblonsky, who liked a joke, to shock a conventional person with the suggestion that if one is going to pride oneself on one's birth, why stop short at Rurik* and repudiate one's earliest ancestors – the apes? Thus Liberalism had become a habit with Oblonsky and he enjoyed his newspaper, as he did his after-dinner cigar, for the slight haze it produced in his brain. He read the leading article, which expounded how quite useless it is in our time to raise the cry that radicalism threatened to swallow up all conservative elements and then maintain that the Government should take measures to crush the hydra of revolution, for, on the contrary, 'in our opinion the danger lies not in an imaginary hydra of revolution but in an obstinate clinging to tradition, which hinders progress', etc. He also read another article, on finance, in which Bentham and Mill were mentioned and hits made at the Ministry. With his natural quickness of

* Rurik, a Varangian chief, invited by the Slav tribes to rule over them; arrived in Novgorod in 862.

perception, he understood the point of each taunt: whence it came, for whom it was intended, and what had provoked it; and this as usual gave him a certain satisfaction. But to-day his satisfaction was marred by the recollection of Matriona Filimonovna's advice and the fact that there was all this trouble in the house. He went on to read that Count Beist was reported to have left for Wiesbaden, that there was no need to have grey hair, that a light carriage was for sale, and a young person offered her services; but these items did not give him the quiet, ironical pleasure they generally did.

Having finished the paper, a second cup of coffee, and a roll and butter, he rose, shook a crumb or two from his waistcoat, and, expanding his broad chest, smiled happily, not because he felt particularly lighthearted – his happy smile was simply the result of a good digestion.

But the happy smile instantly reminded him of everything, and he became pensive.

Two childish voices, which he recognized as those of Grisha, his youngest boy, and Tanya, his eldest daughter, were heard outside the door. They were dragging something along and had upset it.

'I told you not to sit passengers on the roof,' cried the little girl in English. 'Now pick them up!'

'Everything is upside down,' reflected Oblonsky. 'Here are the children running wild.' And going to the door, he called them in. They dropped the box, which they were pretending was a train, and came to their father.

The girl, her father's pet, ran in boldly, hugged him and laughingly clung round his neck, enjoying as she always did the familiar scent of his whiskers. Having kissed his face, which was flushed from stooping and beaming with tenderness, the little girl unclasped her hands and was going to run away, but her father held her back.

'How is Mamma?' he asked, caressing his daughter's smooth, soft neck. 'Hullo,' he said, smiling to the little boy, who had come up to greet him.

He was conscious that he did not care as much for the boy as for the girl and did his best to treat the children alike; but the boy felt this and did not respond to his father's cold smile.

'Mamma? She is up,' replied the girl.

Oblonsky sighed. 'That means she has spent another sleepless night,' he reflected.

'Is she all right?'

The little girl knew that her father and mother had quarrelled and that her mother could not be all right, and that her father must be aware of this, and that he was making believe when he asked about it so lightly. And she blushed for him. He perceived it immediately and blushed too.

'I do not know,' she said. 'She told us we were not to have lessons but go for a walk to Grandmamma's with Miss Hoole.'

'Well, run along, my little Tanyakin. No, wait,' he said, still holding her and stroking her soft little hand.

Taking a box of sweets from the mantelpiece, where he had put it the day before, he selected two of her favourites, a chocolate and a fondant.

'For Grisha?' she asked, pointing to the chocolate.

'Yes, yes.' And with another caress on her tiny shoulder, he kissed the nape of her neck and let her go.

'The carriage is ready,' said Matvey. 'But there is a woman waiting to see you,' he added.

'Has she been waiting long?' asked Oblonsky.

'About half an hour.'

'How many times have I told you to let me know at once when anyone is here?'

'I must give you time to finish your coffee at least,' said Matvey in the rough, friendly tone which made it impossible to get angry.

'Well, ask her in at once,' said Oblonsky, frowning in vexation.

The woman, widow of a staff-captain named Kalinin, had come with an impossible and unreasonable request; but Oblonsky, as was his wont, made her sit down, listened attentively and without interruption, and gave her detailed advice as to whom to apply to, and even briskly dashed off a note in his large, sprawling but fine legible hand to a personage who might be of use. Having dismissed her, he took his hat and paused to consider whether he had forgotten anything. He found that he had forgotten nothing excepting the one thing he wanted to forget – his wife.

'Ye-es!' He hung his head and a gloomy expression came over his handsome face. 'Shall I go and see her or not?' he asked himself. And an inner voice told him that it would be useless to go, that it could only result in hypocrisy, that it was impossible to put right or patch up their relationship because it was impossible to make her attractive and lovable again or to turn himself into an old man incapable of love.

21

Nothing could come of it now, except lies and hypocrisy; and lies and hypocrisy were contrary to his nature.

'All the same, I shall have to sooner or later. Things cannot remain as they are,' he said in an effort to brace himself. He expanded his chest, took out a cigarette, lit it and inhaled once or twice before throwing it into a mother-of-pearl ashtray. Then with quick steps he crossed the sombre drawing-room and opened another door which led into his wife's bedroom.

4

DOLLY was standing before an open chest of drawers, in a dressing-jacket, sorting things out. Her once thick and beautiful hair was pinned in thin little braids on the nape of her neck. Her large apprehensive eyes were made more prominent by the emaciation of her pale wan face. Around her the room was strewn with scattered articles. Hearing her husband's step, she stopped and looked at the door, vainly striving to assume a hard contemptuous expression. She felt that she was afraid of him and afraid of the coming interview. She had just been making another effort to do what she had tried to do a dozen times already in the last three days – sort out her own and the children's clothes to take to her mother's – but she could not bring herself to do it and said to herself now, as she had after each previous attempt, that things could not remain as they were, that she must do something to punish and humiliate him, to pay him back for even a little of the pain he had caused her. She still kept saying that she would leave him but felt that this was impossible. It was impossible because she could not get out of the habit of regarding him as her husband and of loving him. Besides, she felt that if here in her own home it was all she could do to look after her five children, they would be still worse off where she was taking them all. As it was, during the last three days her youngest had fallen ill because he had been given some sour broth, and the others had almost gone without their dinner the day before. She felt that it was impossible to go away; but, deceiving herself, she went on sorting their things and pretending that she really would go.

When she saw her husband, she thrust her arm into the drawer of the chest, as if searching for something, and only glanced round at him when he had come close to her. But instead of appearing stern and determined, as she intended, she looked lost and miserable.

'Dolly!' he said in a subdued, timid voice. He drew his head into his shoulders, hoping to seem pathetic and submissive, but he only radiated freshness and health.

She ran a swift glance over his fresh, healthy figure. 'Yes,' she thought, 'he is happy and content, but what of me? ... And that odious good-nature of his which makes people love and praise him so – how I hate it!' She pressed her lips together, a muscle twitching on the right side of her pale, nervous face.

'What do you want?' she said quickly, her voice hoarse and un-natural.

'Dolly!' he repeated with a quaver. 'Anna is coming to-morrow.'

'Well, what is that to do with me? I cannot receive her!' she exclaimed.

'But you must, Dolly, don't you see? ...'

'Go away, go away, go away!' she cried, without looking at him, as though the cry were torn from her by bodily hurt.

Oblonsky could be calm when he thought about his wife, could hope that things would 'shape themselves', as Matvey expressed it, and could calmly read his newspaper and drink his coffee; but when he saw her worn, suffering face, heard the note of despair and resignation in her voice, he caught his breath, a lump rose in his throat, and his eyes glistened with tears.

'My God, what have I done! Dolly! For Heaven's sake! ... You see ...' He could not go on, the sobs choked him.

She shut the drawer with a bang and looked at her husband.

'Dolly, what can I say? ... Only one thing: forgive me, forgive me. ... Think, nine years. ... Cannot nine years make up for a momentary ... momentary ...'

She lowered her eyes and listened to hear what he would say, as if she were begging him somehow to persuade her that she had made a mistake.

'... a momentary infatuation,' he got out, and would have continued, but at these words her lips tightened again as if with physical pain and the muscle in her right cheek started to twitch again.

'Go away, get out of this room!' she shrieked more piercingly still. 'And do not talk to me about your infatuations and abominations!'

She turned to go, but tottered and clutched the back of a chair for support. His face widened, his lips swelled, and his eyes filled with tears.

'Dolly!' he articulated, now sobbing. 'For God's sake, think of the children; they have done nothing. I am the one to blame. Punish me, make me atone for my sin! Tell me what to do. I will do anything! I am the guilty one, there are no words to express my guilt! But, Dolly, forgive me!'

She sat down. He could hear her loud, heavy breathing and felt un-utterably sorry for her. Several times she tried to speak, but could not. He waited.

'You think of the children, Stiva, when you want to play with them, but I am always thinking of them and I know that now they are ruined,' she said, obviously repeating one of the phrases she had been saying to herself over and over again in the last three days.

She had called him 'Stiva', and he glanced at her gratefully and made a move to take her hand; but she avoided him in disgust.

'I do think of the children, and would do anything in the world to save them; but I am not sure how to save them – whether to take them away from their father or leave them with a father who is dis-solute. Yes, dissolute. ... Tell me, do you suppose it is possible for us to live together after what has happened? Is it possible? Tell me, is it possible?' she repeated, raising her voice. 'When my husband, the father of my children, has an affair with his children's governess ...'

'But what is to be done about it? What can I do?' he pleaded piteously, hardly knowing what he was saying and hanging his head lower and lower.

'You are revolting, disgusting!' she screamed, getting more and more excited. 'Your tears are water! You never loved me; you have no heart, no honour! You are detestable, disgusting, a stranger to me – yes, a perfect stranger!' She pronounced the word *stranger*, which was so dreadful to her own ears, with anguish and hatred.

He looked at her, and the hatred he saw in her face frightened and bewildered him. He did not understand that his pity exasperated her. She saw in him pity for herself, but not love. 'Yes, she hates me. She will not forgive,' he thought.

'This is dreadful, dreadful!' he cried.

At this moment a child who had probably fallen down in the next room started to cry. Dolly listened, and her face suddenly softened.

She seemed to be trying to pull herself together, as if she did not know where she was and what she had to do. Then she rose quickly and moved towards the door.

'At any rate she loves my child,' he thought, noticing the change in her face when the child cried, '*my* child – so how can she hate me?'

'Dolly, one more word,' he said, going after her.

'If you follow me, I shall call the servants, the children! Let them all know what a scoundrel you are! I am going away this very day, and you can live here with your mistress!'

And she went out, banging the door.

Oblonsky sighed, wiped his face, and with soft steps went towards the door. 'Matvey says things will right themselves – but how? I do not see any possibility. Oh dear, how dreadful! And her shouting – it was so vulgar,' he said to himself, recalling her screams and the words *scoundrel* and *mistress*. 'And the maids may have heard! Terribly vulgar, terribly!' He stood still for a second, wiped his eyes, sighed, and, straightening his shoulders, went out of the room.

It was a Friday, and in the dining-room the German clockmaker was winding the clock. Oblonsky remembered a joke he had once made at the expense of this accurate, bald-headed clockmaker and smiled. 'The German,' he had said, 'had been wound up for life to wind up clocks.' Oblonsky was fond of a good joke. 'Well, perhaps things will shape themselves. What a nice expression – *shape themselves!*' he thought. 'I must repeat that.'

'Matvey!' he called. 'You and Maria go and get the little sitting-room ready for Anna Arkadyevna,' he said, when Matvey appeared.

'Yes, sir.'

Oblonsky put on his fur coat and went out on to the porch.

'Will you be home for dinner, sir?' asked Matvey, escorting him.

'It depends. Here – take this for the housekeeping,' he said, giving Matvey a ten-rouble note from his pocket-book. 'Will that be enough?'

'Enough or not, we will have to make it do,' said Matvey, slamming the carriage door and stepping back into the porch.

Meanwhile Dolly, having soothed the child and realizing by the sound of the carriage wheels that her husband had gone, returned to the bedroom. It was her one place of refuge from the household cares which besieged her the moment she appeared. Even during the short time she had spent in the nursery, the English governess and Matriona Filimonovna had succeeded in asking her several questions that could not wait and which only she could answer: 'How were the children to be dressed for their walk? Ought they to have any milk? Should not a new cook be sent for?'

'Oh, be quiet and leave me alone!' she protested; and, returning to the bedroom and the chair where she had sat when talking with her husband, she locked her thin bony fingers, on which the rings hung loosely, and began going over in her mind the conversation they had had.

'He has gone! But has he broken with *her*?' she wondered. 'Is it possible that he is still seeing her? Why did I not ask him? No, no, we can never come together again. If we do go on living in the same house it will be as strangers to each other – strangers for ever!' Once again she repeated with special emphasis the word she found so dreadful. 'And how I loved him! Oh God, how I loved him! ... How I loved – and do I not love him still? Do I not love him more than ever? The most terrible thing of all ...' she began, but did not finish the thought, as Matriona Filimonovna thrust her head in at the door.

'Shall we send for my brother?' asked Matriona Filimonovna. 'After all, he could get dinner ready. Otherwise it will be like yesterday again, and the children will go without food until six o'clock.'

'Yes, all right, I will come and see about it at once. Has the fresh milk been sent for?'

And plunging into her daily cares Dolly for a while drowned her grief in them.

5

OBLONSKY had learned easily at school, thanks to his natural ability, but he was idle and mischievous and so had come out near the bottom of his class. Yet in spite of his dissipated life, not very high rank, and comparative youth, he occupied a distinguished and well-paid post as head of one of Moscow's court-houses. This post he had obtained through his sister Anna's husband, Alexei Alexandrovich Karenin, who held one of the most important positions in the ministry to which this court-house was attached. But even if Karenin had not nominated his brother-in-law for that post, Oblonsky, through one of a hundred other people – brothers, sisters, relations, cousins, uncles, or aunts – would have obtained it or something similar with a salary of some 6,000 roubles a year, which, for all his wife's ample means, he found necessary because his affairs were in an embarrassing condition.

26

Half Moscow and Petersburg were relations or friends of Oblonsky. He was born into the circle of people who were, or who became, the great ones of this earth. A third of the official world, the older men, were his father's friends and had known him from the time he was a baby in petticoats; he was on intimate terms with another third; and the rest were his good acquaintances. Consequently, the distributors of the blessings of this world, in the shape of government posts, grants, concessions, and the like, were all friends of his. They could not pass over one of their own, so Oblonsky had no especial trouble in obtaining a lucrative position. It was only necessary not to raise objections or be envious, not to quarrel or take offence, which in accordance with his natural kindliness he never did. It would have seemed ludicrous if anyone had told him that he would not get the post with the salary he required – the more so as he did not demand anything excessive: he only wanted what other men of his age were getting, and he could perform like functions no worse than they.

Oblonsky was not only liked by everyone who knew him for his good-nature, gay disposition, and undoubted integrity, but there was something in him – in his handsome, bright appearance, his sparkling eyes, black hair and eyebrows, and pink-and-white complexion – that acted like a tonic on the people he met, making them feel friendly and lighthearted. 'Aha! Stiva! Oblonsky! Here he is!' people who saw him would exclaim with a smile of pleasure. And if it occasionally happened that some conversation with him turned out to have been of no especial interest, on the next day or the one after that everyone was as pleased as ever to see him.

In the three years that he had been head of one of the government offices in Moscow, Oblonsky had won not only the affection but also the respect of his colleagues, subordinates, superiors, and all with whom he came in contact. The chief qualities which had earned him this universal esteem in the service were, in the first place, his extreme indulgence with people, which had its roots in the consciousness of his own shortcomings; secondly, a genuine liberalism – not the liberalism of his newspaper but the liberalism which was in his blood and caused him to treat all men alike, whatever their status or position; and thirdly (and of the three the most important), the complete detachment with which he regarded his work, in consequence of which he was never carried away and never made mistakes.

Arriving at the court-house, Oblonsky, followed by a respectful commissionaire who carried his portfolio, crossed into his little private room, put on his uniform, and went into the board-room. Clerks and copyists all rose and bowed with cheerful deference. Oblonsky walked quickly to his place as usual, shook hands with the members of the council and sat down. He jested and chatted for just as long as was seemly, before proceeding to business. No one knew better than Oblonsky how to keep the balance between freedom, simplicity, and formality necessary to make work pleasant. A secretary approached with some papers in the familiar yet respectful manner common to all who surrounded Oblonsky. He spoke in the free-and-easy tone that Oblonsky had introduced.

'At last we have got that information from the Penza provincial office. Would you care …?'

'Got it at last?' said Oblonsky, putting a finger on the paper. 'Well, gentlemen …' And the sitting began.

'If they did but know,' he thought, looking important, with head bowed during the hearing of the report, 'how like a naughty boy their president was half an hour ago!' And his eyes sparkled while the report was being read. The sitting was to continue without interruption until two o'clock, when there would be an adjournment for lunch.

It was not quite two when the great glass doors of the court-room suddenly swung open and someone entered. Glad of the distraction, all the members sitting under the Emperor's portrait or on the farther side of the emblem of justice looked round at the entrance; but the doorkeeper immediately ejected the intruder and closed the glass doors behind him.

When the report was over, Oblonsky stretched himself and then, paying tribute to the liberalism of the times, took out a cigarette before leaving the court-room to go to his private office. Two of his colleagues, the veteran Nikitin and Grinevich, a gentleman of the bed-chamber, followed him.

'There will be time enough to finish after lunch,' remarked Oblonsky.

'Easily,' said Nikitin.

'What a thorough-going scoundrel that Fomin must be!' said Grinevich, referring to one of the men concerned in the case they were considering.

Oblonsky frowned at Grinevich's words, thereby indicating that it was improper to form an opinion prematurely, and made no reply.

28

'Who was it came in?' he asked the doorkeeper.

'Someone, your excellency, got in without permission directly my back was turned. He was asking for you. I said "When the members come out, then …"'

'Where is he?'

'Gone out into the vestibule, most likely; or perhaps he's still here. There he is,' said the doorkeeper, pointing to a strongly-built, broad-shouldered man with a curly beard who, without taking off his sheep-skin cap, was running swiftly and lightly up the worn steps of the stone staircase. A lean official on his way down with a portfolio stepped aside and looked disapprovingly at the feet of the stranger, then glanced in-quiringly at Oblonsky, who was standing at the top of the stairs. Oblonsky's good-natured face beaming over the gold-laced collar of his uniform beamed still more when he recognized who it was running up.

'Why, it's you, Levin, at last!' he said, gazing at the approaching Levin with a friendly, mocking smile. 'How is it you deign to look me up in this den of thieves?' he went on; and, not content with pressing his friend's hand, kissed him. 'Have you been here long?'

'I have just arrived and am very anxious to see you,' replied Levin, looking round shyly and at the same time irately and uneasily.

'Well, let us go into my room,' said Oblonsky, aware of his friend's self-conscious and irritable timidity; and, taking him by the arm, he drew Levin along as if piloting him through danger.

Oblonsky was on an intimate footing with almost all his acquaint-ances: with old men of sixty and youths of twenty, actors, ministers, tradesmen, and adjutants-general; so that a great many of the people on familiar terms with him stood at the two extremes of the social ladder and would have been very much astonished to learn that through Oblonsky they had something in common. He was on fami-liar terms with everyone with whom he took a glass of champagne, and he took a glass of champagne with everyone. But if he chanced to meet in the presence of his subordinates any of his *disreputable* pals, as he jestingly called many of his friends, his natural tact enabled him to minimize any unpleasant impressions that might be made on the minds of his subordinates. Levin was not a disreputable pal, but Ob-lonsky, with his ready tact, felt that Levin imagined that he might not like to parade his intimacy with him in the presence of his staff, and therefore hurried him into his private room.

Levin was about the same age as Oblonsky and their intimacy did not entirely rest on the drinking of champagne. Levin had been Oblonsky's comrade and boyhood friend. They were fond of each other, in spite of the difference in their characters and tastes, as friends who have come together in early youth frequently are. But for all that, as is often the way with men who have chosen different callings, though in discussion each of them might justify the other's career, at heart he despised it. Each believed that the life he himself led was the only real life and the life led by his friend was nothing but an illusion. At the sight of Levin, Oblonsky could not repress a slightly ironical smile. How many times had he seen him appear in Moscow from the country, where he did something or other but what exactly Oblonsky could never quite understand or feel any interest in! Levin always arrived in Moscow in a state of agitation, in a hurry, rather ill at ease, and irritated by his own want of ease, and usually with some totally new and unexpected outlook on things in general. Oblonsky was amused at this and liked it. In just the same way, Levin in his heart despised both his friend's town life and official duties, which he considered futile and which he ridiculed. But the difference lay in the fact that Oblonsky, as he was doing the same as everyone else, laughed with confident good humour, while Levin, not feeling so sure of himself, now and then got angry.

'We have been expecting you for some time,' said Oblonsky, entering his room and releasing Levin's arm, as if to show that the danger was past. 'I am very, very glad to see you,' he continued. 'Well, what are you doing? How are you? When did you arrive?'

Levin was silent, looking at the unfamiliar faces of Oblonsky's two colleagues and especially at the hands of the elegant Grinevich, who had very long, white fingers with very long, yellowish nails curving up at the points and large glittering sleeve-links. These hands apparently absorbed all Levin's attention, depriving him of freedom of thought. Oblonsky at once noticed this and smiled.

'Oh yes, let me introduce you,' he said. 'My colleagues: Philip Ivanich Nikitin, Mihail Stanislavich Grinevich.' Then, turning to Levin, 'And this is my friend Constantine Dmitrich Levin, an active member of the *Zemstvo*,* one of the new order, an athlete who can lift a hundred-and-eighty-pound weight with one hand, a cattle-breeder, a sportsman, and brother to Sergei Ivanich Koznyshev.'

* *Zemstvo* – County Council, founded by Alexander II in 1864.

'Delighted,' said the veteran.

'I have the honour of knowing your brother, Sergei Ivanich,' said Grinevich, holding out his slender hand with its long finger-nails.

Levin frowned, shook hands coldly, and immediately turned to Oblonsky. Although he had a great respect for his half-brother, a writer famous throughout Russia, yet he could not bear to be considered not as Constantine Levin but as a brother of the celebrated Koznyshev.

'No, I am no longer on the *Zemstvo*. I quarrelled with the lot of them and don't go to the meetings any more,' he said, addressing Oblonsky.

'Already?' said Oblonsky with a smile. 'But how? Why?'

'It's a long story – I will tell you some other time,' said Levin, starting to tell it at once. 'Well, to put it in a nutshell: I have come to the conclusion that nothing is or can be done by the *Zemstvo*,' he began, speaking as if someone had just offended him. 'On the one hand, it is nothing but a plaything. They play at being a parliament, and I am neither young enough nor old enough to amuse myself with toys. On the other hand' – he stammered – 'it's a means for the local *coterie* to make a little money. We used to have wardships and courts of justice, now we have the *Zemstvo* – not bribes but unearned salaries,' he concluded, as hotly as if he had just suffered contradiction.

'Oho! Another new phase, I see – a conservative one this time!' said Oblonsky. 'Well, we must talk about this later.'

'Yes, later. But I wanted to see you,' said Levin, staring at Grinevich's hand with aversion.

Oblonsky's smile was hardly perceptible.

'Why, I thought you were never going to wear European clothes again?' he said, surveying Levin's new suit, which was obviously the work of a French tailor. 'That's it! You really are in a new phase!'

Levin suddenly blushed, but not in the way that grown men blush, lightly, without noticing, but like a boy aware that his shyness is ridiculous and in consequence feels ashamed and blushes still more, almost to the point of tears. It was so strange to see that intelligent, masculine face in such a childish plight that Oblonsky left off looking at his friend.

'But where shall we meet? You know, I must have a talk with you,' said Levin.

Oblonsky seemed to reflect.

'I know – suppose we go to Gurin's for lunch and have a talk there? I am free until three.'

'No,' replied Levin after a moment's consideration. 'I have to go somewhere else first.'

'Well then, let us dine together.'

'Dine? I have really nothing particular to say – just a couple of words ... to ask you something. And then we can chat.'

'Well, say your couple of words now and we will talk at dinner.'

'It's like this ... However, it's not very important,' said Levin. His face suddenly took on an almost malicious expression in his efforts to overcome his shyness. 'What are the Shcherbatskys doing? The same as usual?'

Oblonsky had known for some time that Levin was in love with his, Oblonsky's, sister-in-law, Kitty Shcherbatsky. He smiled almost perceptibly and his eyes sparkled merrily.

'A couple of words, you said, but I cannot answer in a couple of words because ... Excuse me a moment ...'

A secretary came in and, with a familiar yet respectful bearing and a certain modest consciousness (common to all secretaries) of his superiority to his chief in knowledge of business matters, approached Oblonsky with a sheaf of papers and, on the plea of asking a question, started to explain some difficulty. Without waiting for him to finish, Oblonsky laid a friendly hand on the secretary's sleeve and, softening his remarks with a smile, said:

'No, do as I asked you to.' With a rapid explanation of the way in which he understood the point, he pushed the papers aside, saying, 'Do it like that, please, Zachary Nikitich.'

The secretary withdrew abashed. Levin had completely recovered his composure during this colloquy. He was standing with his elbows on the back of a chair, a look of ironical attention on his face.

'I don't understand, I don't understand at all,' he said.

'What don't you understand?' asked Oblonsky with a merry smile as he searched for a cigarette. He was expecting Levin to say something odd.

'I can't make out what you do,' said Levin, shrugging his shoulders. 'How can you take this sort of thing seriously?'

'Why not?'

'Why, because there's nothing in it.'

'You think so, but actually we're overwhelmed with work.'

'On paper. But there, you have a gift for that,' added Levin.

'You mean you think there is some failing in me?'

'Perhaps,' said Levin. 'But all the same I can't help being impressed by your importance and am proud of having such a great man for a friend. You've not answered my question, though,' he went on, making a desperate effort to look Oblonsky straight in the face.

'All right! All right! Wait a moment – give me time. It's all very well for you with your six thousand acres in the Karazinsky district and you as fit and fresh as a twelve-year-old girl! But you'll be one of us in the end! ... Now as to what you were asking: nothing has changed, but it is a pity that you stayed away so long.'

'Why?' asked Levin in alarm.

'Oh, nothing,' replied Oblonsky 'We'll talk it over presently. What in particular brings you to town?'

'Oh, we will talk about that, too, presently,' said Levin, again blushing up to his ears.

'All right, I understand!' said Oblonsky. 'Well, you know, I would ask you to come to us, but my wife is not very well. But if you want to see *them*, they are sure to be in the Zoological Gardens from four to five. Kitty skates there. You go, and I will call for you and we will dine somewhere together.'

'Excellent. *Au revoir*, then.'

'Remember now! I know you – you may forget and suddenly go rushing back to the country!' Oblonsky called after him, laughing.

'I won't forget!'

And Levin went out of the room, remembering only when he was in the doorway that he had not taken leave of Oblonsky's colleagues.

'That must be a man full of energy,' said Grinevich, after Levin had gone.

'Yes, my dear fellow,' said Oblonsky, shaking his head. 'He's a lucky beggar! Six thousand acres in the Karazinsky district, everything before him, and as fresh as a daisy! Not like some of us.'

'What have you to complain of, Oblonsky?'

'Oh, things aren't very grand with me,' said Oblonsky with a heavy sigh.

6

WHEN Oblonsky had asked Levin what had brought him to Moscow, Levin had blushed and been angry with himself for blushing, because he could not answer: 'I have come to propose to your sister-in-law,' although he had come solely for that purpose.

The Levins and the Shcherbatskys, belonging to the old nobility of Moscow, had always been on intimate and friendly terms. Their ties were drawn still closer during Levin's university days. He had prepared for and entered the university together with young Prince Shcherbatsky, the brother of Dolly and Kitty. At that time Levin was a frequent visitor to the Shcherbatsky home and fell in love with the family. Strange as it may seem, Levin was in love with the whole family – especially the feminine half of it. He could not remember his mother, and his only sister was older than himself, so that in the Shcherbatskys' house he encountered for the first time the home life of a cultured, honourable family of the old aristocracy, of which he had been deprived by the death of his own father and mother. All the members of the family, in particular the feminine half, appeared to him as though wrapped in some mysterious, poetic veil, and he not only saw no defects in them but imagined behind that poetic veil the loftiest sentiments and every possible perfection. Why the three young ladies had to speak French one day and English the next; why they had, at definite times and each in her turn, to practise the piano (the sound of which reached their brother's room upstairs, where the boys were studying); why those masters of French literature, music, drawing, and dancing came to the house; why at certain hours the three young ladies accompanied by Mademoiselle Linon were driven in a barouche to the Tverskoy boulevard wearing satin pelisses – long for Dolly, shorter for Natalie, and so short for Kitty that her shapely little legs in the tightly-pulled-up red stockings were quite exposed; why they had to walk up and down the Tverskoy boulevard accompanied by a footman with a gilt cockade in his hat – all this and much more that happened in their mysterious world he did not understand; but he knew that everything there was perfect, and he was in love with the very mystery of it all.

In his student days he very nearly fell in love with the eldest daughter, Dolly, but she was soon married to Oblonsky. Then he began being in love with the second. He seemed to feel that he had to be in love with one of the sisters, only he was not sure with which. But as soon as she came out Natalie married the diplomat Lvov. Kitty was still a child when Levin left the university. Young Shcherbatsky entered the navy and was drowned in the Baltic, so that, in spite of his friendship with Oblonsky, Levin's association with the Shcherbatskys became less intimate. When, however, at the beginning of the winter, Levin had come to Moscow after a year's absence in the country and had been to see the Shcherbatskys again, he realized at last which of the three sisters he was really destined to love.

It would seem that nothing could be simpler than for him, a man of good family, rich rather than poor, and thirty-two years of age, to propose to the young Princess Shcherbatsky. In all probability, he would without hesitation have been considered a desirable suitor. But Levin was in love and therefore Kitty appeared to him so perfect in every respect, a being above all earthly beings, while he himself was so earthly and insignificant a creature that there could be no hope of his seeming worthy of her, by others or by himself.

Having spent two months in Moscow, as in a dream, seeing Kitty almost every day in society, which he began to frequent in order to meet her, Levin suddenly decided that the union was impossible, and had gone back to the country.

Levin's conviction that it was impossible was founded on the idea that from the point of view of her relatives he was not a good or worthy match for the delightful Kitty, and that Kitty herself could not love him. In the eyes of her relatives, he reasoned, he had no ordinary, definite career and position in society, whereas all his contemporaries were already colonels, aides-de-camp, professors, directors of banks and railway companies, or presidents of tribunals like Oblonsky. But he (he knew very well how he must appear to others) was just a country squire spending his time breeding cattle, shooting snipe, erecting farm buildings – in other words, a fellow without talent who had not turned out well and was doing just what, according to the ideas of the world, is done by people fit for nothing else.

The mysterious, enchanting Kitty could not love such a dull fellow as he believed himself to be, a man so ordinary and undistinguished. Besides, his former attitude to Kitty – that of a grown-up person to a child, arising from his friendship with her brother – seemed to him an additional obstacle in love's path. He supposed that a plain, kindly man like himself might be liked as a friend, but to be loved with such a love as he felt for Kitty a man would have to be handsome and, above all, remarkable.

He had heard that women often cared for plain, ordinary men but he did not believe it, since he judged by himself and he could not have loved any but beautiful, mysterious, exceptional women.

But after two months alone in the country he was convinced that this was not one of those passions he had experienced in early youth; that this love gave him not a moment's peace; that he could not live without having settled the question whether she would be his wife or not; and that his despair sprang only from his imagination – he had no proof that he would be refused. So now he had come to Moscow with the firm determination to propose to her and marry her if she would accept him. Or ... but he could not conceive what would become of him if he were rejected.

7

ARRIVING in Moscow by the morning train, Levin had gone to the house of his half-brother, Koznyshev, who was older than himself. After changing his clothes, he went to the study, intending to tell his brother why he had come and to ask-his advice; but Koznyshev was not alone. With him was a famous professor of philosophy who had come from Kharkov for the express purpose of clearing up some difference that had arisen between them on a very important philosophical question. The professor was engaged in a fierce polemic against materialists, and Koznyshev, who had been following this polemic with interest, after the Professor's last article had written to reproach him for conceding too much to the materialists; and the professor had immediately come to explain his point of view. They were discussing the fashionable question whether there was a dividing line between the psychological and physiological phenomena in human activity; and, if so, where?

Koznyshev greeted his brother with the coldly affable smile he bestowed on everyone and, having introduced him to the professor, went on with the discussion.

A small, sallow man in spectacles, with a narrow forehead, detached himself from the conversation for an instant to return Levin's bow and, paying him no further attention, went on with what he was saying. Levin sat down to wait for the professor to go, but soon he became interested in the subject under discussion.

Levin had come across the articles they were disputing in magazines and had read them with the interest a man who has studied the natural sciences at the university is likely to take in their development; but he had never connected these scientific deductions as to man's animal origin, as to reflex action, biology, and sociology, with questions concerning the meaning of life and death to himself, which had of late come more and more frequently into his mind.

Listening to his brother's conversation with the professor, he noticed that they linked these scientific questions with the spiritual and several times almost touched on the latter; but every time they got close to what seemed to him the most important point, they promptly beat a hasty retreat and plunged back into the sea of subtle distinctions, reservations, quotations, allusions, and references to authorities; and he had difficulty in understanding what they were talking about.

'I cannot accept it,' said Koznyshev, with his usual clearness, precision of expression, and elegance of phrase. 'I cannot in any way agree with Keiss that my whole conception of the external world is the outcome of impressions. The most fundamental consciousness of *being* is not received through the senses, for there is no special organ to convey that consciousness.'

'Yes, but they – Wurst, and Knaust, and Pripasov – will tell you that your consciousness of existence is derived from the conjunction of all your sensations – is, in fact, the result of your sensations. Wurst even goes so far as to say that where sensation ceases to exist there is no consciousness of existence.'

'I would maintain the contrary,' began Koznyshev.

But here again it seemed to Levin that just as they were reaching the root of the matter they again retreated; and he made up his mind to put a question to the Professor.

'So if my senses are annihilated, if my body dies, no further existence is possible?' he asked.

With displeasure and as if the interruption had caused him mental suffering, the professor surveyed the strange inquirer, who looked more like a barge-hauler than a philosopher, and then turned his eyes to Koznyshev, as if to ask: What's one to say to this? But Koznyshev, who had been talking with far less heat and one-sidedness than the professor, and who had sufficient breadth of mind to answer the professor and at the same time to comprehend the simple and natural point of view which had inspired the question, smiled and answered:

'That question we have as yet no right to determine ...'

'We have not the necessary data,' confirmed the professor and went back to his argument. 'No,' he said, 'I maintain that if, as Pripasov directly asserts, sensation is based on impressions, then we are bound to distinguish sharply between these two conceptions.'

Levin listened no longer, but sat waiting for the professor to go.

8

WHEN the professor had gone, Koznyshev turned to his brother.

'I am so glad that you have come. Are you here for long? How is the estate doing?'

Levin knew that his brother was not very much interested in the estate and that the question was merely a concession; so he just said something about the sale of his wheat and made a mention of money matters.

Levin had meant to tell his brother of his intention to get married and to ask his advice. Indeed he had firmly made up his mind to do so. But after seeing his brother, listening to his conversation with the professor, and now hearing the unconsciously patronizing tone in which his brother inquired about the business of their estate (the property they had inherited jointly from their mother had not been divided, and Levin was managing both their shares), he felt that for some reason or other he could not begin to talk to him of his intention to marry. He felt that his brother would not look at it in the way he would have wished.

'Well, how is your *Zemstvo* doing?' asked Koznyshev, who took a keen interest in these local boards and attached great importance to them.

'I really don't know ...'

'What? Why, surely you are a member of the board?'

'No, I am not a member now. I resigned,' replied Levin, 'and I no longer attend the meetings.'

'A pity!' commented Koznyshev, frowning.

In self-defence Levin began to describe what took place at the meetings in his district.

'But that's how it always is!' Koznyshev interrupted him. 'We Russians are always like that. Perhaps it's our strong point really – this faculty for seeing our own shortcomings; but we overdo it, we comfort ourselves with irony to which we always give ready tongue. All I say is, allow such rights as our local self-government to any other people in Europe – to the Germans or the English – and they would have worked their way to freedom through them, while we simply turn them into ridicule!'

'But how can it be helped?' asked Levin shamefacedly. 'It was my last effort. And I put my whole heart into it. I can't. I'm no good at it.'

'It's not that you're no good at it,' said Koznyshev. 'You just don't look at it as you should.'

'Perhaps not,' replied Levin despondently.

'Oh, do you know brother Nikolai's turned up again?'

Nikolai was Levin's elder brother and Koznyshev's half-brother, a derelict individual who had squandered the greater part of his fortune, who kept the strangest, most ill-favoured company, and who had quarrelled with his brothers.

'What did you say?' cried Levin in horror. 'How do you know?'

'Prokofy saw him in the street.'

'Here in Moscow? Where is he? Do you know?' Levin got up from his chair, as though on the point of starting off at once.

'I am sorry I told you,' said Koznyshev, shaking his head at his younger brother's agitation. 'I sent to find out where he was living and returned him his I.O.U. to Trubin, which I had paid. And this is what he writes to me.'

Koznyshev handed his brother a note which he took from under a paper-weight.

Levin read in the queer, familiar hand: 'I humbly beg you to leave me alone. That is the only favour I ask of my amiable brothers. – Nikolai Levin.'

Levin read it, and without raising his head stood with the note in his hands opposite Koznyshev.

A struggle was going on in his heart between a desire to forget his unfortunate brother for the present and the consciousness that this would be wrong.

'He obviously wants to offend me,' continued Koznyshev, 'but he cannot do that. I wish with all my heart I could help him, but I know it cannot be done.'

'Yes, yes,' repeated Levin. 'I understand and appreciate your attitude to him; but I shall go and see him.'

'If you want to, go by all means; but I shouldn't advise it. That is to say, as far as you and I are concerned I am not afraid of his making mischief between us. But for your own sake, I advise you, better not go. You cannot do anything to help. However, it's as you like.'

'Very likely I can't do any good but I feel – especially at such a moment ... but that is another matter – I feel I could not be easy ...'

'Well, that I don't understand,' said Koznyshev. 'I only know,' he added, 'it's been a lesson in humility. I have come to look differently, more leniently, at what people call rascality since brother Nikolai became what he is ... you know what he did ...'

'Oh, it's awful, awful!' repeated Levin.

Having obtained his brother's address from Koznyshev's footman, Levin was on the point of setting off at once to see him, but on second thoughts he decided to put off his visit till the evening. The first thing to do to set his heart at rest was to accomplish the matter which had brought him to Moscow. So from his brother's Levin went to Oblonsky's office and, having got news of the Shcherbatskys, he drove to the place where he had been told he might find Kitty.

9

AT four o'clock that afternoon Levin stepped out of a hired sleigh at the Zoological Gardens and, with beating heart, turned along the path to the ice-hills and the skating-ground, sure of finding Kitty there, as he had seen the Shcherbatskys' carriage at the entrance.

It was a bright, frosty day. At the gates there were rows of carriages, sleighs, drivers, and policemen. Well-dressed people, their hats shining in the sunlight, crowded about the entrance and along the well-swept little paths between the little old-fashioned Russian châlets with their carved eaves. The old curly birch-trees in the gardens, their branches all laden with snow, looked as though they had been freshly decked in sacred vestments.

He walked along the path towards the skating-ground saying to himself: 'You mustn't get excited. You must keep calm. What is the matter with you? What's wrong? Quiet, fool!' he conjured his heart. And the more he tried to compose himself, the more agitated he grew, until he could hardly breathe. An acquaintance met and hailed him, but Levin did not even notice who it was. He went towards the ice-hills, which resounded with the rattle of chains on sledges being dragged up or sliding down, the rumble of toboggans, and the ring of merry voices. A few steps farther and he saw the skating-rink and, amidst the many skaters, at once recognized her.

He knew she was there by the joy and the terror that seized his heart. She was standing talking to a lady at the opposite end of the rink. There was apparently nothing particularly striking either in her dress or her attitude; but for Levin it was as easy to find her in that crowd as to see a rose among nettles. She made everything bright. She was the smile that shed light on all around her. 'Can I really step on to the ice and go up to her?' he wondered. The spot where she stood seemed to him unapproachable holy ground and there was one moment when he nearly turned away, so filled with awe was he. He had to make an effort and reason with himself that all sorts of people were moving about her and that he too might come there just to skate. He walked down, for a long while averting his eyes from her, as though she were the sun, but seeing her, as one sees the sun, without looking.

On that day of the week and at that hour people belonging to the same set and all acquainted with one another used to meet on the ice. There were crack skaters, parading their skill, and beginners clinging to chairs and making timid, awkward movements, boys, and elderly people skating for their health; and they all seemed to Levin to be fortune's favourites because they were there near her. All these skaters, it appeared, with complete unconcern would skate up to her, skate past her, speak to her even, and were enjoying themselves quite independently of her, delighting in the excellent surface and the fine weather.

Nikolai Shcherbatsky, Kitty's cousin, in a short jacket and tight trousers, was sitting on a bench with his skates on. Seeing Levin, he called out to him:

'Ah, Russia's foremost skater! Have you been here long? The ice is first-rate – get your skates on!'

'I haven't got my skates with me,' replied Levin, marvelling at such boldness and ease in her presence and not for one second losing sight of her, though he did not look at her. He felt the sun approaching him. She was in a corner and, turning out her slender little feet in their high boots, obviously nervous, she skated towards him. A small boy in Russian dress, desperately waving his arms and stooping very low,

41

was overtaking her. She was not skating very steadily. Drawing her hands out of the little muff, that hung on a cord round her neck, she held them ready for emergency and, looking towards Levin, whom she had recognized, she smiled at him and at her own apprehension. When she had got round the turn she gave herself a push off with a springy foot and skated straight up to Shcherbatsky. Clutching his arm, she nodded smilingly to Levin. She was lovelier than he had imagined.

When he thought about her, he could conjure up a vivid picture of her whole appearance and especially the charm of the little fair head, poised so lightly on the shapely girlish shoulders, and the expression of child-like serenity and goodness. That child-like innocence of expression, together with the slender beauty of her figure, made up her special charm, which he always remembered; but what struck him afresh every time was the look of her gentle, tranquil, honest eyes and, above all, her smile, which never failed to transport him into some enchanted world, where his heart softened and he felt full of peace – as he remembered feeling on rare occasions in his early childhood.

'Have you been here long?' she asked, giving him her hand. 'Thank you,' she added as he picked up the handkerchief that had fallen out of her muff.

'I? Not long. I came yesterday ... I mean to-day,' replied Levin, in his agitation not immediately taking in her question. 'I was meaning to come and see you,' he went on; and then, remembering why he was going to see her, was promptly overcome with confusion and blushed. 'I did not know you could skate, and so well.'

She looked observantly at him, as though wishing to make out the reason for his confusion.

'Your praise is praise indeed. The tradition is kept up here that you are a superlative skater,' she said, with a small black-gloved hand brushing some needles of hoar-frost off her muff.

'Yes, once upon a time I used to skate with passion. I wanted to be perfect at it.'

'You seem to do everything with passion,' she said with a smile. 'I should so like to see you skate. Put on your skates and let us skate together.'

'Skate together! Can that be possible?' thought Levin, gazing at her.

'I will go and get some at once,' he said; and went off to hire skates.

42

'It's a long while since we've seen you here, sir,' remarked the attendant, supporting Levin's foot and screwing on the heel of the skate. 'None of the other gentlemen can touch you. Is that all right?' he asked, tightening the strap.

'Fine, fine! Make haste, please,' replied Levin, barely able to restrain the smile of rapture which would spread over his face in spite of himself. 'Yes,' he thought, 'this now is life, this is happiness! *Together*, she said; *let us skate together!* Shall I speak to her now? No, that's why I am afraid to speak – because I'm happy now, happy in my hopes ... But after? ... No, I must! I must! I must! Away with this weakness!'

Levin rose to his feet, took off his overcoat and, after a run over the rough ice round the hut, glided on to the smooth surface of the rink and skated effortlessly, as it were by simple exercise of will quickening and slackening speed and directing his course. He approached her bashfully, but again her smile reassured him.

She gave him her hand and they set off side by side, going faster and faster, and the faster they skated the more tightly she grasped his hand.

'I could soon learn with you. I have confidence in you somehow,' she said to him.

'And I have confidence in myself when you are leaning on me,' he answered, and was immediately panic-stricken at what he had said and blushed. And indeed, no sooner had he uttered the words than all at once, like the sun going behind a cloud, her face lost all its friendliness and Levin recognized the familiar change in her expression that denoted the working of a thought: a wrinkle appeared on her smooth brow.

'Is there anything troubling you? But I have no right to ask,' he said hurriedly.

'Why should there be? ... No, I have nothing to trouble me,' she replied coldly, adding immediately, 'You have not seen Mademoiselle Linon, have you?'

'Not yet.'

'Go over and speak to her, then; she is so fond of you.'

'What's wrong? I have upset her. Lord, help me!' thought Levin, skating swiftly over to the old Frenchwoman with the grey ringlets, who was sitting on one of the benches. Smiling and showing her false teeth, she greeted him as an old friend.

'Yes, you see we are growing up,' she said to him, glancing in Kitty's direction, 'and older. *Tiny bear* has grown big now!' pursued

43

the Frenchwoman with a laugh, and she reminded him of his joke when he had called the three young ladies after the three bears in the English nursery-tale. 'Do you remember when you used to call her that?'

He had not the faintest recollection of it, but she had been laughing at the joke for the last ten years and still enjoyed it.

'Now then, off with you, go and skate. Our Kitty skates nicely now, doesn't she?'

When Levin darted up to Kitty her face was no longer stern and her eyes were friendly and frank again; but he fancied there was something deliberately quiet about her friendliness, and he felt sad. After they had talked of her old governess and her eccentricities, she asked him about his own life.

'Surely you must feel dull in the country in the winter, don't you?' she said.

'No, not a bit, I am very busy,' he answered, conscious that she was subduing him to her own quiet tone, which he would not have the force to break through, just as it had been at the beginning of the winter.

'Are you here for long?' Kitty asked.

'I don't know,' he replied, without thinking of what he was saying. The thought came into his mind that if he submitted to her tone of staid friendliness he would end by going back again with nothing settled, and he resolved to make a struggle.

'How is it you don't know?'

'I don't. It all depends on you,' he said, and was immediately horror-stricken at his own words.

She either did not hear or did not want to hear. She made a sort of stumble, gave a couple of thrusts with her foot against the ice, and hurriedly skated away from him towards Mademoiselle Linon, said something to her, and went in the direction of the little pavilion where the ladies took off their skates.

'Good heavens, what have I done! Merciful God, help me, guide me,' prayed Levin; and at the same time feeling a need of violent exercise, he started doing inside and outside turns at full speed.

Just then a young man, the best of the new generation of skaters, emerged from the coffee-house on his skates, with a cigarette in his mouth. Taking a run, he started down, his skates clattering as he jumped from step to step. Without the least change in the easy way in which he held his arms, he flew down and skated away over the ice.

'Oh, a new trick!' cried Levin and promptly ran up the steps to try it.

'Don't break your neck – it needs practice!' Nikolai Shcherbatsky shouted after him.

Levin climbed the steps, took a run along the top as fast as he could, and then dashed down, his arms poised to balance himself in this unusual movement. On the bottom step his foot caught and one hand almost touched the ice, but he made a violent effort, righted himself, and skated off laughing.

'How good and nice he is!' Kitty was thinking at that very moment, as she came out of the pavilion with Mademoiselle Linon and looked towards him with a smile of quiet affection, as though he were a favourite brother. 'And can it be my fault? Can I have done anything wrong? People would say I am a flirt. I know he isn't the one I love; but all the same I like being with him, and he is so nice. Only what possessed him to say that? ...' she mused.

Seeing Kitty about to depart with her mother, who had come to meet her at the steps, Levin, flushed from his rapid exercise, stood still and considered a moment. Then he took off his skates and caught up with mother and daughter at the entrance of the gardens.

'Delighted to see you,' said Princess Shcherbatsky. 'We are at home on Thursdays, as usual.'

'To-day, then?'

'We shall be delighted,' replied the Princess stiffly.

Kitty was grieved by her mother's manner and could not resist a desire to make amends for it. She turned her head and said with a smile: '*Au revoir.*'

At this point Oblonsky, his hat on one side, face and eyes beaming, strode into the gardens like a conquering hero. But on reaching his mother-in-law he responded with an unhappy, guilty air to her inquiries about Dolly's health. After a few words with her in a subdued and mournful tone, he threw back his shoulders and put his arm in Levin's.

'Well, are you ready? shall we go?' he asked. 'I've been thinking about you all this time and am so glad you've come,' he said, looking him meaningfully in the eye.

'Yes, come along,' replied the happy Levin, still hearing the sound

45

of her voice saying *Au revoir* and seeing the smile that had accompanied it.

'The England or the Hermitage?'

'I don't mind which.'

'Right, the England then,' said Oblonsky, choosing that restaurant because he owed more there than at the Hermitage and consequently considered it not nice to avoid it. 'Have you got a sleigh? Splendid, because I let my carriage go.'

The two friends were silent all the way to the restaurant. Levin was wondering what the change in Kitty's expression had meant, alternately assuring himself that there was hope for him, and falling into despair, clearly seeing that it was madness to hope; but yet feeling himself another man since her smile and the words *Au revoir*.

Oblonsky spent the drive composing the menu for their dinner.

'You like turbot, don't you?' he said to Levin as they were arriving.

'What?' queried Levin. 'Turbot? Oh yes, I am *awfully* fond of turbot.'

10

WHEN they entered the hotel Levin could not help noticing a certain peculiarity in his friend's expression, a sort of suppressed radiance in his face and whole person. Oblonsky took off his overcoat and, his hat over one ear, walked into the dining-room, giving directions to the frock-coated Tartar waiters who, with napkins under their arms, attached themselves to him. Bowing right and left to acquaintances who, here as everywhere else, greeted him with delight, he made his way to the buffet for an appetizer of vodka with a morsel of fish, saying something to the painted, befrizzled Frenchwoman, all ribbons and lace, behind the counter – something that made even her burst into a peal of laughter. Levin did not take any vodka, simply because he felt that this Frenchwoman, all made up, so it seemed to him, of false hair, *poudre de riz*, and *vinaigre de toilette*, was an affront. He turned from her quickly, as from something unclean. His whole heart was filled with memories of Kitty and his eyes shone with a smile of triumph and happiness.

'This way, please, your excellency. Your excellency won't be disturbed here,' said a particularly attentive, white-headed old Tartar, so broad across the hips that his coat-tails gaped behind. 'If you please, your excellency,' he said to Levin; by way of showing his respect for Oblonsky, fussing round his guest as well.

In a twinkling he flung a new cloth over the round table under a bronze chandelier, though it already had a table-cloth on it, pushed up velvet chairs, and came and stood before Oblonsky with a napkin and bill of fare in his hands, awaiting his order.

'If your excellency would prefer a private room, one will be available in a few moments – Prince Golitzin is there with a lady. Fresh oysters are in.'

'Ah, oysters!'

Oblonsky considered.

'How about changing our menu, Levin?' he said, keeping his finger on the bill of fare, his face expressing serious hesitation. 'Are the oysters good? Be sure now!'

'They're Flensburg, your excellency: we've no Ostend.'

'Flensburg or not – are they fresh?'

'They only arrived yesterday, sir.'

'Well then, shall we start with oysters and change the whole programme? What do you think?'

'I don't mind. I like cabbage-soup and *kasha* better than anything; but I don't suppose they have that here.'

'*Kasha à la russe* your excellency would like?' said the Tartar, bending over Levin like a nurse over a child.

'No, seriously though, whatever you choose will suit me. Skating has given me an appetite. But don't imagine,' he added, detecting a look of dissatisfaction on Oblonsky's face, 'that I shan't appreciate your choice. I shall enjoy a good dinner.'

'I should hope so! Say what you like, it is one of the pleasures of life,' said Oblonsky. 'Well then, my good fellow, bring us two – no, three – dozen oysters, clear soup with vegetables …'

'*Printanière*,' prompted the Tartar. But Oblonsky evidently did not care to allow him the satisfaction of giving the dishes their French names.

'Soup with vegetables in it, you know. Then turbot with thick sauce. After that … roast beef (and see that it's good). Followed by capons; and we will finish up with fruit salad.'

Remembering that Oblonsky would not call the dishes by their French names, the Tartar did not repeat the order after him but could not resist the pleasure of rehearsing it to himself according to the

47

menu: '*Soupe printanière, turbot sauce Beaumarchais, poulard à l'estragon, macédoine de fruits ...*' and immediately, as if worked by springs, he laid down the bill of fare in one cardboard cover and, seizing another, the wine list, put it before Oblonsky.

'What shall we drink?'

'Anything you like, only not much. Champagne,' said Levin.

'What? To begin with? After all, why not? You like the white seal?'

'*Cachet blanc*,' put in the Tartar.

'Yes, bring us that with the oysters, and then we'll see.'

'Certainly, sir. And what *vin de table*?'

'You can give us *Nuits* – no, better the classic *Chablis*.'

'Yes, sir. And cheese – your special?'

'Oh yes, Parmesan. Or would you prefer some other kind?'

'No, it's all the same to me,' replied Levin, unable to repress a smile.

And the Tartar darted off, his coat-tails flying, and five minutes later darted in again with a dish of oysters, their pearly shells opened, and a bottle between his fingers.

Oblonsky crumpled his starchy table-napkin and tucked a corner of it inside his waistcoat. Then with his arms comfortably on the table he attacked the oysters.

'Not bad,' he said, tearing the quivering oysters from their pearly shells with a silver fork and swallowing them one after another. 'Not bad,' he repeated, turning his dewy, brilliant eyes from Levin to the Tartar.

Levin ate his oysters, though he would have liked white bread and cheese better. But he looked at Oblonsky with admiration. Even the Tartar, after uncorking the bottle and pouring the sparkling champagne into the delicate, wide-lipped glasses, watched Oblonsky with a smile of evident pleasure, while he adjusted his white cravat.

'You don't care much for oysters?' asked Oblonsky, draining his wine-glass. 'Or are you worried about something? Eh?'

He wanted Levin to be in good spirits. But it was not that Levin was not in good spirits: he felt constrained. The feelings that filled his heart made him ill at ease and uncomfortable in this restaurant with its private rooms where men were dining with ladies, and all this running to and fro and bustle. The bronzes, the mirrors, the gas-light, and the Tartar waiters were all an affront. He was afraid of defiling the love which filled his soul.

'I? Yes, I have got something on my mind – and besides, all this makes me feel uncomfortable,' he said. 'You can't imagine how monstrous all this seems to a country person like myself – like the fingernails of that gentleman I saw in your office ...'

'Yes, I noticed that you were fascinated by poor Grinevich's nails,' laughed Oblonsky.

'I can't help it,' replied Levin. 'Try and put yourself in my place – look at it from a countryman's point of view. Our one object is to have hands that we can use, so we cut our nails; roll up our sleeves. But here people purposely let their nails grow as long as they will and wear studs as big as saucers, so that they can do nothing with their hands.'

Oblonsky smiled merrily.

'Yes, it shows that he does not have to do any rough work. He works with his brain ...'

'Maybe. But it still seems to me monstrous, just as there is something monstrous about what we are doing now. In the country we try to get our meals over as quickly as possible, so as to get on with our work, but you and I are doing our best to make our dinner last as long as we can; we therefore have oysters ...'

'Why, of course,' objected Oblonsky. 'But the whole aim of civilization is to make everything a source of enjoyment.'

'Well, if that is so, I'd rather be a savage.'

'And so you are a savage. All you Levins are savages.'

Levin sighed. He remembered his brother Nikolai and frowned, feeling conscience-stricken and uncomfortable; but Oblonsky introduced a subject which at once distracted his thoughts.

'I say, are you going to see the family this evening – the Shcherbatskys, I mean?' he asked, pushing aside his plate of empty oyster-shells and drawing the cheese towards him, a significant gleam in his eye.

'Yes, I shall certainly go,' replied Levin. 'Though I fancied the princess invited me rather unwillingly.'

'Nonsense! What an idea! It's just her manner ... Come, my good fellow, the soup now ... It's her *grande dame* manner,' said Oblonsky. 'I'm coming too but I shall have to go to the Countess Bonin's rehearsal first. But you really are a savage, aren't you? How do you explain the sudden way in which you vanished from Moscow? The Shcherbatskys kept asking me about you, just as if I ought to know. Yet all I know is that you never behave like anyone else.'

'Yes,' said Levin, slowly and with emotion, 'you're right. I am a savage. Only my outlandishness is not in having gone away then but in coming back now. I have come back now ...'

'Oh, what a lucky fellow you are!' interrupted Oblonsky, looking Levin in the eye.

'Why?'

> ' "By the mark of your steed
> I can tell his fine breed,
> And a young man in love – by his eyes," '

declaimed Oblonsky. 'You have everything before you.'

'What about you – is everything behind you already?'

'No, not exactly, but the future is yours and the present is mine – and the present is not all that it might be.'

'How's that?'

'Oh, things go wrong. However, I don't want to talk about myself – and besides, I can't explain it all,' said Oblonsky. 'Now tell me, why have you come to Moscow? Here, take this away!' he called to the Tartar.

'Can't you guess?' answered Levin, gazing at Oblonsky with eyes that had a light shining in their depths.

'I can guess, but I can't be the first to talk about it, so you can see by that whether my guess is right or wrong,' said Oblonsky, looking at him with a sly smile.

'Well, and what do you say to it?' asked Levin in a trembling voice, feeling that every muscle of his face was quivering. 'What do you think of it?'

Oblonsky slowly emptied his glass of *Chablis*, his eyes fixed on Levin.

'I? There is nothing I should like better – nothing! It would be the best thing that could happen.'

'But you are not making a mistake? You do know what we are speaking of?' asked Levin, with a searching look at his friend. 'You think there is a possibility?'

'Yes. Why shouldn't there be?'

'You really think so? Come – tell me all you are thinking. Oh, but – suppose a refusal is in store for me? ... Indeed, I feel sure ...'

'Why should you think that?' said Oblonsky, smiling at Levin's agitation.

'I don't know, I sometimes think so. And that would be dreadful for me, and for her too.'

'Oh no! In any case, there's nothing dreadful in it for a girl. Every girl is proud of an offer.'

'Yes, girls in general, perhaps, but not she.'

Oblonsky smiled. He knew that feeling of Levin's so well – that for Levin all the girls in the world were divided into two classes: one class included all the girls in the world except Kitty, and they had all the human weaknesses and were very ordinary girls; while Kitty was in a class by herself, without the least imperfection and above the rest of humanity.

'Wait, you must have some sauce,' he said, staying Levin's hand that was pushing the sauce-boat away.

Levin obediently helped himself to sauce, but would not let Oblonsky go on with his dinner.

'No, but listen – listen!' he said. 'Realize that it's a question of life or death for me. I have never spoken to anyone about it. And I could not talk about it to anyone else but you. Of course, you and I are different in every way – we have different tastes, opinions, everything; but I know that you are fond of me and understand me, and that's why I am terribly fond of you. But for God's sake be absolutely frank with me.'

'I am telling you what I think,' said Oblonsky, smiling. 'And I'll tell you something more. My wife, a most wonderful woman ...' Oblonsky sighed, remembering their strained relations, and resumed after a moment's silence: 'She has the gift of second sight. She can see people through and through. But that is not the point – she knows what is going to happen, especially where marriages are concerned. For instance, she foretold that the Shakovskoy girl would marry Brenteln. No one would believe it, but she turned out to be right. And she's on your side.'

'How do you mean?'

'I mean, not only that she likes you – she says Kitty is certain to be your wife.'

At these words Levin's face suddenly lit up with a smile that was not far from tears of emotion.

'She says that?' he cried. 'I always thought she was an angel, your wife! But enough – we have talked enough about it,' and he rose from the table.

'All right, but do sit down!'

Levin, however, could not sit. He strode up and down the little cage of a room, blinking to force back the tears, and only when he had succeeded did he sit again.

'You know,' he said, 'it's not love. I have been in love, but this is not the same thing. It is not my feeling, but a sort of force outside myself has taken possession of me. I went away, you see, because I made up my mind that it could never be – that such happiness does not exist on earth, do you understand? But I have struggled with myself and realize that there's no living without it. And it must be settled ...'

'Why did you go away, then?'

'Stay a moment! Oh, the thoughts that crowd into one's head! The questions one has to ask oneself! Listen. You cannot imagine what you have done for me by saying what you did. I am so happy that I am becoming positively hateful and forgetting everything. I heard today that my brother Nikolai ... you know, he is here ... and I forgot all about him. It seems to me that he's happy too. It is a sort of madness. But there is one awful thing ... You got married, you must know the feeling ... it is awful when we – who are already getting on in years – we have a past ... not of love but of sins ... are suddenly brought close to a pure innocent creature! It is loathsome, and that is why one can't help feeling oneself unworthy.'

'Well, but you can't have much on your conscience!'

'Alas! all the same,' said Levin, 'all the same, looking back on my life "I tremble, and bitterly I curse the day I was born ..." Yes.'

'What's to be done? The world is made that way,' said Oblonsky.

'There is one comfort, just as in that prayer which I have always liked: "Pardon me not according to my deserts but according to Thy lovingkindness ..." She too could only forgive me that way.'

II

LEVIN emptied his glass and they were silent for a while.

'There's just one other thing I ought to tell you. Do you know Vronsky?' Oblonsky asked Levin.

'No, I don't. Why do you ask?'

'Give us another bottle,' Oblonsky directed the Tartar, who was filling up their glasses and fidgeting round them just when he was not wanted.

'Why ought I to know Vronsky?'

'You ought to know Vronsky because he is one of your rivals.'

'Who is this Vronsky?' asked Levin, and his face lost the expression of childlike rapture which Oblonsky had been admiring and suddenly looked angry and disagreeable.

'He is one of Count Kiril Ivanovich Vronsky's sons, and a fine sample of the gilded youth of Petersburg. I got to know him in Tver when I was there on official business and he came for the levy of recruits. Awfully rich, handsome, influential connexions, an aide-decamp to the Emperor and a capital fellow into the bargain. But he is more than just a good fellow. From what I have seen of him here, he is cultured and very intelligent – a man who will go far.'

Levin scowled and was silent.

'Well, he appeared here shortly after you left and, as I understand it, he's head over ears in love with Kitty; and you know that her mother ...'

'Excuse me, but I know nothing,' said Levin, frowning gloomily. And immediately he remembered his brother Nikolai, and thought how hateful it was of himself to have been able to forget him.

'Wait now, wait,' said Oblonsky, smiling and touching Levin's arm. 'I have told you what I know, and I repeat that in this tender and delicate matter, as far as one can judge, I believe the chances are in your favour.'

Levin leaned back in his chair. His face was pale.

'But I should advise you to settle the thing as soon as possible,' pursued Oblonsky, filling up Levin's glass.

'No, thanks, I can't drink any more,' said Levin, pushing his glass aside, 'or it will go to my head. ... Well, and how are you getting on?' he continued, obviously anxious to change the subject.

'Just one word more: in any case, I advise you to settle the question quickly; but I shouldn't speak to-night,' said Oblonsky. 'Go round to-morrow morning, make an offer in the classic manner, and God bless you!'

'You have often talked of coming to me for some shooting. Why not come this spring?' said Levin.

He repented now from the bottom of his heart of ever having started this conversation with Oblonsky. A feeling such as his was profaned by talk of some Petersburg officer as his rival, and by Oblonsky's conjectures and advice.

Oblonsky smiled. He understood what was going on in Levin's heart.

'I will come some day,' he said. 'Yes, my boy, women are the pivot the world turns on. Look at me – I am in a mess, too, and all on account of women. Tell me frankly,' he pursued, picking up a cigar and keeping one hand on his glass, 'give me your advice.'

'What about?'

'It's like this. Suppose you are married, you love your wife, but you are attracted by another woman.'

'Forgive me, but I really find that absolutely incomprehensible. ... It's as if ... as incomprehensible as if, after a good dinner here, I were to go into a baker's shop and steal a roll.'

Oblonsky's eyes sparkled more than usual.

'Why not? Rolls sometimes smell so good that you can't resist them!

> "Himmlisch ist's, wenn ich bezwungen
>   Meine irdische Begier;
> Aber doch wenn's nicht gelungen,
>   Hatt' ich auch recht hübsch Plaisir!" ' *

Oblonsky quoted the verse with a hint of a smile and Levin could not help smiling himself.

'No, seriously,' resumed Oblonsky. 'Imagine a woman, a dear, gentle, affectionate creature, poor and lonely, who has sacrificed everything; and now, when the damage is done – you understand – can one possibly cast her off? We'll allow that it is necessary to part from her, so as not to break up one's family life; but oughtn't one to take pity on her and do something to make amends?'

'Well, you must excuse me there. You know I separate women into two categories ... at least, no ... it would be truer to say: there are women and there are ... I have never seen, nor ever shall see, a fallen woman who was exquisite; and as to that painted Frenchwoman with her ringlets at the counter out there, she and her like are vermin to my mind, and all fallen women are the same.'

'And the woman in the New Testament?'

'Oh, please! Christ would never have spoken those words had He known how they would be abused. They seem to be the only words in the whole of the Gospel that people remember. However, I'm not

---

* 'Splendid if I overcome
   My earthy passion,
 But if I succeed not,
   Still I have known happiness!'

saying so much what I think, as what I feel. I have a horror of fallen women. You are afraid of spiders, and I of these women. Most likely you have not made a study of spiders and their habits, any more than I have studied women of that sort.'

'It is all very well for you to talk like that – just like the character in Dickens who used to fling all embarrassing questions over his right shoulder. But denying facts is no answer. What is to be done? Tell me, what is to be done? Your wife is getting on, while you are full of life. Before you have time to turn round, you feel that you can no longer love your wife, however much you may esteem her. And then all of a sudden love crosses your path and you are done for, done for!' lamented Oblonsky dejectedly and in despair.

Levin smiled.

'Yes, done for,' repeated Oblonsky. 'And what can one do?'

'Don't steal rolls.'

Oblonsky laughed outright.

'Oh, you moralist! But think for a moment; here we have two women: one insists only on her rights, and those rights are your love which you cannot give her; while the other gives you everything and asks for nothing. What are you to do? How are you to act? It is a dreadful conflict.'

'If you want my opinion, I can only tell you that I do not believe there is any conflict about it. For this reason: to my mind, love – both kinds of love (Plato defines them in his *Symposium*) serve as a criterion. Some men only understand one sort, and some only the other. And those who only understand the non-platonic love have no need to talk of conflict. In such love there can be no conflict. "Much obliged for the gratification, my humble respects" – and that is all there is to it. And in Platonic love there can be no conflict because in that love all is clear and pure, because ...'

At that instant, Levin recollected his own sins and the inner conflict he had lived through. And he added unexpectedly:

'However, perhaps you are right. You may very likely be ... But I don't know, I really don't know.'

'There, you see,' said Oblonsky, 'you're very much all of a piece. It's both your strong point and your failing. You are all of a piece and you want the whole of life to be consistent too – but it never is. You scorn public service because you want the reality to correspond all the time to the aim – and that's not how it is. You want man's work, too, always to have a definite purpose, and love and family life to be indivisible. But that does not happen either. All the variety, all the charm, all the beauty of life are made up of light and shade.'

Levin sighed and made no reply. He was thinking of his own affairs and not listening to Oblonsky.

And suddenly both of them felt that though they were friends and had dined and drunk wine together, which should have drawn them closer still, yet each was thinking only of his own affairs and was not concerned with the other. Oblonsky had experienced before this feeling of estrangement instead of *rapprochement* after dining with a friend, and knew what to do in such circumstances.

'The bill!' he cried, and went into the next room, where he immediately saw an aide-de-camp of his acquaintance and dropped into a conversation with him about an actress and her protector. And the talk with the aide-de-camp at once rested and refreshed Oblonsky after the conversation with Levin, who always caused him too great a mental and moral strain.

When the Tartar appeared with a bill for some twenty-six roubles, besides a tip for himself, Levin, who at any other time would have been appalled, like anyone from the country, at his share of fourteen roubles, did not notice it, but paid up and set off homewards to dress and go to the Shcherbatskys', there to decide his fate.

12

THE young Princess Kitty Shcherbatsky was eighteen years old. She had come out that winter and was being more of a success in society than either of her elder sisters, more even than her mother had anticipated. Not only were nearly all the young men who danced at the Moscow balls in love with Kitty, but two serious suitors had presented themselves in her first season: Levin and, immediately after his departure, Count Vronsky.

Levin's appearance at the beginning of the winter, his frequent visits and unconcealed love for Kitty had led to the first serious discussion between Kitty's parents as to her future, and to differences of opinion between them. The prince was for Levin, declaring that he could wish nothing better for Kitty. The princess, in the way women have of going round the question, maintained that Kitty was too young, that Levin had done nothing to prove that he had serious intentions, that Kitty was not particularly attracted to him, and so on; but she did not mention the principal point – that she wanted a better match for her daughter, and that she did not like Levin or understand him. When Levin abruptly departed, the princess was delighted and said to her husband triumphantly: 'You see, I was right!' When Vronsky came on the scene, she was still more delighted, confirmed in her opinion that Kitty was to make not simply a good, but a brilliant match.

In the mother's eyes there could be no comparison between Vronsky and Levin. She did not like Levin's strange, uncompromising opinions, his awkwardness in society (which she put down to conceit), or what she considered his wild sort of life in the country, busy with cattle and peasants. She also did not like the fact that, in love with her daughter, he frequented the house for six weeks on end, in apparent hesitation and looking round as though he were afraid he might be doing them too great an honour by making an offer, and did not realize that a man who constantly visits a house where there is a marriageable daughter ought to make his intentions clear. And then suddenly, without doing so, he had gone away. 'It is fortunate that he is not attractive enough for Kitty to have fallen in love with him,' thought her mother.

Vronsky satisfied all the mother's desires. He was very rich, intelligent, well-born, had a brilliant career before him in the army and at Court, and he was charming. Nothing better could be wished for.

Vronsky was openly attentive to Kitty at balls, danced with her, and was always coming to the house: so there could be no doubt of the seriousness of his intentions. For all that, Kitty's mother had felt anxious and worried the whole winter.

The princess's own marriage thirty years ago had been arranged by an aunt. The young man, about whom everything was known beforehand, had arrived, looked at his intended bride, and been looked at himself. The match-making aunt had ascertained and reported to each the other's impressions, which were favourable. Then, on the appointed day, the expected offer was made to her parents, and accepted. Everything had happened very easily and simply. At least, so it seemed to the princess. But with her two elder girls she had seen how far from easy and simple was the apparently ordinary matter of marrying off one's daughters. The anxiety she had lived through, what there had been to worry over, the money that had been spent, the clashes with her husband when her two elder daughters, Daria and Natalie, were married! Now, since the youngest had come out, she was going through the same fears and doubts, and having even worse disputes with her husband than she had had over the elder two. Like all fathers, the old prince was exceedingly punctilious where his daughters' reputation and honour were concerned. He was unreasonably jealous, especially over Kitty, his favourite, and at every step accused the princess of compromising the girl. The princess had grown used to this in respect of her elder daughters, but this time she felt that there was more justification for her husband's punctiliousness. She saw that of late years much had changed in society, that a mother's responsibilities had become even more difficult. She saw that girls of Kitty's age formed themselves into sets, attended lectures of some sort, made men friends, and drove out alone. Many of them did not curtsey and, worst of all, every one of them was firmly convinced that choosing a husband was her own and not her parents' affair. 'Marriages nowadays are not arranged as they used to be!' all these young girls thought and said, as did even some of their elders. But how exactly marriages were arranged now, the princess could not find out from anyone. The French custom, whereby the parents decided their daughters' fate, was not accepted; it was even condemned. The English custom of giving a girl complete independence was likewise rejected and would have been impossible in Russian society. The Russian way of employing a matchmaker was for some reason considered uncouth and ridiculed by everyone, including the princess herself. But how things should be done nobody knew. Everyone with whom the princess chanced to discuss the subject said the same thing: 'Mercy on us, it's high time in our day to put an end to all that old-fashioned business. It is the young people who are to marry, not their parents; let them arrange their own lives as they think best.' It was all very well for people without daughters to talk like that, but the princess knew that if she allowed Kitty freedom to enjoy the society of young men she ran the risk of her daughter falling in love with someone who had no intention of marrying, or who would not make her a good husband. And however much the princess was advised that the time had come when young people must arrange their future for themselves, she could not believe it, any more than she could believe that a loaded pistol could ever be the best toy for a five-year-old. And so she worried more about Kitty than she had about her elder daughters.

Just at present she was afraid that Vronsky might content himself with paying court to Kitty. She could see that Kitty was already in love with him, but tried to comfort herself with the thought that Vronsky was a man of honour and would not do such a thing. At the same time she knew that the freedom permitted in present-day society made it easy to turn a girl's head and that men in general took a light view of such a crime. The week before, Kitty had recounted to her mother a conversation she had had with Vronsky while they were dancing the mazurka. This conversation had partly reassured the princess; but it did not altogether allay her fears. Vronsky had told Kitty that both he and his brother were so used to obeying their mother that they never made up their minds to any important undertaking without consulting her. 'And just now I am absolutely longing for my mother's arrival from Petersburg,' he had said.

Kitty had repeated this without attaching any significance to the words. But her mother interpreted them differently. She knew that the old lady was expected any day, that she would approve of her son's choice; and, though she thought it strange that he did not make his offer for fear of vexing his mother, she was so anxious for the marriage itself, and more especially for relief from her cares, that she believed this. Bitterly as she felt the unhappiness of her eldest daughter, Dolly, who was thinking of leaving her husband, anxiety as to her youngest daughter's fate, now about to be decided, completely absorbed her attention. The reappearance of Levin that afternoon had added to her worries. She was afraid that her daughter, who had at one time seemed to have an affection for Levin, might refuse Vronsky out of exaggerated loyalty; and that Levin's arrival might complicate and delay matters now nearing conclusion.

'What is he doing – has he been here long?' the princess asked as they returned home, referring to Levin.

'He arrived to-day, *maman.*'

'There is one thing I want to say …' began the princess, and from the disturbed look on her face Kitty guessed what was coming.

'Mamma,' she said, flushing and turning quickly to her mother, 'please, please do not speak! I know – I know all about it.'

She wanted what her mother wanted, but the motives underlying her mother's desire offended her.

'I only want to say that to raise hopes …'

'Mamma, dearest, for heaven's sake, don't speak. It is so dreadful to talk about it.'

'Very well, I won't,' said the mother, seeing the tears in her daughter's eyes. 'But there is just one thing, my love: you have promised to have no secrets from me. You won't, will you?'

'Never, Mamma, none,' replied Kitty, blushing a little and looking her mother straight in the face. 'But I have nothing to tell you at present. I ... I ... if I wanted to, I should not know what to say or how ... I do not know ...'

'No, with those eyes she could never be untruthful,' thought the mother, smiling at her agitation and happiness. The princess smiled to think how important and momentous what was going on in Kitty's heart must appear to her, poor child.

13

DURING the interval between dinner and the arrival of the guests, Kitty felt as a young soldier feels before going into action. Her heart throbbed violently and she could not keep her thoughts fixed on anything.

She felt that this evening, when the two men would meet for the first time, must be the turning-point in her life. And she kept picturing them to herself, first individually, then both together. When she thought of the past, she lingered with pleasure and tenderness on the memories of her relations with Levin. Memories of childhood and of Levin's friendship with her dead brother lent a peculiar poetic charm to her relationship with him. His love for her, of which she felt certain, was flattering and delightful, and she could think of Levin with a light heart. But something uneasy clouded her thoughts of Vronsky, though he was all a well-bred man-of-the-world could be, as if there were a false note – not in him, he was very simple and nice, but in herself; whereas with Levin she felt quite natural and untroubled. On the other hand, directly she started to imagine the future with Vronsky, a dazzling vision of happiness rose up before her, while with Levin the future seemed misty.

Going upstairs to dress for the evening and looking into the mirror, she noticed joyfully that this was one of her good days and that she was at her best, which she needed to be for what lay before her. She felt outwardly serene and that her movements were free and graceful.

At half-past seven, as soon as she got into the drawing-room, the footman announced: 'Constantine Dmitrich Levin!' The princess was still in her room and the prince had not yet come down. 'So be it,' thought Kitty, and the blood rushed to her heart. Glancing at the mirror, she was appalled at her pallor.

She felt certain now that he had come early on purpose to find her alone and make her an offer. And only then for the first time the whole thing appeared to her in a different and entirely new light. Only then did she realize that the question – with whom would she be happy, which was the man she loved – did not concern herself alone but that in a moment she would have to hurt a man she cared for. And hurt him cruelly. Why? Because the dear man loved her, was in love with her. But it could not be helped. What must be, must be.

'Oh God, must I tell him myself?' she thought. 'What shall I say to him now? Must I really tell him that I do not love him? That would not be true. So what am I to say to him? That I love someone else? No, that is impossible! I'm going away, going away.'

She had reached the door when she heard his step. 'No, it would be dishonourable! What have I to be afraid of? I have done nothing wrong. Come what may, I will tell the truth. Besides, one can't feel embarrassed with him. Here he is,' she said to herself, seeing his powerful, diffident figure before her and his shining eyes fixed on her. She looked straight into his face, as though imploring him to spare her, and gave him her hand.

'I don't think I have come at the right time. I am too early,' he said, looking round the empty drawing-room. When he saw that his hopes were realized, that there was nothing to prevent him from speaking, his face clouded over.

'Oh no,' said Kitty, and sat down at a table.

'But this was just what I wanted, to find you alone,' he began, without sitting down or looking at her, lest he lost courage.

'Mamma will be down in a minute. She got very tired yesterday. Yesterday ...' She talked on, not knowing what her lips were saying, and not taking her supplicating, tender eyes off him.

He glanced at her; she blushed and ceased speaking.

'I told you I did not know whether I should be here long ... that it depended on you ...'

She drooped her head lower and lower, not knowing how she would reply to what was coming.

'That it depended on you,' he repeated. 'I meant ... I meant ... I came to say this ... be my wife!' he finished, hardly knowing what he

61

said; but, feeling that the worst was out, he stopped short and looked at her.

She was breathing heavily, not looking at him. She was enraptured. Her heart was bursting with happiness. She had never expected that his declaration of love would have such a powerful effect on her. But this lasted only for a second. She remembered Vronsky. She lifted her clear, honest eyes to Levin and, seeing his desperate face, replied hastily:

'No, that cannot be ... forgive me.'

A moment ago and how near she had been to him, how full of consequence to his life! And how aloof and far-away she had become now.

'It was bound not to be,' he said, without looking at her.

He bowed and turned to leave.

14

BUT at that moment the princess came in. She looked horrified at finding them alone together and at seeing their troubled faces. Levin bowed to her and said nothing. Kitty sat silent with downcast eyes. 'Thank Heaven, she has refused him,' thought the mother, and her face broke into the usual smile with which she greeted her Thursday evening visitors. She sat down and started asking Levin about his life in the country. He too sat down, until the arrival of other guests should enable him to slip away unnoticed.

Five minutes later Kitty's friend the Countess Nordston, married the previous winter, was announced. She was a thin, highly-strung, ailing woman with brilliant black eyes and a sallow complexion. She was fond of Kitty, and her affection, like that of every married woman for a young girl, expressed itself in a desire to see Kitty married in accordance with her own ideal of happiness; so she wanted her to marry Vronsky. She had always disliked Levin, whom she had often met at the Shcherbatskys' in the early part of the winter. Her invariable and favourite pursuit when they met consisted in making fun of him.

'I love it when he looks down at me from the height of his dignity, or breaks off his learned conversation with me because I am too stupid for it, or when he condescends to me. I simply love it. He to condescend! I am very glad he cannot stand me,' she would say of him.

She was right: Levin really could not bear her and despised her for the very thing she was proud of and that put her in conceit with herself – her highly-strung temperament and delicate contempt and disregard for everything coarse and earthy.

The relations between the Countess Nordston and Levin were such as are often encountered in society, when two people, while remaining outwardly on friendly terms, despise each other to such an extent that they are incapable of considering each other seriously or even of giving or taking offence.

The Countess Nordston pounced upon Levin at once.

'Ah, Constantine Dmitrich! Back again in our corrupt Babylon!' she said, holding out her tiny, yellow hand and remembering that at the beginning of the winter he had likened Moscow to Babylon. 'Well, is Babylon reformed or have you been corrupted?' she added, glancing round at Kitty with a simper.

'I am greatly flattered, Countess, that you remember my words so well,' responded Levin, who had had time to recover himself, instantly assuming his usual banteringly hostile tone towards her. 'Decidedly, they make a strong impression on you.'

'Of course! I note down everything you say. Well, Kitty, have you been skating again?' And she began talking to Kitty.

Awkward as it would have been for Levin to leave just then, he would have preferred to be guilty of this awkwardness rather than stay for the rest of the evening watching Kitty, who glanced at him now and again, but avoided catching his eye. He was about to rise when the princess, noticing his silence, turned to him.

'Shall you be long in Moscow? But of course you are busy with your *Zemstvo* and cannot be away long.'

'No, Princess, I am not on the *Zemstvo* now,' he said. 'I have come up for a few days.'

'What is the matter with him?' wondered the Countess Nordston, scrutinizing his stern, grave face. 'Why doesn't he launch into one of his tirades? But I'll draw him out. I love making a fool of him before Kitty, and so I will!

'Constantine Dmitrich,' she began, 'do explain to me, please – you know all about such things – how it is that at home in our village of Kaluga the peasants and their womenfolk have spent their all on drink and now pay us nothing? What is the meaning of that? You are always so full of praise for the peasants.'

At this point another lady entered the room and Levin rose.

'Excuse me, Countess, but I really know nothing about it and cannot give you any explanation,' he said, taking stock of an officer coming in behind the lady.

'This must be Vronsky,' he thought, and looked at Kitty to make sure. Her eyes had involuntarily lighted up at the sight of Vronsky, and one glance from them told Levin that she loved this man. He was as certain of it as if she had said so in so many words. But what kind of a man was he?

Now – for better for worse – Levin could not but remain. He must find out what sort of a man it was that she loved.

Some people when they meet a successful rival, no matter in what, instantly shut their eyes to everything good in him and see only what is bad. Others, on the contrary, endeavour above all to discover in their fortunate rival the qualities which won him success and with an aching heart seek only the good in him. Levin belonged to the latter class. But he had no difficulty in finding what was good and attractive in Vronsky. It was apparent at the first glance. Vronsky was a dark, squarely-built man of medium height, with an exceptionally tranquil and firm expression on his good-natured, handsome face. Everything about his head and figure, from the closely-cropped black hair and freshly-shaven chin to the loosely fitting, brand-new uniform, was simple and at the same time elegant. Having made way for the lady who had come in, Vronsky went up to the princess and then to Kitty.

As he approached Kitty, his fine eyes began to shine with especial tenderness and, bowing carefully and respectfully over her, with a faint, happy, and (so it seemed to Levin) quietly triumphant smile, he held out his small broad hand.

After he had greeted and said a few words to everyone, he sat down without once glancing at Levin, who had not taken his eyes off him.

'Let me introduce you,' said the princess, indicating Levin. 'Constantine Dmitrich Levin, Count Alexei Kirillovich Vronsky.'

Vronsky got up and, looking affably into Levin's eyes, shook hands with him.

'I believe I was to have dined with you earlier this winter,' he said, with his frank. open smile, 'but you had unexpectedly left for the country.'

'Constantine Dmitrich despises and hates town and us townspeople,' said the Countess Nordston.

'My words must make a strong impression on you, you remember them so well,' said Levin; and then, remembering that he had made the same remark before, he reddened.

Vronsky looked from one to the other and smiled.

'And do you live in the country the whole time?' he asked. 'I should think it must be dull in winter?'

'No, not if one has work to do; besides, one is not dull in one's own company,' replied Levin brusquely.

'I like the country,' said Vronsky, noticing but affecting not to notice Levin's tone.

'But I hope, Count, you would not consent to live in the country always,' said Countess Nordston.

'I do not know. I have never tried it for long. I had a curious experience once,' he went on. 'I never felt so homesick for the country – Russian country, with bast shoes and peasants – as I did when I was spending a winter with my mother in Nice. Nice is dull in itself, you know. And indeed, Naples and Sorrento are all right only for a short stay, and even they make one long for Russia, particularly for the countryside. They seem to ...'

He talked on, obviously saying whatever came into his head and directing his quiet, friendly gaze now at Kitty, now at Levin.

Noticing that the Countess Nordston wanted to speak, he stopped without finishing what he had begun, and listened attentively to her.

The conversation did not flag for a moment, so that the old princess, who always kept two heavy guns in reserve – classical versus modern education and universal military service – had no need to move either of them up; and Countess Nordston had no opportunity of chaffing Levin.

Levin wanted to join in the general conversation, but found it impossible and kept saying to himself, 'Now I can go,' yet stayed on, as if waiting for something.

The conversation touched on table-rapping and spiritualism, and the Countess Nordston, who believed in spiritualism, began to describe the miracles she had witnessed.

'Oh, Countess, you must take me next time. For pity's sake take me with you! I have never seen anything supernatural, though I am always on the look-out for it,' said Vronsky with a smile.

'Very well, then, next Saturday,' replied Countess Nordston. 'But do you believe in it, Constantine Dmitrich?' she asked Levin.

'Why do you ask me? You know exactly what I shall say.'

'But I want to hear your opinion.'

'My opinion,' replied Levin, 'is only that this table-rapping proves that our so-called educated class is no better than the peasants. They believe in the evil eye and spells and witchcraft, while we ...'

'Oh, then, you don't believe in it?'

'I cannot believe in it, Countess.'

'But if I have seen it myself?'

'Peasant women say they have seen goblins.'

'So you think I am not telling the truth?'

And she laughed a mirthless laugh.

'Oh no, Masha, Constantine Dmitrich only said he could not believe in spiritualism,' said Kitty, blushing for Levin; and Levin, seeing this, felt still more exasperated and would have answered, but Vronsky with his open, cheerful smile hurried to the rescue of the conversation, which was threatening to become disagreeable.

'But don't you think there might be something in it?' he asked. 'We admit the existence of electricity, of which we know nothing, so why should there not exist some new force, as yet unknown to us, which ...'

'When electricity was discovered,' broke in Levin quickly, 'it was only the phenomenon that was discovered, and its origin and effects were unknown. Centuries passed before anyone thought of applying it. But the spiritualists started with tables writing for them and spirits appearing to them, and only afterwards began saying that it was an unknown force.'

Vronsky listened carefully to Levin, as was his wont, and appeared to be interested in what he said.

'Yes, but the spiritualists say we don't know at present what this force is, but there is a force and these are the conditions in which it functions. Let the scientists find out what the force is. No, I don't see why there should not be a new force, if it ...'

'Why, because with electricity,' interrupted Levin again, 'every time you rub resin against wool you invariably produce a recognized phenomenon; but with spiritualism you do not always get results, and so it cannot be regarded as a natural phenomenon.'

Probably feeling that the conversation was becoming too serious for a drawing-room, Vronsky made no rejoinder, but by way of changing the subject he smiled gaily and turned to the ladies.

'Suppose we try now, Countess,' he began; but Levin wanted to finish explaining what was in his mind.

'I think,' he continued, 'that this attempt on the part of the spiritualists to explain their marvels by some sort of new force is most unsuccessful. They boldly talk of a spiritual force and yet want to subject it to material experiment.'

They were all waiting for him to finish and he was conscious of it.

'And I think you would make a first-rate medium,' said the Countess Nordston. 'There is something so ecstatic about you.'

Levin opened his mouth to reply but blushed and said nothing.

'Do let us try table-turning at once, please, Princess Kitty,' said Vronsky. 'May we, Princess?' he asked her mother and stood up, looking round for a table.

Kitty got up to fetch a table, and as she passed in front of Levin their eyes met. She felt for him with all her heart, the more so since she was pitying him for suffering of which she herself was the cause. 'Forgive me if you can,' pleaded her look. 'I am so happy.'

'I hate them all, and you, and myself,' Levin's eyes replied, and he took up his hat. But he was not destined to escape. Just as the others were arranging themselves round the table and Levin was on the point of leaving, the old prince entered and, after greeting the ladies, turned to Levin.

'Ah,' he cried delightedly. 'Have you been here long? I did not even know you were in town. Very glad to see you.'

He embraced Levin and talking to him did not notice Vronsky, who had risen and was quietly waiting till the prince should turn to him.

Kitty felt that after what had happened her father's cordiality oppressed Levin. She saw, too, how coldly her father responded at last to Vronsky's bow, and that Vronsky looked at him in good-natured perplexity, vainly trying to understand how and why anyone could fail to be friendlily disposed towards himself, and she flushed.

'Prince, let us have Constantine Dmitrich,' said Countess Nordston. 'We want to try an experiment.'

'What experiment? Table-turning? Well, you must excuse me, ladies and gentlemen, but to my mind playing quoits is more amusing,' said the old prince, looking at Vronsky and guessing that the table-turning was his idea. 'There is some sense in that, anyway.'

Vronsky turned his steady gaze upon the old prince in astonishment

and, with a faint smile, at once began talking to the Countess Nordston about the big ball that was to take place the following week.

'I hope you will be there?' he said to Kitty.

As soon as the old prince had left him, Levin got quietly away, and
the last impression he carried with him was of Kitty's smiling, happy
face as she answered Vronsky's inquiry about the ball.

15

At the end of the evening Kitty told her mother of her conversation
with Levin, and, in spite of all the pity she felt for Levin, the thought
that she had received an *offer* delighted her. She had no doubt that she
had acted rightly. Yet she lay in bed for a long while unable to sleep.
She kept seeing Levin's sad face with his kind eyes looking dejectedly
from under his knit brows, as he stood listening to her father and
watching her and Vronsky. And she felt so sorry for him that tears
started into her eyes. But she at once began to think of the other, who
had replaced Levin in her heart. She pictured vividly to herself his
strong, manly face, his quiet serenity, and the kindliness he showed to
everyone. She remembered the love the man she loved bore her, and
joy came back to her soul, and with a smile of happiness she put her
head on the pillow. 'I'm sorry, I'm sorry; but what could I do? It's
not my fault,' she said to herself; but an inner voice spoke otherwise.
Whether she repented of having encouraged Levin or of having refused him, she did not know. But her happiness was troubled with
misgivings. 'Lord, have mercy on us; Lord, have mercy on us; Lord,
have mercy on us!' she repeated to herself till she fell asleep.

Meanwhile, downstairs in the prince's little study, her parents were
having one of their frequent scenes concerning their favourite
daughter.

'What? I'll tell you what!' cried the prince, waving his arms and
then wrapping his squirrel-lined dressing-gown round him again.
'You have no pride, no dignity; and so you bring disgrace and ruin
on your daughter by this vulgar, idiotic match-making!'

'But for heaven's sake, Prince, what have I done?' the princess was
saying, almost in tears.

Pleased and happy after her talk with her daughter, she had come to
say good-night to her husband as usual and, though she had not intended to tell him of Levin's proposal and Kitty's refusal, still she

hinted to the prince that she fancied things were practically settled with Vronsky and that he would declare himself as soon as his mother arrived. And thereupon, at these words, the prince had suddenly flared up and started to shower abuse on her.

'What have you done? Why this: first of all, you are doing your best to hook an eligible young man, which will be the talk of Moscow, and with reason. If you give a party, then you ought to invite everyone, and not pick out possible suitors. Invite all the young bucks,' (as the prince called the young men of Moscow) 'get in a pianist and let them dance. But don't have the sort of thing we had to-night – don't hunt up suitors. It nauseates me, absolutely nauseates me; and you've gone on until you've turned the girl's head. Levin is a thousand times the better man. As for that Petersburg dandy – they turn them out by the dozen, all alike and all trash. And even if he were a prince of the blood, there would be no need for my daughter to run after him.'

'But what have I done?'

'Why, you've ...' the prince began crying wrathfully.

'I know this much – if I were to listen to you,' interrupted the princess, 'we should never see our daughter married at all. We might as well go and live in the country.'

'It would be better if we did!'

'Stop a moment. Do I try to catch them? No, certainly not. But a young man, and a very nice young man, has fallen in love with her, and she, I fancy ...'

'Oh yes, you fancy! And what if she were in love with him and he with no more intention of marrying than I have! ... My eyes boggled! ... Ah! spiritualism! Ah! Nice! Ah! the ball!' And in imitation of his wife the prince curtsied at each word. 'And this is how we shall make our Kitty unhappy – how she will get it into her head to ...'

'Why should you suppose any such thing?'

'I do not suppose, I know. We have eyes for these things, if women haven't. I see one man who has serious intentions – that is Levin; and I see a conceited popinjay who is only amusing himself.'

'Oh well, once you get an idea into your head ...'

'You will remember my words when it's too late, just as you did with our poor Dolly.'

'Very well, very well, we won't talk about it,' the princess stopped him, remembering the unhappy Dolly.

'By all means, and good-night!'

And making the sign of the cross over each other, husband and wife kissed and said good-night, both of them feeling, however, that they remained of their own opinion.

The princess had at first been quite certain that the evening had settled Kitty's fate and that there could be no doubt as to Vronsky's intentions; but her husband's words disturbed her When she reached her room she thought with terror of what the future might have in store, and, just as Kitty had done, repeated several times in her heart, 'Lord, have mercy on us; Lord, have mercy on us; Lord, have mercy on us!'

16

VRONSKY had never had a real home-life. In her youth his mother had been a brilliant society woman, and during her husband's life-time, and still more after his death, had had many love affairs, which everyone knew about. He hardly remembered his father, and he had been educated in the Corps of Pages.

He left the Corps a very young and brilliant officer, and at once entered the circle of wealthy Petersburg army men. Although he did go occasionally into Petersburg society, his love affairs had hitherto been outside it.

In Moscow, after his luxurious and coarse life in Petersburg, he experienced for the first time the charm of friendship with a sweet, innocent girl of his own class, who cared for him. It never entered his head that there could be any harm in his relations with Kitty. At balls he danced mainly with her. He was a constant visitor at her home. He talked to her as people commonly do talk in society – all sorts of nonsense, but nonsense to which he could not help attaching a special meaning in her case. Although he never said anything to her which he could not have said before everybody, he felt that she was growing more and more dependent upon him, and the more he felt this, the better he liked it and the more tender became his feelings for her. He did not know that his mode of behaviour towards Kitty had a label of its own, that it was courting a young girl with no intention of marrying her, and that such courting was one of the worst forms of conduct common among brilliant young men like himself. He thought he was the first to discover this pleasure, and he was enjoying his discovery.

If he could have heard the conversation between her parents that evening, if he could have put himself in her family's place and learned that Kitty would be unhappy if he did not marry her, he would have been greatly astonished and not believed it. He could not believe that what gave such great and enjoyable pleasure to himself, and above all to her, could be wrong. Still less could he have believed that there was any obligation to marry.

Marriage had never presented itself to him as a possibility. Not only did he dislike family life but, in accordance with the views current in the bachelor world in which he lived, he regarded a family, and especially a husband, as something alien, inimical and, worst of all – ridiculous. But although Vronsky had no suspicion of what Kitty's parents were saying, he left the Shcherbatskys' house with the feeling that the secret spiritual bond which existed between him and Kitty had grown so much stronger that evening that some step would have to be taken. But what step could or should be taken, he could not imagine.

'What is so exquisite,' he thought on his way from the Shcherbatskys, bearing away with him, as he always did, a delicious feeling of purity and freshness (partly due to the fact that he had not smoked all the evening), and with it a new sensation of tenderness at her love for him – 'what is so exquisite is that not a word has been said by me or by her, yet we understand each other so perfectly in this subtle language of looks and intonations that to-night she told me more plainly than ever before that she loves me. And how sweetly, simply, and, most of all, trustfully! I feel myself better, purer. I feel I have a heart and that there is much that is good in me. Those dear, loving eyes when she said: "Indeed I do …"'

'Well, and what now? Nothing, of course. I am all right and she is all right.' And he began wondering where he should finish the evening.

He passed in review the places he might go to. 'The Club: a game of bezique and a bottle of champagne with Ignatov? No. The Château des Fleurs – I should find Oblonsky there, and French songs and the cancan. No, I am sick of them. That's what I like about the Shcherbatskys – they uplift me. I shall go home.' He went straight to his room at Dussot's, ordered supper, after which he undressed and had scarcely laid his head on the pillow before he was sound asleep.

17

AT eleven o'clock next morning Vronsky drove to the railway station to meet his mother from Petersburg; and the first person he saw on the great flight of steps was Oblonsky, who was expecting his sister by the same train.

'Hullo, your excellency!' cried Oblonsky. 'Who is it you are meeting?'

'My mother,' Vronsky replied, smiling, as everyone did who met Oblonsky. They shook hands and walked up the steps together. 'She is arriving from Petersburg.'

'And I was looking out for you till two last night. Where did you go after the Shcherbatskys?'

'Home,' replied Vronsky. 'To tell you the truth, I felt in such an agreeable frame of mind when I left the Shcherbatskys' that I did not want to go anywhere else.'

> ' "By the mark of your steed
>   I can tell his fine breed,
>   And a young man in love – by his eyes," '

declaimed Oblonsky, just as he had done earlier to Levin.

Vronsky smiled, as much as to say that he did not deny it, but immediately changed the subject.

'And whom are you meeting?' he asked.

'I? I've come to meet a pretty woman,' said Oblonsky.

'Oh, indeed!'

'*Honi soit qui mal y pense!* My sister Anna.'

'Oh, Karenin's wife?' said Vronsky.

'You know her, don't you?'

'I think so. Or perhaps not ... I really don't remember,' replied Vronsky absent-mindedly, the name Karenin vaguely evoking an impression of something stiff and tedious.

'But surely you must know Alexei Alexandrovich, my illustrious brother-in-law. All the world knows him.'

'Yes, I know him by repute and by sight. I know that he is clever, learned, and rather pious ... But you know he is not ... *not in my line*,' he concluded in English.

'Yes, he's a very remarkable man; a little on the conservative side, but a good man,' observed Oblonsky, 'a good man.'

'Well, so much the better for him,' said Vronsky, smiling. 'Ah, here you are,' he went on, turning to a tall old footman of his mother's, standing at the door. 'Come in here.'

Besides liking Oblonsky, as everyone did, Vronsky had of late felt specially drawn to him because in his imagination he connected him with Kitty.

'Well, what do you say? Shall we give a supper on Sunday for the *diva*?' he asked with a smile, taking Oblonsky's arm.

'By all means. I will collect subscriptions. Oh, by the way, did you meet my friend Levin yesterday?' asked Oblonsky.

'Yes, indeed. Only he left pretty early.'

'He is a splendid fellow,' pursued Oblonsky. 'Didn't you think so?'

'I don't know why it is, but in all Muscovites – present company excepted, of course –' he put in jocosely, 'there is something brusque. They are always getting up on their hind legs and losing their tempers, as if they want to stir people up ...'

'Yes, that's true enough, you are right ...' said Oblonsky, laughing good-humouredly.

'Will the train soon be in?' Vronsky asked a railway official.

'She's signalled,' answered the man.

The approach of the train was made more and more evident by a bustle of preparation in the station, the rush of porters, the appearance of gendarmes and attendants, and the arrival of people meeting the train. Through the frosty vapour could be seen workmen in short sheepskins and soft felt boots crossing the network of rails. The whistle of an engine and the rumble of something heavy could be heard in the distance.

'No,' said Oblonsky, who felt a great inclination to tell Vronsky of Levin's intentions concerning Kitty. 'No, you don't quite appreciate my Levin. He's a very nervous person and sometimes disagreeable, it is true, but he can also be very charming. He has such an honest, straightforward nature, and a heart of gold. But yesterday there were special reasons,' continued Oblonsky with a meaning smile, quite forgetting the genuine sympathy he had felt for his friend the day before and now feeling the same sympathy, only this time for Vronsky. 'Yes, there were reasons why he could not help being either particularly happy or particularly unhappy.'

Vronsky stood still and asked point blank:

'What do you mean? Did he propose to your *belle-sœur* last night?'

73

'He may have,' said Oblonsky. 'I fancied something of the sort was in the wind yesterday. Yes, if he left early and was out of spirits too, it must mean ... He has been in love with her for so long, and I feel very sorry for him.'

'So that's it! ... But I should have thought she could make a better match,' remarked Vronsky, expanding his chest and walking on again. 'However, I do not know him,' he added. 'Yes, that is a painful position. That's why most of us prefer our Claras, the women of the *demimonde*. If you don't succeed with them it only means you've not enough cash; but with the others it's our merits that are weighed in the balance. But here comes the train.'

Indeed, the engine was already whistling in the distance. Soon the platform began to vibrate as the train swung in; puffs of steam were driven downwards by the frosty air; slowly and rhythmically the piston of the middle wheel rose and extended; and the stooping, muffled figure of the engine-driver appeared, covered with hoar-frost. Behind the tender came the luggage-van, with a dog whining inside, gradually slowing down and making the platform shake more than ever. At last the passenger coaches jolted to a standstill.

A sprightly guard jumped out, blowing his whistle as he did so, and then one by one the impatient passengers began to get down: a guards officer, holding himself erect and looking severely about him; a nimble young tradesman with a bag and a merry smile; a peasant carrying a sack over his shoulder.

Standing beside Oblonsky, Vronsky watched the carriages and the passengers getting out, completely forgetting his mother. What he had just heard about Kitty excited and delighted him. Unconsciously he squared his shoulders and his eyes flashed. He felt like a conqueror.

'The Countess Vronsky is in that compartment,' said the sprightly guard, going up to Vronsky.

The guard's words roused Vronsky and reminded him of his mother and his approaching meeting with her. In the depths of his heart he had no great respect for his mother and, though not confessing as much to himself, did not love her; but in accordance with the ideas of his set and with his upbringing, he could not imagine treating her otherwise than dutifully and with the greatest respect, and the more outwardly dutiful and respectful he was, the less he respected and loved her in his heart.

18

VRONSKY followed the guard to the carriage, and at the door of the compartment had to stop and make way for a lady who was getting out. His experience as a man of the world told him at a glance that she belonged to the best society. He begged her pardon and was about to enter the carriage but felt he must have another look at her – not because of her beauty, not on account of the elegance and unassuming grace of her whole figure, but because of something tender and caressing in her lovely face as she passed him. As he looked round, she too turned her head. Her brilliant grey eyes, shadowed by thick lashes, gave him a friendly, attentive look, as though she were recognizing him, and then turned to the approaching crowd as if in search of someone. In that brief glance Vronsky had time to notice the suppressed animation which played over her face and flitted between her sparkling eyes and the slight smile curving her red lips. It was as though her nature were so brimming over with something that against her will it expressed itself now in a radiant look, now in a smile. She deliberately shrouded the light in her eyes but in spite of herself it gleamed in the faintly perceptible smile.

Vronsky stepped into the carriage. His mother, a wizened old lady with black eyes and ringlets, screwed up her eyes to scan her son and her thin lips smiled slightly. Getting up from her seat and passing her bag to her maid, she extended her little wrinkled hand to her son to kiss; then, lifting his head from her hand, she kissed him on the cheek.

'You got my telegram? You are quite well? That's a mercy.'

'Did you have a good journey?' asked her son, sitting down beside her and involuntarily listening to a woman's voice outside the door. He knew it was the voice of the lady he had met as he entered the coach.

'All the same I do not agree with you,' said the lady's voice.

'That's the Petersburg way of looking at it, madame.'

'Not at all, simply a woman's way,' she replied.

'Well, well, allow me to kiss your hand.'

'Good-bye, Ivan Petrovich. And would you see if my brother is here and send him to me,' said the lady right at the door now and coming back into the compartment again.

'Well, have you found your brother?' asked Vronsky's mother, addressing the lady.

Vronsky realized now that this was Madame Karenin.

'Your brother is here,' he said, rising. 'Excuse me, I did not recognize you. Our acquaintance was so short,' he said with a bow, 'that I am sure you do not remember me.'

'Oh yes,' she replied, 'I should have known you – your mother and I seem to have talked of nothing but you the whole journey,' she said, at last allowing the animation which she had been trying to suppress reveal itself in a smile. 'But still no sign of my brother.'

'Do go and call him, Aliosha,' said the old countess.

Vronsky stepped out on to the platform and shouted:

'Oblonsky! Here!'

But Madame Karenin did not wait: as soon as she caught sight of her brother she jumped down from the carriage with a light, sure step. Directly her brother reached her, she flung her left arm round his neck with a gesture that struck Vronsky by its decision and grace, and drawing him quickly to her, kissed him warmly. Vronsky did not take his eyes off her and, without knowing why, smiled. But recollecting that his mother was waiting for him, he went back into the carriage.

'She is very charming, isn't she?' said the countess of Madame Karenin. 'Her husband put her in with me and I was delighted to have her. We talked the whole way. So you, I hear ... *vous filez le parfait amour. Tant mieux, mon cher, tant mieux.*'*

'I do not know what you mean, *maman*,' replied her son coldly. 'Well, shall we go?'

Madame Karenin entered the carriage again to say good-bye to the countess.

'Well, Countess, you have met your son, and I my brother,' she said gaily. 'And I had come to the end of all my gossip and should have had nothing more to tell you.'

'Oh no,' said the countess, taking her hand. 'I could travel round the world with you and never be dull. You are one of those sweet women with whom it is nice to be silent as well as to talk. Now please don't fret over your son; you cannot expect never to be parted.'

Madame Karenin stood still, holding herself extremely erect, her eyes smiling.

'Anna Arkadyevna has a little son of eight, I believe it is,' explained

* ... are living love's young dream. Good, my dear, I'm very glad.

the countess, 'and this is the first time they have ever been parted, and she is fretting at having left him behind.'

'Yes, we have been talking about our sons the whole time, I of mine and the Countess of hers,' said Madame Karenin, and again a smile illumined her face, a caressing smile intended for him.

'It must have been very boring for you,' he said, promptly catching the ball of coquetry she had thrown him. But apparently she did not care to pursue the conversation in that strain, and she turned to the old countess:

'Thank you so much. The time has passed so quickly. Good-bye, Countess.'

'Good-bye, my dear,' replied the countess. 'Let me have a kiss of your pretty little face. I can speak plainly at my age, so let me confess that I have lost my heart to you.'

Stereotyped as the expression was, Madame Karenin obviously took it seriously and was delighted. She blushed, bent down slightly, and put her cheek to the countess's lips. Then she drew herself up again and, with the same smile hovering between lips and eyes, gave her hand to Vronsky. He pressed the little hand offered to him, and the energetic grip with which she boldly and vigorously shook his filled him with joy, as if it were something special. She walked rapidly away, carrying her rather full figure with extraordinary lightness.

'Very charming,' said the old countess.

Her son thought so too. His eyes followed her till her graceful form was out of sight, and still the smile lingered on his face. Through the carriage window he saw her go up to her brother, put her arm in his, and start talking eagerly to him about something – something which obviously had no connexion with him, Vronsky, and he found that vexing.

'Well, and how are you, *maman*, quite well?' he asked a second time, turning to his mother.

'Everything has been splendid. Alexandre was so good and Marie has grown very pretty. She is most interesting.'

And she began telling him of what lay nearest her heart – the christening of her grandson, for which she had gone to Petersburg, and the special favour shown her elder son by the Emperor.

'Here's Lavrenty,' said Vronsky, looking out of the window. 'Now we can go, if you like.'

The old majordomo, who had travelled with the countess, came to the carriage to announce that everything was ready, and the countess rose to go.

'Come, there is not much of a crowd now,' said Vronsky.

The maid took a handbag and the lapdog, the majordomo and a porter the other baggage. Vronsky gave his arm to his mother; but just as they were getting out of the carriage several men ran past with alarmed faces. The station-master too ran by in his strange coloured cap.

Obviously something unusual had happened. Passengers who had left the train were running back.

'What? … What? … Where? … Threw himself under! … Run over! …' people passing by the window were heard saying.

Oblonsky, with his sister on his arm, turned back. They too looked scared, and stopped by the carriage door to avoid the number of people.

The ladies got into the carriage, while Vronsky and Oblonsky followed the crowd to find out about the accident.

A guard, either drunk or too much muffled up against the bitter frost, had not heard the train shunting back and had been crushed.

Even before Vronsky and Oblonsky returned, the ladies heard the facts from the majordomo.

Oblonsky and Vronsky had both seen the mangled body. Oblonsky was visibly affected. His face was puckered up and he seemed ready to burst into tears.

'Oh, how horrible! Oh, Anna, if you had seen it! Oh, how horrible!' he kept saying.

Vronsky did not speak. His handsome face looked serious, but perfectly composed.

'Oh, if you had seen it, Countess,' Oblonsky was saying. 'And his wife was there … It was dreadful to see her! … She flung herself on the body. They say he was the sole support of a huge family. What a dreadful thing!'

'Is there nothing one could do for her?' said Madame Karenin in an agitated whisper.

Vronsky glanced at her and immediately left the carriage.

'I shan't be long, *maman*,' he said, looking round in the doorway.

When he returned a few minutes later Oblonsky was already chatting to the countess about the new *prima donna*, while the countess kept watching impatiently for her son to appear.

'We can be off now,' said Vronsky, coming in.

They went out together, Vronsky walking ahead with his mother, Madame Karenin and her brother following behind. At the exit the stationmaster overtook them and said to Vronsky:

'You gave my assistant two hundred roubles. Would you be so kind as to say whom you intended them for?'

'For the widow,' said Vronsky, shrugging his shoulders. 'I should have thought there was no need to ask.'

'You gave that?' cried Oblonsky from behind and, pressing his sister's arm, he added: 'Very kind, very kind! Isn't he a splendid fellow? My respects to you, Countess.'

And he and his sister waited, looking for her maid.

When they emerged from the station the Vronskys' carriage had already driven off. People coming out were still talking about the accident.

'What a terrible death!' said one gentleman as he passed them. 'They say he was cut in half.'

'On the contrary, I think it was the easiest of deaths – instantaneous,' remarked another.

'How is it they don't take proper precautions?' a third was saying.

Madame Karenin seated herself in the carriage and her brother noticed with surprise that her lips were trembling and that she had difficulty in keeping back her tears.

'What is the matter, Anna?' he asked, when they had driven a few hundred yards.

'It is a bad omen,' she said.

'What nonsense!' replied Oblonsky. 'You've come, that is the chief thing. You cannot imagine how I am counting on you.'

'Have you known Vronsky long?' she asked.

'Yes. You know we're hoping he will marry Kitty.'

'Indeed?' said Anna softly. 'Come now, let us talk about you,' she added, tossing her head as if she wished with a physical gesture to shake off something that troubled and oppressed her. 'Let us talk of your affairs. I got your letter and here I am.'

'Yes, all my hopes are on you,' said her brother.

'Well, tell me all about it.'

And Oblonsky began his story.

When they reached home, he helped his sister out of the carriage, pressed her hand with a sigh, and drove off to the court-house.

19

WHEN Anna entered, Dolly was sitting in the smaller drawing-room with a fair-haired, chubby little boy, already like his father, hearing his French lesson. As he read, the boy kept twisting and trying to pull off a button that was hanging by a thread from his jacket. His mother had several times taken his hand from it but the plump little hand always found its way back to the button. At last she pulled the button off and put it in her pocket.

'Keep your hands still, Grisha,' she said, and took up a coverlet which she had been working on for a long while and which she always turned to at trying times. She knitted with nervous fingers, counting the stitches. Although she had sent word to her husband the day before that it was nothing to her whether his sister came or not, she had made everything ready for Anna's arrival and was awaiting her anxiously.

Dolly was overwhelmed by her sorrow, was utterly swallowed up by it. Still she did not forget that Anna, her sister-in-law, was the wife of one of the most important personages in Petersburg and a *grande dame* of Petersburg society. And so she did not carry out her threat to her husband and ignore the fact that her sister-in-law was coming. 'After all, it is not Anna's fault,' thought Dolly. 'I know nothing but good of her, and she has never shown me anything but kindness and friendship.' True, as far as she could recall her impressions when she had visited the Karenins in Petersburg, she had not liked their home: there was something artificial in the whole framework of their family life. 'But why should I not receive her? So long as she does not take it into her head to try and console me!' thought Dolly. 'Consolation and exhortation and Christian forgiveness – I have gone over all that a thousand times and it's no use.'

All these last days Dolly had been alone with the children. She did not want to talk about her troubles but with them on her mind she could not talk of outside matters. She knew that in one way or another she would tell Anna everything, and she alternately looked forward to telling her and was irritated at the idea of having to speak of her own humiliation to his sister, and hear the set phrases of exhortation and consolation.

She was watching the clock, on the look-out for Anna every

minute, but, as often happens, missed the moment when her visitor arrived and did not hear the bell.

At the sound of light footsteps and the rustle of a skirt in the doorway, she looked round, and her haggard face unconsciously expressed not gladness but surprise. She got up and embraced her sister-in-law.

'What, here already?' she said, kissing her.

'Dolly, I am so glad to see you!'

'I am glad too,' said Dolly with a feeble smile, trying to make out from Anna's expression whether she had been told. 'She must know,' she thought, noticing the look of sympathy on Anna's face.

'Come along, let me take you to your room,' she went on, anxious to defer the moment of confidences as long as possible.

'Is this Grisha? Heavens, how he has grown!' exclaimed Anna, kissing him without taking her eyes off Dolly. Then she paused and flushed a little. 'No, please let us stay here.'

She took off her kerchief and her hat. A lock of her black hair, which was a mass of curls, got caught up and she shook her head to free it.

'Oh, how radiantly happy and well you look!' said Dolly, with a touch of envy.

'Do I? ... Yes,' said Anna. 'Gracious, Tanya! You're the same age as my Seriozha,' she added, turning to the little girl who had run into the room. Anna took her in her arms and kissed her. 'What a sweet child, perfectly sweet! Let me see them all.'

She could remember not only all their names but exactly how old the children were, their characters, and what ailments they had had; Dolly could not help being touched.

'Let us go and see them, then,' she said. 'It is a pity Vassya's asleep.'

After they had looked at the children they returned to the drawing-room and, alone now, sat down to the table for coffee. Anna drew the tray towards her, then pushed it aside.

'Dolly,' she said, 'he has told me.'

Dolly looked coldly at Anna. She was expecting some conventional expression of sympathy, but Anna said nothing of the kind.

'Dolly, my dear,' she began, 'I do not want to speak up for him, or try to console you; that would be impossible. But, dearest, I am just sorry for you - sorry with all my heart!'

Under their thick lashes her brilliant eyes suddenly filled with tears.

She moved closer to her sister-in-law and took her hand in her own strong little one. Dolly did not draw back, but her face kept its frigid expression.

'It is impossible to comfort me,' she said. 'Everything is finished now, after what has happened – it is all over!'

And directly she had said this, her face suddenly softened. Anna lifted Dolly's dry, thin hand, kissed it and said:

'But what is to be done, Dolly, what is to be done? What is the best thing to do in this dreadful situation? That is what we must consider.'

'Everything is at an end and there's nothing more to be said,' Dolly replied. 'And the worst of it is, you see, that I cannot cast him off: there are the children – I am tied. But I cannot live with him: it is torture for me to see him.'

'Dolly, my darling, he told me, but I want to hear it from you. Tell me all about it.'

Dolly looked at her inquiringly.

Unfeigned sympathy and love were written on Anna's face.

'If you like,' she said all at once. 'But I shall begin at the beginning. You know how I was married. With *maman*'s upbringing, I was not merely innocent, I was stupid. I knew nothing. People say, I know, that husbands tell their wives about their past lives, but Stiva ... Stepan Arkadyevich,' she corrected herself, 'told me nothing. You will hardly believe it, but until this happened I supposed I was the only woman he had ever loved. I lived thinking that for eight years. You see, it not only never entered my head to suspect him of being unfaithful to me – I believed such a thing to be impossible, and then ... imagine what it was like with such ideas to find out all this horror, all this vileness. Try to understand. To be fully convinced of one's happiness, and suddenly ...' continued Dolly, holding back her sobs, 'to find a letter ... his letter to his mistress, my children's governess. No, it is too horrible!' She hurriedly drew out her handkerchief and hid her face in it. 'I can imagine being carried away by one's feelings,' she went on after a pause, 'but deliberately, slyly deceiving me ... and with whom? ... To go on being my husband together with her ... that is horrible! You cannot understand ...'

'Oh yes, I do understand! I do understand, Dolly dear, I do,' said Anna, pressing her hand.

'And do you imagine he realizes all the horror of my position?' continued Dolly. 'Not a bit! He is happy and contented.'

'Oh no!' Anna interrupted quickly. 'He's in a pitiful state, weighed down by remorse ...'

'Is he capable of remorse?' broke in Dolly, scrutinizing her sister-in-law's face.

'Yes. I know him. I could not look at him without feeling sorry for him. We both know him. He's good-hearted, but he is proud, too, and now he feels so humiliated. What moved me most of all ...' (and here Anna guessed what would touch Dolly most) 'he is tormented by two things: that he's ashamed for the children's sake and that, loving you – yes, yes, loving you more than anything else in the world,' she went on hurriedly, to prevent Dolly from objecting, 'he has hurt and made you suffer. "No, no, she won't be able to forgive me," he keeps saying.'

Dolly gazed beyond her sister-in-law, listening thoughtfully.

'Yes,' she said, 'I realize that his position must be a terrible one – it is worse for the guilty than the innocent – if he knows he is the cause of all the misery. But how am I to forgive him, how can I be his wife again after her? For me to live with him now would be torture, just because I cherish my past love for him ...'

And sobs cut short her words.

But, as though by design, every time she was softened she began to speak again of what lacerated her.

'Of course, she's young, she's pretty,' she went on. 'You see, Anna, my youth and good looks are gone – taken by whom? By him and his children. I have served my day and all I had went in that service, and now of course any fresh, commonplace creature has more charm for him. Very likely they discussed me when they were together, or, worse, avoided mention of me. You understand?' Again her eyes burned with bitterness. 'And after all that he will come and tell me ... What, and am I to believe him? Never! No, it is all over, everything that once was a comfort to me, a reward for my labours, my sufferings ... all gone. Would you believe it, I was teaching Grisha just now: it used to be a joy to me, now it is torture. What is the good of toiling and striving? What is the use of having children? The terrible thing is that all at once my heart has turned, and instead of love and tenderness, I feel nothing but hatred for him – yes, hatred. I could kill him and ...'

'Dolly, dearest! I understand, but don't torture yourself. You are so distressed, so upset that you see many things in the wrong light.'

Dolly grew calmer, and for a couple of minutes the two were silent.

'What am I to do? Think, Anna, and help me. I have gone over and over it all and can see no way out.'

Anna could not think of anything, but her sister-in-law's every word, every expression went straight to her heart.

'One thing I would say,' began Anna. 'I am his sister, I know his character, that capacity of his for forgetting everything, everything' (she made a gesture with her hand in front of her forehead), 'his capacity for letting himself be completely carried away by his feelings; but he can repent just as wholeheartedly, too. He cannot believe, cannot conceive now how he could have acted as he did.'

'Yes, he understands, he understood!' interrupted Dolly. 'But I ... you are forgetting me ... does that make it any easier for me?'

'Wait. When he told me, I confess I did not realize all the awfulness of your position. I only saw his side, and that the family was disrupted. I felt sorry for him, but now that I have talked to you, as a woman, I see something else: I see your agony, and I can't tell you how sorry I am for you! But Dolly, dearest, I fully appreciate your sufferings, only there is one thing I do not know: I do not know ... I do not know how much love there still is in your heart for him. You alone know whether there is enough for you to be able to forgive. If there is, then forgive him!'

'No,' Dolly was beginning, but Anna stopped her, kissing her hand once more.

'I know the world better than you do,' she said. 'I know how men like Stiva look at things. You speak of his talking about you to *her*. No such thing. Men may be unfaithful but their homes, their wives are sacred to them. Somehow they still look on these women with contempt and do not let them interfere with their feeling for their family. They draw a sort of line that can't be crossed between them and their families. I do not understand it, but it is so.'

'Yes, but he has kissed her ...'

'Dolly, listen, darling. I saw Stiva when he was in love with you. I remember the time when he used to come to me and talk about you with tears in his eyes – what poetry and high ideals you were for him – and I know that the longer he has lived with you the higher you have risen in his esteem. You know we have sometimes laughed at him for adding at every turn: "Dolly is a wonderful woman." You always

84

were and still are a goddess in his eyes, and this has not been an infidelity of the heart …'

'But supposing it should occur again?'

'I don't think it will …'

'Yes, but would you forgive it?'

'I do not know, I cannot tell … Yes, I can,' said Anna, after a moment's consideration, during which her mind took in and weighed up the situation. 'Yes, I can,' she added, 'I can, I can. Yes, I should forgive. I would not be the same, no; but I should forgive, and forgive as utterly as if it had never happened, had never happened at all.'

'Oh, of course,' Dolly broke in quickly, as though saying what she had more than once thought, 'else it would not be forgiveness. If one forgives, it must be completely, completely. Now, come along, let me take you to your room,' she said, rising and putting her arm round Anna as they went. 'My dear, how glad I am you came. I feel better now, ever so much better.'

20

THE whole of that day Anna stayed at home – that is, in the Oblonskys' house, receiving no one, though several acquaintances, hearing of her arrival, came to call. She spent the earlier part of the day with Dolly and the children, merely sending a brief note to her brother to tell him to be sure and dine at home. 'Come,' she wrote, 'God is merciful.'

Oblonsky did dine at home; the conversation was general, and in speaking to him his wife called him 'Stiva' – a thing she had not done since the quarrel. There was the same estrangement in their relations, but nothing more was said about a separation, and Oblonsky saw that explanation and reconciliation might be possible.

Immediately after dinner Kitty arrived. She knew Anna, but only slightly, and came to her sister's in some trepidation as to how this fashionable Petersburg lady whose praise was on everyone's lips would receive her. But she made a favourable impression on Anna – she saw that at once. It was obvious that Anna admired her beauty and youth, and before Kitty knew where she was she felt herself not only under Anna's sway but in love with her, as young girls do fall in love with married women older than themselves. Anna was not like a society lady, nor the mother of an eight-year-old son. Her lithe movements, her freshness, and the persistent animation of her face, which broke out now in her smile, now in her glance, would have made her look more like a girl of twenty, had it not been for the grave and at times mournful expression in her eyes, which struck and drew Kitty to her. Kitty felt that Anna was completely natural and was not trying to conceal anything, but that she had another and higher world of complex and poetic interests beyond Kitty's reach.

After dinner, when Dolly retired to her own room, Anna rose quickly and went up to her brother, who was just lighting a cigar.

'Stiva,' she said with a gay twinkle, making the sign of the cross over him as she indicated the door, 'go to her, and God be with you.'

He understood, threw away his cigar and disappeared through the door.

When Oblonsky had gone, she returned to the couch where she had been sitting, surrounded by the children. Either because they saw that their mother was fond of this aunt, or because they felt her peculiar charm themselves, first the two elder and then the younger ones, as is often the way with children, had attached themselves to their new aunt before dinner and would not leave her side. And they had invented a sort of game which consisted in trying to sit as close as possible to her, touch her, hold her little hand, kiss it, play with her ring, or touch even the flounce of her skirt.

'Now then, as we were sitting before,' said Anna, resuming her place.

And again Grisha poked his little face under her arm and nestled his head on her gown, beaming with pride and happiness.

'And when is the ball to be?' said Anna, turning to Kitty.

'Next week, and it will be a lovely ball. The sort of ball where one always enjoys oneself.'

'And are there balls where one always enjoys oneself?' asked Anna, with tender irony.

'It is odd, but there are! We always enjoy ourselves at the Bobrishchevs', and at the Nikitins' too, but it is always dull at the Mezhkovs'. Surely you have noticed?'

'No, my dear, there are no balls for me now where everything is fun,' said Anna, and Kitty caught a glimpse in her eyes of that peculiar world which was not open to her. 'There are only some which are less tiresome and dull than the rest ...'

'How could *you* be dull at a ball?'

'Why shouldn't *I* be dull at a ball?' asked Anna.

Kitty saw that Anna knew what answer would follow.

'Because you always look nicer than anyone.'

Anna blushed easily. She blushed a little and said:

'In the first place it never is so; and secondly, if it were, what difference would it make?'

'Are you coming to this ball?' asked Kitty.

'I suppose I shall have to. Here, take it,' she said to Tánya, who was pulling at the ring which fitted loosely on her white, tapering finger.

'I do so want you to come. I should so like to see you at a ball.'

'Well, if I have to come, at least I shall be able to console myself with the thought that it will be a pleasure to you ... Grisha, don't pull my hair. It's untidy enough as it is,' she said, tucking in a straying curl which Grisha had been playing with.

'I imagine you in lilac at the ball.'

'Why lilac particularly?' asked Anna, smiling. 'Now, children, off with you, run along. Don't you hear? There's Miss Hoole calling you for your tea,' she said, disengaging herself from the children and despatching them to the dining-room.

'But I know why you press me to come to the ball. You are expecting great things of this ball and you want everyone to be there to have a share in them.'

'Yes. How do you know?'

'Oh, it is good to be your age,' Anna continued. 'I remember that blue haze, like the haze on the mountains in Switzerland. That haze which envelops everything at the blissful time when childhood is just coming to an end and its huge merry circle narrows to a path which one treads gaily yet with dread into life's corridor, bright and splendid as it appears ... Who has not been through it?'

Kitty smiled without speaking. 'How did she go through it? How I should like to know the whole romance of her life!' she thought, recalling the unromantic exterior of Anna's husband.

'I know something – Stiva told me and I congratulate you. I liked him very much,' Anna went on. 'I met Vronsky at the railway station.'

'Oh, was he there?' asked Kitty, blushing. 'What did Stiva tell you?'

'Stiva let it all out. And I should be so glad ... I travelled yesterday with Vronsky's mother,' she continued, 'and his mother talked about him without stopping. He is her favourite son. I know how biased mothers are, but ...'

'What did his mother tell you?'

'Oh, a great deal! And I know that he's her favourite, but even so one can see what a chivalrous nature he has ... For instance, she told me that he wanted to give up all his property to his brother; and that he did something wonderful when he was still quite a boy ... rescued a woman from the water. In fact, he's a hero,' said Anna, smiling and remembering the two hundred roubles Vronsky had given away at the station.

But she did not mention the two hundred roubles. For some reason she did not like thinking about them. She felt that there had been something in the incident to do with her personally, that should not have been.

'She begged me to go and call on her,' Anna went on, 'and I should like to see the old lady again. I shall go to-morrow. Well, thank Heaven, Stiva is being a long time in Dolly's room,' she added, changing the subject and getting up, displeased with something, Kitty fancied.

'No, I'm first! No, me first!' screamed the children, who had finished their tea and were rushing back to their Aunt Anna.

'All together!' cried Anna, laughing and running to meet them; and, putting her arms round them, she tumbled the whole shrieking mob of delighted children on the floor.

21

DOLLY emerged from her room when tea was brought into the drawing-room. Oblonsky did not appear, evidently having left his wife's room by the other door.

'I am afraid you will be cold upstairs,' Dolly remarked to Anna. 'I have a good mind to move you down, and then we shall be nearer one another.'

'Oh, please, you mustn't bother about me,' replied Anna, trying to read in Dolly's face whether there had been a reconciliation or not.

'It would be lighter for you here,' replied her sister-in-law.

'I assure you I can sleep like a dormouse anywhere and at any time.'

'What is it all about?' asked Oblonsky, coming in from the study and addressing his wife.

From his tone both Kitty and Anna knew at once that a reconciliation had taken place.

'I want to move Anna downstairs, but the curtains would have to be changed. No one else knows how to do it, so I must see to it myself,' replied Dolly, turning to him.

'Goodness knows if they have really made it up,' thought Anna, hearing Dolly's cool, quiet tone.

'Oh nonsense, Dolly – you're always making difficulties,' said her husband. 'Come, I'll do it all, if you like ...'

'Yes, they must have made it up,' thought Anna.

'I know how you would do it all,' answered Dolly. 'You would give Matvey all sorts of impossible instructions and then go off and leave him to make a muddle of everything,' and as she spoke the corners of Dolly's mouth creased into her usual ironical smile.

'Yes, their reconciliation is quite complete, quite. Thank God!' Anna thought; and, pleased to have been the means of bringing it about, she went up to Dolly and kissed her.

'Not at all. Why are you so hard on Matvey and me?' said Oblonsky, turning to his wife and almost smiling.

Throughout the evening Dolly lightly bantered her husband as usual, and Oblonsky was happy and cheerful, but not to the extent of seeming to forget his offence now that he was forgiven.

At half-past nine a particularly pleasant and contented family conversation over the tea-table at the Oblonskys' was disturbed by an apparently very ordinary incident, yet which for some reason struck them all as peculiar. They were talking about mutual acquaintances in Petersburg, when Anna rose suddenly.

'I have her in my photograph album,' she said. 'And at the same time I can show you my Seriozha,' she added with a smile of maternal pride.

It was towards ten o'clock – the time she generally said good-night to her son and often tucked him into bed herself before going to a ball – and she felt sad at being so far from him; and whatever they talked about her thoughts kept returning to her curly-headed Seriozha. She longed to look at his photograph and talk about him. Seizing the first pretext, she got up and with her light, resolute step went for the album. The flight of stairs to her room came out on the landing of the large, well-heated main staircase.

Just as she was leaving the drawing-room, there was a ring at the front door.

'Who can it be?' wondered Dolly.

'It is too early for me to be fetched, and too late for a caller,' observed Kitty.

'It must be someone with papers for me,' suggested Oblonsky.

As Anna was passing the top of the staircase, a footman came running up to announce the visitor. The visitor himself was standing under a lamp in the hall. Glancing down, Anna immediately recognized Vronsky, and a strange sensation of pleasure mixed with apprehension suddenly stirred in her heart. He was standing with his overcoat on, searching for something in his pocket. When Anna was halfway across the landing, he raised his eyes, caught sight of her, and an expression of embarrassment and dismay came over his face. With a slight inclination of her head she passed on. Behind her she heard Oblonsky's loud voice inviting him in and the quiet, soft voice of Vronsky gently refusing.

When Anna returned with her album, he had already gone, and Oblonsky was saying that Vronsky had called to inquire about the dinner they were giving next day to a visiting celebrity.

'And nothing would induce him to come up. What a queer fellow he is!' added Oblonsky.

Kitty blushed. She thought that she was the only person who knew why he had called and why he would not come in. 'He must have been to our house,' she thought, 'and, not finding me there, supposed I should be here; but he did not come in because he thought it was late, and Anna's here.'

They all exchanged glances and without a word began looking at Anna's album.

There was nothing out of the ordinary or odd in a man calling on a friend at half-past nine to find out about a dinner they were arranging, and refusing to come in; but it seemed odd to all of them. To Anna in particular it seemed odd and not right.

22

THE ball was just beginning when Kitty and her mother mounted the wide, brilliantly-lit, flower-decked staircase on which stood powdered footmen in red livery. A dull hum of movement came from the ballroom, as from a bee-hive, and while they smoothed their hair and gowns before a mirror on the landing lined with growing plants they could hear the pure note of the violins starting the first waltz. A little old man in civilian dress and smelling of perfume, who had been at another mirror arranging the grey hair on his forehead, brushed against them on the staircase and stepped aside with a look of obvious admiration for Kitty, whom he did not know. A beardless youth in an extremely low-cut waistcoat – one of the society young men whom the old Prince Shcherbatsky called *puppies* – straightening his white necktie as he moved along, bowed to them, and passed, but returned to ask Kitty for the quadrille. The first quadrille was already promised to Vronsky, so she had to give the young man the second. An officer stood near the door buttoning his glove. He looked admiringly at the pink-cheeked Kitty and stroked his moustache.

Although Kitty's toilette, coiffure, and all the preparations for the ball had necessitated a great deal of trouble and thought, she now entered the ballroom in her elaborate gown of tulle with its pink underslip as simply and naturally as if her rosettes, lace, and every other detail had not required a moment of her or her household's attention, as if she had been born in the tulle frock with the lace and the high coiffure which was crowned by a rose and two little leaves.

When her mother tried as they were entering the ballroom to straighten a twisted ribbon in her sash, Kitty drew gently aside. She felt that everything she wore must be right and graceful of its own accord, and that there could be no need to alter anything.

It was one of Kitty's happy days. Her gown was not too tight, her lace bertha was perfect, the rosettes were neither crumpled nor torn off, and her pink slippers with their high, curved heels did not pinch but gladdened her small feet. The thick braids of fair hair kept up as if they had grown naturally so on the little head. The three buttons on the long glove which followed the shape of her arm fastened without strain. The black velvet ribbon of her locket encircled her neck with especial fondness. This velvet ribbon was charming and looking at it round her neck in the mirror at home Kitty felt that it was eloquent. Whatever else one could doubt, the velvet ribbon was charming. Kitty smiled again in the ballroom as she caught sight of it in the mirror. Her bare arms and shoulders felt cool as marble – a sensation which she particularly enjoyed. Her eyes sparkled and she could not keep her red lips from smiling at the consciousness of their own fascination. Before she could enter the ballroom and join the belaced and beribboned throng of ladies in tulle of every hue, who were waiting for partners (Kitty was never long of their number), she was asked for the waltz. And it was the best dancer, the leader in the ballroom hierarchy, the famous *dirigeur* and master of ceremonies, a handsome, stately married man, Yegorushka Korsunsky, who asked her. He had only just left the Countess Bonin, with whom he had opened the ball. Surveying his domain – that is to say, the several couples who had begun to dance – he caught sight of Kitty as she entered and hurried up to her with that easy saunter peculiar to masters of ceremonies and, bowing, held out his arm to clasp the slim waist, without even asking her consent. She looked round for someone to hold her fan and the mistress of the house took it from her with a smile.

'How nice of you to come in good time,' he said, with his arm round her waist. 'Such a bad habit to be late!'

She bent her left arm and put her hand on his shoulder, and her little feet in their rose-coloured slippers began to glide swiftly and lightly over the polished floor, in time with the music.

'It is a rest to dance with you,' he said, falling into the first slow steps of the waltz. 'A delight. What lightness and *précision*!' he remarked, saying to her what he said to nearly all the partners he knew well.

Kitty smiled at his praise and over his shoulder continued to examine the ballroom. She was not a new débutante for whom all faces at a ball merge into a single magical impression. Nor was she so surfeited with balls that all the faces were familiar to dullness. She came between these two extremes and, though elated, was able to notice everything that was going on around her. She saw that the élite of the company was grouped in the left-hand corner of the room. There was the beautiful Lydie, Korsunsky's wife, with an outrageously low décolleté; there was Kitty's hostess; there shone the bald forehead of Krivin, always to be found with the élite. Youths who had not the courage to approach gazed in that direction. And there Kitty's eyes found Stiva and then Anna's lovely head and beautiful figure clad in black velvet. And *he* was there. Kitty had not seen him since the evening she had refused Levin. Her quick eyes recognized him instantly, and even noticed that he was looking at her.

'Shall we have another turn or are you tired?' asked Korsunsky, a little out of breath.

'No more, thank you.'

'Where may I take you?'

'Madame Karenin is over there, I think ... will you take me to her?'

'Wherever you please.'

And, gradually slowing down, Korsunsky waltzed right up to the crowd in the left-hand corner of the room, repeating *'Pardon, mesdames. Pardon, pardon, mesdames,'* as he steered through the sea of lace, tulle, and ribbon, without touching so much as a feather, and then swung his partner suddenly round, revealing her slim ankles in their open-work stockings and causing her train to spread out fan-wise across Krivin's knees. Korsunsky bowed, straightened his broad shirt-front, and offered Kitty his arm to lead her to Madame Karenin. Flushed, Kitty lifted her train off Krivin's knees and, slightly giddy, looked round in search of Anna. Anna was not in lilac, the colour which Kitty was so sure she ought to have worn, but in a low-necked black velvet gown which displayed her full shoulders and bosom, that seemed carved out of old ivory, and her rounded arms with their delicate tiny wrists. Her dress was richly trimmed with Venetian lace. In her black hair, which was all her own, she wore a little wreath of pansies, and there were more pansies on the black ribbon winding through the white lace at her waist. Except for the wilful little curls that always escaped at her temples and on the nape of her neck, adding to her beauty, there was nothing remarkable about her coiffure. She wore a string of pearls round her firmly-modelled neck.

Kitty had been seeing Anna every day and was in love with her, and always imagined her in lilac. But, seeing her now in black, she felt that she had never before realized all her charm. She saw her now in a new and quite unexpected light and realized that Anna could not have worn lilac, and that her charm lay precisely in the fact that she stood out from whatever she was wearing, that her dress was never conspicuous on her. And the black velvet, with its rich lace, was not at all conspicuous but served only as a frame. It was Anna alone, simple, natural, elegant, and at the same time gay and animated, whom one saw.

When Kitty approached the little group, Anna was standing, as usual very erect, talking to her host, her head slightly inclined towards him.

'No, I am not going to throw stones,' she was saying in reply to some question, adding with a shrug of her shoulders, 'although I cannot understand it,' and at once she turned to Kitty with a tender, protective smile. After a swift feminine glance of appraisal, she expressed her approval of Kitty's gown and pretty appearance with a barely perceptible nod, which Kitty understood.

'You even dance into the room,' she said.

'The princess is one of my most faithful helpers,' said Korsunsky, bowing to Anna, whom he had not yet seen. 'She adorns the ballroom and helps to make the ball gay. Anna Arkadyevna, may I have the pleasure?' he said, stooping towards her.

'Oh, you know one another?' asked the master of the house.

'Whom do we not know? My wife and I are like white wolves – everyone knows us,' replied Korsunsky. 'A short waltz, Anna Arkadyevna?'

'I never dance if I can help it,' she said.

'But you must to-night,' replied Korsunsky.

At that moment Vronsky approached.

'Well, if it is impossible not to dance to-night, let us dance, then,' she said, ignoring Vronsky's bow and quickly lifting her hand to Korsunsky's shoulder.

'Why is she displeased with him?' wondered Kitty, seeing that Anna had deliberately refrained from returning Vronsky's bow.

Vronsky came up to Kitty, reminding her about the first quadrille and regretting that he had not seen her for so long. Gazing with admiration at Anna as she danced, Kitty listened, expecting him to ask her to waltz; but he said nothing and she glanced at him in surprise. He coloured and hastily invited her to dance but scarcely had he put his arm round her slender waist and taken the first step when the music stopped. Kitty looked into his face, so close to hers, and for a long time after – for years after – that look, so full of love, which she gave him, and which met with no response, would pierce her heart with tormenting shame.

'*Pardon, pardon!* A waltz – a waltz!' cried Korsunsky from the other end of the room and, seizing the first young girl within reach, he himself started dancing.

23

VRONSKY and Kitty took a few turns round the room, and at the end of the waltz Kitty joined her mother; but she had hardly exchanged a few words with the Countess Nordston before Vronsky fetched her for the first quadrille. Nothing of note was said during the quadrille. They talked in snatches about the Korsunskys, husband and wife, whom Vronsky very amusingly described as dear, forty-year-old children, and about a projected public theatre. Only once did the conversation touch Kitty personally, when he asked about Levin and if he were at the ball, adding that he had liked him very much. But Kitty had not expected more from the quadrille. She was waiting with beating heart for the mazurka. It seemed to her that the mazurka would settle everything. She was not disturbed that he did not ask her for it while they were dancing the quadrille. She was so sure that they would dance it together, as they had at previous balls, that she refused five other partners, saying that she was already engaged. The whole ball up to the last quadrille was for Kitty an enchanted dream of gay colours, music, and movement. She only stopped dancing when she felt too tired and had to beg for a rest. But, while dancing the last quadrille with one of the boring young men whom it would not do to refuse, she found herself face to face with Vronsky and Anna. She had not encountered Anna since the beginning of the ball, and now she suddenly saw her again in a different and unexpected light. She noticed that Anna was elated with success, a feeling Kitty herself knew so well. She saw that Anna was intoxicated with the admiration she had aroused. Knowing the feeling and the signs, she recognized them in Anna. She saw the quivering, flashing light in her eyes, the smile of happiness and excitement that involuntarily curved her lips, and the graceful sureness and ease of her movements.

'Who is the cause?' she wondered. 'Is it all or only one?' And without trying to help her youthful partner, who was struggling to pick up the lost threads of conversation, and mechanically obeying the loudly cheerful directions of Korsunsky, hurling them first into a *grand rond*, then into a *chaîne*, she watched, while her heart sank lower and lower. 'No, it is not the admiration of the crowd that intoxicates her, but the praises of someone in particular. And that someone? Can it be *he*?' Every time he spoke to Anna, her eyes lit up joyously and a smile of happiness parted her red lips. She seemed to be making an effort to restrain these signs of joy but in spite of herself they appeared on her face. 'But what of him?' Kitty looked at him and was filled with dread. What was so plainly mirrored in Anna's face, she saw in him. What had become of his usually quiet, firm manner and tranquil, carefree expression? Now, every time he turned towards Anna, he bowed his head a little, as if wanting to fall at her feet in adoration, and his eyes held only submission and fear. 'I would not offend you,' his every look seemed to say. 'I only want to save myself but I do not know how.' The expression on his face was one Kitty had never seen before.

They were talking about mutual friends, conversing lightly, but to Kitty it seemed that every word they uttered was deciding their fate and hers. And, strange as it may be, although they were indeed only saying how funny Ivan Ivanovich was with his French and that the Eletsky girl ought to make a better match, they felt with Kitty that their words were significant. A mist spread over Kitty's soul, blotting out the ball and all the world. Only her strict upbringing sustained her and forced her to do what was expected of her – to dance, to answer the questions put to her, to talk, even to smile. But before the mazurka began, when the chairs were already being placed for it and several couples moved from the small to the large ballroom, Kitty had a moment of despair and terror. She had refused five partners, and now had no one for the mazurka. She had not even any hope of being asked again: she was too much of a success in society for it to enter anyone's head that she was not already engaged. She would have to tell her mother that she was not feeling well, and go home, but she had not the strength to do so. She felt quite heart-broken.

She went to the far end of a little drawing-room and sank into an arm-chair. The filmy skirt of her gown lifted in a cloud around her slender form. One thin, bare, girlish arm dropped listlessly and sank into the pink folds of her tunic. The other hand held a fan with which she rapidly fanned her flushed face. But, while she looked like a butterfly just settled on a blade of grass and ready at any moment to flutter and unfold rainbow wings, a dreadful despair gripped her heart.

'But perhaps I am mistaken – perhaps it was not so?' And again she recalled all that she had seen.

'Kitty – what does this mean?' asked the Countess Nordston, approaching noiselessly over the carpet. 'I do not understand.'

Kitty's lower lip quivered and she rose quickly.

'Kitty, are you not dancing the mazurka?'

'No, no,' Kitty answered in a voice trembling with tears.

'I heard him ask her for the mazurka,' said the countess, knowing that Kitty would understand whom she meant by *him* and *her*, 'and she said, "Are you not dancing with the Princess Shcherbatsky?"'

'Oh, I don't care,' replied Kitty.

No one but herself realized her situation. No one knew that a few days ago she had refused a man whom she perhaps loved, and had refused him because she trusted another.

The Countess Nordston, who was engaged to Korsunsky for the mazurka, told him to ask Kitty instead.

Kitty danced in the first pair and fortunately was not obliged to talk, as Korsunsky ran about all the time giving directions. Vronsky and Anna were sitting almost opposite to her. She saw them across the room and then she saw them close to, when they met in the dance, and the more she looked at them the surer she was that the blow had fallen. She saw that they felt as if they were alone in the crowded ballroom. And she was struck by the bewildered look of submission on Vronsky's face, usually so firm and self-possessed – an expression like that of an intelligent dog conscious of having done wrong.

If Anna smiled, he smiled in reply. If she grew thoughtful, he looked serious. Some supernatural force drew Kitty's eyes to Anna's face. She was charming in her simple black gown, her rounded arms were charming with their bracelets, charming the firm neck with the string of pearls, charming the unruly curls, charming the graceful, easy movements of her little hands and feet, charming the lovely, animated face: but in that charm there was something terrible and cruel.

Kitty admired her more than ever, and suffered more and more. She felt crushed, and her face showed it. When Vronsky came up against her in the course of the mazurka he did not recognize her at first, so changed was she.

'A delightful ball!' he remarked, for the sake of something to say.

'Yes,' she replied.

Half-way through the mazurka, when they were repeating a complicated figure newly invented by Korsunsky, Anna stepped into the middle of the circle and chose two cavaliers and two ladies, one of whom was Kitty, to join her. Kitty gazed at her in fear and moved forward. Half closing her eyes, Anna smiled and pressed Kitty's hand. But, seeing that Kitty only responded to her smile with a look of surprise and despair, she turned away and started to talk gaily to the other lady.

'Yes, there is something strange, diabolical, and enchanting about her,' thought Kitty.

Anna did not want to stay to supper but the master of the house tried to insist.

'Come, Anna Arkadyevna,' began Korsunsky, taking her bare arm under his. 'I have a wonderful cotillon in mind – *un bijou*!'

And he moved slowly on, hoping to draw her with him. Their host smiled approvingly.

'No, I will not stay,' replied Anna smiling; and despite the smile both Korsunsky and the master of the house realized from the note of determination in her voice that she would not stay.

'No, I have danced more in Moscow at this one ball of yours than I have the whole winter in Petersburg,' said Anna, looking round at Vronsky, who was standing beside her. 'I must rest before my journey.'

'So you really are going to-morrow?' asked Vronsky.

'Yes, I think so,' Anna replied, as if surprised at the boldness of his question. But the uncontrollable radiance of her eyes and her smile set him on fire as she spoke the words.

Anna did not stay for supper, but went away.

24

'YES, there must be something objectionable about me which repels people,' thought Levin as he left the Shcherbatskys' and started walking in the direction of his brother's lodgings. 'I am not popular. They say I am proud. No, I have no pride. If I had any pride, I should not have put myself in such a position as this.' And he pictured Vronsky, happy, kind, clever, and self-possessed – certainly never placed in the awful position in which he had been that evening. 'Yes, she was bound to choose him. It had to be so, and I have no cause to complain of anyone or anything. It was my own fault. What right had I to imagine she would care to go through life with me? Who and what am I? A nobody, not wanted by anyone, no use to anyone.' And he recalled his brother Nikolai and fastened his mind gladly on the thought of him. 'Is he not right when he says that everything in the world is evil and horrid? And have we been fair – are we being fair in judging brother Nikolai? Of course, in Prokofy's eyes, who saw him drunk and in a ragged coat, he is a despicable creature; but I know the other side of him. I know his heart and know that we are alike. Yet, instead of going to see him, I had dinner out and came here.' Levin

P. 98 - 100 .

walked up to a street-lamp to read his brother's address, which he had in his pocket-book, and hailed a sledge. It was a long ride to his brother's and Levin spent the whole time vividly recalling all the circumstances he knew of Nikolai's life. He remembered how at the university, and for a year after, his brother had lived the life of a monk, despite the ridicule of his fellow-students, observing all the rites of religion, attending services and fasting, avoiding pleasure of every sort, especially women; and then how he had suddenly broken loose and started frequenting the dregs of society and giving himself up to the lowest forms of debauch. He recalled the scandal over the little boy his brother had taken from the country to educate and, in a fit of rage, beaten so unmercifully that proceedings had been started against him for crippling the boy. Then there was the cardsharper to whom his brother had lost money and given an I.O.U. and afterwards prosecuted for fraud (It was this I.O.U. that Koznyshev had paid.) Levin went on to recall how his brother had spent a night in the lock-up for disorderly conduct in the street; and the disgraceful action against Koznyshev, whom Nikolai had accused of failing to make over his share of their mother's fortune; and the last adventure – the time his brother had taken an official post in one of the western provinces and there been summoned for assaulting a village elder. ... It was all most disgraceful but to Levin it did not seem nearly so disgraceful as it must to anyone who did not know Nikolai Levin, did not know his story, did not know his heart.

Levin remembered that when Nikolai had been in his devout stage, observing the fasts, frequenting monks and attending church services; when he was seeking help in religion to curb his passionate nature, not only had he been given no encouragement, but everyone, including Levin himself, had made fun of him. They had teased him, called him Noah and 'the monk'; and then, when he had broken out, no one helped him and they had all turned their backs in horror and disgust.

Levin felt that in his soul, in the innermost depths of his soul, his brother Nikolai, in spite of his dissolute life, was no worse than the people who despised him. It was not his fault that he had been born with a tempestuous nature and a kink in his mind. He had always wished to do right. 'I will tell him everything, make him open his heart to me. I will show him that I love him and therefore understand,' Levin decided as towards eleven o'clock he reached the hotel shown in the address.

'At the top, twelve and thirteen,' said the hall-porter in reply to Levin's inquiry.

'Is he in?'

'Sure to be.'

The door of No. 12 was half open and from within, visible in the streak of light, issued dense clouds of cheap, coarse tobacco-smoke. Levin heard an unfamiliar voice but he knew at once that his brother was there by his hacking cough.

As he entered the doorway the unknown voice was saying:

'It all depends on how intelligently and rationally the thing is done.'

Levin looked in and saw that the speaker was a young man with a huge mop of hair, wearing a sleeveless jerkin, and that a rather pock-marked young woman in a woollen dress without collar or cuffs was sitting on the couch. His brother was not to be seen. Levin's heart sank at the thought of his brother associating with such strange people. No one heard him and as he took off his goloshes he listened to what the gentleman in the jerkin was saying. He was talking about some enterprise or other.

'Oh, to the devil with the privileged classes,' his brother's voice responded, with a cough. 'Masha! Get us some supper and bring the wine, if there's any left, or else go and get some.'

The woman rose, came out from behind the partition, and saw Levin.

'There's a gentleman here, Nikolai Dmitrich,' she said.

'What does he want?' said Nikolai Levin's voice angrily.

'It's I,' answered Constantine Levin, coming forward into the light.

'Who's *I*?' demanded Nikolai still more angrily. He could be heard rising hurriedly and stumbling against something, and then Levin saw facing him in the doorway his brother's huge, thin, stooping figure – familiar yet alarming, so wild and ill did he look with his great frightened eyes.

He was even more emaciated than when Levin had seen him last, about three years ago. He was wearing a short coat, and his hands and bony frame seemed bigger than ever. His hair was getting thin but the same straight moustache drooped over his lips and the same eyes looked at the newcomer with their peculiar, naïve gaze.

'Oh, Kostya!' he exclaimed suddenly, recognizing his brother, and his eyes lit up with joy. But the next instant he looked round at the young man and convulsively jerked his head and neck, as if his cravat were too tight – a movement Levin knew so well – and an entirely different expression, wild, suffering, and cruel, settled on his haggard face.

'I wrote both to you and to Sergei Ivanovich that I do not know you and do not wish to know you. What is it – what do you want?'

He was not at all as Levin had been imagining. When he thought of him, Levin would forget the worst and most trying side of his character, the side which made him so difficult to get on with; but now when he saw his face, and especially that convulsive jerking of his head, that other side came back to him.

'I don't want anything,' he ventured timidly. 'I just came to see you.'

His brother's shyness obviously softened Nikolai. His lips quivered.

'Oh, so that's it? Well, come in and sit down. Like some supper? Masha, supper for three. No, wait. Do you know who this is?' he asked, turning to his brother and indicating the gentleman in the jerkin. 'This is Mr Kritsky, my friend from Kiev, a very remarkable man. He's persecuted by the police, of course, because he is not a scoundrel.'

And he glanced round at everyone present, as was his way. Seeing the woman in the doorway make a move to go, he shouted to her: 'Wait, I said.' And in the awkward, incoherent manner Levin knew so well he again looked round at everyone and started telling his brother about Kritsky: how he had been expelled from the university for starting a benefit society for the poorer students and organizing Sunday-schools, and how he had afterwards been a teacher in a peasant school and been driven out of that too, and had then been tried on some charge or other.

'You were at Kiev University?' Levin asked Kritsky, to break the awkward silence that ensued.

'Yes, I was at Kiev,' replied Kritsky curtly, with a frown.

'And this woman,' Nikolai Levin interrupted him, pointing to her, 'is my life's companion, Maria Nikolayevna. I took her out of a brothel,' he continued with another jerk of his neck as he said it. 'But I love and respect her, and anyone who wishes to know me,' he added, raising his voice and scowling, 'must love and respect her too. She is the same as a wife to me, exactly the same. So now you know whom you have to deal with. And if you think you are lowering yourself – there is the door.'

And again his eyes travelled inquiringly over all of them.

'Why I should be lowering myself I don't understand.'

'All right, Masha; supper for three, then, with vodka and wine. ... No, wait a minute. ... No, never mind. ... Go along.'

25

'So you see,' pursued Nikolai Levin, painfully wrinkling his fore-head and twitching. He obviously found it difficult to think of what to say and do. 'Here, look ...' He pointed to a bundle of iron bars tied together with string, lying in a corner of the room. 'Do you see that? That's the beginning of a new enterprise we are embarking upon, a productive association ...'

Levin was scarcely listening. He kept examining his brother's sickly, consumptive face, feeling more and more sorry for him, and he could not bring himself to pay attention to what he was telling him about the association. He realized that this association was merely an anchor to save his brother from self-contempt.

'You know that capitalism is strangling the worker,' Nikolai Levin went on to say. 'The workers in our country, the peasants, bear all the burden of labour but are so placed that, no matter how hard they work, they cannot escape being treated like beasts of burden. All the profits on their labour, by which they might better their lot, gain some leisure for themselves, and then some education – everything over and above their wages is taken from them by the capitalists. And society is so constituted that the harder they work, the more profit they make for the merchants and landowners, while they remain beasts of burden to the end. And this state of affairs must be altered,' he finished up, with an inquiring look at his brother.

'Yes, of course,' said Levin, watching the flush spreading over his brother's prominent cheek-bones.

'And so we are founding a locksmiths' association in which all the production and profit and the chief instruments of production will be common property.'

'Where is the association to be?' asked Levin.

'In the village of Vozdrem, in the Kazan province.'

'But why in a village? I thought that sort of work was done in the villages already. Why start a locksmiths' association in a village?'

'Why, because the peasants are just as much slaves now as they ever were, and because you and Sergei Ivanich don't like people to try and get them out of their slavery,' replied Nikolai Levin, annoyed at the objection.

Levin sighed, looking round at the cheerless, dirty room. The sigh apparently irritated Nikolai still further.

'I know the aristocratic views of men like you and Sergei Ivanich. I know he applies all the power of his intellect to justify the existing evils.'

'That is not so; but why talk about Sergei Ivanich?' said Levin with a smile.

'Sergei Ivanich? I'll tell you why!' Nikolai Levin burst out suddenly at the mention of Sergei Ivanich. 'This is why ... But what is the good? There's only one thing: ... Why have you come here? You despise all this, and you're welcome to, and go away, in God's name go away!' he cried, rising from his chair. 'Go away, go away!'

'I don't despise it in the least,' replied Levin meekly. 'I don't even dispute it.'

At this moment Maria Nikolayevna returned. Nikolai Levin looked round angrily at her. She hurried up to him and said something in a whisper.

'I am not well, I've grown irritable,' said Nikolai Levin, calming down and breathing heavily. 'And then you come talking to me about Sergei Ivanich and his article. It is such rubbish, such moonshine, such self-deception. What can a man write of justice who doesn't know what justice is? Have you read his article?' he asked, turning to Kritsky and sitting down at the table again and clearing a space over half of it by brushing back some cigarettes which lay scattered about.

'I have not,' replied Kritsky morosely, obviously not wishing to enter into the conversation.

'Why not?' demanded Nikolai, now turning irritably on Kritsky.

'Because I don't care to waste my time on it.'

'Allow me to ask how you know it would be a waste of time? Many people could not tackle that article; it would be above their heads. But with me it's another matter: I see through his ideas, and so I know why the article is weak.'

They were all silent. Kritsky got up slowly and reached for his cap.

'Won't you stay to supper? All right, good-bye! Look in tomorrow with the locksmith.'

As soon as Kritsky had gone, Nikolai Levin smiled and winked.

'He's in a bad way, too,' he remarked. 'Of course I can see ...'

But at that instant Kritsky called him from the door.

'What do you want now?' asked Nikolai, joining him in the passage.

Left alone with Maria Nikolayevna, Levin turned to her and asked: 'Have you been with my brother long?'

'Yes, over a year. Nikolai Dmitrich's health has got very bad. Nikolai Dmitrich drinks a good deal,' she said.

'What does he drink?'

'Nikolai Dmitrich drinks vodka, and it's bad for him.'

'Does he really drink much?' asked Levin in a whisper.

'Yes,' she replied, looking timidly towards the door where Nikolai Levin had reappeared.

'What were you talking about?' he asked, frowning and looking from one to the other with alarmed eyes. 'What was it?'

'Oh, nothing,' replied Levin in confusion.

'You needn't tell me if you don't want to. Only it's no good your talking to her. She is a wench and you are a gentleman,' he said, jerking his neck. 'I see you have taken in and sized up everything here, and look with sorrow at the error of my ways,' he began again, raising his voice.

'Nikolai Dmitrich, Nikolai Dmitrich,' whispered Maria Nikolayevna, going up to him again.

'Oh, very well, very well! ... What about that supper? Ah, here it is,' he said, seeing a waiter bringing in a tray. 'Here, put it here,' he added crossly, and immediately picking up the vodka he poured out a glassful and drank it greedily. 'Have a drink?' he turned to his brother, brightening at once.

'Well, that's enough of Sergei Ivanich. I am glad to see you, anyway. After all's said and done, we're not strangers. Have a drink now. Tell me, what are you doing?' he continued, greedily munching a crust of bread and filling himself another glass. 'How are you getting on?'

'I live alone in the country, the way I did before, busy with the estate,' replied Levin, watching with horror the greediness with which his brother ate and drank, and trying not to let it be seen that he noticed.

'Why don't you get married?'

'No luck,' replied Levin, blushing.

'Why not? For me now – everything's all over. I have made a mess of my life. I have said, and always shall say, that if I had been given my share of the property when I needed it, my whole life would have been different.'

Levin hastened to change the conversation.

'Do you know, I have taken your little Vanya into the office at Pokrovsky,' he said.

Nikolai jerked his neck and sank into thought.

'Tell me, what's happening at Pokrovsky? Is the house still standing, and the birch-trees, and our schoolroom? And Philip the gardener, is he still alive? How well I remember the arbour and the seat! Mind, don't alter anything in the house, but make haste and get married and have everything as it used to be again. Then I'll come and see you, if your wife is nice.'

'Come now,' said Levin. 'How well we should get on!'

'I would, if I were sure I should not find Sergei Ivanich there.'

'You would not find him there. I live quite independently of him.'

'Yes, but say what you like, you will have to choose between him and me,' he said, looking timidly into his brother's eyes.

His timidity touched Levin.

'If you want to know what I think on the subject, I'll tell you that I take neither one side nor the other in your quarrel with Sergei Ivanich. You are both in the wrong. You are more to blame according to the letter, and he according to the spirit.'

'Aha! You have realized that, have you, you have realized that!' cried Nikolai delightedly.

'But I, personally, if you want to know, value friendly relations with you more because ...'

'Why, why?'

Levin could not say that it was because Nikolai was unhappy and needed friendship. But Nikolai understood that he meant just that and, scowling, betook himself to the vodka again.

'Enough, Nikolai Dmitrich!' said Maria Nikolayevna, stretching out her plump, bare arm for the decanter.

'Let go! Leave me alone! I'll beat you!' he shouted.

Maria Nikolayevna smiled a gentle, kindly smile, which evoked one from Nikolai, and took away the vodka.

'You think she doesn't understand things?' said Nikolai. 'She understands it all better than any of us. There really is something good and sweet about her, isn't there?'

'You were never in Moscow before?' Levin asked her, for the sake of saying something.

'Only you mustn't be polite and formal with her. It frightens her. No one ever spoke to her like that except the magistrate when they had her up for trying to escape from the brothel. Heavens! how senseless everything is in the world!' he suddenly exclaimed. 'These new institutions, these justices of the peace, these *Zemstvos* – what monstrosities!'

And he began to enlarge on his encounters with the new institutions.

Levin listened to him and the condemnation of all public institutions, although he shared his brother's opinion and had often said the same things himself, was distasteful to him, coming from his brother's lips.

'We shall understand all that in the next world,' he said lightly.

'The next world! Oh, I don't like that next world! I don't like it,' said Nikolai, fixing frightened eyes on his brother's face. 'Yet one would think it would be a good thing to leave all this mess and muddle, one's own and other people's, but I am afraid of death, awfully afraid of death.' He shuddered. 'But do drink something. Would you like some champagne? Or shall we go out somewhere? Let's go and hear the Gypsies! Do you know, I have got so fond of the Gypsies and Russian folk-songs.'

His speech had begun to falter and he started jumping from one subject to another. With Masha's help Levin succeeded in persuading him not to go out anywhere, and they put him to bed, hopelessly drunk.

Masha promised to write to Levin in case of need and to try and get Nikolai to go and stay with him.

26

THE next morning Levin left Moscow and towards evening arrived home. On the way back in the train he chatted politics and the new railways with his fellow-passengers, and felt depressed, just as he had in Moscow, by the confusion in his mind, dissatisfaction with himself, and a vague sense of shame. But when he got out at his station and saw his one-eyed coachman, Ignat, with the collar of his coat turned up; when he caught sight in the dim light from the station windows of his own upholstered sledge, his horses with their plaited tails, and the harness with its rings and tassels; and when Ignat, while they were still getting ready to start, began telling him the village news – how the contractor had arrived and Pava had calved – Levin felt that little by little his confusion was clearing up and his shame and self-dissatisfaction were melting away. He felt this at the mere sight of Ignat and the horses; but when he had put on the sheepskin coat brought for him and, well wrapped up, had seated himself in the sledge and was being driven along, turning over in his mind the work that lay before him in the village and at the same time watching the side-horse (once a saddle-horse, past his prime now, but a spirited animal from the Don), he began to see what had befallen him in quite a different light. He felt himself and did not want to be anyone else. All he wanted now was to be better than he had been before. In the first place, he decided that from that day forth he would give up hoping for any extraordinary happiness such as marriage was to have brought him, and consequently would not so belittle what he really had. Secondly, he would never again let himself give way to low passion, the memory of which had so tortured him when he was making up his mind to propose. Then, remembering his brother Nikolai, he resolved never to allow himself to forget him again but follow up and not lose sight of him, so as to be ready to help when things should go badly. And that would be soon, he felt. Then his brother's talk of communism, to which he had not paid much attention at the time, now made him think. He considered a revolution in economic conditions nonsense; but he had always felt the injustice of his own abundance compared with the poverty of the peasants, and now determined, in order to feel absolutely in the right, that though he had always worked hard and lived by no means luxuriously he would in future work harder still and allow himself still less luxury. And all this seemed to him so easy of fulfilment that he spent the whole drive in the pleasantest of reveries. Manfully looking forward to a new and better life, he reached home before nine o'clock at night.

A light from the windows of Agatha Mihalovna fell on the snow-covered little quadrangle in front of the house. Agatha Mihalovna, his old nurse, now acted as his housekeeper. She was not yet asleep and, roused by her, Kuzma came running out on to the steps, sleepy and barefooted. A setter bitch Laska ran out too, almost throwing Kuzma off his feet, and whined and rubbed herself against Levin's knees, jumping up and longing but not daring to put her forepaws on his chest.

'You have soon come back, sir,' said Agatha Mihalovna.

'I got tired of it, Agatha Mihalovna. Staying with friends is all very well, but there is no place like home,' he replied and went into his study.

A candle was brought in and gradually lit up the study, revealing the familiar details: the antlers, the book-shelves, the stove with its ventilator which had long wanted repairing, his father's sofa, the big table on which lay an open book, a broken ash-tray, a manuscript-book full of his handwriting. As he saw all this, he began to doubt for a moment the possibility of arranging the new life he had been dreaming of during the drive. All these traces of his old life seemed to clutch him and say: 'No, you're not going to get away from us; you're not going to be different. You're going to be the same as you always have been – with your doubts, your perpetual dissatisfaction with yourself and vain attempts to amend, your failures and everlasting expectation of a happiness you won't get and which isn't possible for you'

This was what the things said, but another, inner voice was telling him not to submit to the past, telling him a man can make what he will of himself. And listening to this voice he went to the corner where his two heavy dumb-bells lay and started to do exercises with them, trying to restore his confident mood. There was a creak of footsteps at the door. He hastily put down the dumb-bells.

The bailiff came in and said that everything, heaven be praised, was doing well; but the buckwheat had got a little scorched in the new drying-kiln. This piece of news vexed Levin. The new drying-kiln had been constructed and partly invented by Levin. The bailiff had always been against it, and now with suppressed triumph announced that the buckwheat had been scorched. Levin felt quite certain that if the buckwheat had been scorched it was only because the precautions which he had ordered a hundred times had been neglected. He felt annoyed and reprimanded the bailiff. But there had been one important and happy event: Pava, his best cow, that he had paid a big price for at a cattle-show, had calved.

'Kuzma, give me my sheepskin. And you tell them to bring a lantern,' he said to the bailiff. 'I will come and have a look at her.'

The cowshed for the more valuable cows was just behind the house. Crossing the yard past a snowdrift by the lilac-bush, he went into the cowshed. There was a warm, dungy smell when the frozen door was opened and the cows, startled by the unaccustomed light of the lantern, stirred on the fresh straw. The Friesian cow's smooth, broad, black-and-white back gleamed. Berkut, the bull, was lying down, a ring through his nose. He almost got to his feet, but thought better of it and only gave a snort or two as they passed him. Pava, a perfect beauty, huge as a hippopotamus, with her back turned to them, prevented them from seeing her calf, which she was nuzzling all over.

Levin went into the stall, looked Pava over, and lifted the speckled calf on to its long, tottering legs. Pava, uneasy, was on the point of lowing but quietened down when Levin restored her calf to her and, with a heavy sigh, she began licking it with her rough tongue. The calf pushed its nose under its mother's belly and whisked its little tail.

'Bring the light here, Fyodor, here,' said Levin, examining the calf. 'Like its mother! Although it was sired by the red bull. A beauty. Big-boned and deep-flanked. Isn't it a beauty?' he said to the bailiff, feeling in his satisfaction over the calf quite reconciled about the buckwheat.

'How could it fail to be? Oh, Simon the contractor came the day after you left. You must settle with him, Constantine Dmitrich,' said the bailiff. 'I did inform you about the machine.'

This was enough to draw Levin back to all the business of the estate, which was on a large scale and complicated, and from the cowshed he went straight to the office and after a talk with the bailiff and Simon the contractor he returned to the house and went upstairs to the drawing-room.

27

It was a large, old-fashioned house, and though Levin was living in it alone he used and heated the whole of it. He knew this was foolish and even wrong, and contrary to his present new resolutions, but the house was all the world to Levin. It was the place in which his father and mother had lived and died. They had lived the sort of life which Levin considered the ideal of perfection and which he had dreamed of restoring with a wife and family of his own.

He scarcely remembered his mother. The thought of her was sacred to him, and in his imagination his future wife was to be a repetition of that exquisite and holy ideal of womanhood which his mother had been.

He could not imagine love for woman outside marriage, and he even pictured a family first and then the woman who would give him the family. His ideas about marriage, therefore, did not resemble those of the majority of his acquaintances, for whom getting married was only one of the numerous facts of social life. For Levin it was the principal thing in life, on which its whole happiness turned. And now he had to renounce it.

When he had gone into the little drawing-room where he always had tea and had settled himself in his arm-chair with a book, and Agatha Mihalovna had brought him his cup with her usual remark, 'Well, I'll stay a while, sir,' and had seated herself at the window, he felt that, however strange it might be, he was not parted from his dreams and that he could not live without them. With *her* or with another, they would come true. He read his book, with his mind on what he was reading, pausing to listen to Agatha Mihalovna, who chattered away without ceasing; and at the same time all sorts of pictures to do with the estate and a family life in the future presented themselves disjointedly before his imagination. He felt that in the depths of his heart something was settling down, adjusting and composing itself.

He heard Agatha Mihalovna telling him how Prokhor had forgotten the Lord and was spending on drink the money Levin had given him to buy a horse, and had almost beaten his wife to death. He listened and read his book and kept in mind the whole sequence of ideas inspired by what he was reading. It was Tyndall's *Treatise on Heat*. He remembered how he had criticized Tyndall for being so pleased with himself over his experiments and for his lack of a philosophic outlook. And suddenly he found himself thinking joyfully that in a couple of years he would have two Friesian cows in the herd and Pava herself might still be alive; there would be a dozen young cows by Berkut and with the three others – splendid! He took up his book again.

'All right, let us admit that electricity and heat are the same thing; but can we substitute the one for the other in solving an equation? No. Well, so what then? One can instinctively feel the connexion between all the forces of nature. ... How extraordinarily nice it will be when Pava's calf has grown into a red-speckled cow and the whole herd with those three others. ... Splendid! And I and my wife will go out with our guests to see the herd come in. ... My wife will say "Kostya and I reared that calf like a baby." "How can you be so interested?" one of the guests will ask. "Everything that interests him interests me." But who will *she* be?' And he remembered what had happened in Moscow. ... 'Well, what can I do? ... It's not my fault. But now everything will be different. It is nonsense to believe that life will not allow it, that the past will not allow it. I must struggle to live a better life, a far better life.'

He lifted his head and pondered. Old Laska, who had not yet quite got over her joy at her master's return and had run out to bark in the yard, now came back, wagging her tail and bringing the scent of the fresh air into the room with her, as she crept up to him and thrust her head under his hand, whining plaintively to be stroked.

'She all but speaks,' said Agatha Mihalovna. 'The dog now – why, she understands all right that her master's come home and is in low spirits.'

'Why should I be in low spirits?'

'Do you suppose I don't see, sir? I ought to know gentle-folk by this time. I have grown up with them from a child. Never mind, sir, so long as there's good health and a clear conscience ...'

Levin looked at her intently, surprised that she should understand what was on his mind.

'Shall I fetch you some more tea?' she asked, and went out with his cup.

Laska kept poking her head under his hand. He stroked her and she curled up at his feet, her head on her outstretched hind-paw. And in token that everything was well and all right now, she opened her mouth a little, smacked her flabby lips, and settling them more comfortably over her old teeth she subsided into blissful repose. Levin watched these last movements of hers attentively.

'I shall go and do likewise!' he said to himself. 'I shall go and do likewise! Nothing's amiss ... all is well.'

28

EARLY on the morning after the ball Anna sent her husband a telegram to say that she was leaving Moscow that same day.

'No, I must go, I must go,' she said to her sister-in-law, explaining the change in her plans in a tone that suggested she had suddenly remembered so many things demanding her instant attention that there was no enumerating them. 'No, it had really better be to-day!'

Oblonsky was not dining at home but he promised to be back to take his sister to the station at seven o'clock.

Kitty, too, did not come, sending a note to say that she had a headache. Dolly and Anna dined alone with the children and the English governess. Whether the children were fickle or whether their senses were acute and they felt that Anna was not at all the same now as she had been the day they had lost their hearts to her and that she was no longer interested in them – but they abandoned the game with their aunt and their affection for her, and were not in the least concerned that she was going away. Anna spent the whole morning preparing for her departure: writing notes to her Moscow acquaintances, putting down her accounts, and packing. Altogether she seemed to Dolly to be in a restless state of mind, in that troubled mood which Dolly recognized from her own experience, which does not come without cause and generally cloaks discontent with oneself. After dinner Anna went to her room to dress and Dolly followed her.

'How strange you are to-day!' said Dolly.

'I? Do you think so? I am not strange but I feel queer. I am like that sometimes. I feel like crying all the time. It is very silly but it will pass,' said Anna, speaking quickly and bending her flushed face over the tiny bag into which she was packing her night-cap and some cambric handkerchiefs. Her eyes were peculiarly bright and kept filling with tears. 'I did not want to leave Petersburg and now I don't want to leave here.'

'You came here and did a good deed,' said Dolly, observing her closely.

Anna looked at her with eyes wet with tears.

'Don't say that, Dolly. I have done nothing and could do nothing. I often wonder why people conspire to spoil me. What have I done and what could I do? There was enough love in your heart to forgive …'

'If it had not been for you, God knows what would have happened! How lucky you are, Anna!' said Dolly. 'Everything in your soul is straightforward and good.'

'Most people have a skeleton in their cupboard, as the English say.'

'What skeleton can you have? Everything about you is so straightforward.'

'I have, though!' Anna said suddenly; and unexpectedly after her tears her lips puckered into a sly, ironical smile.

'Well, yours must be a funny skeleton, not a dismal one,' said Dolly, smiling.

'No, it is dismal enough. Do you know why I am going to-day instead of to-morrow? It's a confession that weighs on me and I want to make it to you,' said Anna, resolutely throwing herself into an armchair and looking straight into Dolly's eyes.

And, to her astonishment, Dolly noticed that Anna was blushing to her ears, to the little black curls on her neck.

'Yes,' Anna went on. 'Do you know why Kitty did not come to dinner? She is jealous of me. I have spoiled ... It was because of me that the ball was a torture instead of a joy to her. But truly, truly, I am not to blame, or only a little bit,' she said in a high-pitched voice, drawling the words 'a little bit'.

'Oh, how exactly like Stiva you said that!' laughed Dolly.

Anna was offended.

'Oh no, oh no! I am not Stiva,' she said, with a frown. 'The reason I'm telling you is that I could never let myself doubt myself for an instant.'

But as she was uttering the words she knew they were not true: she not only distrusted herself, but the thought of Vronsky disturbed her, and she was leaving sooner than she had intended solely in order not to meet him again.

'Yes, Stiva told me that you danced the mazurka with him and that he ...'

'You cannot imagine how absurdly it all turned out. I thought I was only going to help along the match, and all at once it happened quite differently. Perhaps in spite of myself I ...'

She crimsoned and did not go on.

'Oh, they sense it directly!' said Dolly.

'But I should be in despair if there were anything serious in it on his side,' Anna interrupted her. 'I am sure it will all blow over and Kitty will leave off hating me.'

'All the same, Anna, to tell you the truth, I am not very keen on this marriage for Kitty. And it would be better for it to come to nothing if Vronsky is capable of falling in love with you in a single day.'

'Oh, heavens above, that would be too idiotic!' said Anna, and again a deep flush of pleasure suffused her face at hearing the thought that filled her mind put into words. 'So here am I going away, having made an enemy of Kitty, whom I liked so much! Oh, how sweet she is! But you'll make it right, Dolly? Say you will?'

Dolly could hardly repress a smile. She loved Anna but it was nice to find that she too had her weaknesses.

'An enemy? That is impossible.'

'I did so want you all to love me, as I love you; and now I love you more than ever,' said Anna with tears in her eyes. 'Oh, how silly I am to-day!'

She dabbed her face with her handkerchief and began to dress.

Just as she was ready to leave, Oblonsky came in, late and smelling of wine and cigars, his face red and jolly.

Anna's emotion had communicated itself to Dolly, who whispered as she embraced her sister-in-law for the last time:

'Remember, Anna, I shall never forget what you have done for me. And remember that I love and always shall love you as my dearest friend!'

'I don't know why,' said Anna, kissing her and struggling with her tears.

'You were so understanding and you understand me. Good-bye, my darling!'

29

'WELL, that's all over, and thank heaven!' was Anna's first thought after she had said the last good-bye to her brother, who stood blocking up the carriage door till the third and final warning bell. She seated herself beside her maid Annushka and peered round the dimly-lit sleeping-car. 'Thank goodness, to-morrow I shall see Seriozha and Alexei Alexandrovich and my life – my nice, everyday life – will go on as before.'

Still in the same worried frame of mind in which she had been all day, Anna arranged herself with pleasure and deliberation for the journey. With small, deft hands she opened a red bag and took out a little cushion, which she laid on her knees before relocking the bag. Then she carefully wrapped a rug round her legs and sat down again. An invalid lady had already settled herself for the night. Two other ladies began talking to Anna, and a stout old woman tucked up her feet and remarked upon the heating of the train. Anna said a few words in reply, but, not foreseeing any entertainment from the conversation, asked Annushka to get a lamp, hooked it on to the arm of her seat, and took a paper-knife and an English novel from her bag. At first she made no progress with her reading. For a while the bustle of people coming and going was disturbing. Then, when the train had started, she could not help listening to the noises. Then the snow beating against the window on her left and sticking to the pane, the guard passing by muffled up and one side of him covered with snow, together with conversation about the terrible blizzard raging outside – all this distracted her attention. And so it went on: the same jolting and knocking, the same snow on the window, the same sudden transition from steaming heat to cold and back again to heat, the same glimpses of the same faces in the semi-darkness, and the same voices, and Anna began to read and to keep her mind on what she read. Annushka was already dozing, her broad hands in their gloves, one of which was split, clutching the red bag on her lap. Anna read attentively but there was no pleasure in reading, no pleasure in entering into other people's lives and adventures. She was too eager to live herself. If she read how the heroine of the novel nursed a sick man, she wanted to be moving about a sick-room with noiseless tread herself; if she read of a member of Parliament making a speech, she wanted to be delivering that speech herself; if she read how Lady Mary rode to hounds and teased her sister-in-law and astonished everyone by her daring – she would have liked to do the same. But there was no possibility of doing anything, so she forced herself to read, while her little hands twisted the smooth paper-knife.

The hero of the novel had nearly attained his Englishman's idea of happiness – a baronetcy and an estate – and Anna was wishing she could go to the estate with him, when she suddenly felt that *he* must be feeling ashamed and that she was ashamed for the same reason. But what had he to be ashamed of? 'What have I to be ashamed of?' she wondered indignantly. She put down her book and leaned back in her seat, gripping the paper-knife in both hands. There was nothing to be ashamed of. She ran through her recollections of her visit to Moscow. They were all good and pleasant. She recalled the ball and Vronsky and the look of slavish adoration in his eyes, recalled what had passed between them: there was nothing to be ashamed of. But just as she got to this point in her recollections the feeling of shame was intensified and some inner voice, when she was thinking about Vronsky, seemed to say to her: 'Warm, very warm, hot!' 'Well, what is it?' she asked herself resolutely, shifting her position on the seat. 'What does it mean? Am I really afraid of looking at the facts? Is there – can there be anything more between me and that officer-lad than there is between me and the rest of my acquaintances?' She laughed contemptuously and took up her book again; but this time she definitely could not follow what she was reading. She traced on the window with the paper-knife, then pressed its smooth cold surface to her cheek and nearly laughed aloud, suddenly and unaccountably overcome with joy. She felt her nerves being stretched more and more tightly, like strings round pegs. She felt her eyes opening wider and wider, her fingers and toes twitching nervously; felt something inside her oppressing her breathing; and all the shapes and sounds in the wavering half-light struck her with unaccustomed vividness. Moments of doubt kept coming upon her when she could not decide whether the train was moving forwards or backwards, or had come to a standstill. Was it Annushka at her side, or a stranger? 'What is that on the arm of the seat, a fur cloak or an animal? And what am I doing here? Am I myself or someone else?' She was terrified of giving way to this nightmare-state. But something seemed to draw her to it and she was free to yield to it or to resist. To rouse herself she stood up, discarded her rug, and took off the cape of her warm dress. She came to her senses for a moment and realized that the thin peasant in a long nankeen coat with a button missing who had entered the carriage was the stoker come to look at the thermometer, and that it was the wind and snow bursting in after him at the door; but then everything became confused again. ... That peasant with the long waist started gnawing at something on the wall; the old woman stretched her legs the whole length of the carriage, which she filled with a black cloud; after that there was a terrible screech and clatter, as though someone were being torn to pieces; then a red light blinded her eyes, and at last a wall rose up and blotted everything out. Anna felt as if she were falling from a height. But all this, far from seeming dreadful, was rather pleasant. The voice of a man muffled up and covered with snow shouted something in her ear. She rose and pulled herself together, realizing that they had stopped at a station and that this was the guard. She asked Annushka to hand her the cape and shawl she had taken off, put them on and moved towards the door.

'Are you getting out?' asked Annushka.

'Yes, I want a breath of air. It is very hot in here.'

She opened the carriage door. The snow and the wind rushed forward and fought with her for the door. And she enjoyed this too. She opened the door and went out. The wind seemed to be waiting for her; it whistled merrily and tried to snatch her up and carry her off but with one hand she felt for the cold handrail and, holding her skirt down, stepped on to the platform and to the lee of the carriage. The wind blew boisterously on the steps of the coach but on the platform sheltered by the train it was quiet. With delight she filled her lungs with deep breaths of snowy, frosty air and standing beside the carriage looked round at the platform and the lighted station.

30

THE terrible storm tore and shrieked between the wheels of the train and round the scaffolding at the corner of the station. The railway carriages, the pillars, the people, and everything that could be seen were covered on one side with snow getting thicker and thicker. Now and then the storm would abate for an instant, and then blow with such gusts that it seemed impossible to stand up against it. Meanwhile people ran along chatting cheerfully together, creaking the boards of the platform and constantly opening and shutting the heavy doors. The stooping shadow of a man glided past her feet and she heard the sound of a hammer upon iron. 'Let me have that telegram!' came an angry voice out of the stormy darkness on the other side. 'This way, please! Number twenty-eight!' other voices shouted, and muffled figures hurried by covered with snow. Two gentlemen with lighted cigarettes between their lips walked past her. She took another deep breath to get her fill of the fresh air and had just drawn her hand out of her muff to take hold of the handrail and get back into the carriage when another man wearing a military overcoat stepped close to her, shutting out the flickering light from the lamp-post. She looked round and instantly recognized Vronsky. Putting his hand to the peak of his cap, he bowed to her and asked if she needed anything and could he be of service to her? For some time she gazed intently at him, making no answer, and, though he stood in the shadow, she saw, or fancied she saw, even the expression of his face and eyes. It was the same expression of reverential ecstasy which had so worked upon her the night before. She had assured herself more than once during the last few days and again a

117

moment ago that Vronsky was no more to her than any of the hundreds of identical young men one came across everywhere, and that she would never allow herself to bestow a thought on him. Yet in the first flash of seeing him again a feeling of joyful pride swept over her. She had no need to ask why he was there. She knew as well as if he had told her that he was there in order to be where she was.

'I did not know you were travelling. What are you coming for?' she asked, letting fall the hand which was about to grasp the handrail. An irrepressible delight and animation shone in her face.

'What am I coming for?' he repeated, looking straight into her eyes. 'You know that I have come to be where you are,' he said. 'I can't help myself.'

At that moment the wind, as if it had surmounted all obstacles, sent the snow flying from the carriage roofs and rattled a loose sheet of iron; while in front the hoarse whistle of the engine began to wail, plaintive and mournful. All the awfulness of the storm now appeared to her more beautiful than ever. He had said what her heart longed to hear, though she feared it with her reason. She made no answer and in her face he saw conflict.

'Forgive me if what I said offends you,' he pleaded.

He spoke courteously, respectfully, but with such firm insistence that it was a long time before she could reply.

'You should not say that, and I beg of you, if you are a gentleman, to forget it, as I will forget it,' she said at last.

'Not one word, not one gesture of yours shall I, could I ever forget ...'

'Stop, stop!' she cried, vainly striving to impart a stern expression to her face, into which he was gazing passionately. And taking hold of the cold handrail, she clambered up the steps and quickly got into the corridor of the train. But there she stopped, going over in her mind what had taken place. Though she could remember neither her own words nor his, she felt instinctively that that brief interchange had drawn them terribly close together; and this both frightened her and made her happy. After a few seconds she went into the carriage and sat down. The tension which had tormented her before not only returned but grew worse, and reached such a pitch that she was afraid every minute that something within her would snap under the intolerable strain. She did not sleep the whole night. But there was nothing unpleasant or sad about that nervous tension or the visions which filled her imagination: on the contrary, they seemed joyful, glowing, and exhilarating. Towards morning Anna sank into a doze, sitting up in her seat. When she awoke it was already broad daylight and the train was nearing Petersburg. At once thoughts of home, of husband and son, of the cares of this day and those that were to follow beset her.

As soon as the train stopped at Petersburg and she got out, the first person she noticed was her husband. 'Good heavens, why are his ears like that?' she thought, looking at his cold, distinguished figure and especially at the cartilages of his ears pressing up against the brim of his round hat. Catching sight of her, he advanced, his lips falling into their habitual sarcastic smile and his large tired eyes looking straight at her. A disagreeable sensation oppressed her heart when she met his fixed and weary gaze, as though she had expected to find him different. She was particularly impressed by the feeling of dissatisfaction with herself which she experienced when they met. It was that old familiar feeling, like a consciousness of hypocrisy, which she experienced in her relations with her husband. But hitherto she had not taken note of the feeling, whereas now she was clearly and painfully aware of it.

'Yes, as you see, here is your devoted husband, as devoted as in the first year of marriage, burning with impatience to see you,' he said in his slow, thin voice and the tone which he almost always adopted with her, a tone of derision for anyone who could talk like that in earnest.

'Is Seriozha all right?' she asked.

'And is that all the reward I get for my ardour?' he said. 'Yes, he is quite all right, quite all right ...'

31

VRONSKY did not even try to sleep that night. He sat in his place, his eyes staring straight before him or scanning the people who got in or out; and if on previous occasions his air of imperturbable composure had struck and upset those who did not know him, he now seemed haughtier and more self-sufficient than ever. He looked at people as if they were things. A nervous young man, a clerk at the local courts, sitting opposite, began to detest him on account of that look. The young man asked him for a light, addressed remarks to him, and even nudged him to make him feel that he was not a thing but a person; but Vronsky paid no more heed to him than to the lamp, and the young man made a wry face, feeling that he was losing his self-control under the stress of this refusal to recognize him as a human being.

Vronsky saw nothing and no one. He felt like a king, not because he believed that he had made an impression on Anna – he did not believe that yet – but because the impression she had made on him filled him with happiness and pride.

What would come of it all he did not know and did not even consider. He felt that all his powers, hitherto dissipated and wasted, were now concentrated and bent with fearful energy on a single blissful goal. And this made him happy. He knew only that he had told her the truth: that he had come where she was, that the whole happiness and meaning of life for him now lay in seeing and hearing her. When he had got out of the train at Bologova to drink a glass of seltzer-water and had caught sight of Anna, involuntarily his first words had told her what was in his heart. And he was glad that he had told her, that she knew it now and was thinking of it. He did not sleep at all that night. When he was back in his carriage he kept going over all the circumstances in which he had seen her and everything she had said; and pictures of what the future might bring floated through his imagination, causing his heart to swoon.

In spite of his sleepless night, when he got out of the train at Petersburg he felt as vigorous and fresh as after a cold bath. He paused near his compartment, waiting for her to appear. 'I shall see her once more,' he said to himself, smiling unconsciously, 'I shall see her walk, her face; she will say something, turn her head, glance at me, even perhaps smile.' But before he caught sight of her, he saw her husband, whom the station-master was deferentially escorting through the crowd. 'Ah, yes! The husband!' And then for the first time did Vronsky clearly realize that there was someone, a husband, attached to her. He knew she had a husband but had hardly believed in his existence, and only fully believed in it when he caught sight of him and saw his head and shoulders and legs in their black trousers; and especially when he saw this husband calmly take her hand with an air of ownership.

Seeing Karenin with his fresh Petersburg face and austere, self-confident figure, his round hat and his slightly-rounded back, Vronsky believed in his existence and experienced the same disagreeable sensation a man tortured by thirst might feel on reaching a spring and finding that a dog, a sheep, or a pig has drunk of it and muddied the water. Karenin's flat feet and the way he swung his hips when he walked were particularly offensive to Vronsky. He acknowledged only his own right to love Anna. But she was still the same, and the sight of her had the same effect on him, physically exhilarating and stimulating him, filling his soul with happiness. He told his German valet, who came running up from the second-class, to get his luggage and take it home; and he himself went up to her. He saw husband and wife meet and noted with a lover's insight the signs of slight reserve with which she spoke to her husband. 'No, she does not love him, she cannot love him,' he decided to himself.

As he drew near her from behind, he noticed with joy that she was aware of his approach and made to look round, and on recognizing him turned to her husband again.

'Did you have a good night?' he inquired, bowing to her and to her husband together, and leaving it to Karenin to take the bow as meant for himself and to acknowledge it or not, as he pleased.

'Excellent, thank you,' she replied.

Her face looked tired and had none of that play of animation which peeped out now in her smile and now in her eyes; but for an instant as she glanced at him her eyes lighted up, and though the fire was at once extinguished, the instant made him happy. She turned to her husband to find out whether he knew Vronsky. Karenin looked at him with displeasure, vaguely recalling who this was. Vronsky's composure and self-confidence thrust like a scythe on stone upon the cold self-confidence of Karenin.

'Count Vronsky,' said Anna.

'Ah, we have met before, I believe,' said Karenin indifferently, holding out his hand. 'You set off with the mother and return with the son,' he said, articulating each syllable as though they were worth a rouble apiece. 'Back from a furlough, I presume?' he remarked to Vronsky; and without waiting for a reply said to his wife in his facetious tone: 'Well, were many tears shed in Moscow when you came away?'

By addressing himself thus to his wife he gave Vronsky to understand that he wished to be left alone and, turning to him, touched his hat. But Vronsky appealed to Anna:

'I hope I may have the honour of calling on you?'

Karenin considered Vronsky wearily.

'Delighted,' he said coldly. 'We are at home on Mondays.' Then, dismissing Vronsky altogether, he said to his wife in his usual bantering manner: 'What a good thing I just had half an hour to spare to meet you and display my devotion!'

'You insist too much on your devotion for me to value it very much,' she responded in the same facetious tone, involuntarily listening to the sound of Vronsky's step behind them. 'But what has it to do with me?' she said to herself and began asking her husband how Seriozha had got on without her.

'Oh, splendidly! Mariette says he has been very good and ... I am sorry to disappoint you ... has not missed you ... unlike your husband. But thank you once again, my dear, for making me the present of a day. Our dear *Samovar* will be in ecstasies.' (He called the celebrated Countess Lydia Ivanovna a samovar because she was always bubbling and boiling with excitement.) 'She was asking after you. And, you know, if I may venture a word of advice, you had better go and see her to-day. She does feel so about everything. Now, on top of all her other cares, she has taken to heart this business of the Oblonskys.'

The Countess Lydia Ivanovna was a friend of her husband's and the centre of that coterie of Petersburg society with which Anna, through her husband, was most closely connected.

'But I wrote to her.'

'Yes, but she wants to hear all the details. Go and see her, if you're not too tired, my dear. Well, Kondraty is here with the carriage for you. I have to go to my committee. Now I shall not have to dine by myself again,' he continued, no longer banteringly. 'You can't imagine how I used ...' And with a long pressure of her hand and a meaning smile he helped her into the carriage.

32

THE first person to meet Anna when she reached home was her son. He rushed down the stairs to her, heedless of his governess's cries, and with wild enthusiasm called out 'Mama! Mama!' He ran to her and clung round her neck.

'I told you it was Mama!' he shouted to the governess. 'I knew!'

Just as her husband had done, her son produced on Anna a feeling akin to disappointment. In imagination she had pictured him nicer than he actually was. She had to descend to reality in order to enjoy him as he was. But as he was, he was charming, with his fair curls, blue eyes, and plump, shapely little legs in tightly dragged-up stockings. Anna felt an almost physical pleasure in his nearness to her, in his caresses, and it was a moral solace to meet his artless, trusting, loving gaze and listen to his naïve questions. She unpacked the presents Dolly's children had sent him and told him what sort of a little girl Tanya was in Moscow and how Tanya could read and was even teaching the other children to read.

'Why – aren't I as nice as she is?' asked Seriozha.

'To me you're nicer than anyone in the world.'

'I know I am,' said Seriozha, smiling.

Before Anna had had time to finish her coffee the Countess Lydia Ivanovna was announced. The Countess Lydia Ivanovna was a tall, stout woman, with an unhealthily sallow skin and handsome, dreamy black eyes. Anna was fond of her, but to-day for the first time she seemed to see all her faults.

'Well, my dear, so you carried the olive branch?' asked the Countess Lydia Ivanovna as soon as she was inside the door.

'Yes, it's all over; but it wasn't as serious as we thought,' replied Anna. 'My *belle sœur* is in general too hasty.'

But the countess, though she was interested in everything that did not concern her, had a habit of never listening to what was of interest to her.

'Yes, there is plenty of sorrow and evil in the world,' she interrupted Anna. 'I am terribly worried to-day.'

'What is the matter?' asked Anna, trying to repress a smile.

'I am beginning to weary of vainly breaking lances for truth and sometimes I feel quite worn out. The "Little Sisters" –' (this was a philanthropic-cum-religious-cum-patriotic society) 'was going along splendidly, but it is impossible to do anything with those gentlemen,' the countess added with an ironical air of resignation to fate. 'They pounced on the idea, distorted it, and now argue in such a trivial, petty way. Two or three people, your husband among them, understand the full import of the work, but the others simply discredit it. Yesterday I had a letter from Pravdin ...'

Pravdin was a well-known Panslavist who lived abroad, and the Countess Lydia Ivanovna proceeded to relate the contents of his letter.

Then she went on to tell Anna of other unpleasantnesses and intrigue against the work for the unification of the churches, after which she hurried away as she had to be at a meeting of another society as well as to attend a Slavonic committee.

'It must always have been the same, of course; but how is it I never noticed before?' Anna said to herself. 'Or was she particularly irritated to-day? But it really is funny: her object is to do good, she is a Christian, and yet she is always angry and she always has enemies, and always enemies in the name of Christianity and doing good!'

After the Countess Lydia Ivanovna had gone, another friend, the wife of a chief secretary, arrived and gave Anna all the news of the town. At three she too went away, promising to return for dinner. Karenin was at the ministry. Left alone, Anna spent the time before dinner in watching her son have his meal (which he had separately by himself), in putting her things in order, and in reading and answering the notes and letters that had accumulated on her table.

The unaccountable feeling of shame she had felt during the journey, and her agitation, had completely vanished. With her life back to normal she again felt steady and irreproachable.

She thought with wonder of the state she had been in on the previous day. 'What had happened? Nothing. Vronsky said something silly, which it was easy to put a stop to, and I answered as I ought to have done. I must not tell my husband about it, and there is no need to. To speak of it would be to give it an importance which it does not have.' She remembered how she had once told her husband about one of his young subordinates in Petersburg who had made her what almost amounted to a declaration, and how Karenin had answered that every woman in society was exposed to that sort of thing, but that he had complete confidence in her tact and could never permit himself to demean himself and her by being jealous. 'So there is no need to say anything, then? No, thank God; and besides, there is nothing to tell!' she said to herself.

33

KARENIN returned from the ministry at four o'clock but, as often happened, he had not time to go up to Anna's room. He went into his study to see the various people waiting for him with petitions and to sign some papers brought him by his private secretary. The Karenins always had three or four guests dining with them and to-day there was an old lady, a cousin of Karenin's, the chief secretary of the department with his wife, and a young man who had been recommended to Karenin for a post. Anna went into the drawing-room to entertain them. Punctually at five – before the bronze Peter the First clock had finished striking – Karenin entered in evening dress with a white tie and two orders on his coat, as he had to go out directly after dinner. Every minute of his life was apportioned and filled. And in order to accomplish all that he had to do each day he observed the strictest punctuality. 'Without haste and without respite,' was his motto. He came into the room, greeted everyone, and quickly sat down, smiling to his wife.

'Yes, my solitude is over. You would not believe how irksome' (he stressed the word *irksome*) 'it is to dine alone!'

During dinner he talked a little to his wife about things in Moscow, asking after Oblonsky with an ironical smile; but for the most part conversation was general and dealt with Petersburg official and social affairs. After dinner he spent half an hour with his guests and then, giving his wife another smile and pressing her hand, he withdrew and drove off to the council. Anna did not go out either to the Princess Betsy Tverskoy who, hearing of her return, had invited her, or to the theatre, where she had a box for that evening. Her chief reason for not going out was that the gown on which she had counted was not ready. When she investigated her wardrobe after the departure of her guests, Anna was very much put out. She had always been very clever at dressing well on comparatively little money and before going to Moscow had left three dresses to be altered to look like new. They should have been finished three days ago but apparently two were not nearly ready, while the third had not been altered as Anna wished. The dressmaker came and explained that it was better the way she had done it, and Anna had so lost her temper that she felt ashamed afterwards. To regain her composure she went into the nursery and spent the whole evening with her son, putting him to bed herself, making the sign of the cross over him, and tucking him up. She was glad she had not gone out anywhere and had spent the evening so agreeably at home. She felt light-hearted and tranquil, saw quite clearly that what had appeared of such consequence in the train was merely one of the ordinary insignificant incidents of society life, and that she had no reason to feel ashamed in her own or anyone else's eyes. Anna sat down by the fire with her English novel and waited for her husband.

Exactly at half past nine she heard his ring and he came into the room.

'Here you are at last!' she said, holding out her hand to him.

He kissed her hand and seated himself beside her.

'On the whole, then, I see your visit was a success,' he remarked.

'Oh yes,' she replied and started telling him about everything from the beginning: her journey with the Countess Vronsky, her arrival, the accident at the railway-station. Then she described the pity she had felt, first for her brother and afterwards for Dolly.

'I don't see how a man like that can be exonerated, even though he is your brother,' said Karenin severely.

Anna smiled. She knew he said that expressly to show that family considerations could not deter him from giving his genuine opinion. She knew this trait in her husband's character and liked it.

'I am glad it has all ended satisfactorily and that you are back again,' he continued. 'Tell me, what are they saying in Moscow about the new measure I have got passed in the council?'

Anna had heard nothing about this measure and she felt conscience-stricken that she could so lightly forget what was of such importance to him.

'Here, on the other hand, it has created quite a stir,' he said with a complacent smile.

She saw that he wanted to tell her something agreeable to himself about the affair and by means of questions she led him on to recount it. With the same complacent smile he told her of the ovations he had received as a result of getting the measure through.

'Of course, I was very pleased. It shows that at last we are beginning to take an intelligent and steady view of the matter.'

Having finished his second glass of tea with cream and his roll, he got up to go to his study.

'And you've not been anywhere this evening? It must have been dull for you,' he said.

'Oh no!' she replied, getting up after him and accompanying him across the room to his study. 'What are you reading now?' she asked.

'At the moment I am reading Duc de Lille – *Poésie des Enfers*,' he replied. 'A most remarkable book.'

Anna smiled, as people smile at the foibles of those they love, and slipping her arm through his walked with him to the study door. She knew his habit, which had grown into a necessity, of reading in the evening. She knew that in spite of his official duties, which swallowed up nearly all his time, he considered it incumbent on him to keep abreast of everything of importance that appeared in the intellectual world. She knew, too, that really he was interested in books on politics, philosophy, and theology and that art was utterly foreign to his nature; yet, in spite of this – or, rather, because of it – he never missed anything which was being discussed in the world of art, but made it his duty to read everything. She knew that in politics, philosophy, and theology he had his doubts and uncertainties; but on questions of art and poetry, and especially music – of which he was totally devoid of understanding – he held the most rigid and fixed opinions. He was fond of talking about Shakespeare, Raphael, and Beethoven, of the significance of new schools of poetry and music, all of which he had classified in his mind with the utmost precision.

'Well, God bless you,' she said at the door of the study, where a shaded candle and carafe of water had been placed ready beside his arm-chair. 'And I must write to Moscow.'

He pressed her hand and kissed it again.

'After all, he's a good man; upright, kind, and remarkable in his own line,' Anna said to herself when she had returned to her room, as though defending him from attack – from the accusation that he was not lovable. 'But why is it his ears stick out so oddly? Or has he had his hair cut too short?'

On the stroke of midnight, when Anna was still sitting at her bureau finishing a letter to Dolly, she heard the even step of Alexei Alexandrovich in his bedroom slippers. He had had his bath and brushed his hair and came in, a book under his arm.

'Time for bed now,' he said with a special smile, crossing into the bedroom.

'And what right had he to look at him like that?' thought Anna, recalling how Vronsky had looked at Karenin.

Undressing, she went into the bedroom; but not only was the animation gone that had sparkled in her eyes and her smile while she was in Moscow – even the fire in her now seemed quenched or hidden far away.

34

On his departure from Petersburg, Vronsky had left his large suite of rooms in Morskaya Street to his friend and favourite comrade Petritsky.

Petritsky was a young lieutenant, not particularly well-connected, and not only not wealthy but up to his ears in debt, drunk every evening, and often under arrest for all sorts of ludicrous and disgraceful escapades; but popular both with his comrades and superior officers. Arriving home about noon from the station, Vronsky saw a familiar hired brougham outside. Even as he rang at the door he heard masculine laughter, a woman's lisping voice, and Petritsky shouting: 'If that's one of the villains, don't let him in!' Vronsky told the servant not to announce him and slipped quietly into the ante-room. The Baroness Shilton, a friend of Petritsky's, resplendent in lilac satin, with a rosy face and flaxen hair, was sitting at the round table making coffee and filling the whole room, like a canary, with her Parisian chatter. Petritsky in his greatcoat and the cavalry captain Kamerovsky in full uniform, probably straight from parade, sat on either side of her.

'Hurrah! Vronsky!' cried Petritsky, jumping up and scraping his chair. 'Our host himself! Baroness, give him some coffee out of the new coffee-pot. Well, we didn't expect you! I hope you are pleased with this ornament to your study,' he said, indicating the baroness. 'You do know each other?'

'I should think so!' replied Vronsky, smiling merrily and pressing the baroness's small hand. 'Yes, indeed! We are old friends.'

'You have returned from a journey?' asked the baroness. 'Then I will run. Oh, I'll be off home this minute if I'm in the way.'

'You are at home wherever you are, Baroness,' said Vronsky. 'How do you do, Kamerovsky,' he added, coldly shaking hands with Kamerovsky.

'There! You never manage to say pretty things like that,' remarked the baroness to Petritsky.

'Oh no? After dinner I will say something quite as good.'

'There is no merit in it after dinner! Well, go and have a wash and tidy yourself up and I will make you some coffee,' said the baroness sitting down again and carefully turning the screw in the new coffee-pot. 'Pierre, pass me the coffee,' she said to Petritsky, calling him Pierre because of his surname and making no secret of her relations with him. 'I want to put some more in.'

'You'll spoil it!'

'No, I shan't. Well, and your wife?' the baroness said suddenly, interrupting Vronsky's conversation with his comrades. 'We here have been marrying you off. Have you brought back a wife?'

'No. Baroness. A Bohemian I was born and a Bohemian I shall die.'

'So much the better, so much the better. Shake hands on it.'

And, detaining him, the baroness began telling Vronsky all her latest plans, interspersed with jokes, and asking his advice.

'He still won't agree to give me a divorce! What am I to do?' (*He* was her husband.) 'I want to begin a suit against him. What would you advise me? Kamerovsky, look after the coffee – it is boiling over. Don't you see, I am busy! I want a lawsuit because I must have my property. You see how absurd it is, that because I am supposed to be unfaithful to him,' she said contemptuously, 'he wants to enjoy my property.'

Vronsky listened with pleasure to this pretty woman's gay prattle, agreed with what she said, and gave her half-playful advice, in general immediately falling into his usual manner with women of her sort. In his Petersburg world people were divided into two quite distinct classes. One – the lower class – commonplace, stupid, and, above all, ridiculous people, who believed that a husband should live with the one woman to whom he was married, that young girls should be virtuous, women chaste, and men virile, self-controlled, and strong; that children should be brought up to earn their bread and pay their debts, and other such nonsense. These were the old-fashioned, ridiculous people. But there was another class: the real people, the kind to which his set belonged, in which the important thing was to be elegant, handsome, broad-minded, daring, gay, and ready to surrender unblushingly to every passion and to laugh at everything else.

For the first few moments only Vronsky felt startled after the impression of a totally different world that he had brought back with him from Moscow; but at once, as he might have put his feet into old slippers, he dropped back into his former jolly, pleasant world.

The coffee never got made but boiled over, splashing everyone and doing just what was required of it – that is, it provided an excuse for noise and laughter and stained the valuable carpet and the baroness's gown.

'Well now, I'll say good-bye, or you will never get washed and I shall have on my conscience the worst sin – uncleanliness – a well-bred person can commit. ... So you advise me to take a knife to his throat?'

'To be sure – only hold it so that your little hand just touches his lips. Then he will kiss it and all will be well,' replied Vronsky.

'At the French theatre to-night, then?' and with a rustle of her skirts she vanished.

Kamerovsky rose too, and Vronsky, without waiting for him to go, shook hands with him and went into his dressing-room. While he was washing, Petritsky gave him a brief outline of his own affairs in so far as there had been any change since Vronsky's departure. He had absolutely no money. His father had said he would neither give him any nor pay his debts. His tailor was trying to get him locked up, and another fellow too was threatening to get him locked up. The colonel of the regiment had announced that if these scandals continued he would have to leave the regiment. He was sick to death of the baroness, especially since she'd taken to offering him money; but he had found a girl – he would let Vronsky see her – a marvel, a beauty, the purest Oriental type, 'a sort of "bondmaid Rebecca", you know'. He had had a row, too, with Berkoshov, and was going to send seconds to him, but of course nothing would come of it. Altogether everything was grand and jolly in the extreme. And without letting his friend go into the details of his position, Petritsky proceeded to recount all the news of interest. Listening to Petritsky's familiar stories in the familiar surroundings of the rooms he had lived in for the last three years, Vronsky experienced a pleasant feeling of having returned to his customary carefree Petersburg life.

'Impossible!' he cried, releasing the pedal of the wash-basin in which he had been sousing his healthy red neck. 'Impossible!' he cried at the news that Laura had thrown over Fertinhof and gone to live with Mileyev. 'And is he still as stupid and self-satisfied as ever? And how's Buzulukov?'

'Oh, there is a lovely story about Buzulukov!' cried Petritsky. 'You know his passion for balls? He never misses a single Court ball. Well, he went to a big ball wearing one of the new helmets. Have you seen the new helmets? They are very good, much lighter than the others. Well, he was standing. ... I say, do listen.'

'I am listening,' answered Vronsky, rubbing himself with a rough towel.

'Up comes the Grand-Duchess on the arm of some ambassador or other and, as ill-luck would have it, she begins talking to him about the new helmets. The Grand-Duchess positively must show the ambassador one of the new helmets. They see our hero standing there.' (Petritsky imitated Buzulukov with the helmet.) 'The Grand-Duchess asks him for the helmet, but he won't let her have it. What do you think of that? The fellows wink at him, nod, frown – give it to her, do! But no! He stands as if turned to stone. Just imagine it! ... Then this ... what's his name, this ambassador ... tries to take it from him, but he won't let go! The other snatches it away and hands it to the Grand-Duchess. "This is one of the new ones," says the Grand-Duchess, turning it over and – just imagine – plop! out tumble a pear and some sweets, a couple of pounds of sweets! ... Our dear boy had pinched them!'

Vronsky shook with laughter. And long afterwards, even when speaking of other things, every time he thought of the helmet he would burst into roars of hearty laughter, showing his strong, even teeth.

Having heard all the news, Vronsky, with the help of his valet, got into his uniform, and went to report himself. He intended when he had done that to go and see his brother and then Betsy and to pay a few calls in order to pave his way into that society where he could meet Madame Karenin. As was usually the case when he was in Petersburg, he left the house only to return in the small hours of the morning.

PART TWO

I

TOWARDS the close of the winter a consultation took place at the Shcherbatskys' in order to pronounce on the state of Kitty's health and decide what should be done to restore her failing strength. She had been ill, and with the approach of spring grew worse. The family doctor prescribed cod-liver oil, then iron, and then nitrate of silver, but as none of them did any good, and as he advised her to go abroad for the spring, a celebrated specialist was called in. The celebrated specialist, an extremely handsome man and still comparatively young, demanded to examine the patient. He insisted, with peculiar satisfaction, it seemed, that maidenly modesty was only a relic of the dark ages and that nothing could be more natural than for a man still in his prime to handle a young girl's naked body. He considered this natural because he did it every day and did not, so he believed, either feel or think anything wrong when he did it. He therefore considered modesty in a girl not merely a relic of the dark ages but an affront to himself.

There was nothing for it but to submit, since, although all the doctors had studied in the same school and from the same books and learned the same science, and though some people said this celebrated man was a bad doctor, in the princess's household and among her set it was for some reason accepted that this celebrated doctor alone possessed some special knowledge, and that he alone could save Kitty. Having attentively examined and sounded the embarrassed patient, who was dazed with shame, the celebrated specialist carefully washed his hands and was now standing in the drawing-room talking to the prince. The prince listened to the doctor with a frown, now and then giving a little cough. As a man who had seen something of life and was neither a fool nor an invalid, he had no faith in doctors, and in his heart was furious at the whole farcical business, the more so as he was probably the only one who really understood the cause of Kitty's illness. 'Jabbering magpie!' he thought, as he listened to the celebrated specialist's chatter about his daughter's symptoms. The specialist was meanwhile finding it hard not to show his contempt for this old fool of a nobleman and had difficulty in coming down to his level of intelligence. He saw that it was waste of time to talk to the old man and that the head of this house was the mother. It was before her that he would scatter the pearls of his wisdom. Just then the princess entered the drawing-room with the family physician. The prince withdrew, trying not to let them see how absurd he thought the whole performance. The princess was distracted and at a loss to know what to do. She felt she had sinned against Kitty.

'Well, doctor, give us your verdict,' she said. 'Tell me everything.' 'Is there any hope?' she meant to say, but her lips quivered and she could not utter the words. 'Well, doctor?'

'In a moment, Princess. I will just confer with my colleague and then I shall have the honour of giving you my opinion.'

'So I had better leave you?'

'If you please.'

The princess sighed and left the room.

When the doctors were alone, the family physician began nervously expounding his opinion, to the effect that it was the beginning of tuberculous trouble but ... etc. The celebrated specialist listened, and half-way through the speech looked at his large gold watch.

'Yes,' he said, 'but ...'

The family physician stopped respectfully in the middle of what he was saying.

'We cannot, as you know, determine the beginning of a tuberculous condition. Till there are cavities, there is nothing definite to go by. But we may suspect it. And there are indications: malnutrition, nervous excitability, and so on. The question is this: when there is reason to suspect tuberculosis, what is to be done to maintain nutrition?'

'But of course you know that in these cases there is always some hidden moral and emotional factor,' the family physician allowed himself to remark with a faint smile.

'Yes, that goes without saying,' replied the celebrated specialist with another glance at his watch. 'Excuse me, am I right in thinking the Yausky bridge is back in place, or shall I have to drive round?' he asked. 'Ah, it's back! So I can do it in twenty minutes. We were saying, then, that the problem is how to maintain nutrition and restore the nervous system. The two are connected and we must see to both.'

'How about a tour abroad?' asked the family physician.

'I am opposed to foreign tours. And mark this: if there are the beginnings of tuberculosis – of which we cannot yet be certain – a foreign tour will be no use. It is essential to find some treatment which would nourish the patient and do no harm.'

And the celebrated specialist explained his plan for a treatment of Soden waters, a remedy obviously prescribed primarily on the grounds that it could do no harm.

The family physician heard him out attentively and respectfully.

'But I would urge in favour of a journey abroad that it would be a complete change and would take her away from all unhappy associations. Besides, it is what the mother wants,' he said.

'Ah! Well, in that case, then, let them go. Only, those German quacks will do mischief. ... They must be got to carry out my instructions. ... However, let them go.'

He looked at his watch again.

'Well, I must be off!' and he moved towards the door.

The celebrated specialist informed the princess (his sense of what was due suggested this to him) that he would have to see the patient once more.

'What – another examination!' exclaimed her mother with horror.

'Oh no, only a few minor points, Princess.'

'As you please, doctor.'

And the mother, followed by the specialist, went back to Kitty, who was standing in the middle of the drawing-room, her thin cheeks flushed and her eyes burning after the ordeal she had endured. When the doctor entered she flushed crimson and her eyes filled with tears. Her illness and the whole treatment seemed to her such a silly, ridiculous business. To try to cure her seemed as ridiculous as trying to piece together a smashed vase. Her heart was broken. Why did they want to dose her with pills and powders? But she could not grieve her mother, especially as her mother considered herself to blame.

'Sit down, please, Princess,' the celebrated specialist said to her.

With a smile he sat down facing her, felt her pulse, and again started asking tiresome questions. She answered him, but suddenly grew angry and stood up.

'Forgive me, doctor, but really this will lead nowhere. This is the third time you've asked me the same thing.'

The celebrated specialist did not take offence.

'Nervous irritability,' he said to the princess, when Kitty had gone from the room. 'However, I had finished ...'

And in learned language the doctor diagnosed Kitty's condition to the princess, as an exceptionally intelligent woman, concluding with directions as to how the unnecessary waters were to be drunk. In reply to the question whether they should go abroad, the specialist pondered deeply, as if considering a weighty problem. Finally he pronounced his decision: they could go abroad, but must not trust to quacks and must always refer to him in any need.

It was just as though something nice had happened after the doctor had gone. The mother in much better spirits rejoined her daughter and Kitty, too, pretended to be more cheerful. She often, almost always, had to pretend now.

'Really, I am quite well, *maman*. But if you want to go abroad, let us go!' she said, and, trying to appear interested in the proposed tour, she began to talk about the preparations for their departure.

2

SOON after the doctor had left, Dolly arrived. She knew there was to be a consultation that day and, though she had only recently got up after a confinement (she had given birth to a girl at the end of the winter), and had trouble and anxiety enough of her own, she had left her baby and another daughter who was ill and called to hear Kitty's fate, which was being decided that day.

'Well, what happened?' she said, coming into the drawing-room without taking off her bonnet. 'You are all in good spirits, so everything must be all right.'

They tried to repeat the specialist's words, but it appeared that though he had spoken very fluently and at great length, it was quite impossible to report what he had said. The only thing of interest was the decision that they should go abroad.

Dolly gave an involuntary sigh. Her dearest friend, her sister, was going away. And as it was, her own life was none too happy. After their reconciliation her relations with her husband had become humiliating. Anna's welding had not held, and domestic harmony had broken again at the same place. There was nothing definite, but Oblonsky was hardly ever at home, there was hardly ever any money, and suspicions that he was being unfaithful continually tortured Dolly, who tried to repel them, fearful of the agonies of jealousy she had been through before. The first onslaught of jealousy, once survived, could not be repeated. Nor even the discovery of infidelities could ever again affect her as it had done the first time. Such a discovery now would only mean breaking up family habits, and she let herself be deceived, despising him and still more herself for such weakness. On top of all this, the care of a large family was a constant worry to her: either something went wrong with the baby's feeding, or the nurse left, or, as at present, one of the children would fall ill.

'And how are you all?' asked her mother.

'Ah, *maman*, you have trouble enough of your own! Lily is not well, and I am afraid it is scarlet fever. I have come out now to hear the news, but if – which God forbid – it is scarlet-fever I shall have to stay at home all the time.'

When the specialist had gone the old prince too came out of his study and after presenting his cheek to Dolly and saying a few words to her, he turned to his wife:

'Well, and what have you decided? Are you going? And what do you intend to do with me?'

'I think you had better stay behind, Alexandre,' said his wife.

'That's as you like.'

'*Maman*, why should not Papa come with us?' said Kitty. 'It would be nicer for him and for us too.'

The old prince got up and smoothed Kitty's hair with his hand. She lifted her face and, forcing a smile, looked up at him. She always felt that he understood her better than the rest of the family, though he did not say much. Being the youngest, she was her father's favourite, and it seemed to her that his love gave him insight. When her gaze now met his kindly blue eyes looking intently at her, it seemed to her that he saw right through her and understood all the trouble that was within her. Blushing, she leaned towards him, expecting a kiss, but he only patted her hair and said:

'These silly chignons! Instead of stroking my child's hair, I stroke the hair of some departed old women. Well, Dolly, my dear,' he said, addressing his eldest daughter, 'what is that hero of yours doing?'

'Nothing much, Papa,' replied Dolly, understanding that he referred to her husband. 'He is always out – I hardly ever see him,' she could not resist adding with an ironical smile.

'What, hasn't he gone to the country yet to see about selling that forest?'

'No, he's still getting ready to.'

'Is he?' said the prince. 'So am I to get ready to go off too? I am all obedience,' he said to his wife, sitting down. 'And as for you, Katya,' he went on to his youngest daughter, 'you must wake up one fine morning and say to yourself: "Why, I'm quite well and happy and Papa and I will go out for a walk in the frost again." Eh?'

Her father's words seemed simple enough, but they threw Kitty into confusion and made her feel like a criminal who has been found out. 'Yes, he knows all about it and understands everything, and in these words he is telling me that, though I feel humiliated, I must get over my shame.' She could not summon up spirit to make any answer. She tried to say something but suddenly burst into tears and ran from the room.

'There, see what you have done with your joking!' the princess flew at her husband. 'You are always …' and she started on a string of reproaches.

The prince listened in silence to her scolding for some time but his face grew darker and darker.

'She is so pitiful, poor little dear, so pitiful, and you can't see that any allusion to what was the cause of it hurts her. Oh, to be so mistaken in anyone!' said the princess, and by the change in her tone Dolly and the prince knew she was speaking of Vronsky. 'I cannot understand why there aren't laws against such vile, odious people.'

'Oh, I can't stand this!' exclaimed the prince gloomily, getting up from his low chair as if wishing to escape but halting at the door. 'There are laws, my dear, and since you've challenged me to it, I'll tell you who is to blame for it all: you and you alone, no one but you. There always were and there still are laws against such young fellows! Yes, and if nothing had been done that ought not to have been done, old as I am, I would have called the young buck out to a duel. Yes, and now you physic her and fetch in these quacks.'

The prince appeared to have a great deal more to say but as soon as the princess heard his tone she subsided at once and became penitent, as she always did when the occasion was serious.

'Alexandre, Alexandre,' she whispered, moving nearer and starting to weep.

As soon as she began to cry the prince, too, calmed down and went up to her.

'There, that will do, that will do! You're wretched, too, I know. It can't be helped. No great harm has been done. God is merciful ... be thankful ...' he said, no longer knowing what he was saying, and after responding to the princess's tearful kiss which he felt on his hand, he went out of the room.

When Kitty had left the room in tears, Dolly's motherly instinct quickly perceived that here was work for a woman, and she prepared to do it. She took off her bonnet and, mentally rolling up her sleeves, prepared for action. While her mother was attacking her father, she tried to restrain her mother in so far as filial respect would allow. During the prince's outburst she kept silent, feeling shame for her mother and tenderness towards her father for his immediate return to kindliness. But when her father left them she prepared for the chief thing that was needed – to go and comfort Kitty.

'I've been meaning to tell you something for a long while, *maman*: do you know that Levin meant to make Kitty an offer the last time he was here? He told Stiva so.'

'What? I do not understand ...'

'Perhaps Kitty refused him? ... She did not tell you?'

'No, she has said nothing about either of them: she is too proud. But I know all this is on account of that ...'

'Yes, but suppose she refused Levin – and she would not have refused him if it hadn't been for the other, I know ... And then the other deceived her so dreadfully.'

It was too awful for the princess to think how much wrong she had done her daughter, and she broke out angrily:

'Oh, I don't understand a thing! Nowadays every girl wants to go her own way, as she pleases, and mothers are told nothing, and then ...'

'*Maman*, I will go to her.'

'Do, then. Am I stopping you?' said her mother.

3

When she went into Kitty's little boudoir – a pretty, pink room full of knick-knacks in *vieux saxe*, as fresh, pink, and gay as Kitty herself had been two months earlier – Dolly recalled how happily and lovingly they had arranged that room together the year before. Her heart turned cold when she saw Kitty sitting on a low chair near the door, her eyes fixed on a corner of the carpet. Kitty glanced at her sister and the cold, rather harsh expression on her face did not change.

'I am going home now, and I shall have to stay in, and you won't be able to come and see me,' said Dolly, sitting down beside her. 'I want to talk to you.'

'What about?' asked Kitty quickly, raising her head in dismay.

'About your troubles, of course.'

'I have no troubles.'

'Now, Kitty. Do you really imagine I could help knowing? I know all about it. And believe what I say, it's of so little consequence ... We've all been through it.'

Kitty was silent and her face looked stern.

'He is not worth suffering for,' pursued Dolly, going straight to the point.

'No, because he has slighted me,' Kitty said, her voice breaking. 'Don't talk about it! Please, don't talk about it!'

'But who can have told you that? No one has said that. I am sure he was in love with you, and would still be in love with you if it hadn't ...'

'Oh, this sympathizing is the most awful thing of all!' cried Kitty, suddenly flaring up.

She turned in her chair, flushed crimson, and began rapidly moving her fingers, pressing first with one hand, then with the other the buckle of a belt she was holding. Dolly knew this trick her sister had of clutching at something when she was excited; she knew how capable Kitty was in moments of excitement of forgetting herself and saying things that were disagreeable and better left unsaid. She tried to soothe her, but it was too late.

'What do you want me to feel – what is it?' Kitty said quickly. 'That I was in love with a man who did not care a straw for me and that I am dying for love of him? And it is my own sister who says this to me, my sister who thinks that ... that ... that she is sympathizing with me! ... No, I don't want this pity and humbug of yours!'

'Kitty, you are unfair.'

'Why do you torment me?'

'On the contrary, I ... I see you're unhappy ...'

But Kitty in her anger did not listen.

'There is nothing for me to grieve over and be comforted about. I have enough pride never to let myself care for a man who does not love me.'

'But I am not suggesting ... Only – tell me the truth,' said Dolly, taking her by the hand, 'tell me, did Levin speak to you? ...'

Mention of Levin seemed to deprive Kitty of the last fragments of self-control. She jumped up from her chair, flung the buckle on the floor, and, hands rapidly gesticulating, she began:

'What has Levin to do with it? I can't understand what you want to torment me for. I've told you, and I say it again, that I have some pride and never, *never* would I do what you do – go back to a man who has betrayed you, who loves another woman. I can't understand you, I can't understand you! You may do it, but I cannot!'

Having said these words, she looked at her sister and, seeing that Dolly sat silent, her head bowed sadly, instead of running out of the room as she had meant to, Kitty sat down near the door and, burying her face in her handkerchief, hung her head.

For a minute or two there was silence. Dolly was thinking about herself. The humiliation of which she was always conscious was peculiarly painful when her sister reminded her of it. She had not expected such cruelty from her and was angry with her. But suddenly she heard the rustle of a skirt and the sound of smothered sobbing. Two arms encircled her neck from below, and Kitty was kneeling before her.

'Dolly, dearest, I am so, so wretched!' she pleaded in a whisper. And the sweet, tear-stained face hid itself in the folds of Dolly's skirt.

As if tears were the necessary lubricant without which the mechanism of mutual confidence could not work successfully, after having had a cry the two sisters started talking not of what was uppermost in their minds, but of indifferent matters, and in so doing understood one another. Kitty knew that what she had said in a fit of anger about Stiva's unfaithfulness and her sister's humiliation had cut her poor sister to the quick, but that she was forgiven. Dolly for her part learned all that she wanted to know: she felt certain that her conjectures were correct and that Kitty's misery – her inconsolable misery – was really because Levin had made her an offer and she had refused him, but now that Vronsky had played her false she was ready to love Levin and detest Vronsky. Kitty did not say a word of all this: she spoke only of her state of mind.

'I have nothing to make me miserable,' she said when she had grown calmer, 'but can you understand that everything seems vile, odious, coarse to me, myself most of all? You cannot imagine what vile thoughts I have about everything.'

'Why, whatever vile thoughts can you have?' asked Dolly, smiling.

'The most utterly vile and coarse: I can't tell you. It's not unhappiness, not depression, but something much worse. It's as though all the good in me had disappeared, leaving only the evil. How can I explain to you?' she went on, noticing the puzzled look in her sister's eyes. 'Papa began saying something to me just now … and it seems to me he is thinking that all I need is to get married. Mamma takes me to a ball: and I think she is only taking me there to marry me off as quickly as possible and be free of me. I know it is not true, but I cannot get rid of these ideas. I can't bear to see so-called eligible young men. They seem to me to be taking my measure. Before it was a positive pleasure to go anywhere in a ball-dress, I used to delight in myself; now I feel ashamed and uncomfortable. What am I to do? And then, the doctor …'

Kitty hesitated. She wanted to continue that ever since this change had taken place in her, Oblonsky had become unbearably distasteful, and that she could not set eyes on him without having the grossest and ugliest thoughts.

'So you see, everything appears vile and odious,' she went on. 'That is my illness. Perhaps it will pass …'

'But you mustn't think about it.'

'I can't help it. It is only when I am with the children at your house that I feel all right.'

'What a pity you cannot come to us.'

'But I will come. I have had scarlet fever, and I will persuade *maman* to let me.'

Kitty insisted on having her own way, and moved to her sister's and nursed the children all through the scarlet fever, for scarlet fever it turned out to be. The two sisters brought all six children successfully through it, but Kitty's health did not improve and in Lent the Shcherbatskys went abroad.

4

THE top circle of Petersburg society is really one whole: everyone knows everyone else and all are on visiting terms with each other. But this large circle has its subdivisions. Anna Arkadyevna Karenin had friends and close connexions in three different sets. One of these was her husband's official, Government set, consisting of his colleagues and subordinates, who were linked or separated in the most diverse and capricious fashion by social conditions. Anna found it difficult now to recall the almost religious awe she had at first felt for these people. Now she knew them all as well as people know one another in a country town. She knew each one's habits and weaknesses and where the shoe pinched this or that foot. She knew their relations with one another and with the head authorities, knew who sided with whom, and how and by what means each supported himself, and who agreed or disagreed with whom and why. But despite what the Countess Lydia Ivanovna had to say, this bureaucratic circle of masculine interests had never interested Anna, and she avoided it.

Another circle with which Anna was closely connected was the one through which Karenin had made his career. The centre of this coterie was the Countess Lydia Ivanovna. It consisted of elderly, plain, benevolent, pious women and clever, learned, and ambitious men. One of the clever people who belonged to it called it 'the conscience of Petersburg society'. Karenin had the highest esteem for this circle, and Anna, with her special gift for getting on with everyone, in the early days of her life in Petersburg had made friends in this circle too. But now, since her return from Moscow, this circle had become unbearable. It seemed to her that she and all of them were insincere, and she began to feel so bored and ill at ease with them that she visited the Countess Lydia Ivanovna as little as possible.

The third circle with which Anna had ties was society proper – the world of balls, dinner-parties, brilliant toilettes, which clung on to the Court with one hand, lest it sink to the level of the *demi-monde* which the members of that fashionable world affected to despise, though their tastes were not only similar but identical. Her link with this circle was the Princess Betsy Tverskoy, her cousin's wife, who had an income of 120,000 roubles, and who had taken a great fancy to Anna on Anna's first appearance in society, made much of her, and drawn her into her own set, making fun of the Countess Lydia Ivanovna's coterie.

'When I am old and ugly, I shall become like her,' Betsy would say, 'but for a young and beautiful woman like you it's early yet for that house of charity.'

At first Anna had avoided the Princess Tverskoy's set as much as she could, because it meant living beyond her means and also because she really preferred the other; but since her visit to Moscow all this was reversed. She avoided her serious-minded friends and went into high society. There she saw Vronsky and experienced a tremulous joy every time she met him. She met him most frequently at Betsy's, who had been born a Vronsky herself and was his cousin. Vronsky went wherever there was a chance of meeting Anna and whenever he could spoke to her of his love. She gave him no encouragement, but every time they met her heart quickened with the same feeling of animation that had seized her in the train the day she first saw him. She knew that at the sight of him joy lit up her eyes and drew her lips into a smile, and she could not quench the expression of that joy.

At first Anna sincerely believed that she was displeased with him for daring to pursue her; but soon after her return from Moscow, having gone to a party where she expected to meet him but to which he did not come, she distinctly realized, by the disappointment that overcame her, that she had been deceiving herself and that his pursuit was not only not distasteful to her, but was the whole interest of her life.

The famous *prima-donna* was giving her second performance, and all the fashionable world was at the opera house. Catching sight of his cousin from his seat in the front row of the stalls, Vronsky went to her box, without waiting for the interval.

'Why didn't you come to dinner?' she asked, adding with a smile so that only he could hear, '*she was not there either.* But come after the opera.'

Vronsky looked at her inquiringly. She nodded. He thanked her with a smile and sat down beside her.

'And how you used to laugh at others!' continued the Princess

143

Betsy, who took particular pleasure in following the progress of this passion. 'What has become of all that? You are caught now, my dear.'

'That is all I want – to be caught,' replied Vronsky with his serene, good-humoured smile. 'To tell you the truth, my only complaint is that I am not caught enough! I am beginning to lose hope.'

'Whatever hope can you have?' said Betsy, offended on behalf of her friend. '*Entendons-nous* ...' But little lights danced in her eyes which said that she understood very well, and just as he did, what hope he might have.

'None,' said Vronsky, laughing and showing his compact teeth. 'Excuse me,' he added, taking the opera-glasses out of her hand and proceeding to scan over her bare shoulder the row of boxes opposite. 'I am afraid I am becoming ridiculous.'

He was very well aware that he ran no risk of appearing ridiculous in Betsy's eyes or in the eyes of fashionable people generally. He was very well aware that in their eyes the role of the disappointed lover of a young girl or of any single woman might be ridiculous; but the role of a man pursuing a married woman, who has made it the purpose of his life at all costs to draw her into adultery – that role had something fine and grand about it and could never be ridiculous; and so it was with a proud, glad smile lurking under his moustache that he lowered the opera-glasses and looked at his cousin.

'But why didn't you come to dine?' she said, contemplating him with admiration.

'I must tell you about that. I was busy, and doing what, do you suppose? If I give you a hundred guesses – a thousand, even – you'd never guess it. I was making peace between a husband and a fellow who had insulted the husband's wife. Yes, it's a fact!'

'Well, and did you succeed?'

'Nearly.'

'You must tell me all about it,' she said, getting up. 'Come back in the next interval.'

'I can't. I'm going on to the French theatre.'

'What? Deserting Nilsson?' asked Betsy in horror, though she could not for the life of her have distinguished Nilsson's voice from that of any chorus-girl.

'Can't help it. I have an appointment there, all to do with my mission of peace.'

' "Blessed are the peace-makers, for they shall be saved," ' said Betsy, vaguely remembering that she had heard someone say something of the sort. 'Well then, sit down and tell me all about it.'

5

And she sat down again.

It is rather indiscreet, but it's so good that it's an awful temptation to tell the story,' said Vronsky, looking at her with his laughing eyes. 'I shan't mention names.'

All the better. I shall guess.'

'Listen then: two gay young fellows were out driving ...'

'Officers of your regiment, of course?'

'I didn't say they were officers – simply two young men who had been lunching ...'

In other words, drinking.'

Possibly. They are on their way to dine with a comrade, and are in the gayest of spirits. They see a pretty woman passing them in a hired sledge and looking round and laughing and nodding to them – at least, so they fancy. Of course off they go after her, driving for all they are worth. To their surprise, their beauty stops at the door of the very house they are going to. The fair one darts upstairs to the top storey. They just manage to get a glimpse of red lips under a short veil and a pair of pretty little feet.'

'You describe it with such feeling that it seems to me you were one of the party.'

'And after what you said to me just now! Well, the young men go up to their comrade's rooms. He is giving a farewell dinner. There they really may have drunk a little too much, as one always does at farewell dinners. During dinner they inquire who lives at the top of the house. No one knows; only their host's valet, in answer to their inquiry whether there are any "mam'selles" upstairs, replies that a lot of them live round about. After dinner the young men go into their host's study to compose a letter to the fair stranger. It was a passionate epistle – a declaration, in fact. They take the letter upstairs themselves, in order to explain anything that might not be quite clear in it.'

'Why do you tell me such disgusting things? Well?'

'They ring. A maid comes to the door. They hand her the missive

145

and assure her that they are both so much in love that they are ready to die. The bewildered girl carries in their message. All at once out comes a gentleman with whiskers like sausages, red as a turkey-cock, and informs them that no one lives in that flat except his wife, and sends them both packing.'

'How do you know he had whiskers like sausages, as you say?'

'You just listen. I called there to-day to make peace.'

'Well, what happened?'

'This is the most interesting part of the story. It turns out that the happy couple are a Titular Councillor and his Titular wife. The Titular Councillor lodges a complaint and I am nominated peace-maker – and what a peace-maker! ... I assure you Talleyrand couldn't hold a candle to me.'

'What was the difficulty?'

'Just listen. ... We duly apologized. "We are desperately sorry. We beg you to overlook our unfortunate mistake." The Titular Councillor with his sausages begins to melt, but he, too, wishes to express his sentiments and immediately he begins to express them he starts getting heated and saying unpleasant things; and again I have to bring all my diplomatic talents into action. "I quite agree that their behaviour was reprehensible, but may I beg you to take into account that it was a mistake and make allowances for their youth? Besides which, the young men had only just been lunching together, do you see? They regret it deeply and entreat your forgiveness." The Titular Councillor again softens. "I agree with you, Count, and I am ready to forgive them; but you must understand that my wife – my wife, a respectable woman – has been subjected to the persecution, insults, and insolence of these young louts, these scoundrels ..." And you realize that one of the young louts is standing by my side and I am there to make peace! Again my diplomacy comes into action and I am once more on the point of bringing the whole matter to a happy conclusion when my Titular Councillor loses his temper, grows red in the face, his sausages stick out – and I again launch into diplomatic finesse.'

'Oh, you must hear this!' cried Betsy, laughing and turning to a lady who was just coming into the box. 'He has been making me laugh so.'

'Well, *bonne chance*,' she added, giving Vronsky a finger that was not engaged in holding her fan, and with a shrug of her shoulders making the bodice of her dress, which had ridden up a little, slip down again that she might be befittingly naked when she moved forward to the front of her box and into the glare of gas-light and the gaze of all eyes.

Vronsky drove to the French theatre, where he did in fact have to see the colonel of his regiment (who never missed a single performance there) to report on his work as peace-maker, which had occupied and amused him for the last three days. Petritsky, whom he was fond of, was implicated in the affair, and so was young Prince Kedrov, a capital fellow and first-rate comrade who had lately joined the regiment. But, most important of all, the interests of the regiment itself were involved.

Both the young men concerned were in Vronsky's squadron. Titular Councillor Venden had gone to the colonel of the regiment with a complaint against his officers who had insulted his wife. His young wife, so Venden said – he had been married six months – was in church with her mother and, suddenly feeling unwell, owing to her interesting condition, could not stand any longer, and had engaged the first sledge she could find on the spot, a smart-looking one, to take her home. The officers had chased after her; she had taken fright and, feeling still more unwell, had run up the stairs to her flat. Venden himself had just returned from his office when he heard a ring at the bell and the sound of voices. He had gone to the door and, seeing two drunken officers with a letter, had pitched them out. He demanded that they should be severely punished.

'Yes, it's all very well,' remarked the colonel to Vronsky, whom he had invited to come and see him. 'Petritsky is becoming impossible. Not a week passes without some scandal. That Councillor will not let the matter drop: he'll take it further.'

Vronsky saw that things looked bad – that there could be no question of a duel, and that everything must be done to appease the Titular Councillor and hush up the affair. The colonel had consulted Vronsky precisely because he knew him to be well-bred, able, and, above all, a man who had the honour of the regiment at heart. They had discussed the matter and decided that Petritsky and Kedrov should go with Vronsky and apologize to the Titular Councillor. The colonel and Vronsky were both aware that Vronsky's name and insignia of aide-de-camp to the Emperor would be sure to contribute greatly to pacifying the Titular Councillor. And indeed they did have a partial effect, though the result of the peace-making still remained in doubt, as Vronsky had explained.

Arriving at the French theatre, Vronsky retired to the foyer with his colonel and reported his success, or lack of success. After considering the whole question, the colonel decided to let the matter rest; but, for his own amusement, went on to cross-examine Vronsky about his interview, and for a long time could not help laughing as he listened to Vronsky's description of how the Titular Councillor, after subsiding for a while, would suddenly flare up again at the recollection of some detail, and how Vronsky, at the last syllable of conciliation, had manoeuvred a retreat, shoving Petritsky out before him.

'A wretched business, but killing. Kedrov really can't fight the gentleman! Did he get so awfully heated?' he asked for the second time, laughing. 'But how do you like Claire this evening? Isn't she wonderful!' he went on, speaking of the new French actress. 'However often one sees her, every day she's different. You only get that with the French.'

6

PRINCESS BETSY left the theatre without waiting for the end of the last act. She had scarcely time to go to her dressing-room, dust her long, pale face with powder, rub it off again, tidy herself, and order tea to be served in the big drawing-room, before carriages started driving up one after the other to her huge house in Bolshaya Morskaya Street. Her guests stepped into the broad porch, and the stout hall-porter, who in the mornings would read a newspaper behind the glass panels of the front door, to the edification of passers-by, now noiselessly opened this enormous door to admit them.

Almost at the same instant the hostess, freshly combed and powdered, walked in at one door and her guests at the other door of the large drawing-room, with its dark walls, thick carpets and brightly-lit table, the white cloth, silver samovar and transparent china gleaming in the candle-light.

The hostess sat down by the samovar and took off her gloves. Moving their chairs with the help of unobtrusive footmen, the company arranged themselves in two groups: one round the samovar near the hostess, the other at the opposite end of the room round the wife of an ambassador, a beautiful woman in black velvet with sharply-outlined black eyebrows. In both groups the conversation wavered, as it always does for the first few minutes, broken up by new arrivals, greetings, offers of tea, feeling about as it were for something to settle on.

'She is an extraordinarily good actress: one can see she's studied Kaulbach,' remarked a diplomatic attaché in the group round the ambassador's wife. 'Did you notice how she fell? ...'

'Oh, please don't let us talk about Nilsson! No one can possibly say anything new about her,' said a stout, red-faced, fair-haired lady who wore an old silk dress and had no eyebrows or chignon. This was the Princess Myagky, notorious for her naïveté and the roughness of her manners, who was nicknamed the *Enfant terrible*. The Princess Myagky sat half-way between the two circles, listening to both and taking part in the conversation first of one and then of the other. 'Three different people have made that same remark about Kaulbach to me to-day already, as if they had a conspiracy about it. And I can't see why they should be so pleased with the remark.'

The conversation was cut short by this observation, and it became necessary to find another topic.

'Tell us something amusing, but not spiteful,' said the ambassador's wife, an adept at that art of polite conversation which the English call 'small talk', turning to the attaché, who was also at a loss for a subject.

'They say that's very difficult, that only what is spiteful is amusing,' he began, with a smile. 'But I will try if you give me a theme. The theme is everything. Once one has a theme, it is easy enough to embroider it. I often think that the great conversationalists of the last century would find it difficult to talk cleverly nowadays. We have got so tired of what is clever ...'

'That was said long ago,' interrupted the ambassador's wife, laughingly.

The conversation had started amiably, but just because it was too amiable it came to a stop again. They had to have recourse to the one sure and never-failing expedient – scandal.

'Don't you think there's something Louis Quinze about Tushkevich?' said the attaché, glancing towards a handsome, fair-haired young man standing near the tea-table.

'Oh yes! He matches the drawing-room: that is why he comes here so often.'

This conversation did not flag, since it rested on allusions to what could not be talked of in this room – namely, the relations existing between Tushkevich and their hostess.

Round the samovar and the hostess the conversation, after flickering for some time between the three inevitable topics – the latest piece of news, the theatre, and ill-natured gossip – also caught on when it got to the last of these subjects, scandal.

'Have you heard? That Maltyshchev woman – the mother, not the daughter – is having a *diable rose* colour costume made for herself!'

'You don't mean it! No, that's delicious!'

'I wonder that with her intelligence – for she's not a fool – she doesn't see how ridiculous she makes herself.'

Everyone had something disparaging and derisive to say about the unfortunate Madame Maltyshchev, and the conversation began crackling merrily like a blazing wood-pile.

Princess Betsy's husband – a stout, good-natured man, an ardent collector of prints – hearing that his wife had visitors, came into the drawing-room for a moment before going to his club. Stepping silently over the thick carpet, he went up to the Princess Myagky.

'How did you like Nilsson?' he asked.

'Oh dear, why do you steal up on a person like that! How you startled me!' she replied. 'Please don't talk to me about the opera: you don't know a thing about music. I had better meet you on your own ground and talk about your majolica and your prints. Tell me, what treasures have you picked up lately in the junk shops?'

'Would you like me to show you? But you don't understand them.'

'Oh, do let me see them! I have been learning all about that sort of thing at those – what is their name? – those banker people. ... They have some marvellous engravings. They showed them to us.'

'Why, have you been at the Schützburgs'?' asked the hostess from her place by the samovar.

'I have, *ma chère*. They asked my husband and me to dine, and I was told that the sauce alone cost a thousand roubles,' said the Princess Myagky loudly, conscious that everybody was listening. 'And a very nasty sauce it was, too: some green mess. We had to invite them back, and I made a sauce for eighty-five kopecks and everyone was quite satisfied. I can't afford thousand-rouble sauces.'

'She is incredible!' said the hostess.

'Marvellous!' said someone else.

The effect produced by anything the Princess Myagky said was always the same, the secret of that effect being that, though she was often, as now, beside the point, what she said was simple and contained sense. In the society in which she lived such plain-speaking passed for the greatest wit. The Princess Myagky could never understand why this was so, but she knew that it was, and took advantage of it.

Seeing that while the Princess Myagky was speaking everyone listened and conversation round the ambassador's wife stopped, the hostess turned to her in the hope of drawing the whole party together.

'Won't you really have any tea? You should come over here by us.'

'No, we are very comfortable where we are,' replied the ambassador's wife with a smile, and she resumed the interrupted conversation.

It was a very pleasant conversation. They were disparaging the Karenins, husband and wife.

'Anna is quite changed since her trip to Moscow. There is something strange about her,' said a friend of Anna's.

'The great change is that she has brought back with her the shadow of Alexei Vronsky,' said the ambassador's wife.

'Well, what of it? Grimm has a fable – *The Man without a Shadow* – about a man who loses his shadow, as a punishment for something or other. I never could understand why it was a punishment. But it must be disagreeable for a woman to be without a shadow.'

'Yes, but women who have shadows generally come to a bad end,' said Anna's friend.

'Hold your tongues!' suddenly remarked the Princess Myagky, hearing these words. 'Madame Karenin's a fine woman. I don't like her husband, but I'm very fond of her.'

'Why don't you like her husband? He is such a remarkable man,' said the ambassador's wife. 'My husband says there are few statesmen like him in Europe.'

'And my husband says the same, only I don't believe it,' replied the Princess Myagky. 'If our husbands were not so fond of talking, we should see things as they are; and it's my opinion that Karenin is simply a fool. I say it in a whisper ... but does not that explain everything? Before, when I was told to consider him clever, I kept looking for his ability and thought I must be too stupid myself to see his cleverness; but directly I said to myself, *he's a fool* – only in a whisper, of course – it all became quite clear. Don't you agree?'

'How spiteful you are to-day!'

'Not at all. I'd no alternative. One of us had to be a fool. And, well, you know one can't say that of oneself.'

'No man is satisfied with his fortune, but every man is satisfied with his wit,' remarked the attaché, quoting the French saying.

'That's just it,' the Princess Myagky said to him quickly. 'But the point is that I won't abandon Anna to your mercies. She is such a dear, sweet person. How can she help it if everyone is in love with her and follows her about like a shadow?'

'Oh, I was not thinking of blaming her,' Anna's friend said in self-defence.

'If we have no one following us about like a shadow, it doesn't prove that we have the right to condemn her.'

And having disposed of Anna's friend, the Princess Myagky got up and, together with the ambassador's wife, joined the group round the table, where the conversation was dealing with the King of Prussia.

'Whom were you back-biting over there?' asked Betsy.

'The Karenins. The Princess was analysing Alexei Alexandrovich's character for us,' replied the ambassador's wife with a smile as she seated herself at the table.

'A pity we didn't hear it!' said the hostess, glancing towards the door. 'Ah, here you are at last!' she greeted Vronsky, who was just coming into the room.

Vronsky not only knew everybody present but saw them all every day; and so he entered in the quiet way of one coming back to a room full of people from whom one has only just parted.

'Where do I come from?' he said in answer to the ambassador's wife. 'Well, there's no help for it, so I must confess. From the *opéra bouffe*. I do believe I've seen a hundred performances, and always with fresh enjoyment. It's enchanting! I know it's a disgrace, the opera sends me to sleep, but I sit out the *opéra bouffe* to the very end and enjoy every minute of it. To-night ...'

He mentioned a French actress and was just going to tell some story about her when the ambassador's wife interrupted in mock alarm.

'Please don't talk about that fright.'

'All right, I won't – especially as of course you all know about frights!'

'And we should all go to see them if it were considered the correct thing, like the opera,' put in the Princess Myagky.

7

STEPS were heard outside the door and the Princess Betsy, knowing it was Madame Karenin, glanced at Vronsky. He was looking towards the door with a strange new expression on his face. Joyfully, intently, and at the same time timidly, he gazed at the approaching figure and slowly rose to his feet. Anna walked into the drawing-room. Holding herself very erect as usual and looking straight before her, she came up to her hostess, moving with the quick, firm, yet light step which distinguished her from other society women. She shook hands, smiled, and with the same smile looked round at Vronsky. Vronsky gave a low bow and pushed a chair forward for her.

She responded only by an inclination of her head, flushed a little, and frowned. But immediately, while nodding rapidly to her acquaintances and pressing the hands extended to her, she addressed herself to her hostess.

'I have just been at the Countess Lydia's. I meant to come earlier, but could not get away. Sir John was there. A very interesting man.'

'Oh, that's this missionary?'

'Yes. It was very interesting – he was telling us about life in India.'

The conversation, interrupted by her arrival, flickered into life again, like the flame of a lamp that has been blown about.

'Sir John? Oh yes, Sir John. I've met him. He talks well. The Vlassiev girl is quite in love with him.'

'Is it true that the younger Vlassiev girl is going to marry Topov?'

'Yes, they say it's quite settled.'

'I am surprised at her parents. I heard it was a love match.'

'A love match? What antediluvian ideas you have! Who talks of love nowadays?' said the ambassador's wife.

'What is to be done about it? That foolish old custom has not gone out of fashion yet,' said Vronsky.

'So much the worse for those who follow the fashion! The only happy marriages I know of are *mariages de convenance*.'

'Yes, but how often the happiness of a *mariage de convenance* falls to pieces just because the very passion that was disregarded asserts itself later!' said Vronsky.

'But by a *mariage de convenance* we mean a marriage where both parties have already sown their wild oats. Love is like scarlet fever – one has to go through it and get it over.'

'Then they ought to find a way of being inoculated against love, like being vaccinated for smallpox.'

'In my young days I was in love with a deacon,' said the Princess Myagky. 'I don't know that it did me any good.'

'No, joking apart, I believe that before one can know what love really is one must have a fall and then pick oneself up,' said the Princess Betsy.

'Even after marriage?' said the ambassador's wife archly.

'It's never too late to mend,' said the attaché, quoting the English proverb.

'Exactly,' Betsy put in. 'One has to have a fall and pick oneself up. What do you think?' she asked Anna, who was listening to the conversation with a faint but resolute smile on her lips.

'I think,' replied Anna, toying with the glove she had pulled off, 'I think ... that if there are as many minds as there are heads, then there are as many kinds of love as there are hearts.'

Vronsky was gazing at Anna, waiting anxiously to hear what she would say. He sighed as if a danger had passed with these words of hers.

Suddenly Anna addressed him:

'I have just had a letter from Moscow. They say that Kitty Shcherbatsky is very ill.'

'Indeed?' said Vronsky, frowning.

Anna looked at him sternly.

'You don't seem to be interested?'

'On the contrary, I am, very much. What exactly do they write, if I may know?' he asked.

Anna got up and went to Betsy. 'May I have a cup of tea?' she said, stopping behind Betsy's chair.

While Betsy was pouring out the tea, Vronsky approached Anna.

'What do they write?' he asked again.

'I often think men do not understand the meaning of honour, though they are always talking about it,' said Anna, without answering him. 'I have been wanting to tell you for a long time,' she added, and, moving a few steps towards a corner table on which lay some albums, she sat down.

'I do not quite understand you,' he said, handing her the cup.

She glanced at the sofa beside her, and he at once sat down.

'Yes. I have been wanting to tell you,' she said, not looking at him. 'You behaved badly, very badly indeed.'

'Do you suppose I don't know that I behaved badly? But who was the cause of it?'

'Why do you say that to me?' she asked, looking at him severely.

'You know why,' he answered boldly and joyously, meeting her look and not lowering his eyes.

It was not he, but she who became confused.

'That only shows you have no heart,' she said. But her eyes said that she knew he had a heart, and for that very reason she feared him.

'What you have just referred to was a mistake, and not love.'

'Remember, I have forbidden you to mention that word, that hateful word,' said Anna, with a shudder; but at once she felt that by the very word 'forbidden' she had shown that she admitted some proprietorship over him, and thereby was encouraging him to speak of love. 'I have long meant to say that to you,' she went on, looking resolutely into his eyes, her face all aflame with a burning blush, 'and I came here on purpose this evening, knowing I should meet you. I came to tell you that this must stop. I have never had to blush in front of anyone before, but you make me feel as if I were guilty of something.'

He looked at her, and was struck by a new spiritual beauty in her face.

'What do you wish of me?' he asked, simply and seriously.

'I want you to go to Moscow and beg Kitty's forgiveness,' she said.

'You don't wish that,' he replied.

He saw that she was saying what she forced herself to say, not what she wanted to say.

'If you love me as you say you do,' she whispered, 'then do what will give me peace.'

His face brightened.

'Don't you know that you are my life? But I know no peace and cannot give it you. My whole being, my love ... yes. I cannot think of you and myself apart. To me, you and I are one. And I do not see any possibility of peace ahead, either for me or for you. I see the possibility of despair, unhappiness ... or happiness, what happiness! ... Can it be there's no chance of it?' he murmured with his lips; but she heard.

She tried with all her strength of mind to say what ought to be said. But instead of that her eyes rested on him, full of love, and made no answer.

'At last!' he thought with rapture. 'Just as I was beginning to despair and it seemed as though nothing could come of it – here it is! She loves me! She confesses it!'

'Then do this for me – never utter such words again, and let us be good friends,' said her lips; but her eyes said something very different.

'Friends we shall never be; you know that yourself. But whether we shall be the happiest people on earth or the most wretched – that's in your hands.'

She was about to say something, but he interrupted her.

'I ask only one thing: I ask for the right to hope, to suffer as I do now. But if even that cannot be, command me to disappear, and I disappear. You shall not see me if my presence is distasteful to you.'

'I don't want to drive you away.'

'Only don't change anything. Leave everything as it is,' he said in a trembling voice. 'Here is your husband.'

Indeed, just at that moment Karenin entered the drawing-room with his quiet, awkward gait.

Glancing at his wife and Vronsky, he went up to his hostess and, sitting down with a cup of tea, started talking in his deliberate, always audible voice, in the ironical way he had, as if he were deriding someone.

'Your Rambouillet is in full muster,' he said, looking round at the whole company. 'The Graces and the Muses!'

But the Princess Betsy could not endure that tone of his – 'sneering', as she called it in English; and so, like a skilful hostess, she at once led him into a serious conversation touching universal conscription. Karenin was immediately carried away by the subject and began earnestly defending the new imperial decree against the Princess Betsy, who had attacked it.

Vronsky and Anna still sat on at the little table.

'This is becoming improper,' whispered one lady, with an expressive glance at Anna, Vronsky, and Anna's husband.

'What did I tell you?' replied Anna's friend.

Not only those two ladies, but almost everyone in the drawing-room, even the Princess Myagky and Betsy herself, looked more than once across at the couple who had withdrawn from the general circle, as if their having done so were a disturbing fact. Karenin was the only person who did not once glance in that direction and was not distracted from the interesting discussion in which he was engaged.

Noticing the disagreeable impression being made on everyone, the Princess Betsy slipped someone else into her place to listen to Karenin, and she herself went up to Anna.

'I always marvel at your husband's lucidity and accuracy of expression,' she said 'The most transcendental ideas become within my reach when he's speaking.'

'Oh yes!' said Anna, radiant with a smile of happiness, and not taking in a single word of what Betsy was saying. She crossed over to the big table and joined in the general conversation.

After staying half an hour, Karenin went up to his wife and suggested that they should go home together; but, without looking at him, she answered that she was staying to supper. Karenin bowed to the company and left.

The Karenins' fat old Tartar coachman, in his shiny leather coat, was finding it difficult to hold the near grey horse, which had grown restive with the cold and was rearing up at the portico. A footman waited with his hand on the carriage door. The hall-porter stood holding the great door of the house. With deft little fingers Anna was disengaging the lace of her sleeve, which had caught on a hook of her fur cloak, and with bent head was listening rapturously to the words Vronsky murmured as he escorted her down.

'You have promised nothing, of course, and I ask nothing,' he was saying; 'but you know that it is not friendship I want. There's only one happiness in life for me – the word you dislike so … yes, love! …'

'Love,' she repeated slowly to herself, and suddenly, as she disentangled the lace, she added: 'I dislike the word because it means too much to me, far more than you can understand,' and she glanced into his face. 'Au revoir!'

She gave him her hand and with her quick, elastic step went past the hall-porter and vanished into the carriage.

Her look and the touch of her hand set him on fire. He kissed the palm of his hand where she had touched it and went home, happy in the knowledge that this evening had brought him nearer to the attainment of his dreams than the past two months.

8

KARENIN had seen nothing peculiar or improper in his wife sitting at a separate table and talking animatedly with Vronsky; but he noticed that the rest of the party considered it peculiar and improper, and for that reason it seemed to him, too, to be improper. He decided that he must speak to his wife about it.

When he reached home he went to his study, as usual, seated himself in his arm-chair, and opened a book on the Papacy at the place marked by a paper-knife. He read until one o'clock, just as he usually did, only now and again rubbing his high forehead and jerking his head, as though to drive something away. At his usual hour he rose and made his toilet for the night. Anna had not yet returned. With his book under his arm he went upstairs; but this evening, instead of the usual thoughts and calculations about his official duties, his mind was full of his wife and something disagreeable connected with her. Contrary to his habit, he did not get into bed, but fell to pacing up and down the rooms with his hands clasped behind his back. He felt that he could not go to bed until he had thought over the new situation that had arisen.

When Karenin had decided to speak to his wife, it had seemed to him easy and simple enough; but now, when he began considering this new situation which had arisen, it appeared to him very complicated and difficult.

He was not jealous. Jealousy, in his opinion, was an insult to one's wife, and a man should have confidence in his wife. Why he ought to have confidence – in other words, a full and firm conviction that his young wife would always love him – he never stopped to ask himself. But he had had no experience of distrust, because he had confidence in her and told himself that it was right to have it. Now, however, though his conviction had not broken down that jealousy was a shameful feeling and that one ought to have confidence, he felt face to face with something illogical and irrational, and he did not know what to do. Karenin was face to face with life – with the possibility of his wife's loving someone else – and this seemed to him very irrational and incomprehensible because it was life itself. All his life he had lived and worked in official spheres, having to do with the reflection of life. And every time he had come up against life itself he had stepped aside.

Now he experienced a sensation such as a man might feel who, quietly crossing a bridge over a chasm, suddenly discovers that the bridge is broken and the abyss yawns below. The abyss was real life; the bridge, that artificial existence Karenin had been leading. For the first time the possibility of his wife's falling in love with anybody occurred to him, and he was horrified.

He did not undress, but paced up and down with his even step over the echoing parquet floor of the dining-room, lit by a single lamp, over the carpet of the dark drawing-room, where a solitary light shone upon the large, recently-painted portrait of himself hanging above the sofa, and on through her sitting-room, where two candles burned, illuminating the portraits of her parents and women friends and the pretty knick-knacks on her writing-table, so familiar to him. Through her room he reached the door of their bedroom and turned back again.

At each turn in his walk, especially at the parquet floor of the lamp-lit dining-room, he halted and said to himself: 'Yes, this thing must be settled and put a stop to. I must frankly tell her my decision.' And he would turn back again. 'But tell her what – what decision?' he would ask himself in the drawing-room, and find no answer. 'But, after all,' he reflected before turning into her room, 'what has occurred? Nothing. She had a long conversation with him. Well, what harm is there in that? Is it unusual for a woman in society to talk to someone? Besides, to be jealous means lowering both myself and her,' he told himself as he went into her sitting-room. But this argument, which had always had so much weight with him before, now had neither weight nor meaning. At the bedroom door he would turn back, and as soon as he re-entered the dark drawing-room a voice would whisper that it was not so, and that if others noticed, that showed there was something to notice. And again he repeated to himself in the dining-room: 'Yes, I must come to a decision and put a stop to this and declare myself...' And again, as he turned about in the drawing-room, he would ask himself: 'Decide what?' and again, 'What had occurred?' and reply, 'Nothing,' and remember that jealousy was a feeling which insults a wife; but in the drawing-room he would once again be convinced that something had happened. His thoughts, like his body, went full circle, without arriving at anything new. He noticed this, rubbed his forehead, and sat down in her boudoir.

Here, as he looked at her table, at the malachite cover of her blotter, and an unfinished letter lying on it, his thoughts suddenly underwent a change. He began to think of her, of what she was thinking and feeling. For the first time he really pictured to himself her personal life, her ideas, her desires; and the notion that she could and should have a separate life of her own appeared to him so dreadful that he hastened to drive it away. This was the abyss into which he was afraid to look. To put himself in thought and feeling into another being was a mental exercise foreign to Karenin. He considered such mental exercise harmful and dangerous romancing.

'And the worst of it all,' he thought, 'is that now, just as my work is nearing completion' (he was thinking of the project he was bringing forward at the time), 'when I need peace of mind and all my energies, this idiotic anxiety has to fall on me. But what is to be done? I am not one to suffer anxiety and trouble without having the courage to face them.

'I must think it over and come to a decision, and put it out of my mind.' he said aloud.

'The question of her feelings, of what has taken place or may take place in her heart, is not my affair but the affair of her conscience, and comes under the head of religion,' he said to himself, feeling relieved at having found the category of regulating principles to which the newly-arisen situation rightly belonged.

'So then,' continued Karenin to himself, 'the question of her feelings and so on is a question for her conscience, with which I can have nothing to do. My duty becomes clear. As head of the family I am the person whose duty it is to guide her and who is, therefore, partly responsible; I must point out the danger I see, warn her, even use my authority. I must speak plainly to her.'

And what he would say to his wife took shape in Karenin's head. As he thought it over, he grudged having to expend his time and intellect on such domestic matters. But, in spite of that, the form and sequence of the speech he had to make shaped themselves in his head as clearly and precisely as if it were a ministerial report.

'I must make the following points quite plain: first, an exposition of the importance of public opinion and propriety; secondly, an exposition of the religious significance of marriage; thirdly, if need be, a reference to the unhappiness that may result to our son; fourthly, a reference to her own unhappiness.' And, interlacing his fingers, palms downwards, he stretched them and the joints cracked.

This trick – the bad habit of clasping his hands and cracking his fingers – always soothed him, and restored the mental balance so needful to him at this juncture. There was the sound of a carriage driving up to the front door and Karenin stood still in the middle of the room.

He heard a woman's step ascending the stairs. Ready to deliver his speech, Karenin stood, pressing his interlocked fingers and wondering whether there would be another crack. One joint did crack.

The sound of her light step on the stair told him that she was close and, though he was satisfied with his speech, he felt frightened of the interview confronting him.

9

ANNA walked in with bent head, playing with the tassels of her hood. Her face shone with a vivid glow; but it was not a joyous glow – it suggested the terrible glow of a fire on a dark night. On seeing her husband, Anna raised her head and smiled, as if waking from a dream.

'Not in bed? What a wonder!' she said, throwing off her hood and, without pausing, she crossed into the dressing-room. 'It is late, Alexei Alexandrovich,' she called from the other side of the door.

'Anna, I must have a talk with you.'

'With me?' she said wonderingly, coming out from behind the door and looking at him. 'What is it? What about?' she asked, sitting down. 'Well, let us talk, if we must. But it would be better to get to sleep.'

Anna was saying the first thing that came into her head and hearing herself marvelled at her own capacity for lying. How simple and natural her words sounded, and how likely that she was simply sleepy! She felt herself clad in an impenetrable armour of falsehood. She felt that some invisible power had come to her aid and was supporting her.

'Anna, I must put you on your guard,' he said.

'Put me on my guard? What about?'

She looked at him so innocently and gaily that anyone who did not know her as her husband knew her could have detected nothing unnatural either in the intonation or the meaning of her words. But for him, knowing her, knowing that when he was five minutes late in going to bed she would remark on it and ask the reason – who knew that she always immediately told him all her joys, pleasures, and sorrows – for him her reluctance now to notice his state of mind or say a word about herself signified a great deal He saw that the depths of her soul, always before open to him, were now closed against him. More than that, he knew by the tone of her voice that she was not even troubled by this but seemed to be saying straight out to him: 'Yes, my heart is closed, and so it should be and will be in future.' Now he felt like a man who returns home to find his own house locked against him. 'But perhaps the key may yet be found,' thought Karenin.

'I want to warn you,' he said in a quiet voice, 'that by thoughtlessness and indiscretion you may cause yourself to be talked about in society. Your too animated conversation this evening with Count Vronsky' (he enunciated the name firmly and with deliberate emphasis) 'attracted attention.'

As he spoke he looked at her laughing eyes, which now alarmed him with their impenetrability, and felt the utter uselessness and idleness of his words.

'You are always like that,' she replied, as though completely misapprehending him and intentionally taking note only of the last part of what he said. 'First you don't like me to be dull, then you don't like me to enjoy myself. I was not dull this evening. Does that offend you?'

Karenin started, and bent his fingers to make the joints crack.

'Oh, please don't do that! I do dislike it so,' she said.

'Anna, is this you?' said Karenin softly, trying to control himself and stopping the movement of his hands.

'But what is all this?' she asked in a tone of comical surprise and sincerity. 'What do you want of me?'

Karenin was silent for a moment and passed his hand over his forehead and eyes. He saw that, instead of doing what he had intended, and warning his wife against making a mistake in the eyes of the world, he was involuntarily getting excited about a matter that concerned her conscience, and was struggling against some barrier of his imagination.

'This is what I wanted to say,' he went on coldly and calmly, 'and I ask you to listen to me. As you know, I look upon jealousy as a humiliating and degrading emotion and I shall never allow myself to be influenced by it; but there are certain laws of propriety which one cannot disregard with impunity. I did not notice it this evening but, judging by the impression created on all present, everyone noticed that you were behaving and acting in a not altogether desirable manner.'

'I really don't understand at all,' said Anna, shrugging her shoulders. 'He does not care,' she thought. 'But other people noticed and that's what upsets him.'

'You are not well, Alexei Alexandrovich,' she added, rising and making for the door; but he moved forward as though he would stop her.

His face was more ugly and forbidding than she had ever seen it. She stopped and, bending her head back and to one side, with quick fingers began taking out her hairpins.

'Well, I'm listening for what's to come!' she said quietly and mockingly. 'And indeed I listen with interest, for I should like to understand what it is all about.'

She wondered as she spoke at her confident natural tone and at her choice of words.

'I have not the right to enter into the details of your feelings, and besides I consider that futile and even harmful,' began Karenin. 'Ferreting into our souls, we often ferret out something that might have lain there unnoticed. Your feelings are the affair of your own conscience; but I am in duty bound to you, to myself, and to God to point out to you your duties. Our lives have been joined not by man but by God. Only a crime can sever that union, and a crime of that nature brings its own heavy punishment.'

'I don't understand a thing you're saying. And, oh dear, I am desperately sleepy!' she said, rapidly running her fingers through her hair in search of any remaining hairpins.

'Anna, for God's sake, don't speak like that!' he said gently. 'Perhaps I am mistaken but, believe me, what I say, I say as much for my own sake as for yours. I am your husband, and I love you.'

For an instant her face fell and the mocking light in her eyes died away; but the word 'love' roused her into revolt again. 'Love?' she thought. 'Can he love? If he hadn't heard there was such a thing as love he would never have used the word. He does not know what love is.'

'Alexei Alexandrovich, really I don't understand,' she said. 'Explain what it is you think …'

'Allow me to finish. I love you. But I am not speaking of myself.

163

The people principally concerned are our son and yourself. It is quite possible, I repeat, that my words may seem to you idle and misplaced; perhaps they result from a mistake on my part. In that case, I ask your pardon. But if you are conscious yourself of even the smallest grounds for them, then I beg you to reflect and, if your heart prompts you, to tell me ...'

Karenin did not notice that he was saying something quite different from the speech he had prepared.

'I have nothing to say. Besides,' she added quickly, with difficulty restraining a smile, 'it really is bed-time.'

Karenin sighed and, without saying more, went into the bedroom.

When she came, he was already in bed. His lips were sternly compressed and his eyes did not look at her. Anna got into her bed and lay expecting every moment that he would begin to speak again. She both feared his speaking and wanted it. But he remained silent. She waited motionless for a long while and then forgot him. She thought of that other; she pictured him and felt her heart fill with excitement and guilty delight at the thought of him. Suddenly she heard an even, tranquil snore. For a moment the sound seemed to have appalled Karenin, and he stopped; then, after a couple of breaths, the snoring began afresh with quiet regularity.

'It's late, it's late, it's late,' she whispered to herself with a smile. She lay for a long time not moving, with wide-open eyes, the brightness of which she almost fancied she could herself see in the darkness.

10

FROM that evening a new life began for Karenin and for his wife. Nothing particular happened. Anna went into society as usual, frequently visiting Princess Betsy and meeting Vronsky wherever she went. Karenin saw this but could do nothing. She opposed an impenetrable wall of light-hearted perplexity to all his efforts to draw her into a discussion. There was no outward change in their life but their intimate relations with one another were completely altered. Karenin, who was such a forceful person when dealing with affairs of state, felt himself helpless in this. Like an ox with head bent, he waited submissively for the axe which he felt raised above him. Each time he began to think about it, he felt he must make one more effort, that by kindness, tenderness, and persuasion there was still a hope of saving her, of bringing her to her senses; and every day he made up his mind to talk to her. But every time he began talking to her, he felt the same spirit of evil and deceit which had taken possession of her lay hold of him, too, and he neither said the things he meant to nor spoke in the tone he had meant to use. He would involuntarily assume his usual bantering tone, which jeered at those who spoke like that. And in that tone it was impossible to say what needed to be said to her.

II

THAT which for nearly a year had been the one absorbing desire of Vronsky's life, supplanting all his former desires; that which for Anna had been an impossible, terrible, but all the more bewitching dream of bliss, had come to pass. Pale, with trembling lower jaw, he stood before her and besought her to be calm, himself not knowing how or why.

'Anna! Anna!' he said in a choking voice. 'Anna, for pity's sake!...'

But the louder he spoke the lower she drooped her once proud, gay, but now shame-stricken head, and she crouched down and sank from the sofa where she was sitting to the floor at his feet. She would have fallen on the carpet if he had not held her.

'Oh God, forgive me!' she said, sobbing and pressing his hands to her breast.

She felt so sinful, so guilty, that nothing was left to her but to humble herself and beg forgiveness; but she had no one in the world now but him, and so to him she even addressed her prayer for forgiveness. Looking at him, she had a physical sense of her degradation and could not utter another word. He felt what a murderer must feel when he looks at the body he has robbed of life. The body he had robbed of life was their love, the first stage of their love. There was something frightful and revolting in the recollection of what had been paid for by this terrible price of shame. Shame at her spiritual nakedness crushed her and infected him. But in spite of the murderer's horror before the body of his victim, that body must be hacked to pieces and hidden, and the murderer must make use of what he has obtained by his crime.

And, as with fury and passion the murderer throws himself upon the body and drags it and hacks at it, so he covered her face and shoulders with kisses. She held his hand and did not stir. 'Yes, these kisses – these are what have been bought by my shame! Yes, and this hand, which will always be mine, is the hand of my accomplice!' She lifted his hand and kissed it. He sank on his knees and tried to see her face; but she hid it and did not speak. At last, as though making an effort over herself, she sat up and pushed him away. Her face was as beautiful as ever but all the more pitiful for that.

'Everything is over,' she said. 'I have nothing but you left. Remember that.'

'I can never forget what is life itself to me. For one moment of happiness like this ...'

'Happiness!' she said with disgust and horror, and her horror was involuntarily communicated to him. 'For pity's sake, do not speak of it – do not speak of it again!'

She rose quickly and moved away from him.

'Do not speak of it,' she repeated and, with a look of cold despair, incomprehensible to him, she left him.

She felt that at that moment she could not put into words her sense of shame, rapture, and horror at this stepping into a new life, and she did not want to talk about it and profane this feeling by inappropriate words. But later on, the next day and the next, she still not only found no words to express the complexity of her feelings but could not even find thoughts with which to reflect on all that was in her soul.

She said to herself: 'No, I can't think about it now; by and by, when I am calmer.' But that calm for reflection never came. Every time she thought of what she had done and of what would become of her and of what she ought to do, horror descended on her and she drove these thoughts away.

'By and by,' she would say to herself. 'By and by, when I am calmer.'

But in dreams, when she had no control over her thoughts, her position appeared to her in all its ugly nakedness. One dream she had almost every night. She dreamed that she was the wife of both of them and that both lavished their caresses on her. Alexei Alexandrovich was weeping, kissing her hands, and saying, 'How happy we are now!' And Alexei Vronsky was there too, and he, too, was her husband. And she was marvelling that this had once seemed impossible to her, and she would explain to them, laughing, that it was ever so much simpler this way and that now both of them were contented and happy. But this dream weighed on her like a nightmare and she awoke from it in terror.

12

WHEN Levin first returned from Moscow, and while he still started and grew red every time he remembered the ignominy of being refused, he had said to himself: 'I blushed and started like this, and thought the world had come to an end, when I was ploughed in physics and did not get my remove; and it was the same when I bungled that affair my sister entrusted to me. And what happened? Now that years have gone by I recall it and wonder that I could have grieved so much. So it will be with this grief. Time will go by and I shall not mind about this either.'

But three months had passed and he had not left off minding and it was as painful to think of it as it had been those first days. He could not be at peace because after dreaming so long of family life and feeling so ready for it, he was still single and farther than ever from marriage. He was painfully conscious himself, as were all around him, that it was not good for a man of his age to be alone. He remembered how, just before leaving for Moscow, he had said to his cowman Nikolai, a simple-hearted peasant, with whom he liked to talk: 'Well, Nikolai, I mean to get married,' and how Nikolai had promptly replied, as on a matter about which there could be no doubt: 'And high time, too, Constantine Dmitrich.' But now he was farther from marriage than ever. The place in his heart was taken and whenever he tried to imagine there any of the girls he knew, he felt that it was quite impossible. Moreover, the memory of Kitty's refusal and of the part he had played in the affair tormented him with shame. However much he told himself that he was in no wise to blame, the memory of it, like other humiliating memories of the same nature, made him start and blush. There had been in his past, as in every man's, actions which he acknowledged were wrong and for which his conscience ought to have tormented him; but the recollection of these evil actions tormented him far less than these trivial yet humiliating memories. These wounds never healed. And with these memories was now ranged his rejection and the pitiful spectacle he must have presented to others that evening. But time and work did their part. Painful memories became more and more blurred by the ordinary but important incidents of country life. With every week he thought less often of Kitty. He was impatiently looking forward to the news that she was married or just going to be married, hoping that such news, like having a tooth out, would bring healing.

Meanwhile, spring had come, beautiful, tender, without the longings and disappointments of spring – one of those rare springs which rejoice plants, beasts, and man alike. This lovely spring stimulated Levin still more and confirmed him in his determination to renounce all that had been before, in order firmly and independently to fashion his solitary life. Though he had not carried out many of the plans with which he had returned to the country, he had held to his most important resolution – that of living a pure life – and he was free from that shame which had usually harassed him after a fall ; he could look people boldly in the face. In February he had received a letter from Maria Nikolayevna to say that his brother Nikolai's health was getting worse but that he refused to have treatment. In consequence of this letter, Levin went to Moscow, saw his brother, and succeeded in persuading him to consult a doctor and to go to a watering-place abroad. He was so successful in persuading his brother, and in lending him money for the journey without irritating him, that in this respect Levin was satisfied with himself. In addition to his reading and his work on the estate, which required special attention in springtime, Levin had that winter begun writing a book on agriculture, the idea of which was that the temperament of the agricultural labourer was to be treated as a definite factor, like climate and soil, and that therefore the conclusions of agronomic science should be deduced not from data supplied by soil and climate only, but from data of soil, climate, and the immutable character of the labourer. Thus, in spite of his solitary life, or rather because of it, his days were extraordinarily full. Only now and again did he feel an unsatisfied desire to share with someone besides Agatha Mihalovna the thoughts that wandered through his head – although even with her he often discussed physics, the theory of agriculture, and especially philosophy; philosophy was Agatha Mihalovna's favourite subject.

Spring was slow in unfolding. For the last weeks of Lent the weather had been clear and frosty. It thawed by day in the sun but at night there were seven degrees of frost. The crust on the snow was so hard that carts could go anywhere without keeping to the road. Easter found snow still on the ground. Then suddenly, on Easter Monday, a warm wind began to blow, the clouds gathered, and for three days and three nights there was wild, warm rain. On Thursday the wind fell and a thick grey mist overspread the land, as if to hide the changing mysteries that were taking place in nature. Hidden by the mist, the snow-waters rushed down, the ice on the river began to crack and slide away, and the turbid, frothing torrents flowed more swiftly, until on the following Monday evening the mist lifted, the clouds split up into fleecy cloudlets, the sky cleared, and spring was really come. In the morning the sun rose brilliant and quickly melted the thin ice on the water, and the warm air all around vibrated with the vapour given off by the awakening earth. Last year's grass grew green again and the young grass thrust up its tiny blades; the buds swelled on the guelder-rose and the currant-bushes, and on the sticky, resinous birch-trees, and the honey-bee hummed among the golden catkins of the willow. Invisible larks broke into song above the velvety green fields and the ice-covered stubble-land; peewits began to cry over the low lands and marshes, still bubbly with water not yet swept away; cranes and wild geese flew high across the sky, uttering their spring calls. The cattle, bald in patches where they had shed their winter coats, began to low in the pastures; lambs with crooked legs frisked round their bleating mothers who were losing their fleece; swift-footed children ran about the paths drying with imprints of bare feet; there was a merry chatter of peasant women over their linen at the pond and the ring of axes in the yard, where the peasants were repairing their ploughs and harrows.

Spring had really come.

13

LEVIN put on his big boots and, for the first time, a cloth jacket instead of his fur coat and went about his farm, stepping over streams of water that flashed in the sunshine and hurt his eyes, treading one minute on ice and the next into sticky mud.

Spring is the time of plans and projects. And, like a tree in spring which does not yet know where and how its young shoots and twigs, still imprisoned in swelling buds, will develop, Levin hardly knew what work on his beloved estate he was going to begin upon. But he felt full of the most splendid plans and projects. First of all he went to have a look at the cattle. The cows had been let out into the yard and were warming themselves in the sunshine, their glossy coats glistening, and were lowing to go to the meadow. Having admired his cows for a little – he knew them intimately down to the smallest detail – Levin gave instructions for them to be driven into the meadow and for the calves to be let into the yard. The herdsman ran off merrily to make ready. The dairy-maids, with switches in their hands, picking up their petticoats over their bare, white legs, not yet sunburned, splashed through the mud chasing the lowing calves, mad with the joy of spring, into the yard.

After admiring the unusually fine calves born that year – the early calves were as big as a peasant's cow, and Pava's calf at three months was the size of a yearling – Levin gave orders for a trough to be brought out and for hay to be put into the racks. But it appeared that the racks, which had been put up in the yard in the autumn and not used during the winter, were broken. He sent for the carpenter, who according to his orders ought to have been at work on the thrashing-machine, but it appeared that the carpenter was mending the harrows which should have been mended back at Shrovetide. This was very annoying to Levin. It was annoying to come upon that everlasting slovenliness in the farm work, against which he had struggled with all his might for so many years. He found out that the racks which were not wanted in the winter had been taken into the cart-horses' stable, and there had got broken, as they were lightly made, being meant for the calves. In addition, it appeared that the harrows and all the agricultural implements which he had ordered to be looked over and repaired during the winter, and for which purpose three carpenters had been specially hired, had not been touched, and that the harrows were now being mended when they ought to be out in the fields in use. Levin sent for his bailiff but, instead of waiting, immediately went to look for him himself. The bailiff, as radiant as everything else that day, was coming out of a barn in a sheepskin bordered with astrakhan, twisting a bit of straw in his hands.

'Why isn't the carpenter on the thrashing-machine?'

'Oh, I meant to tell you yesterday, the harrows want mending. It is time to be ploughing, you know.'

'Why wasn't that done during the winter?'

'But what would you be wanting the carpenter for?'

'Where are the racks for the calves' yard?'

'I gave orders for them to be got ready. What is one to do with those peasants!' said the bailiff, with a wave of his hand.

'It's not those peasants but this bailiff!' said Levin, flaring up.

'Why, what do I keep you for?' he shouted; but bethinking himself that this would not help matters, he stopped short in the middle of a sentence and merely sighed. 'Well, can we start sowing?' he asked, after a pause.

'We might, round behind Turkino, to-morrow or the day after.'

'And the clover?'

'I've sent Vassily and Mishka: they're sowing. Only I don't know if they will get through, it's so muddy.'

'How many acres?'

'About fifteen.'

'Why not the lot?' cried Levin.

That they were only sowing fifteen acres of clover instead of fifty was still more annoying. Clover, as he knew from books as well as by his own experience, never did well unless it was sown as early as possible – almost before the snow had finished melting. And Levin could never get this done.

'There are not enough men. What are you to do with such people? Three haven't turned up. And there's Simeon ...'

'Well, you should have taken some men from the thatching.'

'So I have.'

'Where are the men, then?'

'Five of them are making compot' (he meant compost), 'four are turning the oats over. Otherwise they might begin sprouting, Constantine Dmitrich.'

Levin knew very well that 'might begin sprouting' meant that his English oats were already done for. Here again his orders had not been obeyed.

'Why, I told you back in Lent to put in the ventilating chimneys!' he shouted.

'Don't worry, we shall get it all done in time.'

Levin waved his hand angrily and went to the barn to look at the oats, before returning to the stable. The oats were not yet spoiled. But the men were turning them over with spades, whereas they could simply have let them slide down from the loft. Levin arranged for this to be done, told off a couple of the men to help sow clover, and recovered from his vexation with the bailiff. Indeed, it was impossible to be angry on such a lovely day.

'Ignat!' he called to the coachman who, with sleeves rolled up, was washing the barouche at the well. 'Saddle me ...'

'Which, sir?'

'Oh, Kolpik will do.'

'Right, sir.'

While the horse was being saddled, Levin again called the bailiff, who was hanging about within sight so as to make it up with him, and began talking to him about the spring work that lay before them and his plans for the estate. He wanted the manure carted early, to have it all done before the first mowing. And the far field was to be ploughed continually, so as to keep it fallow. The hay would be got in by outside labour, not by their own men, who would want half the harvest.

The bailiff listened attentively, making visible efforts to approve his master's plans; but he wore the hopeless, despondent look which Levin knew so well and which always irritated him. His expression seemed to say, 'That is all very well, but it will be as God wills.'

Nothing chagrined Levin so much as this manner; but it was one common to all the bailiffs he had ever employed. They all took up the same attitude to his plans, and so now he was not angered by it, but chagrined, and felt all the more stimulated to struggle against this kind of elemental force, for which he could find no other name than 'as God wills', and which he was always up against.

'If we can manage it, Constantine Dmitrich,' said the bailiff.

'Why ever shouldn't you manage it?'

'We must hire at least fifteen more labourers. But you see they won't come. There were some here to-day asking seventy roubles for the summer.'

Levin was silent: always this same force opposing him. He knew that, try as they would, they had never managed to hire more than thirty-seven or thirty-eight labourers – forty at the most – at the proper wages. Some forty had been taken on, and there were no more. Yet all the same he could not help continuing the struggle.

'Send to Sury, to Chefirovka. If they don't come we must look for them.'

'I'll send all right,' said Vassily Fedorovich despondently. 'But there are the horses too – they're not good for much.'

'We will buy some more. But I know you,' he added laughingly, 'you always want to make do with as little as possible, and poor quality. However, this year I'm not going to let you have your own way. I shall see to everything myself.'

'Why, I don't think you spend much time asleep as it is. It is nicer for us to work under the master's eye …'

'So they're sowing clover the other side of the Birch Dale? I'll ride over and have a look at them,' said Levin, mounting the little bay cob, Kolpik, which the coachman had led up.

'You won't get across the streams, Constantine Dmitrich,' the coachman called out.

'All right, I'll go through the woods, then.'

And Levin rode through the muddy yard and out of the gate into the field at a brisk amble, his good little horse, who had been inactive too long, snorting at the puddles and pulling at the bridle.

If Levin had felt happy before in the cattle-sheds and farmyard, his spirits rose still higher in the open country. Peacefully swinging along on his good little cob and drinking in the warm, fresh scent of the snow and the air, he rode through the wood here and there over crumbling, sinking snow, covered with dissolving tracks, and delighted in every one of his trees with their swelling buds and the moss growing green again on their bark. When he came out of the wood, a vast expanse of smooth, velvety green spread before him without a single bare place or swamp and only stained here and there in the hollows with patches of melting snow. He was not put out of temper either by the sight of a peasant's horse and colt trampling his young grass (he told a peasant he met to drive them off), or by the impudent and stupid answer the peasant Ipat, whom he happened to meet, gave in reply to his question: 'Well, Ipat, shall we be sowing soon?' 'We must get the ploughing done first, Constantine Dmitrich,' said Ipat.

The farther he went, the happier he became, and all kinds of plans for the farm, each better than the last, presented themselves to his mind. He would plant trees along the south side of all the fields so that the snow should not lie long under them; divide the fields, manuring six and keeping three for pasture; put up a cattle-yard at the far end of the field; and dig a pond and make movable pens for the cattle, so as to get the land manured. And then he would have 800 acres of wheat, some 300 of potatoes, and 400 of clover, and not a single acre exhausted.

With such dreams as these, carefully guiding his horse along the borders of the fields so as not to trample the young growth, he rode up to the men who were sowing clover. The cart with the seed was standing not on the side but in the middle of a field of winter-wheat, which was being cut up by the wheels and trampled by the horse. Both the men were sitting at the side of the field, probably sharing a pipe of tobacco. The earth in the cart, with which the seed was mixed, was not rubbed fine but caked or frozen into lumps. Seeing the master, the labourer, Vassily, moved towards the cart, while Mishka set to work sowing. This was all wrong but Levin seldom got angry with the men. When Vassily came up, Levin told him to take the horse and cart to the side of the field.

'It's all right, sir, the wheat will recover.'

'Please don't argue,' said Levin, 'but do as you are told.'

'Yes, sir,' replied Vassily, and he took the horse's head. 'But the sowing is getting on first-rate, Constantine Dmitrich,' he said ingratiatingly. 'Only it is dreadfully hard going! You pick up half a hundred-weight with each step.'

'And why isn't your earth sifted?' asked Levin.

'Oh we crumble it up as we go along,' replied Vassily, taking up a handful of seed and rubbing the earth between his palms.

It was not Vassily's fault that they had given him unsifted earth, but still it was annoying.

Having more than once successfully tested a method he knew for stifling his annoyance and making right again all that seemed wrong, Levin applied it now. He watched how Mishka strode along, dragging the huge lumps of earth that stuck to each foot, dismounted from his horse, took the seed-basket from Vassily and prepared to sow.

'Where did you leave off?'

Vassily pointed to a spot with his foot and Levin went forward, as best he could, scattering the seed. It was hard going, like wading through a marsh, and by the time Levin had done a row he was wet with perspiration. He stopped and handed the basket back to Vassily.

'Well sir, don't blame me for that row when summer comes,' said Vassily.

'Why?' asked Levin cheerily, already feeling the efficacy of his remedy.

'You will see in the summer. It'll look different. You just look now where I sowed last spring. How I worked at it! Why, Constantine Dmitrich, I believe I try as hard for you as I would for my own father. I don't like bad work myself, nor would I let the others do it. What's good for the master's good for us too. To look out yonder now,' said Vassily, pointing to the field, 'it does your heart good.'

'It's a lovely spring, Vassily.'

'Yes, it's a spring the old men don't remember the like of. I was up home and one old man has sown wheat too – about an acre of it. He was saying you wouldn't know it from rye.'

'Have you been sowing wheat long?'

'Why, sir, it was you taught us the year before last. You gave me two bushels of seed yourself. We sold a quarter of it and sowed the rest.'

'Well, mind you crumble up the lumps,' said Levin, going towards his horse. 'And keep an eye on Mishka. And if there's a good crop you shall have half a rouble for every acre.'

'Thank you kindly. We are well content as it is, sir.'

Levin mounted his horse and rode to the field where clover had been sown the year before and then to the field which had been ploughed ready for the spring wheat.

The clover was coming up splendidly in the stubble-field. It was already sturdy and looked quite green among the broken stalks of last year's wheat. The horse sank fetlock-deep into the mud and drew each hoof out of the half-thawed earth with a sucking noise. It was utterly impossible to ride across the ploughland: the ground bore only where there was ice and in the thawing furrows the mud came over the horse's pasterns. The ploughland was in excellent condition: a couple of days and they would be able to harrow and sow. Everything was capital, everything was cheering. Levin rode back across the streams, hoping the water would have gone down. And indeed he did manage to ford them, startling two ducks as he did so. 'There should be some snipe too,' he thought, and just at the turning to the house he met the keeper, who confirmed his supposition.

Levin rode home at a trot so as to have time to eat his dinner and get his gun ready for the evening.

14

As Levin, in the best of spirits, was nearing the house, he heard the tinkling of a bell approaching the main entrance.

'That must be someone from the railway station,' he thought. 'Just the time the Moscow train arrives ... Who can it be, I wonder? What if it's brother Nikolai? He did say, "Maybe I'll go to a watering-place, or maybe I'll come down to you." ' For a moment he felt dismayed

175

and disturbed lest his brother Nikolai's presence should upset his happy mood of spring. But he felt ashamed of this feeling, and immediately, as it were, opened out his spiritual arms and with tender joy and expectation now hoped with his whole soul that it was his brother. He spurred on his horse and, coming round the acacia-tree, saw the troika from the station and in it a gentleman in a fur coat. It was not his brother. 'Oh, if only it's some nice person I can talk to a little!' he thought.

'Ah!' cried Levin joyfully, flinging up both his hands. 'What a welcome guest! Ah, how glad I am to see you!' he exclaimed, recognizing Oblonsky.

'I shall find out for certain now whether she's married, or when she's going to be married,' he thought.

And on this lovely spring day he felt that the memory of her did not hurt at all.

'You didn't expect me, I suppose?' said Oblonsky, climbing out of the sledge, splashes of mud on the bridge of his nose, his cheek, and his eyebrows, but beaming with cheerfulness and health. 'I've come to see you – one,' he said, embracing and kissing Levin, 'to get some shooting – two, and three, to sell the Yergushovo forest.'

'Splendid! And what do you think of the spring we are having? However did you manage to get here in a sledge?'

'It would have been worse still on wheels, Constantine Dmitrich,' said the driver, whom Levin knew.

'Well, I am very, very pleased to see you,' said Levin, smiling his frank smile, happy as a child's.

He led his guest into the spare bedroom, where Oblonsky's things – his bag, a gun-case, and a satchel for cigars – were also brought. Leaving him to wash and change, Levin went off to the office to speak about the ploughing and clover. Agatha Mihalovna, who always had the honour of the house very much at heart, met him in the hall with queries about dinner.

'Do just as you like, only make haste about it,' he said, and went out to see the bailiff.

When he returned, Oblonsky, washed and brushed and beaming, was coming out of his room, and they went upstairs together.

'How glad I am to have got away to you! Now I shall understand what the mysteries are that you perpetrate here! No, but seriously, I envy you. What a house! How nice it all is – so light and gay,' said

Oblonsky, forgetting that it was not always spring and that the days were not always bright. 'And what a dear your old nurse is! A pretty maid in an apron would be preferable; but with your severe monastic style the old nurse fits in better.'

Oblonsky had much interesting news to tell and one item of especial interest to Levin was that his brother, Sergei Ivanich, intended to pay him a visit in the summer.

Not one word did Oblonsky say in reference to Kitty or the Shcherbatskys, except to deliver greetings from his wife. Levin was grateful to him for his delicacy and was very glad of his visitor. As usual during his solitude, a mass of ideas and impressions which he could not communicate to those about him had collected in his mind; and now he poured out to Oblonsky the romantic joy he felt in the spring, his failures, his plans for the estate, his opinions and thoughts about the books he had been reading and, in particular, the idea of his own book, the basis of which, though he was unaware of it himself, was a criticism of all previous works on agriculture. Oblonsky, always kind and quick to understand everything – a hint was enough – was especially kind on this visit. There was a new trait which Levin noticed and was flattered by – an undertone of respect and a sort of tenderness.

The efforts of Agatha Mihalovna and the cook to prepare a specially good dinner only ended in the two hungry friends sitting down to the preliminary course and filling themselves up with bread and butter, smoked goose, and pickled mushrooms, and in Levin's ordering the soup to be served without waiting for the little pies with which the cook had particularly meant to impress their visitor. But Oblonsky, though he was accustomed to very different dinners, found everything delicious: the herb brandy, the bread and the butter, and, above all, the smoked goose and the mushrooms, the nettle soup and the chicken in white sauce, the Crimean white wine – everything was superb and marvellous.

'Excellent, excellent!' he said, lighting a fat cigarette after the joint. 'Coming to you I feel as if I had landed on a peaceful shore after the noise and jolting of a steamer. So you maintain that the labourer himself is an element to be studied and taken as a governing factor in the choice of agricultural methods. Of course, I am ignorant about these matters; but I should imagine that theory and its application will have an influence on the labourer too.'

'Yes, but wait a moment. I'm not talking of political economy – I mean the science of agriculture. Like the natural sciences, it ought to observe existing phenomena and the labourer in his economic, ethnographical ...'

At this point Agatha Mihalovna came in with jam.

'Ah, Agatha Mihalovna,' said Oblonsky, kissing the tips of his plump fingers, 'what smoked goose, what herb brandy! ... But what do you think, Kostya? Isn't it time to start?' he added to Levin.

Levin glanced out of the window at the sun sinking behind the bare tree-tops of the forest.

'Yes, high time!' he said. 'Kuzma, get the trap ready,' and he ran downstairs.

Oblonsky followed and carefully took the canvas cover off his varnished gun-case with his own hands, opened it, and set to work to put together his expensive gun, which was of the latest type. Kuzma, already scenting a generous tip, never left Oblonsky's side, putting on his stockings and his boots for him, which Oblonsky willingly allowed.

'Kostya, tell them that if Ryabinin the dealer appears – I told him to come to-day – they're to ask him in and make him wait ...'

'Do you mean to say you're selling the forest to Ryabinin?'

'Yes. Do you know him?'

'Of course I know him. I have done business with him, "positively and finally".'

Oblonsky laughed. 'Positively and finally' was the dealer's favourite expression.

'Yes, it's terribly funny the way he talks. She knows where her master is going,' he added, patting Laska, who was whining and jumping round Levin, licking now his hand, now his boots and his gun.

The trap was already at the steps when they went out.

'I told them to bring the trap round, though it is not far, but we can walk if you like?'

'No, let us drive,' said Oblonsky, getting into the trap. He sat down, tucked the tiger-skin rug round his legs, and lit a cigar. 'How is it you don't smoke? A cigar is not just a pleasure – it's the crown and hall-mark of pleasure. Ah, this is life! How lovely! This is how I should like to live.'

'And who prevents you?' asked Levin, smiling.

'No, but you are a lucky fellow! You've got everything you like.

You like horses – and you have them; dogs – you have them; shooting – you get it; farming – you have that too.'

'Perhaps it is because I enjoy what I have and don't fret for what I have not,' said Levin, thinking of Kitty.

Oblonsky understood and glanced at him but said nothing.

Levin was grateful to Oblonsky for noticing, with his usual tact, that he dreaded conversation about the Shcherbatskys, and therefore not mentioning them; but now Levin was longing to find out about the matter that tormented him, yet he had not the courage to begin.

'Well, and how are your affairs?' he asked, bethinking himself that it was not nice of him to be thinking only of himself.

Oblonsky's eyes began to sparkle merrily.

'You don't admit, I know, that one may like a roll when one's ration of bread is there for one – to your mind it is a crime; but I don't count life as life without love,' he said, interpreting Levin's question in his own fashion. 'It can't be helped: I was born that way. And besides, it does so little harm to anyone else but gives so much pleasure to oneself ...'

'The old story, or is there something new?' queried Levin.

'Yes, my boy, there is! You know the Ossian type of woman ... such as one only sees in dreams? ... Well, such women do exist ... and they are terrible. Woman, don't you know, is the sort of subject that study it as much as you will it is always quite new.'

'In that case then, better not study it.'

'Oh no! Some mathematician has said that happiness lies in the search for truth, not in finding it.'

Levin listened in silence and, in spite of all his efforts, he could not even begin to enter into the feelings of his friend and understand his sentiments and the charm of studying women of that kind.

15

THE place where they were going to shoot was not far off, in a little aspen-grove by a stream. Reaching the copse, Levin got down and led Oblonsky to a corner of a mossy, swampy glade, already clear of snow. He himself returned to a double birch on the other side and, leaning his gun against the fork of a dead lower branch, took off his coat, tightened his belt, and worked his arms to see if he could move them freely.

Grey old Laska, following close on his heels, sat down warily opposite him and pricked up her ears. The sun was setting behind the great forest and the birch trees dotted about in the aspen-grove stood out clearly in the evening glow with their drooping branches and their swollen buds ready to burst into leaf.

From the thicket, where the snow had not all melted, the water flowed almost noiselessly in narrow, winding streamlets. Tiny birds chirped and occasionally fluttered from tree to tree.

The intervals of profound silence were broken by the rustle of last year's leaves, stirred by the thawing earth and the grass growing.

'Why, one can hear and see the grass growing!' thought Levin, noticing a wet, slate-coloured aspen leaf moving beside a blade of young grass. He stood listening, and gazing down now at the wet, mossy ground, now at the watchful Laska, now at the sea of bare tree-tops that stretched on the slope below him, now at the darkening sky streaked with little white clouds. Slowly sweeping its wings, a hawk flew high over the distant forest; another followed unhurriedly in the same direction and vanished. In the thicket the birds chirped louder and more busily. Nearby a brown owl hooted, and Laska gave a start, took a few cautious steps, and, putting her head on one side, pricked up her ears again. A cuckoo was heard on the other side of the stream. It called twice on its usual note, and then gave a hoarse, hurried call and broke down.

'Fancy, the cuckoo already!' said Oblonsky, appearing from behind a bush.

'Yes, I can hear,' replied Levin, reluctantly disturbing the silence of the wood, his voice sounding disagreeable to himself. 'It won't be long now.'

Oblonsky's figure went behind the bush again and Levin saw nothing but the flare of a match, followed by the red glow of a cigarette and a spiral of blue smoke.

'Tchk! tchk!' came the clicking sound of Oblonsky cocking his gun.

'What's that cry?' he asked, drawing Levin's attention to a long-drawn whine like the high-pitched whinnying of a colt in play.

'Don't you know? It's a hare. But no more talking! Listen, they're coming!' Levin almost shouted, cocking his gun.

They heard a shrill whistle in the distance and, two seconds later – the interval the sportsman knows so well – another followed and then a third, and after the third whistle the sound of a hoarse cry.

Levin looked to right and left, and there, straight in front of him against the dusky blue sky, above the blurred tops of the tenderly sprouting aspen-trees, he saw a bird. It was flying straight towards him: the guttural cry, like the even tearing of some strong fabric, sounded close to his ear; the long beak and neck of the bird were already visible and, just as Levin was taking aim, there was a red flash from behind the bush where Oblonsky was standing and the bird dropped like an arrow, then fluttered up again. Another flash, followed by the sound of a hit, and beating its wings as though trying to keep up in the air, the bird stopped, remained stationary for a moment and then fell with a heavy thud on the muddy ground.

'Did I miss it?' shouted Oblonsky, who could see nothing for smoke.

'Here it is!' said Levin, pointing to Laska, who, with one ear raised, wagging the tip of her shaggy tail, moving slowly as if to prolong the pleasure and almost smiling, was bringing the dead bird to her master. 'Well, I'm glad you got it,' said Levin, at the same time feeling envious that he had not shot the snipe himself.

'A wretched miss with the right barrel,' replied Oblonsky, loading his gun. 'Ssh … here's one coming.'

Indeed, they could hear a quick succession of shrill whistles. Two snipe, playing and chasing one another, and whistling but not crying, flew right above the sportsmen's heads. Four shots rang out and the snipe turned swiftly like swallows and vanished from sight.

The sport was excellent. Oblonsky shot another brace and Levin got two, of which one was not recovered. It began to get dark. Bright, silvery Venus was already shining her gentle light low in the west behind the birch-trees and sombre Arcturus was spilling his red fires high in the east. Overhead Levin made out the stars of the Great Bear and lost them again. There were no more snipe now; but Levin decided to stay a little longer, until Venus, whom he could see below a branch of a birch-tree, should climb above it and all the stars of the Great Bear should be quite visible. Venus had risen above the branch, the chariot of the Great Bear with its shaft showed clearly against the dark blue sky, yet still he waited on.

'Isn't it time to go?' asked Oblonsky.

It was quiet now in the copse, not a bird stirred.

'Let's stay a little longer,' answered Levin.

'As you like.'

They were standing now some fifteen paces apart.

'Stiva!' said Levin suddenly and unexpectedly. 'Why don't you tell me whether your sister-in-law is married yet, or when she is going to be?'

Levin felt so calm and steady that he thought the answer, whatever it might be, could not affect him. But he did not at all expect the reply Oblonsky gave him.

'She has not thought, and is not thinking of getting married; but she's very ill and the doctors have sent her abroad. They're even afraid she may not live.'

'What did you say?' cried Levin. 'Very ill? What is the matter with her? How did she ...?'

While they were talking, Laska, ears cocked, kept looking at the sky and then reproachfully at them.

'What a time to choose to talk!' she seemed to be thinking. 'And here comes one flying. ... Yes, here it is. They'll miss it ...'

But at that very instant both men suddenly heard a shrill whistle that seemed to pierce their ears; both suddenly seized their guns and there were two flashes and two reports. The snipe that was flying high above at once folded its wings and fell into a thicket, bending down the tender grass.

'Well done! Both together!' cried Levin, and he ran into the thicket with Laska to look for the bird. 'Oh yes – what was it that was distressing me?' he wondered. 'I know, Kitty is ill. ... Well, it can't be helped. I am very sorry,' he thought.

'Found it? Clever girl!' he said, taking the warm bird from Laska's mouth and packing it into the game-bag that was almost full. 'I've got it, Stiva!' he shouted.

16

ON the way home Levin asked all about Kitty's illness and the Shcherbatskys' plans and, though he would have been ashamed to admit it, he was pleased at what he heard. He was pleased that there was still hope for him and even more pleased that she, who had made him suffer so much, should be suffering herself. But when Oblonsky began to speak of the cause of Kitty's illness and mentioned Vronsky's name, Levin cut him short.

'I have no right whatever to know these family matters and, to tell the truth, no interest in them either.'

Oblonsky smiled almost perceptibly, catching the instantaneous change he knew so well in Levin's face, as gloomy now as it had been bright a moment ago.

'Have you quite settled with Ryabinin about the forest?' asked Levin.

'Yes, quite. I'm getting a magnificent price for it: thirty-eight thousand. Eight down and the rest in six years. I have been trying to sell it for a long time. No one would give more.'

'The fact is, you are giving the forest away,' said Levin gloomily.

'How do you mean – giving it away?' said Oblonsky with a good-humoured smile, knowing that nothing would be right in Levin's eyes now.

'Because the forest is worth at least a hundred and eighty-five roubles an acre,' replied Levin.

'Oh, you country landowners!' said Oblonsky playfully. 'And your tone of contempt for us townsfolk! ... But when it comes to business, we do it better than anyone. I assure you I have reckoned it all out,' he went on, 'and the forest is fetching a very good price – so much so that I'm afraid the fellow may cry off. You know it's not "timber", so much as stuff for burning,' said Oblonsky, hoping by this distinction to convince Levin finally of the unfairness of his doubts. 'And it won't run to more than thirty-five yards of faggots per acre, and he is paying me at the rate of seventy roubles the acre.'

Levin smiled contemptuously. 'I know this manner,' he thought. 'It is not only his but all city people's who visit the country a couple of times in ten years, pick up two or three expressions, use them in season and out, and are firmly persuaded they know everything. "*Timber ... run to so many yards the acre.*" He uses the words without understanding a thing about the business.'

'I wouldn't attempt to teach you what you write about in your office,' he said, 'and if need arose I should come to you for advice. But you're so positive you know all there is to know about selling the forest. It is not easy. Have you counted the trees?'

'How can you count the trees?' said Oblonsky, laughing, still anxious to draw his friend out of his ill-humour. 'Count the sands of the seas, number the planets. Even a great mind ...'

'Well, Ryabinin's great mind can. And no dealer ever buys a forest without counting the trees, unless someone's giving him the forest for nothing, as you are doing. I know your forest. I go shooting there every year and it's worth a hundred and eighty-five roubles an acre, cash down, while he's paying you seventy in instalments. So that in fact you have made him a present of about thirty thousand roubles.'

'Don't exaggerate!' pleaded Oblonsky piteously. 'Why was it no one would offer more?'

'Because he and the other dealers are in league: he's bought them off. I've had to do with all of them: I know them. They're not genuine dealers but speculators. He would not look at a deal that brought him ten or fifteen per cent profit: he waits till he can buy a rouble for twenty kopecks.'

'Come now! You are in a bad mood.'

'Not at all,' said Levin gloomily, as they drove up to the house.

At the porch stood a trap tightly bound with iron and leather, with a sleek horse tightly harnessed with broad straps. In the trap sat Ryabinin's clerk (who also served as coachman), red-faced and tightly belted. Ryabinin himself was already in the house and met the two friends in the hall. Ryabinin was a tall, spare, middle-aged man, with a moustache, a prominent clean-shaven chin, and prominent dull eyes. He wore a long-tailed dark blue coat, with buttons below the waist at the back, high boots crinkled round the ankles and straight over the calf, and on top of them a large pair of goloshes. He rubbed his face with his handkerchief and wrapping his coat round him – although it hung very well as it was – he greeted them with a smile, holding out his hand to Oblonsky, as if he were trying to catch something.

'So here you are,' said Oblonsky, giving him his hand. 'Capital!'

'I dared not disregard your excellency's commands, although the road was really too bad. I positively walked the whole way but I am here on time. Constantine Dmitrich, my respects to you,' he said, turning to Levin and trying to seize his hand too.

But Levin, scowling, pretended not to see and began taking the snipe out of the game-bag.

'Your honours have been pleased to amuse yourselves with shooting? What kind of bird would that be, pray?' added Ryabinin, looking contemptuously at the snipe. 'A great delicacy, I suppose,' and he shook his head disapprovingly, as if he had grave doubts whether this game were worth the candle.

'Would you like to go into my study?' Levin said in French to

Oblonsky, scowling moodily. 'Go into my study; you can talk business there.'

'Quite so, wherever you please,' said Ryabinin with scornful dignity, as though wishing to make it felt that others might have difficulty in knowing how to behave but that he could never be in difficulty about anything.

When he entered the study, Ryabinin looked round instinctively, as though to find the ikon, but when he discovered it he did not cross himself. He scanned the bookcases and bookshelves with the same dubious air with which he had regarded the snipe, smiled contemptuously and shook his head in disapproval, quite sure that this game was not worth the candle.

'Well, have you brought the money?' asked Oblonsky. 'Take a seat.'

'There won't be any difficulty about the money. I have come to see you to talk matters over.'

'What is there to talk over? But do take a seat.'

'I don't mind if I do,' said Ryabinin, sitting down and leaning his elbows on the back of the chair in the most uncomfortable fashion. 'You must give way a bit, Prince. It would be a sin not to. The money is positively ready to the last kopeck. There will be no hitch about the money.'

Levin, who had been putting his gun away in the cupboard, was just going out of the door but catching the dealer's words he stopped.

'As it is, you are getting the forest for nothing,' he said. 'He came to me too late, or I'd have fixed the price for him.'

Ryabinin rose and, smiling, silently looked Levin up and down.

'Very close about money is Constantine Dmitrich,' he said with a smile, addressing Oblonsky. 'There is positively no doing business with him. I wanted to buy his wheat off him, and a pretty price I offered too.'

'Why should I make you a present of my goods? I didn't pick it up on the ground, nor steal it either.'

'Mercy on us! Nowadays there is positively no chance of stealing. With the open courts and everything done in style nowadays there's no question of stealing. We are just talking things over like gentlemen. The forest is too dear: I can't make both ends meet over it. I must ask for a little something to be knocked off the price.'

'But is the thing settled or not? If it is, it's useless haggling; but if not,' said Levin, 'I'll buy the forest myself.'

The smile vanished from Ryabinin's face, leaving a hawk-like, predatory, cruel expression in its place. With swift, bony fingers he unbuttoned his coat, revealing a shirt, brass waistcoat buttons, and a watch-chain, and quickly pulled out a fat old pocket-book.

'Pardon, the forest is mine,' he said, crossing himself quickly and holding out his hand. 'Take your money; it's my forest. That's the way Ryabinin does business, no haggling over kopecks,' he added, scowling and flourishing his pocket-book.

'I wouldn't be in a hurry if I were you,' said Levin.

'But I've given my word, you know,' exclaimed Oblonsky in surprise.

Levin went out of the room, slamming the door. Ryabinin looked at the door and shook his head with a smile.

'That's youth all over – he's positively only a boy. Now, believe me, I'm buying just for the honour of the thing – so that Ryabinin, and no one else, should have bought the Oblonsky forest. But I shall have to rely on God for my profit. We must trust in Him. If you would kindly sign the agreement now ...'

An hour later the dealer, his overcoat carefully patted into place and the hooks of his jacket fastened, with the agreement in his pocket, seated himself in his iron-bound trap and drove homewards.

'Ugh, these gentry!' he remarked to his clerk. 'They're a nice lot!'

'That's so,' responded the clerk, handing over the reins and buttoning up the leather apron of the trap. 'But can I congratulate you on a good bargain, Mihail Ignatich?'

'Not too bad ...'

17

OBLONSKY went upstairs, his pocket bulging with notes which the dealer had paid him for three months in advance. The business of the forest was over, he had the money in his pocket; the shooting had been excellent, he himself was in the best of spirits and therefore all the more anxious to dispel the ill-humour that had fallen on Levin. He wanted to finish the day at supper as pleasantly as it had begun.

Levin certainly was in a bad mood and however much he desired to be affectionate and cordial to his dear guest, he could not master his mood. The intoxication of the news that Kitty was not married had gradually begun to work on him.

Kitty not married but ill – ill for love of a man who had slighted her. This affront somehow rebounded on him. Vronsky had slighted her and she had slighted him, Levin. Consequently Vronsky had the right to despise Levin and was therefore his enemy. But Levin did not think all this out. He vaguely felt that there was something insulting to him in it and was angry not with what had upset him but with everything that came to his mind. The ridiculous sale of the forest, the fraud practised upon Oblonsky, which had taken place under his roof, exasperated him.

'Well, finished?' he said, meeting Oblonsky upstairs. 'What about supper?'

'I won't say no. What an appetite I get in the country – it's incredible! Why didn't you offer Ryabinin a snack?'

'Oh, he can go to the devil!'

'The way you treat him, though!' said Oblonsky. 'You didn't even shake hands with him. Why not shake hands with him?'

'Because I don't shake hands with my footman, and my footman's worth a hundred of him.'

'What a reactionary you are, really! How about the merging of classes?' said Oblonsky.

'Anyone who likes that is welcome to it, but it sickens me.'

'You're a regular reactionary, I see.'

'To tell you the truth, I have never considered what I am. I am Constantine Levin, that's all.'

'And Constantine Levin very much out of temper,' said Oblonsky, smiling.

'Yes, I am out of temper, and do you know why? Because – forgive my saying so – of that idiotic sale ...'

Oblonsky frowned good-humouredly, like one who feels himself teased and attacked for no fault of his own.

'Oh, do stop!' he said. 'When did anybody ever sell anything without being told immediately afterwards that it was worth much more? But when one wants to sell, no one will give anything. ... Yes, I see you've got your knife into that unfortunate Ryabinin.'

'Maybe I have. And do you know why? You will call me a reactionary again, or some other dreadful name; but all the same it does annoy and upset me to see on all sides the impoverishing of the nobility to which I belong and, to which in spite of your merging of classes, I am very glad to belong. ... And their impoverishment is not due to extravagance – that would not matter: living like a lord is the proper thing for them and only the nobility knows how to do it. Now the peasants about us are buying land, and I don't mind that. The gentleman does nothing, the peasants works and squeezes out the idler. That's as it should be, and I am very glad for the peasant. But it hurts me to see this impoverishment happening as a result of – I don't know what to call it – of artlessness. Here a Polish speculator buys for half its value a superb estate from a lady who lives in Nice. There land which is worth five roubles an acre is leased to a merchant for less than half a rouble. Here you go and make that rogue a present of thirty thousand roubles for no reason at all.'

'What should I have done? Count every tree, one by one?'

'Of course. You didn't count them but Ryabinin did. Ryabinin's children will have means of livelihood and education, while yours may not!'

'Well, you must forgive me, but there is something mean about this counting. We have our business and they have theirs, and they must make their profit. However, the thing's done, and there's an end of it. Ah, here come the poached eggs, my favourite dish. And Agatha Mihalovna will give us some of that marvellous herb-brandy ...'

Oblonsky sat down to the table and began joking with Agatha Mihalovna, assuring her that he had not tasted such a dinner and supper for a long time.

'You appreciate it at least,' said Agatha Mihalovna, 'but Constantine Dmitrich now, whatever you gave him – if it were only a crust of bread – would just eat it and be off.'

Though Levin made every effort to master his mood, he remained morose and silent. There was one question he wanted to put to Oblonsky but he could not bring himself to ask it, and could not find the words or the moment in which to put it. Oblonsky had gone down to his room, undressed, washed himself again, arrayed himself in his night-shirt with goffered frills and got into bed, but Levin still lingered in his room, talking various trifles and unable to ask what he wanted to know.

'How wonderfully they make this soap,' he said, examining and turning over in his hands a cake of soap which Agatha Mihalovna had put ready for the visitor but which Oblonsky had not used. 'Just look: it is quite a work of art.'

'Yes, everything's brought to such a pitch of perfection nowadays,' said Oblonsky, with a moist and blissful yawn. 'The theatre, for instance, and those amusement places ... ah-h-h!' he yawned. 'The electric light everywhere ... ah-h!'

'Yes, the electric light,' said Levin. 'Yes. Oh, and where's Vronsky now?' he asked, suddenly laying down the soap.

'Vronsky?' said Oblonsky, checking his yawn. 'He's in Petersburg. He left shortly after you did, and he's not been in Moscow once since then. And you know, Kostya, I will be frank with you,' he went on, leaning his elbow on the table and propping his handsome, rosy face on one hand, his moist, good-natured, sleepy eyes shining like stars. 'It was your own fault. You took fright at the sight of your rival. But as I told you at the time, I couldn't say which of you had the better chance. Why didn't you fight it out? I told you at the time that ...' He yawned with his jaws only, without opening his mouth.

'Does he know, or doesn't he, that I did make an offer?' Levin wondered, gazing at him. 'Yes, there is something sly and diplomatic in his face,' and feeling himself blushing he looked Oblonsky straight in the eyes without a word.

'If there was anything on her side at that time, it was just that she was attracted by his appearance,' pursued Oblonsky. 'His being the perfect aristocrat and his future position in society, don't you know, had an influence not with her, but with her mother.'

Levin scowled. The humiliation of his rejection stung him to the heart, as though it were a fresh wound he had only just received. But he was at home, and at home the very walls are a support.

'Stay, stay,' he began, interrupting Oblonsky. 'You talk of his being an aristocrat. But I should like to ask you what is Vronsky's or anyone else's aristocracy that I should be looked down upon because of it? You consider Vronsky an aristocrat: I don't. A man whose father intrigued and crawled up from nothing, whose mother has had relations with heaven knows whom.... No, forgive me, I consider myself and people like me aristocrats, people who can point back to three or four honourable generations, all with the highest degree of breeding (talent and intelligence are a different matter), who have never curried favour with anyone, never depended on anyone, but have lived like my father and my grandfather before him. And I know many such. You think it mean of me to count the trees in my forest, while you make Ryabinin a present of thirty thousand; but you get rents from your lands and I don't know what else, while I don't, and so I prize what's come to me from my ancestors or been won by hard work. ... We are the aristocrats – not those who only manage to exist on the favour of the mighty of this world, and who can be bought for a copper coin.'

'Well, but whom are you attacking? I agree with you,' said Oblonsky, sincerely and genially, though he felt that Levin included him among those who could be bought for a copper coin. Levin's vehemence genuinely pleased him. 'Whom are you attacking? Though a good deal of what you say of Vronsky is not true, but I won't talk about that. I tell you candidly that if I were you I should come back with me to Moscow and ...'

'No. I don't know if you know it or not, and I don't care, but I will tell you – I did make an offer and was rejected, and Katerina Alexandrovna is now nothing to me but a painful and humiliating memory.'

'Why? What nonsense!'

'But we won't talk about it. Please forgive me if I've been churlish,' said Levin. Now that he had opened his heart, he became once more as he had been in the morning. 'You are not angry with me, Stiva? Please don't be angry,' he said and, smiling, took his hand.

'Of course not! Not a bit, and no reason to be. I am glad we've had this talk. And do you know, shooting in the early morning is often very good. Shall we? I would not go to bed again afterwards, but drive straight to the station.'

'Capital!'

18

THOUGH Vronsky's whole inner life was absorbed in his passion, its outward course ran unalterably and inevitably along the old accustomed lines of social and regimental ties and interests. The regiment occupied an important place in Vronsky's life, both because he was fond of his regiment and still more because the regiment was fond of him. Not only were they fond of him in the regiment, they respected him, too, and were proud of him: proud that this man, with his vast wealth, his brilliant education and abilities, the path open before him to every kind of success dear to ambition and vanity, disregarded all that and of all life's interests had nearest to his heart those of his regiment and his comrades. Vronsky was aware of his comrades' view of him and, in addition to liking the life, he felt bound to live up to the reputation they had given him.

It goes without saying that he never spoke of his love to any of his comrades, nor did he betray his secret even in the wildest drinking bouts (indeed, he was never so drunk as to lose control of himself). And he silenced any of his irresponsible comrades who attempted to allude to his liaison. But in spite of that, his love was known to all the town – everybody guessed more or less correctly at his relations with Madame Karenin. Most of the younger men envied him precisely on account of what was the most irksome factor in his love – the exalted position of Karenin and the consequent publicity given to the liaison in society.

The majority of the young women, who envied Anna and had long been weary of hearing her virtue praised, rejoiced at the fulfilment of their predictions and were only waiting to be sure that public opinion had turned before falling upon her with all the weight of their scorn. They were already preparing the lumps of mud they would fling when the time came. Most of the older people and certain highly-placed personages were annoyed at the impending social scandal.

Vronsky's mother was at first pleased when she heard of his liaison: nothing, to her mind, gave such a finishing touch to a brilliant young man as an affair in the highest society. She was pleased, too, that Madame Karenin, who had so taken her fancy and who had talked so much of her son, was, after all, just like all other pretty and well-bred women – at least, according to the Countess Vronsky's ideas. But latterly she had heard that her son had refused a post of great importance to his career merely in order to remain in the regiment and constantly see Madame Karenin. She learned that exalted personages were displeased with him on this account, and so she altered her opinion. She was vexed, too, that, as far as she could gather, it was not the brilliant, graceful, worldly liaison such as she would have approved of, but a sort of desperate, Werther-like passion, so she was told, which might well lead him into doing something foolish. She had not seen him since his abrupt departure from Moscow and through her elder son she sent him word to come and see her.

The elder brother, too, was displeased with the younger. He did not analyse what kind of love it was, great or small, passionate or otherwise, guilty or pure (he kept a ballet-girl himself, though he was the father of a family, so he was disposed to be lenient on that score); but he knew that this love affair was viewed with displeasure by those whom it was necessary to please, and therefore he did not approve of his brother's conduct.

Besides the service and society, Vronsky had still another interest – horses. He was passionately fond of horses.

This year there was to be an officers' steeplechase and Vronsky had entered for it, bought a thoroughbred English mare, and, in spite of his love affair, was looking forward to the races with intense, though reserved, excitement.

These two passions did not interfere with one another. On the contrary, he needed occupation and distraction apart from his love, to refresh himself and find rest from the violent emotions that agitated him.

19

ON the day of the Krasnoe Selo races, Vronsky went earlier than usual to eat his beefsteak in the officers' mess. It was not necessary for him to train strictly, as his weight was just the regulation eleven and a half stone; but he had to be careful not to put on flesh and so he avoided sweets and starchy foods. He sat with his coat unbuttoned over a white waistcoat, resting both elbows on the table and looking at a French novel that lay open on his plate as he waited for the steak he had ordered. He was only looking at the book in order not to have to talk to the officers coming in and out while he was thinking.

He was thinking of Anna's promise to meet him that day after the races. But he had not seen her for three days and as her husband had just returned from abroad he did not know whether they would be able to see each other that day, nor did he know how to find out. He had seen her last at his cousin Betsy's summer villa. He went to the Karenins' summer villa as seldom as possible but now he wanted to go there and was considering how to do it.

'Of course I can say that Betsy sent me to ask whether she is coming to the races. I don't see why I shouldn't go,' he decided, lifting his eyes from the book, his face radiant as he imagined the happiness of seeing her.

'Send to my house and tell them to get the troika ready at once,' he said to the waiter who had brought him a steak on a hot silver dish, and moving the dish up he began eating.

From the adjoining billiard-room came the click of balls and the sound of talk and laughter. Two officers appeared in the doorway: one, a young fellow with a weak, thin face, who had recently joined the regiment from the Corps of Pages; the other, a plump, elderly officer with a bracelet on his wrist and sunken little eyes.

Vronsky glanced at them, frowned, and, as if he had not noticed them, bent over his book and proceeded to eat and read at the same time.

'What? Fortifying yourself for the job?' asked the plump officer, taking a seat beside him.

'As you see,' responded Vronsky with a frown, wiping his mouth and not looking at the speaker.

'Not afraid of getting fat?' said the latter, turning a chair round for the young officer.

'What?' said Vronsky angrily, making a grimace of disgust and showing his even teeth.

'Not afraid of getting fat?'

'Waiter, sherry!' said Vronsky, without replying, and moving his book over to the other side he went on reading.

The plump officer took up the wine-list and addressed his young companion.

'You choose what we're to drink,' he said, handing him the wine-list and looking at him.

'Suppose we have some Rhine wine,' said the young man, looking out of the corner of his eye at Vronsky while his fingers tried to catch hold of his budding moustache. Seeing that Vronsky did not turn round, he rose. 'Let's go to the billiard-room,' he said.

The plump officer got up obediently and they made their way towards the door.

At that moment Captain Yashvin, a tall cavalry officer with a fine figure, walked into the room. He gave a contemptuous backward nod to the two officers and came up to Vronsky.

'Ah, here you are!' he cried, slapping him heavily on the shoulder with his large hand.

Vronsky looked up angrily but his face brightened at once into its characteristic look of quiet, genial kindliness.

'That's right, Alexei,' said the captain in his loud baritone. 'Have just a mouthful now and drink only one small glass.'

'I'm not hungry.'

'There go the inseparables,' added Yashvin, glancing ironically at the two officers who were just going out of the room. He sat down beside Vronsky, and his legs, encased in tight riding-breeches, being too long for the chair, bent at a sharp angle at the hip and knee. 'Why didn't you turn up at the Red Theatre last night? Numerova was not at all bad. Where were you?'

'I stayed late at the Tverskoys'.'

'Ah!' said Yashvin.

Yashvin, a gambler and a rake, a man not merely without moral principles but of immoral principles – Yashvin was Vronsky's greatest friend in the regiment. Vronsky liked him both for his extraordinary physical strength, which he demonstrated for the most part by his ability to drink like a fish and go without sleep without being in the slightest degree affected, and for his great strength of character, which he showed in his relations with his comrades and superior officers, commanding both fear and respect, and also at cards, when he would play for tens of thousands and, however much he might have drunk, play with such skill and assurance that he was reckoned the best player in the English Club. Vronsky liked and respected Yashvin particularly because he felt Yashvin liked him, not for his name and money but for himself. And Yashvin was the one person of his acquaintance with whom Vronsky would have liked to speak of his love. He felt that Yashvin, though apparently despising any kind of emotion, was the only man who could, so he fancied, have understood the power of the passion which now filled his whole life. Besides, he was convinced that Yashvin certainly found no pleasure in gossip and scandal but interpreted his feeling in the right way – that is, knew and believed that this love was not a joke or a pastime but something more serious and important.

Vronsky had never spoken to him of his love but he was aware that he knew all about it and that he put the right interpretation on it, and it was pleasant to him to read this in Yashvin's eyes.

'Ah, yes!' said Yashvin to the announcement that Vronsky had been at the Tverskoys'. His black eyes twinkled and he began plucking at one side of his moustache and twisting it into his mouth – a foolish habit he had.

'Well, and what were you doing yesterday? Win anything?' asked Vronsky.

'Eight thousand. But three don't count: I don't expect he will pay up.'

'Oh, then you can afford to lose on me,' said Vronsky, laughing. (Yashvin had staked heavily on Vronsky.)

'No chance of my losing. Mahotin's the only danger.'

And the conversation turned to forecasts of the day's races, the only thing Vronsky could think of just now.

'Come along, I've finished,' said Vronsky and, getting up, he moved towards the door.

Yashvin got up, too, stretching his long legs and his long back.

'It is too early for me to dine but I must have a drink. I'll come along directly. Hey, wine!' he shouted in his rich voice, so famous on the parade-ground, that here made the glasses shake. 'No, it doesn't matter,' he shouted again immediately after. 'You are going home, so I'll come with you.'

And he and Vronsky went out together.

20

VRONSKY was lodged in a roomy, clean, Finnish hut, divided into two by a partition. Petritsky lived with him in camp too. Petritsky was asleep when Vronsky and Yashvin came into the hut.

'Get up, you've slept long enough!' said Yashvin, stepping behind the partition and giving the tousled Petritsky, who was lying with his nose buried in the pillow, a prod on the shoulder.

Petritsky jumped suddenly to his knees and looked round.

'Your brother's been here,' he said to Vronsky. 'Woke me up, confound him, and said he would come back.' And, pulling up the blanket, he threw himself on to the pillow again. 'Shut up, Yashvin!' he said, getting angry with Yashvin, who was pulling the blanket off him. 'Shut up!' He turned over and opened his eyes. 'You'd better tell me what to drink: I've got such a vile taste in my mouth that ...'

'Brandy's better than anything,' boomed Yashvin. 'Tereshchenko! Brandy for your master, and cucumbers,' he shouted, obviously enjoying the sound of his own voice.

'Brandy do you think? Eh?' queried Petritsky, blinking and rubbing his eyes. 'And will you have a drink? All right, then, we'll have a drink together! Vronsky, a drink for you?' he added, getting up and wrapping a tiger-skin rug round himself, leaving his arms free.

He went to the door of the partition, held up his hands and started singing in French, 'There was a king in Thu-u-le.' 'Vronsky, will you have a drink?'

'Get away!' said Vronsky, putting on the coat his valet handed him.

'Where are you off to?' asked Yashvin. 'Oh, here's your troika,' he added, seeing the calèche drive up.

'To the stables, and then I've got to see Bryansky about the horses,' said Vronsky.

Vronsky had indeed promised to call at Bryansky's, some seven miles from Peterhof, and to settle with him for the horses; and he hoped to make time to get that in too. But his comrades understood at once that he was not only going there.

Petritsky, still humming, winked an eye and pouted his lips, as much as to say, 'We all know what going to see Bryansky means.'

'Mind you're not late!' was all Yashvin said and, to change the subject, 'How's my roan? Is he doing all right?' he inquired, looking out of the window at the middle horse which he had sold to Vronsky.

'Wait!' cried Petritsky to Vronsky as he was going out. 'Your brother left a letter for you, and a note. Wait! Where are they?'

Vronsky stopped. 'Well, where are they then?'

'Where are they? That is the question!' proclaimed Petritsky solemnly, pointing a forefinger upwards from his nose.

'Come on, tell me. This is silly!' said Vronsky smiling.

'I did not light the fire. They must be somewhere here.'

'That's enough – come along! Where is the letter?'

'No, honestly I've forgotten. Or did I dream it? Wait, wait! What's the use of getting in a rage? If you had emptied four bottles drinking toasts last night, as I did, you'd forget even the bed you were lying in. Just a second – I'll remember directly.'

Petritsky went behind the partition and lay down on his bed.

'Let me see! I was lying like this and he was standing there. Yes – yes – yes ... Here it is!' – and Petritsky pulled a letter out from under the mattress, where he had hidden it.

Vronsky took the letter and his brother's note. It was just what he was expecting: a letter from his mother reproaching him for not having been to see her – and the note was from his brother to say that he must have a talk with him. Vronsky knew that it all referred to the same thing. 'What business is it of theirs!' he thought, and crumpling up the letters he thrust them in between the buttons of his coat, to be read more attentively on the road. In the passage he met two officers, one from his own, the second from another regiment.

Vronsky's quarters were always the haunt of all the officers.

'Whither away?'

'I have to go to Peterhof.'

'Has the mare arrived from Tsarskoe?'

'Yes, but I've not seen her yet.'

'They say Mahotin's Gladiator has gone lame.'

'Rubbish! But how will you race in this mud?' said the other.

'Here are my rescuers!' cried Petritsky, seeing them come in. Before him stood an orderly with a tray of brandy and pickled cucumbers. 'Yashvin here's ordering me to have a drink to freshen myself up.'

'What a time you gave us last night!' said one of the officers. 'We didn't get a wink of sleep all night.'

'Oh, didn't we finish up prettily!' said Petritsky. 'Volkov climbed out on to the roof and began telling us how melancholy he felt. I said, "Let us have music – a funeral march!" And he fell asleep up there on the roof to the sound of the funeral march.'

'Go on, drink up your brandy and then seltzer water with plenty of lemon,' said Yashvin, standing over Petritsky like a mother making a child take medicine. 'And after that a little champagne – just a small bottle.'

'That sounds sense all right. Wait, Vronsky, have a drink with us.'

'No, good-bye, gentlemen. I am not drinking to-day.'

'What, afraid of putting on weight? All right, then, we'll drink by ourselves. Pass the seltzer water and lemon.'

'Vronsky!' shouted someone when Vronsky was already outside. 'What?'

'You'd better get your hair cut, or it'll weigh you down, especially at the top.'

Vronsky was in fact beginning to get prematurely bald. He laughed cheerfully, showing his regular teeth, and pulling his cap over the place that was thin went out and got into the carriage.

'To the stables!' he said and was about to take out the letters to read but thought better of it, not wanting to be upset before inspecting his mare. 'Later will do!' he said to himself.

21

THE temporary stable, a wooden shed, had been put up close to the race-course and it was there his mare was to have been taken the day before. He had not yet been to see her. These last few days he had not exercised her himself but had handed the job over to the trainer, and so now he had no idea in what condition his mare had arrived or how she was. Hardly had he stepped out of the calèche before his stable-boy, or groom, as the boy was called, who had recognized the carriage some way off, summoned the trainer. A lean Englishman in top boots and a short jacket, with only a tuft of beard left under his chin, came to meet him, walking with the awkward gait of a jockey, turning his elbows out and swaying from side to side.

'Well, how's Frou-Frou?' Vronsky asked in English.

'All right, sir,' the Englishman's voice responded from somewhere inside his throat. 'Better not go in,' he added, touching his cap. 'I've put a muzzle on her and the mare's fidgety. Better not go in; it excites the mare.'

'Oh yes, I'm going in. I want to have a look at her.'

'Come along, then,' said the Englishman, frowning and speaking as before, without opening his mouth. He led the way, swinging his elbows and walking with his loose gait.

They entered a little yard in front of the wooden stable. A smart lad in a clean jacket met them with a broom in his hand and followed them. In the shed there were five horses in their separate stalls and Vronsky knew that his chief rival, Mahotin's sixteen-hand chestnut, Gladiator, was to have been brought in that day and must be there too. Even more than his own mare, Vronsky longed to see Gladiator, whom he had never seen; but he knew that racing etiquette not only forbade his seeing Gladiator but made it improper for him even to inquire about Mahotin's horse. As he was passing along the passage, the lad opened the door into the second horse-box on the left and Vronsky caught a glimpse of a big chestnut with white legs. He knew that this was Gladiator but, like a man who looks away from another man's open letter, he turned round and went into Frou-Frou's stall.

'We've got here the horse that belongs to Mah ... Mah ... I never can say that name,' said the Englishman over his shoulder, pointing a big finger with a black nail towards Gladiator's stall.

'Mahotin? Yes, he's my only serious rival,' said Vronsky.

'If you were riding him, I'd back you,' said the Englishman.

'Frou-Frou has more spirit and the chestnut is the more powerful horse,' said Vronsky, smiling at the compliment to his riding.

'In a steeplechase everything depends on riding and on pluck,' said the Englishman.

Pluck – in other words, energy and courage – Vronsky felt he had in abundance and, much more important, he was firmly convinced that no one in the world could have more of this pluck than he had.

'Are you quite sure more training wasn't necessary?'

'Quite unnecessary,' answered the Englishman. 'Please don't speak loud. The mare's fidgety,' he added, jerking his head towards the horse-box before which they were standing and from which came the sound of restless stamping in the straw.

He opened the door and Vronsky went into the box, which was dimly lighted by one small window. In the horse-box stood a dark bay mare, with a muzzle on, picking at the fresh straw with her hooves. Looking round him in the twilight of the horse-box, Vronsky automatically took in at one comprehensive glance all the points of his favourite mare. Frou-Frou was of medium build, not altogether free from reproach, from a breeder's point of view. She was small-boned; her chest, though well arched, was narrow. Her hind-quarters tapered slightly and in her fore-legs, and still more in her hind-legs, there was a noticeable curvature. Neither her fore nor her hind legs were particularly muscular; but across the saddle she looked exceptionally broad, owing to the training she had undergone and the leanness of her belly. Seen from the front her cannon-bones seemed no thicker than a finger but from the side they looked extraordinarily thick. Except for the ribs, she gave the impression of being all squeezed in at the sides and drawn out in depth. But she possessed in the highest degree that quality which made one forget her defects – that quality was *blood*, the blood *that tells*, as the English expression has it. The muscles showed sharply under the network of sinews covered with delicate, mobile skin, smooth as satin, and seemed as hard as bone. Her lean head with the prominent fiery eyes broadened out from the nose to the nostrils with their blood-red membranes. Her whole appearance, and in particular her head, was spirited yet gentle. She was one of those creatures who seem as if they would certainly speak if only the mechanism of their mouths allowed them to.

To Vronsky, at any rate, it seemed that she understood all he was feeling while he looked at her.

Directly Vronsky went towards her, she drew in a deep breath and, turning back her prominent eye till the white looked bloodshot, she stared from the other side of the box at the two who had come in, shook her muzzle, and shifted springily from leg to leg.

'There, you see how excited she is,' said the Englishman.

'Oh, you beauty, you!' said Vronsky, moving up to the mare and trying to soothe her.

But the nearer he came, the more excited she grew. Only when he reached her head did she suddenly quieten down, while the muscles quivered under her fine, soft skin. Vronsky stroked her powerful neck, straightened a lock of mane that had got on to the wrong side of her sharply defined withers, and brought his face to her dilated nostrils, transparent as a bat's wing. Her tense nostrils drew in and snorted out a loud breath, she gave a start, set back one of her pointed ears, and stretched out a firm black lip towards Vronsky, as though she would nip hold of his sleeve. But remembering the muzzle, she shook it and began restlessly pawing the ground again with her finely-chiselled hooves.

'Quiet, sweet, quiet!' he said, stroking her flank again; and in the happy knowledge that his mare was in the best possible condition he left the horse-box.

The mare's excitement had infected Vronsky. He felt the blood rushing to his heart and that, like the horse, he, too, wanted to move about and attack. It was a sensation both disgraceful and delicious.

'Well then, I rely on you,' he said to the Englishman. 'Half-past six on the course.'

'All right,' said the man. 'But where are you going, my lord?' he asked unexpectedly, addressing him as 'my lord', which he scarcely ever did.

Vronsky raised his head in astonishment and stared, as he knew how to, not into the Englishman's eyes but at his forehead, astounded at the impertinence of the question. But realizing that in asking it the fellow had been regarding him not as an employer but as a jockey, he replied:

'I have to see Bryansky, but I shall be home in an hour.'

'How many times have I been asked that question to-day!' he

thought, and blushed – a thing he rarely did. The other looked gravely at him; and, as if he knew where Vronsky was going, added:

'The great thing is to keep calm before a race. Don't get put out or upset about anything.'

'All right,' said Vronsky smiling and, jumping into the calèche, he told the man to drive to Peterhof.

He had not gone many yards before the clouds, which had been threatening since morning, broke and there was a downpour.

'Too bad!' thought Vronsky, putting up the hood of the carriage. 'It was muddy before, now it will be a perfect swamp.'

In the privacy of the closed carriage he took out his mother's letter and his brother's note and read them through.

Yes, it was the same story over and over again. They all – his mother, his brother, everybody – thought fit to interfere in the affairs of his heart. This interference roused him to a feeling of anger and hate – a feeling he rarely experienced. 'What business is it of theirs? Why does everybody feel called upon to worry about me? And why do they hang on to me? Because they see that this is something they can't understand. If it were an ordinary, vulgar. society intrigue, they would have let me alone. They feel that this is something different, that it is not a mere pastime, that this woman is dearer than life itself to me. That is incomprehensible, and therefore it annoys them. Whatever our destiny is or may be, we have made it ourselves and we do not complain,' he said, in the word *we* linking himself with Anna. 'No, they must needs teach us how to live. They haven't the remotest idea of what happiness is; they don't know that without our love, for us there is neither happiness nor unhappiness – there would be no life at all,' he thought.

He was angry with them all for their interference, just because in his heart he felt that they were all of them right. He felt that the love which bound him to Anna was not a momentary infatuation, which would pass, as worldly attachments do pass, without leaving any trace in the lives of one or the other of them, except a few pleasant or unpleasant memories. He felt all the torment of his own and her position, all the difficulty there was for them, conspicuous as they were to the eyes of the world, in concealing their love, in lying and deceiving; and having to lie, deceive, scheme, and constantly think about others when the passion which united them was so intense that they were both oblivious of everything but their love.

All the oft-repeated occasions when the lying and deceit so foreign to his nature had been necessary rose vividly to his mind. He recalled most vividly the shame he had more than once detected in her at this necessity for deceit and lies. And he experienced the strange feeling which had sometimes come upon him since his liaison with Anna. It was a feeling of revulsion against something: against Karenin, or himself, or the whole world – he hardly knew which. But he always drove away this strange feeling. Now, too, he gave himself a shake and continued the current of his thoughts.

'Yes, she was unhappy before, but proud and at peace; but now she cannot be at peace and secure in her dignity, though she does not show it. Yes, this must stop,' he decided.

And for the first time the idea presented itself clearly that it was essential to put an end to this false position, and the sooner the better.

'We must throw up everything, both of us, and go and hide ourselves somewhere alone with our love,' he said to himself.

22

THE rain did not last long and by the time Vronsky reached his destination – with the shaft-horse at full trot, pulling the side-horses through the mud, their traces loose – the sun had peeped out again, the roofs of the summer villas and the old lime-trees in the gardens on both sides glistened with wet brilliance, and the water dripped merrily from the branches and ran down from the roofs. He thought no more of the shower spoiling the race-course but was rejoicing now that, thanks to the rain, he would be sure to find her at home and alone, for he knew that Karenin, who had recently returned from a foreign watering-place, had not moved from Petersburg.

Hoping to find her alone, Vronsky alighted, as he always did, to avoid attracting attention, before crossing the bridge and walked the rest of the way. He did not go to the porch but round into the courtyard.

'Has your master come?' he asked a gardener.

'Oh no, sir. The mistress is at home. Will you go to the front? The servants are there and will open the door to you,' answered the man.

'No, I will go through the garden.'

And feeling satisfied that she was alone, and eager to take her by surprise – he had not promised to come that day and she would certainly not expect him before the races – he walked, holding his sword and stepping cautiously along the sandy, flower-bordered path to the terrace that looked out over the garden. Vronsky had now forgotten all the thoughts he had had on the way about the hardships and difficulties of his position. He was thinking of one thing only – that he would see her directly, not merely in his imagination but living, all of her, as she was in reality. He was just going in, stepping on the whole of his foot so as not to make a noise, up the worn steps of the terrace, when he suddenly remembered what he was always forgetting, the most painful side of his relations with her – her son with his (as he fancied) questioning, hostile eyes.

This boy was more often than anyone else a check upon their freedom. When he was present, neither Vronsky nor Anna would allow themselves to speak of anything – or even refer by hints to anything – the boy would not have understood. They had made no agreement about this: it had come about of itself. They would have considered it unworthy of themselves to deceive the child. In his presence they talked like acquaintances. Yet, in spite of their caution, Vronsky often noticed the child's attentive, bewildered gaze fixed upon him and a strange timidity and uncertainty in the boy's manner to him – at one time affectionate, at another cold and reserved. It was as if the child felt that between this man and his mother there was some important bond which he could not understand.

The child did in fact feel that he could not understand this relation; and he tried but could not make out what feeling he ought to have for this man. With a child's sensitiveness to feeling in others, he saw distinctly that his father, his governess, and his nurse all not only disliked Vronsky but regarded him with aversion, though they never said anything about him, while his mother looked on him as her greatest friend.

'What does it mean? Who is he? How ought I to love him? If I don't know, it's my fault: it means I am a silly boy, or a bad boy,' thought the child. And this was what caused his scrutinizing, inquiring, and to some extent hostile expression and the shyness and uncertainty which so embarrassed Vronsky. The child's presence invariably called up in Vronsky that strange feeling of inexplicable revulsion which he had experienced of late. The child's presence called up both in Vronsky and in Anna a feeling akin to that of a sailor who can see by the compass that the direction in which he is swiftly sailing is wide of the proper course, but is powerless to stop. Every moment takes him farther and farther astray, and to admit to himself that he is off his course is the same as admitting final disaster.

This child, with his innocent outlook upon life, was the compass which showed them the degree to which they had departed from what they knew but did not want to know.

This time Seriozha was not at home, and she was quite alone, sitting on the terrace waiting for the return of her son, who had gone for a walk and been caught in the rain. She had sent a manservant and a maid to look for him, and sat waiting. She wore a white gown with deep embroidery, and was sitting in a corner of the terrace behind some flowers, and did not hear him. Her dark curly head bent, she was pressing her forehead against a cool watering-can that stood on the parapet, and both her lovely hands, with the rings he knew so well, were clasping the can. The beauty of her whole figure, her head, her neck, her arms, struck Vronsky every time with surprise. He stood still, gazing at her in ecstasy. But just as he would have stepped towards her, she felt his presence, pushed away the watering-can, and turned her flushed face to him.

'What is the matter? Are you not well?' he said in French, going up to her.

He wanted to rush to her but remembering there might be someone about he looked round towards the balcony door and reddened a little, as he always did when he felt that he had to be afraid and on his guard.

'No, I am all right,' she said, getting up and pressing his outstretched hand tightly. 'I did not expect … you.'

'Gracious! What cold hands!'

'You startled me,' she said. 'I'm alone and I was waiting for Seriozha. He's out for a walk. They will be returning this way.'

But, though she was trying to be calm, her lips were quivering.

'Forgive me for coming but I could not let the day pass without seeing you,' he went on, in French.

He always spoke French to her, to avoid using the word *you*, which sounded so impossibly cold in Russian, or the dangerously intimate *thou*.

'Forgive you? I'm so glad to see you!'

'But you are ill or worried,' he went on, not letting go her hands but bending over her. 'What were you thinking of?'

'Always of the same thing,' she said with a smile.

She spoke the truth. If ever at any moment she had been asked what she was thinking of, she could have answered with perfect truth that she was always thinking of the same thing, of her happiness and her unhappiness. Just now when he came upon her she was wondering why for others – Betsy, for instance, whose secret relations with Tushkevich she knew about – it was all so easy, while for her it was such torture. For certain reasons, this thought tormented her particularly to-day. She asked him about the races. He answered her questions and, seeing that she was agitated, to distract her he began telling her all about the preparations, in the most matter-of-fact tone.

'Shall I tell him or not tell him?' she thought, looking into his calm, caressing eyes. 'He is so happy, so full of his races, that he would not understand properly, would not understand all the gravity of it for us.'

'But you haven't told me what you were thinking of when I came in,' he said, interrupting his account. 'Please tell me!'

She did not answer and, bending her head a little, looked inquiringly at him from under her brows, her eyes shining beneath their long lashes. Her hand, toying with a leaf she had pulled off, shook. He noticed this and the look of humble, slavish devotion which so captivated her came over his face.

'I can see something has happened. Do you suppose I could have a moment's peace, knowing that you have some trouble I am not sharing? Tell me, for God's sake!' he repeated imploringly.

'Yes, I should never forgive him if he did not realize all the gravity of it. Better not say anything. Why put him to the test?' she thought, still staring at him in the same way and feeling the hand which held the leaf trembling more and more.

'For God's sake!' he repeated, taking her hand.

'Shall I?'

'Yes, yes, yes ...'

'I am with child,' she whispered slowly.

The leaf in her hand shook more violently but she did not remove her eyes from his face, watching to see how he would take her news. He turned pale, tried to say something but stopped, dropped her hand and sank his head on his breast. 'Yes, he realizes all the gravity of it,' she thought, and gratefully pressed his hand.

But she was mistaken in thinking he realized the gravity of the fact as she, a woman, understood it. Her words gave him that strange feeling of revulsion for someone with tenfold force. But at the same time he realized that the turning-point he had been longing for was now near, that they could no longer go on concealing their relations from her husband, and that somehow or other they would inevitably have to put an end to their unnatural situation. But, besides this, her agitation communicated itself to him physically. He gave her a tender, submissive look, kissed her hand, got up, and in silence paced up and down the terrace.

'Yes,' he said, going up to her resolutely. 'Neither you nor I have looked on our relations lightly, and now our fate is sealed. It is essential to put an end' – he looked round as he spoke – 'to the deception in which we are living.'

'Put an end? How put an end, Alexei?' she said softly.

She was calmer now, and her face lighted up with a tender smile.

'Leave your husband and unite our lives.'

'They are united as it is,' she replied, almost inaudibly.

'I know, but I mean completely – completely.'

'But how, Alexei, tell me how?' she said in mournful mockery at the hopelessness of her position. 'Is there really any way out of such a position? Am I not the wife of my husband?'

'There is a way out of every position. We must make our decision,' he said. 'Anything would be better than the way in which you are living. Don't I see how you torture yourself over everything – the world, your son, your husband?'

'Oh, not my husband, please,' she said, with a quiet smile. 'I don't know, I never think of him. He doesn't exist.'

'You are not speaking sincerely. I know you. You torment yourself about him too.'

'Oh, he does not even know,' she said, and suddenly her face flushed a vivid red. Her cheeks, her forehead, her neck crimsoned, and tears of shame welled into her eyes. 'But we won't talk of him.'

23

VRONSKY had tried several times before, though not so resolutely as now, to get her to consider her position, and each time he had encountered the same superficiality and lightness of judgement with which his appeal met now. It was as though there were something in it which she could not or would not face, as though directly she began to speak of it she, the real Anna, retreated somewhere inside herself and another woman appeared, a stranger to him, whom he did not love and whom he feared, and who was in opposition to him. But to-day he was determined to have it out.

'Whether he knows or not,' said Vronsky in his usual firm, quiet tone – 'whether he knows or not, that is not our business. We cannot … you cannot go on like this, especially now.'

'What's to be done, according to you?' she asked with the same frivolous irony. She, who had so feared he might take her condition too lightly, was now vexed with him for deciding from it the necessity for action.

'Tell him everything, and leave him.'

'Very well; suppose I do so,' she said. 'Do you know what the result will be? I can tell you it all in advance,' and a spiteful light gleamed in her eyes, which a moment ago had been so tender. ' "Ah, so you love another man and have entered into guilty relations with him?" ' (She was mimicking her husband and throwing an emphasis on the word 'guilty' exactly as Karenin did.) ' "I warned you of the consequences from the religious, the civil, and the domestic points of view. You have not listened to me. Now I cannot let you disgrace my name" ' – 'and my son,' she had meant to say, but about her son she could not jest – ' "disgrace my name", and some more in the same vein,' she added. 'In general terms, he will say in his official manner, with all distinctness and precision, that he cannot let me go but will take all measures in his power to prevent a scandal. And he will quietly and punctiliously do what he says. That is what will happen. He's not a human being but a machine, and a cruel machine when he is angry,' she added, picturing Karenin to herself as she spoke, with every detail of his personality and his manner of speaking, setting against him every defect she could find, forgiving nothing because of the great wrong she was doing him.

'But Anna,' said Vronsky in a persuasive, gentle voice, trying to soothe her, 'he must be told, all the same, and afterwards we will be guided by what he does.'

'What, shall we run away?'

'And why not run away? I don't see how we can keep on like this. And not on my account – I see that you are suffering.'

'Yes, run away, and for me to become your mistress,' she said maliciously.

'Anna!' he reproached her tenderly.

'Yes,' she went on, 'become your mistress and complete the ruin of ...'

Again she was going to say 'my son', but could not utter the word.

Vronsky could not understand how, with her strong, upright nature, she could endure this state of deceit and not long to escape from it; but he did not guess that the chief cause of it was the word *son*, which she could not bring herself to pronounce. When she thought of her son, and his future attitude to his mother, who had cast off his father, she was too terrified at what she had done to reason but, woman-like, only tried to reassure herself with false arguments and words in order that everything should remain as before and that she might forget the dreadful question of what would happen with her son.

'I beg you, I implore you,' she said suddenly, taking his hand and speaking in a quite different tone, sincere and tender, 'never speak to me of that!'

'But, Anna ...'

'Never. Leave it to me. I know all the degradation, all the horror of my position; but it is not so easy to arrange as you think. Leave it to me, and do what I say. Never speak to me about it. Do you promise? ... No, no, promise! ...'

'I promise anything, but I cannot be easy, especially after what you have told me. I cannot be easy when you are not ...'

'I?' she repeated. 'Yes, I do torment myself sometimes; but that will pass if you never speak to me about it. It is only when you talk about it that I suffer.'

'I don't understand,' he said.

'I know,' she interrupted him, 'how hard it is for your truthful nature to lie, and I grieve for you. I often think that you have ruined your whole life on my account.'

'I was just thinking the same thing,' he said, 'and wondering how you could sacrifice everything for my sake. I cannot forgive myself that you are unhappy.'

'I unhappy?' she said, drawing near him and gazing at him with a rapturous smile of love. 'I feel like a starving man who has been given food. He may be cold, his clothes may be in rags, and he may feel ashamed, but he is not unhappy. I unhappy? No, this is my happiness. ...'

She heard the sound of her son's voice coming towards them and, glancing quickly round the terrace, she rose hurriedly to her feet. Her eyes lit up with the light he knew so well; with a swift movement she raised her lovely hands, covered with rings, took his head, gave him a long look, and, putting her face near his, with parted, smiling lips, quickly kissed his mouth and both eyes, and pushed him away. She would have gone but he held her back.

'When?' he murmured in a whisper, looking at her with ecstasy.

'To-night, at one o'clock,' she whispered and, giving a heavy sigh, walked with her light, rapid step to meet her son.

Seriozha had been caught in the park by the rain and he and his nurse had taken shelter in an arbour.

'Well, *au revoir*,' she said to Vronsky. 'It will soon be time to start for the races. Betsy has promised to call for me.'

Vronsky looked at his watch and hurried away.

24

WHEN Vronsky looked at his watch on the Karenins' balcony, he was so agitated and preoccupied with his thoughts that he saw the figures on the dial but could not take in what time it was. He went out into the road, stepping carefully through the mud, and made his way to the carriage. He was so full of his feeling for Anna that he did not even think about the time and whether he could still get to Bryansky's. As often happens, he only retained the external faculty of memory which indicated what he had decided to do next. He approached his coachman, who was dozing on the box in the already lengthening shadow of a thick lime-tree; glanced with pleasure at the swaying columns of midges hovering over the perspiring horses and, waking the coachman, jumped into the carriage and told him to drive to Bryansky's. It was only after they had gone some five miles that he recovered himself sufficiently to look at his watch and realize that it was half-past five and he was late.

There were to be several races that day: the Mounted Guards' race, then the officers' mile-and-a-half, a three-mile race, and then the one for which he was entered. He could be in time for his own race but if he went to Bryansky's first he could only just manage it and would arrive when the whole Court was already there. That was not the correct thing. But he had promised Bryansky to come, and so he decided to drive on, telling the coachman not to spare the horses.

He reached Bryansky's, stayed with him five minutes, and drove back at a gallop. The quick drive soothed him. All that was painful in his relations with Anna, all the uncertainty left by their conversation, slipped out of his mind. He was thinking now with delight and excitement of the race and that after all he would be there in time, and now and again the thought of the blissful meeting awaiting him that night flashed vividly across his imagination.

The excitement of the approaching race gained upon him as he drove farther and farther into the atmosphere of the races, overtaking carriages making their way to the course from Petersburg and the surrounding country.

No one was left at his quarters – they had all gone to the races and his valet was looking out for him at the door. While he was changing, the valet told him that the second race had begun already, that a number of gentlemen had been to inquire for him, and that a lad had twice run over from the stables.

Dressing without hurry (he never hurried and never lost his self-possession), Vronsky ordered the coachman to drive to the stables. From there he could see a perfect sea of carriages, pedestrians, soldiers surrounding the race-course and pavilions thronged with people. The second race must be on, for as he drew near he heard a bell ringing. On his way he met Mahotin's white-legged chestnut, Gladiator, in a blue-bordered orange horse-cloth with what looked like huge ears edged with blue, being led on to the course.

'Where's Cord?' he asked the stable-boy.

'In the stables, saddling.'

In her open stall Frou-Frou stood ready saddled. They were just going to lead her out.

'I am not late?'

'All right! All right!' answered the Englishman. 'Don't get excited.'

Vronsky cast another look at the exquisite lines of his favourite mare, who was quivering all over, and tearing himself with an effort from the sight of her, he went out of the stable. He went towards the pavilions at the most favourable moment for escaping attention. The mile-and-a-half was just finishing and all eyes were fixed on an officer of the Horse Guards in front and a Light Hussar behind, urging their horses to the last limits of their strength as they neared the winning-post. From within and without the ring everyone was crowding towards the winning-post, and a group of Horse Guards – officers and men – were shouting their joy at the expected victory of their officer and comrade. Vronsky slipped unnoticed into the heart of the crowd almost at the very moment that the bell rang to announce the finish of the race and the tall, mud-spattered Guards officer who had come in first was bending down in the saddle and letting go the reins of his panting grey stallion, dark with sweat.

Checking its pace with difficulty, the big horse slowed down and the officer of the Horse Guards looked round him like a man waking from a heavy sleep and just managed to smile. A crowd of friends and strangers surrounded him.

Vronsky purposely avoided the select, fashionable throng which was moving and chattering with restrained freedom in front of the pavilions. He knew that Madame Karenin was there, and Betsy, and his brother's wife, and he did not go near them for fear of something distracting his attention. But he continually met acquaintances, who stopped him, telling him about the races that had been run and asking why he was so late.

When the winners were called to the pavilion to receive their prizes and everyone was looking that way, Vronsky's elder brother, Alexander, a colonel with heavy fringed epaulets, came up to him. He was not tall, but as thick-set as Alexei, and handsomer and ruddier than he; he had a red nose and an open, drunken-looking face.

'Did you get my note?' he asked. 'One can never get hold of you.'

Alexander Vronsky, in spite of his dissolute and, in particular, drunken life, for which he was notorious, was very much one of the Court circle.

Now, as he talked to his brother of a matter extremely disagreeable to him, knowing that many eyes might be fixed upon them, he kept a smiling expression, as though he were joking with his brother about something of little import.

'Yes, I got it, and I really can't make out what *you* are worrying yourself about,' said Alexei.

'I'm worrying because it has just been pointed out to me that you were not here, and that you were seen in Peterhof on Monday.'

'There are matters which only concern those directly interested in them, and the matter you are so worried about is one of them. ...'

'Yes, but if so you may as well get out of the army. ...'

'I ask you not to interfere; that is all I have to say.'

Alexei Vronsky's frowning face turned pale and his prominent lower jaw twitched, which rarely happened with him. Being a very good-natured man, he seldom got angry; but when he did, and when his chin twitched, then he was dangerous, as Alexander Vronsky knew. Alexander Vronsky smiled gaily.

'I only wanted to deliver Mama's letter. Write to her, and don't upset yourself before the race. *Bonne chance,*' he added smiling and went off.

His brother had no sooner gone than another friendly greeting stopped Vronsky.

'So you won't recognize your friends! How are you, *mon cher*?' said Oblonsky, his ruddy face and glossy, well-combed whiskers sparkling here, amid all the Petersburg brilliance, no less than in Moscow. 'I arrived yesterday and I'm delighted that I shall see your triumph. When shall we meet?'

'Come to the mess to-morrow,' said Vronsky, and apologetically squeezing the sleeve of Oblonsky's coat he moved away to the middle of the race-course, where the horses were already being led out for the steeplechase.

The steaming, exhausted animals which had run in the last race were being led away by their grooms and one after another the fresh horses made their appearance for the next race, for the most part English horses, looking like huge weird birds in their cloths with their bellies tightly girthed. On the right Frou-Frou was being led in, lean and beautiful, lifting up her elastic, rather long pasterns, as though moved by springs. Not far from her they were taking the horse-cloth off the lop-eared Gladiator. The perfect symmetry of the strong, exquisite stallion, with its superb hind-quarters and exceptionally short pasterns almost over its hooves, arrested Vronsky's attention in spite of himself. He was about to go up to his mare when another acquaintance detained him.

'Ah, there's Karenin!' said the acquaintance with whom he was chatting. 'He's looking for his wife, and she's in the centre of the pavilion. Didn't you see her?'

'No,' replied Vronsky, and without so much as a glance round at the pavilion where his friend was pointing out Madame Karenin, he went to his mare.

Vronsky had hardly had time to examine the saddle, which needed some adjustment, before the competitors were summoned to the pavilion to draw their numbers and places. With serious, stern, and in many cases pale faces, seventeen officers assembled at the pavilion and drew their numbers. Vronsky drew the number seven. The cry was heard: 'Mount!'

Feeling that with the other riders he was the focus of all eyes, Vronsky approached his mare in that state of nervous tension which generally made his movements deliberate and composed. Cord, in honour of the races, had put on his best clothes – a black coat buttoned-up, a stiffly starched collar, which propped up his cheeks, a black bowler hat and top-boots. He was calm and dignified as usual and, standing in front of the mare, was himself holding Frou-Frou by both reins. Frou-Frou continued to tremble as though in a fever. Her fiery eye glanced sideways at Vronsky. Vronsky slipped a finger under the saddle-girth. The mare rolled her eyes, showed her teeth, and put back her ears. The Englishman pursed his lips, intending to indicate a smile that anyone should test his saddling.

'Get up: you won't feel so nervous.'

Vronsky took a last look round at his rivals. He knew that once the race started he would not see them. Two were already riding forward to the starting-point. Galtsin, a friend of Vronsky's and a formidable competitor, was struggling with a bay horse that would not let him mount. A short Hussar in tight riding-breeches was coming along at full gallop, crouching over his horse like a cat, in imitation of an English jockey. Prince Kuzovlov sat pale-faced on his thoroughbred mare from the Gravobsky stud, while an English groom led her by the bridle. Vronsky and all his comrades knew Kuzovlov and his peculiarity of 'weak' nerves and terrible vanity. They knew he was afraid of everything, afraid of riding a spirited horse; but now, just because it was dangerous, because people broke their necks and there was a doctor standing at each obstacle, and an ambulance with a red cross on it and a Sister of Mercy, he had made up his mind to take part in the race. Their eyes met and Vronsky gave him a friendly, encouraging wink. The only one Vronsky did not see was his principal rival, Mahotin on Gladiator.

'Don't be in a hurry,' said Cord to Vronsky, 'and remember one thing: don't hold her back at the fences and don't urge her over. Let her go as she likes.'

'Very well, very well,' said Vronsky, taking the reins.

'Take the lead if you can; but don't lose heart till the last minute if you happen to be behind.'

Before the mare had time to stir, Vronsky, with a powerful, agile movement, put his foot into the notched steel stirrup, and seated himself lightly and firmly on the creaking leather of the saddle. Getting his right foot in the stirrup, he smoothed the double reins between practised fingers, and Cord let go. As if not knowing which foot to put forward first, Frou-Frou stretched the reins with her long neck and started, as though on springs, balancing her rider on her supple back. Cord quickened his step to keep up with them. The excited mare pulled at the reins, first from one side, then from the other, trying to take her rider off his guard, and Vronsky vainly sought with voice and hand to soothe her.

They were just reaching the dammed-up stream on their way to the starting-post. Several of the riders were in front and several behind, when suddenly Vronsky heard a horse galloping through the mud behind him and he was overtaken by Mahotin on his white-legged, lop-eared Gladiator. Mahotin smiled, showing his long teeth, but Vronsky looked at him angrily. He did not like him and considered him now as his most dangerous rival. He was annoyed with him for galloping past and startling his mare. Frou-Frou kicked up her left leg and broke into a canter, leaped forward twice and, fretting at the tightened reins, changed into a jerky trot, jolting her rider up and down. Cord, too, scowled, and followed Vronsky almost at a run.

25

ALTOGETHER there were seventeen officers competing in the steeplechase, which was to take place over a large three-mile elliptical course in front of the pavilion. Nine jumps had been arranged on the course: the stream; a barrier nearly five feet high just before the pavilion; a dry ditch; a water-jump; an incline; an Irish bank (one of the most difficult obstacles), consisting of an embankment with brushwood on top and a ditch on the other side which the horse could not see, so that the animal had to clear both obstacles or come to grief; then two more water-jumps and another dry ditch. The winning-post was opposite the pavilion again. But the start was not in the ring, but some two hundred or more yards to one side of it, and the first obstacle – the dammed-up stream seven feet wide – was there. The riders could either jump or ford it at their own discretion.

Three times the riders got into line but each time some horse made a false start and they had to begin again. The starter, Colonel Sestrin, was beginning to get impatient but at last, at the fourth try, he shouted 'Off!' – and the race began.

Every eye, every field-glass was turned on the parti-coloured little group of riders while they were getting into line.

'They're off! There they go!' was heard on all sides after the hush of expectation.

And people, in groups and singly, began running from place to place to get a better view. In the first minute the field spread out and could be seen approaching the brook in twos and threes and one behind another. It had looked to the spectators as though they had all started simultaneously; but the riders were aware of seconds of difference which were of great importance to them.

The excited and over-nervous Frou-Frou fell behind in the first moment and several horses started ahead of her but even before they reached the stream Vronsky, who was holding in the mare with all his strength as she pulled at the reins, easily overtook three riders and before him there was only Mahotin's chestnut Gladiator (whose hindquarters were moving lightly and rhythmically up and down in front of him), and, leading them all, the exquisite Diana, bearing Kuzovlov more dead than alive.

For the first instant Vronsky was master neither of himself nor of the mare. Up to the first obstacle, the stream, he could not control her movements.

Gladiator and Diana approached the stream together and almost at the same moment; simultaneously they rose and soared across to the other side. Lightly, as if on wings, Frou-Frou rose up behind them but just when Vronsky felt himself in the air he suddenly saw, almost under his mare's hooves, Kuzovlov floundering with Diana on the farther side of the stream. (Kuzovlov had let go the reins after Diana had jumped, and the mare had sent him flying over her head.) These details Vronsky learned later: at the time all he saw was that right under him, where Frou-Frou must alight, Diana's legs or head might be in the way. But Frou-Frou, like a cat falling, made an effort of legs and back while in the air and, clearing the other mare, sped on.

'Oh, you beauty!' thought Vronsky.

After the stream Vronsky had complete control of his mount and started holding her in, intending to cross the big barrier behind Mahotin and try to overtake him only on the flat five hundred yards before the next obstacle.

The big barrier was right in front of the imperial pavilion. The Emperor and the whole Court and a crowd of people were all looking at them – at him and at Mahotin, a length ahead – as they approached the 'devil' (as the solid barrier was called). Vronsky felt eyes directed on him from all sides but he saw nothing except the ears and neck of his mare, the ground racing towards him and Gladiator's rump and white legs rhythmically beating the ground before him, always the same distance ahead. Gladiator rose, without touching anything, swished his short tail and disappeared from Vronsky's sight.

'Bravo!' cried a voice.

At the same instant the planks of the barrier flashed close before Vronsky's eyes. Without the slightest change in her action the mare rose under him; the planks vanished and he heard only a knock behind him. Excited by Gladiator in front, the mare had risen too soon at the barrier and had grazed it with a hind hoof. But her pace never changed and Vronsky, hit in the face by a lump of mud, realized that he was still the same distance from Gladiator. Once more he could see Gladiator's rump and short tail before him and the swift white feet the same distance off.

Just when Vronsky was thinking that it was time to pass Mahotin, Frou-Frou herself, already understanding what was in his mind, without any urging, considerably increased her speed and began to draw nearer Mahotin on the inside, the most favourable way to overtake him. Mahotin was not leaving the ropes. Vronsky had just time to think of trying to overtake on the outside, when Frou-Frou changed course and started to do exactly that. Frou-Frou's shoulder, now beginning to grow dark with sweat, drew level with Gladiator's hindquarters. They ran side by side for a few lengths. But before the obstacle they were approaching, Vronsky, anxious not to have to circle out widely, started working at the reins and got ahead of Mahotin on the slope. He caught a glimpse of his mud-spattered face as he flashed by. He even fancied he saw him smile. Vronsky passed Mahotin but was aware that Mahotin was close upon him, and he kept hearing at his back the regular rhythm of Gladiator's hooves and the still quite fresh breathing of his nostrils.

The next two obstacles – a ditch and a fence – were taken easily but Vronsky heard Gladiator galloping and snorting closer upon him. He urged on his mare and to his delight felt how easily she increased her pace and he heard the thud of Gladiator's hooves again the same distance away as before.

Vronsky now had the lead, as he had wanted to and as Cord had advised, and he felt confident of success. His excitement, his happiness, and his affection for Frou-Frou grew keener and keener. He longed to look round but dared not do so and tried to keep calm and not urge his mare, so as to let her retain the same reserve of strength as he felt Gladiator still had. There remained only one more obstacle – the most difficult one; if he could clear it ahead of the others he would come in first. He was flying towards the Irish bank. He and Frou-Frou both together saw the bank in the distance and both the man and the mare felt a momentary misgiving. He noticed the hesitation in the mare's ears and lifted his whip but immediately felt that his fears were groundless: the mare knew what was wanted. She quickened her pace and took off at the right moment, just as he had expected she would. Giving a thrust from the ground, she surrendered herself to the impetus of her leap, which carried her far beyond the ditch. Then, in the same rhythm, without effort and without changing feet, Frou-Frou continued her gallop.

'Bravo, Vronsky!' he heard shouts from a knot of people – he knew they were brother-officers and friends – who were standing by the obstacle. He could not fail to recognize Yashvin's voice, though he did not see him.

'Oh, my beauty!' he said inwardly to Frou-Frou, at the same time listening for what was happening behind. 'He's over!' he thought, as he heard Gladiator galloping behind him.

There remained only the last water-jump, a yard and a half across. Vronsky did not even look at it but, anxious to get in first by a long way, began sawing on the reins with a circular movement, raising the mare's head and letting it go in time with her stride. He felt she was using her last reserve of strength; not merely her neck and shoulders were wet, but on her mane, her head, her pointed ears the sweat stood out in drops and her breath came in short, harsh gasps. But he knew that her reserve of strength was more than enough for the remaining five hundred yards. Only because he felt himself nearer the ground and by the peculiar smoothness of her motion did Vronsky know how greatly the mare had increased her pace. She cleared the ditch as if she did not notice it, flying over like a bird; but at that very instant Vronsky, to his horror, felt that, instead of keeping up with the mare's pace, for some inexplicable reason he had made a dreadful, unforgivable blunder and dropped back into the saddle. All at once his position had shifted and he knew that something horrible had happened. Before he could tell what it was, the white legs of a chestnut horse flashed by him and Mahotin dashed past at a swift gallop. Vronsky was touching the ground with one foot and his mare was sinking on that foot. He had scarcely time to free his leg before she fell on one side, gasping painfully and making vain efforts of her slender, sweat-soaked neck to rise, and began fluttering on the ground at his feet like a wounded bird. Vronsky's clumsy movement had broken her back. But this he only knew much later. Now all that he saw was Mahotin disappearing ahead while he stood staggering alone on the muddy, stationary ground and Frou-Frou lay breathing heavily before him, bending her head back and gazing at him with her beautiful eyes. Still unable to realize what had happened, Vronsky tugged at the rein. Again she writhed, like a fish, creaking the flaps of the saddle, put out her forelegs but, unable to lift her back, immediately collapsed and fell on her side again. His face distorted with passion, pale, and with lower jaw trembling, Vronsky kicked her in the belly with his heel and again fell to tugging at the rein. But she did not stir and, her nose nuzzling the ground, only gazed at her master with her eloquent eyes.

'A-a-ah!' groaned Vronsky, his hands to his head. 'A-a-ah! What have I done!' he cried. 'The race lost! And it was my own shameful, unforgivable fault! And this dear, unfortunate mare done for! A-a-ah! What have I done!'

Onlookers – a doctor and his assistant and officers of his regiment – ran up to him. To his misery, he felt that he was sound and unhurt. The mare had broken her back and it was decided to shoot her. Vronsky could not answer questions, could not speak to anyone. He turned away and, without picking up the cap that had fallen from his head, walked off the race-course, not knowing where he was going. He felt wretched. For the first time in his life he knew the bitterest kind of misfortune – misfortune beyond remedy, caused by his own fault.

Yashvin hastened after him with his cap and took him home, and half an hour later Vronsky had come to himself. But the memory of that steeplechase long remained in his heart, the cruellest and bitterest memory of his life.

26

OUTWARDLY Karenin's relations with his wife remained the same. The sole difference was that he was even more occupied than before. As in former years, with the coming of spring he had gone to a foreign watering-place to repair his health, which suffered from his winter's work, heavier each year. And as usual he returned in July and at once took up his customary activities with increased energy. As usual, too, his wife had moved to their summer villa, while he remained in Petersburg.

Since their conversation on the night of the Princess Tverskoy's party he had never spoken to Anna again of his suspicions and jealousy, and that habitual tone of his, as if he were mocking someone, could not have been better suited to his present attitude to his wife. He was a little colder to her. He simply appeared to be slightly displeased with her for that first midnight conversation which she had resisted. In his manner there was a shade of vexation, but nothing more. 'You would not be open with me,' he seemed to say, mentally addressing her; 'so much the worse for you. The time will come when you will beg me to be open with you and I shall not listen. So much the worse for you!' he said mentally, like a man who, having vainly tried to extinguish a fire, might be annoyed at his vain exertions and say to it: 'Go on and burn then; it is your own fault!'

He, who was so intelligent and shrewd where official affairs were concerned, did not realize the insanity of such an attitude to his wife. He did not realize it because it was too dreadful to him to face the true situation, and he shut down and locked and sealed that compartment of his soul which contained his feelings for his family – that is, for his wife and son. He who had been a considerate father had, since the end of the winter, turned particularly cold towards his son and treated him in the same bantering way he did his wife. 'Aha, young man!' was the greeting with which he addressed him.

Karenin believed and declared that in no previous year had he so much official business as this year; but he was not conscious of the fact that this year he invented work for himself, that this was one of the ways of keeping closed the compartment where lay his feelings for his wife and son, and his thoughts about them which became more terrible the longer they lay there. If anyone had had the right to ask Karenin what he thought of his wife's conduct, the mild and peaceable Karenin would have made no answer, but would have been greatly angered with the man who put such a question. For this reason Karenin's face bore a stern, haughty expression whenever anyone inquired after his wife's health. He did not want to think at all about his wife's conduct and feelings, and actually succeeded in not thinking about them.

Karenin's permanent summer villa was in Peterhof and as a rule the Countess Lydia Ivanovna used to spend the summer there, close to Anna and in constant touch with her. This year the Countess Lydia Ivanovna declined to settle in Peterhof, did not once come to see Anna, and in conversation with Karenin hinted at the unsuitability of Anna's intimacy with Betsy and Vronsky. Karenin sternly checked her, roundly declaring his wife to be above suspicion, and from that time began to avoid the Countess Lydia Ivanovna. He did not want to see, and did not see, that many people in society were already looking askance at his wife; he did not want to understand, and did not understand, why his wife had so particularly insisted on moving to Tsarkoe, where Betsy was staying and which was not far from Vronsky's camp. He did not allow himself to think about it, and he did not think about it; but all the same, in the depths of his heart, though he never admitted it to himself or had any proofs or even suspicious evidence, he knew beyond all doubt that he was a wronged husband, and he was profoundly unhappy about it.

How many times during those eight years of happy married life had Karenin looked at other men's unfaithful wives and other deceived husbands and asked himself: 'How could they let it come to that? Why don't they put an end to such a hideous situation?' But now that the disaster had fallen on his own head, he not only did not think of how to end it but would not recognize it at all – would not recognize it just because it was too dreadful, too unnatural.

Since his return from abroad Karenin had been down to their country villa twice, once to dinner and the other time he spent the evening there with a party of friends, but he never stayed the night, as he had been in the habit of doing formerly.

The day of the races was a very busy one for Karenin; but in the morning when he made his plans for the day he decided that immediately after an early dinner he would go to see his wife at their country house and from there to the races, at which the whole Court would be present and where he ought to appear. He was going to see his wife because he was determined to do so once a week to keep up appearances. Besides, it was the fifteenth – the day he gave her money for the housekeeping expenses.

With his habitual mental control, having once deliberated these matters to do with his wife, he did not let his thoughts stray further in regard to her.

He had a very busy morning. The evening before, Countess Lydia Ivanovna had sent him a pamphlet by a famous traveller in China, who was now in Petersburg, with a note begging him to see the traveller himself, an extremely interesting man, and important, for various reasons. Karenin had not had time to read the pamphlet through in the evening, and finished it in the morning. Then people began arriving with petitions and there were reports, interviews, appointments, dismissals, allotting of rewards, pensions, and grants, and correspondence to be attended to – the work-a-day round, as Karenin called it, which took up so much of his time. After that there came business of his own, a visit from his doctor and one from the steward who managed his property. The steward did not take long. He simply handed Karenin the money he needed together with a brief account of the state of his affairs, which was not too satisfactory, for it happened that, owing to their having been away from home a good deal that year, more had been spent than usual, and there was a deficit. But the doctor, a distinguished Petersburg doctor, who was on intimate terms with Karenin, took up a great deal of time. Karenin had not expected him that day and was surprised to see him, and still more so when the doctor plied him with searching questions about his health, sounded his chest, and tapped and probed his liver. Karenin did not know that his friend Lydia Ivanovna, noticing that he was not as well as usual that year, had begged the doctor to go and see him. 'Do it for my sake,' the Countess Lydia Ivanovna had said.

'I will do it for the sake of Russia, Countess,' the doctor had replied.

'An invaluable man!' the Countess Lydia Ivanovna had exclaimed.

The doctor was most dissatisfied with Karenin. He found the liver considerably enlarged, the digestive powers impaired: taking the waters had done him no good whatever. He prescribed as much physical exercise and as little mental strain as possible and, above all, no worry – which for Karenin was just as impossible as not to breathe. He withdrew, leaving Karenin with the disagreeable impression that something was wrong with him which could not be put right.

On his way out the doctor ran into a good acquaintance of his on the steps, Slyudin, Karenin's private secretary. They had been at the university together and, though they very seldom met, they thought highly of each other and were excellent friends; and so there was no one to whom the doctor would have expressed his opinion of the patient so freely as to Slyudin.

'How glad I am that you have been seeing him!' said Slyudin. 'He is not well, and I fancy ... Well, what do you think of him?'

'I will tell you,' said the doctor, signalling over Slyudin's head to his coachman to bring the carriage round. 'It's like this,' said the doctor, taking a finger of his kid glove in his white hands and pulling it. 'Try to break a violin string that is not taut and you'll find it a difficult job; but strain the string to its utmost, and the weight of a finger will snap it. And with his assiduity, his conscientious devotion to his work, he is strained to the utmost; and there's some outside burden weighing on him, weighing heavily,' concluded the doctor, raising his eyebrows significantly. 'Will you be at the races?' he added, descending the steps to the brougham which had drawn up. 'Yes, yes, to be sure, it does waste a lot of time,' he said vaguely, in reply to some remark of Slyudin's he had not caught.

Immediately after the doctor, who had taken up so much time, the famous explorer arrived, and Karenin, thanks to the pamphlet he had just finished reading and his previous acquaintance with the subject, impressed the traveller by the extent of his knowledge and the breadth and enlightenment of his outlook.

At the same time as the traveller, a marshal of the nobility from one of the provinces was announced. He was on a visit to Petersburg and Karenin had various matters to discuss with him. After his departure, he had to finish the routine business of the day with his secretary and had also to drive round to call on a certain important personage on a grave and urgent affair. Karenin just managed to be back by five – his hour for dinner – and after dining with his secretary he invited him to drive with him to his country villa and go to the races.

Though he did not acknowledge it to himself, Karenin always tried nowadays to secure the presence of a third person at his interviews with his wife.

27

ANNA was upstairs, standing before a looking-glass, pinning, with Annushka's help, a final bow to her gown, when she heard the noise of wheels crunching the gravel in front of the house.

'It is too early for Betsy,' she thought and, glancing out of the window, caught sight of a carriage and, sticking out of it, a black hat and Karenin's familiar ears. 'How unfortunate! Can he be going to stay the night?' she wondered, and the consequences that might result therefrom struck her as so awful and terrible that, without a moment's hesitation, she went to meet him with a gay and smiling face; and conscious of the presence within herself of the already familiar spirit of falsehood and deceit, she immediately abandoned herself to it and began talking, hardly knowing what she was saying.

'Oh, how nice!' she said, extending her hand to her husband and greeting Slyudin, who was like one of the family, with a smile. 'You are staying the night, I hope?' were the first words the devil of deceit prompted her to utter. 'And now we can go together. Only it's a pity I promised Betsy. She's calling for me.'

Karenin frowned at the mention of Betsy's name.

'Oh, I won't separate the inseparables,' he said in his usual bantering tone. 'Slyudin and I will go together. The doctors have ordered me exercise. I will walk part of the way and imagine myself at the springs again.'

'There is no hurry,' said Anna. 'Would you like tea?'

She rang.

'Tea, please, and tell Seriozha that his father is here. Well, and how are you?' she asked. 'I don't think you have been here before,' she said, turning to Slyudin. 'See how lovely it is out on my terrace.'

She spoke very simply and naturally, but she was saying too much and saying it too quickly. She was made the more aware of this by Slyudin's inquiring look, which seemed to be watching her.

Slyudin at once went out on the terrace.

She sat down beside her husband.

'You are not looking very well,' she said.

'No,' he replied. 'The doctor came to-day and wasted an hour of my time. I have a feeling one of our friends must have sent him: my health is so precious apparently ...'

'Yes, but what did he say?'

She asked him about his health and what he had been doing, and tried to persuade him to take a rest and come and stay in the country.

It was all said lightly, rapidly, and with a peculiar brilliance in her eyes; but Karenin did not now attach any significance to this tone of hers. He heard her words and gave them only their literal meaning. And he answered simply, though banteringly. In all this conversation there was nothing of note, yet never afterwards could Anna recall this brief scene without an agonizing pang of shame.

Seriozha came in, preceded by his governess. Had Karenin cared to, he might have noticed the timid, lost look which the child cast first at his father and then at his mother. But he was unwilling to see anything and so saw nothing.

'Aha, young man! He has grown. Really, he's getting quite a man. How do you do, young man?'

And he held out his hand to the scared boy.

Seriozha had always been shy of his father and now, ever since Karenin had taken to calling him 'young man' and since he had begun to worry over the problem whether Vronsky were friend or enemy, he shrank from his father. He looked round at his mother, as if seeking protection. Only with his mother did he feel at ease. Karenin, meanwhile, was talking to the governess with his hand on his son's shoulder, and Seriozha was so miserably uncomfortable that Anna could see he was on the verge of tears.

Anna, who had flushed a little when the boy came in, noticing that Seriozha was wretched, got up hurriedly, lifted Karenin's hand off her son's shoulder, kissed the boy as she led him out on to the terrace and came back at once.

'It's time to start, though,' she said, glancing at her watch. 'I wonder why Betsy doesn't come? ...'

'By the way,' said Karenin and, rising, he interlocked his fingers to make the joints crack. 'I also came to bring you some money, since we know nightingales don't live on fables,' he said. 'You need it, I expect?'

'No, I don't ... yes, I do,' she replied, not looking at him and crimsoning to the roots of her hair. 'But you'll be coming back after the races, I suppose?'

'Oh, yes!' answered Karenin. 'And here is the ornament of Peterhof, Princess Tverskoy,' he went on, looking out of the window at the

224

approaching carriage of English design, with the tiny body placed extremely high. 'What elegance! Charming! Well, we must be off too.'

Princess Tverskoy did not get out of her carriage; but her footman, in high boots, a cape, and black hat, jumped down at the front door.

'I am going, good-bye!' said Anna, and giving her son a kiss she went up to Karenin and held out her hand to him. 'It was very nice of you to come.'

Karenin kissed her hand.

'Well, *au revoir*, then! You will come back for some tea afterwards; splendid!' she said and went out, gay and radiant. But as soon as she no longer saw him she became conscious of the spot on her hand that his lips had touched and gave a shudder of repulsion.

28

WHEN Karenin reached the race-course, Anna was already sitting beside Betsy in the pavilion: the pavilion where the élite of society had gathered. She caught sight of her husband in the distance. Two men, her husband and her lover, were the two centres of her existence, and without the aid of her external senses she was aware of their nearness. She was conscious of her husband approaching a long way off, and involuntarily followed him with her eyes in the surging crowd through which he was moving. She watched him making his way towards the pavilion, saw him now condescendingly acknowledging an obsequious bow, now exchanging friendly, nonchalant greetings with his equals, now assiduously trying to catch the eye of some great one of this world and raising his big round hat that pressed on the tips of his ears. She knew all these ways of his, and they were all hateful to her. 'Nothing but ambition, nothing but the desire to get on – that is all there is in his soul,' she thought; 'and as for those lofty ideals of his, his passion for culture, religion, they are only so many tools for advancement.'

She realized by the glances he cast towards the ladies' pavilion (he was staring straight at her but did not recognize his wife in the sea of muslin, ribbons, feathers, parasols, and flowers) that he was looking for her but she purposely avoided noticing him.

'Alexei Alexandrovich!' the Princess Betsy called to him. 'I am sure you don't see your wife: here she is!'

He smiled his chilly smile.

'There is so much splendour here that one's eyes are dazzled,' he said, and approached the pavilion. He smiled to his wife as a husband should smile on meeting his wife after they had only just parted, and greeted the princess and other acquaintances, giving to each what was due – that is, talking nonsense to the ladies and bestowing greetings among the men. Below, by the side of the pavilion, stood an adjutant-general respected by Karenin and noted for his wit and culture. Karenin began a conversation with him.

It was during an interval between two races, so nothing hindered conversation. The adjutant-general expressed disapproval of racing. Karenin replied, defending it. Anna heard his high, measured tones, not missing one word, and every word he uttered struck her as false and grated painfully on her ear.

When the three-mile steeplechase was about to begin she leaned forward and did not take her eyes off Vronsky. She watched him go up to his horse and mount, and at the same time she heard the loathsome, never-ceasing voice of her husband. She was in an agony of anxiety for Vronsky but a still greater agony was what seemed to her the never-ceasing flow of her husband's shrill voice with its familiar intonations.

'I'm a bad woman, a wicked woman,' she thought; 'but I don't like lying, I cannot stand falsehood, while *he*' – (her husband) – 'lives on it. He knows all about it, he sees it all – what does he care, if he can talk so calmly? If he were to kill me, if he were to kill Vronsky, I might respect him. But no. All he cares about is pretence and propriety,' Anna said to herself, without considering what it was she wanted of her husband, or what she would have liked to see him do. Nor did she understand that Karenin's peculiar loquacity that day, which so exasperated her, was merely the expression of his inner distress and uneasiness. As a child that has been hurt skips about, making his muscles move to drown the pain, so Karenin needed mental activity to drown the thoughts of his wife, which in her presence and in Vronsky's, and with the continual iteration of his name, would force themselves on his attention. And it was as natural for him to talk well and cleverly as it is natural for a child to skip about. He was saying:

'Danger in army racing – that is, in the racing of cavalry men – is an essential element. If England can boast the most brilliant cavalry charges in military history, it is simply owing to the fact that historically she has developed this daring in her horses and riders. Sport has, in my opinion, a deep value and, as is always the case, we see only its superficial aspect.'

'It's not superficial,' said the Princess Tverskoy. 'They say one of the officers has broken two ribs.'

Karenin smiled his smile which uncovered his teeth but expressed nothing.

'We will admit, Princess,' he said, 'that that is not superficial but internal. However, that is not the point,' and he returned to the serious conversation with the general. 'Do not forget that those who go in for racing are military men who have chosen that career, and one must allow that every calling has its reverse side. It forms an integral part of the duty of a soldier. The ugly sports of prize-fighting and Spanish bull-fights are a sign of barbarism. But specialized trials of skill are a sign of progress.'

'No, I shan't come another time; it is too upsetting,' said the Princess Betsy. 'Don't you think so, Anna?'

'It is upsetting, but one cannot tear oneself away,' said another lady. 'If I'd been a Roman I should never have missed a single circus.'

Anna said nothing and, keeping her binoculars raised, gazed steadily at the same spot.

At that moment a highly-placed general made his way through the pavilion. Interrupting what he was saying, Karenin rose hurriedly, though with dignity, and bowed low to the general as he passed.

'You are not racing?' the general chaffed him.

'My race is a more difficult one,' replied Karenin respectfully.

And though the answer meant nothing, the general looked as if he had heard a witty repartee from a witty man and fully relished *la pointe de la sauce*.

'There are two sides to it,' Karenin resumed: 'that of those who take part and that of those who look on; and a passion for such spectacles is unmistakable proof of a low degree of development in the spectator, I admit, but ...'

'Princess, a wager!' came the voice of Oblonsky from below, addressing Betsy. 'What's your favourite?'

'Anna and I are betting on Prince Kuzovlov,' replied Betsy.

'I'm for Vronsky. A pair of gloves?'

'Agreed!'

'But it is a pretty scene, isn't it?'

Karenin was silent while others were talking round him but he began again directly.

'I admit that manly sports do not ...' he was continuing.

But at that moment the race began and all conversation ceased. Karenin, too, fell silent as everyone stood up and turned towards the stream. Karenin was not interested in the race and so did not watch the riders but began listlessly scanning the spectators with his weary eyes. His eyes rested on Anna.

Her face was pale and set. She was obviously seeing nothing and nobody but one man. Her hand convulsively clutched her fan and she held her breath. He looked at her and hurriedly turned away, scrutinizing other faces.

'Yes, that lady there – and those others are excited too: it's very natural,' Karenin told himself. He tried not to look but his eyes were involuntarily drawn to her. He examined Anna's face again, striving not to read what was so plainly written on it, and against his own will with horror read on it what he did not want to know.

The first fall – Kuzovlov's at the stream – agitated everyone, but Karenin saw clearly by Anna's pale, triumphant face that the man she was watching had not fallen. When Mahotin and Vronsky had leaped the big barrier, and the officer following them fell on his head, nearly killing himself, a shudder of horror ran through the whole crowd; but Karenin saw that Anna had not even noticed it and had some difficulty in understanding what those about her were talking of. He looked at her more and more often, and with greater persistence. Anna, wholly engrossed as she was with the sight of the galloping Vronsky, became aware of her husband's cold eyes fixed upon her from one side.

Glancing round for an instant, she gave him a look of inquiry and, with a slight frown, turned away again.

'Ah, I don't care!' she seemed to say to him, and she did not look at him again.

The steeplechase was an unlucky one: more than half of the field of seventeen were thrown and hurt. Towards the end of the race everyone was in a state of agitation, intensified by the fact that the Emperor was displeased.

29

EVERYONE was loudly expressing his disapproval and repeating a phrase someone had uttered: 'Lions and gladiators will be the next thing,' and everyone was feeling horrified; so that when Vronsky fell and Anna moaned aloud there was nothing very out of the way in it. But immediately after, a change came over Anna's face which was positively unseemly. She completely lost her head. She began fluttering like a caged bird, at one moment getting up to go, at the next turning to Betsy.

'Let us go, let us go!' she said.

But Betsy did not hear her. She was leaning over and talking to a general who had come up to her.

Karenin approached Anna and courteously offered her his arm.

'We can go if you like,' he said in French; but Anna was listening to what the general was saying and did not notice her husband.

'He's broken his leg too, they say,' said the general. 'This is beyond everything.'

Without replying to her husband, Anna lifted her binoculars and gazed towards the place where Vronsky had fallen; but it was so far off and so many people had crowded there that it was impossible to distinguish anything. She laid down her glasses and was about to go, but at that moment an officer galloped up and made some announcement to the Emperor. Anna craned forward to listen.

'Stiva! Stiva!' she called to her brother.

But her brother did not hear her. She was once more on the point of going.

'I again offer you my arm if you want to be going,' said Karenin, touching her arm.

She shrank from him with aversion and, without looking at him, answered:

'No, no, let me be; I shall stay.'

She saw now an officer running across the course towards the pavilion, from the place of Vronsky's accident. Betsy waved her handkerchief to him. The officer brought news that the rider was not killed but the horse had broken its back.

On hearing this Anna sat down hurriedly and hid her face behind her fan. Karenin saw that she was weeping and that she was unable to keep back either her tears or the sobs shaking her bosom. He stepped forward so as to screen her, giving her time to recover herself.

'For the third time I offer you my arm,' he said after a little while, turning to her.

Anna looked at him and did not know what to say. The Princess Betsy came to her rescue.

'No, Alexei Alexandrovich,' she put in. 'I brought Anna and promised to take her home.'

'Excuse me, Princess,' he said, smiling courteously but looking her firmly in the eye, 'but I see that Anna is not very well and I wish her to come back with me.'

Anna looked about her in a frightened way, got up obediently, and laid her hand on her husband's arm.

'I'll send to him and find out, and let you know,' Betsy whispered to her.

As they left the pavilion, Karenin, as usual, exchanged remarks with those he met and Anna, as usual, had to reply and make conversation; but she was beside herself and walked as in a dream, holding her husband's arm.

'Is he killed or not? Is it true what they said? Will he come or not? Shall I see him to-night?' she was thinking.

She took her seat in her husband's carriage in silence and in silence they drove out of the crowd of vehicles. In spite of all he had seen, Karenin would still not allow himself to think of his wife's real state. He merely saw the outward signs. He saw that she had behaved unbecomingly, and considered it his duty to tell her so. But it was very difficult for him to say that and nothing more. He opened his mouth to tell her she had behaved in an unseemly fashion but against his will said something quite different.

'What an inclination we all have, though, for these cruel spectacles!' he said. 'I notice ...'

'What? I don't understand,' said Anna contemptuously.

He was offended and at once began to say what he had intended.

'I am obliged to tell you ...' he began.

'It's coming – now we are to have a scene!' she thought, and was filled with dread.

'I am obliged to tell you that your behaviour was unbecoming today,' he said in French.

'In what way was my behaviour unbecoming?' she asked loudly, turning her head quickly and looking him straight in the eyes, not with the former mask of gaiety but with a determined air which concealed with difficulty the dismay she was feeling.

'Be careful,' he said, pointing to the open window behind the coachman's back.

He rose and pulled up the window.

'What did you consider unbecoming?' she repeated.

'The despair you were unable to hide when one of the riders fell.'

He waited for her to answer but she was silent, looking straight before her.

'I have asked you before to conduct yourself in public so that malicious tongues can find nothing to say against you. There was a time when I spoke of our private relations; now I do so no longer. I speak now only of appearances. Your conduct was unseemly, and I do not wish it to occur again.'

She did not hear half of what he was saying; she felt afraid before him, and was wondering whether it was true that Vronsky was not killed. Was it of him they were speaking when they said the rider was not hurt but the horse had broken its back? She merely smiled with a pretence of irony when he finished, and made no reply because she had not heard what he said. Karenin had begun to speak boldly but, when he realized plainly what he was speaking of, the dismay she was feeling communicated itself to him. He saw her smile and a strange delusion possessed him.

'She is smiling at my suspicions. In a moment she will tell me what she told me the other time: that there is no foundation for my suspicions, that it's ridiculous.'

Now that the revelation of everything was hanging over him, there was nothing he wanted so much as that she would answer derisively, as she had before, that his suspicions were ridiculous and groundless. What he knew was so terrible that now he was ready to believe anything. But the expression of her frightened, sombre face did not now hold out hope even of deception.

'Possibly I am mistaken,' he said. 'In that case, I beg your pardon.'

'No, you were not mistaken,' she said slowly, looking despairingly into his cold face. 'You were not mistaken. I was, and I could not help being in despair. I listen to you, but I am thinking of him. I love him, I am his mistress; I cannot endure you, I am afraid of you and I hate you. … You can do what you like with me.'

And throwing herself back in the corner of the carriage she broke into sobs, hiding her face in her hands. Karenin did not stir and continued to look straight in front of him. But his whole face suddenly assumed the solemn immobility of the dead, and that expression did not alter throughout the drive home. As they reached the house he turned his face to her, still with the same expression.

'Very well! But I must insist that you conform outwardly to propriety until such time' – his voice shook – 'as I take measures to secure my honour and inform you of them.'

He alighted first and helped her out. In the presence of the servants he pressed her hand in silence, reseated himself in the carriage, and drove back to Petersburg.

He had no sooner gone than a footman came bringing Anna a note from the Princess Betsy.

'I sent to Alexei to find out how he was,' it said, 'and he writes that he is safe and sound, but in despair.'

'So *he* will be here,' she thought. 'What a good thing I told him everything!'

She glanced at her watch. She had still three hours to wait, and the memories of their last meeting fired her blood.

'Heavens, how light it is! It's dreadful but I do love to see his face and I do love this fantastic light. ... My husband! Oh, yes! ... Well, thank God, everything's over with him.'

30

As always happens where people are gathered together, the little German watering-place to which the Shcherbatskys had betaken themselves saw the usual crystallization, as it were, of society, assigning to each member of that society his particular and immutable place. As definitely and inevitably as a drop of water exposed to the frost is transformed into a snow-crystal of a certain shape, so each newcomer at the springs was immediately established in his special place.

Fürst Shcherbatsky, *seine Gemahlin und Tochter* – Prince Shcherbatsky with his wife and daughter – by the lodgings they took, by their name, and by the people they were acquainted with were immediately crystallized into a definite place marked out for them.

There was a real German Fürstin at the watering-place that year, in consequence of which the crystallizing process went on more energetically than ever. Princess Shcherbatsky was very eager to present her daughter to this German princess and on the day after their arrival duly performed this rite. Kitty made a deep and graceful curtsey in the *very simple*, that is to say, very elegant summer gown ordered from Paris. The German princess said: 'I hope the roses will soon come back to this pretty little face,' and for the Shcherbatskys certain definite lines of existence were at once laid down from which there was no departing. The Shcherbatskys made the acquaintance of the family of a titled English lady, of a German countess and her son, wounded in the last war, of a Swedish *savant*, and of Mr Canut and his sister. But inevitably the Shcherbatskys found themselves mainly in the company of a Moscow lady, Maria Yevgenyevna Rtishchov, and her daughter, whom Kitty disliked because her illness was also due to a love affair; and a Moscow colonel, whom Kitty had known from her childhood and always seen in uniform and epaulets and who looked indescribably comical here, with his little eyes and his open neck and flowered cravat, and who was tedious because there was no getting away from him. When they had quite settled down to all this, Kitty began to feel very dull, the more so as the prince went away to Carlsbad and she was left alone with her mother. She was not interested in the people she knew, feeling that nothing fresh would come of them. Her chief private interest at the watering-place consisted in observing the people she did not know and making guesses about them. It was a characteristic of Kitty's always to expect to find all the most excellent qualities in people, especially in those who were strangers to her. And now, when making surmises as to who was who, what relation they stood in to one another, and what they were like, Kitty endowed them with the most marvellous and beautiful characters and found confirmation in her observations.

Of these people, the one that attracted her most was a Russian girl who had come to the watering-place with an invalid Russian lady – Madame Stahl, as everyone called her. Madame Stahl belonged to the highest society, but she was so ill that she could not walk and only on exceptionally fine days made her appearance at the springs in an invalid carriage. But it was not so much from ill-health as from pride – so the Princess Shcherbatsky interpreted it – that Madame Stahl had not made the acquaintance of any of the Russians there. The Russian girl looked after Madame Stahl, and besides that, as Kitty observed, made friends with all the people who were seriously ill – and there were many of them at the springs – and waited on them in the most natural way. This Russian girl, Kitty decided, was not related to Madame Stahl, but neither was she a paid companion. Madame Stahl called her 'Varenka', and other people addressed her as 'Mademoiselle Varenka'. Apart from the interest Kitty took in this girl's relations with Madame Stahl and with other unknown persons, Kitty, as often happens, felt an inexplicable attraction to this Mademoiselle Varenka and was aware, when their eyes met, that Mademoiselle Varenka liked her too.

Of Mademoiselle Varenka one would not say that she had passed her first youth, but that she was, as it were, someone without youth: she might be nineteen or she might be thirty. If one analysed her features separately, she was pretty rather than plain, in spite of her unhealthy colour. She would have had a good figure, too, had she not been too thin and her head too large for her medium height; but she was not likely to be attractive to men. She was like some beautiful flower already past its bloom and without fragrance, though its petals had not dropped. Another reason why she could not be attractive to men was because she lacked just what Kitty had too much of – the suppressed fire of vitality and a consciousness of her own attractiveness.

She always seemed to be absorbed in work about which there could be no doubt, and so it seemed that she could have no time for anything else. This contrast to herself especially attracted Kitty, who felt that in her, in her manner of life, she might find the pattern she herself was so painfully seeking: interest in life, a dignity in life – apart from the social relations of girls with men, which now seemed repulsive to Kitty, like infamous exhibitions of goods for sale. The more Kitty observed her unknown friend, the more convinced she was that this girl really was the perfect creature she imagined her to be, and the more she longed to make her acquaintance.

The two girls would pass each other several times a day, and every time they met, Kitty's eyes said: 'Who are you? What are you? Are you the delightful being I imagine you to be? But for goodness' sake,' her look added, 'don't think that I would force myself on you. I simply admire you and like you.' 'I like you, too, and you are very, very sweet. And I should love you still more if I had time,' answered the unknown girl's eyes. And Kitty saw, indeed, that she was always busy: either taking the children of a Russian family home from the springs, or fetching an invalid's shawl and wrapping it round her, or trying to interest an irritable patient, or selecting and buying biscuits for someone's coffee.

Soon after the arrival of the Shcherbatskys, two new-comers who provoked universal and unfavourable attention began to appear at the springs in the mornings. They were a very tall man with a stooping figure and huge hands, who wore an old coat too short for him and had black, naïve, yet terrible eyes, and a slightly pock-marked, pleasant-faced woman, very badly and tastelessly dressed. Recognizing them as Russians, Kitty at once began to weave a beautiful and touching romance about them. But when the princess ascertained from the visitors' list that this was Nikolai Levin and Maria Nikolayevna, she soon explained to Kitty what a bad man this Levin was, and all her fancies about these two people vanished. Not so much because of what her mother told her as because the man was Constantine's brother did this pair suddenly seem extremely disagreeable to Kitty. This Levin, with his habit of jerking his head, now inspired in her an insuperable feeling of aversion.

It seemed to her that his big, terrible eyes, which followed her persistently, expressed hatred and derision, and she tried to avoid encountering him.

31

IT was a wet day, raining the whole morning, and the invalids with their umbrellas had crowded into the arcades.

Kitty was walking there with her mother and the Moscow colonel, swaggering jauntily in his European coat, bought ready-made in Frankfort. They kept to one side of the arcade, trying to avoid Levin, who was walking on the other side. Varenka, in her dark dress and a black hat with a turned-down brim, was walking up and down the whole length of the arcade with a blind Frenchwoman, and every time she met Kitty they exchanged friendly glances.

'Mama, couldn't I speak to her?' asked Kitty, following her unknown friend with her eyes and noticing that she was moving towards the spring and that they might meet there.

'Oh, if you want to so much I will find out about her first and speak to her myself,' replied her mother. 'What is it you see in her particularly? I expect she is only a lady's-companion. If you like I will make Madame Stahl's acquaintance. I used to know her *belle-sœur*,' added the princess, lifting her head haughtily.

Kitty knew that her mother was offended that Madame Stahl had seemed to avoid making her acquaintance. Kitty did not insist.

'What a wonderfully sweet person she is!' she said, gazing at Varenka just as she was handing a tumbler to the Frenchwoman. 'Look how naturally and sweetly she does everything.'

'You are so funny with your infatuations,' said the princess. 'Come, we had better turn back,' she added, noticing Levin coming towards them with his companion and a German doctor, to whom he was talking loudly and angrily.

They turned to go back, when suddenly they heard, not noisy talk, but shouting. Levin, stopping short, was shouting at the doctor and the doctor, too, was excited. The princess and Kitty hastily moved away, while the colonel joined the crowd to find out what it was all about.

A few minutes later the colonel caught them up.

'What was the matter?' inquired the princess.

'Shameful! Scandalous!' answered the colonel. 'The one thing to beware of is meeting Russians abroad. The tall gentleman was abusing the doctor, flinging insults at him because he wasn't treating him quite as he liked. He began waving his stick at him. Perfectly disgraceful!'

'How very unpleasant!' said the princess. 'Well, and how did it end?'

'Luckily that … you know that girl in the mushroom hat intervened. She's Russian, I think,' said the colonel.

'Mademoiselle Varenka?' asked Kitty, pleased.

'Yes, yes. She was quicker than anyone else – took the fellow by the arm and led him away.'

'There, Mama,' said Kitty. 'And you wonder that I admire her.'

The next day, watching her unknown friend, Kitty noticed that Mademoiselle Varenka was already on the same terms with Levin and his companion as with her other protégés. She went up and talked to them, and served as interpreter for the woman, who only spoke Russian.

Kitty entreated her mother still more urgently to let her make friends with Varenka. And, disagreeable as it was to the princess to appear to be taking the first step towards getting acquainted with Madame Stahl, who thought fit to give herself airs, she made inquiries about Varenka and, having ascertained particulars which allowed her to conclude that, though there might be little good, there would be no harm in the acquaintance, she herself approached Varenka.

Choosing a time when her daughter had gone to the spring, while Varenka had stopped outside a confectioner's, the princess went up to her.

'Allow me to introduce myself,' she said, with her dignified smile. 'My daughter has lost her heart to you. Possibly you do not know me. I am ...'

'It is more than reciprocal, Princess,' Varenka answered hurriedly.

'What a real service you did yesterday to our poor fellow-countryman!' said the princess.

Varenka blushed. 'I don't remember. I don't think I did anything,' she said.

'Of course you did – you saved that Levin from disagreeable consequences.'

'Yes, *sa compagne* called me and I tried to pacify him; he is very ill and was dissatisfied with his doctor. I am so used to looking after invalids.'

'I hear you live in Mentone with your aunt – I think – Madame Stahl. I used to know her *belle-sœur*.'

'No, she is not my aunt. I call her *maman* but we are not related. I was brought up by her,' replied Varenka, again flushing a little.

It was said so simply, and so sweet was the truthful and candid expression of her face, that the princess saw why Kitty had taken such a fancy to this Varenka.

'Well, and what is this Levin going to do?' asked the princess.

'He is leaving,' answered Varenka.

Just then Kitty came up from the spring, beaming with delight that her mother had become acquainted with her unknown friend.

'Well, see, Kitty, your passionate wish to know Mademoiselle ...'

'Varenka,' prompted Varenka, smiling, 'that is what everyone calls me.'

Kitty blushed with happiness, long and silently pressing her new friend's hand, which did not return her pressure but lay passively in hers. The hand did not respond to her pressure but Mademoiselle

Varenka's face glowed with a soft, pleased, though rather sad smile, which disclosed large but fine teeth.

'I have long wished for this too,' she said.

'But you are so busy ...'

'Oh no, I'm not at all busy,' answered Varenka; but at that very moment she had to leave her new friends because two little Russian girls, the children of one of the invalids, ran up to her.

'Varenka, Mama's calling!' they cried.

And Varenka went after them.

32

THE particulars the princess had learned in regard to Varenka's past and her relations with Madame Stahl, and in regard to Madame Stahl herself, were these:

Madame Stahl, of whom some people said that she had harried her husband to his grave, while others said that it was he who had made her life wretched by his loose behaviour, had always been an ailing and hysterical woman. She was already divorced from her husband when her first child was born, and the baby had died almost immediately. Madame Stahl's family, knowing her emotional nature and fearing the news might kill her, had substituted in place of the dead baby another child, born the same night and in the same house in Petersburg, the daughter of the head cook of the Imperial Household. This child was Varenka. Madame Stahl learned afterwards that Varenka was not her own child, but continued to bring her up, the more readily as very soon Varenka was left without a relation in the world.

For more than ten years Madame Stahl had been living continuously abroad, in the south, never leaving her couch. And some people said that Madame Stahl had made her social position as a philanthropic and highly religious woman; others said she really was the highly ethical being, living for nothing but the good of her fellow-creatures, which she represented herself to be. No one knew what her faith was – Catholic, Protestant, or Orthodox. But one thing was certain: she was on terms of friendship with the highest dignitaries of all the churches and denominations.

Varenka lived with her all the while abroad, and everyone who knew Madame Stahl knew and liked Mademoiselle Varenka, as they all called her.

Having learned all these facts, the princess found nothing to object to in a friendship between her daughter and Varenka, especially as Varenka's breeding and education were of the best – she spoke admirable French and English – and, what was of the most weight, she brought a message from Madame Stahl expressing her regret that illness deprived her of the pleasure of making the princess's acquaintance.

After getting to know Varenka, Kitty became more and more fascinated by her friend and every day discovered new virtues in her.

When she heard that Varenka had a good voice, the princess asked her to come and sing to them one evening.

'Kitty plays, and we have a piano – not a good one, it's true – but you would give us so much pleasure,' said the princess with her affected smile, which was especially distasteful to Kitty, for she noticed that Varenka had no inclination to come and sing.

Varenka came, however, in the evening and brought a roll of music with her. The princess had invited Maria Yevgenyevna and her daughter and the colonel.

Varenka seemed quite unconcerned that there were people there she did not know, and went straight to the piano. She could not accompany herself but she sang at sight beautifully. Kitty, who played well, accompanied her.

'You have an exceptional talent,' the princess said to her after Varenka had sung her first song extremely well.

Maria Yevgenyevna and her daughter thanked her and were full of praise.

'Come and see what an audience has collected to listen to you,' said the colonel, looking out of the window. And indeed there was quite a considerable crowd under the windows.

'I am very glad it gives you pleasure,' Varenka answered simply.

Kitty looked at her friend with pride. She was enraptured by her talent, her voice, and her face, but, most of all, by her manner – by the fact that Varenka obviously thought nothing of her singing and was quite unmoved by their praises. She seemed only to be asking: 'Am I to sing again, or is that enough?'

'If it were I,' thought Kitty, 'how proud I should feel! How delighted I should be to see that crowd under the windows! But she is quite indifferent. She is only anxious not to refuse, and to please Mama.

What is it in her? What gives her this power to disregard everything, to be so quietly independent of everything? How I should like to know it, and learn it from her!' thought Kitty, gazing into her serene face.

The princess asked Varenka to sing again and Varenka sang another song, with equal care and perfection, standing erect by the piano and beating time on it with her thin, brown hand.

The next song in the book was an Italian one. Kitty played the opening bars and glanced round at Varenka.

'Let us skip this one,' said Varenka, flushing a little.

Kitty let her eyes rest anxiously and inquiringly on Varenka's face. 'Very well, the next one, then,' she said hurriedly, turning over the pages, immediately realizing that there was something connected with that song.

'No,' answered Varenka, laying her hand on the music and smiling. 'No, let's have this one.' And she sang it just as quietly, coolly, and well as the others.

When she had finished, they all thanked her again and went to drink tea. Kitty and Varenka walked out into the little garden at the side of the house.

'Am I right – you have some memory attached to that song?' said Kitty. 'Don't tell me,' she added hastily, 'only say if I'm right.'

'Why shouldn't I tell you?' said Varenka simply and, without waiting for an answer, went on: 'Yes, it does bring back memories, painful ones at one time. I cared for someone once, and used to sing that song to him.'

Kitty gazed wide-eyed at Varenka, silently and sympathetically.

'I cared for him and he cared for me; but his mother did not wish it, and he married someone else. He is living not far from us now and I see him sometimes. You didn't think I had a love-story too, did you?' she said, and on her handsome face there was a faint gleam of the fire which Kitty felt must once have lighted her whole being.

'Why not? Why, if I were a man, I could never care for anyone else after knowing you. Only I can't understand how, to please his mother, he could forget you and make you unhappy: he had no heart.'

'Oh no, he is a very good person and I am not unhappy. Well, we shan't be singing any more to-day,' she added, turning towards the house.

'How good you are, how good!' exclaimed Kitty and, stopping her, she kissed her. 'If I could only be even a little bit like you!'

'Why should you be like anyone? You're nice as you are,' said Varenka, smiling her gentle, weary smile.

'No, I'm not at all nice. But tell me ... Stop a minute, let's sit down,' said Kitty, making Varenka sit down again on a garden bench beside her. 'Tell me, isn't it humiliating to think that a man has disdained your love, that he didn't want it? ...'

'But he didn't disdain it; I believe he cared for me but he was a dutiful son ...'

'Yes, but if it hadn't been on account of his mother, if it had been his own doing? ...' said Kitty, feeling she was giving away her secret and that her face, burning with a flush of shame, had betrayed her already.

'In that case he would have behaved badly and I should not regret him,' replied Varenka, evidently realizing that they were now talking not of her but of Kitty.

'But the humiliation,' said Kitty, 'the humiliation one can never forget, can never forget,' she said, remembering the look she had given Vronsky at the last ball when the music stopped.

'Where is the humiliation? You did nothing wrong?'

'Worse than wrong – shameful.'

Varenka shook her head and laid her hand on Kitty's.

'But what is there shameful?' she said. 'You didn't tell a man who did not care for you that you loved him, did you?'

'Of course not; I never said a word, but he knew. No, no; there are looks, there are ways. If I live to be a hundred I shall never forget.'

'But why? I don't understand. The point is whether you love him now or not,' said Varenka, calling everything by its name.

'I hate him; I cannot forgive myself.'

'Why, what for?'

'The shame, the humiliation!'

'Oh, if everyone were as sensitive as you are!' said Varenka. 'There isn't a girl who hasn't experienced the same sort of thing. And it is all so unimportant.'

'Then what is important?' asked Kitty, examining her face in surprise and curiosity.

'Oh, there's so much that's important,' said Varenka, smiling.

'What?'

241

'Oh, so much that's more important,' replied Varenka, not knowing what to say.

But at that instant they heard the princess's voice from the window. 'Kitty, it is chilly! Either get a shawl, or come in.'

'Yes, I really must be going!' said Varenka, getting up. 'I have to look in on Madame Berthe; she asked me to.'

Kitty held her by the hand and with passionate curiosity and entreaty questioned Varenka with her eyes: 'What is it – what is it that is so important? What gives you such tranquillity? You know, tell me!'

But Varenka did not even understand what Kitty's eyes were asking her. She only knew that now she had to call in and see Madame Berthe and hurry home for *maman*'s midnight tea. She went indoors, collected her music and, having said good-bye to everybody, turned to go.

'Allow me to see you home,' said the colonel.

'Yes, how can you go alone at night like this?' agreed the princess. 'At any rate, I will send Parasha with you.'

Kitty saw that Varenka could scarcely contain a smile at the idea that she needed an escort.

'Oh no, I always go about alone, and nothing ever happens to me,' she said, taking up her hat. And kissing Kitty once more, without having told her what was important, she stepped out fearlessly with her music under her arm and disappeared into the twilight of the summer night, bearing away her secret of what was important and what gave her her enviable calm and dignity.

33

KITTY made the acquaintance of Madame Stahl, too, and this acquaintance, together with her friendship with Varenka, not only had a great influence on her, it was also a comfort in her mental distress. She found this comfort through a completely new world being opened to her by means of this acquaintance, a world that had nothing in common with her past, an exalted, noble world, from the heights of which she could contemplate her past calmly. It was revealed to her that besides the instinctive life to which she had given herself up hitherto there was a spiritual life. This life was disclosed in religion, but a religion having nothing in common with the religion Kitty had known since childhood and which found expression in morning and evening service at the Widows' Home, where one might meet one's friends, and in learning Slavonic texts by heart with the priest. This was a lofty, mysterious religion connected with a whole series of noble thoughts and feelings, a religion one could do more than merely believe in because one was told to – it was a religion one could love.

Kitty did not find all this out from words. Madame Stahl talked to Kitty as to a dear child who gives pleasure by reminding one of one's own youth, and only once she said in passing that in all human sorrows love and faith alone bring consolation and that no sorrow is too trifling for Christ's compassion – and immediately changed the subject. But in every gesture of Madame Stahl, in every word, in every heavenly – as Kitty called it – look, and above all in the whole story of her life, which she heard from Varenka, Kitty discovered 'what was important', of which, till then, she had known nothing.

Yet, elevated as was Madame Stahl's character, touching as was her story, and exalted and moving as was her speech, Kitty could not help noticing certain traits which perplexed her. She noticed that Madame Stahl, when questioning her about her family, had smiled disdainfully, which did not accord with Christian charity. Another time, when she had found a Catholic priest with her, Madame Stahl had been at pains to keep her face in the shadow of the lampshade and had smiled in a peculiar manner. Trivial as these two observations were, they perplexed her and she had her doubts about Madame Stahl. Varenka, on the other hand, alone in the world, without friends or relations, with a sad disappointment in the past, desiring nothing and regretting nothing, personified that perfection of which Kitty hardly dared dream. In Varenka she saw that it was only necessary to forget oneself and love others in order to be at peace, happy, and good. And that was what Kitty longed to be. Having once clearly understood what was *the most important*, Kitty was not content merely to admire it: she at once devoted herself with her whole soul to the new life which had opened out before her. From Varenka's accounts of the works of Madame Stahl and others whom she named, Kitty had already constructed the plan of her own future life. Like Madame Stahl's niece, Aline, of whom Varenka had talked to her a great deal, Kitty would seek out those who were in trouble, wherever she might be living, help them to the best of her ability, distribute and read the Gospel to the sick, to criminals, to the dying. The idea of reading the Gospel to criminals, as Aline did, particularly fascinated Kitty. But all these were secret dreams, which Kitty did not speak of either to her mother or to Varenka.

While awaiting the time when she could put her plans into practice on a larger scale, however, Kitty, here at the watering-place where there were so many sick and unhappy people, readily found opportunities to apply her new principles in imitation of Varenka.

At first the princess noticed nothing but that Kitty was strongly under the influence of her *engouement*, as she called it, for Madame Stahl and still more for Varenka. She saw that Kitty not only imitated Varenka in her activities but was unconsciously copying her manner of walking, of talking, of blinking her eyes. But later the princess noticed that, apart from this infatuation, a serious spiritual transformation was taking place in her daughter.

The princess saw that at night Kitty read a French testament that Madame Stahl had given her – a thing she had never done before; that she avoided her society acquaintances and associated with the invalids under Varenka's protection, and especially with the family of a poor sick artist named Petrov. Kitty was unmistakably proud of playing the part of a sister-of-mercy to that family. This was all very well, and the princess had nothing against it, especially as Petrov's wife happened to be a lady, and the German princess, noticing Kitty's activities, praised her, calling her a ministering angel. All this would have been very well if it had not been overdone. But the princess saw that her daughter was rushing to extremes and spoke to her about it.

'*Il ne faut jamais rien outrer*,' she said to her.

But her daughter made no reply; only in her heart she thought that one could not talk about exaggeration where Christianity was concerned. What extremes could there be in the practice of a doctrine wherein one was bidden to turn the other cheek when one was smitten and give one's cloak if one's coat were taken? But the princess disliked this excess, and still more did she dislike the fact that she felt her daughter did not care to open her heart to her. Kitty did indeed conceal her new views and feelings from her mother. She concealed them not because she did not respect and love her mother but simply because it was her mother. She would have revealed them to anyone sooner than to her mother.

'It seems a long time since Anna Pavlovna was here,' the princess said one day, referring to the artist Pavlov's wife. 'I've asked her to come but she appears to be put out about something.'

'I have not noticed anything, *maman*,' said Kitty, colouring up.

'Have you been to see them lately?'

'We are planning an expedition to the mountains to-morrow,' replied Kitty.

'I see no objection,' said the princess, looking intently into her daughter's embarrassed face and trying to fathom the cause of her embarrassment.

That day Varenka came to dinner and said that Anna Pavlovna had changed her mind about going to the mountains on the morrow. And the princess noticed that Kitty went red again.

'Kitty, haven't you had some misunderstanding with the Petrovs?' the princess asked as soon as they were alone. 'Why has she given up sending the children here and coming to see us herself?'

Kitty answered that nothing had happened and that she did not understand at all why Anna Pavlovna seemed displeased with her. It was perfectly true. She did not know the reason Anna Pavlovna had changed to her, but she could guess. She guessed at something which she could not tell her mother, which she could not put into words to herself. It was one of those things which one knows but which one can never speak of even to oneself, so dreadful and shameful would it be to be mistaken.

Again and again she went over in her mind all the relations she had had with the family. She remembered the naïve pleasure that had shone on Anna Pavlovna's round, good-humoured face whenever they met; she remembered their secret consultations about the invalid, their schemes to draw him away from work which the doctor had forbidden and to get him out of doors; the attachment of the youngest boy, who called her 'my Kitty' and who would not go to bed without saying good night to her. How nice it all was! Then she recalled Petrov's emaciated figure in his brown coat, with his long neck, his thin, curly hair, his inquiring blue eyes that Kitty had found so terrible at first, and his feverish efforts to appear hearty and animated in her presence. She recalled her own efforts in the early days to overcome the repugnance she felt for him, as for all consumptive people, and her struggles to think of something to say to him. She recalled the timid, touching way he gazed at her and the strange feeling of compassion and awkwardness, and later a consciousness of her own goodness, which she had felt at it. How nice it all was! But all that was at first. Now, a few days ago, everything was suddenly spoiled. Anna Pavlovna had greeted Kitty with feigned cordiality and had kept watching her and her husband.

Could his touching joy at seeing her be the cause of Anna Pavlovna's coolness?

'Yes,' she mused, 'there was something unnatural about Anna Pavlovna, and quite unlike her usual good nature, when she said angrily the day before yesterday: "There, he would wait for you! Wouldn't drink his coffee till you came, though he's grown so dreadfully weak."

'Yes, and perhaps she didn't like it when I gave him the rug. It was such a natural thing to do but he took it so awkwardly, and was so long thanking me that I began to feel awkward myself. And then that portrait of me he did so well. And most of all that look of confusion and tenderness! Yes, yes, that's it!' Kitty repeated to herself with horror. 'No, it can't be, it mustn't be! He's so pathetic!' she said to herself directly after.

This doubt poisoned the charm of her new life.

34

BEFORE the end of the course of drinking the waters, Prince Shcherbatsky, who had gone on from Carlsbad to Baden and Kissingen to see some Russian friends – to get a breath of Russian air, as he expressed it – came back to his wife and daughter.

The views of the prince and princess on life abroad were diametrically opposed. The princess found everything admirable and, in spite of her established position in Russian society, she tried abroad to be like a European lady, which she was not – for the simple reason that she was typically Russian. And because she was being artificial she did not feel altogether at ease. The prince, on the contrary, considered everything foreign detestable and life abroad unendurable, clung to his Russian habits and purposely tried to show himself abroad less European than he was in reality.

The prince returned looking thinner, with the skin in loose bags on his cheeks, but in the gayest of spirits. His spirits were still better when he saw Kitty completely recovered. The news of Kitty's friendship with Madame Stahl and Varenka, and the princess's accounts of the change she had observed in Kitty, disturbed the prince and aroused his habitual feeling of jealousy of everything that drew his daughter away from him, and a dread lest his daughter might escape from his influence into regions he could not enter. But these unpleasant matters were soon drowned in the sea of kindliness and good-humour which was always within him, and more so than ever since his course of Carlsbad waters.

The day after his arrival the prince, in his long overcoat and with his Russian wrinkles and baggy cheeks propped up by a starched collar, set off with his daughter to the spring in the greatest good humour.

It was a lovely morning: the neat, cheerful houses with their little gardens, the sight of the red-faced, red-armed, beer-drinking German waitresses, working away merrily, and the clear sunshine did the heart good. But the nearer they got to the springs the oftener they encountered sick people, whose appearance seemed more pitiable than ever in those well-ordered German surroundings. Kitty was no longer struck by this contrast. The bright sun, the brilliant green of the foliage, the strains of the music were for her the natural setting of all these familiar faces, with their changes for worse or for better, for which she watched. But to the prince the glittering radiance of the June morning, the sound of the band playing a gay waltz then in fashion, and, above all, the appearance of the robust-looking attendants, seemed somehow unseemly and monstrous in conjunction with these slow-moving, dying figures from every corner of Europe.

In spite of his pride and sense of renewed youth, as it were, which he felt with his favourite daughter on his arm, he was uncomfortable and almost ashamed of his firm step and sturdy, stout limbs – almost like a man with no clothes on in a crowd.

'Present me – present me to your new friends,' he said to his daughter, squeezing her hand with his elbow. 'I even like your nasty Soden for the good it has done you. Only it is depressing, very depressing, this place of yours. Who's that?'.

Kitty told him the names of all the people they met, with some of whom she was acquainted and some not. Right at the entrance of the garden they met the blind lady, Madame Berthe, with her guide, and the prince was delighted to see the tender look on the old Frenchwoman's face when she heard Kitty's voice. With exaggerated French politeness she at once began talking to him, complimenting him on having such a charming daughter, praising her to the skies before her face, and calling her a treasure, a pearl, and a ministering angel.

'Then she must be angel number two,' said the prince, smiling. 'She calls Mademoiselle Varenka angel number one.'

'Oh, Mademoiselle Varenka! She's a real angel, *allez*,' Madame Berthe agreed.

In the arcade they met Varenka herself. She was walking rapidly towards them carrying an elegant little red bag.

'See, Papa has arrived,' Kitty said to her.

Simply and naturally as she did everything, Varenka made a movement between a bow and a curtsey and immediately began talking to the prince, naturally and without shyness, as she talked to everyone.

'Of course I know you; I know you very well,' the prince said to her with a smile, by which Kitty detected with joy that her father liked her friend. 'Where are you off to in such a hurry?'

'*Maman*'s here,' she said, turning to Kitty. 'She did not sleep all night and the doctor advised her to go out. I'm taking her her work.'

'So that is angel number one?' said the prince when Varenka had gone.

Kitty saw that he had meant to make fun of Varenka but was quite unable to because he liked her.

'Well, let us see all your friends,' he went on, 'including Madame Stahl, if she deigns to recognize me.'

'Why, do you know her, Papa?' asked Kitty apprehensively, catching the ironical twinkle in the prince's eyes when he mentioned Madame Stahl.

'I used to know her husband, and I knew her slightly, in the days before she'd joined the Pietists.'

'What is a Pietist, Papa?' asked Kitty, already dismayed to find that what she prized so highly in Madame Stahl had a name.

'I'm not quite sure myself. I only know that she thanks God for everything, for every misfortune ... and thanks God too that her husband died. And that's rather droll, as they did not get on well together.'

'Who's that? What a sad face!' he asked, noticing a sick man of medium height sitting on a bench, wearing a brown overcoat and white trousers that fell in strange folds about his fleshless legs. The man lifted his straw hat, showing his thin, curly hair and high forehead, with an unhealthy red mark where the hat pressed.

'That's Petrov, an artist,' answered Kitty, blushing. 'And there's his wife,' she added, indicating Anna Pavlovna, who, as though on purpose, at the very instant they approached walked away after a child that had run off along a path.

'Poor man! And what a nice face he has!' said the prince. 'Why didn't you go up to him? He looked as if he wanted to speak to you.'

'Well, let us go back, then,' said Kitty, turning round resolutely. 'How are you feeling to-day?' she asked Petrov.

Petrov got up, leaning on his stick, and looked shyly at the prince.

'This is my daughter,' said the prince. 'Allow me to introduce myself.'

The artist bowed and smiled, showing strangely dazzling white teeth.

'We were expecting you yesterday, Princess,' he said to Kitty.

He staggered as he said this, and then repeated the movement, trying to make it seem as if it had been intentional.

'I would have come, but Varenka said that Anna Pavlovna sent word you were not going.'

'Not going?' said Petrov, flushing and immediately beginning to cough, and looking round for his wife. 'Annetta! Annetta!' he said loudly, while the swollen veins stood out like cords on his thin white neck.

Anna Pavlovna came up.

'How is it you sent word to the princess that we weren't going?' he whispered to her angrily, losing his voice.

'Good morning, Princess,' said Anna Pavlovna, with an assumed smile totally unlike her former manner. 'Very glad to make your acquaintance,' she went on, turning to the prince. 'You have long been expected, Prince.'

'How is it you sent word to the princess that we weren't going?' hoarsely whispered the artist once again, still more angrily, obviously exasperated that his voice had failed him so that he could not give his words the expression he would have liked to.

'Oh, good gracious! I thought we weren't going,' his wife answered crossly.

'What, when ...' He was seized by a fit of coughing and waved his hand.

The prince raised his hat and moved away with his daughter.

'Oh dear!' he sighed deeply. 'Poor things!'

'Yes, Papa,' replied Kitty. 'And you know they have three children, no servant, and scarcely any money. He gets something from the Academy,' she explained animatedly, trying to stifle the distress aroused by the sudden change in Anna Pavlovna's manner towards her.

'Oh, here's Madame Stahl,' said Kitty, indicating an invalid carriage in which something in grey and blue was lying under a sunshade, propped up by pillows.

It was Madame Stahl. Behind her was a sullen-looking, muscular German workman who pushed the carriage. At her side stood a fair-haired Swedish count, whom Kitty knew by name. Several invalids were lingering near the low carriage, staring at the lady as if she were a curiosity.

The prince went up to her and Kitty detected that disconcerting gleam of irony in his eyes. He went up to Madame Stahl and addressed her with extreme courtesy and affability in that excellent French that so few speak nowadays.

'I don't know if you remember me but I must recall myself to you to thank you for your kindness to my daughter,' he said, taking off his hat and not putting it on again.

'Prince Alexander Shcherbatsky,' said Madame Stahl, lifting upon him her heavenly eyes, in which Kitty discerned a shade of annoyance. 'I am very pleased to meet you again. I have taken a great fancy to your daughter.'

'Your health is still not good?'

'No, but I am accustomed to it now,' said Madame Stahl, and she introduced the prince to the Swedish count.

'You are scarcely changed at all,' the prince said to her. 'It's ten or eleven years since I had the honour of seeing you.'

'Yes; God sends the cross and sends the strength to bear it. I often wonder why my life drags on. ... The other side!' she said irritably to Varenka, who had arranged the rug over her feet not to her satisfaction.

'To do good, probably,' said the prince, with a twinkle in his eye.

'That is not for us to judge,' said Madame Stahl, perceiving the gleam on the prince's face. 'So you will send me that book, my dear count? Thank you very much,' she added, addressing the young Swede.

'Ah!' cried the prince, catching sight of the Moscow colonel standing nearby, and with a bow to Madame Stahl he moved away with his daughter and the Moscow colonel, who had joined them.

'That is our aristocracy, Prince!' remarked the Moscow colonel, wishing to appear sarcastic. He was piqued with Madame Stahl for not making his acquaintance.

'She's just the same as ever,' replied the prince.

'Did you know her before her illness, Prince? I mean, before she took to her bed?'

'Yes, I knew her when she first became an invalid.'

'They say it's ten years since she has stood on her feet.'

'She doesn't get up because her legs are too short. She has a very ugly figure ...'

'Papa, it's not possible!' cried Kitty.

'Spiteful tongues say so, my love. And your Varenka catches it too,' he added. 'Oh, these invalid ladies!'

'Oh no, Papa!' Kitty objected warmly. 'Varenka worships her. And besides, she does so much good! Ask anyone! Everyone knows her and Aline Stahl.'

'Maybe,' said the prince, squeezing her hand with his elbow. 'But it is better to do good in such a way that you may ask everyone and no one knows.'

Kitty was silent, not because she had nothing to reply but because she did not want to reveal her secret thoughts even to her father. Yet, strange to say, although she had made up her mind not to be influenced by her father's views, not to let him into her inmost sanctuary, she felt that the divine image of Madame Stahl which she had carried for a whole month in her heart had vanished, never to return, just as the fantastic figure made by some clothes flung aside vanishes when one realizes that it is only the way the clothes are lying. All that was left was a woman with short legs, who lay on couches because she had a bad figure, and who martyrized poor patient Varenka for not arranging her rug to her liking. And by no effort of imagination could Kitty bring back the former Madame Stahl.

35

THE prince imparted his good spirits to his own family and his friends, and even to the German landlord in whose house the Shcherbatskys were staying.

When he and Kitty returned from the springs, the prince, who had invited the colonel and Maria Yevgenyevna and Varenka all to come and have coffee with them, had a table and chairs brought into the garden under the chestnut tree and lunch laid there. The landlord and the servants grew brisker under the influence of his cheerfulness. They knew his open-handedness; and half an hour later the invalid doctor from Hamburg, who lived on the top floor, was looking enviously out of the window at the jolly party of healthy Russians gathered under the chestnut tree. Beneath the trembling circles of shadow from the leaves, at one end of a table covered with a white cloth and set with coffee-pot, bread-and-butter, cheese, and cold game, sat the princess in a high cap with lilac ribbons, handing out cups of coffee and sandwiches. At the other end sat the prince, eating heartily, and talking loudly and merrily. The prince had spread out in front of him his purchases: carved boxes, little ornaments, paper-knives of all kinds, of which he had bought a heap at every watering-place, and was giving them away to everybody, including Lieschen, the servant-girl, and the landlord, with whom he jested in his comically bad German, assuring him that it was not the waters that had cured Kitty but his splendid cooking, especially his prune soup. The princess laughed at her husband for his Russian ways but was more lively and gay than she had been all the time at the spa. The colonel smiled, as he always did, at the prince's jokes; but when it came to Europe, of which he believed himself to be making a careful study, he sided with the princess. The simple-hearted Maria Yevgenyevna shook with laughter at everything absurd the prince said, and even Varenka succumbed to helpless but infectious laughter at his jokes, which was something Kitty had never seen before.

Kitty was glad of all this but she could not be light-hearted. She could not solve the problem her father had unconsciously set her by his jocular view of her friends and of the life that had so attracted her. To this problem was added the change in her relations with the Petrovs, which had been so conspicuously and unpleasantly marked that morning. Everybody was gay, but Kitty could not feel gay and this increased her distress. She felt the feeling she had known in childhood, when she had been shut in her room as a punishment and had heard her sisters' happy laughter outside.

'Now what made you buy all those things?' asked the princess, smiling and handing her husband a cup of coffee.

'Well, one goes for a walk, looks in a shop, and they ask you to buy something. It's *"Erlaucht, Excellenz, Durchlaucht."* By the time they get to *"Durchlaucht"* I can't hold out any longer and ten thalers are gone.'

'It's only because you are bored,' said the princess.

'Of course it is! The time hangs so heavy, my dear, that one doesn't know what to do with oneself.'

'How can you be bored, Prince? There is so much that is interesting in Germany now,' said Maria Yevgenyevna.

'Yes, I know all that is interesting: prune soup and pea-sausages, I know. I know them all.'

'No, say what you like, Prince, there's the interest of their institutions,' said the colonel.

'What is there interesting about them? They are so mighty self-satisfied. They've conquered the world. Tell me what there is for me to be pleased about in that? I haven't conquered anybody; here I'm obliged to take off my own boots, yes, and put them outside the door myself, too. In the morning I have to get up and dress at once and go to the dining-room to drink execrable tea! How different it is at home! There you can wake up when you please, get a bit cross about something, grumble a bit, recover yourself properly and turn things over in your mind. You've no need to hurry about anything.'

'But time's money; you forget that,' said the colonel.

'It all depends! There are times when one would give a whole month for sixpence and others when you wouldn't sell half-an-hour at any price. Isn't that so, Katinka? What is the matter – why are you so quiet?'

'I'm all right.'

'Where are you off to? Stay a little longer,' he said to Varenka.

'I must get home,' said Varenka, getting up and again subsiding into a giggle. When she had recovered, she said good-bye and went into the house for her hat.

Kitty followed her. Even Varenka seemed different now. She was not less good, but different from what she had imagined her before.

'Oh dear, I haven't laughed like that for a long time!' said Varenka, gathering up her parasol and her bag. 'What a dear your father is!'

Kitty was silent.

'When shall I see you?' asked Varenka.

'*Maman* was going to call in on the Petrovs. You won't be there?' said Kitty, trying to sound Varenka.

'Oh, yes, I shall,' answered Varenka. 'They're getting ready to go away, so I promised to help them pack.'

'Well, I'll come too, then.'

'No; why should you?'

'Why not? Why not? Why not?' Kitty broke out, opening her eyes wide and clutching at Varenka's parasol to prevent her going. 'No, wait a moment; tell me why not.'

'Oh, nothing. Your father has come, and besides, they feel awkward with you.'

'No, tell me why you don't want me to be often at the Petrovs'. You don't want me to, do you? Why?'

'I didn't say that,' replied Varenka quietly.

'No, please tell me!'

'Tell you everything?' asked Varenka.

'Everything, everything!' Kitty assented.

'Well, there's really nothing special to tell; only that Mihail Alexeyevich' – (that was Petròv's name) – 'had meant to leave earlier and now he doesn't want to go away,' said Varenka, smiling.

'Well, go on!' urged Kitty, looking darkly at Varenka.

'Well, and for some reason Anna Pavlovna told him he didn't want to go because you are here. Of course that was nonsense; but there was a quarrel over it – over you. And you know how irritable these sick people are.'

Kitty, frowning more than ever, kept silent, and only Varenka spoke, trying to soften and soothe her, and seeing a storm gathering – of tears or words, she did not know which.

'So you'd better not go. ... And you understand? You won't be offended? ...'

'It serves me right! It serves me right!' said Kitty quickly, snatching the parasol out of Varenka's hand and looking past her friend's eyes.

Varenka felt like smiling at her friend's childish fury but she was afraid of wounding her.

'How does it serve you right? I don't understand,' she said.

'It serves me right because it was all sham; because it was all artificial and did not come from my heart. What business had I to interfere with others? And now it's come about that I am the cause of a quarrel and that I've been doing what nobody asked me to do. Because it was all a sham, a sham, a sham! ...'

'A sham? But with what object?' asked Varenka gently.

'Oh, it's so idiotic! So hateful! There was no need whatever for me to. ... Nothing but sham!' she said, opening and shutting the parasol.

'But with what object?'

'To appear better to people, to myself, to God – to deceive everyone. No, I won't descend to that again! I'll be bad; but at any rate not a liar, a humbug!'

'But who is a humbug?' said Varenka reproachfully. 'You speak as if ...'

But Kitty was in one of her gusts of fury. She would not allow Varenka to finish.

'I am not talking about you, not about you at all. You are perfection. Yes, yes, I know you are all perfection; but how can I help it if I am wicked? This would never have happened if I weren't wicked. So let me be what I am, but I won't be a sham. What is Anna Pavlovna to me? Let them go their way and me go mine. I can't be different. ... And yet it's not that, it's not that.'

'What is not that?' asked Varenka in bewilderment.

'Everything. I can't act except from the heart, but you act from principle. I liked you simply, but you most likely only wanted to save me, to improve me.'

'You are unfair,' said Varenka.

'But I am not speaking of other people: I'm speaking of myself.'

'Kitty!' called her mother's voice. 'Come here and show Papa your necklace.'

Kitty took the necklace in its little box from the table and with a haughty air, without having made it up with her friend, went to her mother.

'What is the matter? Why are you so flushed?' her mother and father said to her with one voice.

'Nothing,' she replied. 'I will be back in a moment,' and she ran into the house again.

'She is still here,' she thought. 'What am I to say to her? Oh dear, what have I done, what have I said? Why was I rude to her? What am I to do? What am I to say to her?' thought Kitty, and stopped at the door.

Varenka, with her hat on, was sitting at the table, examining the spring of her parasol which Kitty had broken. She lifted her head.

'Varenka, forgive me, do forgive me!' whispered Kitty, going up to her. 'I don't remember what I said. I ...'

'I really didn't mean to upset you,' said Varenka, smiling.

Peace was made. But with her father's coming all the world in which she had been living was completely changed for Kitty. She did not give up everything she had learned, but she realized that she had deceived herself in supposing she could be what she wanted to be. Her eyes were opened, as it were; she felt without hypocrisy or boastfulness all the difficulty of maintaining herself on the pinnacle to which she had wished to rise. Moreover, she became aware of all the dreariness of the world of sorrow, of sick and dying people, in which she had been living. The efforts she had made to like it seemed intolerable to her now and she longed to get back quickly into the fresh air, to Russia, to Yergushovo, where, as she knew from letters, her sister Dolly had already moved with the children.

But her affection for Varenka did not wane. When she said goodbye, Kitty begged her to come and stay with them in Russia.

'I'll come when you get married,' said Varenka.

'I shall never marry.'

'Well, then, I shall never come.'

'Well, then, I will marry just for that. Mind now, remember your promise!' said Kitty.

The doctor's prediction was fulfilled. Kitty returned home to Russia cured. She was not so carefree and light-hearted as before, but she was at peace. The misery she had felt in Moscow had become only a memory to her.

PART THREE

I

SERGEI IVANICH KOZNYSHEV wanted a rest from intellectual work and, instead of going abroad as he usually did, he arrived at his brother's house in the country towards the end of May. In his judgement the best sort of life was a country life. He had come now to enjoy such a life at his brother's. Constantine Levin was very glad to have him, especially as he did not expect his brother Nikolai that summer. But in spite of his affection and respect for Sergei Ivanich, Constantine Levin was uncomfortable with his brother in the country. His brother's attitude to the country made him uncomfortable and positively irritated him. To Constantine Levin the country was the background of life – that is to say, the place where one rejoiced, suffered, and laboured; but to Koznyshev the country meant on one hand rest from work, on the other a valuable antidote to the corrupt influences of town, which he took with satisfaction and a sense of its efficacy. To Levin beyond all the country was good because it was the scene of labour, of the usefulness of which there could be no doubt. To Koznyshev the country was particularly good because there one could and should do nothing. And then, Koznyshev's attitude to the peasants jarred on Levin. Koznyshev was wont to say that he knew and liked the peasantry, and he often chatted to the peasants – which he did very well, without affectation or condescension – and from every such conversation he would deduce general conclusions in favour of the peasantry and in confirmation of his knowing them. Levin did not like this kind of attitude to the peasants. He regarded the peasant merely as the chief partner in their common labour, and in spite of all the respect and the affection that was in his blood for the peasant (imbibed probably, as he said himself, with the milk of his peasant nurse), he, as partner in their common labour, while sometimes enthusiastic over the strength, gentleness, and fairness of these men, was often, when their common labours called for other qualities, exasperated with the peasant for his carelessness, dirt, drunkenness, and lying. If he had been asked whether he liked the peasants, Levin would certainly not have known what to answer. He both liked and did not like the peasants, just as he liked and did not like men in general. Of course, being a good-hearted person, he liked people rather than disliked them, and so, too, with the peasants. But like or dislike 'the people' as something apart he could not, not only because he lived among them and all his interests were bound up with theirs but also because he regarded himself as part of 'the people', did not see any special qualities or failings distinguishing himself from 'the people', and could not contrast himself with them. Moreover, though he had lived so long in the closest relations with the peasants, as their master, arbitrator, and, what was more, adviser (the peasants trusted him and would come from thirty miles around to consult him), he had no definite views concerning them, and would have been as much at a loss to answer the question whether he knew 'the people' as the question whether he liked them. For him to say that he knew the peasants would have been the same as to say he knew men. He was always observing and getting to know people of all sorts, peasants among them, whom he considered as good, interesting people, and he was continually discovering new traits in them and altering his opinions accordingly. With Koznyshev it was quite the reverse. Just as he liked and praised a country life as opposed to the life he did not like, so he liked the peasantry as opposed to the class of men he did not like, and so, too, he knew the peasantry as something distinct from and opposed to men generally. His methodical mind had formulated definite ideas about peasant life, deduced partly from that life itself but chiefly from contrast with other modes of life. He never altered his opinions about the peasantry or his sympathetic attitude towards them.

In the discussions which took place between the brothers on their views of the peasantry, Koznyshev was always victorious, precisely because he had definite ideas about the peasant – his character, his qualities, and his tastes – while Levin had no definite and fixed views on the subject, and so in their arguments Levin was readily convicted of contradicting himself.

Koznyshev thought his younger brother a capital fellow, *with his heart in the right place* (as he expressed it in French), but with a mind, though fairly quick, apt to be swayed by the impressions of the moment and consequently full of contradictions. With an elder brother's condescension, he would sometimes try to explain to him the true import of things but he derived little satisfaction from arguing with him because he got the better of him too easily.

Levin regarded his brother as a man of vast intellect and culture, as generous in the highest sense of the word and endowed with a special faculty for working for the public good. But in the depths of his heart, the older he grew and the more intimately he knew his brother, the oftener the thought struck him that this faculty for working for the public good, of which he felt himself completely devoid, was perhaps not so much a quality as a lack of something – not a lack of kindly honesty and noble desires and tastes but a lack of the vital force, of what is called heart, of the impulse which drives a man to choose some one out of all the innumerable paths of life and to care for that one only. The better he knew his brother, the more he noticed that Koznyshev, and many other people who worked for the welfare of the public, were not led by an impulse of the heart to care for the public good, but had reasoned out in their minds that it was a right thing to take interest in public affairs, and consequently took interest in them. Levin was confirmed in this supposition by observing that his brother did not take questions affecting the public welfare, or the question of the immortality of the soul, a bit more to heart than he did chess problems or the ingenious design of a new machine.

Another thing which made Levin feel ill at ease with his brother was that in the country, in summer especially, Levin was continually busy with the farm, and the long summer day was not long enough to get through all there was to do, while Koznyshev was taking a holiday. But though he was taking a holiday now – that is to say, he was doing no writing – he was so used to intellectual activity that he liked to put into concise and elegant shape the ideas which occurred to him, and to have someone to listen to him. His most usual and natural listener was his brother. And so, in spite of the friendliness and directness of their relations, Levin felt uncomfortable at leaving him alone. Koznyshev liked to stretch himself on the grass in the sun, basking and chatting lazily.

'You can't imagine what a joy this rural laziness is to me,' he would say to his brother. 'Not the trace of an idea in one's brain, as empty as a drum!'

But Levin found it tedious to sit and listen to him, especially when he knew that in his absence they would be carting manure on to fields not ploughed ready for it and heaping it all anyhow if he were not there to see; and they would not screw the shares in the ploughs, but let them come off, and then tell him that the new ploughs were a silly invention and there was nothing like the old peasant plough, and so on.

'Haven't you done enough trudging about in the heat?' Koznyshev would say to him.

'No, I must just run round to the office for a minute,' Levin would answer, and he would run off to the fields.

2

EARLY in June it happened that Agatha Mihalovna, Levin's old nurse and housekeeper, slipped as she was carrying to the cellar a jar of mushrooms she had just pickled, and fell and sprained her wrist. The district doctor, a talkative young man who had only just qualified, came to see her. He examined the wrist, said it was not dislocated, and applied fomentations. He stayed to dinner, evidently delighted to have a chance of talking to the celebrated Sergei Ivanich Koznyshev and, to show off his enlightened views, told him all the scandal of the country-side, complaining of the poor state into which the District Council had fallen. Koznyshev listened attentively, asked questions, and, roused by a new listener, talked fluently and made some keen and weighty observations, which were respectfully appreciated by the young doctor, and was soon in that eager frame of mind his brother knew so well, which generally followed a brilliant and lively conversation. After the young doctor's departure, Koznyshev said he would like to go to the river with a line. He was fond of angling and seemed proud of being able to like such a stupid occupation.

Levin, whose presence was needed in the plough-land and the meadows, offered to drive his brother in the trap.

It was the time of year – the turn of the summer – when the crops of the present year are assured and the farmer begins to think about sowing for next year, and the mowing is at hand; when the grey-green rye waves yet unswollen ears lightly in the wind; when the green oats, interspersed with tufts of yellow grass, droop irregularly over the late-sown fields; when the early buckwheat spreads out and hides the ground; when the fallow-land, trodden hard as stone by the cattle, is half-ploughed, leaving long strips untouched by the plough; when the fields smell night and morning of dried heaps of manure mingled with the honeyed perfume of the grasses; and the lowland meadows, waiting for the scythe, stretch vigilant as the sea, with here and there blackening heaps of weeded sorrel-stalks.

It was the time of that brief lull in the toil of the fields before the harvest, that great yearly event that strains every nerve of the peasants. The crops promised to be superb and the clear, hot days were followed by short, dewy nights.

The brothers had to drive through the woods to reach the meadows. Koznyshev kept going into raptures over the beauty of the woods, which were a tangled mass of foliage, pointing out to his brother first an old lime-tree, looking so dark on the shady side, covered with yellow stipules, and ready to burst into flower; then the brilliant emerald-green of this year's saplings. Levin did not like talking and hearing about the beauty of nature. Words for him detracted from the beauty of what he saw. He assented to what his brother said, but could not help beginning to think of other things. When they came out of the woods all his attention was engrossed by the sight of the fallow-land on the slope of a hill, yellow with grass or trampled and chequered with furrows, in some parts dotted with heaps of manure, or even ploughed. A string of carts was moving across the field. Levin counted the carts and was pleased that all that were wanted were being brought, and at the sight of the meadows his thoughts passed to mowing. A special feeling of exhilaration always came over him at the hay-making. When they reached the meadow Levin stopped the horse.

The morning dew still lingered at the roots of the thick undergrowth of grass, and Koznyshev, afraid of getting his feet wet, asked his brother to drive him across the meadow to the willow clump near which carp were caught. Although Levin was sorry to crush his grass, he drove across the meadow. The tall grass twisted lightly round the wheels and the horse's legs, leaving seeds on the wet hubs and spokes of the wheels.

His brother sat down under a bush, arranging his tackle, while Levin led the horse away, tethered her and stepped into the vast grey-green sea of grass, unruffled by the wind. The silky grass with its ripe seeds reached almost to his waist in places where the meadow had been flooded in spring.

Crossing the meadow, Levin came out on to the road and met an old man with a swollen eye, carrying a swarm of bees in a skep.

'What, found one, Fomich?' he asked.

'Found one indeed, Constantine Mitrich! All we can do to keep our own! This is the second time a swarm has got away. Luckily the lads caught them. They were ploughing your field. They unharnessed a horse and galloped after them …'

'Well, what do you say, Fomich? Shall we start mowing, or wait a bit?'

'What's that? Our way's to wait till St Peter's Day. But you always mow earlier. Why not, God willing? The hay's fine. There'll be more room for the cattle.'

'And what about the weather?'

'That's in the Lord's hands. Maybe it will keep fine.'

Levin went back to his brother. Koznyshev had caught nothing, but he was not bored and seemed in the best of spirits. Levin saw that he had been stimulated by his conversation with the doctor and now wanted to talk. Levin, on the other hand, was impatient to get home to give orders for collecting the mowers for next day and to set at rest his doubts about the hay-making, which was much on his mind.

'Well, let's be going,' he said.

'What is the hurry? Let's sit here a little. How wet you are, though! Even though nothing bites, it is pleasant here. Any kind of sport is good that brings you in touch with nature. Look how lovely this steely water is!' he said. 'These grassy banks always remind me of that riddle – do you know it? The grass says to the water: we quiver and we quiver.'

'I don't know that riddle,' answered Levin wearily.

3

'Do you know, I've been thinking about you,' said Koznyshev. 'From what the doctor told me – and he's no fool – what goes on round here seems pretty bad. I've told you all along and I say it again: it is wrong of you not to go to the meetings and altogether keep out of *Zemstvo* activities. If decent people stop away, of course it's bound not to go right. We pay the money and it all goes in salaries, and there are no schools, no district nurses, no midwives, no dispensaries – nothing!'

'I did try, you know,' Levin replied slowly and unwillingly, 'but I just can't, and so there's no help for it.'

'Why can't you? I confess I can't make it out. It can't be indifference or incapacity: surely it's not simply laziness?'

'None of those things. I have tried, and I see I can do nothing,' said Levin.

He was not paying much attention to what his brother was saying. Scanning the ploughland on the other side of the river, he discerned something black but could not distinguish whether it was a horse or the bailiff on horseback.

'Why is it you can do nothing? You made an attempt and because it did not turn out to your satisfaction, you give up. I wonder you haven't more self-respect!'

'Self-respect?' said Levin, stung by his brother's words; 'I don't see what that has to do with it. If they'd told me at college that other men understood the integral calculus, and I didn't, that would have touched my self-respect. But in this case one wants first to be convinced that one has the necessary ability and, above all, that the business is of some particular importance.'

'What! Do you mean to say it is not important?' said Koznyshev, nettled that his brother should regard as unimportant something that interested him, and still more that he was obviously only half listening.

'I don't think it important. Say what you like, it does not interest me,' answered Levin, now certain that what he saw was the bailiff, who seemed to be taking the peasants off the ploughing, for they were turning the ploughs over. 'Can they really have finished ploughing already?' he wondered.

'Listen to me now,' continued the elder brother, with a frown on his handsome, clever face, 'there's a limit to everything. It's all very well to be original and outspoken and to dislike everything conventional – I know all about that; but really what you are saying either has no sense in it or very bad sense. How can you think it a matter of no importance whether the peasant, whom you love, so you say …'

'I never said any such thing,' thought Levin.

'– dies without help? Ignorant peasant-women starve their children and the people are steeped in ignorance, at the mercy of every village clerk, while it is in your power to remedy it all, yet you don't help because you don't consider it worth while.'

And Koznyshev confronted his brother with a dilemma: 'Either you are so undeveloped that you can't see all that you could do, or you won't sacrifice your ease, your vanity, or whatever it is, to do it.'

Levin felt that there was nothing for it but to submit, or own to a lack of zeal for the common good. And this mortified him and hurt his feelings.

'It's both,' he said resolutely. 'I don't see that it is possible ...'

'What? Not possible to provide medical aid, if the money were properly laid out?'

'It seemed impossible to me. ... For the three thousand square miles of our district, what with the deep slush when the snow starts melting, our snow-storms, and the pressure of work at busy seasons, I don't see how it is possible to provide a public medical service. And besides, I have no great faith in medicine anyway.'

'Come now, that's not fair! ... I could quote you thousands of instances. ... And how about schools?'

'Schools? What for?'

'What do you mean? Can there be two opinions on the advantage of education? If it's a good thing for you, it's a good thing for everyone.'

Levin felt himself morally pinned against a wall, and so he flew into a passion and involuntarily blurted out the main reason for his indifference to social questions.

'All this may be a good thing; but why should I bother myself about establishing dispensaries which I should never make use of, and schools to which I should never send my children, to which the peasants would not want to send theirs either – and to which I am not at all sure they ought to send them?' he said.

This unexpected view of the matter took Koznyshev by surprise for a minute; but he promptly formed a new plan of attack.

He paused in silence, drew out his line, cast it again, and then turned to his brother with a smile.

'Now let's see. ... In the first place, there is need of a dispensary. We had this very day to send for the district doctor for Agatha Mihalovna.'

'And I fancy her hand will stay crooked all the same.'

'That remains to be seen. ... Next, a peasant who can read and write is more useful to you and is worth more.'

'Not at all! Ask anyone you like,' replied Levin decidedly. 'A peasant who can read and write is far worse as a labourer. And mending the high-roads is an impossibility; and as soon as a bridge is put up it's stolen.'

'However, all that's not the point,' frowned Koznyshev, who did not like to be contradicted, especially when he was met with arguments that continually shifted their ground, introducing new considerations without the slightest relevance, so that there was no knowing which to answer first. 'Listen. Do you admit that education is a good thing for the people?'

'I do,' said Levin unguardedly, and at once realized that he had said what he did not think. He felt that, since he made this admission, it would be proved to him that he was talking meaningless nonsense. How it would be proved he did not know; but he knew that it certainly would be proved logically to him, and he awaited the proofs.

The argument turned out to be far simpler than Levin had anticipated.

'If you admit it to be a good thing,' said Koznyshev, 'then, as an honest man, you cannot help caring about it and sympathizing with the idea, and so wishing to work for it.'

'But I am not yet prepared to say that it is a good thing,' objected Levin, reddening a little.

'What! Why you said just now ...'

'I mean, I don't admit its being good or practical.'

'You cannot tell without having tried it.'

'Well, supposing that's so,' said Levin, though he did not suppose so at all – 'supposing that is so, still I don't see why I should be bothered with it.'

'Not bothered with it?'

'No; but since we have started on the subject, perhaps you had better explain it to me from the philosophical point of view,' said Levin.

'I don't see what philosophy has to do with it,' observed Koznyshev in a tone, Levin fancied, as though he did not admit his brother's right to talk about philosophy. And this irritated Levin.

'I'll tell you, then,' he began with heat. 'I believe the mainspring of all our actions is, after all, self-interest. Now I, as a nobleman, see nothing in our local institutions that could contribute to my prosperity. The roads are not better and could not be better; besides, my horses carry me well enough over bad ones. Doctors and dispensaries are no use to me. An arbitrator of disputes is no use to me – I never have applied to him and don't expect to. I not only do not require schools: they would even do me harm, as I have explained. To me the *Zemstvo* means nothing but a tax of three-halfpence an acre, my having to spend a night in town eaten by bugs and listening to rubbish and loathsomeness of every kind; and my personal interests do not prompt me to it!'

'One moment,' interrupted Koznyshev with a smile. 'It was not self-interest that induced us to work for the emancipation of the serfs, but we did work for it.'

'No!' Levin broke in with still greater heat. 'The emancipation of the serfs was quite a different matter. There self-interest did come in. We longed to throw off that yoke that crushed all decent people alike. But to be a town councillor and discuss how many dustmen are needed, and how the drains should be laid in a town in which I don't live – to serve on a jury and try a peasant who's stolen a flitch of bacon, and listen for six hours on end to all the nonsense jabbered by counsel and prosecutor and hear the president ask my half-witted old Alioshka, "Prisoner in the dock, do you plead guilty to the indictment of having removed the bacon?" "Eh-h-h?"'

Quite carried away, Levin began mimicking the president and the half-witted Alioshka: it seemed to him that it was all to the point.

But Koznyshev shrugged his shoulders.

'Well, what do you mean to say, then?'

'I simply mean to say that those rights which touch me … my personal interests, I shall always defend to the best of my ability; that when the police came and searched us students and read our letters, I was ready to defend to the last drop of my blood my right to education and liberty. I can understand compulsory military service which affects my children, my brothers, and myself; I am ready to discuss what concerns me; but deliberate on how to spend forty thousand roubles of district council money, or try the village idiot Alioshka – I neither understand nor can take part in it.'

Levin's words came pouring out as if the floodgates of his speech had burst open. Koznyshev smiled.

'And suppose you were to be arrested to-morrow: would you rather be tried in the old criminal tribunal?'

'I'm not going to be tried. I am not going to cut anyone's throat, so I've no need to be tried. Do you know what' – he went on, flying off again to something quite beside the point – 'our district self-government and all the rest of it put me in mind of the little birch branches we stick in the ground on Trinity Sunday to look like a copse which has grown up of itself in Europe, and I can't for the life of me gush over those birch branches and believe in them.'

Koznyshev only shrugged his shoulders, as much as to say that he really could not see how birch branches came into their discussion, although he had at once grasped what his brother meant.

'Oh, come; one really can't argue in that way,' he observed.

But Levin was anxious to justify himself for the failing, of which he was conscious – his indifference to the general welfare – and he went on:

'I believe that no sort of activity is likely to be lasting if it is not based on self-interest. That is a universal principle, a philosophical principle,' he said, emphasizing the word *philosophical*, as though wishing to show that he had as much right as anyone else to talk of philosophy.

Koznyshev smiled again. 'He, too, has a philosophy of his own at the service of his natural tendencies,' he thought.

'You had better leave philosophy out of it,' he said. 'The great task of philosophy has always, in all ages, been to find the essential link existing between individual and social interests. But that is not the point, though I have a word or two to say about your comparison. The birches are not simply stuck in: some of them are planted, and others are sown and have to be tended more carefully. It's only those peoples that have an intuitive sense of what is of importance and significance in their institutions, and know how to value them, that have a future before them – it's only those peoples that can be called historical.'

And to prove the error of Levin's views Koznyshev carried the discussion into the regions of philosophical history, which was beyond Levin's reach.

'As for your dislike of it, excuse my saying so, that's simply our Russian indolence and fastidiousness, and I'm convinced that in your case it's a temporary error and will pass.'

Levin was silent. He felt himself routed on all sides, but he felt all the same that what he wanted to say was unintelligible to his brother. Only he could not make up his mind whether it was unintelligible because he was not capable of expressing his meaning clearly, or because his brother would not or could not understand him. But he did not pursue the speculation and, without replying, fell to musing on a quite different and personal matter.

Koznyshev wound up the last line, untied the horse, and they drove back.

4

THE personal matter that absorbed Levin during his conversation with his brother was this: the year before, during hay-making, he had lost his temper with the bailiff, and to calm himself had had recourse to a remedy of his own – he had taken a scythe from one of the peasants and himself started to mow.

He had enjoyed the work so much that he had several times tried his hand at mowing since. He had cut the whole of the meadow in front of the house, and this year ever since the early spring he had cherished a plan for mowing with the peasants for whole days together. Since his brother's arrival, however, he had been hesitating whether to go mowing or not. He did not like to leave his brother alone for days on end, and he was afraid his brother would laugh at him. But walking across the meadow he recalled the impressions mowing had made on him and almost decided that he would go. After his irritating conversation with his brother, he again remembered this intention.

'I must have some physical exercise, or my temper will certainly go to pieces,' he thought, and determined to do some mowing, however awkward he might feel about it with his brother or the peasants.

Towards evening Levin went to the office and gave orders about the work, sending round the village to summon the mowers for next day to cut the hay in Kalinov meadow, the largest and best of his grass-lands.

'And send my scythe, please, to Titus for him to set, and tell him to bring it round to-morrow. I may do some mowing myself,' he said, trying not to be embarrassed.

The bailiff smiled and said, 'Very well, sir.'

At tea that evening Levin said to his brother:

'It looks as if the weather will last; to-morrow we begin mowing.'

'It is work I like very much,' said Koznyshev.

'I am terribly fond of it. I have mown with the peasants now and then, and to-morrow I want to try mowing the whole day.'

Koznyshev looked up at his brother with interest.

'How do you mean? Just like one of the peasants, all day long?'

'Yes, it's very enjoyable,' said Levin.

'It is a splendid form of exercise, only you'll hardly be able to stand it,' said Koznyshev, without a hint of irony.

'I've tried it. At first it's hard work but afterwards you get into it. I dare say I shall manage to keep up ...'

'Really, what an idea! But tell me, how do the peasants look at it? They must laugh up their sleeves at their master's being such a queer fish?'

'No, I don't think so; but it's such jolly work, and at the same time so hard, that there is no time for thinking.'

'But how can you have your dinner with them? You could hardly have turkey and a bottle of Lafitte brought to you in the field.'

'No, I shall come home when they knock off for their noonday rest.'

Next morning Levin got up earlier than usual, but giving directions on the farm delayed him, and when he reached the meadow the men were already at their second row.

From the hill he could get a view below of the shady part of the field that had been cut, with the greyish ridges of mown grass and dark piles of coats thrown down by the mowers when they started mowing.

Gradually, as he rode nearer, the peasants came into sight, some with coats on, some in their shirts, following one behind another in a long string, each swinging his scythe in his own manner. He counted forty-two of them.

They moved slowly over the uneven, low-lying part of the meadow, where there had been an old dam. Levin recognized some of his own men. There was old Yermil in a very long white smock, bending forward to swing his scythe; there was a young fellow, Vaska, who had been a coachman of Levin's, going for every swath with all his might; and Titus, too, who had taught Levin to scythe, a thin little peasant, walking erect in front and cutting a wide swath, wielding his scythe as though it were a toy.

Levin dismounted and, tethering his horse by the roadside, went up to Titus, who fetched a second scythe out of a bush and gave it to him.

'Here it is, master; 'tis sharp as a razor, cuts of itself,' said Titus, taking off his cap and smiling as he handed the implement.

Levin took the scythe and began trying it. As they finished their rows, the peasants, perspiring and good-humoured, came out into the road one after another and, laughing a little, greeted their master. They all stared at him but no one made any remark, till a tall old man with a wrinkled, beardless face, wearing a sheepskin jacket, stepped out on to the road and addressed him.

'Look'ee now, master; once take hold of the rope there's no letting go!' he said, and Levin heard smothered laughter among the mowers.

'I'll try not to let go,' he said, taking his place behind Titus and waiting for the signal to begin.

'Mind'ee,' repeated the old man.

Titus made room and Levin started behind him. The grass was short close to the road, and Levin, who had not done any mowing for a long time and was disconcerted by so many eyes upon him, mowed badly at first, though he swung his scythe with vigour. He heard voices behind him:

'The handle's not right; it's too high; look how he has to stoop,' said one.

'Ought to press more on the heel,' said another.

'Never mind, it's all right – he'll get into it,' said the old man. 'Off you go. ... You swing it too wide, you'll tire yourself out. ... Doesn't matter how he does it, he's the master; he's working for himself! But look at that one! Us fellows would catch it for that!'

They came to softer grass, and Levin, listening without answering, followed Titus, trying to mow as well as possible. They advanced a hundred paces. Titus kept on, without stopping or showing the slightest sign of fatigue; but Levin was already beginning to be dreadfully afraid he would not be able to keep up: he felt so tired.

He swung his scythe, using the last ounce of his strength, and was making up his mind to ask Titus to stop. But at that very moment Titus stopped of his own accord, bent down and picked up a handful of grass, wiped his scythe, and began whetting it. Levin straightened his back and looked round with a sigh of relief. The peasant behind him was still mowing and evidently he, too, was tired, for he stopped without coming even with Levin, and started to whet his scythe. Titus sharpened his blade and Levin's, and they went on.

The same thing happened the next time. Titus moved on with

sweep after sweep of his scythe, not stopping and not tiring. Levin followed, trying to keep up, and finding it harder and harder, until the moment came when he felt he had no strength left, but at that very moment Titus stopped and whetted the scythes.

So they finished the first row. And this long row seemed particularly hard work to Levin; but when the end was reached and Titus, with his scythe over his shoulder, turned about and slowly retraced his steps, placing his feet in the tracks left by his heels in the cut grass, and Levin walked back in the same way along his tracks, in spite of the large drops of sweat that rolled down his face and dripped from his nose, and though his back was as drenched as if he had been soaked in water, he felt very happy. What delighted him particularly was that now he knew he would be able to hold out.

His satisfaction was marred only by the fact that his row was not good. 'I must swing less with my arms and use my body more,' he thought, comparing Titus's swath, cut straight as a thread, with his own uneven and irregularly lying grass.

Levin noticed that Titus had mowed the first row specially quickly, probably to see what his master could do, and it happened to be a long one. The next rows were easier, but still Levin had to strain every nerve not to drop behind the peasants.

He thought of nothing, wished for nothing, except not to be left behind and to do his work as well as possible. He heard nothing save the swish of the knives, saw the receding upright figure of Titus in front of him, the crescent curve of the cut grass, the grass and flower-heads slowly and rhythmically falling about the blade of his scythe, and ahead of him the end of the row, where would come rest.

Suddenly, without understanding what it was or whence it came, in the midst of his toil, he felt a pleasant sensation of chill on his hot, perspiring shoulders. He glanced up at the sky while his scythe was being sharpened. A dark cloud was hanging low overhead and big drops of rain were falling. Some of the peasants went to put their coats on; others, like Levin, merely moved their shoulders up and down, enjoying the refreshing coolness.

Swath followed swath. They mowed long rows and short rows, good grass and poor grass. Levin lost all count of time and had no idea whether it was late or early. A change began to come over his work which gave him intense satisfaction. There were moments when he forgot what he was doing, he mowed without effort and his line was almost as smooth and good as Titus's. But as soon as he began thinking what he was doing and trying to do better, he was at once conscious how hard the task was, and would mow badly.

He finished yet another row and would have gone back again to begin the next but Titus stopped and went up to the old man and said something in a low voice. They both looked at the sun. 'What are they talking about, and why doesn't he start another row?' thought Levin. It did not occur to him that the peasants had been mowing for four hours on end and it was time for their breaskfast.

'Breakfast time, master,' said the old man.

'Already? All right, breakfast, then.'

Levin handed his scythe to Titus and together with the peasants, who were going to their coats for their bread, walked over the long stretch of mown grass, slightly spattered with rain, to his horse. Only then he suddenly awoke to the fact that he had been wrong about the weather and the rain was wetting his hay.

'The hay will be spoiled,' he said.

'It won't hurt, sir. Mow in the rain and you'll rake in the sun!' said the old man.

Levin untied his horse and rode home to his coffee.

Koznyshev had only just got out of bed. Before he had had time to dress and come to the dining-room, Levin had drunk his coffee and ridden back to the meadow.

5

AFTER breakfast Levin was not in the same place in the string of mowers as before, but found himself between the old man who had accosted him quizzically, and now invited him to be his neighbour, and a young peasant who had only been married in the autumn and who was mowing this summer for the first time.

The old man, holding himself erect, went in front, moving with long, regular strides, his feet turned out and swinging his scythe as precisely and evenly, and apparently as effortlessly, as a man swings his arms in walking. As if it were child's play, he laid the grass in a high, level ridge. It seemed as if the sharp blade swished of its own accord through the juicy grass.

Behind Levin came the lad Mishka. His pleasant, boyish face, with a twist of fresh grass bound round his hair, worked all the time with effort; but whenever anyone looked at him he smiled. He would clearly sooner die than own it was hard work for him.

Levin kept between them. In the very heat of the day the mowing did not seem such hard work. The perspiration with which he was drenched cooled him, while the sun, that burned his back, his head, and his arms, bare to the elbow, gave a vigour and dogged energy to his labour; and more and more often now came those moments of oblivion, when it was possible not to think of what one was doing. The scythe cut of itself. Those were happy moments. Still more delightful were the moments when they reached the river at the end of the rows and the old man would rub his scythe with a thick knot of wet grass, rinse the steel blade in the fresh water of the stream, ladle out a little in a tin dipper, and offer Levin a drink.

'What do you say to my home-brew, eh? Good, eh?' he would say with a wink.

And truly Levin had never tasted any drink so good as this warm water with bits of grass floating in it and a rusty flavour from the tin dipper. And immediately after this came the blissful, slow saunter, with his hand on the scythe, during which he could wipe away the streaming sweat, fill his lungs with air, and look about at the long line of mowers and at what was happening around in the forest and the country.

The longer Levin mowed, the oftener he experienced those moments of oblivion when it was not his arms which swung the scythe but the scythe seemed to mow of itself, a body full of life and consciousness of its own, and as though by magic, without a thought being given to it, the work did itself regularly and carefully. These were the most blessed moments.

It was only hard work when he had to interrupt this unconscious motion and think; when he had to mow round a hillock or a tuft of sorrel. The old man did this easily. When he came to a hillock he would change his action and go round the hillock with short strokes first with the point and then with the heel of the scythe. And while he did this he noted everything he came to: sometimes he would pick a wild berry and eat it, or offer it to Levin; sometimes he threw a twig out of the way with the point of the steel, or examined a quail's nest, from which the hen-bird flew up from right under the scythe; or caught a snake that crossed his path, lifting it on the scythe as though on a fork, showed it to Levin, and flung it away.

For both Levin and the young lad on the other side of him such changes of position were difficult. Repeating over and over again the same strained movement, they found themselves in the grip of feverish activity and were quite incapable of altering the motion of their bodies and at the same time observing what was before them.

Levin did not notice how time was passing. Had he been asked how long he had been working he would have answered, 'Half an hour' – and it was getting on for dinner-time. As they were walking back over the cut grass, the old man drew Levin's attention to the little girls and boys approaching from different sides, along the road and through the long grass – hardly visible above it – carrying the haymakers' pitchers of rye-beer stoppered with rags, and bundles of bread which dragged their little arms down.

'Look'ee, little lady-birds crawling along!' he said, pointing to them and glancing at the sun from under his hand.

They completed two more rows; the old man stopped.

'Come, master, dinner-time!' he said briskly. And on reaching the stream the mowers moved off across the cut grass towards their pile of coats, where the children who had brought their dinners sat waiting for them. The men who had driven from a distance gathered in the shadow of their carts; those who lived nearer went under a willow bush, over which they threw grass.

Levin sat down beside them; he did not want to go away.

All constraint in the presence of the master had disappeared long ago. The peasants began preparing for dinner. Some had a wash, the young lads bathed in the stream, others arranged places for their after-dinner rest, untied their bundles of bread and unstoppered their pitchers of rye-beer.

The old man crumbled up some bread in a cup, pounded it with the handle of a spoon, poured water on it from the dipper, broke up some more bread and, having sprinkled it with salt, turned to the east to say his prayer.

'Come, master, have some of my dinner,' he said, squatting on his knees in front of the cup.

The bread and water was so delicious that Levin changed his mind about going home. He shared the old man's meal and chatted to him about his family affairs, taking the keenest interest in them, and told him about his own affairs and all the circumstances that could be of interest to the old peasant. He felt much nearer to him than to his brother, and could not help smiling at the affection he felt for this man. When the old chap got up again, said his prayer, and lay down under a bush, putting some grass under his head for a pillow, Levin did the same and, in spite of the clinging flies that were so persistent in the sunshine and the insects that tickled his hot face and body, he fell asleep at once, and only woke when the sun had gone the other side of the bush and reached him. The old man had been awake some time and sat whetting the scythes of the younger lads.

Levin looked about him and hardly recognized the place, everything was so altered. A wide expanse of meadow was already mown and the sweet-smelling hay shone with a peculiar fresh glitter in the slanting rays of the evening sun. And the bushes by the river had been cut down, and the river itself, not visible before, its curves now gleaming like steel, and the peasants getting up and moving about, the steep wall of yet uncut grass, and the hawks hovering over the stripped meadow – all was completely new. Rousing himself, Levin began calculating how much had been done and how much more could still be done that day.

The forty-two men had got through a considerable amount. They had cut the whole of the big meadow, which used to take thirty men two days in the time of serf labour. Only the corners remained to be done, where the rows were short. But Levin wanted to get as much mowing done that day as possible, and was vexed with the sun for sinking so quickly. He did not feel the least bit tired and was only eager to go on and finish as much as he could.

'What do you think – could we do Mashkin hill to-day too?' he said to the old man.

'If God wills. The sun's getting low, though. Would there be a drop of vodka for the lads?'

About tea-time, when they were sitting down again and those who smoked were lighting their pipes, the old man told the men that there would be vodka if they mowed Mashkin hill.

'What, not mow that? Come on, Titus! We'll do it in no time! We can eat our fill after dark. Come on!' cried voices, and the mowers went back to work, eating up their bread as they went.

'Now then, lads, keep going!' said Titus, and ran on ahead almost at a trot.

'Get along, get along!' said the old man, hurrying after him and easily catching him up. 'I'll mow you down, you watch!'

And young and old mowed away, as if they were racing each other. Yet, however fast they worked, they did not spoil the grass and the swaths fell as neatly and exactly as before. The little patch left in the corner was whisked off in five minutes. The last of the mowers had scarcely finished their swaths before those in front had slung their coats over their shoulders and were crossing the road towards Mashkin hill.

The sun was already sinking into the trees when they entered the woody little ravine of Mashkin hill, their dippers rattling as they walked. The grass in the middle of the hollow was waist-high, tender, soft, and feathery, speckled here and there among the trees with wild pansies.

After a brief consultation – whether they should take the rows lengthwise or diagonally – Prohor Yermilin, also a renowned mower, a huge, black-haired peasant, went on ahead. He went up to the top, turned back again and started mowing, and they all proceeded to fall into line behind him, going downhill through the hollow and uphill right to the edge of the trees. The sun sank behind the forest. The dew was falling by now. The mowers were in the sun only on the ridge; below, where the mist was rising, and on the opposite side, they were in the fresh, dewy shade. The work progressed briskly.

The grass cut with a juicy sound and fell in high, fragrant rows. On the short rows the mowers bunched together, their tin dippers rattling, their scythes ringing when they touched, the whetstones whistling upon the blades, and their good-humoured voices resounding as they urged each other on.

Levin still kept between the young peasant and the old man. The old man, who had put on his sheepskin jacket, was just as jolly, chaffing, and free in his movements as before. In the wood their scythes were continually cutting birch-mushrooms, grown plump in the succulent grass. But the old man bent down every time he came across a mushroom, picked it up, and put it inside his smock. 'Another little treat for my old woman,' he said as he did so.

It was easy enough to mow the wet, soft grass but going up and down the steep slopes of the ravine was hard work. But this did not trouble the old man. Swinging his scythe just as usual, taking short, firm steps with feet shod in large plaited shoes, he climbed slowly up the slope, and though his whole frame and the breeches below his smock shook with effort, he did not miss one blade of grass or let a single mushroom escape him, and never ceased joking with the other peasants and Levin. Levin followed him and often thought he must fall, as he climbed up a steep cliff that would have been difficult going even without the scythe in his hand. But he managed to clamber up and do what he had to do. Some external force seemed to propel him on.

6

MASHKIN hill was mown, the last swath finished. The peasants put on their coats and were gaily trudging home. Levin got on his horse and, partingly regretfully from the mowers, rode homewards. On the hillside he looked back; he could not see them in the mist rising from the valley; he could only hear their rough, happy voices, boisterous laughter, and the sound of clanking scythes.

Koznyshev had long ago finished dinner and was drinking iced lemon and water in his own room, looking through the newspapers and magazines just arrived by post, when Levin burst in, his hair matted and sticking to his forehead and his back and chest grimed and moist.

'We've done the whole meadow!' he cried joyfully. 'Oh, it's so good! Marvellous! And how have you been getting on?' Levin had completely forgotten their disagreeable conversation of the previous day.

'Heavens! What a sight you are!' said Koznyshev, turning to his brother with a momentary look of disapproval. 'And the door, do shut the door!' he cried. 'You must have let in a dozen at least.'

Koznyshev could not bear flies and in his own room he never opened the window except at night, and carefully kept the door shut.

'Not one, I'll swear! But if I have, I'll catch them. You can't imagine how delightful it was! How did you spend the day?'

'Quite well. But have you really been mowing the whole day? You must be as hungry as a wolf. Kuzma has everything ready for you.'

'No, I don't want to eat. I had something there. But I'll go and wash.'

'Yes, go along, and I'll join you directly,' said Koznyshev, shaking

277

his head as he looked at his brother. 'Hurry up,' he added with a smile, and collecting up his books prepared to follow. He suddenly felt in good spirits, too, and disinclined to part from his brother. 'But what did you do while it was raining?'

'What rain was that? There was scarcely a drop. Well, I'll be back directly. So you had a nice day? That's capital.' And Levin went off to change his clothes.

Five minutes later the brothers met in the dining-room. Although Levin had fancied he was not hungry, and sat down to dinner simply not to hurt Kuzma's feelings, yet when he began eating everything struck him as extraordinarily appetizing. Koznyshev watched him with a smile.

'Oh, by the way, there's a letter for you,' he said. 'Kuzma, go and get it, please. And mind you shut the door.'

The letter was from Oblonsky. Levin read it aloud. Oblonsky wrote from Petersburg: 'I have had a letter from Dolly; she's at Yergushovo, and everything seems to have gone wrong there. Do please ride over and see her, and help her with your advice – you know all about it. She will be so glad to see you. She's quite alone, poor thing. My mother-in-law and the others are still abroad.'

'That's splendid! I will certainly go and see her,' said Levin. 'Or we could go together. She is such a nice person, don't you think?'

'It's not far from here, then?'

'About twenty-five miles. Or perhaps it's thirty. But a capital road. We could get there in no time.'

'I should like it very much,' said Koznyshev, still smiling. The sight of his younger brother had immediately put him in good humour.

'Well, you have an appetite!' he said, looking at his dark-red, sun-burnt face and neck bent over the plate.

'Haven't I? You would hardly believe how good this kind of thing is for every sort of foolishness. I am thinking of enriching medicine with a new term: *Arbeitskur* – health through work!'

'Well, certainly you don't need it much, it seems to me.'

'No, but those who suffer with their nerves do.'

'Yes, it ought to be tried. You know, I was coming to have a look at you mowing but it was so unbearably hot that I got no farther than the forest. I sat there a little while and then went on to the village, met your old nurse, and sounded her as to what the peasants think of you. As far as I could gather, they don't approve of your working in

278

the fields. "It's not work for the gentry," she said. Altogether, I fancy that the peasantry have very definite ideas as to what the gentry should and should not do. And they don't like the gentry moving outside the bounds they set for them.'

'It may be so; but I've never enjoyed anything more in my life. And there's no harm in it, you know. Is there?' replied Levin. 'I can't help it if they don't like it. And besides, I don't think it matters, do you?'

'Altogether,' pursued Koznyshev, 'I see you're satisfied with your day.'

'Quite satisfied! We cut the whole meadow. And I made friends with such a fine old man. You can't imagine what a delightful fellow he is!'

'Well, so you're content with your day. And so am I. First of all, I solved two chess problems – one is a beauty, it opens with a pawn. I must show you. And afterwards I thought over our conversation of yesterday.'

'Eh? Our conversation of yesterday?' said Levin, who had finished dinner and sat blissfully blinking and puffing, absolutely incapable of recalling what yesterday's conversation had been about.

'I came to the conclusion that you are partly right. Our difference of opinion amounts to this: that you make self-interest the mainspring, while I assume that interest in the common weal is bound to exist in every man with a certain degree of education. You may be right in thinking that activity with a material interest behind it would be preferable. Your nature is altogether too *primesautière*, as the French say: you must have intense, energetic action, or nothing.'

Levin listened to his brother and understood absolutely nothing and did not try to understand. He was only afraid his brother might ask him some question which would make it evident that he was not paying attention.

'That's what it is, my dear boy,' said Koznyshev, touching him on the shoulder.

'Yes, of course. But what does it matter? I don't insist on my view,' answered Levin, with a guilty, childlike smile. 'Whatever was it I was disputing about?' he wondered. 'Of course, I'm right, and he's right, and everything's excellent. Only I must go round to the office and see to things.' He stood up, stretching and smiling.

Koznyshev smiled too.

'If you want to take a turn, let's go out together,' he said, unwilling to be parted from his brother, who radiated freshness and energy. 'Come along! We could even call in at the office, if need be.'

'Oh, heavens!' exclaimed Levin so loudly that Koznyshev was startled.

'What is it? What is the matter?'

'How's Agatha Mihalovna's wrist?' said Levin, clapping his hand to his head. 'I had positively forgotten her.'

'It's much better.'

'Well, I'll run down to her all the same. I'll be back before you have time to get your hat on.'

And he ran downstairs, clattering his heels like a rattle.

7

OBLONSKY had gone to Petersburg to perform the most natural and essential duty – so familiar to everyone in Government service, yet so incomprehensible to outsiders, and neglect of which makes it impossible to be in Government service – the duty of reminding the ministry of his existence. And having, for the due performance of this rite, taken away with him practically all the money there was in the house, he was gaily and agreeably spending his days at the races and visiting at summer villas. Meanwhile Dolly and the children had moved into the country, to cut down expenses as much as possible. She had gone to Yergushovo, the estate that had been her dowry – the forest which had been sold in the spring had belonged to it. It was about thirty-five miles from Levin's Pokrovskoe.

The big old house at Yergushovo had been pulled down long ago and the old prince had had the lodge done up and built on to. Twenty years before, when Dolly was a child, the lodge had been roomy and comfortable, though, like all lodges, it stood sideways to the drive and did not face south. But now it was old and dilapidated. When Oblonsky had gone down in the spring to sell the forest, Dolly had begged him to look over the house and have the necessary repairs done. Oblonsky, like all unfaithful husbands, indeed, was very solicitous for his wife's comfort. He had looked over the house himself and given instructions about everything that he considered necessary. According to him it was necessary to re-cover all the furniture with new cretonne, put up curtains, weed the garden, build a little bridge by the pond, and plant flowers. But he forgot many other things which were essential, the want of which harassed Dolly later on.

Try as he would to be an attentive father and husband, he never could keep in his mind that he had a wife and children. He had bachelor tastes and understood no others. On his return to Moscow he told his wife with pride that he had seen to everything, that the house would be a little paradise, and that he strongly advised her to go. His wife's departure to the country suited Oblonsky in every way: it would be good for the children, it would cut down expenses, and it would leave him freer. Dolly regarded a move to the country for the summer as essential for the children, especially for the little girl, who was very slow in recovering after the scarlet fever; and also as a means of escaping the petty humiliations, the little bills owing to the wood-merchant, the fishmonger, the shoe-mender, which made her miserable. Besides this, she liked the idea of going away to the country because she hoped to entice her sister Kitty, who was to return from abroad at midsummer, and who had been ordered bathing, to join her. Kitty wrote from her watering-place that no prospect was so alluring as to spend the summer with Dolly at Yergushovo, full of childhood memories for both of them.

The first days Dolly found life in the country very difficult. She used to stay in the country as a child and the impression she had retained was of the country as a place of refuge from all the trials of town; that life there, if not luxurious (and Dolly was easily reconciled to that), was cheap and comfortable; that there was plenty of everything, everything was cheap and easy to get, and children were happy. But now, coming to the country as mistress of the house, she saw that it was all utterly unlike what she had fancied.

The day after their arrival it poured in torrents, and in the night the rain came through in the corridor and the nursery, so that the children's beds had to be carried into the drawing-room. There was no kitchen-maid to be found. Of the nine cows, according to the dairy-maid, some were about to calve, others had just calved for the first time, some were old and the rest hard-uddered, so there was scarcely enough butter or milk even for the children. There were no eggs. It was impossible to get any fowls and they were obliged to boil and roast tough, old, purplish roosters. No women to scrub the floors – they were all out in the potato-fields. Driving was out of the question because one of the horses was restive and bolted in the shafts. There was no place where they could bathe: the whole of the river-bank was trampled by the cattle and open to the road; even walks were impossible, for the cattle strayed into the garden through a gap in the hedge, and there was one terrible bull who bellowed and might therefore be expected to gore somebody. There were no proper cupboards for their clothes; such as there were would not shut at all, or else burst open when anyone passed. There were no pots or pans, no copper in the wash-house, and not even an ironing-board in the maids' room.

At first, instead of finding peace and rest, Dolly was driven to despair by what, from her point of view, were dreadful calamities. She bustled about and did her utmost but, feeling the hopelessness of the situation, had every minute to struggle with the tears that kept starting to her eyes. The bailiff, a retired sergeant, whom Oblonsky had taken a fancy to and promoted from hall-porter on account of his handsome and respectful appearance, showed no sympathy for his mistress's tribulations but simply said respectfully: 'It's no use, the peasants are such a wretched lot,' and did nothing to help her.

The position seemed hopeless. But in the Oblonskys' household, just as in all families, indeed, there was one inconspicuous yet most important and useful person – Matriona Filimonovna. She soothed her mistress, assured her that everything would *right itself* (it was her expression and Matvey had borrowed it from her), and set to work herself without hurry or fuss.

She had immediately made friends with the bailiff's wife, and on the very first day she drank tea with her and the bailiff under the acacias, and talked things over. Soon a sort of club was established under the acacias, consisting of the bailiff's wife, the village elder, and the clerk from the office; and there it was that the difficulties of existence were gradually smoothed away, so that within a week everything had in fact *righted itself*. The roof was mended, a kitchen-maid – a crony of the village elder's – was found, the cows began to give milk, the garden hedge was stopped up with stakes, the carpenter made a mangle, hooks were put in the cupboards and they ceased to burst open when not meant to, and an ironing-board covered with army cloth lay across the arm of a chair and the chest of drawers, and a smell of flat-irons soon pervaded the maids' room.

'There, you see! And you were quite in despair,' said Matriona Filimonovna, pointing to the ironing-board.

Even a bathing-hut was rigged up made of straw hurdles. Lily began to bathe, and part at least of Dolly's expectations were fulfilled, if not of a peaceful, at least of a comfortable life in the country. Peace with six children was next to impossible. One would fall ill, another would threaten to fall ill, a third would be without something necessary, a fourth would show symptoms of a bad disposition, and so on, and so on. Rare indeed were the brief intervals of peace. But these cares and anxieties were for Dolly the sole happiness possible. Had it not been for them, she would have been left alone to brood over her husband who did not love her. And besides, hard though it was for the mother to bear the dread of illness, the illnesses themselves and the grief of seeing signs of evil tendencies in her children – the children themselves were even now repaying her in small joys for her sufferings. Those joys were so small that they passed unnoticed, like gold in sand, and in trying moments she could see nothing but the pain, nothing but sand; but there were good moments, too, when she saw nothing but the joy, nothing but gold.

Now, in the solitude of the country, she began to be more and more frequently aware of these joys. Often, looking at them, she would make great efforts to persuade herself that she was mistaken, that, being their mother, she was prejudiced in their favour; all the same, she could not help saying to herself that she had charming children, all six of them in different ways, but a set of children such as is seldom met with, and she was happy in them and proud of them.

8

TOWARDS the end of May, when everything was more or less in order, she received a letter from her husband in answer to her complaints of the disorganized state of things in the country. He wrote asking her to forgive him for not having thought of everything, and promised to come down at the first opportunity. This opportunity did not present itself, and till the beginning of June Dolly stayed alone in the country.

On the Sunday before St Peter's Day, Dolly drove to Mass for all her children to take the sacrament. Dolly in her intimate, philosophical talks with her sister, her mother, and her friends often astonished them by the freedom of her views in regard to religion. She had a strange religion of transmigration of souls all her own, in which she had firm faith, troubling herself little about the dogmas of the Church. But in her family she was punctilious – not merely in order to set an example, but with her whole heart – about carrying out all that was required by the Church. She was genuinely concerned because the children had not been to communion for nearly a year. So, with the full approval and sympathy of Matriona Filimonovna, she resolved to take them now in the summer.

For several days before, Dolly was busy deliberating on how the children should be dressed. Frocks were made, or altered and washed, hems let down and gathers let out, buttons sewn on, and ribbons pressed. Only Tanya's frock, which the English governess had undertaken, caused Dolly much anxiety. The English governess in altering it had put the darts in the wrong place, cut the arm-holes too big, and altogether spoilt the dress. It was so tight across Tanya's shoulders that it was quite painful to look at her. But Matriona Filimonovna had the happy thought of putting in gussets and adding a little shoulder-cape to wear on top. The frock was set right, but there was nearly a quarrel with the English governess. However, on the morning everything was all right, and towards nine o'clock – the hour till which the priest had been asked to defer the service – the children in their new dresses, with beaming faces, stood on the steps before the carriage, waiting for their mother.

Instead of the restive Raven, the bailiff's horse Brownie had been harnessed, as a result of Matriona Filimonovna's intervention, and Dolly, delayed by anxiety over her own *toilette*, came out in a white muslin gown and took her seat in the carriage.

Dolly had done her hair and dressed with care and excitement. There was a time when she used to dress for her own sake to look pretty and be admired. Later on, as she got older, she took less and less pleasure in clothes: she saw that she was losing her good looks. But now she began to feel pleasure and interest in dress again. Now she did not dress for her own sake, not for the sake of her own beauty, but simply that as the mother of those charming children she might not spoil the general effect. And looking for the last time in the looking-glass she was satisfied with herself. She looked nice. Not nice in the way she used to wish to look nice in the old days at a ball, but nice for the object she now had in mind.

In the church there was no one except the peasants, the servants, and their women-folk. But Dolly saw, or fancied she saw, the admiration aroused by her children and herself. The children were not only lovely to look at in their fine clothes, but they were charming in the way they behaved. Aliosha, to be sure, did not stand very well: he kept turning round and trying to see the back of his jacket; but all the same he was wonderfully sweet. Tanya stood like a grown-up person, and looked after the little ones. And the smallest, Lily, was bewitching in her naïve wonder at everything, and it was difficult not to smile when, after taking the sacrament, she said in English, 'Please, some more.'

On the way home the children were very quiet, feeling that something solemn had happened.

All went well at home, too; but at lunch Grisha began whistling and, what was worse, was disobedient to the English governess, and had to go without pudding. Dolly would not have let things go so far on such a day had she been present; but she was obliged to uphold the English governess, and confirmed her decision that Grisha should have no pudding. This rather spoiled the general happiness.

Grisha cried, declaring that Nikolinka had whistled, too, but they did not punish him, and that he was not crying about the pudding – he didn't mind that – but because it wasn't fair. This was too pathetic, and Dolly decided to speak to the governess and get her to forgive Grisha, and went to find her. But as she was passing the drawing-room she beheld a scene which filled her heart with such joy that tears came into her eyes and she pardoned the little delinquent herself.

The culprit was sitting in the corner by the window; beside him stood Tanya with a plate. On the plea of wanting to give her dolls some dinner, she had obtained the governess's permission to take her pudding to the nursery, and had brought it instead to her brother. Still weeping over the unfairness of his punishment, he was eating the pudding, and kept saying through his sobs, 'You have some too ... let's eat it together ... together.'

Tanya, affected at first by her pity for Grisha, and then by a sense of her own noble action, also had tears in her eyes; but she did not refuse, and ate her share.

When they caught sight of their mother, they were dismayed; but, looking into her face, they saw they were not doing wrong and, with their mouths full, began to laugh and wipe their smiling lips with their hands, smearing their beaming faces all over with tears and jam.

'Mercy! Your new white frock! Tanya! Grisha!' exclaimed their mother, trying to save the frock but, with tears in her eyes, smiling a blissful, rapturous smile.

The new clothes were taken off, the little girls were told to go and have their blouses put on and the boys their old jackets, and orders were given for the wagonette to be harnessed, with Brownie again – to the bailiff's vexation – for the whole family to go mushroom-picking and bathing. A chorus of delighted squeals arose in the nursery and did not subside until they set out for the bathing-place.

They gathered a whole basketful of mushrooms; even Lily found a birch-mushroom. Before, Miss Hoole had always found one and pointed it out to her; but this time she found a fine big one all by herself, and there was a general shout of triumph, 'Lily's found a mushroom!'

After that they drove to the river, left the horses under the birch-trees, and went to the bathing-place. Terenty the coachman tied the horses to a tree – they kept swishing their tails to whisk away the flies – and, treading down the grass, stretched himself full length in the shade of a birch and smoked his shag, while the children's continuous shrieks of delight floated across to him from the bathing-place.

Although it was busy work to look after all the children and restrain their wild pranks, though it was difficult to remember whose were all those little stockings and drawers, not to mix up the shoes for the different feet, and to untie, unbutton, and then do up again all the tapes and buttons, Dolly, who had always been fond of bathing herself and considered it good for the children, was never happier than when bathing with all the children. To go over all those chubby little legs, pulling on their stockings, to take the naked little bodies in her arms and dip them in the water, to hear their squeals of delight and alarm; and to see these little cherubs of hers gasping and splashing, their merry eyes wide with fright, was a great joy.

When half the children were dressed again, some peasant women in their Sunday best, out picking herbs, came up to the bathing-hut and stopped shyly. Matriona Filimonovna called to one of them to give her a sheet and a shirt to dry that had dropped into the water, and Dolly began to talk to the others. The women, who had started by laughing behind their hands and not understanding her questions, soon grew bolder and more talkative, and immediately won Dolly's heart by their frank admiration for the children.

'My, what a little beauty! As white as sugar!' said one, admiring Tanya and nodding her head. 'But thin ...'

'Yes, she has been ill.'

'And they've been bathing you, too, have they?' said another to the baby.

'Oh no; he's only three months old,' replied Dolly with pride.

'You don't say!'

'And have you any children?'

'I've had four; I've two living – a boy and a girl. I weaned her last carnival.'

'How old is she?'

'Just turned two.'

'Why did you nurse her so long?'

'It's our custom: for three fasts …'

And the conversation was launched upon topics that interested Dolly more than any other: what sort of confinement did she have? What was the matter with the boy? Where was her husband? Did it often happen?

Dolly was loath to part with the peasant women, so interesting to her was their conversation, so completely identical were all their interests. What pleased her most of all was that she clearly saw how all the women admired more than anything the fact that she had so many and such fine children. The peasant women even made Dolly laugh, and offended the English governess, because she was the cause of the laughter she did not understand. One of the younger women was watching the governess, who was dressing after all the rest, and when she put on her third petticoat she could not refrain from remarking: 'My, look at her! She keeps putting on and putting on, and she hasn't done yet!' and they all went off into roars.

9

WITH her children round her, their heads still wet from their bathe, and a kerchief tied round her own head, Dolly was nearing home, when the coachman said:

'There's a gentleman coming – looks like the gentleman from Pokrovskoe.'

Dolly peeped out in front and was delighted to see Levin's familiar figure in a grey hat and grey coat coming to meet them. She was glad to see him at any time but at this moment she was specially glad he should see her in all her glory. No one was better able to appreciate her splendour than Levin.

As he looked at her, he found himself face to face with one of the pictures of the family life of his dreams.

'You're like a hen with her chicks.'

'Ah, I am so glad to see you,' she said, holding out her hand to him.

'Glad to see me, but you didn't send me word. My brother's staying with me. I got a note from Stiva telling me you were here.'

'From Stiva?' Dolly asked in surprise.

'Yes, he wrote that you were here, and he thought you might allow me to be of use to you,' said Levin and, having said it, suddenly became embarrassed.

He did not finish but walked on in silence by the wagonette, snapping off twigs from the lime-trees and biting them in half. He was embarrassed because he fancied Dolly might not like to accept from an outsider help that should by rights have come from her own husband. Dolly certainly did not like Oblonsky's little way of burdening other people with his domestic duties. And she was at once aware that Levin was aware of this. It was precisely for this fineness of perception, for this delicacy of feeling, that Dolly liked Levin.

'Of course I realize,' said Levin, 'that that simply means that you would like to see me, and I'm exceedingly glad. I can well imagine, though, that used to housekeeping in town you must feel in the wilds here, and if there is anything I can do, I'm entirely at your disposal.'

'Oh no!' said Dolly. 'At first things were rather uncomfortable, but now we've settled everything nicely – thanks to my old nurse,' she added, indicating Matriona Filimonovna who, perceiving that they were speaking of her, gave Levin a bright, cordial smile. She knew him, and knew that he would be a good match for her young lady, and hoped the affair would come off.

'Won't you get in, sir? We can squeeze up this side,' she said to him.

'No, I'll walk. Children, who'd like to race the horses with me?'

The children hardly knew Levin and did not remember when they had seen him, but they did not show towards him any of that strange shyness and hostility children so often feel for grown-up people who 'pretend', and for which they are so often miserably punished. Pretence about anything whatever may deceive the cleverest and shrewdest of men, but the dullest child will see through it, no matter how artfully it may be disguised. Whatever failings Levin had, there was not an atom of pretence in him, and so the children showed him the same friendliness that they read in their mother's face. At his invitation the two eldest at once jumped down and ran along with him as naturally as they would have done with their nurse or Miss Hoole or their mother. Lily begged to go, too, and her mother handed her to him; he sat her on his shoulder and ran on.

'Don't be afraid, don't be afraid!' he said to Dolly, with a merry smile. 'I won't hurt her or let her fall.'

And when she saw his strong, agile, careful, and ultra-cautious movements, the mother lost her fears and looked at him with a bright smile of approval.

Here, in the country, with children, and in Dolly's congenial company, Levin dropped into a mood, not infrequent with him, of child-like light-heartedness, that Dolly particularly liked in him. He ran about with the children, taught them gymnastic feats, set Miss Hoole laughing with his broken English, and talked to Dolly of his rural pursuits.

After dinner, when they were sitting alone on the balcony, Dolly began to speak of Kitty.

'You know, Kitty's coming here to spend the summer with me.'

'Really,' he said, colouring up; and at once, to change the subject, he added: 'So I'll send you a couple of cows, shall I? If you insist on squaring accounts you can pay me five roubles a month; but it's really too bad of you.'

'No, thank you. We can manage all right now.'

'In that case, then, I'll have a look at your cows and, with your permission, tell your people about their food. Everything depends on the feeding.'

And Levin, to turn the conversation, went on to explain to Dolly the theory of dairy-farming, based on the principle that the cow is simply a machine for converting fodder into milk, and so on.

He was saying all this and at the same time passionately longing, yet dreading to hear more of Kitty. He was in terror lest the peace of mind he had acquired with such difficulty be destroyed.

'Yes, but all that has to be looked after, and who is there to do it?' replied Dolly reluctantly.

Now that she had got her household matters satisfactorily in order, thanks to Matriona Filimonovna, she was disinclined to make any change; besides, she had no confidence in Levin's knowledge of farming. She was suspicious of arguments about cows being milk-producing machines. She thought that such arguments could only be a hin-drance in farming. It all seemed to her much simpler: you only had, as Matriona Filimonovna had explained, to give Spotty and Whiteflank more food and drink and see that the cook did not carry all the kitchen slops to the laundry-woman's cow. That was clear. But propositions as to feeding on meal and on grass were doubtful and obscure. Most important of all, she wanted to talk about Kitty.

10

'KITTY writes to me that there is nothing she longs for so much as seclusion and quiet,' said Dolly after the silence that had followed.

'And how is she – better?' Levin asked in agitation.

'Thank God, she's quite well again. I never did believe there was anything wrong with her lungs.'

'Oh, I am very glad!' said Levin, and Dolly fancied there was something pathetic, helpless, in his face as he said this and looked silently at her.

'Let me ask you, Constantine Dmitrich,' said Dolly, with her kindly but slightly mocking smile, 'why are you angry with Kitty?'

'I? I'm not angry with her,' said Levin.

'Yes, you are. Why was it you did not come to see us, or them, when you were in Moscow?'

'Darya Alexandrovna,' he said, blushing to the roots of his hair, 'I wonder really that with your kind heart you don't feel this. How is it you feel no pity for me, if nothing else, when you know …'

'What do I know?'

'You know that I made an offer and was refused,' said Levin, and all the tenderness he had been feeling for Kitty a minute before was replaced by a feeling of anger at the humiliation he had suffered.

'What makes you suppose I know?'

'Because everyone knows.'

'That is where you are mistaken; I did not know, although I had my suspicions.'

'Well, now you know.'

'All I knew was that something had happened that made her dread-fully unhappy, and that she begged me never to speak of it. And if she would not tell me, she would certainly not speak of it to anyone else. But what did pass between you? Tell me.'

'I have told you.'

'When was it?'

'When I was at their house the last time.'

'Do you know,' said Dolly, 'I am awfully, awfully sorry for her. You only suffer in your pride …'

'That may be,' said Levin, 'but …'

She interrupted him.

'But for her, poor girl … I am awfully, awfully sorry. Now I see it all.'

'Well, Darya Alexandrovna, you must excuse me,' he said, getting up. 'Good-bye, Darya Alexandrovna, till we meet again.'

'No, wait,' she said, clutching him by the sleeve. 'Wait a minute; sit down.'

'Please, please, don't let us talk about it,' he said, sitting down and conscious as he did so that a hope he had believed dead and buried was rising and stirring within his heart.

'If I were not fond of you,' Dolly went on, and tears started into her eyes; 'if I did not know you, as I do know you …'

The feeling that had seemed dead revived more and more, sprang up and took possession of Levin's heart.

'Yes, I understand it all now,' continued Dolly. 'You can't understand it; for you men, who are free and make your own choice, it's always clear whom you love. But a girl's in a state of suspense, with her feminine, maidenly modesty, a girl who sees you men from afar, who takes everything on trust – a girl may and often does feel something, and not know what to say.'

'Yes, if her heart does not speak …'

'No, the heart does speak; but just think for a moment: you men are interested in a girl, you come to the house, you make friends, you watch her, you wait to see if you have found what you love, and then, when you are quite sure you love her, you make an offer …'

'Well, it isn't quite like that.'

'Never mind! You make an offer, when your love is ripe or when the scales have turned in favour of one of your two choices. But a girl is not consulted. She is expected to make her choice, and yet she cannot choose, she can only answer "yes" or "no".'

'Yes, and the choice was between me and Vronsky,' thought Levin, and the dead hope that had quickened to life within him died again, and only made his heart ache painfully.

'Darya Alexandrovna,' he said, 'that's the way people choose a new dress or some other purchase or other, not love. The choice has been made, and so much the better. ... And there can be no repeating it.'

'Ah, pride, pride!' said Dolly, as though despising him for the baseness of this feeling in comparison with that other feeling which only women know. 'At the time you made Kitty an offer she was just in that state when she could not give an answer. She was wavering – wavering between you and Vronsky. She was seeing him every day, you she had not seen for some while. Supposing she had been older ... I, for instance, in her place could not have hesitated. To me he was always nauseous, and so he has proved to be in the end.'

Levin recalled Kitty's answer. She had said: 'No, *that cannot be* ...'

'Darya Alexandrovna,' he said dryly, 'I appreciate your confidence in me; I believe you are mistaken. But whether I am right or wrong, that pride you so despised makes any thought of Katerina Alexandrovna out of the question for me – you understand, utterly out of the question.'

'I will only say one thing more: you know that I am speaking of my sister, whom I love as I love my own children. I don't say she cared for you; all I meant to say is that her refusal at that moment proves nothing.'

'I don't know!' said Levin, jumping to his feet. 'If you only knew how you are hurting me! It's just as if a child of yours were dead and people kept saying to you, "He would have been like this and like that, and he might have lived, and how happy you would have been in him." But he's dead, dead, dead! ...'

'How absurd you are!' said Dolly, giving a mournful smile in spite of Levin's agitation. 'Yes, I see it all more and more clearly,' she went on thoughtfully. 'So you won't come to see us, then, when Kitty is here?'

'No, I shan't come. Of course I won't avoid meeting Katerina Alexandrovna, but as far as I can I shall try to spare her the affliction of my presence.'

'You are very, very absurd!' Dolly repeated, tenderly looking into his face. 'Very well, then, let it be as though we had not spoken a word about it. What is it, Tanya?' she said in French to the little girl who had come in.

'Where's my spade, Mama?'

'I am speaking French, and you must answer in French.'

The little girl tried to, but she could not remember the French for spade; her mother prompted her, and then told her in French where to look. All this made a disagreeable impression on Levin.

Everything in Dolly's house and children struck him now as by no means so charming as before.

'Why does she talk French with the children?' he thought. 'It's so affected and unnatural. And the children sense it. Learning French and unlearning sincerity,' he thought to himself, unaware that Dolly had reasoned over and over again in the same fashion and yet had decided that, even at the cost of some loss of sincerity, the children must be taught French in that way.

'But why must you be going? Do stay a little.'

Levin stayed to tea, but his good humour had vanished and he felt ill at ease.

After tea he went out into the hall to order his horses to be harnessed, and when he came back he found Dolly upset, with a troubled look on her face and tears in her eyes. While Levin had been outside, an incident had occurred which had suddenly shattered all the happiness she had been feeling that day, and her pride in the children. Grisha and Tanya had come to blows over a ball. Hearing a scream in the nursery, Dolly had run in and been met by a terrible sight. Tanya had got Grisha by the hair, while he, his face distorted with rage, was pounding her with his fists wherever he could reach her. Something snapped in Dolly's heart when she saw this. A black cloud seemed to have descended upon her life; she recognized that these children of hers, of whom she was so proud, were not merely most ordinary, but positively bad, ill-bred children, with coarse, brutal propensities – wicked children, in fact.

She could not talk or think of anything else, and could not help telling Levin of her misery.

Levin saw she was unhappy and tried to comfort her, saying that it showed nothing bad, that all children fight; but even as he spoke, he was thinking in his heart: 'No, I won't give myself airs and talk French with my children. But my children won't be like that. All one has to do is not spoil children, not contort them, and they're sure to be delightful. No, my children won't be like that.'

He said good-bye and drove away, and she did not try to keep him.

11

In the middle of July the elder of the village on Levin's sister's estate, about fifteen miles from Pokrovskoe, came to Levin to report on how things were going there and on the hay harvest. The principal income on his sister's estate came from the meadows which were flooded every spring. In former years the peasants had bought the standing hay for twenty roubles the three acres. When Levin took on the management of the estate, he had looked over the grass-lands and come to the conclusion that this was too cheap, and fixed the price at twenty-five roubles the three acres. The peasants would not pay that price and, as Levin suspected, kept off other buyers. Then Levin had driven over himself and arranged to have the meadows mown partly by hired labour, partly by peasants paid in kind. His own men did all in their power to oppose this innovation but the arrangement was carried out and the first year the meadows brought in almost double. Last year – which was the third year – the peasants still held out and the hay harvest was got in by the same means. This year the peasants had agreed to do all the mowing for a third of the crop, and the village elder had arrived now to announce that the hay had been cut and that for fear of rain they had invited the clerk from the office to come, had divided the hay in his presence and had raked together eleven stacks as the owner's share. From the vague answers to his question how much hay the big meadow had given, from the elder's haste to apportion the hay without waiting for leave, from the whole tone of the peasant, Levin perceived that there was something wrong about the division of the hay, and made up his mind to drive over and investigate the matter himself.

Arriving at the village at dinner-time, he left his horse at the cottage of an old friend of his, the husband of his brother's wet-nurse, and went to see the old man in his bee-house, wanting to find out from him the truth about the hay. Parmenich, a loquacious, comely old man, was delighted to see Levin, showed him all he was doing, told him everything about his bees and the swarms of that year; but to Levin's inquiries about the hay harvest he gave vague and reluctant answers. This still further confirmed Levin in his suspicions. He went down to the hayfields and examined the stacks. There could not possibly be fifty cart-loads in each. To catch the peasants Levin ordered the carts that had carried the hay to be fetched directly, to lift one stack and bring it to the barn. There were only thirty-two loads in the stack. Notwithstanding the village elder's protestations that the hay had been loose and had settled in the stacks, and his oath that everything had been done in the fear of God, Levin stuck to his point that the hay had been divided without his orders and that, therefore, he would not accept this hay as fifty loads to a stack. After a lengthy dispute it was agreed that the peasants should take these eleven ricks, reckoning them as fifty loads each, and that the owner's share should be measured afresh. These discussions and the apportioning of the hay-cocks lasted the whole afternoon. When the last of the hay had been apportioned, Levin entrusted the rest of the supervision to the clerk from the office and seated himself on a haycock marked off by a stake of willow, looking with enjoyment at the meadow teeming with peasants.

Before him, in the bend of the river beyond the marsh, moved a line of gaily-clad peasant women chattering merrily as they rapidly raked the scattered hay into grey, winding ramparts over the pale green stubble. Men with hayforks followed the women, and the ridges grew into tall, broad, soft haycocks. To the left carts were rumbling over the meadow that had already been cleared, and one after another the haycocks vanished, flung up in huge forkfuls, and their places were taken by heavy wagon-loads of sweet-smelling hay hanging over the horses' hind-quarters.

'Make hay while the sun shines! What hay it'll be!' said an old man, squatting down beside Levin. 'It's more like tea, not hay! Like scattering grain to the ducks, the way they pick it up!' he added, pointing to the growing haycocks. 'They've carted a good half of it since dinner-time. … Is that the last?' he shouted to a young peasant who was driving by, standing up in the front of the wagon, flicking the end of the cord reins.

'The last one, Dad!' the lad shouted back, pulling in the horse and looking round with a smile to a bright, rosy-cheeked peasant girl who sat in the cart smiling too, and drove on.

'Who's that? Your son?' asked Levin.

'My youngest,' said the old man with a fond smile.

'A fine lad!'

'He's all right.'

'Married already?'

'Yes, two years last St Philip's day.'

'You don't say! Any children?'

'Children indeed! Why, for over a year he was innocent as a babe himself, aye and bashful into the bargain,' answered the old man. 'Well, this is hay! Regular tea!' he said again, anxious to change the subject.

Levin looked more attentively at Vanka Parmenich and his wife. They were loading their cart not far from him. Vanka stood on the cart, receiving, arranging, and stamping down the huge bales of hay which his pretty young wife deftly handed up to him, at first in armfuls and then on the pitch-fork. The young woman worked easily, cheerfully, and with skill. The fork could not at once penetrate the close-packed hay. She would start by loosening it with the prongs, stick the fork in, then with a rapid, supple movement, leaning the whole weight of her body behind the fork, at once with a bend of her back under the red belt she drew herself up, and, arching her full bosom under the white smock, with an adroit turn of the fork she pitched the hay high on to the cart. Vanka, obviously anxious to spare her every minute of unnecessary exertion, made haste to catch the hay in his widespread arms, and smoothed it evenly in the cart. When she had raked together what was left of the hay, the young wife shook off the bits that had fallen on her neck and, straightening the red kerchief that had slipped forward over her white, unsunburned forehead, crawled under the cart to fasten the load. Vanka was telling her how to tie the cord to the cross-piece and burst into a roar of laughter at something she said. Strong, young, freshly-awakened love showed in both their faces.

12

THE load was fastened. Vanka jumped down and took the quiet, well-fed horse by the bridle. His wife flung her rake on to the cart and, with a bold step, swinging her arms, went over to the other women, who had gathered into a circle to sing. Vanka reached the road and took his place in the line of loaded carts. The women, carrying their rakes over their shoulders, gay in their bright colours, fell in behind the carts, their voices ringing merrily. One of the women with a wild, untrained voice started a song and sang it as far as the refrain, when half a hundred powerful voices, some gruff, others soft, took it up from the beginning again.

The singing women were drawing nearer Levin and he felt as if a thunder-cloud of merriment were swooping down upon him. The cloud swooped down and enveloped him; and the haycock on which he was lying, the other haycocks, the carts, the whole meadow and the distant fields all seemed to advance and vibrate and throb to the rhythm of this madly-merry song with its shouting and whistling and clapping. Levin felt envious of this health and mirthfulness, and longed to take part in this expression of joy at being alive. But he could do nothing except lie and look on and listen. When the peasants and their song had disappeared out of sight and hearing, a weary feeling of despondency at his own isolation, his physical inactivity, his alienation from this world, came over him.

Some of the very peasants who had most disputed with him over the hay – whom he had been hard on or who had tried to cheat him – those very peasants had nodded happily to him, evidently not feeling and unable to feel any rancour against him, any regret, any recollection even of having intended to cheat him. All that had been swallowed up in the sea of cheerful common toil. God gave the day, God gave the strength for it. And the day and the strength were consecrated to labour, and that labour was its own reward. For whom the labour? What would be its fruits? These were idle considerations beside the point.

Levin had often admired this life, had often envied the men who lived it; but to-day for the first time, especially under the influence of what he had seen of the relations between Vanka Parmenich and his young wife, the idea came into his mind that it was in his power to exchange the onerous, idle, artificial, and selfish existence he was leading for that busy, honourable, delightful life of common toil.

The old man who had been sitting beside him had gone home long ago; the peasants had all dispersed. Those who lived near had ridden home, while those from a distance had gathered into a group for supper and to spend the night in the meadow. Levin, unnoticed by them, still lay on the haycock, looking round, listening, and thinking. The peasants who had remained for the night in the meadow scarcely slept all the short summer night. At first Levin heard merry chatter and general laughter over supper, then singing again and more laughter. The whole long day of toil had left upon them no trace of anything but gaiety.

Before dawn all grew quiet. Only the sounds of night were heard –

the incessant croaking of frogs in the marsh and the horses snorting in the mist rising over the meadow before the morning. Rousing himself, Levin got up from the haycock and, looking at the stars, he saw that the night was over.

'Well, then, what am I going to do? How am I to set about it?' he said to himself, trying to put into words all he had been thinking and feeling in that brief night. All the thoughts and feelings he had passed through fell into three separate trains of thought. The first was the renunciation of his old life, of his utterly useless education. The idea of this renunciation gave him satisfaction, and was easy and simple. Another series of thoughts and mental images related to the life he longed to live now. The simplicity, the integrity, the sanity of this life he felt clearly, and he was convinced he would find in it the content, the peace, and the dignity, of the lack of which he was so painfully conscious. But the third line of thought brought him to the question of how to effect this transition from the old life to the new. And here nothing was clear. 'Take a wife? Have work and the necessity to work? Leave Pokrovskoe? Buy land? Join a peasant community? Marry a peasant girl? How am I to set about it?' he asked himself again, and could find no answer. 'I haven't slept all night, though, and can't think it out now,' he said to himself. 'I'll work it out later. One thing is certain: this night has decided my fate. All my old dreams of family life were nonsense, not the real thing,' he told himself. 'It's all ever so much simpler and better …

'How beautiful!' he thought, looking up at some fleecy white clouds poised in the middle of the sky right above his head, like a strange mother-of-pearl shell. 'How lovely everything is in this lovely night! And when did that shell have time to form? I was looking at the sky a moment ago and only two white streaks were to be seen. Yes, and my views of life changed in the same imperceptible way!'

He left the meadow and walked along the highway towards the village. A slight breeze was blowing up and it became grey and overcast with the moment of gloom that usually precedes daybreak and the final victory of light over darkness.

Shrinking from the cold, Levin walked fast, with his eyes fixed on the ground.

'What's that? Someone coming,' he thought, catching the jingle of bells, and lifting his head. Forty paces from him a four-in-hand with luggage on top was driving towards him along the grassy high-road on which he was walking. The wheelers pressed in towards the pole away from the ruts, but the skilful driver, seated on one side of the box, kept the pole over the ruts, so that the wheels ran on the smooth part of the road.

That was all Levin noticed, and without wondering who it could be he glanced absently at the coach.

An elderly woman was dozing in one corner, while at the window, evidently only just awake, sat a young girl holding the ribbons of her white nightcap in both hands. Serene and thoughtful, full of a subtle, complex inner life, remote from Levin, she was gazing beyond him at the glow of the sunrise.

At the very instant when this vision was vanishing, the candid eyes fell on him. She recognized him, and a look of wonder and delight lit up her face.

He could not be mistaken. There were no other eyes like those in the world. There was only one creature in the world that could concentrate for him all the light and meaning of life. It was she. It was Kitty. He realized she must be on her way to Yergushovo from the railway station. And everything that had been stirring Levin during that sleepless night, all the resolutions he had made, all vanished at once. He recalled with disgust his ideas of marrying a peasant girl. There alone, in the rapidly disappearing carriage that had crossed to the other side of the road, was the one possible solution to the riddle of his life, which had weighed so agonizingly upon him of late.

She did not look out again. The sound of the carriage springs could no longer be heard, the jingle of bells grew fainter. The barking of dogs told him the carriage had reached the village, and all that was left were the empty fields, the village in the distance, and he himself, solitary and apart from it all, making his lonely way along the deserted high-road.

He looked up at the sky, expecting to find there the cloud-shell he had delighted in and which had seemed to him the symbol of the ideas and feelings of that night. There was nothing in the sky in the least like a shell now. There, in the remote heights above, a mysterious change had been accomplished. No trace was to be seen of the shell; but spread half across the sky was a smooth tapestry of fleecy cloudlets, growing tinier and tinier. The sky had turned blue and clear; and met with the same tenderness but with the same remoteness his questioning gaze.

'No,' he said to himself, 'however good that simple life of toil may be, I cannot go back to it. I love *her*.'

13

NONE but those who knew Karenin most intimately was aware that, while on the surface the coldest and most rational of men, he had one weakness quite inconsistent with the general trend of his character. Karenin could not with equanimity see or hear a child or woman crying. The sight of tears upset him and made him lose all power of reflection. The chief of his department and his private secretary knew this and would warn women who came with petitions on no account to give way to tears, if they did not want to ruin their chances. 'He will get angry and will not listen to you,' they would say. And it was a fact that in such cases the emotional disturbance set up in Karenin by the sight of tears found expression in hasty anger. 'I can do nothing, nothing. Kindly go away!' he would commonly cry on these occasions.

When Anna had informed him, on their way back from the races, of her relations with Vronsky, and immediately afterwards had burst into tears, hiding her face in her hands, Karenin, for all the fury aroused in him against her, was aware at the same time of a rush of that emotional turmoil always produced in him by tears. Conscious of it, and conscious that any expression of his feelings at that moment would be ill-adapted to the situation, he endeavoured to suppress every manifestation of life in himself, and so neither stirred nor looked at her. This was what had caused that strange deathlike appearance which had so struck Anna.

When they reached the house he helped her out of the carriage, and, making an effort to master himself, took leave of her with his usual urbanity, and pronounced that phrase that bound him to nothing – he said that to-morrow he would inform her of his decision.

His wife's words, confirming his worst suspicions, had sent a cruel pang to his heart. That pang was made more acute by the strange feeling of physical compassion for her evoked by her tears. But when he was all alone in the carriage, to his surprise and delight he felt completely freed both from this pity and from the doubts and agonies of jealousy that had been torturing him of late.

He felt like a man who has had a tooth out that has been aching for a long time. After excruciating pain and a sensation of something enormous, bigger than his whole head, being wrenched out of his jaw, the sufferer, scarcely able to believe in his good fortune, feels that what has so long poisoned his existence and claimed all his attention is no longer there, and he can once more live and think and be interested in other things besides his tooth. Such was the feeling Karenin was experiencing. The agony had been strange and terrible but now it was over; he felt he could live again and think of something other than his wife.

'No honour, no heart, no religion; a depraved woman. I knew it and have seen it all along, though I tried out of pity for her to deceive myself,' he thought. And he really believed that he had seen it all along. He went on to recall incidents of their past life, and things in which he had never seen anything wrong before now plainly showed that she had always been a depraved woman. 'I made a mistake when I linked my life to hers; but there was nothing blameworthy in my mistake, and therefore I am not to be unhappy. I am not the guilty one,' he told himself, 'but she is. However, she is no concern of mine. She does not exist for me ...'

Whatever might befall her and his son, towards whom his sentiments were as much changed as towards her, ceased to interest him. His only thought now was the question in what way he could best, with most propriety and comfort for himself, and consequently with most justice, shake off the mud with which she had spattered him in her fall, and then proceed along his path of active, honourable, and useful existence.

'I cannot be made unhappy because a despicable woman has committed a crime. I merely have to find the best way out of the painful situation in which she has placed me. And find it I shall,' he said to himself, his face growing darker and darker. 'I am not the first, and I shall not be the last.' And leaving out historical instances dating from Menelaus and *La Belle Hélène*, recently revived and fresh in everyone's memory, a whole list of contemporary cases of husbands with unfaithful wives in the highest society occurred to his mind. 'Daryalov, Poltavsky, Prince Karibanov, Count Paskudin, Dram. ... Yes, even Dram, such an upright, capable fellow. ... Semeonov, Tchagin, Sigonin,' Karenin remembered. 'Admitting that a certain irrational *ridicule* falls to the lot of these men, yet I never saw anything but a misfortune in it and always felt nothing but sympathy,' Karenin said to himself, though this was not true: he had never sympathized with misfortunes of that kind but had always plumed himself the more whenever he heard of wives betraying their husbands. 'It is a misfortune that may befall anyone. And this misfortune has befallen me. The only thing to be done is to make the best of the situation.' And he began passing in review the different methods of procedure of other men who had found themselves in the same position.

'Daryalov fought a duel ...'

In his youth the idea of a duel had particularly fascinated Karenin, for the very reason that he was physically a coward and quite aware of it. He could not think without horror of a pistol being levelled at him, and had never handled a firearm in his life. This horror had in his youth set him pondering on duelling and picturing himself in a situation in which he would have to expose his life to danger. Having attained success and an established position in the world, he had long ago forgotten this feeling; but the old habitual feeling reasserted itself, and dread of his own cowardice proved even now so strong that Karenin spent a long time considering the question of duelling in all its aspects, and fondling the idea of a duel, though he knew beforehand that in no circumstances would he fight.

'There's no doubt our society is still so uncivilized (it's not the same in England) that a great many' – and among the many were those whose opinion Karenin particularly valued – 'would regard a duel with approval; but what object would be attained? Suppose I call him out,' Karenin went on to himself, and conjuring up a vivid picture of the night he would spend after the challenge, and the pistol pointed at him, he shuddered, and knew that he would never do it – 'suppose I call him out. Suppose I learn to shoot,' he went on musing, 'they put us in position; I pull the trigger,' he said to himself, closing his eyes, 'and it turns out that I kill him.' He shook his head to dispel such foolish thoughts. 'What sense is there in murdering a man in order to define one's relation to an erring wife and her son? I should still have to decide what I ought to do with her. But what is more likely and what would doubtless happen – I should be the one to be killed or wounded. I, the innocent person, would be the victim – killed or wounded. That would be more senseless still. And this is not all. A challenge to fight on my part would be hardly honest. Don't I know beforehand that my friends would never allow me to fight a duel – would never allow the life of a statesman, whom Russia needs, to be exposed to danger? What, then, would happen? Knowing beforehand that the matter would never reach the stage of being dangerous, it would amount to my simply trying to gain the sort of false glory that a challenge would give me. That would be dishonourable; it would be false; it would be deceiving myself and others. A duel is out of the question, and no one expects it of me. My aim is to safeguard my reputation, which is essential for the unhampered pursuit of my work.' His official duties, which had always been of great importance in Karenin's eyes, now appeared to him of extraordinary importance.

Having considered and rejected the idea of a duel, Karenin turned to divorce – another expedient resorted to by several of the husbands he could think of. Passing in review all the cases he knew of divorce (there were plenty of them in the very highest society with which he was familiar), Karenin could not find a single example in which the purpose of the divorce was the one he had in view. In each case the husband had relinquished or practically sold his unfaithful wife, and the very party which, being in fault, had no right to contract a fresh marriage, entered into counterfeit, pseudo-matrimonial ties with a new partner. In his own case, Karenin saw that a legal divorce – that is to say, one in which the guilty wife would only be repudiated – was impossible of attainment. He saw that the complex conditions of the life they led made the coarse proofs of his wife's guilt, required by the law, out of the question; he saw that a certain convention of refinement in that life would not admit of such proofs being brought forward, even if he had them, and that to bring forward such evidence would damage him in public estimation more than it would her.

An attempt at divorce could lead to nothing but a scandal which would be a god-sent opportunity to his enemies for calumny and attacks on his high position in society. His chief object, that of arranging matters with the least possible amount of disturbance, could not be secured by divorce either. Moreover, in the event of a divorce, or even of an attempt to obtain a divorce, it was obvious that the wife severed all relations with the husband and threw in her lot with the lover. And in spite of the complete and contemptuous indifference he imagined he felt for his wife, at the bottom of his heart there was one feeling left in regard to her – a disinclination to see her free to throw in her lot with Vronsky, thus letting her profit by her crime. The mere notion of this so stung Karenin that directly he thought of it he groaned with inward agony, and got up and changed his place in the carriage, and for a long while after he sat scowling darkly, wrapping his numbed and bony legs in the fleecy rug.

'Apart from formal divorce, one might do the same as Karibanov, Paskudin and that good fellow Dram – just separate,' he resumed, when he had regained his composure. But this step, too, presented the same drawback of public scandal as a divorce and – and this was the main objection – a separation would throw his wife into the arms of Vronsky quite as much as a formal divorce. 'No, it's out of the question, out of the question!' he said aloud, wrapping his rug about him again. 'I am not to be unhappy, but neither she nor he must be happy.'

The jealousy which had tortured him during the period of uncertainty had left him the moment the tooth had been with agony extracted by his wife's words. But jealousy had given place to another feeling: the desire, not merely that she should not triumph, but that she should be punished for her crime. He did not acknowledge it to himself, but in the depths of his soul he wanted her to suffer for having destroyed his peace of mind and his honour. And reviewing once again the conditions inseparable from a duel, a divorce, a separation, and once again rejecting them, Karenin felt convinced that there was only one solution – to keep her with him, concealing what had happened from the world, and using every measure in his power to break off the intrigue and, above all – though this he did not admit to himself – to punish her. 'I must inform her of my conclusion, tell her that, after thinking over the terrible position in which she has placed her husband and son, I hold that any other expedient would be worse for both sides than a nominal *status quo*, and that such I am prepared to retain, on the strict condition of obedience on her part to my wishes, that is to say, cessation of all intercourse with her lover.' When this decision had been finally adopted, a further weighty argument occurred to Karenin in support of it. 'That is the only course in keeping with the dictates of religion,' he told himself. 'In adopting this solution, I am not casting off a guilty wife, but giving her a chance to mend her ways; and indeed, difficult as the task will be to me, I shall devote part of my energies to her reformation and salvation.'

Though Karenin was perfectly aware that he could not exert any moral influence over his wife, that such an attempt at reformation could lead to nothing but lies; though in passing through these painful moments he had not once thought of seeking guidance in religion, now that his decision corresponded, as it seemed to him, with the requirements of religion, this religious sanction to his decision afforded him complete satisfaction and a measure of comfort. He was pleased to think that, even in such an important crisis in his life, no one would be able to say that he had not acted in accordance with the principles of that religion whose standard he had always held aloft in the midst of universal apathy and indifference. Pondering in further detail, Karenin could not see, indeed, why his relations with his wife should not remain practically the same as before. Of course, she could never regain his esteem; but there was and could be no reason for him to spoil his own life and suffer personally because she was a bad and faithless wife. 'Yes, time will pass, time which arranges all things, and the old relations will be restored,' Karenin told himself; 'restored, that is, in so far that I shall not be sensible of a break in the continuity of my life. She is bound to be unhappy, but I am not to blame, and so I cannot be unhappy.'

14

By the time he neared Petersburg, Karenin was not only resolved on his decision, but had even composed in his head the letter he would write to his wife. Going into the porter's room, Karenin glanced at the letters and papers sent from his office and directed them to be brought to him in his study.

'The horses can be taken out and I will see no one,' he said in answer to the hall porter's inquiry, accentuating with a certain pleasure the words 'see no one'. It was a sign that he was in a good temper.

In his study Karenin took a couple of turns up and down, and halted at an immense writing-table, on which six candles had already been lighted by the valet who had preceded him. Cracking his knuckles, he sat down, arranging his writing materials. Then, with his elbows on the table and leaning his head to one side, he reflected for a moment before beginning to write without pausing for a second. He wrote without using any form of address to her, in French, making use of the plural 'you', which has not the same note of coldness as the corresponding Russian form.

'At our last conversation, I notified you of my intention to communicate to you my decision in regard to the subject of that conversation. Having carefully considered everything, I write now with the object of fulfilling that promise. My decision is as follows. Whatever your conduct may have been, I do not consider myself justified in severing the ties with which a Higher Power has bound us. The family cannot be broken up at the caprice, discretion, or even the sin of one of the partners of that marriage, and our life must continue as before. This is essential for me, for you, and for our son. I am fully persuaded that you have repented and do repent of what has called forth the present letter, and that you will co-operate with me in eradicating the cause of our estrangement and forgetting the past. In the event to the contrary, you can conjecture what awaits you and your son. All this I hope to discuss more in detail in a personal interview. As the season is drawing to a close, I would request you to return to Petersburg as soon as possible, not later than Tuesday. All necessary preparations shall be made for your arrival here. I beg you to note that I attach particular importance to compliance with this request.

A. KARENIN

'*P.S.* I enclose money which may be needed for your expenses.'

He read the letter through and was satisfied with it, and especially that he had remembered to enclose money; there was not a harsh word, not a reproach in it, nor was there undue indulgence. Above all, it provided a golden bridge for return. Having folded the letter, smoothed it with a massive ivory paper-knife, and put it in an envelope with the money, he rang the bell with the gratification the use of his well-arranged writing materials always aroused in him.

'Give this to the courier to be delivered to Anna Arkadyevna tomorrow at the summer villa,' he said, getting up.

'Yes, your excellency. Shall tea be served in your study?'

Karenin ordered tea to be brought to the study and, toying with the massive paper-knife, moved to his easy-chair, near which a lamp had been placed ready for him, with a French work on the Eugubine tables that he had begun. Over the easy-chair hung a portrait of Anna in an oval gilt frame, a fine painting by a celebrated artist. Karenin glanced at it. The impenetrable eyes gazed mockingly and insolently back at him, as they had that last evening he had seen her. To Karenin the black lace about the head, admirably touched in by the painter, the black hair and beautiful white hand with its fourth finger covered with rings seemed unbearably insolent and challenging. After looking at the portrait for a minute or two, he shuddered so that his lips quivered, and he uttered a sound like 'brrr' and turned away. Hurriedly seating himself in his easy-chair, he opened the book. He tried to read but could not revive the very lively interest he had felt before in the

Umbrian inscriptions. His eyes were on the page but he was thinking of something else. He was thinking not of his wife, but of a complication that had recently arisen in his official life and at present constituted the chief interest of it. He felt that he could penetrate more deeply than ever before into this intricate affair, and that a capital idea – he might say it without flattering himself – had occurred to him calculated to clear up the whole business, advance him in his official career, discomfit his enemies and thereby be of the greatest benefit to the Government. Directly the footman had set the tea and left the room, Karenin got up and went to the writing-table. Moving into the middle of the table the portfolio containing current business papers, with a scarcely perceptible smile of self-satisfaction, he took a pencil from the stand and plunged into the perusal of the intricate documents he had sent for, relating to the present complication. The complication was of this nature: Karenin's characteristic quality as a statesman – that special individual qualification that every rising functionary has – the qualification that with his unflagging ambition, his reserve, his probity, and his self-confidence had made his career, was his contempt for red tape, his cutting down of correspondence, his direct contact, wherever possible, with the root of the matter in hand, and his economy. It so happened that the famous Commission of the 2nd of June had set on foot an inquiry into the irrigation of lands in the Zaraisky province, which came under Karenin's department, and was a glaring example of waste of money and of paper reforms. Karenin was aware of the truth of this. The irrigation of these lands in the Zaraisky province had been initiated by Karenin's predecessor. Vast sums had been spent and were still being spent, and quite unproductively, and it was obvious that the whole business could lead to nothing whatever. Karenin had perceived this at once on taking office, and would have liked to lay hands on the affair; but at first, until he felt secure in his position, he knew it would be injudicious to do so, as too many interests were involved. Later on he had been occupied with other questions and had simply forgotten the business. Like all such matters, it carried on of itself, by the mere force of inertia. (Many people gained their livelihood by it, in particular one very upright and musical family, in which all the daughters played stringed instruments. Karenin knew the family and had stood godfather at the wedding of one of the elder girls.) For a hostile department to raise this question was, in Karenin's opinion, a dishonourable proceeding, seeing that in every department there were still graver matters which, for recognized reasons of official etiquette, no one inquired into. However, now that the gauntlet had been thrown down, he would pick it up boldly and demand the appointment of a special commission to investigate and report upon the working of the Board of Irrigation of the lands in the Zaraisky province; but at the same time he would give no quarter to the enemy either. He would demand that another special commission be set up to inquire into the question of the Native Tribes Organization Committee. The question of the Native Tribes had been brought up incidentally in the Commission of the 2nd of June, and had been pressed forward energetically as a matter of urgency in view of the deplorable condition of the native tribes. In the commission this question had been a ground of contention between several departments. The department opposed to Karenin had argued that the condition of the tribes was most flourishing, that the proposed reorganization might be the ruin of their prosperity, and that if there were anything unsatisfactory, it was entirely due to failure on the part of Karenin's department to carry out measures prescribed by law. Now Karenin intended to demand: first, that a new commission be formed to investigate locally the condition of the native tribes; secondly, should their condition prove such as it appeared to be from official documents in the hands of the committee, that another scientific commission be appointed to study the causes of these deplorable conditions from the (1) political, (2) administrative, (3) economic, (4) ethnographical, (5) material, and (6) religious points of view; thirdly, that evidence should be required from the rival department concerning the measures that had been taken during the last ten years by the department to avert the disastrous conditions in which the native tribes now found themselves; and fourthly and finally, that that department be called upon to explain why it had, as appeared from the evidence before the committee – No. 17015 and No. 18308 of December 5th, 1863, and June 7th, 1864 – acted in direct contravention of the intention of the fundamental and organic law, Vol. —, Art. 18 and footnote to Art. 36. A flush of excitement suffused the face of Karenin as he rapidly wrote out a summary of these ideas for his own benefit. Having covered a sheet of paper, he got up, rang, and sent a note to the chief secretary of his department, asking for some necessary references to be looked up. Getting up and walking about the room, he glanced again at the portrait, frowned, and smiled contemptuously. After reading a little more of the book on the Eugubine tables and renewing his interest in it, at eleven o'clock Karenin retired, and, recollecting as he lay in bed the incident with his wife, he saw it now in by no means such a gloomy light.

15

THOUGH Anna had obstinately and with exasperation contradicted Vronsky when he said that her position was an impossible one and tried to persuade her to tell her husband everything, at the bottom of her heart she regarded her position as false and dishonourable, and longed with her whole soul to put an end to it. On the way back from the races, in a moment of agitation she had told her husband the truth, and, in spite of the agony it had caused her, she was glad she had done so. After her husband had left her, she told herself that she was glad, that now everything would be straight, and at least there would be no more lying and deception. It seemed to her beyond doubt that her position would now be made clear for ever. It might be bad, this new state of things, but it would be clear; and not false and equivocal. The pain she had inflicted on herself and her husband in uttering those words would be compensated now by everything being made clear, she thought. That evening she saw Vronsky, but she did not tell him of what had passed between her and her husband, though, to make the position definite, he would have to be told.

When she woke next morning the first thing that came into her mind was what she had said to her husband, and those words seemed to her so awful that she could not conceive now how she could have brought herself to utter such strange, coarse words, and could not imagine what would come of it. But the words were spoken, and Karenin had departed without saying anything. 'I saw Vronsky and did not tell him. At the very instant he was leaving I wanted to call him back and tell him, but I changed my mind, because it would have looked so strange that I had not told him in the beginning. Why didn't I tell him, since I wanted to do so?' And in answer to this question a burning flush of shame spread over her face. She knew what had stopped her; she knew that she had been ashamed. Her position, which the night before had seemed simplified, suddenly struck her now as not only anything but simple, but as absolutely hopeless. She dreaded the disgrace, which she had not even thought of before. Directly she thought of what her husband would do, the most terrible ideas came to her mind. She fancied that presently the bailiff would arrive and turn her out of the house, and that her disgrace would be proclaimed to all the world. She asked herself where she should go when she was turned out of the house, and she could not find an answer.

When she thought of Vronsky, it seemed to her that he did not love her, that he was already beginning to find her a burden, that she could not go and offer herself to him, and she felt bitter against him for it. It seemed to her that the words she had spoken to her husband, which she kept repeating in her imagination, she had said to everyone, and everyone had heard them. She could not bring herself to look into the eyes of her household. She could not bring herself to ring for her maid, and still less to go downstairs and see her son and his governess.

The maid, who had long had an ear at the door, at last came in unsummoned. Anna glanced inquiringly into her face, and blushed with alarm. The girl excused herself for coming in, saying that she thought she had heard the bell ring. She brought a gown and a note. The note was from Betsy. Betsy reminded her that she was expecting Liza Merkalov and Baroness Shtoltz with their adorers, Kaluzhsky and old Stremov, for a game of croquet that morning. 'Do come, if only as a study in manners and customs. I shall expect you,' she finished.

Anna read the note and gave a deep sigh.

'Nothing, I need nothing,' she said to Annushka, who was rearranging the bottles and brushes on the dressing-table. 'You can go. I will get dressed and come down at once. I need nothing, nothing at all.'

Annushka went out, but Anna did not start dressing, and continued sitting in the same attitude, her head and arms hanging listlessly. Every now and then her whole body shuddered as she tried to make some gesture, utter some word, and she would sink back into lifelessness again. She repeated continually, 'My God! My God!' but neither word had any meaning to her. The idea of seeking help in her trouble in religion was as remote as seeking help from Karenin himself would have been, though she had never doubted the faith in which she had been brought up. She knew beforehand that she could find no help in religion unless she were prepared to renounce that which made up for her the whole meaning of life. She was not only miserable, she was beginning to feel frightened by the new spiritual condition, never experienced before, in which she found herself. She felt as though everything in her soul were beginning to be double, just as objects sometimes appear double to over-tired eyes. She hardly knew at times what it was she feared, and what she hoped for. Whether she feared or desired what had happened, or what was going to happen, and exactly what she did want, she could not have said.

'Oh, what am I doing!' she said to herself, feeling a sudden pain in both sides of her head. She recovered herself to find that both hands had hold of her hair at the temples and were pulling it. She jumped to her feet and began pacing up and down.

'The coffee is ready, and Ma'm'selle and Seriozha are waiting,' said Annushka, coming back again and finding Anna in the same position.

'Seriozha? What about Seriozha?' Anna asked, with sudden eagerness, recollecting her son's existence for the first time that morning.

'He's been naughty, I think,' answered Annushka with a smile.

'In what way?'

'There were some peaches lying on the table in the corner room. I think he crept in and ate one of them on the quiet.'

The thought of her son suddenly roused Anna from the helpless condition in which she found herself. She remembered the partly sincere, though greatly exaggerated role of the mother living for her child, which she had assumed during the last few years, and she felt with joy that in the plight in which she was now she had a support, quite apart from her relation to her husband or to Vronsky. This support was her son. No matter what might happen to her, she could not give up her son. Let her husband put her to shame and turn her out, let Vronsky grow cold towards her and go on living his own life apart (she thought of him again with bitterness and reproach), she could not leave her son. She had an aim in life. And she must act; act to secure this relation to her son, so that he might not be taken away from her. There was no time to lose – she must act quickly, before they took him away from her. She must take her son and go away. Here was the one thing she had to do now. She must be calm, and get out of this torturing situation. The idea of decided action, binding her to her son, of going away somewhere with him immediately, made her feel calmer.

She dressed quickly, went downstairs and with resolute steps walked into the drawing-room, where Seriozha and his governess were waiting breakfast for her, as usual. Seriozha, all in white, was standing at a table under a looking-glass, and, with bent head and back, and an expression of intense concentration which she knew well and in which he resembled his father, was doing something to some flowers he had brought in.

The governess was looking exceptionally stern. Seriozha called out in a shrill voice, as he often did, 'Oh, Mama!' and stopped, hesitating whether to go and greet his mother and leave the flowers, or to finish the garland he was making and take it to her.

The governess said good-morning and began a long and detailed account of Seriozha's naughtiness, but Anna did not hear her. She was considering whether to take her with her or not. 'No, I won't take her,' she decided. 'I'll go alone with my child.'

'Yes, that was very naughty,' said Anna, and taking her son by the shoulder she looked at him, not severely but with a timid face that bewildered and delighted the boy, and she kissed him. 'Leave him to me,' she said to the astonished governess, and not letting go of her son she sat down at the table, where coffee was set ready for her.

'Mama! I ... I ... didn't ...' he said, trying to make out from her expression what was in store for him for eating the peach.

'Seriozha,' she said, as soon as the governess had gone out of the room, 'that was naughty, but you'll never do it again, will you? You love me?'

She felt the tears coming into her eyes. 'Could I help loving him?' she said to herself, looking deeply into his scared and at the same time delighted face. 'Is it possible that he could take sides with his father in punishing me? Will he not feel for me?' The tears were now streaming down her cheeks and to hide them she jumped up abruptly and almost ran out on to the terrace.

Cold, clear weather had followed the thundery rain of the last few days. In spite of the bright sunshine filtering through the rain-washed leaves, the air was cold out of doors.

She shivered, both from the cold and from the terror within her that had clutched her with fresh force in the open air.

'Run along; go to Mariette,' she said to Seriozha, who was coming out after her, and she began walking up and down on the straw matting of the terrace. 'Can it be that they won't forgive me, won't understand how none of it could be helped?' she said to herself.

Standing still and looking at the tops of the aspen-trees waving in the wind, with their rain-washed leaves glistening brightly in the cold sunshine, she knew they would not forgive her, that everything and everybody would be merciless to her now as was this sky, these green trees. And again she felt that duality in her soul. 'No, no, I mustn't think,' she said to herself. 'I must get ready. To go where? When? Whom shall I take with me? Yes, to Moscow by the evening train. Take Annushka and Seriozha, with just the most necessary things. But first I must write to them both.' She hurried indoors to her boudoir, sat down at the table and wrote to her husband:

'After what has happened, I cannot remain any longer in your house. I am going away, and taking my son with me. I don't know the law, and so I don't know which of the parents should have the child; but I take him with me because I cannot live without him. Be generous and let me have him.'

Up to this point she wrote rapidly and naturally, but the appeal to the generosity she did not recognize in him, and the necessity of winding up the letter with something affecting, checked her.

'Mention my wrong-doing and remorse – I cannot, because ...'

She stopped again, unable to connect her thoughts. 'No,' she said to herself, 'there's no need,' and tearing up the letter she wrote it again, leaving out the allusion to generosity, and sealed it.

Another letter had to be written to Vronsky. 'I have told my husband,' she began, and sat for a long time unable to go on. It seemed so coarse, so unfeminine. 'Besides, what can I write to him?' she said to herself. Again a flush of shame spread over her face. She recalled his calm self-possession, and a feeling of anger against him impelled her to tear the sheet of paper with the one sentence written on it into tiny bits. 'There is no need,' she said to herself and, closing her blotting-case, she went upstairs to tell the governess and the servants that she was going that day to Moscow, and at once set to work to pack her things.

16

In all the rooms of the summer villa porters, gardeners, and footmen went to and fro carrying things out. Cupboards and chests of drawers stood open; twice someone had to be sent to the shop for cord; the floor was strewn with newspapers. Two trunks, several bags, and a bundle of rugs had been taken down to the hall. The carriage and two hired cabs were waiting at the steps. Anna, who had forgotten her agitation in the work of packing, was standing at a table in her boudoir, packing her travelling-bag, when Annushka called her attention to the noise of carriage-wheels approaching. Anna looked out of the window and saw Karenin's courier on the steps, ringing at the front door bell.

'Go and find out what it is,' she said and, calmly prepared for anything, she sat down in a low chair and folded her hands in her lap.

A footman brought in a thick envelope addressed in Karenin's hand.

'The courier has orders to wait for an answer,' he said.

'Very well,' she replied and, as soon as he had left the room, she tore open the envelope with trembling fingers. A flat packet of banknotes in a paper band fell out. She disengaged the letter and began reading it from the end first. 'All necessary preparations shall be made for your arrival. ... I attach particular importance to compliance with my request ...' she read. Her eyes ran on farther, then back, she read it all through, and once more read it right through again from the beginning. When she had finished she felt cold all over and that a terrible, unlooked-for calamity had fallen on her.

In the morning she had regretted having told her husband and wished for nothing so much as to unsay all she had said. And here was this letter treating her words as unspoken and giving her what she had wanted. But now this letter seemed to her more awful than anything she could have imagined.

'He's in the right!' she muttered. 'Of course, he's always in the right; he's a Christian, he's magnanimous! Yes, the mean, odious creature! And no one understands it except me, and no one ever will; and I can't explain it. People say he's so religious, so high-principled, so upright, so clever; but they don't see what I've seen. They don't know how for eight years he has crushed my life, crushed everything that was living in me – he has never once thought that I'm a live woman in need of love. They don't know how at every step he's humiliated me and remained self-satisfied. Haven't I striven, striven with all my might, to find something to give meaning to my life? Haven't I struggled to love him, to love my son when I could no longer love my husband? But the time came when I realized I couldn't deceive myself any longer, that I was alive, that I was not to blame, that God had made me so that I need to love and live. And now what? If he'd killed me, if he'd killed him, I could have borne anything, I could have forgiven anything. But no! He ... How was it I didn't guess what he would do? He'll do what's consistent with his mean nature. He'll keep himself in the right, while he sees to it that I, poor lost woman, sink still farther, am still more disgraced ...'

'You can conjecture what awaits you and your son ...' – she recalled the words from the letter. 'That's a threat to take my son from me, and I dare say with their stupid laws he can. But don't I know why he says it? He doesn't even believe in my love for my child, or he despises it (he always did make fun of it). He despises that feeling in me, but he knows that I would not give up my son, that I can't give him up, that there could be no life for me without my child, even with him whom I love – that if I ran away and abandoned my son, I should be behaving like the most infamous and wickedest of women. He knows that, and knows I could never do it.'

She recalled another sentence in the letter. 'Our life must continue as before ...' 'That life was miserable enough in the past; it has been awful of late. What will it be now? And he knows all that; knows that I can't repent that I breathe, that I love; he knows that nothing but lies and deceit can come of it, but he must needs go on torturing me. I know him; I know that he's at home and happy in deceit, like a fish swimming in water. No, I won't let him have that happiness. I'll tear down the spider-web of lies in which he wants to catch me, come what may. Anything is better than lying and deceit.

'But how? Oh God! Oh God! Was ever a woman so unhappy as I am? ...

'No, I will tear it down, tear it down!' she cried, jumping up and forcing back her tears. And she went to the writing-table to write him another letter, though she already knew at the bottom of her heart that she would not have the strength to tear down anything, nor to escape from the old situation, however false and dishonourable it might be.

She sat down at the writing-table but instead of writing she clasped her hands on the table and, laying her head on them, burst into tears, sobbing and heaving her breast like a child crying. She wept because her dream of having her position cleared up and made definite had been destroyed for ever. She knew beforehand that everything would go on as it was – would, in fact, be far worse than before. She felt that the position she enjoyed in society, which had seemed of so little consequence that morning, was precious to her after all, and that she would not have the strength to exchange it for the shameful one of a woman who has deserted husband and child to join her lover; that, however much she might struggle, she could not be stronger than herself. She would never know freedom in love, but would always be the guilty wife continually threatened with exposure, deceiving her husband for the sake of a disgraceful liaison with a man living apart and away from her, whose life she could never share. She knew that this was how it would be, and yet it was so awful that she could not even conceive what it would end in. And she wept unrestrainedly, as children weep when they are punished.

The sound of the footman's step forced her to rouse herself and, hiding her face from him, she pretended to be writing.

'The courier is asking for the answer,' the footman announced.

'The answer? Oh yes,' said Anna. 'Let him wait. I will ring.'

'What can I write?' she thought. 'What can I decide by myself? What do I know? What do I want? What is there I care for?' Again she felt that schism in her soul and again was terrified by the sensation; so she seized the first pretext for action that occurred to her to distract her thoughts. 'I must see Alexei,' (so she called Vronsky to herself). 'No one but he can tell me what to do. I'll drive over to Betsy's; perhaps I shall see him there,' she said to herself, completely forgetting that when she had told him the day before that she was not going to the Princess Tverskoy's, he had said that in that case he would not go either. She went to the table, wrote to her husband, 'I have received your letter. – A.', rang, and gave the note to the footman.

'We are not going,' she said to Annushka, who had just come in.

'Not going at all?'

'No; don't unpack till to-morrow, and let the carriage wait. I am driving over to the princess's.'

'Which dress shall I put out?'

17

THE croquet party to which the Princess Tverskoy had invited Anna was to consist of two ladies and their adorers. The two ladies were the leading representatives of a select new Petersburg circle, nicknamed, in imitation of some imitation, *les sept merveilles du monde*. These ladies belonged to a circle which, though of the highest society, was entirely hostile to the one in which Anna moved. Moreover, Stremov, one of the most influential people in Petersburg, and the elderly admirer of Liza Merkalov, was Karenin's enemy in the political world. These considerations had made Anna reluctant to accept, and the remarks in the Princess Tverskoy's note referred to her refusal. Now, however, Anna was eager to go, in the hope of seeing Vronsky.

Anna arrived at the Princess Tverskoy's before the other visitors.

As she was mounting the steps, Vronsky's footman, with side-whiskers combed out like a Gentleman of the Bedchamber, also came up. He stopped at the door and, taking off his cap, let her pass. Anna recognized him, and only then remembered that Vronsky had told her the day before that he was not coming. Most likely he was sending a note now to say so.

As she was taking off her outdoor things in the hall she heard the footman – who even pronounced his '*r*'s' like a Gentleman of the Bedchamber – say, 'From the count for the princess,' as he delivered the note.

She longed to inquire of him where his master was. She longed to go home and send him a letter to come and see her, or to go to see him herself. But neither the first nor the second nor the third course was possible. Already she heard bells ringing ahead of her to announce her arrival and Princess Tverskoy's footman was standing half-turned at the open door, waiting for her to go forward into the inner apartments.

'The princess is in the garden; they will inform her immediately. Would Madam care to go into the garden?' said another footman in the next room.

She was in the same state of irresolution and uncertainty as she had been at home – indeed, it was worse, because she could do nothing; she could not see Vronsky, and she had to stay here among outsiders, in company so uncongenial to her present mood. But she was wearing a dress that she knew suited her, she was not alone; around her was that luxurious setting of idleness that she was used to, and she felt less wretched than at home. She was not forced to consider what she was to do. Everything did itself. When she met Betsy coming towards her in a white gown that impressed her by its elegance, Anna smiled to her just as she always did. Princess Tverskoy came up, accompanied by Tushkevich and a young girl, a relation, who, to the vast delight of her parents in the provinces, was spending the summer with the famous princess.

There must have been something strange about Anna, for Betsy noticed it at once.

'I had a bad night,' answered Anna, gazing at the footman who came to meet them with, Anna supposed, Vronsky's note.

'I am so glad you've come,' said Betsy. 'I am tired and was just longing to have a cup of tea before the others arrive. Won't you and Masha go and try the croquet-lawn over there, where they've been cutting it?' she said, turning to Tushkevich. 'We shall have time to have a little talk over our tea. We'll have a cosy chat, won't we?' she added in English, smiling to Anna and pressing the hand with which she held a parasol.

'Yes, especially as I can't stay long. I simply must go and see old Madame Vrede. I promised to, ages ago,' said Anna, to whom lying, so foreign to her by nature, had become not merely simple and natural in society but a positive source of satisfaction. Why she had said this, which she had not thought of a second before, she could not have explained. She had said it for the sole reason that, as Vronsky was not coming, she had better secure her own freedom and try to see him in some other way. But why exactly she had spoken of old Madame Vrede, to whom, among many other people, she owed a visit, she could not have explained; but as it turned out afterwards, had she tried to invent the most cunning of devices to meet Vronsky, she could have thought of nothing better.

'No, I'm not going to let you go on any account,' replied Betsy, fixing her eyes intently on Anna. 'Really, I should feel quite hurt, if I were not fond of you. Anyone would think you were afraid my company might compromise you. Tea in the little salon, please,' she said, half closing her eyes as she always did when addressing the footman.

Taking the note from him, she read it.

'Alexei's played us false,' she said in French. 'He writes that he can't come,' she went on in a tone as natural and matter-of-fact as though it could never enter her head that Vronsky was of any more interest to Anna than a game of croquet.

Anna knew that Betsy knew everything, but when she heard her speak of Vronsky before her she was always persuaded for a minute that she knew nothing.

'Oh,' said Anna indifferently, as if not greatly interested, and continued with a smile: 'How could your company compromise anyone?' This playing with words, this hiding of a secret, had a great fascination for Anna, as it has for all women. And it was not the necessity for secrecy, nor its purpose, but the process itself that attracted her.

'I can't be more Catholic than the Pope,' she said. 'Stremov and Liza Merkalov – why, they're the very cream of society. Besides, they are received everywhere, and *I*' – she laid special stress on the I – 'have never been rigid and intolerant. I simply haven't the time.'

'No; perhaps you don't care to meet Stremov? Let him and your husband tilt at each other in the committee room – that's no affair of ours. But in society he's the most amiable man I know, and a devoted croquet-player. You will see. And, in spite of his ridiculous position as Liza's lovesick swain at his age, you ought to see how he carries it off! He is very nice. Sappho Shtoltz you don't know? She is quite the latest thing.'

While Betsy was saying all this, Anna saw by her bright, shrewd glance that she partly guessed her plight and was hatching something for her benefit. They were in the little boudoir.

'But I must write to Alexei,' and Betsy sat down to the table, scribbled a few lines and put them in an envelope. 'I've asked him to come and dine. I've one lady too many. See if I've made it persuasive enough. Excuse me, I must leave you for a minute. Would you seal it up, please, and send it off?' she said from the door. 'I have something to see to.'

Without a moment's hesitation, Anna sat down at the table with Betsy's letter and, without reading it, added at the foot: 'I must see you. Come to the Vrede garden. I shall be there at six o'clock.' She sealed it up, and, Betsy returning, in her presence handed the note to be taken.

Over tea, which was brought to them on a little tea-table in the cool little drawing-room, the two women really did have the cosy chat promised by Princess Tverskoy before the arrival of her visitors. They discussed the people who were expected, and the conversation fell upon Liza Merkalov.

'She is very sweet, and I always liked her,' said Anna.

'So you ought to: she raves about you. Yesterday she came up to me after the races and was in despair that she had missed you. She says you are like a real heroine out of a novel, and that if she were a man she would do all sorts of mad things for your sake. Stremov tells her she does that as it is!'

'But do tell me, I never could make it out,' began Anna after a pause, speaking in a tone that clearly showed she was not putting an idle question and that what she was asking was of more importance to her than it should have been; 'do tell me – what are her relations with Prince Kaluzhsky, Mishka, as they call him? I come across them very little. What exactly is their relation?'

Betsy's eyes twinkled, and she looked keenly at Anna.

'It is the new fashion,' she said. 'They've all adopted it. They have kicked over the traces. But there are ways and ways of doing it.'

'Yes, but what are her relations with Kaluzhsky?'

Betsy unexpectedly broke into a peal of merry, uncontrollable laughter, with her a thing that rarely happened.

'You are encroaching on Princess Myagky's domain now! That is a question the *enfant terrible* might ask!' and Betsy obviously tried to but could not contain herself and went off into another peal of infectious laughter characteristic of people who do not laugh often. 'You'd better ask them!' she brought out between tears of laughter.

'No, you laugh,' said Anna, laughing too, in spite of herself, 'but I never could understand it. I don't understand what part the husband plays in it.'

'The husband? Liza Merkalov's husband carries her rugs after her and is always at her beck and call. But what there is besides that, no one cares to inquire. As you know, in decent society one doesn't talk or think even of certain details of the toilet. That's how it is with this.'

'Will you be at Madame Rolandak's party?' asked Anna, to change the subject.

'I don't think so,' replied Betsy and, without looking at her friend, she began carefully filling the little translucent cups with fragrant tea. Putting a cup before Anna, she took out a cigarette and, fitting it into a silver holder, she lit it.

'It's like this, you see: I'm in a fortunate position,' she began, quite serious now, as she took up her cup. 'I understand you, and I understand Liza. Liza's one of those naïve natures who no more understand the difference between right and wrong than a child. At least, she did not comprehend it when she was very young. And now she's aware that the role of not understanding suits her. Now, perhaps, she doesn't know on purpose,' said Betsy with a faint smile. 'Still, it suits her, just the same. You see, you can look at a thing tragically and turn it into a misery, or you can take it simply and even humorously. Possibly you are inclined to look on the tragic side.'

'How I wish I knew other people as I know myself!' said Anna gravely and thoughtfully. 'Am I worse than others, or better? Worse, I think.'

'*Enfant terrible, enfant terrible!*' repeated Betsy. 'But here they are.'

18

STEPS were heard, and a man's voice, then a woman's voice and laughter, and immediately after the expected visitors walked in – Sappho Shtoltz and a young man, brimming over with good health, known as Vaska. It was evident that a diet of beefsteak, truffles, and Burgundy agreed with him. Vaska bowed to the two ladies and glanced at them, but only for a second. He had come into the drawing-room behind Sappho, and followed her about as though he were chained to her, keeping his sparkling eyes fastened on her as if he would like to eat her. Sappho Shtoltz was a blonde beauty with black eyes. She walked with brisk little steps in high-heeled shoes, and shook hands with the ladies vigorously like a man.

Anna had not met this new star of fashion before, and was struck by her beauty, the extravagant extreme of her dress, and the boldness of her manners. On her head there was such a superstructure of soft, golden hair – her own and false mixed – that her head looked as large as her shapely, well-developed, and much-exposed bust. The impulsive abruptness of her movements was such that at every step the lines of her knees and thighs were clearly visible under her dress, and one involuntarily wondered where in the undulating, bolstered-up mountain of material at the back the real body of the woman, so small and slender, so naked in front and so hidden behind and below, really came to an end.

Betsy hastened to introduce her to Anna.

'Just fancy – we all but ran over two soldiers,' she began telling them at once, using her eyes and smiling as she twitched back her skirt, which she immediately jerked all on one side. 'I was driving with Vaska. ... Oh, but you don't know each other.' And she introduced the young man by his surname, blushing and bursting into a ringing laugh at her mistake in speaking of him as Vaska to a stranger.

Vaska bowed to Anna a second time but did not say a word.

'You've lost the wager,' he said, turning to Sappho. 'We got here first. Pay up,' he added, smiling.

Sappho laughed more festively than ever.

'Not just now,' she said.

'All right, I'll have it later.'

'Very well, very well. Oh yes!' She turned suddenly to Princess Betsy. 'I'm a nice one ... I positively forgot ... I've brought you a visitor. Here he is.'

The unexpected young visitor, whom Sappho had invited and whom she had forgotten, was, nevertheless, a personage of such consequence that, in spite of his youth, both ladies rose to greet him.

He was a new admirer of Sappho's. Like Vaska, he now followed at her heels.

Soon after, Prince Kaluzhsky arrived, and Liza Merkalov with Stremov. Liza Merkalov was a thin brunette, with a languid, Oriental type of face and – everyone said – exquisite enigmatic eyes. The tone of her dark dress (as Anna immediately observed and appreciated) was in perfect harmony with her style of beauty. Liza was as soft and droopy as Sappho was hard and compact.

But to Anna's taste Liza was by far the more attractive. In speaking of her to Anna, Betsy had said that Liza had adopted the pose of an ingenuous child, but when Anna saw her she felt that this was not the truth. She really was ingenuous, a spoiled but sweet and irresponsible woman. To be sure, her case was the same as Sappho's: she also had two admirers, one young and one old, tacked on to her and devouring her with their eyes; but there was something about her that made her seem superior to her surroundings – she had the sparkle of a real diamond among glass imitations. This sparkle shone out in her exquisite, truly enigmatic eyes. The weary and at the same time passionate gaze of those eyes, ringed with dark circles, was striking in its absolute sincerity. Everyone looking into those eyes fancied he knew her wholly and, knowing her, could not but love her. At the sight of Anna her whole face suddenly lighted up with a smile of delight.

'Oh, I am so glad to see you!' she said, going up to Anna. 'Yesterday at the races I was just trying to get near you when you went away. And I did so want to see you yesterday especially. Wasn't it awful?' she said, looking at Anna with eyes that seemed to lay bare her whole soul.

'Yes, I had no idea it would be so exciting,' said Anna, blushing.

The company rose at this moment to go into the garden.

'I'm not coming,' said Liza, smiling and sitting down beside Anna. 'You won't go either, will you? Who wants to play croquet?'

'Oh, I like it,' said Anna.

'Tell me, how do you manage not to feel bored? It's delightful to look at you. You're alive, while I am bored.'

'You bored? Why, yours is the gayest set in Petersburg,' said Anna.

'Maybe those who are not in our set are even more bored; but we – I at any rate – do not feel gay but awfully, awfully bored.'

Sappho lit a cigarette and went out into the garden with the two young men. Betsy and Stremov stayed at the tea-table.

'How can you say that?' exclaimed Betsy. 'Sappho said they had a very jolly time at your house yesterday.'

'Oh dear, it was so dreary!' said Liza Merkalov. 'We all went back to my place after the races. The same everlasting crowd doing the same everlasting things! Nothing's ever any different. We spent the whole evening lolling about on sofas. What was there jolly about that? No, do tell me how you manage not to get bored,' she asked Anna again. 'One has only to look at you to see here's a woman who may be happy or unhappy, but who isn't bored. Tell me how you do it.'

'I don't do anything,' answered Anna, blushing at these searching questions.

'That's the best way,' Stremov put in.

Stremov was a man of fifty, getting grey but still vigorous-looking, very ugly but with a clever face full of character. Liza Merkalov was his wife's niece, and he spent all his leisure hours with her. An enemy of Karenin's in the Government, he endeavoured, like a shrewd man and a man of the world, to be particularly cordial with her, the wife of his enemy.

' "Don't do anything," ' he repeated with a subtle smile, 'that's the best way. I have always told you,' he said, turning to Liza Merkalov, 'that if you don't want to be bored, you mustn't think you're going to be bored, just as you mustn't be afraid of not being able to fall asleep if you fear insomnia. That's just what Madame Karenin has just said.'

'I should be very pleased if I had said it, for it's not only wise but true,' said Anna, smiling.

'No, but tell me why it is one can't go to sleep and can't help being bored?'

'To sleep well one ought to work, and to enjoy oneself one ought to have some work too.'

'Why should I work when my work is no use to anyone? And I can't and won't make believe.'

'You are incorrigible,' said Stremov, not looking at her and turning to Anna again.

As he rarely met Anna, he could say nothing but commonplaces to her, but he said the commonplaces as to when she was returning to Petersburg, and how fond the Countess Lydia Ivanovna was of her, in a way that expressed his whole-hearted desire to be agreeable to her and show his regard for her, and even more.

Tushkevich came in to say that everybody was waiting for the other players to begin croquet.

'No, please don't go,' begged Liza Merkalov, hearing that Anna was leaving.

Stremov joined in her entreaties.

'It's too violent a transition,' he said, 'to go from such company to old Madame Vrede. And besides, you will only give her a chance for talking scandal, while here, on the contrary, you arouse very different feelings of the highest and most opposite kind,' he said to her.

Anna hesitated for a moment, undecided. This clever man's flattering words, the naïve, child-like affection which Liza Merkalov displayed towards her, the social atmosphere she was used to – it was all so easy, while what awaited her was so difficult, that for a moment she was in uncertainty whether to stay and put off a little longer the painful moment of explanation. But remembering what was in store for her alone at home if she did not come to some decision, remembering that gesture – terrible even in memory – when she had clutched her hair with both hands, she said good-bye and went away.

19

In spite of his apparently frivolous life in society, Vronsky was a man who hated disorder. While quite young and still in the Corps of Pages, he had the humiliation of being refused a loan he asked for to get him out of some difficulty, and never again had he allowed himself to get into such a position.

In order to keep his affairs straight, he was in the habit, some four or five times a year, according to circumstances, of shutting himself up alone and putting all his affairs into shape. He called it his day of reckoning or '*faire la lessive*'.

On the morning after the races he awoke late and, without shaving or taking his bath, he got into a linen tunic, distributed about the table moneys, bills, and letters, and set to work. When Petritsky – who knew Vronsky was apt to be irritable on such occasions – awoke and saw his comrade at the writing-table, he dressed quietly and went out without disturbing him.

Every man who is familiar down to the last detail with all the complexity of his own circumstances involuntarily assumes that these complexities and the difficulty of clearing them up are peculiar to himself, and never supposes that other people are surrounded by just as complicated an array of personal affairs as his. So it seemed to Vronsky. And not without a certain inward pride, nor without reason, did he feel that any other man would have got into a mess long ago and been forced into some dishonourable course, had he found himself in such a difficult position. But Vronsky felt that now especially it was more essential than ever to investigate and clear up his affairs if he were to keep out of trouble.

He began by attacking his financial problems, as the easiest to settle. Having made a list of all he owed in his minute hand on a sheet of notepaper, he added it up and found that it came to seventeen thousand and some odd hundreds, which he left out for the sake of simplicity. Reckoning up his ready money and looking over his bank-book, he found he had 1,800 roubles, and nothing coming in before the New Year. Going over his list of debts, he copied it, dividing it into three categories. In the first he put the debts which he would have to pay at once, or the money for which had at any rate to be kept handy so that they could be paid on demand without a moment's delay. These debts amounted to about 4,000: 1,500 for a horse, and 2,500 as surety for a young comrade, Venovsky, who had lost that sum to a card-sharper in Vronsky's presence. Vronsky had wanted to pay the money at the time – he had that amount then – but Venovsky and Yashvin had insisted that they would pay, and not Vronsky, who had not even been playing. That was all very fine but Vronsky knew that in this dirty business, his only share in which had been to give a verbal guarantee for Venovsky, it was essential for him to have the 2,500 roubles to throw at the swindler's head without any further talk. Thus for this first category of urgent debts he must have 4,000 roubles. The 8,000 roubles in the second category were less important: these were mainly owed on his stable account, for oats and hay, to his English trainer, to the saddler, and so on. Of these, too, he would have to pay out some 2,000 immediately, in order to be quite free from anxiety. In the last column were debts to shops, hotels, to his tailor, and they could wait. In all, then, he needed at least 6,000 roubles for current expenses, and he only had 1,800. For a man with an income of 100,000 a year, which was what everyone supposed Vronsky to have, it would seem that such debts could hardly be embarrassing; but the trouble was that he was far from having the 100,000. His father's immense estate, which alone brought in a yearly revenue of 200,000, was left undivided between the brothers. At the time his elder brother, having a pile of debts, married the Princess Varya Tchirkov, the daughter of a penniless Decembrist, Alexei had given up to his elder brother practically the whole income from their father's estate, reserving for himself only 25,000 a year from it. Alexei had told his brother at the time that this would be enough for him till he married, which he probably never would do. And his brother, who was in command of one of the most expensive regiments, and newly-married, could not decline the gift. Alexei had a further allowance of some 20,000 roubles a year from his mother, who had her own private fortune, in addition to the 25,000, and Alexei got through it all. Latterly, his mother, incensed with him on account of his love-affair and his departure from Moscow, had left off sending him the money. Consequently, Vronsky, who was in the habit of living at the rate of 45,000 a year, having this year received only 25,000, now found himself in difficulties. He could not apply to his mother for help. Her last letter, which had come the day before, had particularly irritated him with its hints that she was quite ready to further his success in the world and in the army, but not to lead a life which was a scandal to all good society. His mother's attempt to buy him offended him to the bottom of his soul, and made him feel still cooler towards her. Yet he could not go back on his generous promise when once it was made, even though he felt now, dimly foreseeing certain eventualities in his liaison with Madame Karenin, that this generous word had been spoken thoughtlessly, and that even though he was not married he might need all the 100,000 of income. But it was impossible to draw back. He had only to think of his brother's wife and recall how that dear, sweet Varya never lost an opportunity of letting him know that she remembered his generosity and appreciated it to realize the impossibility of withdrawing what he had given. It was just as impossible as beating a woman, stealing or lying. There was only one thing he could and must do, and Vronsky determined upon it without a moment's hesitation: he would borrow 10,000 from a money-lender, a procedure which presented no difficulty, cut down his expenses generally, and sell his race-horses. Having decided on this, he immediately wrote a note to Rolandak, who had made more than one offer to buy horses from him. Then he sent for his English trainer and the money-lender, and divided what money he had according to the different accounts he intended to pay. This done, he wrote a cold and cutting answer to his mother. Then he took out of his pocket-book three notes of Anna's, read them again, burned them and, remembering their conversation the evening before, he fell into a reverie.

20

VRONSKY's life was particularly happy in that he had a code of principles, which defined with unfailing certitude what should and what should not be done. This code of principles covered only a very small circle of contingencies, but in return the principles were never obscure, and Vronsky, as he never went outside that circle, had never had a moment's hesitation about doing what he ought to do. This code categorically ordained that gambling debts must be paid, the tailor need not be; that one must not lie to a man but might to a woman; that one must never cheat anyone but one may a husband; that one must never pardon an insult but may insult others oneself, and so on. These principles might be irrational and not good, but they were absolute and in complying with them Vronsky felt at ease and could hold his head high. Only quite lately, in regard to his relations with Anna, Vronsky had begun to feel that his code did not quite meet all circumstances and that the future presented doubts and difficulties for which he could find no guiding thread.

His present relations to Anna and to her husband were to his mind perfectly clear and simple. They were clearly and precisely defined in the code of principles which guided him.

She was an honourable woman who had bestowed her love upon

him, and he loved her; therefore she was in his eyes a woman who had a right to the same, or even more respect than a lawful wife. He would have let his hand be cut off sooner than permit himself a word, a hint that might humiliate her, or fail to show her all the regard a woman could expect.

His attitude to society also was clear. Everyone might know or suspect it but no one must dare to speak of it. At the first hint he was ready to silence the speaker and make him respect the non-existent honour of the woman he loved.

Clearest of all was his attitude to her husband. From the moment that Anna gave Vronsky her love, he had considered his own right over her unassailable. Her husband was merely a superfluous person and a hindrance. No doubt he was in a pitiable position but how could that be helped? The only right a husband had was, weapon in hand, to demand satisfaction, and Vronsky had been prepared for that from the first moment.

But of late something new had arisen in his inner relations with Anna, which frightened Vronsky by their vagueness. Only the day before she had told him that she was with child. And he felt that this fact and what she expected of him called for something not fully defined in his code of principles. He had indeed been taken by surprise, and at the first moment when she told him of her condition his heart had prompted him to beg her to leave her husband. He had said so, but now, on reflection, he saw clearly that it would be better to manage without it; and yet while he told himself so, he was afraid that this might be wrong.

'If I urged her to leave her husband, that must mean uniting her life with mine. Am I prepared for that? How can I take her away now, when I have no money? Supposing I could arrange ... But how could I go away with her while I'm in the service? If I say that – I must be ready to do it, that is, I ought to have the money and to retire from the army.'

And he pondered. The question whether to retire from the service or not brought him to the other and perhaps the chief interest of his life, of which none knew but he.

Ambition was the old dream of his youth and boyhood, a dream he did not confess even to himself, though it was so strong that even now this passion was doing battle with his love. His first steps in society and in the service had been successful, but two years ago he had made a great mistake. Anxious to show his independence and to advance, he had refused a post that was offered him, hoping that this refusal would enhance his value; but it turned out that he had been too confident and he was passed over. And having perforce taken up the position of an independent man, he carried it off with tact and good sense, behaving as though he bore no grudge against anyone, and did not feel at all injured, and cared for nothing but to be left in peace, since he was enjoying himself. Actually, he had ceased to enjoy himself as long ago as the year before, when he went away to Moscow. He felt that this independent attitude of a man who might have done anything but cared to do nothing was already beginning to pall, and that many people were beginning to fancy that he was not really capable of anything but being a straightforward, good-natured fellow. His connexion with Madame Karenin, which had created such a stir and attracted general attention, by investing him with fresh glamour had for a while lulled the gnawing worm of ambition within him, but a week before that worm had been roused up again with renewed vigour. A playmate of his childhood, a man of the same set, of the same coterie, his comrade in the Corps of Pages, Serpuhovskoy, who had graduated with him and had been his rival in class, at gymnastics, in mischief, and their dreams of glory, had just returned from Central Asia, where he had been twice promoted and had won a distinction seldom awarded to so young a general.

As soon as he arrived in Petersburg, people began to talk about him as a newly-risen star of the first magnitude. A schoolfellow of Vronsky's and of the same age, he was a general and was expecting a command which might have influence on the course of political events; while Vronsky, though independent and brilliant, and beloved by a charming woman, was merely a cavalry captain, allowed to remain as independent as he pleased. 'Of course I don't envy Serpuhovskoy and never could envy him; but his advancement proves that a man like me has only to watch his opportunity for his career to be made in no time. Three years ago he and I were in the same position. If I resign my commission, I burn my boats. If I remain in the service, I lose nothing. She said herself she did not wish to change her position. And with her love I cannot feel envious of Serpuhovskoy.' And slowly twirling his moustaches he got up from the table and began to walk about the room. His eyes shone particularly brightly, and he was conscious of that confident, calm, and happy frame of mind which always came after he had put his affairs in order. Everything was clear and straight, just as after his former days of reckoning. He shaved, took a cold bath, dressed and went out.

21

'I've come to fetch you. Your *lessive* took a long time to-day,' said Petritsky. 'Well, is it done?'

'Yes, it's done,' answered Vronsky, smiling with his eyes only and twisting the ends of his moustaches as circumspectly as though any over-bold or abrupt movement might upset the order into which he had brought his affairs.

'After the operation you always look as if you had emerged straight from a bath,' said Petritsky. 'I've come from Gritsky's' (as they called their colonel); 'they're expecting you.'

Vronsky looked at his comrade without answering, thinking of something else.

'Yes; is that where the music is?' he said, listening to the familiar strains of brass instruments playing polkas and waltzes that floated across to him.

'Serpuhovskoy's arrived.'

'Aha!' said Vronsky. 'Why, I didn't know.'

The smile in his eyes gleamed more brightly than ever.

Once having made up his mind that he was happy in his love, that he sacrificed his ambition to it – having, at any rate, assumed this role, Vronsky was incapable of feeling either envious of Serpuhovskoy or hurt that he had not come first to him on reaching the regiment. Serpuhovskoy was a good friend, and he was delighted he had come.

'Ah, I'm very glad.'

The colonel, Demin, had taken a large country-house. The whole party were on the wide lower balcony. In the courtyard the first objects that met Vronsky's eyes were a band of singers in white linen coats, standing near a cask of vodka, and the hale, jovial figure of the colonel surrounded by officers. He had gone out on to the top step of the balcony and his loud voice could be heard above the music of the band (which was playing a quadrille of Offenbach's). He was waving his arms and giving some orders to a few soldiers standing on one side. A group of men, a quartermaster and several subalterns came up to the balcony with Vronsky. The colonel returned to the table, went out again on to the steps with a glass in his hand and proposed a toast, 'To the health of our old comrade, the gallant general, Prince Serpuhovskoy. Hurrah!'

The colonel was followed by Serpuhovskoy, who came out on to the steps smiling, champagne-glass in hand.

'You get younger every day, Bondarenko,' he said to the ruddy-cheeked, smart-looking quartermaster, doing his second term of service, who was standing just before him.

It was three years since Vronsky had seen Serpuhovskoy. He was more mature, had let his whiskers grow, but his figure was still just as good and he was just as striking – not so much for his handsome features as for a certain gentleness and nobility in his face and bearing. The only change Vronsky detected in him was that subdued, continual radiance which settles on the faces of men who are successful and feel assured that their success is recognized by everyone. Vronsky knew that radiant air and immediately observed it in Serpuhovskoy.

As Serpuhovskoy came down the steps he caught sight of Vronsky. A smile of pleasure lit up his face. He jerked his head backwards and waved the glass in his hand, greeting Vronsky and showing him by the gesture that he must go first to the quartermaster, who had drawn himself up and was already pursing his lips ready to be kissed.

'Ah, here he is!' shouted the colonel. 'Yashvin told me you were in one of your gloomy moods.'

Serpuhovskoy planted a kiss on the dashing quartermaster's moist, fresh lips and, wiping his mouth with his handkerchief, went up to Vronsky.

'Well, I am glad!' he said, squeezing his hand and drawing him on one side.

'Look after him!' the colonel shouted to Yashvin, pointing to Vronsky; and he went down below to the soldiers.

'Why weren't you at the races yesterday? I expected to see you there,' said Vronsky, taking stock of Serpuhovskoy.

'I did go, but late. Excuse me,' he added, and turned to the adjutant: 'Please see this is divided among the men.'

And he hastily took three one-hundred-rouble notes from his pocket-book, blushing a little.

'Vronsky! Have anything to eat or drink?' asked Yashvin. 'Hi! Bring the count something to eat! Ah, here it is: have a drink!'

The fête at the colonel's lasted a long while. There was a great deal of drinking. They tossed Serpuhovskoy in the air and caught him again several times. Then they did the same to the colonel. Then, to the accompaniment of the band, the colonel himself danced with Petritsky. After that, the colonel, feeling a trifle worn, sat down on a bench in the courtyard and began demonstrating to Yashvin the superiority of Russia over Prussia, especially in cavalry attack, and there was a lull in the revelry for a moment. Serpuhovskoy went indoors to the cloakroom to wash his hands, and found Vronsky there. Vronsky was drenching his head with water. He had taken off his coat and put his sunburnt, hairy neck under the tap and was rubbing it and his head with his hands. When he had finished, Vronsky went and sat beside Serpuhovskoy on a little sofa in the dressing-room, and a conversation began of great interest to both of them.

'I used to hear all about you from my wife,' said Serpuhovskoy. 'I'm glad you've been seeing a good deal of her.'

'She is friendly with Varya, and they are the only women in Petersburg I care about seeing,' answered Vronsky with a smile. He smiled because he foresaw the turn the conversation would take and it pleased him.

'The only ones?' Serpuhovskoy queried, smiling.

'Yes; and I heard news of you, but not only through your wife,' said Vronsky, checking the hint by a stern look. 'I was delighted at your success, but not a bit surprised. I expected even more.'

Serpuhovskoy smiled. Such an opinion was obviously agreeable to him and he saw no reason to hide the fact.

'I, on the contrary, expected less – I'll own frankly. But I'm glad, very glad. I'm ambitious: that's my weakness and I confess to it.'

'Perhaps you wouldn't confess to it if you weren't successful,' said Vronsky.

'I don't suppose so,' and Serpuhovskoy smiled again. 'I won't say life wouldn't be worth living without it, but it would be dull. Of course I may be mistaken, but I fancy I have a certain ability for the career I've chosen, and that power of any sort in my hands, if it is to be, will be better than in the hands of a good many people I know,' said Serpuhovskoy, with beaming consciousness of success. 'And so the nearer I get to it, the better pleased I am.'

'Perhaps that is true for you, but not for everyone. I used to think the same, yet here am I living and finding life worth living for other reasons too.'

'There it's out! Here it comes!' said Serpuhovskoy, laughing. 'I began by saying that I used to hear about you, I heard about your refusal. ... Of course, I approved of it. But there are ways of doing everything. And I think that though your action was good in itself, you didn't do it in quite the right way.'

'What's done can't be undone, and you know I never go back on what I've done. And besides, I'm quite happy as I am.'

'Yes, for a time. But you won't be for long. I wouldn't say this to your brother. He's a nice boy, like our host here. Hark at him!' he added, listening to the roar of 'Hurrah!' – 'He goes about enjoying himself, but that wouldn't satisfy you.'

'I didn't say it would.'

'Yes, and that's not the only thing. Men like you are wanted.'

'By whom?'

'By whom? By society, by Russia. Russia needs men; she needs a party – without it everything goes and will go to the dogs.'

'How do you mean? Bertenev's party against the Russian communists?'

'No,' said Serpuhovskoy, frowning with vexation at being suspected of such an absurdity. '*Tout ça est une blague.* That's always been and always will be. There are no communists. But scheming people always have to invent some noxious, dangerous party. It's an old trick. No, what's wanted is a powerful party of independent men like you and me.'

'But why?' Vronsky named several influential men with power. 'Why aren't they independent men?'

'Simply because they have not, or have not had from birth, an independent position – they've not had a name; they weren't born as near the sun as we were. They can be bought either by money or by favour. To keep in power they have to invent some sort of policy. And they bring forward some notion, some policy they don't believe in themselves and which does harm; and the whole policy is really only a means to a government house and so much income. *Cela n'est plus fin que ça* – that's all it amounts to – when you get a peep at their cards. I may be inferior to them, stupider perhaps, though I don't see why I should be. Anyhow, you and I have one important advantage over them: we are more difficult to buy. And such men are more needed than ever.'

Vronsky listened attentively, but it was not so much the content of

333

Serpuhovskoy's words that interested him as his attitude, for Serpuhovskoy was already contemplating a struggle with the powers-that-be and already had his likes and dislikes in the great world, whereas his own interest did not go beyond the interests of his regiment. Vronsky realized, too, how powerful Serpuhovskoy might become with his undoubted faculty for thinking things out and understanding them, with his intelligence and gift of words, so rare in the circle in which he moved. And, ashamed as he was of it, he felt envious.

'All the same I lack the one essential,' he answered. 'I haven't the desire for power. I had it once, but it's gone.'

'Excuse me, that's not true,' said Serpuhovskoy smiling.

'Yes, it is true, it is true ... now,' Vronsky added, to be quite frank.

'Yes, true now, that's another matter; but that *now* will not last for ever.'

'Maybe,' replied Vronsky.

'You say *maybe*,' Serpuhovskoy went on, as if guessing his thoughts, 'but I say *for certain*. And that's why I wanted to see you. You acted rightly. I quite understand that. But I don't think you ought to keep it up. I only ask you to give me *carte blanche*. I'm not going to patronize you ... though, indeed, why shouldn't I? Think of the times you've been my patron! I should hope our friendship rises above all that sort of thing. Come,' he said with a smile tender as a woman's, 'give me *carte blanche*, retire from the regiment, and I'll advance you imperceptibly.'

'But don't you see, I want nothing,' said Vronsky, 'except that things should remain as they are.'

Serpuhovskoy rose and stood facing him.

'You say you want things to remain as they are. I understand what that means. But listen: we're the same age, you've known more women than I have, perhaps.' Serpuhovskoy's smile and gestures told Vronsky that he needn't be afraid, that he would be tender and careful in touching the sore place. 'But I am married and, believe me, in getting to know your wife, if one loves her, as someone has said, a man gets to know all women better than if he knew thousands of them.'

'We're just coming!' Vronsky shouted to an officer, who looked in at the door to call them to the colonel.

Vronsky was now eager to hear the rest of what Serpuhovskoy had to say.

'And here's my opinion. Women are the chief stumbling-block in a man's career. It's difficult to love a woman and do anything. There's only one way of having love conveniently without its being a hindrance – and that is to marry. How can I explain – how can I tell you what I mean?' said Serpuhovskoy, who was fond of similes. 'Wait, I have it! Yes, you can only carry a *fardeau* and do something with your hands at the same time if the *fardeau* is tied on your back: and that's marriage. I discovered that when I married. I suddenly had my hands free. But if you drag that *fardeau* about with you without marriage, your hands will always be so full that you can do nothing. Look at Mazankov, look at Krupov. They have ruined their careers for the sake of women.'

'But what women!' said Vronsky, recalling the Frenchwoman and the actress with whom the two men he had mentioned were connected.

'So much the worse! The firmer the woman's footing in society, the worse it is! That's much the same as not merely carrying the *fardeau* in your arms but having to wrench it away from someone else.'

'You have never loved,' murmured Vronsky, gazing straight before him and thinking of Anna.

'Perhaps not. But you remember what I've told you. And another thing – women are all more materialistic than men. We make something immense out of love, but they are always *terre-à-terre*.'

'Coming, coming!' he said to a footman who approached. But the footman had not come to call them again, as he supposed. The footman brought Vronsky a note.

'From the Princess Tverskoy.'

Vronsky opened the note and flushed crimson.

'My head aches; I'm going home,' he said to Serpuhovskoy.

'Well, good-bye, then. You give me *carte blanche*?'

'We'll talk it over another time. I will look you up in Petersburg.'

22

IT was already well past five and, in order not to be late and at the same time not use his own horses, known to everyone, Vronsky got into Yashvin's hired fly and told the driver to drive as fast as possible. It was a spacious old vehicle with room for four. He sat in one corner, stretched his legs out on the front seat, and sank into thought.

A vague sense of the order into which his affairs had been brought, a vague sense of Serpuhovskoy's friendship and flattery in considering him a man that was needed, and, most of all, the anticipation of the coming rendezvous, all blended into one general joyous impression of life. This impression was so strong that he could not help smiling. He dropped his legs, crossed one leg over the other knee and, taking it in his hand, felt the springy muscle of the calf, where he had bruised it in his fall the day before, and then, leaning back, he drew several deep breaths.

'Good, splendid!' he said to himself.

He had often had this sense of physical joy but he had never felt so fond of himself, of his own body, as at that moment. He enjoyed the slight ache in his strong leg, he enjoyed the muscular sensation of movement in his chest as he breathed. The bright, cold August day which had made Anna feel so hopeless seemed exhilarating to him and refreshed his face and neck that still tingled after the drenching he had given them under the tap. The scent of brilliantine on his moustaches struck him as peculiarly pleasant in the fresh air. Everything he saw through the carriage window, everything in that cold pure air, in the pale light of the sunset, was as fresh and jolly and vigorous as he was himself : the roofs of the houses shining in the rays of the setting sun, the sharp outlines of fences and angles of buildings, the figures of passers-by, other carriages, the motionless green of the trees and grass, the fields with evenly drawn furrows of potatoes, and the slanting shadows that fell from the houses and trees and bushes, and even from the rows of potatoes – everything was beautiful, like a lovely landscape fresh from the artist's brush and lately varnished.

'Faster! faster!' he said to the driver, putting his head out of the window; and taking a three-rouble note from his pocket he thrust it into the man's hand as the latter looked round. The driver fumbled with something at the lamp, the whip cracked, and the carriage whirled rapidly over the smooth high-road.

'I want nothing, nothing but this happiness,' he thought, staring at the ivory knob of the bell in the space between the windows, while his imagination pictured Anna as he had seen her last time. 'And as I go on, I love her more and more. Well, here's the park of the Vredes' country-house. Whereabouts will she be? Where? How shall I find her? Why did she fix on this place for a meeting, and why does she write in Betsy's letter?' he wondered for the first time, but there was now no time for wonder. He called to the driver to stop before reaching the avenue and, opening the door, jumped out while the carriage was moving, and went into the avenue that led up to the house. There was no one in the avenue; but looking round to the right he caught sight of her. Her face was hidden under a veil, but he drank in with glad eyes that special manner of walking, peculiar to her alone, the slope of her shoulders, the poise of her head; and at once a thrill ran through his body like an electric current. With new intensity he felt conscious of himself from the elastic spring of his legs to the rise and fall of his lungs as he breathed, and something set his lips twitching.

Joining him, she pressed his hand tightly.

'You're not angry that I sent for you? I absolutely had to see you,' she said; and at the sight of the grave, set line of her lips under the veil his mood changed at once.

'I angry! But how did you get here – where shall we go?'

'Never mind,' she said, laying her hand on his arm. 'Come, I must talk to you.'

He saw that something had happened, and that this meeting would not be a happy one. In her presence he had no will of his own: without knowing the grounds for her distress, he already felt himself involuntarily infected by it.

'What is it? What has happened?' he asked, squeezing her hand with his elbow and trying to read her face.

She walked on a few steps in silence, gathering up her courage, and then suddenly stopped.

'I did not tell you last night,' she began, breathing quickly and painfully, 'that coming home with Alexei Alexandrovich I told him everything ... told him I could no longer be his wife, that ... and told him everything.'

He listened, unconsciously bending his whole figure down to her as though hoping in this way to soften the painfulness of the position for her. But directly she had said this he suddenly drew himself up and a proud, stern expression came over his face.

'Yes, yes, that's better, a thousand times better! I know how hard it must have been for you,' he said.

But she was not listening to his words, she was reading his thoughts from his face. She could not guess that that expression arose from the first idea that presented itself to him – that a duel was now inevitable.

The possibility of a duel had never crossed her mind, and so she put a different interpretation on this fleeting look of severity.

When she got her husband's letter, she knew then in the depths of her heart that everything would go on in the old way, that she would not have the courage to forego her position, to abandon her son and join her lover. The morning spent at the Princess Tverskoy's had further confirmed this. But this meeting was still of the utmost importance. She hoped that it would transform their position and save her. If on hearing this news he were to say to her firmly, passionately, without a moment's hesitation: 'Throw up everything and come with me!' she would give up her son and go away with him. But the news had not produced the effect she had expected in him: he only looked as though he were resenting some affront.

'It was not in the least hard for me. It happened of itself,' she said irritably. 'And here ...' She pulled her husband's letter out of her glove.

'I understand, I understand,' he interrupted, taking the letter, but not reading it, and trying to soothe her. 'The one thing I longed for, the one thing I prayed for, was to put an end to this situation, so as to devote my life to your happiness.'

'Why do you tell me that?' she said. 'Do you suppose I could doubt it? If I doubted ...'

'Who's that coming?' said Vronsky suddenly, pointing to two ladies walking towards them. 'They may know us!' and he hastily drew her into a side-walk.

'Oh, I don't care!' she said. Her lips were quivering. And he fancied that her eyes looked with strange malevolence at him from under her veil. 'I tell you that's not the point – I cannot doubt that; but see what he writes to me. Read it.' She stood still again.

Again, just as at the first moment of hearing of her rupture with her husband, Vronsky, on reading the letter, was unconsciously carried away by the natural sensation aroused in him by his own relation to the injured husband. As he held the letter in his hand he could not help picturing the challenge which he would most likely find at home to-day or to-morrow, and the duel itself, in which, with the same cold, haughty expression that his face was assuming at this moment, he would await the injured husband's shot, after having discharged his own weapon in the air. And at this point there flashed across his mind the thought of what Serpuhovskoy had just been saying to him, and what he himself had been thinking in the morning – that it was better not to tie himself down – and he knew that this thought he could not tell her.

Having read the letter, he raised his eyes, and there was no determination in them. She realized at once that he had been thinking about it before by himself. She knew that whatever he might say to her, he would not say all he thought. And she knew that her last hope had failed her. This was not what she had been reckoning on.

'You see what sort of man he is,' she said in a trembling voice, 'he ...'

'Forgive me, but I rejoice at it,' Vronsky interrupted. 'For God's sake, let me finish!' he added, his eyes beseeching her to give him time to explain. 'I rejoice, because things cannot, cannot possibly remain as he supposes.'

'Why can't they?' muttered Anna, forcing back her tears and obviously attaching no sort of consequence to what he would say. She felt that her fate was sealed.

Vronsky meant that after the duel – inevitable, he considered – things could not go on as before, but what he said was:

'It can't go on. I hope that now you will leave him. I hope' – he was confused, and reddened – 'that you will let me arrange and plan our life. To-morrow ...' he was beginning.

She did not let him go on.

'And my son?' she cried out. 'You see what he writes! I should have to leave him, and I can't and won't do that.'

'But, for God's sake, which is better? To leave your child or keep up this degrading position?'

'Degrading for whom?'

'For everyone, and most of all for you.'

'You say degrading ... don't say that. Such words have no meaning for me,' she said tremulously. She did not want him now to say what was untrue. She had nothing left but his love, and she wanted to love him. 'Try to understand that from the day I loved you everything has changed for me. For me there is one thing, and one thing only – your love. If that's mine, I feel so uplifted, so strong, that nothing can be humiliating to me. I am proud of my position, because ... proud of being ... proud ...' She could not say what she was proud of. Tears of shame and despair choked her. She stood still and sobbed.

He, too, was conscious of a smarting in his nose and something swelling in his throat and for the first time in his life felt on the point of weeping. He could not have said exactly what it was that moved him so. He felt sorry for her, and he felt he could not help her, and with that he knew that he was to blame for her wretchedness, that he had done wrong.

'Is a divorce really not possible?' he said feebly. She shook her head, not answering. 'Couldn't you take your son, and still leave him?'

'Yes; but it all depends on him. Now I must go to him,' she said drily. Her foreboding that everything would remain as it was had not deceived her.

'On Tuesday I shall be in Petersburg, and everything can be settled.'

'Yes,' she said. 'But don't let us talk about it any more.'

Anna's carriage, which she had sent away, and ordered to come back to the little gate of the Vrede garden, drove up. Anna said good-bye to him and drove home.

23

ON Monday there was the usual sitting of the Commission of the 2nd of June. Karenin walked into the hall where the sitting was held, greeted the members and the president, as usual, and sat down in his place, putting his hand on the papers laid ready before him. Among these papers were the necessary references and a draft of the speech he intended to make. But he did not really require these documents. He remembered every point, and did not consider it necessary to run over in his mind what he would say. He knew that when the time came and he saw his opponent facing him, vainly trying to look indifferent, his speech would flow of itself better than he could prepare it now. He felt that the import of his speech was of such magnitude that every word of it would have weight. Meanwhile, as he listened to the usual report, he wore the most innocent and inoffensive air. No one, looking at his white hands with their accentuated veins and long fingers so softly stroking the edges of the white paper that lay before him, and at his head inclined wearily to one side, would have suspected that in a few minutes a torrent of words would pour from his lips that would arouse such a fearful storm as would cause the members to shout each other down and the president to call for order. When the report was over, Karenin announced in his quiet, thin voice that he had certain considerations to submit in regard to the Commission for the Re-organization of the Native Tribes. All attention was turned upon him. Karenin cleared his throat and, not looking at his opponent but selecting, as he always did while he was delivering his speeches, the first person sitting opposite him, a peaceful little old man who never had any opinion to express in the Commission, began to expound his views. When he reached the point about the fundamental and organic law, his opponent jumped up and began to protest. Stremov, who was also a member of the Commission, and also stung to the quick, began defending himself, and altogether a stormy sitting followed. But Karenin won the day and his motion was carried. Three new commissions were appointed, and on the morrow in a certain Petersburg circle nothing else was talked of but this sitting. Karenin's success had been even greater than he had anticipated.

Next morning, Tuesday, when he awoke, Karenin recollected with satisfaction his triumph of the previous day, and he could not help smiling, though he tried to appear indifferent, when the chief secretary of his department, anxious to flatter him, told him of the reports that had reached him of what had taken place in the Commission.

Busy with the chief secretary, Karenin had completely forgotten that it was Tuesday, the day fixed by him for Anna's return, and he was disagreeably surprised when a footman came in to inform him of her arrival.

Anna got to Petersburg early in the morning; the carriage had been sent to meet her in accordance with her telegram, and so Karenin might have known of her arrival. But he did not come out when she arrived. She was told that he had not yet gone out, but was busy with his secretary. She sent word to her husband that she was back, went to her boudoir and set to work unpacking her things, expecting that he would come to her. But an hour passed and he did not come. She went into the dining-room on the pretext of giving some directions and purposely spoke in a loud voice, expecting him to come out there; but, although she heard him accompany his secretary to the study door, he did not come out to her. She knew that in the usual way he would soon be going to his office, and she wanted to see him first, that their attitude to one another might be defined.

She crossed the drawing-room and went resolutely to him. When she entered his study he was sitting in his official uniform, evidently ready to start, with his elbows on the table, looking wearily in front of him. She saw him before he saw her, and knew that he was thinking about her.

On seeing her, he half rose but changed his mind, and his face flushed – a thing Anna had never seen before. Then he got up quickly and came forward, looking not at her eyes, but above them at her forehead and hair. He came up to her, took her by the hand, and asked her to sit down.

'I am very glad you have come,' he said, sitting down beside her, and, obviously wishing to say something, he faltered. Several times he tried to speak but stopped. Although, in preparing for this interview, she had been schooling herself to despise and reproach him, she did not know what to say, pitying him. And so the silence lasted for some time.

'Seriozha quite well?' he said, and without waiting for a reply he added: 'I shall not be dining at home to-day, and I have got to go out directly.'

'I had thought of going to Moscow,' she said.

'No, you did quite right, quite right to come,' he said, and fell silent again.

Seeing that he was powerless to begin, she began for him.

'Alexei Alexandrovich,' she said, looking at him and not dropping her eyes under his persistent gaze at her hair, 'I am a guilty woman, I'm a bad woman, but I am the same as I was, as I told you then, and I have come to say that I cannot alter anything.'

'I did not ask you about that,' he said, suddenly resolutely and with hatred looking her straight in the face. 'It is what I supposed.' Under the influence of anger he apparently regained complete possession of all his faculties. 'But I repeat again what I told you then, and have subsequently written to you,' he went on in a thin, shrill voice, 'I repeat now, that I am not obliged to know it. I ignore it. Not all wives are as good as you in hastening to communicate such *agreeable* news to their husbands.' He stressed the word 'agreeable'. 'I shall ignore it so long as the world knows nothing of it, so long as my name is not disgraced. And therefore I simply warn you that our relations must remain as they have always been, and that only if you let yourself be *compromised* shall I be forced to take measures to secure my honour.'

'But our relations cannot be the same as always,' murmured Anna in a timid voice, looking at him with dismay.

When she saw once more those composed gestures, heard that shrill, childish, sarcastic voice, loathing for him extinguished her former pity and she now felt nothing but fear and anxiety to make her position clear at all costs.

'I cannot be your wife while I ...' she began.

He gave a cold, spiteful laugh.

'The kind of life you have chosen is reflected, I suppose, in your ideas. I have so much respect and contempt – respect for your past and contempt for your present – that I was far from the interpretation you put on my words.'

Anna sighed and hung her head.

'Though indeed I fail to comprehend how, with the independence you show,' he went on, getting heated, '– informing your husband outright of your infidelity and seeing nothing reprehensible in it, apparently – you can find anything reprehensible in performing a wife's duties in relation to your husband.'

'Alexei Alexandrovich! What is it you want of me?'

'I want not to meet that man here, and for you to conduct yourself so that neither society nor the servants can find anything to say against you ... for you not to see him. I think that is not much to ask. In return you will enjoy all the privileges of a respectable wife without fulfilling the duties of one. That is all I have to say to you. Now it is time for me to go. I shall not be back for dinner.'

He got up and moved towards the door. Anna got up too. Bowing to her in silence, he let her pass.

24

THE night Levin spent on the haycock was not without effect. The way in which he had been managing his land became repugnant and lost all interest for him. In spite of the magnificent harvest, he had never, or thought he had never encountered so many mishaps, or so much ill-feeling between himself and the peasants, as he had that year; and the origin of those mishaps and that hostility was now perfectly comprehensible to him. The delight he had felt in the work itself, and the consequent greater intimacy with the peasants, his envy of them and their life, his desire to adopt that way of living, which had been to him that night not a dream but an intention, the execution of which he had considered in detail – all this together had so transformed his outlook on the farming of his estate that he could not take his former interest in it, and could not help seeing that disagreeable relation between himself and the peasants underlying everything. A herd of line-bred cattle like Pava, the land all dressed and ploughed, the nine level fields hedged round with hurdles of willow, the 240 acres heavily manured, the seed-drills and all the rest of it would have been splendid if they could be done by himself alone, or with the help of friends and people in sympathy with him. But he saw clearly now (his work on a book on agriculture, in which the labourer was to have been the chief element in husbandry, greatly assisted him in this) that his present method of farming was one bitter, obstinate struggle between himself and the men, in which on one side – his side – there was a continual striving to remodel everything to a pattern he considered better; on the other side the natural order of things. And in this struggle he saw that with the greatest efforts on his part, and with no effort or even intention on theirs, all that resulted was that the work did not go to the liking of either side, and fine implements and splendid cattle and soil were uselessly spoiled. Worst of all, not only was the energy expended on this work wasted, but he could not help feeling now, when he saw the meaning of his system laid bare before him, that the aim of his energy was a most unworthy one. In reality, what was the struggle about? He was fighting for every farthing of his share (and he could not do otherwise: he had only to relax his efforts and he would not have had the money to pay his labourers), whereas they were only anxious to be left to do their work lazily and comfortably, in other words, to work the way they always had done. It was to his interest that every man should work as hard as possible and at the same time keep his wits about him and not break the winnowing-machines, the horse-rakes, the thrashing-machines, that he should attend to what he was doing. What the labourer wanted was to take it as easy as possible, with rests, and, especially, not have the trouble of worrying and thinking. That summer Levin noticed this at every step. He sent the men to mow some clover for hay, picking out the worst patches where the clover was overgrown with grass and hemlock and no good for seed; and time and again they mowed the best seed clover, justifying themselves by saying that the bailiff had told them to, and trying to pacify him with the assurance that it would be splendid hay; while he knew that they had done it because those acres were easier to mow. He sent out the tedder to pitch the hay – it got broken in the first few rows because the peasant found it dull sitting on the seat in front with

344

the blades swinging over his head. And he was told, 'Don't worry, master; sure the women will toss it in no time.' The ploughs were practically useless because it never entered the peasant's head to raise the share at the end of the furrow – the horses were forced to wrench the plough round, straining themselves and tearing up the ground; and Levin was begged not to mind about it. The horses were allowed to stray into the wheat because not a single man would consent to be night-watchman and, in spite of this having been forbidden, the labourers took turns for night duty, and Vanka, after working all day long, fell asleep, and confessed his guilt, saying 'Do what you will to me, sir.' Three of his best calves died through over-feeding – they had been let into the meadow where the clover had been cut, without any water to drink; and nothing would make the men believe that they had been blown out by the clover. They told him by way of consolation that one of his neighbours had lost 112 head of cattle in three days. All this happened, not because anyone wished ill to Levin or his farm; on the contrary, he knew that they liked him and considered him a homely gentleman (the highest praise they could bestow). It happened simply because all they wanted was to work light-heartedly and irresponsibly, and his interests were not only remote and incomprehensible to them but fatally opposed to their own most just claims. Levin had long felt dissatisfaction with his own position in regard to the land. He saw that his ship leaked, but he did not look for the hole, perhaps purposely deceiving himself. But now he could deceive himself no longer. The farming of the land, as he was managing it, had not only ceased to interest him, but had become distasteful, and he could no longer give his mind to it.

Added to this there was the presence, not twenty miles off, of Kitty Shcherbatsky, whom he longed to see, yet could not. When he was over there Dolly had asked him to come; to come with the object of once more making his offer to her sister, who would, so she gave him to understand, accept him now. Levin himself knew from the glimpse he had caught of Kitty that he had never ceased to love her; but he could not go over to Dolly's, knowing she was there. The fact that he had proposed and she had refused him had placed an insuperable barrier between them. 'I cannot ask her to be my wife merely because she can't be the wife of the man she wanted to marry,' he said to himself. The thought of this made him cold and hostile towards her. 'I should not be able to speak to her without a feeling of reproach; I could not look at her without resentment; and she would only hate me all the more – and rightly! And besides, how can I now, after what Darya Alexandrovna told me, go to see them? Could I help showing that I know what she told me? And for me to go magnanimously to forgive her and have pity on her! For me to stand before her in the role of one who forgives her and deigns to bestow his love on her! ... What induced Darya Alexandrovna to tell me that? I might have met her accidentally, then everything would have followed naturally; but as it is, it's out of the question, out of the question!'

Dolly sent him a note, asking for the loan of a side-saddle for Kitty's use. 'I'm told you have a side-saddle,' she wrote. 'I hope you will bring it over yourself.'

This was more than he could stand. How could a woman of any intelligence, of any delicacy, put her sister in such a humiliating position! He wrote a dozen notes and tore them all up, eventually sending the saddle without any reply. To say that he would come was impossible, because he could not go; to say that something prevented him from coming, or that he would be away, was still worse. He sent the saddle without an answer, conscious of doing something disgraceful; and next day, handing over all the now disagreeable business of the estate to the bailiff, he set off to a remote district to visit his friend Sviazhsky, who had splendid snipe marshes in his neighbourhood, and had lately written inviting him to keep a long-standing promise to pay him a visit. The snipe-marshes in the Surovsky district had long tempted Levin but he had continually put off this visit on account of the work on the estate. Now, however, he was glad to get away from the proximity of the Shcherbatskys, and still more from his farm work, especially on a shooting expedition, which always served as the best solace in all his troubles.

25

THERE was no railway or service of post-horses in the Surovsky district, so Levin drove there with his own horses in his *tarantas*, a large four-wheeled vehicle with leather top.

He stopped half-way at a well-to-do peasant's to feed his horses. The bald-headed, well-preserved old man, with a broad, red beard going grey round his cheeks, opened the gate, squeezing against the post to let the three horses pass. Directing the coachman to a place in a lean-to in the big, clean, tidy, newly-constructed yard, where stood some charred old-fashioned ploughs, the old man invited Levin indoors. A cleanly-dressed young woman, her unstockinged feet in goloshes, was scrubbing the floor in the new outer room. The dog running in behind Levin frightened her and she uttered a shriek, but at once began laughing at her fears when told that the dog would not hurt her. Pointing Levin with her bare arm to the parlour door, she bent down again, hiding her pretty face, and resumed her scrubbing.

'Would you like the samovar?' she asked.

'Yes, please.'

The parlour was a big room, with a Dutch stove and a partition dividing it in two. Under the shelf in the corner with the ikons was a table decorated with a painted pattern, a bench, and two chairs. By the door stood a dresser full of crockery. The shutters were closed, there were not many flies, and it was so clean that Levin was anxious that Laska, who had been running along the road and rolling in puddles, should not muddy the floor, and told her to lie down in the corner by the door. After looking round the room, Levin went out in the backyard. The good-looking young woman in goloshes, swinging the empty pails on the yoke, ran on in front of him to the well for water.

'Look lively, my girl!' the old man shouted after her good-humouredly, and went up to Levin. 'Well, sir, is it to Nikolai Ivano-vich Sviazhsky you are going? He stops at our place too,' he began garrulously, leaning his elbows on the railing of the steps. In the middle of the old man's account of his acquaintance with Sviazhsky, the gates creaked again, and in drove the farm-hands with their ploughs and harrows from the fields. The horses harnessed to the ploughs and harrows were sleek and sturdy. The men obviously belonged to the house: two young fellows wore print shirts and peaked caps; the others, an old man and a lad in homespun shirts, were labourers. Moving off from the steps, the old master of the house went up to the horses and began unharnessing them.

'What have they been ploughing?' asked Levin.

'They've been earthing up the potatoes. We rent a bit of land too. Fedot, don't let the gelding out, but take him to the trough. We can harness the other. ...'

'I say, Father, have those ploughshares I ordered come?' asked a tall, healthy-looking young fellow, evidently the old man's son.

347

'They're there ... in the outer room,' answered the old man, coiling up the reins he had taken off and throwing them on the ground. 'You can put them on while they are having dinner.'

The good-looking young woman returned, her shoulders weighed down with the two brimming buckets of water, and went into the house. More women appeared from somewhere, young and comely, middle-aged, old and ugly, some with children, others without.

The water in the samovar was beginning to sing. The labourers and the family, having attended to the horses, came in to dinner. Levin took some provisions out of his carriage and invited the old man to take tea with him.

'Why, I don't know, I have had some to-day already,' said the old man, obviously pleased to accept the invitation. 'Well, just for company, then.'

Over their tea Levin heard all about the old man's farming. Ten years before, he had rented 300 acres from the lady who owned them, and a year ago had bought them outright and rented another 700 from a neighbouring landowner. A small portion of the land – the poorest – he let, while with the help of his family and two hired men he cultivated 100 acres of arable land. The old man complained that things were doing badly. But Levin could see that he only did so as a matter of course, and that his farm was in a flourishing condition. Had his affairs been in a bad way, he would not have bought land at thirty-five roubles an acre, would not have married three of his sons and a nephew, would not have rebuilt twice after fires, and each time on a larger scale. In spite of the old man's grumbling, it was obvious that he was proud, and justly proud, of his prosperity, proud of his sons, his nephew, his sons' wives, his horses, and his cows, and especially of the fact that he could keep it all going. From his conversation with the old man, Levin gathered he was not averse to new methods either. He had planted a good many potatoes, and his potatoes had already flowered and were beginning to set, as Levin had noticed when passing the fields on the way, whereas Levin's were only just coming into flower. He earthed up his potatoes with a new kind of plough borrowed from a neighbouring landowner. He sowed wheat. One small point particularly struck Levin: the old man used the thinnings from the rye as fodder for the horses. Many a time Levin had seen this valuable food wasted, and tried to have it gathered up, but had never succeeded. The peasant got this done, and could not praise it enough as fodder.

'What have the young women to do? They carry it out in little heaps to the roadside, and the cart comes and picks them up.'

'We landowners don't manage well with our labourers,' said Levin, handing him a tumbler of tea.

'Thank you,' replied the old man, and he took the tea but refused sugar, pointing to a little nibbled lump he had left. 'How can you run a farm with hired labourers?' he said. 'They're simple destruction. Take Sviazhsky's, now. We know what sort of soil his is, black as poppy-seed, yet his harvests are nothing to boast of. It's not looked after enough – that's all it is!'

'But you use hired labour on your farm?'

'Yes, but we're all peasants together. We see to everything ourselves. If a man's no use, he can go, and we can manage by ourselves.'

'Father, Finogen wants some tar,' said the young woman in goloshes, coming in.

'That's how it is, sir!' said the old man, getting up; and, after crossing himself several times, he thanked Levin and went out.

When Levin went into the back room to call his coachman he found the whole family of menfolk at dinner. The women were standing up waiting on them. The young, sturdy-looking son with his mouth full of buckwheat porridge was saying something funny, and they were all laughing, the woman in the goloshes most merrily of all as she refilled his bowl with cabbage soup.

Very probably the comely face of the young woman in the goloshes had a good deal to do with the impression of well-being this peasant household made upon Levin, but the impression was so strong that Levin could never get rid of it. And all the way from the old peasant's to Sviazhsky's his thoughts kept returning to this peasant farm as though there were something in this impression that demanded his special attention.

26

SVIAZHSKY was the marshal of his district. He was five years older than Levin, and had been married some time. His sister-in-law, a young girl Levin liked very much, lived in his house. And Levin knew that Sviazhsky and his wife would have greatly liked to marry the girl to him. He knew this with certainty, as so-called eligible young men always know it, though he could never have brought himself to speak of it; and he knew, too, that, although he wanted to get married, and although by every token this very attractive girl would make an excellent wife, he could no more have married her than fly, even had he not been in love with Kitty Shcherbatsky. And this knowledge marred the pleasure he hoped to find in the visit.

Levin had immediately thought of this when he got Sviazhsky's letter with the invitation for shooting, but in spite of it he had made up his mind that Sviazhsky's having such views for him was simply an unfounded supposition on his side, and so he would go all the same. Besides, at the bottom of his heart he was eager to test his feelings about the girl. The Sviazhskys' home life was exceedingly pleasant, and Sviazhsky himself, the best type of man taking part in local affairs that Levin knew, was very interesting to him.

Sviazhsky was one of those people – always a source of wonder to Levin – whose very logical if unoriginal convictions find no reflection in their lives, which are most definite and stable in their direction and go their way quite independently and as a rule in diametric contradiction to their convictions. Sviazhsky was an extreme liberal. He despised the nobility, and believed the majority of them to be secretly in favour of serfdom, only too cowardly to express their views openly. He regarded Russia as a ruined country, after the style of Turkey, and the government of Russia too bad to criticize seriously, and yet he was a functionary of that Government and a model marshal of nobility, when he drove about always wearing the cockade of office and the cap with the red band. He held that a civilized life was only possible abroad, and went abroad at every opportunity; yet at the same time he carried on a complex and improved system of agriculture in Russia, and with deep interest followed everything and knew everything that was being done in Russia. He considered the Russian peasant in the transitional stage between monkey and man, yet in the local assemblies he was the first to shake a peasant by the hand and listen to his opinions. He believed neither in God nor the devil, yet he was much concerned about the question of improving the condition of the clergy and the maintenance of their revenues, and took special trouble to keep up the church in his village.

On the woman question he sided with the extremists who advocated the fullest freedom for women, and especially their right to work. But he lived with his wife on such terms that their affectionate child-less home-life was the admiration of everyone, and arranged his wife's life so that she did nothing and could do nothing except share her husband's efforts to pass their time as happily and as agreeably as possible.

Had it not been Levin's nature to put the most favourable inter-pretation on people, Sviazhsky's character would have presented no doubt or difficulty to him: he would have said to himself, 'a fool or a knave,' and everything would have been plain. But he could not call him a fool, because Sviazhsky was unmistakably clever and, more-over, a highly cultivated man, exceptionally modest about himself. There was no subject with which he was not acquainted; but he never displayed his knowledge unless obliged to do so. Still less could Levin say that he was a knave, as Sviazhsky was unquestionably an upright, kind-hearted, sensible man, always cheerfully and energetically en-gaged on work highly esteemed by all around him, and certainly a man who could never consciously do anything base.

Levin tried but invariably failed to understand him, and regarded him and his life as a living enigma. He and Levin were great friends, and so Levin used to venture to sound Sviazhsky, to try to get to the very roots of his philosophy of living; but always in vain. Every time Levin tried to penetrate below the surface of Sviazhsky's mind, which was hospitably open to all, he noticed that Sviazhsky seemed slightly disconcerted: faint signs of alarm were visible in his eyes, as though he were afraid Levin would understand him, and he would give him a kindly, good-humoured rebuff.

Just now, since his disillusionment with farming, Levin looked for-ward with particular pleasure to staying with Sviazhsky. Apart from the fact that the sight of this happy, affectionate couple, so pleased with themselves and everyone else, and their well-ordered home al-ways had a cheering effect on Levin, he felt a longing, dissatisfied as he was with his own life, to get at the secret which gave Sviazhsky such clarity, definiteness, and courage in life. Moreover, Levin knew that at Sviazhsky's he would be sure to meet the landowners of the neighbourhood, and it would be particularly interesting for him just now to hear and take part in those rural conversations concerning crops, labourer's wages, and so on, which, he was aware, are con-ventionally regarded as matters beneath dignity, but which seemed to him just now to be the one subject of importance. 'It was not, perhaps, of importance in the days of serfdom, and it may not be of importance in England. In both cases, the conditions of agriculture were or are firmly established; but with us now, when everything has been turned upside down and is only just taking shape, the question of how to regulate things is the one important question in Russia,' thought Levin.

The shooting did not prove as good as Levin had expected. The marsh was dry and there were no snipe at all. He walked about the whole day and only brought back three birds, but to make up for that he brought back, as he always did after a day's sport, an excellent appetite, excellent spirits, and that feeling of intellectual excitement which with him always accompanied physical exertion. And while out shooting, when he seemed to be thinking of nothing at all, again and again he found himself remembering the old man and his family, and the impression of them seemed to claim not merely his attention, but the solution of some question connected with them.

In the evening at tea a very interesting conversation sprang up, just as Levin had hoped, in the company of two landowners who had driven over about some business connected with a wardship.

Levin was sitting beside his hostess at the tea-table, and was obliged to keep up a conversation with her and her sister, who was sitting opposite. The hostess was a short, fair, round-faced woman, all dimples and smiles. Levin tried through her to find the answer to the weighty enigma her husband presented to his mind; but he had not full freedom of thought because he was in an agony of embarrassment. He was in an agony of embarrassment because her sister was sitting opposite him in a dress, specially put on, as he fancied, for his benefit, with a particularly low square-cut *décolletage* showing her white bosom. Though her bosom was so white, or perhaps because it was so white, this square-cut *décolletage* deprived Levin of the full use of his faculties. He imagined, probably mistakenly, that this bodice had been cut low on his account, and felt that he had no right to look at it; but he felt to blame for the very fact that it was cut so. It seemed to Levin that he had deceived someone, that he ought to explain something, but that to explain it was quite impossible, and for that reason he was continually blushing, and was ill at ease and awkward. His awkwardness infected the pretty sister, too. But the hostess appeared not to notice this, and made a point of drawing her sister into the conversation.

'You say,' she said, pursuing the subject that had been started, 'that my husband cannot feel an interest in what's Russian. On the contrary, though he is happy abroad, he is never so happy as he is here. Here, he feels in his proper place. He has so much on hand, and he has the gift of interesting himself in everything. Oh, you've not been to see our school, have you?'

'I saw it. ... The little house covered with ivy, isn't it?'

'Yes; that's Nastia's work,' she said, indicating her sister.

'You teach in it yourself?' asked Levin, trying to look beyond the open neck but feeling that wherever he looked in that direction he must see it.

'Yes; I have been and still am teaching there, but we have a first-rate schoolmistress now. And we have started gymnastics.'

'No, thanks, I won't have any more tea,' said Levin, and conscious of behaving rudely but incapable of keeping up the conversation any longer he rose, blushing. 'I hear a very interesting conversation over there,' he added, and went to the other end of the table, where Sviazhsky was sitting with the two landowners. Sviazhsky sat sideways, leaning his elbow on the table and twisting his cup round with one hand, while with the other he gathered his beard into his fist, lifted it to his nose as if smelling it and let it drop again. His brilliant black eyes were fixed on the excited country gentleman with grey whiskers, whose remarks evidently amused him. The landowner was complaining of the peasants. It was plain to Levin that Sviazhsky had an answer to this gentleman's complaints which would at once demolish his whole argument, but that in his position he could not give utterance to this answer, and listened, not without pleasure, to the landowners' absurd discourse.

The gentleman with the grey whiskers was evidently an inveterate believer in serfdom and a passionate farmer, who had spent all his life in the country. Levin saw proofs of this in his dress, in the old-fashioned threadbare coat, obviously not his everyday attire, in his shrewd, beetle-browed eyes, in his well-turned Russian, in the authoritative tone that had become habitual from long use, and in the imperious gestures of his large, red, sunburnt hands, the right one having an old betrothal ring on the little finger.

27

'I F I'd only the heart to throw up what's been set going ... such a lot of trouble wasted ... I would turn my back on the whole business, sell up and go off like Nikolai Ivanovich ... to hear *La Belle Hélène,*' the landowner was saying, a pleasant smile lighting up his shrewd old face.

'But as you don't,' said Nikolai Ivanovich Sviazhsky, 'there must be some advantages.'

'Just one: I live in my own house, which is neither bought nor rented. And there is always the hope that people will learn sense. Though, instead of that, you'd hardly believe the drunkenness, the immorality there is! They keep chopping and changing their bits of land. Not a sight of a horse or a cow. The peasant's dying of hunger, but just go and take him on as a labourer, he'll do his best to spoil and break everything you possess, and end by bringing you before the justice of the peace.'

'But you can make complaints to the justice, too, if you like,' ventured Sviazhsky.

'I lodge a complaint? Nothing on earth would induce me to! I should never hear the end of it! At the mill, for instance, they pocketed money in advance and made off. And what did the justice do? Why, acquitted them. Nothing keeps them in order but their own communal tribunal and their village elder. He'll thrash them in the good old style! But for that there'd be nothing for it but to throw it all up and fly to the other side of the world!'

The old man was evidently chaffing Sviazhsky, who, far from resenting it, was obviously amused.

'Well, now, we manage our estates without such measures,' said he, smiling: 'Levin and I and our neighbour.' He indicated the other landowner.

'Oh yes, Mihail Petrovich manages, but ask him how it's done. Do you call his rational farming?' demanded the landowner, ostentatiously using the word 'rational'.

'My system's very simple, thank the Lord!' said Mihail Petrovich. 'My whole management rests on getting the money ready for the autumn taxes. The peasants come along and say, "Be a father to us and help us out!" Well, the peasants are my own people, my neighbours, and I feel sorry for them. So I advance 'em the first third, only

I say: "Remember, lads, I have helped you, and you must lend me a hand when I need it – whether it's sowing the oats, or hay-making or the harvest." And so we agree for so much work from each family. True, there are some among them who haven't any conscience.'

Levin, who had long been familiar with these patriarchal methods, exchanged a glance with Sviazhsky and, interrupting Mihail Petrovich, addressed the landowner with the grey whiskers again.

'What are your ideas, then?' he asked. 'How would you manage an estate these days?'

'Just the way Mihail Petrovich does: either let the land for half the crop or rent it to the peasants. That one can do – but that's just how the general prosperity of the country is being ruined. Land which with serf-labour and good management used to yield ninefold now on the half-crop system yields threefold. Emancipation of the peasants has been the ruin of Russia!'

Sviazhsky looked at Levin with a twinkle in his eye and even made a just perceptible sign of scornful amusement; but Levin did not think the landowner's words absurd – he understood them better than he did Sviazhsky. Much of what the landowner went on to say to show that Russia was ruined by the emancipation even appeared to him very true, new, and undeniable. The landowner was plainly expressing his own thought – which people rarely do – and a thought to which he had been led not by a desire to find some occupation for an idle brain but which had grown up out of the conditions of his life; a thought which he had brooded over in his rural solitude and had considered from every angle.

'The fact of the matter is, don't you see, that progress of every sort can be achieved only by the use of authority,' he said, evidently wishing to show that education was not foreign to him. 'Take the reforms of Peter, Catherine, Alexander. Take European history. And progress in agriculture more than anything else – the potato, for instance, had to be forced on us. The wooden plough, too, wasn't always used. It was probably introduced in the earliest days of Russian history, and no doubt brought in by force. Now, in our own day, we landowners under serfdom applied various improved methods of farming: drying-kilns and thrashing-machines and carting manure and all the modern implements – which we introduced because we had the power, and the peasants resisted at first and afterwards copied. Now that serfdom has been abolished and authority taken out of our hands, our husbandry, where it had been raised to a high level, is bound to sink back again to the most savage and primitive condition. That's how I see it.'

'But why? If it's rational, you'll be able to keep up the same system with hired labour,' remarked Sviazhsky.

'Not without the power. How are you to do it, allow me to ask?'

'There it is – the question of labour – the chief element in agriculture,' thought Levin.

'Hired labourers.'

'Hired labourers won't work well. Nor do they want to use decent implements. The Russian worker understands one thing only – how to drink like a hog, and when he's drunk he ruins everything you put into his hands. He will water your horses to death, spoil good harness, barter the tyres off your wheels for drink, drop a bolt into the thrashing-machine so as to break it. He loathes the sight of anything that's not after his fashion. That is why the whole standard of husbandry has fallen. Land gone out of cultivation, overgrown with weeds, or given over to the peasants, and where millions of bushels were once raised you get a few hundred thousand. The wealth of the country has declined. If the same thing had been done, but with care that …'

And he proceeded to unfold his own scheme of emancipation by which these drawbacks might have been avoided.

This did not interest Levin who, as soon as he had finished, returned to his first point and, addressing Sviazhsky, tried to get him to express his serious opinion.

'It is perfectly true that the standard of agriculture is dropping and that with our present relations to the peasants it is impossible to farm on a rational system and get a profit,' he observed.

'I don't agree,' objected Sviazhsky quite seriously. 'All I see is that we don't know how to cultivate the land and that our system of agriculture in the serf-days was by no means too high, but too low. We have no machinery, no good stock, no proper supervision; we don't even know how to keep accounts. Ask any landowner – he won't be able to tell you what crop's profitable and what is not.'

'Italian book-keeping!' said the landowner scornfully. 'Keep any accounts you like, but if they ruin everything you've got, there won't be any profit.'

'Why should they ruin everything? They will break one of your miserable thrashing-machines, or a Russian presser, but my steam-

press they don't break. A wretched Russian nag, what d'you call it?...
the breed you have to drag along by the tail – can be spoiled for you;
but provide yourself with Flemish drays or good cart-horses – they
won't harm them. And so it is with everything. We must raise the
standard of agriculture all round.'

'Yes, if one can afford it, Nikolai Ivanich! It's all very well for you;
but I have a son to keep at the university, lads to educate at the high
school – how am I going to buy these dray-horses?'

'That's what the banks are for.'

'Yes, and end by being sold up under the hammer? No, thanks!'

'I don't agree that it's necessary or possible to raise the level of agriculture still higher,' said Levin. 'I devote myself to farming, and I
have means, but I never could accomplish a thing. And as for banks, I
don't see the use of them. For my part, anyway, no matter what I've
spent money on in the way of farming, it's always been a loss: stock –
a loss, machinery – a loss.'

'That's true enough,' confirmed the landowner with the grey
whiskers, positively laughing with satisfaction.

'And I am not the only one,' pursued Levin. 'I mix with all the
neighbouring landowners who are cultivating their land on a rational
system and, with rare exceptions, all of them are making a loss. Come,
tell us how your land does – does it pay?' said Levin, and at once detected in Sviazhsky's face that fleeting expression of alarm which he
had observed before, whenever he had tried to penetrate below the
surface of Sviazhsky's mind.

Moreover, this question on Levin's part was not altogether in good
faith. His hostess had just told him at tea that they had that summer engaged a German expert from Moscow and paid him 500 roubles to
investigate the management of their property, and found that they
were losing 3,000 roubles odd a year on their farming. She did not
remember the exact figure, though the German had worked it out to
the last fraction apparently.

The landowner with the grey whiskers smiled at the mention of
profit on Sviazhsky's farming, evidently aware of the sort of profits
his neighbour and marshal was likely to be making.

'Possibly it does not pay,' answered Sviazhsky. 'That only shows
that either I'm a bad farmer or that I spend capital on increasing my
rental value.'

'Oh, rental value!' Levin exclaimed with horror. 'There may be such a thing in Europe, where the land has been improved by the labour put into it; but in this country the land is deteriorating from the labour put into it – in other words, from being worked out. So there can be no such thing as rental value.'

'No rental value? But that's a natural law.'

'Then we are outside the law; rental value explains nothing for us but simply muddles us. No, tell me how the theory of rental value can ...'

'Will you have some junket? Masha, pass us some junket or raspberries.' He turned to his wife. 'Extraordinary how long the raspberries are lasting this year.'

And in the most excellent spirits Sviazhsky got up and moved away, apparently supposing the conversation to have ended at the very point where to Levin it seemed to be just beginning.

Having lost his interlocutor, Levin continued the conversation with the grey-whiskered landowner, trying to prove to him that the whole trouble arises from the fact that we don't want to understand the peculiarities and habits of our labourer; but the landowner, like all men who think independently and in isolation, was slow in taking in another point of view, and was tenacious of his own. He stuck to it that the Russian peasant was a swine and liked being a swine, and that it needed authority to get him out of his swinishness, and there was none. One must have the stick, but we had got so liberal that we had all of a sudden exchanged the traditional rod for lawyers and model prisons, where the worthless, stinking peasants were fed on good soup and provided with so many cubic feet of air.

'What makes you think,' said Levin, trying to get back to the question, 'that it's impossible to find some relation to the labourer which would make the work productive?'

'That could never be done with the Russian peasantry; we've no power over them,' answered the landowner.

'What new conditions could be discovered?' said Sviazhsky. Having eaten his junket and lighted a cigarette, he came back to the discussion. 'All possible relations to labour have been studied and defined,' he said. 'The relic of barbarism, the primitive commune with each a guarantee for all, is disappearing of itself; serfdom has been abolished, and there is nothing left but free labour – and its forms are fixed and ready made, and we must accept them. The farm hand, the day labourer, the farmer – you can't get away from that.'

'But Europe is not satisfied with this system.'

'No, and is looking for new methods. And will find them, in all probability.'

'That's just what I was meaning,' answered Levin. 'Why shouldn't we seek them for ourselves?'

'Because it would be much the same as inventing afresh the way to construct a railway. It is already invented and there.'

'But if it doesn't do for us? If it's stupid?' said Levin.

And again he noticed the expression of alarm in Sviazhsky's eyes.

'Oh yes, we'll throw our caps in the air! We've found the secret Europe was looking for! I know all that; but, begging your pardon, are you aware of all that's been done in Europe on the question of the organization of labour?'

'No, very little.'

'The question is at present occupying the best brains in Europe. There is the Schulze–Delitsch movement. ... And then all that mass of literature on the labour question, with the most liberal Lassalle tendency ... the Mulhausen experiment – that is already a fact, as you probably know.'

'I have some idea of it, but very vague.'

'Oh, you only say that: I'm sure you know as much about it as I do! I'm not a professor of sociology, of course, but it interested me, and really if it interests you it would be worth your while to study it.'

'But what have they arrived at?'

'Excuse me ...'

The two neighbouring landowners had risen, and Sviazhsky, once more checking Levin in his inconvenient habit of prying beyond the outer chambers of his mind, went to see his visitors out.

28

LEVIN felt insufferably bored by the ladies that evening; he was stirred as never before by the idea that the dissatisfaction he was feeling with his system of managing his land was not an exceptional case, but the general condition of things in Russia; that some arrangement that would make the labourers work as they did for the peasant he had visited on the way was not an idle dream but a problem it was essential to solve. And it seemed to him that the problem could be solved, and that an attempt ought to be made to do so.

After saying good-night to the ladies, and promising to stay the whole of the next day, so as to make an expedition on horseback with them to see an interesting landslide in the crown forest, Levin before going to bed dropped into his host's study to borrow the books on the labour question that Sviazhsky had recommended. Sviazhsky's study was a huge room lined with bookcases and having two tables – one a massive writing-table, standing in the middle of the room, and the other a round one on which lay a number of newspapers and periodicals in different languages, ranged like the rays of a star round the lamp in the centre. By the writing-table was a little stand of drawers labelled with gilt lettering full of papers of various sorts.

Sviazhsky got the books, and sat down in a rocking-chair.

'What are you looking at?' he asked Levin, who had stopped by the round table and was turning over the periodicals. 'Oh yes, there's a very interesting article there,' said Sviazhsky of the review Levin was holding in his hand. 'It appears that the chief agent in the partition of Poland was not Frederick, after all,' he continued with eager animation. 'It appears ...'

And, with characteristic clearness, he summed up those new and very important and interesting discoveries. Though at present Levin was more taken up with his ideas about the problem of the land, he wondered as he listened to Sviazhsky: 'What is there in his mind? And why, why is he interested in the partition of Poland?' When Sviazhsky had finished, Levin could not help asking: 'Well, and what of it?' But there was nothing to follow. It was simply interesting that it 'appeared' to be so and so. But Sviazhsky did not explain, and saw no need to explain why he found it interesting.

'Yes, but I was very much interested by your irascible old neighbour,' said Levin, sighing. 'He's a clever fellow and said a good deal that was true.'

'Oh, get away with you! An inveterate supporter of serfdom at heart, like the rest of them!' said Sviazhsky.

'Whose marshal you are.'

'Yes, only I marshal them in the other direction,' retorted Sviazhsky, laughing.

'I'll tell you what interests me very much,' said Levin. 'He's right that our system – our rational farming – doesn't answer, that the only thing that answers is the money-lender system, like that quiet fellow's, or else the most elementary methods. ... Whose fault is it?'

'Our own, of course. Besides, it's not true that it doesn't answer. It answers with Vasiltchikov.'

'A mill ...'

'But I don't see what it is you are surprised at. The people are at such a low stage of material and moral development that naturally they're bound to oppose everything that's strange to them. In Europe, a rational system answers because the people are educated: it follows that we must educate our people – that's all.'

'But how are we to educate them?'

'To educate the people three things are needed: schools, schools, schools!'

'But you said yourself that the people are at such a low stage of material development: how would schools help that?'

'You know, you put me in mind of that story of the advice given to the sick man: "You should try an aperient." "I have, and it made me worse." "Try leeches." "I have, and they made me worse." "Well, there is nothing for it but to say your prayers." "I have – and that made me worse." That's just how it is with you and me. I mention political economy; you say it makes things worse. I mention socialism; you say, "Still worse." Education? Worse and worse.'

'But how would schools help?'

'By giving the people fresh wants.'

'Now that's a thing I never could understand,' objected Levin vehemently. 'In what way could schools help the people to improve their material position? You say schools, education, will give them fresh wants. So much the worse, since they won't be able to satisfy them. And in what way knowledge of addition and subtraction and the catechism is going to better their material position, I never could make out. The other evening I met a peasant woman with a baby in her arms, and asked her where she was going. She replied that she was going to the "wise woman", because the baby had convulsions and she was taking him to be cured. I asked her what cure the "wise woman" had for convulsions. "She puts the child on the hen-roost and repeats something ..." '

'Exactly, there's your answer! In order to teach them they can't cure babies of convulsions by sitting them on the hen-roost, you must ...' began Sviazhsky with a merry smile.

'Oh no, not at all!' Levin interrupted crossly. 'I meant that sort of doctoring seems to me just like your remedy of schools for the people.

The people are poor and ignorant – we see that as surely as the peasant woman sees the baby is ill because it screams. But why schools should cure the ills of poverty and ignorance is as incomprehensible as the idea that hens on their perches cure convulsions. You must first remedy the cause of their poverty.'

'Well, there, at any rate, you're in agreement with Spencer, whom you dislike so much. He, too, says that education may result from greater prosperity and comfort, from more frequent washing, as he says, but not from being able to read and write ...'

'I am very glad, then – or rather, very sorry to be in agreement with Spencer; only I've known it a long while. Schools will not help – what we want are economic conditions in which the people will be better off and have more leisure. Then schools would follow.'

'Yet all over Europe education is now compulsory.'

'And how is it you agree with Spencer yourself about it?' asked Levin.

But the look of alarm flashed into Sviazhsky's eyes and he said with a smile:

'Yes, that cure for convulsions is marvellous! Did you really hear it yourself?'

Levin saw that he was not to discover the connexion between this man's life and his ideas. It was evidently a matter of indifference to him what conclusions his reasoning led to: it was simply the process of reasoning that appealed to him. And he did not like it when the process of reasoning brought him to a blind alley. That was the only thing he disliked and avoided by changing the conversation to something agreeable and amusing.

All the impressions of the day, beginning with the peasant he had visited on the way, which served as a basis for all the other impressions and ideas, threw Levin into violent excitement. There was this good fellow Sviazhsky, keeping a stock of opinions simply for social purposes, and obviously having some other principles Levin could not fathom, while with the crowd whose name is legion he guided public opinion by means of ideas he did not share; that testy old landowner, perfectly correct in the conclusions that he had been worried into by life, but wrong in his exasperation with a whole class, and that the best class in Russia; his own dissatisfaction with the work he had been doing, and his vague hope of finding a remedy for all this – all merged into a sense of inward turmoil and anticipation of some solution near at hand.

Left alone, in his room, lying on a spring mattress that gave unexpectedly whenever he moved an arm or a leg, Levin did not fall asleep for a long while. Not one of the talks with Sviazhsky, though he had said a great deal that was clever, had interested Levin; but the conclusions of the irascible landowner required consideration. Levin found himself recalling every word he had said and in imagination amending his own replies.

'Yes, I ought to have said to him: You say that our husbandry is not a success because the peasants detest improvements, and that these should be introduced by force. If no system of farming answered at all without these improvements, you would be right. But the only system that does answer is where the labourer is working in conformity with his habits, just as on the old peasant's land half-way here. Our common dissatisfaction with the system shows that either we are to blame or the labourers. We have pushed on in our own way – the European way – a long time, without stopping to consider the nature of labour. Let us try seeing labour not as abstract man power, but as the *Russian peasant* with his instincts, and organize our system of agriculture accordingly. Imagine, I ought to have said to him, that you run your farm like that old man's; that you have discovered a method of interesting your labourers in the success of the work, and have hit upon the happy mean in the way of improvements that they are willing to recognize – then, without impoverishing the soil, you will get double and treble the crops you got before. Divide equally and give half the produce to labour, and the surplus left you will be larger and labour will receive more too. And to do this we must lower the standard of husbandry and interest the peasants in the success of the work. How this can be done is a question of detail; but undoubtedly it can be done.'

This idea threw Levin into a state of great excitement. He lay awake half the night, thinking over in detail the putting of his idea into practice. He had not meant to go away next day, but he now determined to leave early in the morning. Besides, there was that sister-in-law with the low-cut bodice who occasioned in him a feeling akin to shame and remorse for some utterly base action. Most important of all, he was anxious to get home without delay and lose no time in presenting his new plan to the peasants before the sowing of the winter wheat, so that the sowing might be undertaken on a new basis. He had made up his mind to revolutionize his whole system.

29

THE carrying out of Levin's plan presented many difficulties; but he struggled on, doing his utmost, and attained, if not what he desired, at any rate enough to enable him to believe, without self-deception, that the thing was worth doing. One of the chief difficulties was that the cultivation of the land was in full swing, that it was impossible to stop everything and start afresh. The machine had to be overhauled while it was working.

When he reached home in the evening and informed the bailiff of his new plans, the bailiff with undisguised satisfaction agreed with what he said so long as he was pointing out that all that had been done hitherto was absurd and unproductive. The bailiff remarked that he had said so a long while ago but no one would listen to him. But Levin's proposal that he and the peasants should participate as shareholders in the farm occasioned an expression of profound dejection and he offered no definite opinion, but at once began talking of the urgent necessity of carting the last sheaves of rye the next day, and of starting the men on the second ploughing, so that Levin felt that this was not a propitious moment for discussing his plans.

On speaking to the peasants of the matter, and offering them land on new terms, he ran up against the same great difficulty: they were so busy with the current work of the day that they had no time to deliberate upon the advantages or disadvantages of the venture.

One simple-hearted peasant – the cowman, Ivan – seemed thoroughly to grasp Levin's proposal to let him and his family have a share in the profits from the dairy-farm, and thoroughly approved of the plan. But when Levin hinted at the benefits that would accrue to him in the future, a look of anxiety and regret that he could not stop to listen to it all appeared on Ivan's face, and he quickly found himself some task that must be done immediately: he either seized a pitchfork to remove the hay from the stalls, or ran to fill the troughs, or swept up manure.

Another stumbling-block was the insurmountable distrust of the peasants: they could not believe that the master could have any other aim than to squeeze all he could out of them. They were firmly convinced that his real aim (whatever he might say) would always be hidden in what he did not tell them. And they themselves, in giving their opinion, said a great deal but never what they really meant. Moreover (Levin came to the conclusion that the irascible landowner had been right) the first and indispensable condition the peasants insisted on in any new arrangement was that they should not be compelled to adopt any new methods or use any new kinds of agricultural machinery. They agreed that the new-fashioned plough ploughed better, that a scarifier did the work more quickly, but they found a thousand reasons why they could not use them; and though he was convinced that he would have to lower his standard of cultivation he was sorry to give up improvements, the advantages of which were so obvious. Yet, in spite of all these difficulties he got his way, and by autumn the new arrangements began to work, or at any rate so it seemed to him.

At first Levin had thought of letting the whole of the farm as it stood to the peasants, the labourers, and the bailiff on the new co-partnership lines, but he very soon saw that this was impossible, and decided to divide it up. The cattle-yard, the fruit and vegetable gardens, the hay-fields and arable land, divided into several parts, had to be made into separate lots. The simple-hearted Ivan, who looked after the cattle and who had grasped the idea better than the rest, Levin fancied, got together a company of his own, consisting mainly of members of his own family, and became partner in the dairy section. The far field that had lain fallow for eight years, with the aid of the intelligent carpenter, Fiodor Rezunov, was taken over by six families of peasants, and the peasant Shuraev took the kitchen-gardens, all on the new co-operative terms. The rest of the estate remained as before; but these three associated partnerships were the first step to a new order, and occupied all Levin's attention.

It is true that in the cattle-yard things went no better than before, and Ivan strenuously opposed heating the cow-sheds and making butter from fresh cream, maintaining that cows required less food when kept in the cold and that butter made from sour cream went further; and he expected his wages to be paid as before, not being at all interested in the fact that the money he received was not wages in the old sense but an advance out of his future share in the profits.

It is true that Fiodor Rezunov's group did not plough their land over twice before sowing, as had been agreed, pleading as their excuse that time was short. It is true that the peasants of this same group, though they had agreed to work the land on the new conditions, always spoke of it not as co-operatively held land but as land rented for half the crop, and more than once the peasants and Rezunov himself said to Levin: 'If only you would take a rent for the land, it would save you trouble and we should feel more free.' Moreover, the same peasants kept finding all sorts of excuses to put off the building of the new cattle-yard and barn they had agreed upon, and dragged the matter on till winter.

It is true that Shuraev would have liked to sub-let the kitchen gardens in small lots to the other peasants. He evidently quite misunderstood, and apparently intentionally misunderstood, the conditions on which the land had been given to him.

It is true that often, when talking to the peasants and explaining to them the advantages of the new arrangement, Levin felt that they were only listening to the sound of his voice and were quite determined, whatever he might say, not to let themselves be taken in. Especially did he feel this when he talked to the most intelligent of them, Rezunov, and detected the gleam in Rezunov's eye which showed so plainly both ironical amusement at Levin and a firm resolve that if anyone were to be taken in, it should not be he, Rezunov.

But in spite of all this Levin was hopeful and thought that by keeping strict accounts and insisting on his own way he would eventually be able to prove to them the advantages of the new arrangement, and then the system would go of itself.

These matters, together with the management of the remainder of the estate still on his hands, and his work indoors on the book he was writing so filled Levin's whole summer that he scarcely ever went out shooting. At the end of August he heard from a servant of theirs, who brought back the side-saddle, that the Oblonskys had returned to Moscow. He felt that in not answering Dolly's letter – he could not remember his rudeness without a flush of shame – he had burned his boats and could never visit there again. He had been just as rude to the Sviazhskys, leaving them without saying good-bye. But he would never go to see them again either. That made no difference to him now. The new arrangements on his farm absorbed him as completely as though there would never be anything else in his life. He read the books lent him by Sviazhsky and, having ordered various others that he required, he read political economy and socialistic works on the same subject, but, as he had expected, found nothing in them related to his undertaking. In the political economy books – in Mill, for instance, whom he studied first and with great ardour, hoping every minute to find an answer to the questions that were engrossing him – he found only certain laws deduced from the state of agriculture in Europe; but he could not for the life of him see why these laws, which did not apply to Russia, should be considered universal. It was the same with the socialistic books: either they were beautiful but impracticable fantasies which had fascinated him when he was a student, or they were attempts at improving, patching up the economic order existing in Europe, with which the system of land tenure in Russia had nothing in common. Political economy told him that the laws by which Europe had developed and was developing her wealth were universal and absolute. Socialist teaching told him that development along those lines leads to ruin. And neither of them offered the smallest enlightenment as to what he, Levin, and all the Russian peasants and landowners were to do with their millions of hands and millions of acres, to make them as productive as possible for the common good.

Having once taken the subject up, he conscientiously read everything bearing on it, and intended to make a journey abroad in the autumn in order to study land systems further, on the spot, so that what had frequently happened to him with other questions should not be repeated. Often, just as he was beginning to understand the idea in his interlocutor's mind and to explain his own, he would suddenly be asked: 'And what about Kauffmann, and Jones, and Dubois, and Miccelli? You haven't read them. You should do so – they've thrashed that question out thoroughly.'

He now saw clearly that Kauffmann and Miccelli had nothing to tell him. He knew what he wanted. He saw that Russia possessed splendid soil and splendid labour, and that in certain cases (such as at the peasant's on the way to Sviazhsky's) the men and the land could produce abundantly; but that in the majority of cases, where capital was expended in the European fashion, little was produced, and that this happened simply because the labourers were willing to work and work well only in the way natural to them, and that their resistance was not accidental but invariable, having its roots in the spirit of the people. He thought that the Russian people whose task it was consciously to occupy and cultivate enormous tracts of uninhabited land, so long as any land remained unoccupied, clung to the methods suitable to their purpose, and that these methods were by no means so bad as was generally supposed. And he wanted to demonstrate this theoretically in his book and practically on his land.

30

By the end of September the timber had been carted for building the cattle-yard on the land allotted to the peasant-group, and the butter from the cows was sold and the profits divided. In practice the system was running capitally, at least so it seemed to Levin. To work out the whole subject theoretically and to finish his book, which, in Levin's day-dreams, would not merely revolutionize political economy but annihilate that science altogether and lay the foundation of a new one – the science of the relation of the people to the soil – all that was left was to make a tour abroad and there study what had been done in the same direction, and collect conclusive evidence that what had been done there was not what was needed. Levin was only waiting for the wheat to be delivered and to get the money for it before taking his departure. But rain set in, making it impossible to harvest what remained of the corn and potatoes, brought all work to a standstill and even prevented delivery of the wheat. Mud made the roads impassable, two mills were carried away by floods, and the weather was steadily getting worse.

On the morning of the 30th of September the sun showed itself, and, hoping for fine weather, Levin began making serious preparations for his journey. He gave orders for the grain to be sacked ready for carting, sent the bailiff to collect the money from the merchant who was buying it, and went out himself to give final instructions about the estate before leaving.

Having finished all his business, soaked through with the streams of water that kept running in at the neck of his leather coat and the tops of his gaiters, but in the most cheerful and lively temper, Levin returned homewards in the evening. The weather had grown worse since the morning; the sleet lashed the drenched mare so cruelly that she walked sideways, shaking her head and ears; but Levin under his hood was all right, and he looked cheerfully about him at the turbid streams running under the wheels, at the drops hanging on every bare twig, at the whiteness of the patch of unthawed hailstones on the planks of the bridge, at the heaps of still juicy, fleshy leaves lying in a thick layer round a denuded elm. In spite of the gloomy aspect of nature around him, he felt extraordinarily elated. The talks he had been having with the peasants in the outlying village showed that they were beginning to get used to their new position. The old servant to whose hut he had gone to get dry evidently approved of Levin's plan and of his own accord offered to join a group to buy cattle.

'I need only push on steadily towards my goal, and I shall get what I want,' thought Levin; 'and it's worth working and striving for. It is not a personal affair of my own but one that concerns the general welfare. The entire system of farming and, above all, the condition of the people as a whole must be completely transformed. In the place of poverty we must have universal prosperity and contentment; instead of hostility – harmony and unity of interests. In short, a bloodless revolution, but a mighty revolution, beginning in the little circle of our district, then reaching the province, Russia, the whole world! A just idea cannot help bearing fruit. Yes, it's a goal worth working for. And the fact that the author of it is I, Kostya Levin, the same fellow who went to a ball in a black tie and was refused by the Shcherbatsky girl, and who seems so pitiful and insignificant a creature to himself – is neither here nor there. I am sure Franklin felt just as insignificant and distrusted himself just as I do, when he summed himself up. All that does not matter. He too, most likely, had his Agatha Mihalovna to whom he confided his secrets.'

With such thoughts Levin reached home in the dark.

The bailiff, who had been to the merchant's, had returned with part of the money for the wheat. An agreement had been made with the old servant, and the bailiff had learned on the way that everywhere the corn was still standing in the fields, so that his 160 shocks still in the fields were a trifle compared to what others were losing.

After dinner Levin as usual sat down in an easy-chair with a book, and while he read continued to think of the journey before him in connexion with his book. To-day the importance of his work presented itself to him with special distinctness, and whole sentences ranged themselves in his mind, expressing the essence of his thought. 'I must write that down,' he said to himself. 'That will make a short introduction, though I had wanted to dispense with a preface.' He got up to go to his writing-table, and Laska, who had been lying at his feet, stretched herself, got up too, and looked round at him as if asking where she was to go. But there was no time to make notes: the peasants' foremen came for the next day's orders, and Levin went out into the hall to talk to them.

When he had finished giving them their instructions, or rather, making arrangements for the next day, and had seen the various other peasants who had business with him, Levin went back to his study and sat down to work. Laska lay under the table; Agatha Mihalovna settled herself in her usual place with a stocking she was knitting.

After writing for a while, Levin suddenly thought with extraordinary vividness of Kitty, her refusal and their last meeting. He got up and began walking about the room.

'What's the use of fretting?' said Agatha Mihalovna. 'Come, why do you stay on at home? You should go to a watering-place especially now you've made all the preparations for a journey.'

'I am going the day after to-morrow, Agatha Mihalovna. I must finish my business first.'

'There, there, this business of yours! Haven't you done enough for the peasants? As it is, they're saying, "Your master will be getting some favour from the Tsar for it." Indeed, and it is a strange thing: why should you bother yourself about the peasants?'

'I'm not bothering about them: I'm doing it for my own good.'

Agatha Mihalovna knew every detail of Levin's plans for his land. Levin often put his ideas before her in all their complexity, and frequently argued with her and did not agree with her comments. But this time she completely misinterpreted him.

'Of course one must think of one's soul's salvation before everything else,' she remarked with a sigh. 'Parfen Denisich now, for all he was no scholar, he died a death God grant every one of us the like of,' she said, referring to a servant who had lately died. 'Took the sacrament and all.'

'I did not mean that,' he said. 'I meant that I'm working for my own profit. It's more profitable for me if the peasants do their work better.'

'Well, no matter what you do, if he's a lazy good-for-nought, everything'll be at sixes and sevens. If he has a conscience he'll work, and if not, there's no doing anything.'

'Oh come, you say yourself that Ivan looks after the cattle better than he used to.'

'All I say is,' replied Agatha Mihalovna, evidently not speaking at random but in strict sequence of ideas, 'that you ought to get married. That's what it comes to.'

Agatha Mihalovna's allusion to the very subject he had been thinking about a moment ago grieved and wounded him. Levin scowled and without answering her sat down to his work again, repeating to himself all that he had been thinking about its importance. Only occasionally he gave an ear in the stillness to the click of Agatha Mihalovna's needles and, remembering what he did not want to remember, he frowned again.

At nine o'clock they heard the sound of a bell and the heavy rumbling of a carriage through the mud.

'There now! Here's visitors come to see you, so you won't be dull any more,' said Agatha Mihalovna, getting up and going to the door. But Levin ran out ahead of her. His work was not going well now, and he was glad of a visitor, whoever it might be.

31

RUNNING half-way down the stairs, Levin caught a familiar sound of coughing in the hall; but the noise of his own steps prevented his hearing it clearly, and he hoped he was mistaken. Then he saw a long, bony, familiar figure, and now it seemed there was no further room for doubt; and yet he still went on hoping he was mistaken and that this tall man taking off his fur coat and coughing was not his brother Nikolai.

Levin was fond of his brother but being with him was always a torture. Just now, when Levin, under the influence of the thoughts that had come to him and Agatha Mihalovna's advice, was in an unsettled and uncertain state of mind, the forthcoming meeting with his brother seemed particularly difficult. Instead of a cheerful, healthy visitor, some newcomer who would, he hoped, divert him from his mental perplexity, there was his brother, who knew him through and through, who would read his innermost thoughts and force him to come out with his views.

Angry with himself for so base a feeling, Levin ran down into the hall. The moment he saw his brother close, this feeling of selfish disappointment vanished, giving way to pity. Dreadful as his emaciation and illness had made Nikolai before, now he looked still more emaciated, still more wasted. He was a skeleton covered with skin.

He stood in the hall, jerking his long thin neck, pulling a scarf from it, and smiling in an oddly pitiful manner. When he saw that meek, submissive smile, Levin felt his throat contract.

'There – I *have* come to see you,' said Nikolai in a thick voice, without for a second taking his eyes off his brother's face. 'I've been meaning to for a long time but I never felt well. Now I'm ever so much better,' he said, wiping his beard with the palms of his large, thin hands.

'Yes, yes!' answered Levin. And he felt more frightened still when his lips touched his brother's dry skin as they kissed and he saw close to him his big, unnaturally glittering eyes.

A few weeks before, Levin had written to his brother that a small part of the property, that had not been divided, had been sold and there was a sum of about 2,000 roubles to come to him as his share.

Nikolai said that he was now here to fetch this money and, what was more important, to stay awhile in the old nest and touch his native soil, so as to renew his strength like the heroes of old for the work that lay before him. In spite of the fact that he was more round-shouldered than ever and that being so tall his emaciation was startling, his movements were as quick and abrupt as before. Levin led him into his study.

His brother changed his clothes with particular care – a thing he never used to do – combed his thin, straight hair and, smiling, went upstairs.

He was in the most affectionate and happy mood, just as Levin often remembered him in childhood. He even referred to Koznyshev without rancour. When he saw Agatha Mihalovna, he chaffed her and asked about the old servants. The news of Parfen Denisich's death made a painful impression on him. A look of fear crossed his face but he recovered his composure at once.

'Of course he was quite old,' he remarked, and changed the subject. 'Well, I'll spend a month or two with you, and then I'm off to Moscow. Do you know, Myakov has promised me a post, and I'm going into the service. Now I shall arrange my life quite differently,' he went on. 'You know I got rid of that woman, don't you?'

'Maria Nikolayevna? Why, what for?'

'Oh, she was an awful woman! She caused me no end of trouble.' But he did not say what the trouble had been. He could not explain that he had driven Maria Nikolayevna away because she made his tea too weak and, above all, because she would look after him like an invalid.

'Besides, I want to turn over a new leaf now. Of course, like everyone else, I've done silly things, but money's the last consideration: I don't regret it. The thing is to have one's health, and my health, thank God, has mended.'

Levin listened and racked his brains, but could think of nothing to say. Nikolai was probably feeling the same; he began questioning his brother about his affairs, and Levin was glad to talk about himself, because he could do so without hypocrisy. He told his brother of his plans and his doings.

His brother listened, but evidently was not interested.

These two men were so akin, so near each other, that the slightest gesture, the tone of voice, told both more than could be said in words.

At this moment both of them had only one thought – Nikolai's illness and approaching death – which stifled all else. But neither dared speak of it, and so, not uttering the one thing on both their minds, whatever they said rang false. Never had Levin felt so glad when the evening was over and it was time to go to bed. Never with any outside person, never on any formal visit had he been so constrained and unnatural as he was that evening. And the consciousness of this, and the remorse he felt at it, made him more unnatural still. He wanted to weep over his beloved brother who was dying, and he had to listen and keep on talking of how he meant to live.

As the house was damp and Levin's bedroom was the only one that was kept heated, Levin put his brother to sleep there behind a screen.

His brother got into bed and whether he slept or not tossed about like a sick man, coughed and when he could not get his throat clear muttered something. Sometimes, when his breathing was painful he said: 'Oh God!' Sometimes when he was choking he would mutter angrily: 'Ah, the devil!' For a long time Levin lay listening to him. His thoughts were many and varied, but they always returned to the one theme – death.

Death, the inevitable end of everything, confronted him for the first time with irresistible force. And death, which was here in this beloved brother who groaned in his sleep and from force of habit invoked without distinction both God and the devil, was not so remote as it had hitherto seemed to him. He felt it in himself too. If not to-day, then to-morrow; if not to-morrow, then in thirty years' time – wasn't it all the same? And what this inevitable death was, he not only did not know, not only had never considered, but could not and dared not consider.

'Here am I working, wanting to accomplish something, and completely forgetting it must all end – that there is such a thing as death.'

He sat up in bed in the dark, crouched and hugging his knees, holding his breath from strain as he thought. But the more mental effort he made, the clearer it became to him that it was indubitably so, that in looking upon life he had indeed forgotten one little fact – that death comes and puts an end to everything, that nothing was even worth beginning and that there was no help for it. Yes, it was awful, but it was so.

'But I am alive still. Now what's to be done? What's to be done?' he said in despair. He lighted a candle, got up cautiously and went to the looking-glass, and began examining his face and hair. Yes, there were grey hairs about his temples. He opened his mouth. His back teeth were beginning to decay. He bared his muscular arms. Yes, he was still very strong. But Nikolai, who lay there breathing with what was left of his lungs, had once had a strong healthy body too. And suddenly he recalled how they used to go to bed when they were children and wait till Fiodor Bogdanich was out of the room before throwing pillows at each other and laughing, laughing so helplessly that even fear of Fiodor Bogdanich could not check their overflowing, bubbling consciousness of life and happiness. 'And now that sunken, hollow chest … and I, not knowing what will become of me, or wherefore …'

'K … ha! Kha! Damnation!' coughed his brother. 'What are you fidgeting about for? Why aren't you asleep?' he called.

'Oh, I don't know; I'm not sleepy.'

'I have had a good sleep. I'm not in a sweat now. See, feel my night-shirt: not wet, is it?'

Levin felt, withdrew behind the screen, and put out the candle, but it was a long while before he could get to sleep. Just as he was beginning to find out how to live, he was confronted with the new insoluble problem of – death.

'Why, he is dying – he will be dead before the spring, and how can I help him? What can I say to him? What do I know about it? I had even forgotten there was such a thing!'

32

LEVIN had long ago observed that after people have made one uncomfortable by their excessive docility and submissiveness they soon become intolerably exacting and quarrelsome. He foresaw that this would happen with his brother. And indeed Nikolai's meekness did not last long. The very next morning he started being irritable and attacking him on his most sensitive spots.

Levin felt himself to blame but could not mend matters. He felt that if they both stopped keeping up appearances and spoke straight from the heart, as it is called – that is to say, said just what they were thinking and feeling – they would simply have looked into each other's eyes, and Constantine could only have said, 'You're dying, you're dying!' and Nikolai could only have answered, 'I know I am, but I'm afraid, afraid, afraid!' That is all they would have said, had they spoken only what was in their hearts. But that would make life impossible, and so Constantine tried to do what he had been trying to do all his life, and never could learn to do, though, as far as he could observe, many people knew so well how to do it, and without it life was impossible: he tried to say something different from what he was thinking, and he felt all the time that it sounded false and that his brother saw through him and was exasperated.

On the third day of his stay Nikolai challenged his brother to explain his new plans to him once more, and not only found fault with them but purposely confused them with communism.

'You've simply borrowed someone else's idea and distorted it, and you want to apply it where it's not applicable.'

'But I tell you the two have nothing in common! Communists deny the right to private property, capital, or inheritance, while I do not. I look upon them as the main *stimuli* ...' (Levin felt disgusted with himself for using such expressions but ever since he had become engrossed in his work he found himself unconsciously using foreign words more and more frequently.) 'All I want is to regulate labour.'

'Precisely! You've borrowed an idea, stripped it of all that gives it force, and then want to pass it off as something new,' said Nikolai, with an angry tug at his necktie.

'But I tell you my idea has nothing in common ...'

'The other, at any rate,' interrupted Nikolai, with a sarcastic smile, his eyes flashing malignantly, 'has the charm of – one might say – geometrical symmetry, of clarity, of infallibility. It may be utopian. But granting the possibility of making *tabula rasa* of all the past – no private property, no family – then labour comes into its own. But you have nothing …'

'Why will you persist in mixing things up? I have never been a communist.'

'But I have, and I believe it's premature, but rational, and it has a future, as Christianity had in the first centuries.'

'I merely consider that the labour force ought to be investigated from the point of view of natural science; that is, it ought to be studied, its properties ascertained and …'

'But that's complete waste of time! That force finds a certain form of activity of itself, in accord with its degree of development. First there were slaves everywhere, then villeins; and we have the half-crop system, rent, and day-labourers. What more do you want?'

Levin flared up at these last words, for in his secret soul he feared that it was true – true that he was trying to hedge between communism and the existing forms, and that this was hardly possible.

'I am trying to find a way of making labour profitable for myself and for the labourer,' he answered hotly. 'I want to organize …'

'You don't want to organize anything. You simply want to be original, as you always have done, and to show that you are not simply exploiting the peasants, but have some idea in mind.'

'Oh, all right, that's what you think – and leave me alone!' answered Levin, feeling a muscle twitching uncontrollably in his left cheek.

'You have no convictions, and you never have had. All you want is to flatter your self-esteem.'

'Oh, very well; then let me alone!'

'I certainly will! And high time too! You can go to the devil! And I'm very sorry I ever came!'

In spite of all Levin's efforts to pacify his brother afterwards, Nikolai would not listen, but persisted in saying that it was better to part. And Constantine saw that it simply was that life had become unbearable to his brother.

Nikolai had already packed his things when Levin went to him again and in an unnatural manner begged his forgiveness if he had hurt his feelings in any way.

'What magnanimity!' said Nikolai, and smiled. 'If you want to feel yourself in the right, I can let you have that satisfaction. You're in the right; but I'm going all the same.'

At the last moment, however, Nikolai kissed him and suddenly said, with a strange, serious look at his brother:

'Don't think too badly of me, Kostya, will you?' And his voice trembled.

These were the only sincere words that had passed between them. Levin understood that they were meant to say, 'You see, and you know, that I am in a bad way, and perhaps we shall never see each other again.' Levin understood this, and tears gushed from his eyes. He kissed his brother once more, but could not say anything.

Three days after his brother's departure, Levin too set off for his foreign tour. Happening to meet young Shcherbatsky, Kitty's cousin, at the railway station, Levin greatly astonished him by his moroseness.

'What's the matter with you?' asked Shcherbatsky.

'Oh, nothing; there's not much to be cheerful about in the world.'

'Not much to be cheerful about? You come with me to Paris, instead of going to some old Mulhausen. You'll see how jolly life can be.'

'No, thanks, I've done with it all. It's time I was dead.'

'What an idea!' said Shcherbatsky, laughing. 'Why, I'm only just getting ready to begin.'

'Yes, I thought the same not long ago, but now I know I shall soon be dead.'

Levin said what he had genuinely been thinking of late. He saw death or the advance towards death in everything. But the scheme he had started upon only engrossed him the more. After all, he had to live his life somehow till death did come. Darkness had fallen upon everything for him; but just because of this darkness he felt that the one thread to guide him through the darkness was his work, and he clutched at it and clung to it with all his might.

PART FOUR

I

THE Karenins, husband and wife, continued living in the same house and met every day, but they were wholly estranged. Karenin made it a rule to see his wife each day, so as to give the servants no grounds for conjecture, but avoided dining at home. Vronsky never came to the Karenins' house, but Anna met him away from home, and her husband was aware of it.

The situation was one of misery for all three, and not one of them could have endured it for a single day, had it not been for the expectation of change: that it was merely a temporary, painful ordeal which would pass. Karenin hoped that this passion like everything else in the world would pass, that people would forget about it, and his name would remain unsullied. Anna, who was the cause of all the trouble and on whom it weighed most heavily, bore it because she not only hoped but firmly believed that everything would very soon be settled and come right. She had not the least idea what would settle the situation, but she was quite certain that something would very soon turn up now. Vronsky, against his own will following her lead, hoped, too, that something apart from any action of his would surely clear up all these difficulties.

In the middle of the winter Vronsky spent a very tiresome week. He was delegated to show a foreign prince on a visit to Petersburg the sights of the city. Vronsky had a distinguished appearance; he possessed, moreover, the art of carrying himself with respectful dignity, and was used to such exalted personages. And so he was chosen to attend the prince. But he found his duties very irksome. The prince was anxious not to miss seeing anything about which he might be asked at home; and on his own account he wanted to enjoy as many Russian forms of amusement as possible. Vronsky had to act as his guide in satisfying both these inclinations. In the mornings they drove out sight-seeing; the evenings they spent taking part in national entertainments. The prince enjoyed unusually good health even for a prince. Thanks to athletics and training he was so physically fit that in spite of the excesses he indulged in when taking his pleasures he looked as fresh as a big shiny green Dutch cucumber. The prince had travelled a great deal, and in his opinion one of the chief advantages of the modern facilities of communication was that they made the delights of all nations accessible. He had been to Spain, where he had serenaded and made friends with a Spanish girl who played the guitar. In Switzerland he had killed chamois. In England he had hunted in a pink coat and shot two hundred pheasants for a bet. He had penetrated a harem in Turkey, ridden an elephant in India, and now in Russia wished to sample all the typically Russian forms of amusement.

Vronsky, as chief master-of-ceremonies, so to speak, was at great pains to arrange all the Russian entertainments recommended to the prince by various people: trotting-races and pancakes, bear-hunts and troikas and gypsies and carousals with the Russian accompaniment of breaking glasses. And the prince entered into the Russian spirit with surprising ease, smashed trays of plates and dishes, sat with a gypsy girl on his knee, while his eyes seemed to be asking, 'What next – or does the whole pleasure of Russians consist in just this?'

In actual fact, of all the Russian forms of gaiety, the prince preferred French actresses, a ballet-dancer, and white-seal champagne. Vronsky was used to princes but either because he himself had changed of late, or he had had too much of this one, that week seemed fearfully wearisome. Throughout the time he felt like a man placed in charge of a dangerous lunatic, who fears the proximity may affect his own reason. Vronsky was obliged to be on his guard the whole time, never for a second to relax the tone of stern official respectfulness, that he might not himself be insulted. The prince's manner of treating the very people who, to Vronsky's astonishment, were ready to go to any lengths to provide him with Russian entertainment, was disdainful. His criticisms of Russian women, whom he wished to study, more than once made Vronsky crimson with indignation. But the real reason why Vronsky disliked the prince so much was that in him he could not help seeing himself. And what he saw in this mirror did not gratify his self-esteem. The prince was a very stupid, very self-satisfied, very healthy and immaculate man, and nothing else. He was a gentleman – that was true, and Vronsky could not deny it. He was easy and dignified with his superiors, free and simple with his equals, and contemptuously indulgent with his inferiors. Vronsky was the same, and was proud of it; but in his relations with the prince he was an inferior, and the latter's good-natured condescension roused his resentment.

'Beefy ass! Am I really like that?' he wondered.

However this may have been, at the end of the week, when he parted from the prince (who was going on to Moscow) and received his thanks, he was glad to be delivered from an uncomfortable position and the distasteful reflection of himself. He said good-bye to him at the station after their return from a bear-hunt, followed by a whole night of Russian revels.

2

WHEN he got home, Vronsky found a note from Anna. 'I am ill and unhappy,' she wrote. 'I cannot come out, but I cannot go on any longer without seeing you. Come in this evening. Alexei Alexandrovich goes to the council at seven and will be there till ten.' Wondering for an instant at the strangeness of her bidding him come straight to her, in spite of her husband's injunctions, he decided to go.

Vronsky had that winter been promoted to the rank of colonel and, no longer quartered with the regiment, was living alone. Immediately after lunch he lay down on the sofa and five minutes later memories of the disreputable scenes he had witnessed during the last few days became confused and merged with a mental image of Anna and of a peasant who had played an important part as a beater in the bear-hunt; and Vronsky fell asleep. He awoke in the dark, trembling with horror, and hurriedly lighted a candle. 'What was it? What was the dreadful thing I dreamed? Yes, I know. The peasant-beater – a dirty little man with a matted beard – was stooping down doing something, and all of a sudden he began muttering strange words in French. Yes, there was nothing else in the dream,' he said to himself. 'But why was it so awful?' He vividly recalled the peasant again and the incomprehensible French words the man had muttered, and a chill of horror ran down his spine.

'What foolishness!' thought Vronsky, and glanced at his watch.

It was half-past eight already. He rang for his servant, dressed in haste, and went out on to the steps, completely forgetting his dream and only worried at being late. As he drove up to the Karenins' porch he looked at the time and saw that it was ten minutes to nine. A high, narrow carriage with a pair of greys stood at the door. He recognized Anna's carriage. 'She is coming to me,' thought Vronsky, 'and better she should. I don't like going into this house. But no matter! I can't hide myself.' And with the manner, habitual to him since childhood, of one who has nothing to be ashamed of, Vronsky got out of his sledge and went to the door. The door opened, and the hall-porter with a rug on his arm called the carriage. Vronsky, though not in the habit of noticing details, nevertheless noticed the look of surprise with which the porter glanced at him. In the doorway Vronsky almost ran up against Karenin. The gas jet lit up his bloodless, worn face under the black hat, and his white neck-tie brilliant against the beaver collar of his coat. Karenin's steady, dull eyes were fastened upon Vronsky's face. Vronsky bowed, and Karenin, pressing his lips together, lifted his hand to his hat and went out. Vronsky saw him get into the carriage without looking round, take the rug and a pair of opera-glasses through the carriage window, and disappear. Vronsky went into the hall. His brows met in a frown and there was a proud, angry gleam in his eye.

'What a position!' he thought. 'If he would fight, would stand up for his honour, I could do something, could express my feelings; but this weakness or abjectness ... He puts me in the position of a snake in the grass, which I never meant and never mean to be.'

Vronsky's ideas had changed a good deal since the day of his conversation with Anna in the Vrede garden. Involuntarily submitting to the weakness of Anna – who had given herself up to him entirely, and placed her fate in his hands, ready to accept anything – he had long ceased to think that they might part, as he had thought then. His ambitious plans had receded to the background again and, feeling that he had stepped outside that circle of activity in which everything was definite, he had completely abandoned himself to his passion, and that passion was binding him more and more closely to her.

He was still in the hall when he caught the sound of her retreating footsteps. He realized that she had been waiting for him, had listened for him, and was now going back to the drawing-room.

'No,' she cried, when she saw him, and at the sound of her voice tears filled her eyes. 'No; if things are to go on like this, it will happen much, much too soon!'

'What is it, my dear?'

'What? I wait in agony an hour, two hours. ... No, I won't ... I can't quarrel with you. Of course you couldn't come. No, I won't.'

She laid her hands on his shoulders, and gave him a long, searching look, her eyes full of love. She was studying his face, making up for the time she had not seen him, comparing, as she did every time they met, the picture of him in her imagination (incomparably superior, impossible in reality) with him as he actually was.

3

'You met him?' she asked, when they had sat down at a table under the lamp. 'You're punished, you see, for being late.'

'Yes, but how was it? I thought he had to be at the council?'

'He had been there and come back, and was going out somewhere else. But it does not matter. Don't let us talk about it. Where have you been? With the prince all the time?'

She knew every detail of his existence. He was going to say that he had been up all night and had dropped asleep, but the sight of her excited, happy face made him feel conscience-stricken. And he said he had had to go and report the prince's departure.

'But it's over now? He has gone?'

'Yes, thank heaven! You have no idea how insufferable it was.'

'Why? All you young men are accustomed to that kind of life, aren't you?' she observed with a frown, taking up her crochet-work from the table and disentangling the hook, without looking at Vronsky.

'I gave up that existence long ago,' he said, wondering at the change in her face, and trying to divine its meaning. 'And I confess,' he added, smiling and showing his fine, white teeth, 'this week I've been looking at myself in a glass, as it were, seeing that kind of life, and I didn't like it.'

She held her work in her hands, but did not crochet, and gazed at him with strange, glittering, hostile eyes.

'This morning Liza came to see me – they're not afraid to call on me, in spite of the Countess Lydia Ivanovna,' she put in, 'and she told me about your Athenian evening. How disgusting!'

'I was about to say ...'

She interrupted him.

'And that Thérèse you used to know – was she there?'

'I was just saying …'

'How odious you men are! How is it you don't understand that a woman can never forget these things,' she said, getting more and more angry, and thus betraying the cause of her irritation, 'especially a woman who cannot share your life. What do I know? What have I ever known?' she said. 'Only what you tell me. And how do I know whether you tell me the truth? …'

'Anna, you hurt me. Don't you trust me? Haven't I told you over and over again that I haven't a single thought I would not share with you?'

'Yes, yes,' she said, evidently trying to suppress her jealousy. 'But if only you knew how wretched I am! I believe you, I do believe you … Now tell me what you were going to say!'

But he could not immediately remember what he had been going to say. These fits of jealousy, which of late had been more and more frequent, horrified him and, however much he tried to disguise the fact, estranged him from her, although he knew the cause of her jealousy was her love for him. How often he had told himself that to be loved by her was happiness; and now that she loved him as only a woman can love for whom love outweighs all that is good in life, he was much farther from happiness than when he had followed her from Moscow. Then he had considered himself unhappy, but happiness was before him; now he felt that his best happiness was already behind. She was utterly unlike the woman she had been when he first saw her. Both morally and physically she had changed for the worse. She had grown stouter, and when she spoke of the actress a spiteful expression had distorted her face. He looked at her as a man might look at some faded flower he had picked, in which it was difficult to trace the beauty that had made him pick and so destroy it. Yet in spite of this he felt that though at first, when his love was stronger, he could, had he earnestly desired, have torn that love out of his heart, now, at this moment when it seemed to him that he felt no love for her, he knew that the bond between them could not be broken.

'Well, what were you going to tell me about the prince? I have driven away the demon,' she added. (The demon was the name they had given her jealousy.) 'Yes, what did you begin to say about the prince? Why did you find it so disagreeable with him?'

'Oh, it was unbearable!' he said, trying to pick up the lost thread of his thought. 'He does not improve on closer acquaintance. If I had to describe him I should compare him to one of those prime, well-fed beasts who take first prize at cattle-shows, and nothing more,' he concluded in a tone of vexation which interested her.

'But in what way?' she objected. 'Isn't he an educated man who has travelled a great deal?'

'It's an entirely different kind of education – their education. One can see he's been educated simply to be able to despise education, as they despise everything except animal pleasures.'

'But don't all of you like those animal pleasures?' she asked, and again he noticed on her face that morose look which evaded his.

'Why are you so anxious to take his part?' he asked, with a smile.

'I'm not taking his part – it's nothing to me. Only I can't help thinking that if you had not cared for such pleasures yourself you might have got out of them. But you enjoy seeing Thérèse dressed as Eve ...'

'There's the demon again,' Vronsky said, taking the hand she had laid on the table and kissing it.

'I know, but I can't help it. You can't imagine what torture it has been waiting for you. I don't think I am jealous. I'm not jealous: I trust you when you are here but when you are away somewhere leading your life, so incomprehensible to me ...'

She turned away from him and, managing at last to disentangle her crochet-hook, with the aid of her forefinger began to draw the loops of white wool, shining in the lamp-light, through each other, her slender wrist twisting rapidly, nervously in its embroidered cuff.

'Well, and what happened? Where was it you met Alexei Alexandrovich?' she suddenly asked in an unnatural tone.

'We ran into each other at the door.'

'And did he bow to you like this?' She pulled a long face, half-closed her eyes and quickly transformed her expression, folding her hands; and upon her beautiful face Vronsky saw at once the very look with which Karenin had bowed to him. He smiled, and she laughed with her merry, delightfully deep laugh that was one of her greatest charms.

'I can't understand him at all,' said Vronsky. 'Had he left you after what you told him in the country, or challenged me – yes! But this sort of thing I can't understand. How can he put up with such a position? He feels it, that's obvious.'

'He?' she said scornfully. 'He's perfectly satisfied.'

'Why do we all go on tormenting ourselves when everything might be so happy?'

'He doesn't torment himself! Don't I know him – he's steeped in falsehood, through and through! If he had any feeling, could he possibly live with me as he does? He understands nothing, feels nothing. Could a man with any feelings live in the same house with a wife whom he knows is unfaithful? Could he talk to her, call her "My dear"?'

And without meaning to, she began mimicking him again: ' "Anna *ma chère*; Anna, dear!" '

'He's not a man, not a human being – he's a ... puppet! No one knows him, but I do. Oh, if I'd been in his place, I should long ago have murdered and torn in pieces a wife like me. I shouldn't be calling her "*ma chère*"! He's not a man, he's an automaton. He doesn't understand that I am your wife, that he's a stranger, in our way. ... Don't let us talk of him!'

'You are unfair, unfair, dearest,' said Vronsky, trying to soothe her. 'But never mind, we won't talk about him. Tell me what you have been doing. What is the matter? What is this illness of yours, and what did the doctor say?'

She looked at him with a mischievous light in her eyes. She had evidently remembered other ridiculous and grotesque sides to her husband and was waiting for an opportunity to come out with them. But he continued:

'I expect it is not illness at all, but your condition. When is it to be?'

The mocking light in her eyes faded, but a different smile, a consciousness of something, he did not know what, and gentle sadness spread over her face.

'Soon, soon. You were saying that our position is miserable, that we must put an end to it. If you knew how terrible it is to me, what I would give to be able to love you freely and openly! I should not torture myself and torture you with my jealousy. ... And it will happen soon, but not in the way we expect.'

And at the thought of how it would happen, she felt so sorry for herself that tears came into her eyes and she could not go on. She laid her lovely white hand on his sleeve, her rings sparkling in the lamplight.

'It won't happen in the way we suppose. I did not mean to tell you, but you made me. Soon – soon everything will come right and we shall all, all be at peace, and suffer no more.'

'I don't understand,' he said, understanding her.

'You asked when? Soon. And I shall not live through it. Don't interrupt me!' and she made haste to speak. 'I know it; I know it for certain. I shall die, and I am very glad I shall die, and set you free and myself as well.'

Tears rolled down her cheeks. He bent over her hand and began kissing it, trying to hide his agitation, which he knew had no foundation, though he could not control it.

'Yes, it's better so,' she said, convulsively gripping his hand. 'That's the only way, the only way left to us.'

He recovered and lifted his head.

'What rubbish! What utter rubbish you talk!'

'No, it's the truth.'

'What is – what is the truth?'

'That I shall die. I had a dream about it.'

'A dream?' repeated Vronsky, and instantly remembered the peasant in his own dream.

'Yes, a dream,' she said. 'A dream I had a long time ago. I dreamed that I ran into my bedroom to fetch something or find out something – you know how it is in dreams,' she said, her eyes wide with horror. 'And in the bedroom, in the corner, stood something.'

'Oh, what nonsense! How can you believe …'

But she would not let him interrupt. What she was saying was too important to her.

'And the something turned round, and I saw it was a peasant with a tangled beard, little and dreadful-looking. I wanted to run away, but he stooped down over a sack and was fumbling about in it with his hands …'

She showed how he had fumbled in the sack. There was terror in her face. And Vronsky, remembering his own dream, felt the same terror fill his being.

'And all the time he was rummaging, he kept muttering very quickly, in French, you know, rolling his r's: *Il faut le battre, le fer; le broyer, le pétrir*★ … And I was so terrified I tried to wake up … and I did wake up but it was still part of the dream. And I began asking myself what

★ It must be beaten, must the iron; pound it, knead it.

it meant. And Korney said to me: "In childbirth you'll die, in child-birth, ma'am ..." And then I woke up.'

'What nonsense, what nonsense!' said Vronsky, but he himself felt that there was no conviction in his voice.

'But don't let us talk of it. Ring the bell; I will order tea. And stay a little, now; it's not long I shall ...'

But all at once she stopped. The expression of her face changed in a flash. Horror and agitation suddenly gave way to a look of gentle, grave, blissful attention. He could not comprehend the meaning of the change. She was listening to the stirring of the new life within her.

4

AFTER meeting Vronsky at his own door, Karenin drove, as he had intended, to the Italian opera. He sat through two acts and saw every-body it was necessary for him to see. On his return home he carefully looked at the coat-stand and, noticing that no military greatcoat hung there, proceeded to his own room as usual. Contrary to habit, how-ever, he did not go to bed but paced up and down his study until three in the morning. The feeling of anger with his wife, who would not observe the rules of propriety and fulfil the one condition he had laid on her – not to receive her lover in his house – gave him no rest. She had not complied with his stipulation, and he must punish her and carry out his threat to divorce her and take the boy away. He knew all the difficulties connected with such a course, but he had said he would do it and must keep to his word. The Countess Lydia Ivanovna had hinted that this would be the best way out of the situation, and of late the procedure of divorce had been so perfected that Karenin saw a possibility of overcoming the formal difficulties. Moreover, mis-fortunes never come singly, and the affair of the reorganization of the native tribes, and the irrigation of the Zaraisky province, had caused Karenin so much worry in his official capacity that for some time he had been in a perpetual state of extreme irritability.

He did not sleep the whole night, and his fury, growing in a sort of vast, arithmetical progression, reached its peak in the morning. He dressed in haste, and, as though carrying his cup of wrath full to the brim and fearing to spill any – fearing to lose with his wrath the energy necessary for an interview with his wife – he went to her room directly he heard she was up.

Anna, who thought she knew her husband so well, was amazed at his appearance when he entered. His brow was dark, and his eyes glowered before him, avoiding her look; his lips were tightly and contemptuously pressed together. In his walk, in his gestures, in the sound of his voice were such determination and firmness as his wife had never seen in him. He came in without greeting her, went straight to her writing-table and, taking her keys, unlocked the drawer.

'What do you want?' she cried.

'Your lover's letters.'

'They're not here,' she said, shutting the drawer; but her action told him he had guessed aright, and roughly pushing away her hand he quickly snatched a portfolio in which he knew she kept her most important papers. She tried to grab it from him, but he thrust her aside.

'Sit down! I have something to say to you,' he said, putting the portfolio under his arm and squeezing it so tightly with his elbow that his shoulder was forced up.

Amazed and intimidated, she gazed at him in silence.

'I told you that I would not allow you to receive your lover in this house.'

'I had to see him to …'

She stopped, unable to invent a reason.

'I do not enter into details as to why a woman wants to see her lover.'

'I meant, I only …' she said, flushing hotly. His coarseness angered her and gave her courage. 'It is easy enough for you to insult me, isn't it?' she said.

'An honest man and an honest woman may be insulted, but to tell a thief he's a thief is simply *la constatation d'un fait*.'

'This cruelty is something new I did not know in you.'

'You call it cruelty for a husband to give his wife freedom, give her the honourable protection of his name, on the one condition that she should observe the proprieties. Is that cruelty?'

'It's worse than cruelty – it's base, if you want to know!' Anna cried, in a burst of hatred, and got up to go.

'No!' he shrieked in his shrill voice, that had risen a note higher even than usual, and gripping her so tightly with his large fingers that her bracelet left red marks on her wrist he forced her back into her chair.

'Base? If that's the word you want to use, what is base is to abandon husband and son for a lover, while you continue to eat your husband's bread!'

She bowed her head. She did not say what she had said the evening before to her lover, that *he* was her husband, and her husband the stranger in the way; she did not even think of it. She felt all the justice of his words, and only said softly:

'You cannot paint my position any worse than I feel it to be myself; but what are you saying all this for?'

'What am I saying it for? What for?' he went on, as angrily as before. 'That you may know that since you have not carried out my wishes that propriety be observed, I shall take steps to put an end to this state of things.'

'Soon, very soon, it will come to an end of itself,' she said, and again, at the thought of the nearness of death, which she now longed for, tears filled her eyes.

'It will end sooner than you and your lover have planned! You want the gratification of your animal passions …'

'Alexei Alexandrovich! This is not only ungenerous – it's not even gentlemanly to hit one who is down.'

'Yes, you think only of yourself! But the sufferings of a man who was your husband have no interest for you. What do you care that his whole life is in ruins! What does it matter to you what he has thuf … thuff … thuffered!'

Karenin was speaking so rapidly that he stammered, and was utterly unable to articulate the word 'suffered'. In the end he pronounced it 'thuffered'. She wanted to laugh, and immediately was ashamed that anything could seem funny to her at such a moment. And for the first time, for an instant, she felt for him, put herself in his place, and was sorry for him. But what could she say or do? She bowed her head and sat silent. He, too, was silent for a while, and then began again coldly, in a less shrill voice, emphasizing random words that had no special significance.

'I came to tell you …' he said.

She looked at him. 'No, it was only my fancy,' she thought, recalling the expression of his face when he had stumbled over the word 'suffered'. 'No; as if a man with those dull eyes, with that self-satisfied air, could have any feelings!'

'I cannot change anything,' she whispered.

'I came to tell you that I am going to Moscow to-morrow and shall not return to this house again, and you will hear what I decide through the lawyer to whom I shall entrust the divorce. My son will go to my sister's,' said Karenin, remembering with an effort what he had meant to say about the boy.

'You want Seriozha in order to hurt me,' she said, looking at him from under her brows. 'You don't love him. ... Leave me Seriozha!'

'Yes, I have lost even my affection for my son, because he is associated with my loathing for you. But all the same I shall take him. Good-bye!'

And he turned to go, but this time she stopped him.

'Alexei Alexandrovich, leave me Seriozha!' she whispered again. 'I have nothing else to say. Leave me Seriozha till my ... I shall soon be confined, leave him with me!'

Karenin lost his temper and, snatching his hand from her, left the room without a word.

5

THE famous Petersburg lawyer's waiting-room was full when Karenin entered it. Three women – an old lady, a young one, and a merchant's wife – and three gentlemen – one a German banker with a ring on his finger, the second a bearded merchant, and the third an irate official in uniform with an order hanging from his neck – had evidently been waiting a long time already. Two clerks sat at their tables writing, their pens scratching. The writing-table accessories, of which Karenin was a connoisseur, were exceptionally good, as he could not help observing. One of the clerks, without rising from his seat, screwed up his eyes and addressed Karenin ill-humouredly.

'What do you want?'

'I have to see the lawyer on business.'

'He is engaged,' replied the clerk severely, indicating with his pen the people who were waiting, and went on writing.

'Can he not find time to see me?' said Karenin.

'He has no spare time; he is always busy. Kindly wait your turn.'

'Then I must trouble you to give him my card,' Karenin said with dignity, seeing the impossibility of preserving his incognito.

The clerk took the card and, obviously not approving of what he read on it, went to the door.

In theory Karenin was in favour of publicity for legal proceedings, though for certain high official considerations he disliked the application of the principle in Russia, and criticized it in so far as he could criticize anything instituted by the authority of the Emperor. His whole life had been spent in administrative activity, and consequently when he did not approve of anything his disapproval was mitigated by a recognition of the inevitability of mistakes and the possibility of reform in every department. In the new public law-courts he disliked the restrictions laid on the lawyers conducting cases. But till now he had had nothing to do with the law-courts, and so his objections to their publicity were of a purely theoretical nature. Now, however, his objections were strengthened by the disagreeable impression made on him by the lawyer's waiting-room.

'He will be out in a moment,' said the clerk; and indeed a minute or two later the tall figure of an elderly solicitor who had been consulting with the lawyer appeared in the doorway, followed by the lawyer himself.

The lawyer was a short, thick-set, bald-headed man, with a dark, reddish beard, fair bushy eyebrows, and a prominent forehead. He was as spruce as a bridegroom, from his necktie and double watch-chain to his patent-leather boots. He had a clever, rustic face, while his clothes were dandified and in bad taste.

'Come in, please,' said the lawyer, addressing Karenin; and, gloomily ushering Karenin in before him, he closed the door.

'Won't you sit down?' He indicated an arm-chair by the writing-table stacked with papers, and ensconced himself behind the desk, rubbing his little hands together with their short fingers covered with white hairs, and bending his head to one side. But hardly had he settled down before a moth flew over the table. The lawyer, with a swiftness that could never have been expected of him, caught the moth between his hands, and resumed his former attitude.

'Before beginning to explain my business,' said Karenin, who had followed the lawyer's movements with astonishment, 'I must mention that the matter about which I have to speak to you must remain strictly private.'

A scarcely perceptible smile parted the lawyer's drooping reddish moustaches.

'I should not be a lawyer if I could not keep the secrets confided to me. But if you would like proof ...'

Karenin glanced at his face, and saw that the shrewd grey eyes were laughing, and seemed to know everything already.

'You know my name?' Karenin resumed.

'I know you and the valuable work' – he caught another moth – 'you are doing, like every Russian,' said the lawyer, bowing.

Karenin sighed, plucking up his courage. But having once made up his mind he went on in his shrill voice, without timidity or hesitation, emphasizing a word here and there.

'I have the misfortune,' he began, 'to have been deceived in my marriage, and I wish to break off all relations with my wife by legal means – that is, to obtain a divorce, but in such a way that my son should not remain with his mother.'

The lawyer's grey eyes did their best not to laugh, but they were dancing with irrepressible glee, and Karenin could see that it was not simply the glee of a man at the prospect of a profitable job – there was triumph and delight, there was a gleam like the malignant gleam he had seen in his wife's eyes.

'You desire my assistance in securing a divorce?'

'Exactly! But I ought to warn you that I may be wasting your time. I have only come for a preliminary consultation. I want a divorce, but it is the form in which it can be obtained that is important to me. It is quite possible that if that form does not correspond with my requirements I may forego my legitimate desire.'

'Oh, that is always so,' said the lawyer, 'and that is always open to you.'

The lawyer looked down at Karenin's feet, feeling that the sight of his overwhelming pleasure might offend his client. He glanced at a moth that flew past his nose, and put out a hand to catch it, but refrained out of respect for Karenin's position.

'Although the general outline of our laws relating to this subject is familiar to me,' pursued Karenin, 'I should be glad to have an idea of the usual practice.'

'You would like me,' said the lawyer, without lifting his eyes, and adopting, with a certain satisfaction, the tone of his client's remarks, 'to lay before you the various ways in which you could secure what you desire?'

And on receiving an assenting nod from Karenin he continued, only occasionally stealing a glance at Karenin's face, which had grown red in patches.

'Divorce by our laws,' he said, with a slight shade of disapprobation for our laws, 'is possible, as you are aware, in the following circumstances ... You must wait a little!' he exclaimed to the clerk, who had put his head in at the door, but he rose all the same, spoke a few words to him, and sat down again. '... in the following circumstances: physical defect in either party, desertion without communication for five years,' he said, crooking a short, hairy finger, 'and adultery' (this word he pronounced with obvious satisfaction), 'subdivided as follows' (he continued to crook his fat fingers, though the three cases and their subdivisions could plainly not be classified together): 'physical defect of husband or wife, adultery of the husband or wife.' As by now all his fingers were used up, he straightened them and went on: 'That is the theoretical side; but I presume you have done me the honour of coming to consult me on the practical application of the law. And therefore, guided by precedents, I must inform you that in practice cases of divorce may all be reduced to the following – I take it there is no question of physical defect, or desertion? ...'

Karenin nodded in assent.

'– may be reduced to the following: adultery of one of the parties, and the detection of the guilty party by mutual agreement, or, failing such agreement, involuntary detection. It must be admitted that the latter case is seldom met with in practice,' said the lawyer, and stealing a glance at Karenin he paused, with the air of a gunsmith who, having explained to his customer the advantages of this weapon and that, waits for him to make his choice. But Karenin said nothing, and so he began again: 'The most usual, simple, and sensible course, in my opinion, is adultery by mutual consent. I should not venture so to express myself were I not talking to a man of the world,' said the lawyer, 'but I take it you follow me.'

Karenin was so perturbed, however, that he did not immediately grasp all the wisdom of adultery by mutual consent, and his eyes expressed his perplexity; but the lawyer promptly came to his assistance.

'Two people cannot go on living together – here you have a fact. And if both are agreed about it, the details and formalities become a matter of no importance. And at the same time it is the simplest and surest method.'

Karenin fully understood now. But he had religious scruples, which stood in the way of such a course.

'It is out of the question in the present case,' he said. 'Only one alternative is possible: undesigned detection, supported by letters which I have in my possession.'

At the mention of letters the lawyer pursed his lips and uttered a high-pitched note of pity and contempt.

'I beg you not to forget,' he began, 'cases of that kind, as you are aware, come under ecclesiastical jurisdiction; the reverend fathers like to investigate such cases down to the minutest detail,' he said with a smile which showed his sympathy with the reverend fathers' taste. 'Letters may certainly serve as partial confirmation; but direct evidence is required – that is, of eye-witnesses. In fact, if you do me the honour of giving me your confidence, you will do well to leave me the choice of the measures to be employed. If one wants the result, one must not be shy of the means.'

'If it is so …' Karenin began, suddenly turning pale; but at this point the lawyer got up and went to the door to speak to his clerk, who had again come to interrupt him.

'Tell her we don't haggle over fees!' he said, and returned to Karenin.

Before taking his seat again, he furtively caught another moth. 'A fine state my furniture will be in by the summer!' he thought with a frown.

'You were just saying …' he said.

'I will communicate my decision to you by letter,' said Karenin, rising and holding on to the table. After a short pause he added: 'From what you say, then, I may conclude that a divorce is possible. I should be obliged if you would let me know your fees?'

'Quite possible if you allow me entire freedom of action,' said the lawyer, ignoring his question. 'When may I expect to hear from you?' he asked, moving towards the door, his eyes and patent-leather boots shining.

'In a week's time. And have the goodness to let me know whether you are willing to undertake the case, and on what terms.'

'Certainly.'

The lawyer bowed his client out respectfully and, left alone, abandoned himself to his sense of amusement. He felt in such good humour that, contrary to his rules, he lowered his fee to the lady who haggled, and gave up catching moths, having finally decided that next winter he would have his furniture re-upholstered in plush, like Sigonin's.

6

KARENIN had won a brilliant victory at the sitting of the Commission of the 17th of August, but the sequel to this victory proved his undoing. The new commission for the inquiry into the condition of the native tribes in all its branches had been formed and despatched to its field of operations with unusual speed and energy inspired by Karenin. Within three months a report was presented. The condition of the native tribes had been investigated in its political, administrative, economic, ethnographic, material, and religious aspects. All these questions had received admirably drafted answers – answers admitting no shade of doubt, since they were not a product of human thought, always liable to error, but were the outcome of official labours. The answers were all based on official data furnished by governors and prelates, founded on reports from district authorities and ecclesiastical superintendents, founded in their turn on the reports of rural administrative officers and parish priests. Consequently these answers left no possible room for doubt. Such questions, for instance, as to why crops failed, or why certain tribes adhered to their own creeds, and so on – questions which without the convenience of the official machine do not and cannot get solved for centuries – received clear and convincing answers. And these answers were in favour of Karenin's contention. But Stremov, who had been stung to the quick at the last sitting, had, on the reception of the commission's report, resorted to tactics which Karenin had not anticipated. Stremov suddenly went over to Karenin's side, carrying several other members with him, and was not only enthusiastic in his support of the measures advocated by Karenin but proposed others along the same lines, even more radical. These measures, going beyond Karenin's original idea, were adopted, and then the meaning of Stremov's tactics became apparent. Carried to an extreme, these measures proved so ridiculous that the highest authorities, and public opinion, and intellectual ladies, and the press all together fell in a torrent of indignation both on the measures and their begetter, Karenin. Stremov withdrew to the background, making it appear that he had but blindly followed Karenin's lead and now was astounded and distressed at what had been done. This proved fatal to Karenin. But in spite of ill-health and his domestic troubles, he did not give in. There was a split in the commission.

Some members, with Stremov at their head, tried to justify their mistake on the ground that they had put their faith in Karenin's revisory commission, and maintained that the report of the commission was rubbish and simply so much waste paper. Karenin and a number of others who saw the danger of so revolutionary an attitude to official documents persisted in upholding the findings of the said revisory commission. In consequence of this, in the higher spheres, and even in society, all was chaos and, although everyone was deeply interested, no one could make out whether the native tribes really were falling into poverty and ruin, or were flourishing. Karenin's position, owing to this and partly owing to the contempt lavished on him as a result of his wife's infidelity, became very precarious. And in these circumstances he took an important resolution. To the surprise of the commission, he announced his intention of applying for leave to go and investigate the matter personally. And having obtained permission, Karenin set out for the distant provinces.

Karenin's departure created a great sensation, the more so as just before starting he formally returned the money advanced to him for travelling expenses, to cover the cost of twelve horses all the way to his destination.

'I consider it very noble of him,' the Princess Betsy observed, discussing it with the Princess Myagky. 'Why pay for post-horses when everyone knows there are railways everywhere now?'

But the Princess Myagky did not agree, and was even annoyed by the Princess Tverskoy's opinion.

'It's all very well for you to talk when you possess I don't know how many millions,' she said. 'But I am very glad when my husband goes on a tour of inspection in the summer. It is very good for his health and he enjoys travelling about; and we have an arrangement by which the money goes to keep a carriage and coachman for me.'

On his way to the distant provinces Karenin stopped three days in Moscow.

The day after his arrival he was driving back from calling on the Governor-General. At the Gazetny lane crossing, where there is always a crowd of vehicles, Karenin suddenly heard his name called in such a loud and cheerful voice that he could not help looking round. At the corner of the pavement, in a short, stylish overcoat and a low-crowned stylish hat on the side of his head, white teeth gleaming between smiling red lips, young, gay, and beaming stood Oblonsky, vigorously and insistently shouting and demanding that Karenin should stop. He had one hand on the window of a carriage that had stopped at the corner of the street, and the heads of a lady in a velvet bonnet and two little children were thrust out of the window. With his other hand Oblonsky gaily beckoned to his brother-in-law. The lady smiled a kindly smile and she, too, waved to Karenin. It was Dolly with her children.

Karenin did not want to see anyone in Moscow, and least of all his wife's brother. He raised his hat and would have driven on, but Oblonsky told his coachman to stop, and ran across the snow to him.

'What a shame not have let us know! Been here long? And I was at Dussot's yesterday and saw "Karenin" on the board, but it never entered my head it could be you!' said Oblonsky, sticking his head in at the carriage window. 'Otherwise I should have looked you up. I am so glad to see you!' and he kicked one foot against the other to shake off the snow. 'What a shame of you not to let us know!' he repeated.

'I had no time: I am very busy,' Karenin replied dryly.

'Come over and speak to my wife. She is so anxious to see you.'

Karenin unwrapped the rug that was wound round his chilly legs, got out of the carriage, and made his way over the snow to Dolly.

'Why, what has happened, Alexei Alexandrovich? Why are you avoiding us like this?' said Dolly, smiling.

'I was very busy. Delighted to see you,' he said in a tone that plainly denoted the reverse. 'How are you?'

'Tell me, how is my darling Anna?'

Karenin mumbled something and made to go. But Oblonsky stopped him.

'I tell you what we'll do to-morrow. Dolly, ask him to dinner. We'll invite Koznyshev and Pestsov, to give him a sample of our Moscow intelligentsia.'

'Yes, please, do come,' said Dolly. 'We shall expect you at five, or six o'clock, just as you like. Well, how is my darling Anna? It is so long …'

'She is quite well,' mumbled Karenin, frowning. 'Glad to have met you!' and he moved away towards his carriage.

'You will come?' Dolly called after him.

Karenin made some reply which Dolly could not catch in the noise of the traffic.

'I shall look in to see you to-morrow!' Oblonsky shouted to him.

Karenin got into his carriage, and leaned back, so as neither to see nor be seen.

'Queer chap!' said Oblonsky to his wife and, glancing at his watch, made a motion of his hand before his face to indicate a caress to his wife and children, and walked jauntily away along the pavement.

'Stiva! Stiva!' Dolly called, reddening.

He turned round.

'You know I must get coats for Grisha and Tanya. Do give me some money.'

'Never mind! Tell them I'll settle the bill!' and, gaily nodding his head to an acquaintance who drove by, he disappeared from view.

7

THE next day was Sunday. Oblonsky went to the Bolshoy Theatre to a rehearsal of the ballet, and gave Masha Tchibisov, a pretty dancing-girl whom he had just taken under his protection, the coral necklace he had promised her the evening before, and in the wings in the dim light of the theatre contrived to plant a kiss on her pretty little face, radiant over her present. Besides giving her the necklace, he had come to arrange with her about meeting after the ballet. Explaining that he could not be there at the beginning of the performance, he promised to arrive in time for the last act and take her to supper. From the theatre Oblonsky drove to the poultry market and himself selected the fish and asparagus for dinner; and by noon he was at Dussot's, where he had to see three people, fortunately for him all staying at the same hotel: Levin, who had recently returned from abroad and was putting up there; the new head of his department, who had just been promoted to that position and was on a tour of inspection in Moscow; and his brother-in-law, Karenin, whom he wanted to secure for dinner.

Oblonsky liked a good dinner, but what he liked better still was a dinner-party at his own house: not a big affair, but very choice, both as regards the food and drink, and the guests. He was well satisfied with the programme for that day's dinner: there would be perch (brought alive to the kitchen), asparagus, and *la pièce de résistance* – a superb but quite plain joint of roast-beef, and the appropriate wines: so much for the food and drink. As for the guests, Kitty and Levin

398

would be of the party, and that this might not be obtrusively evident there would be a girl-cousin too, and young Shcherbatsky. Here the *pièce de résistance* was to be Koznyshev and Karenin – the first a Muscovite and a philosopher, the second a Petersburg man of affairs. He was asking, too, the well-known eccentric and enthusiast, Pestsov, a liberal, a great talker, a musician, a historian, and the dearest of fifty-year-old boys, who would be a sauce or garnish for Koznyshev and Karenin. He would provoke them and set them by the ears.

The second instalment of the money for the forest had been received and was not yet all spent. Dolly had been very amiable and good-humoured of late, and the thought of his dinner-party was in every respect pleasing to him. He was in the most light-hearted mood. There were just two circumstances that were not quite satisfactory, but they were drowned in the ocean of happy gaiety which overflowed his heart. The first was that he had noticed that Karenin had been very cold and stiff when they met in the street the day before, and, coupling this with the fact that he had not come to see them, or let them know of his arrival, with the rumours that had reached him about Anna and Vronsky, Oblonsky guessed that all was not well between husband and wife.

This was one disagreeable thing. The other slightly disagreeable fact was that his new chief, like all new heads, already had the reputation of being a terrible person who got up at six in the morning, worked like a horse, and expected his subordinates to do the same. Besides which, he was further reputed to have the manners of a bear, and to hold views diametrically opposed to those of his predecessor, and which till now Oblonsky had shared. On the previous day Oblonsky had appeared at the office in uniform, and the new chief had been very affable and had chatted with him as with an old acquaintance. Consequently Oblonsky deemed it his duty to call upon him in a morning coat. The thought that the new chief might not give him a warm reception was the other disturbing element. But Oblonsky instinctively felt that everything would *right itself* splendidly. 'They're all human beings, all men, like us poor sinners: what is there to get angry and quarrel about?'

'Halloa, Vassily!' he greeted a footman he knew as he walked down the corridor, his hat tilted to one side. 'You've let your whiskers grow? Levin, number 7, is it? Take me up, please. And find out if Count Anitchkin' (this was his new chief) 'is in.'

'Yes, sir,' Vassily replied with a smile. 'It's a long time since you've been to see us.'

'I was here yesterday, but I came in at the other door. Is this number 7?'

Levin was standing in the middle of the room with a peasant from Tver, measuring a new bearskin, when Oblonsky entered.

'I say, did you kill him?' cried Oblonsky. 'What a fine specimen! A she-bear? Morning, Arhip.'

He shook hands with the peasant and sat down on the edge of a chair, without removing his coat and hat.

'Do take your things off and stay a little,' said Levin, taking his hat.

'No, I haven't time. I've only looked in for half a second,' answered Oblonsky, throwing open his coat. In the end he did take it off, and sat on for a whole hour, talking to Levin about hunting and all sorts of very personal matters.

'Now tell me what you did abroad. Where have you been?' said Oblonsky, when the peasant had gone.

'Well, I stayed in Germany, in Prussia, in France, and in England – not in the capitals but in the manufacturing towns, and saw a great deal that was new to me. And I'm glad I went.'

'Yes, I know your idea about settling the labour question.'

'Oh no! In Russia there can be no labour question. In Russia the question turns on the relation of the worker to the land: the problem exists there too, but with them it's a case of patching up what has been ruined, while here …'

Oblonsky listened to Levin attentively.

'Yes, yes,' he said, 'very likely you're right. But I am delighted to find you are in good spirits, and go bear-hunting and work and are full of enthusiasm. Young Shcherbatsky told me another story – he met you and said you were down in the mouth and kept talking of death …'

'Well, what of it? I never stop thinking of death,' said Levin. 'It's true that it's high time I was dead and that all this is vanity. I will tell you frankly: I do value my idea and my work awfully; but in reality – just think! This whole world of ours is nothing but a speck of mildew, which has grown up on a tiny planet. And for us to suppose we can have something great – ideas, work – it's all dust and ashes.'

'But, my dear fellow, what you say is as old as the hills!'

'That may be, but you know, when once you realize it, somehow everything becomes of no consequence. When you think that to-morrow, if not to-day, you may be dead and nothing will be left of you, what does anything matter? And I look upon my ideas as very important, but they turn out to have no more significance, even if it were possible to carry them out, than the act of walking round this bear-skin. So one passes one's life, amusing oneself with hunting, with work – anything so as not to think of death!'

Oblonsky smiled affectionately as he listened to Levin.

'Well, of course! So you have come round to my way of thinking at last. Do you remember how you used to fall on me for seeking enjoyment in life? Be not so severe, O moralist!'

'But of course, what's fine in life is ...' Levin became confused. 'Oh, I don't know. All I know is that we shall soon be dead.'

'Why soon?'

'And you know, there's less charm in life, when one thinks of death, but it is more peaceful.'

'On the contrary, it is much more fun towards the end! However, I must be going,' said Oblonsky, getting up for the tenth time.

'No, stay a little longer!' said Levin, trying to detain him. 'Now, when shall we see each other again? I'm leaving to-morrow.'

'I'm a nice one! I came on purpose to ... You simply must come and dine with us to-day. Your brother's coming, and Karenin, my brother-in-law.'

'You don't mean to say he's here?' said Levin, and he wanted to inquire about Kitty. He had heard that at the beginning of the winter she had gone to Petersburg to stay with her sister, the wife of a diplomat, and he did not know whether she had come back or not, but he changed his mind and did not ask. 'Whether she comes or not will make no difference,' he thought.

'So you'll come?'

'Yes, of course.'

'At five o'clock, then, and not evening dress.'

And Oblonsky rose and went downstairs to call on the new head of his department. Instinct had not misled Oblonsky. The terrible new head turned out to be an extremely amenable person, and Oblonsky lunched with him and stayed on, so that it was nearly four o'clock by the time he got to Karenin.

8

AFTER returning from church, Karenin spent the rest of the morning indoors. He had two matters to see to that morning: first, to receive and send on a deputation from the native tribes which was now in Moscow, on its way to Petersburg; secondly, to write the promised letter to the lawyer. The deputation, though it had been summoned on Karenin's initiative, presented many difficulties, even dangers, and he was very glad he had chanced to meet it in Moscow. The members of the deputation had not the slightest conception of their role or of their duties. They were naïvely convinced that their business consisted in explaining their needs and the existing state of affairs, and of asking for help from the Government. They could not be got to understand that some of their statements and demands would play into the hands of the hostile party, and so ruin the whole business. Karenin had a prolonged tussle with them, drew up a programme from which they were not to deviate, and, having dismissed them, wrote several letters to Petersburg with instructions regarding the deputation. He looked to the Countess Lydia Ivanovna to be his chief support in the matter. She was a specialist in the art of handling deputations, and no one knew better than she how to pilot a deputation and put it in the way it should go.

Next, Karenin wrote the letter to the lawyer. Without the slightest hesitation he gave him authority to act as he thought best. In the letter he enclosed three of Vronsky's notes to Anna, which were in the portfolio he had taken away.

Ever since Karenin had left home with the intention of not returning to his family again, and ever since he had been to the lawyer's and spoken, though only to one man, of his intention, especially since he had converted this matter of life into an affair of ink and paper, he had grown more and more accustomed to his own intention, and by now its execution seemed to him distinctly feasible.

He was sealing the envelope to the lawyer, when he heard the loud tones of Oblonsky's voice. Oblonsky was disputing with Karenin's servant, and insisting on being announced.

'No matter,' thought Karenin. 'I may as well see him and inform him at once of my position in regard to his sister, and explain why it is I cannot dine at his house.'

'Let the gentleman in!' he said in a loud voice, gathering up his papers and pushing them in the blotter.

'There, you see, you were lying and he is at home!' Oblonsky was heard saying to the servant, who had been trying to stop him, and, taking off his coat as he went, Oblonsky walked into the room. 'I'm awfully glad to find you in! So I hope ...' began Oblonsky gaily.

'I cannot come,' Karenin said coldly, standing and not asking his visitor to sit down.

Karenin had thought at once to pass into those frigid relations proper with the brother of a wife against whom he was starting a suit for divorce; but he had not reckoned with that ocean of kindliness brimming over in the heart of Oblonsky.

Oblonsky opened wide his clear, bright eyes.

'Why can't you? What do you mean?' he asked perplexedly, speaking in French. 'Oh no, you promised. And we're all counting on you.'

'I want to tell you that I cannot come to your house because the relations that have existed between us must be severed.'

'What? I mean, how? Why?' said Oblonsky with a smile.

'Because I am about to take divorce proceedings against your sister, my wife. I ought to have ...'

But before Karenin could finish his sentence, Oblonsky did something quite unexpected. He uttered a groan and sank into an armchair.

'No, Alexei Alexandrovich! What are you talking about?' cried Oblonsky, a look of pain appearing on his face.

'It is true.'

'Excuse me, I can't – I can't believe it ...'

Karenin sat down, feeling that his words had not had the effect he had anticipated, and that he would be obliged to give an explanation, and that whatever that explanation might be it would not alter his relations to his brother-in-law.

'Yes, I am under the painful necessity of applying for a divorce.'

'I will say one thing, Alexei Alexandrovich. I know you for a first-rate fellow and a man of principle; I know Anna – forgive me, I cannot change my opinion of her – for a fine, splendid woman; and so, forgive me, I cannot believe it. There must be some misunderstanding,' said he.

'I only wish it were a misunderstanding!'

'Of course, I quite see ...' Oblonsky interrupted him. 'But really ... One thing: you must not act in haste. You must not, you really must not act in haste!'

'I am not acting in haste,' Karenin replied coldly, 'but one cannot ask advice of anyone in such a matter. My mind is made up.'

'This is awful!' said Oblonsky, sighing deeply. 'I would do one thing, Alexei Alexandrovich. I implore you to do it. Proceedings have not yet been begun, if I understand rightly. Before doing anything, see my wife, talk it over with her. She loves Anna like a sister, she loves you, and she's a wonderful woman. For God's sake, talk it over with her! Do me that favour, I beseech you!'

Karenin considered, and Oblonsky looked at him sympathetically, without breaking the silence.

'You will go and see her?'

'I really don't know. That was why I did not call at your house. I supposed our relations must change.'

'But why should they? I don't see it. Allow me to believe that apart from our family relationship you have for me, at least to some extent, the same friendly feelings I have always had for you ... And sincere esteem,' said Oblonsky, pressing his hand. 'Even if your worst suppositions were correct, I don't – and never would – take on myself to judge either side, and see no reason why our relations should be affected. But now, do this, come and see my wife.'

'Well, we look at the matter differently,' said Karenin coldly. 'However, we won't discuss it.'

'But why not come, if only to dinner to-night? My wife's expecting you. Do come. And, above all, talk it over with her. She is a wonderful woman. For God's sake – I implore you on my bended knee!'

'If you wish it so much, I will come,' said Karenin with a sigh.

And, anxious to change the subject, he began inquiring about a matter of interest to them both – Oblonsky's new chief, a man who though still young had suddenly been given so high a post.

Karenin had never liked Count Anitchkin and had always differed from him in his opinions. But now he could not repress a feeling of hatred, comprehensible to anyone in an official position, from one who has suffered a set-back in the service for one who had received promotion.

'Well, and have you seen him?' asked Karenin with a venomous smile.

'Oh yes, he came to the sitting yesterday. He seems to know his business perfectly, and to be very energetic.'

'Yes, but what is his energy directed to?' said Karenin. 'Towards getting things done, or undoing what's been done? The curse of our country is its scribbling bureaucracy, of which he is a worthy representative.'

'Really, I don't know what fault one could find with him. I have no idea what his policy is, but one thing – he's a capital fellow,' replied Oblonsky. 'I have just been in to see him, and really he's an excellent chap. We had lunch together, and I showed him how to make that drink – you know, wine and orange-juice. It's most refreshing. I was surprised he didn't know it. He liked it very much. Yes, he certainly is a jolly good fellow.'

Oblonsky glanced at his watch.

'Dear me, it is after four, and I have still to go to Dolgóvushin's! So you'll come to dinner? You can't imagine how you will grieve my wife and me if you don't.'

Karenin parted from his brother-in-law in a manner very different from that in which he had greeted him.

'I have promised, and I'll come,' he answered dejectedly.

'Believe me, I appreciate it, and I hope you won't regret it,' Oblonsky replied with a smile.

As he put on his overcoat while walking away, his arm touched the footman's head. He chuckled, and went out.

'Five o'clock, and not evening dress, please,' he called out once more, returning to the door.

9

IT was past five, and some of the guests had already arrived, when the master of the house got home. He came in with Koznyshev and Pestsov, who had met on the doorstep. These two were the leading representatives of the Moscow intellectuals, as Oblonsky called them. Both were men respected for their character and intelligence. They respected each other, but upon almost every subject were in complete and hopeless disagreement, not because they belonged to opposite schools of thought but for the very reason that they belonged to the same camp (their enemies confused them one with the other); but in that camp each had his own special shade of opinion. And since nothing is less conducive to agreement than disagreement on semi-abstract themes, they not only disagreed in their opinions but had long been accustomed without anger to make fun of each other's incorrigible aberrations.

They were just entering the door, talking of the weather, when Oblonsky overtook them. Prince Alexander Shcherbatsky, Oblonsky's father-in-law, young Shcherbatsky, Turovtsyn, Kitty, and Karenin were already sitting in the drawing-room.

Oblonsky saw at a glance that without him things were not going well in the drawing-room. Dolly in her gala grey silk gown, obviously worried about the children who would have to have their dinner by themselves in the nursery, and because her husband was late, had not managed in his absence to bring the company together. They all sat straight and prim, 'like so many clergymen's daughters out calling' (as the old prince expressed it), evidently wondering why they were there, and pumping out remarks to avoid being silent. The good-natured Turovtsyn clearly felt like a fish out of water, and the smile with which his thick lips greeted Oblonsky said as plainly as words: 'Well, old boy, you have planted me in a learned set! A drinking-party now, or the Château des Fleurs, would be more in my line!' The old prince sat silent, his shining eyes every now and then casting a sidelong look at Karenin, and Oblonsky saw that he had already hit upon some phrase to polish off that state dignitary of whom people were invited to partake as of a special dish of sturgeon. Kitty was looking at the door, calling up all her energies to keep from blushing when Levin should enter. Young Shcherbatsky, who had not been introduced to Karenin, was trying to look as if this did not make him feel in the least awkward. Karenin himself was wearing evening dress with a white tie, as is the Petersburg fashion when ladies are present, and Oblonsky could tell by his face that he had come merely to keep his word, and was performing a disagreeable duty in being in this company. He indeed was the chief cause of the icy chill which had frozen the other guests before Oblonsky's arrival.

Entering the drawing-room, Oblonsky apologized for being late, explaining that he had been detained by a certain prince, who was his usual scapegoat whenever he was unpunctual or absent, and in a moment he had introduced everyone all round, and, bringing Karenin and Koznyshev together, started them on a discussion of the Russification of Poland, into which they immediately plunged with Pestsov.

Clapping Turovtsyn on the shoulder, he whispered something funny in his ear, and installed him near Dolly and the old prince. Then he told Kitty how pretty she was looking that evening, and presented young Shcherbatsky to Karenin. In a moment he had so kneaded together that society dough that the company began enjoying themselves and the drawing-room was filled with animated conversation. Constantine Levin was the only person who had not arrived. However, that was all for the best, as on looking in at the dining-room Oblonsky saw to his horror that the port and sherry were from Depret and not from Levé. Directing that the coachman should be sent off as speedily as possible to Levé's, he turned to go back to the drawing-room.

At the door he met Levin.

'I'm not late?'

'As if you could ever help being late!' said Oblonsky, taking his arm.

'Have you a lot of people? Who's here?' asked Levin, unable to help blushing, and knocking the snow off his cap with his glove.

'All our own set. Kitty's here. Come along, I'll introduce you to Karenin.'

For all his liberal views, Oblonsky was well aware that to meet Karenin could not but be a flattering distinction, and so treated his best friends to that honour. But at that instant Levin was not in a condition to appreciate the gratification of such an acquaintance. He had not seen Kitty since that memorable evening when he had met Vronsky, not counting, that is, that one moment when he had had a glimpse of her in the carriage on the high road. He had known at the bottom of his heart that he would see her here to-day. But to maintain his freedom of thought, he had been trying to persuade himself that he did not know it. Now, when he heard that she was here, he was suddenly conscious of such joy and at the same time such dread that he caught his breath and could not say what he wanted to.

'How will she seem, I wonder? The same as before, or as she was in the carriage that morning? What if what Darya Alexandrovna had said was true? Why shouldn't it be true?' he thought to himself.

'Oh, do introduce me to Karenin!' he brought out with an effort, and with a desperately determined step he walked into the drawing-room and beheld her.

She was not the same as before, nor as he had seen her in the carriage. She was quite different.

She was scared, shy, shame-faced, and therefore all the more charm-ing. She saw him the instant he entered the room. She had been wait-ing for him. She was filled with joy, and so confused at her own joy, that there was a moment – the moment when he went up to his host-ess and glanced again at her – when she, and he, and Dolly, who saw it all, thought she would break down and burst into tears. Blushing and going pale by turns, she sat rigid, waiting with quivering lips for his approach. He went up to her, bowed, and silently held out his hand. Except for the slight quiver of her lips and the moist film that came over her eyes, making them appear brighter, her smile was almost calm as she said:

'What a long time it is since we met!' and with desperate resolve her cold hand pressed his.

'You've not seen me, but I've seen you,' said Levin, with a beaming smile of happiness. 'I saw you coming from the station on your way to Yergushovo.'

'When?' she asked, wondering.

'You were driving to Yergushovo,' said Levin, feeling ready to sob with the rapture that was flooding his heart. 'And how could I have imputed anything not-innocent to this touching creature? And yes, I do believe it's true, what Darya Alexandrovna told me,' he thought.

Oblonsky took him by the arm and led him over to Karenin.

'Let me introduce you,' and he gave their names.

'Very glad to meet you again,' said Karenin coldly, shaking hands with Levin.

'You know each other?' asked Oblonsky in surprise.

'We spent three hours together in a railway carriage,' said Levin with a smile, 'but we parted filled with curiosity, like people at a masked ball – at any rate, I was.'

'Really! Please, come along,' said Oblonsky with a gesture in the direction of the dining-room.

The men went into the dining-room and walked up to a table on which stood half a dozen different kinds of vodka and as many kinds of cheese, with and without little silver scoops, caviare, herrings, pre-serves of various kinds, and plates with thin slices of French bread.

The men stood round the fragrant vodka and the delicacies, and the conversation about the Russification of Poland between Koznyshev, Karenin, and Pestsov began to flag in anticipation of dinner.

Koznyshev, who was unequalled in his skill in winding up the most abstract and serious argument by some unexpected grain of Attic salt that changed his interlocutors' frame of mind, did so now.

Karenin had been maintaining that the Russification of Poland could be achieved only as a result of larger measures which ought to be introduced by the Russian Government.

Pestsov insisted that one nation could assimilate another only when it had a larger population.

Koznyshev, with certain limitations, agreed with both. In order to terminate the discussion, he remarked with a smile as they were leaving the drawing-room:

'So there is only one way of Russifying alien nationalities – have as many children as possible. My brother and I are badly at fault, I see; while you married gentlemen, especially you, Oblonsky, are the real patriots. How many have you?' he asked, smiling genially at their host and holding out a tiny wine-glass to him.

Everyone laughed, and Oblonsky with particular good-humour.

'Oh yes, that's the best method!' he said, munching a piece of cheese and filling the wine-glass held out to him with a special sort of vodka. The conversation came to an end with that sally.

'This cheese is not at all bad. May I help you to some?' said the master of the house. 'Why, have you been going in for gymnastics again?' he asked Levin, with his left hand pinching Levin's muscles. Levin smiled, bent his arm, and under Oblonsky's fingers a lump like a Dutch cheese and hard as steel bulged the fine cloth of his coat.

'What biceps! A regular Samson!'

'I suppose you need great physical strength for bear-hunting?' observed Karenin, whose notions about hunting were of the vaguest, as he spread some cheese on a wafer of bread thin as a cobweb.

Levin smiled.

'Not at all. On the contrary, a child can kill a bear,' he said, standing aside, with a slight bow, for the ladies who were approaching the table with the hostess.

'You have killed a bear, I hear?' said Kitty, vainly trying to stick her fork into a perverse mushroom that would slip away, and setting the lace quivering over her white arm. 'I did not know you had bears in your part of the world,' she added, turning her lovely little head to him and smiling.

There was, it would seem, nothing extraordinary in what she said, but what unutterable meaning there was for him in every sound, in every turn of her lips, her eyes, her hand as she said it! There was entreaty for forgiveness, there was trust in him and a caress – a tender, timid caress – and promise and hope and love for him, which he could not but believe in and which suffocated him with happiness.

'No, we went up to Tver. It was on my way back that I met your brother-in-law in the train – or rather, your brother-in-law's brother-in-law,' he said with a smile. 'It was a funny meeting.'

And he gave a lively and amusing description of how, in a short sheepskin coat and dishevelled after a sleepless night, he had broken into Karenin's compartment.

'Regardless of the proverb, the guard wanted to chuck me out on account of my clothes, but I there and then assumed a high and mighty air, and … you, too,' he said, addressing Karenin (whose Christian name and patronymic he had forgotten), 'were suspicious of my peasant coat and would have done likewise, but in the end you took my part, for which I am extremely grateful.'

'The rights of passengers in the choice of seats are altogether too indefinite,' said Karenin, wiping the tips of his fingers on his handkerchief.

'I could see you were not quite sure what to make of me,' continued Levin, with a good-natured smile, 'so I hastened to start an intellectual conversation to make you forget my sheepskin.'

Koznyshev, who was talking to his hostess and at the same time listening with one ear to his brother, glanced at him sideways and thought: 'What has happened to him to-day? Why such a conquering hero?' He did not know that Levin was feeling as though he had grown a pair of wings. Levin knew she was listening to him and taking pleasure in hearing him. And that was the only thing he cared about. Not only in that room but in the whole world there existed for him only himself, with enormously increased importance and dignity, and Kitty. He felt on a pinnacle that made him dizzy, and there, somewhere far below, were all those good, excellent Karenins, Oblonskys, and the rest of humanity.

Quite casually, without looking at them, and as though there were no other place to put them, Oblonsky sat Levin and Kitty beside each other.

'You might sit here,' he said to Levin.

The dinner was as choice as the dinner-service, and Oblonsky was a connoisseur of china. The soup *Marie-Louise* had succeeded to perfection, the tiny patties melted in the mouth and were flawless. Matvey and two footmen in white ties manipulated the dishes and wines unobtrusively, noiselessly, and skilfully. On the material side the dinner was a success; it was no less so on the non-material side. The conversation, sometimes general and sometimes tête-à-tête, never flagged, and towards the end became so animated that the men got up from the table still talking, and even Karenin was completely thawed.

10

Pestsov liked thrashing an argument out to the end, and had not been satisfied with Koznyshev's remark, the more so as he was aware of the fallacy of his own opinion.

'I did not mean,' he began over the soup, addressing Karenin, 'that we should set about absorbing other nations on principle, but that it would come about naturally if our population were the larger.'

'It seems to me,' said Karenin languidly, and with no haste, 'that that amounts to the same thing. In my opinion, only a nation with a superior culture can hope to influence another. A culture that ...'

'But that is precisely the question,' interrupted Pestsov in his deep voice – he was always in a hurry to speak and always seemed to be staking his whole soul on what he was saying. 'How is one to recognize this superior culture? The English, the French, the Germans – which of them is at the highest stage of development? Which is to nationalize the other? We see that the Rhine provinces have turned French – is this a proof of inferiority on the part of the Germans?' he cried. 'There must be some other law at work.'

'I believe that the advantage is always on the side of true culture,' observed Karenin, raising his eyebrows slightly.

'But what are the signs of this true culture?' Pestsov asked.

'I should have thought such signs were generally well known,' said Karenin.

'But are they fully known?' put in Koznyshev with a subtle smile. 'It is the accepted view at the present time that real culture depends on a purely classical education; but we hear violent arguments on both sides, and there is no denying that the opposite camp has some strong points in its favour.'

'You are a classical scholar, Sergei Ivanich! Will you take red wine?' said Oblonsky.

'I am not speaking of my personal opinions,' replied Koznyshev with a condescending smile, as though to a child, and holding out his glass. 'All I say is that there are strong arguments on both sides,' he went on, addressing himself to Karenin. 'I had a classical education, but personally can find no place in the controversy. I see no clear reason why the classics should be preferred to a modern education.'

'The natural sciences have just as great an educational value,' Pestsov joined in. 'Take astronomy, take botany, or zoology with its system of general principles ...'

'I cannot quite agree with you there,' answered Karenin. 'It seems to me that one must admit that the very process of studying the forms of a language has a peculiarly beneficial effect on intellectual development. Moreover, it cannot be denied that the influence of the classical authors is in the highest degree a moral one, whereas, unfortunately, with the study of the natural sciences are associated the false and noxious doctrines which are the curse of our times.'

Koznyshev was about to say something when Pestsov's deep bass interrupted him. He began warmly contesting the justice of such a view. Koznyshev quietly waited to put in a word, evidently ready with some crushing retort.

'But,' said Koznyshev with his subtle smile, addressing Karenin, 'one cannot help allowing that to weigh all the pros and cons of classical and scientific studies is a difficult task, and the question, which form of education is to be preferred, would not have been so quickly and conclusively decided had not classical education had on its side the advantage, as you expressed it just now, of its moral – *disons le mot* – anti-nihilist influence.'

'Exactly.'

'Were it not for the advantage of this anti-nihilistic influence on the side of classical education, we should have given longer consideration to the question, and weighed the arguments on both sides,' said Koznyshev, subtly smiling. 'We should have given elbow-room to both systems. But as it is we know that these little pills of classical learning possess the medicinal property of anti-nihilism, and we boldly prescribe them to our patients. ... But what if they had no such medicinal property?' he concluded, adding the grain of Attic salt.

At Koznyshev's little pills, everyone laughed, and Turovtsyn in particular roared loudly and jovially, having at last heard something funny, all he ever looked for in listening to conversation.

Oblonsky had made no mistake in inviting Pestsov. With Pestsov there, intellectual conversation could not flag for an instant. Hardly had Koznyshev with his joke put an end to the discussion of one question before Pestsov promptly raised another.

'I can't agree even,' said he, 'that the Government had that aim. The Government obviously is guided by general considerations, and remains indifferent to the influence its measures may exercise. For instance, the education of women ought to be considered as likely to be harmful, yet we find the Government opening schools and universities for women.'

And the conversation at once veered to a new topic – the education of women.

Karenin expressed the opinion that the education of women was apt to be confounded with the emancipation of women, and on that account alone could be considered dangerous.

'I consider, on the contrary, that the two questions are interdependent,' observed Pestsov. 'It is a vicious circle. Women are deprived of rights from lack of education, and the lack of education results from the absence of rights. We must not overlook the fact that the subjection of women is so complete, and dates so far back, that we are often unwilling to recognize the abyss that separates them from us.'

'You speak of rights,' began Koznyshev, who had been waiting for Pestsov to finish. 'Did you mean the right of serving on a jury, of voting, of presiding at local government boards, of entering the civil service, of sitting in parliament? ...'

'Certainly.'

'But if women, in some rare exceptional cases, can fill such posts, it seems to me you are wrong in using the expression "rights". It would be more correct to say duties. Every man will agree that when we fill the office of juryman, witness, telegraph clerk, we feel we are performing duties. So it would be more correct to say that women are seeking duties, and quite legitimately. And we cannot but sympathize with this desire of theirs to assist man in his work for the community.'

'Quite so,' Karenin assented. 'The question, I imagine, resolves itself into this: are they fitted for such duties?'

'In all probability they will be perfectly fitted when education becomes general among them,' Oblonsky put in. 'We see this...'

'And how about the proverb?' said the old prince, who had long been listening to the conversation with a twinkle in his comical little eyes. 'My daughters won't mind my repeating it: long hair, short wit ...'

'People thought the same of the Negroes before their emancipation,' interrupted Pestsov angrily.

'The thing that seems strange to me is that women should be seeking fresh duties,' observed Koznyshev, 'while, as we see, unfortunately, men usually try to avoid them.'

'Duties are bound up with rights – power, money, honours: that is what women are after,' said Pestsov.

'Exactly as though I demanded the right to be a wet-nurse, and felt injured because women are paid for the work, while no one would take me,' said the old prince.

Turovtsyn burst into loud laughter, and Koznyshev felt a touch of envy that he had not made the comparison himself. Even Karenin smiled.

'Yes, but a man can't nurse a baby,' said Pestsov, 'while a woman...'

'Oh yes, there was an Englishman who did rear his baby on board ship,' said the old prince, allowing himself this licence in his speech in the presence of his daughters.

'There would be about as many women fitted to be officials as there are Englishmen of that kind,' said Koznyshev.

'Yes, but what is a girl to do who has no family?' asked Oblonsky, who, in agreeing with Pestsov and taking his part, had been thinking all the time of the ballet-girl, Masha Tchibisov.

'If you look closely into the story of a girl like that, you would find she has left her family – her own or a sister's, where she might have found a woman's duties,' said Dolly, unexpectedly breaking into the conversation with a certain amount of irritation, probably guessing the girl her husband had in mind.

'But we take our stand on a principle, an ideal!' replied Pestsov in his sonorous bass. 'Women want the right to be independent, educated. They are hampered, oppressed by the consciousness of their disabilities.'

'And I'm hampered and oppressed that they won't take me as a wet-nurse at the Foundling Hospital,' the old prince said again, to the huge delight of Turovtsyn, who laughed so much that he dropped his asparagus with the thick end in the sauce.

11

EVERYONE took part in the general conversation except Kitty and Levin. At first, when the influence that one nation has on another was being discussed, there rose to Levin's mind what he had to say on the subject; but these ideas, once so important to him, now only flashed through his brain as in a dream, and had not the slightest interest for him. It even struck him as strange that they should be so eager to talk of something that made no difference to anyone. In the same way, what was being said of the rights and education of women should have interested Kitty. How often had she considered the question, thinking of Varenka, her friend abroad, of her painfully dependent position, how often had she wondered what would be her own fate if she did not marry, and how many times had she argued with her sister on the subject! But now it did not interest her in the least. She and Levin had a conversation of their own – not a conversation but a sort of mystic communion which every moment bound them more closely together, and stirred in both a sense of fear and joy before the unknown upon which they were entering.

They began by Kitty asking how he came to see her last year in the carriage, and Levin explaining how he had been coming home from the mowing along the high-road and had met her.

'It was very, very early in the morning. You were probably only just awake. Your mother was asleep in the corner. It was a lovely morning. I was walking along wondering who it could be in a four-in-hand. It was a splendid team with bells, and in a second you flashed by, and I saw you at the window sitting like this and holding the ribbons of your cap with both hands, and thinking awfully deeply about something,' he said, smiling. 'How I wish I knew what you were thinking then! Was it something very important?'

'Wasn't I dreadfully untidy?' she wondered to herself, but seeing the rapturous smile these reminiscences called up she felt that the impression she had made must have been a very pleasing one. She blushed and laughed with delight: 'Really I don't remember.'

'What a jolly laugh Turovtsyn has!' said Levin, admiring his glistening eyes and shaking body.

'Have you known him long?' asked Kitty.

'Oh, everyone knows him!'

'And I see you think he's a horrid man?'

'Not horrid, but not of much account.'

'Oh, you're wrong! And you must change your opinion at once!' said Kitty. 'I used to have a very poor opinion of him, too, but he's an awfully dear and wonderfully good-hearted man. He has a heart of gold.'

'How could you find out what sort of heart he has?'

'He and I are great friends. I know him very well. Last winter, soon after ... soon after you came to see us,' she said, with a guilty and at the same time confiding smile, 'Dolly's children all had scarlet fever, and he happened to call. And just fancy,' she went on in a whisper, 'he felt so sorry for her that he stopped and helped her nurse them. Yes, for three weeks he stayed in the house and looked after the children like a nurse.

'I am telling Constantine Dmitrich about Turovtsyn and the scarlet fever,' she said, leaning over to her sister.

'Yes, it was wonderful! He is splendid!' said Dolly, glancing towards Turovtsyn, who had become aware they were talking of him, and giving him a gentle smile. Levin looked at Turovtsyn again, and wondered how it was he had failed to appreciate this man's goodness before.

'I'm sorry, I'm sorry, and I'll never think ill of people again!' he said gaily, giving expression to what he genuinely felt at the moment.

12

IN the conversation that had sprung up on the rights of women, certain questions were touched upon, to be discussed with reserve in the presence of ladies, concerning the inequality of the rights of women in marriage. Pestsov flew at these questions more than once during dinner, but Koznyshev and Oblonsky carefully headed him off.

However, when they rose from the table and the ladies had gone, Pestsov did not follow them, but turned to Karenin and began to expound the chief ground of inequality. In his opinion, the inequality in marriage lay in the fact that infidelity of the wife and infidelity of the husband were not punished alike, either by the law or by public opinion.

Oblonsky hurried over to Karenin and offered him a cigar.

'No, I don't smoke,' Karenin answered calmly, and, as though purposely wishing to show that he was not afraid of the subject, he turned to Pestsov with a chilly smile.

'I imagine that the root of such a view is in the very nature of things,' he said, and was about to go on to the drawing-room, but Turovtsyn suddenly and unexpectedly broke into the conversation, addressing Karenin.

'Have you heard about Pryatchnikov?' said Turovtsyn, exhilarated by the champagne he had drunk and eager to break the silence that had weighed on him. 'Vasya Pryatchnikov,' he said with a good-natured smile on his moist, red lips, addressing himself mainly to Karenin, the most important guest of the evening. 'I heard to-day that he fought a duel in Tver with Kvitsky and killed him.'

Just as one always seems to knock on a bruise, so the conversation, Oblonsky felt, was fated to touch on Karenin's sensitive spot. He made another attempt to draw his brother-in-law away, but Karenin himself inquired with curiosity:

'What did Pryatchnikov fight about?'

'His wife. Acted like a man, he did! Called him out and shot him!'

'Really!' said Karenin indifferently, and, lifting his eyebrows, he went into the drawing-room.

'I am so glad you came,' said Dolly with a scared smile, meeting him in the anteroom. 'I must have a talk with you. Let us sit here.'

Karenin, with the same look of indifference which his lifted eyebrows gave him, sat down beside Dolly and feigned a smile.

'Yes,' he said, 'especially as I was about to ask you to excuse me and let me take my leave at once. I have to start to-morrow.'

Dolly was firmly convinced of Anna's innocence, and she felt herself growing pale and her lips trembling with anger at this cold, unfeeling man, who was so calmly intending to ruin her innocent friend.

'Alexei Alexandrovich,' she began, looking into his eyes with desperate determination, 'I asked you about Anna; you did not answer me. How is she?'

'She is, I believe, quite well, Darya Alexandrovna,' replied Karenin, not looking at her.

'Alexei Alexandrovich, forgive me, I have no right ... but I love and esteem Anna like a sister. I beg, I beseech you to tell me what is wrong between you? What do you accuse her of?'

Karenin frowned, half shut his eyes, and bowed his head.

'I presume your husband has told you the grounds on which I

consider it necessary to change my attitude to Anna Arkadyevna?'
he said, avoiding her eye and casting a look of annoyance at Shcherbatsky, who was walking across the drawing-room.

'I don't believe it, I don't believe it, I can't believe it!' Dolly said, clasping her bony hands before her with an energetic movement. She rose quickly, and laid her hand on Karenin's sleeve. 'We shall be disturbed here. Come with me, please.'

Dolly's agitation had an effect on Karenin. He got up and obediently followed her to the schoolroom. They sat down to a table covered with a piece of oilcloth cut all over by pen-knives.

'I don't believe it, I don't believe it!' repeated Dolly, trying to catch his eye which avoided hers.

'One cannot deny facts, Darya Alexandrovna,' he said, emphasizing the word 'facts'.

'But what has she done?' asked Dolly. 'What exactly is it she has done?'

'She has treated her duty with contempt and betrayed her husband. That is what she has done,' he said.

'No, no, it can't be! Don't say that, for God's sake; you must be mistaken,' Dolly exclaimed, putting her hands to her temples and closing her eyes.

Karenin smiled coldly, merely with his lips, meaning to signify to her and to himself the firmness of his conviction; but this passionate defence of Anna, though it did not shake him, reopened his wound. He began to speak with greater heat.

'It is extremely difficult to be mistaken when a wife informs her husband herself – informs him that eight years of married life, and a son, have all been an error, and that she wants to begin life again,' he said angrily, with a snort.

'Anna and transgression – I cannot connect the two, I cannot believe it!'

'Darya Alexandrovna,' he said, now looking straight into Dolly's kind, troubled face, and feeling his tongue involuntarily loosened, 'I would give a great deal still to be able to have any doubts. While I was in doubt, I was miserable, but it was not so hard as it is now. When I doubted, I could hope, but now there is no hope, and still I doubt everything. I am in such doubt of everything that I cannot bear my son, and sometimes do not believe he is my son. I am very unhappy.'

He had no need to say that. Dolly had seen it as soon as he glanced into her face; and she felt sorry for him, and her faith in her friend's innocence began to totter.

'Oh, this is awful, awful! But can it be true that you are resolved on a divorce?'

'I am resolved on the final step. There is nothing else for me to do.'

'Nothing else to do, nothing else to do ...' she muttered, with tears in her eyes. 'Oh no, don't say nothing else to do!' she said.

'That is the terrible part about a trouble of this kind – one cannot just bear one's cross as one does in other troubles, like loss, or death. It becomes necessary to act,' he said, as though divining her thought. 'One must get out of the humiliating position in which one is placed: one can't live *à trois*.'

'I understand, I quite understand that,' said Dolly, and her head sank. She was silent for a little, thinking of herself and her own domestic troubles, and all at once, with an impulsive movement, she raised her head and clasped her hands beseechingly. 'But wait! You are a Christian! Think of her! What will become of her if you cast her off?'

'I have thought, Darya Alexandrovna. I have thought a great deal,' said Karenin. His face became mottled, and his dim eyes looked straight into hers. Dolly at that moment pitied him with all her heart. 'I did that very thing when she herself informed me of my humiliation; I left everything as of old. I gave her a chance to reform, I tried to save her. And with what result? She would not heed the easiest of demands – that she should observe the proprieties,' he went on, getting heated. 'You can only save a person who wants to be saved. But if the whole nature is so corrupt, so depraved, that ruin itself seems to her salvation, what can one do?'

'Anything, only not divorce!' answered Dolly.

'But what is anything?'

'No, it is awful. She will be nobody's wife; she will be lost!'

'But what can I do?' said Karenin, shrugging his shoulders and raising his eyebrows. The recollection of his wife's latest conduct had so incensed him that he became as cold as he had been at the beginning of the conversation. 'I am very grateful for your sympathy, but I must be going,' he said, getting up.

'No, wait a minute. You must take pity on her. Listen, I will tell you my own story. I was married, and my husband betrayed me. In

my anger and jealousy I wanted to throw up everything, I wanted to
... But I came to my senses; and who did it? It was Anna who saved
me. And here am I living on. The children are growing up, my husband is coming back to his family, and feels his fault, is growing
nobler, better, and I live on ... I have forgiven, and you ought to forgive!'

Karenin listened, but now her words had no effect on him. All the
bitterness of that day when he had resolved on a divorce sprang up
again in his soul. He shook himself, and began in a shrill, loud voice:

'Forgive I cannot; I do not want to, and do not think it would be
right. I have done everything for this woman, and she has trampled it
all in the mud, which is her natural element. I am not a spiteful man,
I have never hated anyone, but I hate her with all my soul, and I cannot even forgive her because I hate her too much for all the wrong she
has done me!' he said, and tears of anger trembled in his voice.

'Love them that hate you ...' whispered Dolly timidly.

Karenin smiled contemptuously. He knew that long ago, but it
could not apply to his case.

'Love them that hate you, but you can't love those you hate. Forgive me for having upset you. Sufficient unto every man is his own
grief!' And having regained his self-control, Karenin quietly bade her
good-bye and departed.

13

WHEN they rose from table, Levin would have liked to follow Kitty
into the drawing-room; but he was afraid she might not like this, as
too markedly paying her attention. He remained with the men, taking
part in the general conversation, and, without looking at Kitty, he was
aware of her movements, her looks, and where she was sitting in the
drawing-room.

He began at once, and without the smallest effort, to keep the promise he had made her – always to think well of everyone, and to love
all men. The conversation fell on the village commune, in which
Pestsov saw a sort of special principle, which he called the 'choral'
principle. Levin did not agree with Pestsov, nor with his brother, who
had a special attitude of his own, both admitting and not admitting
the significance of the Russian commune. But he talked simply with
the idea of getting them to agree and modifying their differences. He

was not in the least interested in what he said himself, still less in what they were saying: all he wanted was to see them and everybody happy and contented. He knew now what was the one important thing. And that one importance was at first there, in the drawing-room, but afterwards began moving about and came to a standstill at the door. Without looking round he felt the eyes fixed on him, and the smile, and he could not help turning round. She was standing in the doorway with Shcherbatsky, looking at him.

'I thought you were going to the piano,' he said, walking over to her. 'That's something I miss in the country – music.'

'No, we only came to fetch you and thank you,' she said, rewarding him with a smile that was like a gift, 'for coming. What do they want to argue for? No one ever convinces anyone.'

'Yes, that's true,' said Levin. 'People mostly argue warmly just because they cannot make out what their opponent wants to prove.'

Levin had often noticed in discussions between the most intelligent people that after enormous efforts, and endless logical subtleties and talk, the disputants finally became aware that what they had been at such pains to prove to one another had long ago, from the beginning of the argument, been known to both, but that they liked different things, and would not define what they liked for fear of its being attacked. He had often had the experience of suddenly in the middle of a discussion grasping what it was the other liked and at once liking it too, and immediately he found himself agreeing, and then all arguments fell away useless. Sometimes the reverse happened: he at last expressed what he liked himself, which he had been arguing to defend and, chancing to express it well and genuinely, had found the person he was disputing with suddenly agree. He tried to say this.

She wrinkled her forehead, striving to understand. But directly he began to illustrate his meaning, she understood at once.

'I see: you have to find out what your adversary is arguing for, what is precious to him, then you can ...'

She had completely caught and found the right words for his badly expressed idea. Levin gave a smile of pleasure: he was so struck by the transition from the confused, verbose discussion with his brother and Pestsov to this laconic, clear, almost wordless communication of a very complex idea.

Shcherbatsky left them, and Kitty, going up to a card-table, sat down and, taking a piece of chalk, began drawing diverging circles on the new green cloth.

They resumed the conversation started at dinner – the emancipation and occupations of women. Levin agreed with Dolly that a girl who did not marry could always find some feminine occupation in the family. He supported this view by saying that no family can get along without women to help them, that every family, poor or rich, had to have nurses, either paid or belonging to the family.

'No,' said Kitty, blushing, but looking at him all the more boldly with her truthful eyes, 'a girl may be so placed that it is humiliating for her to live in the family, while she herself ...'

He understood her allusion.

'Oh yes,' he said. 'Yes, yes, yes – you're right; you're right!'

And he saw all that Pestsov had been driving at at dinner about the freedom of women, simply because he got a glimpse of the terror in Kitty's heart of the humiliation of remaining an old maid; and, loving her, he felt that terror and humiliation, and at once gave up his contention.

A silence followed. She continued scribbling on the table with the chalk. Her eyes shone with a soft light. Surrendering to her mood he felt a continually growing tension of happiness throughout his whole being.

'Oh, I've scribbled all over the table!' she exclaimed, and, putting down the chalk, made a movement to get up.

'What! Shall I be left alone – without her?' he thought, with terror, and took the piece of chalk. 'Don't go,' he said, sitting down at the table. 'I've wanted to ask you a question for a long time.' He looked straight into her caressing, though frightened eyes.

'What is it?'

'Here,' he said, and wrote down the initial letters, *w, y, t, m, i, c, n, b – d, t, m, n, o, t*? These letters stood for, 'When you told me it could not be – did that mean never, or then?' There seemed no likelihood that she would be able to decipher this complicated sequence; but he looked at her as though his life depended on her understanding the words.

She gazed up at him seriously, then leaned her puckered forehead on her hand and began to read. Once or twice she stole a look at him, as though asking, 'Is it what I think?'

'I know what it is,' she said, flushing a little.

'What is this word?' he asked, pointing to the *n* which stood for *never*.

'That means *never*,' she said, 'but it's not true!'

He quickly rubbed out what he had written, handed her the chalk, and stood up. She wrote: *T, I, c, n, a, d.*

Dolly felt consoled for the grief caused by her conversation with Karenin when she caught sight of the two together: Kitty with the chalk in her hand, gazing up at Levin with a shy, happy smile, and his fine figure bending over the table, his radiant eyes directed now on the table, now on her. He was suddenly radiant: he had understood. The letters meant: 'Then I could not answer differently.'

He glanced at her questioningly, timidly.

'Only then?'

'Yes,' her smile answered.

'And n... – and now?' he asked.

'Well, read this. I'll tell you what I should like, what I should like so much!' She wrote the initial letters: *i, y, c, f, a, f, w, h,* meaning, 'If you could forget and forgive what happened.'

He seized the chalk, breaking it with his nervous, trembling fingers, and wrote the first letters of the following sentence: 'I have nothing to forget and forgive; I have never ceased to love you.'

She looked at him with a smile that did not waver.

'I understand,' she said in a whisper.

He sat down and wrote a long sentence. She understood it all and, without asking if she was right, took the chalk and at once wrote the answer.

For a long time he could not make out what it was, and kept looking up into her eyes. He was dazed with happiness. He could not fill in the words she meant at all; but in her lovely eyes, suffused with happiness, he saw all he needed to know. And he wrote down three letters. But before he had finished writing she read them over his arm, and herself finished and wrote the answer, 'Yes.'

'Playing secrétaire?' said the old prince, coming up to them. 'But we ought to be going if you want to be in time for the theatre.'

Levin rose and escorted Kitty to the door.

In their conversation everything had been said: it had been said that she loved him, and that she would tell her father and mother that he would come in the morning.

14

WHEN Kitty had gone and Levin was left alone, he felt so restless without her and so impatient to get quickly – as quickly as possible – through the hours till morning, when he would see her again and be plighted to her for ever, that he dreaded like death the fourteen hours he would have to spend away from her. He must have someone to be with and talk to, to avoid being alone, to kill time. Oblonsky would have been the most congenial company for him now, but he was going out, he said, to a soirée – in reality to the ballet. Levin had just time to tell him he was happy, and that he loved him and would never, never forget what he had done for him. Oblonsky's look and smile showed Levin that he comprehended that feeling rightly.

'Oh, so it's not time to die yet?' said Oblonsky, pressing Levin's hand affectionately.

'N-n-no!' said Levin.

Dolly, too, when saying good-bye to him, gave him a sort of congratulation. 'I am so glad you and Kitty have met again,' she said. 'One must treasure old friends.'

Levin did not like her remark. She could not understand how lofty and beyond her it all was, and she should not have dared to refer to it. Levin took leave of them, but, not to be left alone, he attached himself to his brother.

'Where are you going?'

'I'm going to a meeting.'

'Well, I'll come with you. May I?'

'What for? Yes, come along,' said Koznyshev, smiling. 'What has come over you to-day?'

'Me? Happiness!' said Levin, letting down the window of the carriage in which they were driving. 'You don't mind? It's stifling in here. It's happiness that's come over me! Why is it you never married?'

Koznyshev smiled.

'I am very glad, she seems a nice gi ...' he began.

'Don't say it, don't say it!' exclaimed Levin, clutching at the collar of his brother's fur coat with both hands and lapping it over his face. 'She's a nice girl,' were such simple, humble words, so out of harmony with his feeling.

Koznyshev burst into a merry laugh, which was rare with him.

'At any rate you'll let me say how glad I am?'

'That you may do to-morrow, to-morrow, and not another word now, not another word, nothing, silence! ...' said Levin, and muffling him once more in his fur coat, he added: 'I am very fond of you! Will they really let me in at the meeting?'

'Of course they will.'

'What is the discussion about to-night?' asked Levin, still smiling.

They arrived at the meeting. Levin listened to the secretary stammering through the minutes which he evidently did not understand himself; but Levin saw from this secretary's face what a nice, kind, splendid fellow he was. That was plain from the way he stumbled and hesitated in reading the minutes. Then followed the debate. They were discussing the misappropriation of certain sums of money and the laying of certain pipes, and Koznyshev attacked and stung two other members and said something at great length with an air of triumph. Another member, scribbling a few notes on a bit of paper, after a tentative start went on to answer him very venomously and neatly. And then Sviazhsky (he was there too) also made a grand, high-flown speech. Levin listened, and saw clearly that these missing sums of money and the sewer pipes and the rest had no real existence for them, and that they were not really quarrelling but were all the nicest, kindest people, enjoying themselves immensely. They were doing no one any harm, and everybody was pleased. What surprised Levin so much was that he seemed to be able to see through them all to-day, and from little signs he had never noticed before recognized the soul of each, and saw distinctly that they were all good at heart, and were all specially fond of him that day. That was obvious from the way they spoke to him and the kindness and affection with which they all, even those he did not know, looked at him.

'Well, how do you like it?' asked Koznyshev.

'Very much. I had no idea it would be so interesting! First-rate! Splendid!'

Sviazhsky came up and invited Levin to come round to tea with him. Levin was utterly at a loss to understand or remember what it was he had disliked in Sviazhsky, what he had failed to find in him. He was an intelligent and astonishingly kind-hearted fellow.

'Thank you very much,' he said, and asked after his wife and sister-in-law. And by a queer association of ideas – as Sviazhsky's sister-in-law was connected in his mind with the idea of marriage – it occurred to him that there was no one to whom he could more suitably speak of his happiness than Sviazhsky's wife and sister-in-law, and he was very glad of an opportunity to go and see them.

Sviazhsky questioned him about his agricultural ventures, as usual presupposing that there was no discovering anything that had not already been tried in Europe. But Levin did not mind this in the least now. On the contrary, he felt that Sviazhsky was right, that the whole business was of little consequence, and he noticed the extraordinary gentleness and consideration with which Sviazhsky avoided saying, I told you so. The Sviazhsky ladies were particularly charming. It seemed to Levin that they already knew everything and shared his joy but said nothing out of delicacy. He stayed with them one hour, two, three hours, talking of all sorts of subjects but thinking only of the one thing that filled his heart, and not noticing that they were dreadfully weary of him and that it was long past their time for retiring. Sviazhsky accompanied him to the hall, yawning and wondering at the strange state his friend was in. It was past one. Levin went back to his hotel, and the thought that he was all alone now with his impatience and ten hours to get through dismayed him. The servant on duty lighted his candles and was going away, but Levin stopped him. This man, Yegor, to whom Levin had not paid any attention before, turned out to be a very intelligent, good, and, above all, kind-hearted fellow.

'I say, Yegor, don't you find it hard work keeping awake?'

'We have to put up with it! It's part of our job. In private service it's easier; but we make more money here.'

It appeared that Yegor had a family, three sons and a daughter, a seamstress, whom he wanted to marry to a harness-maker's assistant.

Levin took this opportunity of informing Yegor that, in his opinion, love was the great thing in marriage, and that with love one would always be happy, because happiness lay only in yourself.

Yegor listened with attention, and obviously quite understood Levin's meaning, but by way of assent brought out the unexpected reflection that he had always been satisfied in the service of good masters, and was perfectly satisfied with his present employer, although he was a Frenchman.

'What an extraordinarily good fellow he is!' thought Levin.

'Well, and you, Yegor, when you married your wife, did you love her?'

'Ay, and why not?' replied Yegor.

And Levin saw that Yegor, too, was in an exalted state and eager to express all his most heartfelt emotions.

'My life, too, has been a remarkable one. From a child I ...' he began, with shining eyes, apparently catching Levin's excitement, just as people catch yawning.

But at that moment a bell rang. Yegor departed, and Levin was left alone. He had scarcely eaten anything at dinner, had refused tea and supper at the Sviazhskys', but he could not think of eating. He had not slept the previous night, but could not think of sleep either. It was cool in his room but he felt oppressively hot. He opened both the little panes in the window and sat down on a table in front of them. Beyond a snow-covered roof he could see a cross adorned with chains and above it the rising triangle of the Charioteer, and bright yellow Capella. He gazed at the cross, then at the stars, drank in the keen frosty air that steadily filled the room, and followed as in a dream the images and memories that rose in his imagination. Towards four o'clock he heard steps in the corridor and peeped out at the door. It was a gambler named Myaskin, whom he knew, returning from the club. He walked gloomily, frowning and coughing. 'Poor, unfortunate fellow!' thought Levin, and tears of affection and pity for the man filled his eyes. He wanted to speak to him and comfort him, but remembering that he had nothing on but his shirt, he changed his mind and sat down again in front of the open window to bathe in the cold air and gaze at the exquisite lines of the cross, silent, but full of meaning for him, and at the bright yellow mounting star. Soon after six o'clock he heard the floor-polishers begin their work, and bells ringing somewhere in the servants' quarters, and realized that he was nearly frozen. He shut the little window, washed, dressed, and went out into the street.

15

THE streets were still empty. Levin went to the house of the Shcherbatskys. The front door was locked and everything was quiet. He walked back to his room, and ordered coffee. A day-waiter, not Yegor this time, brought it up to him. Levin would have liked to start a conversation, but a bell rang and the man had to go. Levin tried to drink his coffee and put a piece of roll into his mouth, but his mouth had no idea what to do with it. Levin spat out the roll, put on his coat and went out to walk again. It was past nine when he reached the Shcherbatskys' steps for the second time. The inmates of the house were only just up, and the cook came out to go marketing. Levin had to get through at least two hours more.

All that night and morning Levin had lived quite unconsciously, quite lifted out of the conditions of material existence. He had not eaten for a whole day, he had not slept for two nights, had spent several hours half-dressed and exposed to the frosty air, and he felt not only fresher and better than ever, but completely independent of his body: he moved without any effort of his muscles, and felt capable of anything. He was sure he could fly upwards or lift the corner of a house, if need be. He spent the rest of the time walking about the streets, every other minute consulting his watch, and gazing about him.

And what he saw that morning, he never saw again. He was moved in particular by the children going to school, the silvery-grey pigeons that flew down from the roof to the pavement, and the little loaves of bread, powdered with flour, that some invisible hand had put outside a baker's shop. Those loaves, the pigeons, and the two little boys seemed not of this earth. It all happened at the same time: one of the boys ran towards a pigeon and looked smilingly up at Levin; the pigeon fluttered its wings and flew off, flashing in the sun amid the quivering snow-dust in the air, while from a little window came the smell of fresh-baked bread, and the loaves were put out. All this together was so extraordinarily nice that Levin laughed and cried with delight. After making a long round by Gazetny lane and Koslovka street, he returned to the hotel again, placed his watch before him, and sat down to wait for twelve o'clock. In the next room they were saying something about machines and fraud, and coughing as people do in the morning. They did not realize that the watch hand was nearing twelve. The hand reached twelve. Levin went out on to the steps. The cabmen evidently knew all about it. With happy faces they surrounded Levin, disputing among themselves and offering their services. He chose one, and not to offend the others promised to engage them some other time. He told the man to drive to the Shcherbatskys'. The sledge-driver looked charming with the white shirt-band sticking out over his coat and fitting tightly round his full, sturdy red neck. The sledge was high and comfortable, and never after did Levin drive in one like it, and the horse was a good one and tried its best to go fast but did not seem to move. The driver knew the Shcherbatskys' house, and rounding his elbows and calling 'Whoa!' in a manner especially indicative of respect for his fare drew up at the entrance. The Shcherbatskys' hall-porter certainly knew all about it. That was obvious from the smile in his eyes and the way he said:

'Well, it's a long time since you were here last, Constantine Dmitrich!'

Not only did he know all about it but he was unmistakably delighted, making efforts to conceal his joy. Glancing into his kindly old eyes, Levin felt something new even in his happiness.

'Are they up?'

'This way, sir! Leave it here, please,' said he, smiling, as Levin turned back for his fur cap. That meant something.

'To whom shall I announce you, sir?' a footman asked.

The footman, though a young man and one of the new school of footmen, a dandy, was very obliging and attentive, and he too understood the situation.

'The princess ... I mean, the prince ... the young princess ...' said Levin.

The first person he saw was Mademoiselle Linon. She was passing through the hall and her ringlets and her face shone. He had barely exchanged a few words with her when he heard the rustle of a skirt at the door, and Mademoiselle Linon vanished from Levin's eyes, and his heart stood still at the nearness of his happiness. Mademoiselle Linon hurriedly left him and went towards the other door. Directly she had gone out, swift, swift light little steps sounded on the parquet, and his bliss, his life, his self – the better part of himself, which he had so long been seeking and hoping for – came rapidly towards him. She did not walk but was borne along by some invisible force.

He saw only her clear, truthful eyes, timid with the same bliss of love that flooded his own heart. Those eyes were shining nearer and nearer, dazzling him with their light of love. She stopped still close to him, touching him. She raised her arms and her hands dropped on to his shoulders.

She had done everything she could – she had run up to him and yielded herself entirely, shy and happy. He put his arms round her and pressed his lips to her mouth that sought his kiss.

She, too, had passed a sleepless night, and had been waiting for him all the morning.

Her mother and father had given their consent without demur, and were happy in her happiness. She had been on the watch for him. She wanted to be the first to tell him of her happiness and his. She had got ready to see him alone, and had rejoiced at the idea, and had felt shy and confused and had not known herself what she would do. She had heard his step and his voice, and had waited at the door for Mademoiselle Linon to go. Mademoiselle Linon had gone away. Without thinking, without asking herself how and what, she had gone up to him and acted in the way she had.

'Let us find Mama!' she said, taking him by the hand.

For a long while he could not speak, not so much because he was afraid that words might desecrate the loftiness of his emotion, as because every time he tried to say something he felt that, instead of words, tears of happiness would rush out. He took her hand and kissed it.

'Is it really true?' he said at last in a husky voice. 'I cannot believe you love me, dear!'

She smiled at that 'dear', and at the timidity with which he glanced at her.

'Yes!' she said significantly and slowly. 'I am so happy!'

Not letting go his hand, she entered the drawing-room. On seeing them the princess became rather breathless and immediately began to cry and then immediately began to laugh, and, running up to them with a vigorous step Levin had not expected, she took his head in both her hands and kissed him, wetting his cheeks with her tears.

'So it is all settled! I am glad. Love her. I am glad … Kitty!'

'You didn't take long arranging matters,' said the old prince, trying to appear indifferent; but Levin noticed that his eyes were moist when he turned to him.

'I have always hoped for this,' he said, taking Levin by the arm and drawing him towards himself. 'Even when this little feather-brain thought of …'

'Papa!' cried Kitty, and shut his mouth with her hands.

'All right, I won't!' he said. 'I am very, very … plea … Oh, what a fool I am …!'

He took Kitty in his arms, kissed her face, her hand, her face again, and made the sign of the cross over her.

And Levin was seized with a new feeling of affection for this old man, who had been a stranger to him before, when he saw how fervently and tenderly Kitty kissed his strong hand.

16

THE princess was sitting in her arm-chair, silent and smiling; the prince seated himself beside her. Kitty stood by her father's chair, still holding his hand. No one spoke.

The princess was the first to put everything into words, and bring all their thoughts and feelings back to the practical side of life. And for a moment this seemed strange and even painful to them all.

'When is it to be? We must have the betrothal and announce it. And when's the wedding to be? What do you think, Alexander?'

'There's the hero,' said the old prince, pointing to Levin. 'He's the principal person concerned.'

'When?' said Levin, blushing. 'To-morrow. If you ask me, I should say, the betrothal to-day and the wedding to-morrow.'

'Come now, *mon cher*, that's nonsense!'

'Well then, next week.'

'He's quite mad.'

'Why not?'

'Upon my word!' said the mother, with a pleased smile at this haste. 'And how about the trousseau?'

'Must there really be a trousseau and all that?' Levin thought with horror. 'However ... as if a trousseau and a betrothal ceremony and the rest could spoil my happiness! Nothing can spoil it!' He glanced at Kitty, and noticed that she was not in the least, not in the very least, disturbed at the idea of a trousseau. 'Then it must be necessary,' he thought.

'Oh, I know nothing about it; I only said what I should like,' he said apologetically.

'We'll talk it over, then. We can have the betrothal now and make the announcement. That will be all right.'

The princess went up to her husband, kissed him, and was about to go away, but he stopped her, put his arm round her and tenderly, like a young lover, kissed her several times, smiling. The two old people were evidently confused for a moment, and did not quite know whether it was they who were in love again or only their daughter. When the prince and princess had gone, Levin went up to his betrothed and took her hand. He had now regained his self-possession and could speak, and there was much he had to say to her. But what he said was not at all what he had intended.

'How well I knew it would happen! I never dared hope, yet at the bottom of my heart I was always certain,' he said. 'I believe it was pre-ordained.'

'And I!' she said. 'Even when ...' She stopped and went on again, looking at him resolutely with those truthful eyes of hers, '... even when I drove my happiness from me. I never loved anyone except you, but I was carried away. I must ask you: can you forget it?'

'Perhaps it was for the best. You have much to forgive me. I ought to tell you ...'

This was one of the things he had made up his mind to speak about. He had resolved from the first to tell her two things – that he was not chaste as she was, and that he was an agnostic. It was agonizing, but he considered he ought to tell her both these facts.

'No, not now, later!' he said.

'All right, later, but you must certainly tell me. I'm not afraid of anything. I want to know everything. Now it is settled.'

He finished the sentence. 'Settled that you'll take me whatever I may be – you won't go back on your word, will you?'

'Oh no!'

They were interrupted by Mademoiselle Linon, who with an artificial but affectionate smile came to congratulate her favourite pupil. Before she had gone, the servants came in with their congratulations. Then relations arrived, and there began that blissful hubbub which went on until the day after the wedding. Levin continually felt uncomfortable and awkward but the intensity of his happiness kept increasing all the while. He felt all the time that a great deal was being expected of him – what, he did not know; and he did everything he was told, and it all gave him joy. He had thought his courtship would have nothing in common with other courtships, that the ordinary conditions of engaged couples would spoil his peculiar happiness; but it ended in his doing exactly as other people did, and his happiness was thereby only increased, becoming more and more personal and unlike anyone else's ever was.

'Now we shall have bonbons to eat,' Mademoiselle Linon happened to say, and off Levin went to buy bonbons.

'Well, I'm very glad,' said Sviazhsky. 'I advise you to go to Fomin's for the flowers.'

'Oh, are they wanted?' And he drove to Fomin's.

His brother told him he ought to borrow money, as there would be a great many expenses, presents to give ...

'Oh, are presents wanted?' And he galloped to buy jewellery at Foulde's.

And at the confectioner's, and at Fomin's, and at Foulde's he saw that he was expected, that they were pleased to see him and rejoiced in his happiness, just like everyone else with whom he had to do during those days. What was extraordinary was that everyone not only liked him but even people who had formerly been unfriendly, cold, or indifferent now delighted in him, gave way to him in everything, treated his feelings with delicate consideration, and shared his conviction that he was the happiest man on earth because his betrothed was the height of perfection. Kitty, too, felt the same thing. When the Countess Nordston ventured to hint that she had hoped for something better, Kitty got so heated and proved so conclusively that nothing in the world could be better than Levin that Countess Nordston had to admit it, and thereafter in Kitty's presence never failed to greet Levin with a smile of ecstatic admiration.

The confession he had promised was the one painful episode of this time. He consulted the old prince and with his sanction gave Kitty his diary, wherein were written the facts that tormented him. He had kept this diary purposely to show his future wife. Two things caused him anguish: his lack of purity and his lack of faith. His confession of unbelief passed unnoticed. She was religious and had never doubted the truths of religion, but his external unbelief did not affect her in the least. Through her love she knew his whole soul, and in his soul saw what she wanted; and the fact that his spiritual condition was called agnosticism troubled her not at all. The other confession, however, caused her to shed bitter tears.

Levin had not handed her his diary without an inner struggle. He knew that between him and her there could and should be no secrets, and therefore he had decided that it was his duty; but he did not realize the effect the confession might have on her: he had not put himself in her place. It was only when he called that evening before going to the theatre and on entering her room saw in her sweet, pitiful, tear-stained face the irremediable sorrow he had caused that he felt the abyss that separated his tainted past from her dove-like purity, and was appalled at what he had done.

'Take them, take these dreadful books away!' she said, pushing aside the notebooks lying before her on the table. 'Why did you give them to me? No, it is better that you did, after all,' she added, moved to pity by the despair on his face. 'But it's awful, awful!'

He hung his head and was silent. He could say nothing.

'You can't forgive me,' he whispered.

'Yes, I have forgiven you. But it's terrible!'

However, his happiness was so great that this confession did not mar it but only added another shade to it. She forgave him; but from that time he considered himself more than ever unworthy of her, morally bowed still lower before her and prized still more highly his undeserved happiness.

17

INVOLUNTARILY reviewing the impressions left on his mind by the conversations at dinner and after, Karenin returned to his lonely room. What Dolly had said about forgiveness had merely annoyed him. Whether or not the Christian precept was applicable to his own case was too difficult a question to be discussed lightly, and had long ago been answered by Karenin in the negative. Of all that had been said, the remark of the silly, good-natured Turovtsyn had sunk deepest into his memory – 'Acted like a man, he did! Called him out and shot him!' Apparently they had all agreed with that, though they had refrained from saying so out of politeness.

'Anyway, that point is settled and it's no use thinking about it,' Karenin told himself. And with nothing on his mind but his impending departure and tour of inspection, he went into his room and asked the porter, who followed him, where his valet was. The man replied that the valet had only just gone out. Karenin ordered tea, sat down at a table, took up a railway-guide, and began planning his journey.

'Two telegrams,' said his man-servant, coming into the room. 'I beg your pardon, your excellency – I'd only just that minute run out.'

Karenin took the telegrams and opened them. The first contained the news that Stremov had received the very appointment Karenin had coveted for himself. Karenin flung the telegram down and, flushing a little, rose and began to pace the room. '*Quos vult perdere demen-*

tat,' he said, by *quos* meaning those who had had a hand in the appointment. He was annoyed not so much at having missed the post himself, at having been so conspicuously passed over, as at the incomprehensible, astonishing fact that they did not see that that babbling phrase-monger Stremov was the last man fitted for it. How was it they did not understand that they were ruining themselves and their own *prestige* by this appointment?

'More news of the same kind,' he said to himself bitterly, opening the second telegram. This was from his wife. The signature, 'Anna', written in blue pencil, was the first word that caught his eye. 'I am dying. I beg, I implore you to come. I shall die easier with your forgiveness,' he read. He smiled contemptuously and threw down the telegram. That this was false, that it was a trick, at first thought he had not the remotest doubt.

'There is no deception she would stick at. It is getting near her confinement. Perhaps it is the confinement. But what can be their object? To make the child legitimate, to compromise me and prevent the divorce,' he thought. 'But it says something about dying ...' He re-read the telegram, and suddenly the plain meaning of what it said struck him. 'Supposing it's true?' he said to himself. 'If it were true – that in the moment of agony and the nearness of death she is genuinely penitent, and I, taking it for a trick, refuse to go? It would not only be cruel, and everyone would condemn me, but it would be foolish on my part.'

'Piotr, keep the carriage! I am going to Petersburg,' he told his servant.

Karenin decided that he would go to Petersburg and see his wife. If her illness were a trick, he would say nothing and go away again. If she were really ill and dying, and wanted to see him before her death, he would forgive her if he arrived in time, and perform his last duty to her if he came too late.

On the journey he gave no more thought to what he should do.

Feeling tired and dirty after a night in the train, Karenin drove through the early-morning Petersburg mist along the deserted Nev-sky, staring straight ahead, not thinking of what awaited him. He dared not think of it, because when he imagined what would happen he could not drive away the reflection that her death would at once solve the whole situation. Bakers, closed shops, night-cabmen, house-porters sweeping the pavements, flashed past his eyes, and he watched it all, trying to stifle the thought of what lay before him, and what he dared not hope for and yet was hoping for. The carriage drove up to the steps. A sledge and a carriage with a coachman asleep on the box stood at the entrance. As he entered the hall, Karenin wrested his resolve as it were from a remote corner of his brain and mastered it. Its meaning ran: 'If it's a trick, then calm contempt and departure. If true, do what is proper.'

The hall-porter opened the door before Karenin rang. The porter, Petrov, otherwise Kapitonich, presented a strange appearance in an old coat, without a tie, and wearing slippers.

'How is your mistress?'

'Safely delivered yesterday.'

Karenin halted and turned pale. He clearly realized now how intensely he had desired her death.

'And how is she?'

Korney, in his morning apron, came running downstairs.

'Very bad,' he answered. 'There was a consultation yesterday, and the doctor's here now.'

'Take my things,' said Karenin and, with a slight feeling of relief at the news that there was still some hope of her dying, he went into the hall.

A military overcoat was hanging on the hall-stand. Karenin noticed it and asked:

'Who is here?'

'The doctor, the midwife, and Count Vronsky.'

Karenin crossed into the inner apartments.

There was no one in the drawing-room; at the sound of his foot-steps the midwife came out of Anna's boudoir in a cap with lilac ribbons.

She went up to Karenin and with the familiarity that the approach of death permits took his arm and drew him towards the bedroom.

'Thank God you've come! She keeps on about you, always you,' she said.

'Make haste with the ice!' came the doctor's peremptory voice from the bedroom.

Karenin entered the boudoir. By her writing-table, sitting sideways in a low chair, was Vronsky, his face hidden in his hands, weeping. He jumped up at the doctor's voice, took his hands from his face, and saw Karenin. The sight of her husband filled him with such confusion that he sat down again, drawing his head between his shoulders, as if he wanted to disappear; but he made an effort over himself, got up and said:

'She is dying. The doctors say there is no hope. I am entirely in your hands, only let me be here … though I am in your hands, I …'

Karenin, seeing Vronsky's tears, became aware of a rush of that nervous emotion that the sight of suffering in others always aroused in him. He turned his head away and hurried towards the door without waiting to hear the end of what Vronsky was saying. From the bedroom came the sound of Anna's voice – gay, animated, with exceedingly distinct intonations. Karenin went into the bedroom and up to the bed. She was lying with her face towards him. Her cheeks were flushed, her eyes glittered, her little white hands thrust out from the cuffs of her dressing-jacket were playing with the corner of the counterpane, twisting it about. She seemed not only fresh and well but in the best of spirits. She was talking rapidly, in a ringing voice, exceptionally distinct and full of feeling.

'Because Alexei – I am speaking of Alexei Alexandrovich (how strange and terrible that they should both be Alexei, is it not?) – Alexei would not refuse me. I should forget, he would forgive … But why doesn't he come? He is good, he doesn't know himself how good he is. Oh God, what anguish! Give me some water, quick! Oh, that would be bad for her, for my little girl! Very well, then, give her to nurse. Yes, I agree, it's better in fact. He'll be coming: it will hurt him to see her. Give her to nurse.'

'Anna Arkadyevna, he has come. Here he is!' said the midwife, trying to attract her attention to Karenin.

'Oh, what nonsense!' Anna went on, not seeing her husband. 'No, give her to me; give me my little girl! He has not come yet. You say he won't forgive me, because you do not know him. No one knows him. I'm the only one, and even for me it has become hard. One must know his eyes … Seriozha's are just the same – that is why I can't bear to see them. Has Seriozha had his dinner? I know they will all forget. He would not forget. Seriozha must be moved into the corner room, and Mariette told to sleep with him.'

All of a sudden she shrank back and was silent. In terror she put her arms before her face, as though expecting and warding off a blow. She had seen her husband.

'No, no!' she began. 'I am not afraid of him. I am afraid of death.

437

Alexei, come here. I am in a hurry, because I've no time. I have not much longer to live. The fever will be on me directly, and I shall understand nothing more. Now I understand. I understand it all, I see it all!'

A look of suffering came over Karenin's drawn face. He took her hand and tried to say something but could not utter a word. His lower lip quivered but he still went on struggling with his agitation, and only now and then glanced at her. And each time he glanced at her, he saw her eyes gazing at him with such tender and ecstatic affection as he had never seen in them.

'Wait a moment, you don't know ... Stay a little, stay! ...' She stopped, as if trying to collect her thoughts. 'Yes,' she began; 'yes, yes, yes. This is what I wanted to say. Don't be surprised at me. I am still the same. But there is another woman in me, I'm afraid of her: it was she who fell in love with that man, and I tried to hate you, and I could not forget the self that had once been. I'm not that woman. Now I'm my real self, all myself. I'm dying now, I know I am; you ask him. I feel it already. My hands and feet are as heavy as lead, and my fingers – look at them: see how huge they are! But it will soon be over ... I only want one thing – for you to forgive me, forgive me completely! I am wicked, but my nurse used to tell me: the holy martyr – what was her name? – she was worse. And I'll go to Rome; there's a wilderness there, and I shan't be in anybody's way, only I'll take Seriozha and the little one ... No, you can't forgive me! I know, it can't be forgiven! No, no, go away, you're too good!' With one burning hand she held his, while with the other she tried to push him away.

Karenin grew more and more upset, until his emotion now reached such a point that he gave up struggling against it. He suddenly felt that what he had regarded as nervous agitation was on the contrary a blissful spiritual condition that gave him all at once a new happiness he had never known. He was not thinking that the Christian law which he had been trying to follow all his life enjoined on him to forgive and love his enemies; yet a glad feeling of love and forgiveness for his enemies filled his heart. He knelt down and laying his head in the curve of her arm, which burned like fire through her sleeve, he sobbed like a child. She put her arm round his head that was growing bald, moved closer towards him, and raised her eyes defiantly.

'There, I knew he would be like that! Now good-bye, everyone, good-bye! ... They've come again – why don't they go away? ... Oh, take these furs off me!'

The doctor moved her arms, carefully laying her back on the pillow, and covered her shoulders. She lay down submissively and gazed before her with radiant eyes.

'Remember one thing: that I only wanted your forgiveness, nothing more ... Why doesn't *he* come?' she cried, turning to Vronsky at the door. 'Come in, come in! Give him your hand.'

Vronsky approached the side of the bed and, seeing Anna, buried his face in his hands again.

'Uncover your face! Look at him! He is a saint,' she said. 'Yes, yes, uncover your face!' she cried angrily. 'Alexei Alexandrovich, uncover his face! I want to see him.'

Karenin took Vronsky's hands and drew them away from his face, terrible with its look of agony and shame.

'Give him your hand. Forgive him.'

Karenin held out his hand, not attempting to restrain the tears that streamed down his cheeks.

'Thank God, thank God!' she cried, 'now everything is ready. I will just stretch my legs a little. There, that's nice. How badly these flowers are drawn – not a bit like violets,' she said, pointing to the hangings. 'Oh God, oh God, when will it end? Give me some morphia! Doctor, give me morphia! Oh God, oh God!'

And she began tossing about in the bed.

The doctor and his colleagues said it was puerperal fever, which in ninety-nine cases out of a hundred was fatal. All day she was feverish, delirious, and unconscious. Towards midnight she lay insensible, and with hardly any pulse.

The end was expected every moment.

Vronsky went home, but returned in the morning to inquire how she was. Karenin met him in the hall and said: 'You had better stay: she may ask for you,' and himself led him into his wife's boudoir. Towards morning she became agitated and excited again, and her thoughts and words flowed rapidly; but she soon relapsed into unconsciousness. The following day it was the same, and the doctors said there was hope. That day Karenin went into the boudoir where Vronsky was sitting and, closing the door, sat down opposite him.

'Alexei Alexandrovich,' said Vronsky, feeling that the time for plain speaking approached. 'I can't say anything, I am unable to comprehend. Spare me! However painful it is for you, I assure you it is more terrible for me.'

He would have risen but Karenin took him by the hand and said:

'Pray hear me: it is necessary. I must explain to you my feelings, the feelings that have guided and will continue to guide me, so that you may not be in error regarding me. You know I had decided on a divorce, and had even begun to take proceedings. I won't conceal from you that when I first took action I was in a state of uncertainty. I was in misery. I confess that I was pursued by a desire to be revenged on you and on her. When I got the telegram, I came here with the same sentiments – I will say more: I hoped for her death. But ...' He paused, hesitating whether to disclose his feelings. 'But I saw her and forgave her. And the happiness of forgiving has revealed to me my duty. I forgive her completely – I would turn the other cheek, I would give my cloak if my coat be taken. I only pray God not to deprive me of the joy of forgiving!'

Tears filled his eyes, and the luminous, serene look in them impressed Vronsky.

'That is my position. You may trample me in the mire, make me the laughing-stock of the world, I will not forsake her and will never utter a word of reproach to you,' Karenin went on. 'My duty is plain to me: I ought to remain with her, and I will. Should she want to see you, I will let you know, but now I think you had better go.'

He rose, and sobs choked his voice. Vronsky rose, too, and in a stooping, not yet erect posture, looked up at him from under his brows. He could not understand Karenin, but he felt that there was something lofty and inaccessible to him in Karenin's outlook on life.

18

AFTER the conversation with Karenin, Vronsky went out on to the steps of the Karenins' house and stood still, with difficulty recalling where he was and where he had to go. He felt ashamed, humiliated, guilty, and deprived of all possibility of washing away his humiliation. He felt thrust from the ordered way he had hitherto trodden so proudly and lightly. All the seemingly solid habits and maxims of his life suddenly appeared false and inapplicable. The deceived husband – who had figured till now as a pitiful object, an incidental and somewhat ludicrous obstacle to his happiness – had suddenly been summoned by her herself, elevated to an awe-inspiring pinnacle, and on the pinnacle that husband had shown himself not vindictive, not false, not ludicrous, but kind, straightforward, and dignified. Vronsky could not help being aware of this. They had suddenly exchanged roles. Vronsky felt Karenin's elevation and his own abasement, Karenin's integrity and his own untruth. He felt that the husband was magnanimous even in his sorrow, while he had been mean and petty in his deceit. But this sense of his own humiliation before the man he had unjustly despised accounted for only a small part of his distress. He was unutterably wretched because his passion for Anna, which had seemed to him of late to be cooling, now that he knew her to be lost to him for ever, was stronger than at any time. During her illnesss he had learned to know her through and through, to see into her very soul; and it seemed to him that he had never loved her until then. And just when he had discovered her, had come to love her as she should be loved, he had been humiliated before her and had lost her for ever, leaving with her nothing of himself but a shameful memory. Most terrible of all had been the ridiculous, shameful figure he had cut when Karenin had pulled his hands away from his burning face. He stood on the steps of the Karenins' house like one distraught, and did not know what to do.

'A sledge, sir?' inquired the hall-porter.

'Yes, a sledge.'

On getting home, after three sleepless nights, Vronsky threw himself full-length on the sofa without undressing, his head on his folded arms. His head was heavy. Images, memories, and ideas of the strangest description followed one another with extraordinary rapidity and vividness: now he saw himself pouring out medicine for the patient and overflowing the spoon, now he could see the midwife's white hands, then Karenin's queer posture on the floor beside the bed.

'To sleep! To forget!' he said to himself with the calm confidence of a healthy man that if he is tired and drowsy he will fall asleep at once. And in fact at that instant his thoughts became confused and he began to sink into oblivion. The waves of the sea of unconsciousness were closing over his head, when all at once it was as if a violent electric shock shot through him. He started so fiercely that his whole body jerked the springs of the sofa and, leaning on his hands, he jumped to his knees in terror. His eyes were wide open, as though he had never been asleep. The heaviness of his head and the weariness in his limbs, of which he had been aware a moment previously, had suddenly vanished.

'You may trample me in the mire,' he heard Karenin's words, and saw him standing before him, and saw Anna's feverish face and brilliant eyes gazing with love and tenderness not at him, but at Karenin; he saw his own, as he fancied, foolish and ludicrous figure when Karenin took his hands away from his face. He stretched out his legs again and flung himself on the sofa, where he lay without moving and shut his eyes.

'To sleep, to sleep!' he repeated to himself. But with his eyes closed he could see more distinctly than ever Anna's face as it had been on that memorable evening before the races.

'All that is over now, and will never be again, and she wants to wipe it from her memory. But I cannot live without it. How can we be reconciled, then – however can we be reconciled?' he said aloud, unconsciously repeating the words again and again. This reiteration held back other images and recollections which he felt rising to throng his brain. But repeating words did not check his imagination for long. Again, following each other with extraordinary rapidity, his happiest moments rose before his mind, and with them his recent humiliation. 'Take away his hands,' Anna's voice says. He takes away his hands, and is conscious of the shamed, ridiculous expression on his face.

He still lay trying to fall asleep, though he knew there was not the slightest hope of it, and kept repeating in a whisper random words from some chain of thought, trying to keep back the influx of new images. He listened, and heard in a strange, mad whisper, 'You did not appreciate her, you did not make enough of her. You did not appreciate her, you did not make enough of her,' repeated over and over again.

'What's this? Am I going out of my mind?' he asked himself. 'Perhaps I am. What makes men lose their reason? What makes them shoot themselves?' he replied to his own thought and, opening his eyes, he saw with wonder near his head a cushion embroidered by Varya, his brother's wife. He touched the tassel of the cushion, and tried to think of Varya, of when he had seen her last. But to think of anything extraneous was painful. 'No, I must sleep!' He pulled the cushion towards him and pressed his head against it, but he had to make an effort to keep his eyes shut. He jumped up and sat down.

'That's ended for me,' he said to himself. 'I must think what to do. What is left?' His mind rapidly ran through his life apart from his love of Anna.

'Ambition? Serpuhovskoy? Society? The Court?' He could not come to a pause anywhere. They had all had meaning for him once, but they had none now. He got up from the sofa, took off his coat, loosened his belt and, baring his hairy chest in order to breathe more freely, began striding up and down the room. 'This is how people go mad,' he said again, 'and shoot themselves ... to escape humiliation,' he added slowly.

He went to the door and closed it; then with fixed gaze and clenched teeth approached the table, took up his revolver, examined it, turned it to a loaded chamber, and pondered. For a minute or two he stood motionless, head bent forward, holding the revolver in his hand and thinking, a strained expression of effort on his face. 'Of course,' he said to himself, as though a logical, clear-cut sequence of ideas had brought him to an indubitable conclusion. But in reality that convinced (as he thought) 'Of course!' was merely the outcome of the same round of memories and images that he had already gone over a dozen times during the last hour. There were the same memories of happiness lost for ever, the same sense of the meaninglessness of all that life might have in store for him, the same consciousness of humiliation. Even the sequence of these impressions and feelings was the same.

'Of course,' he repeated, when for the third time he started on the same spellbound circle of memories and ideas, and, putting the revolver to the left side of his chest, with a powerful jerk of his whole hand, as though to clench his fist, he pulled the trigger. He did not hear the report, but a violent blow on his chest sent him reeling. He tried to clutch at the edge of the table, dropped the revolver, staggered, and sat down on the floor, looking about him in astonishment. He did not recognize his room, looking up at the curved legs of the table, the waste-paper-basket, and the tiger-skin rug. The hurried, squeaking step of his servant coming through the drawing-room brought him to his senses. He made an effort to think, found that he was on the floor, and, seeing blood on the tiger-skin and on his hand, realized that he had tried to shoot himself.

'Fool! I missed!' he muttered, fumbling for the revolver. The revolver was beside him – he sought it further off. Still feeling for it, he leaned over to the other side, and unable to keep his balance fell, bathed in blood.

The elegant servant with side-whiskers, who frequently complained to his acquaintances of his weak nerves, was so terrified when he saw his master lying on the floor, that he left him bleeding to death while he ran for help. An hour later Varya, his brother's wife, had arrived, and with the assistance of three doctors, whom she had summoned from every quarter, and who all appeared at the same moment, she got the wounded man to bed, and remained to nurse him.

19

THE mistake Karenin had made when preparing for the meeting with his wife – in overlooking the possibility that her repentance might be sincere, and he might forgive her, and she might recover – this mistake faced him in all its seriousness two months after his return from Moscow. But this mistake of his had arisen not simply from his having overlooked that contingency: it was also due to the fact that it was not until he saw his dying wife that he knew his own heart. By his sick wife's bedside he had given way for the first time in his life to that feeling of sympathetic compassion which the suffering of others produced in him, and which he had hitherto been ashamed of, as of a pernicious weakness; and pity for her, and remorse at having desired her death, and, most of all, the joy of forgiving suddenly gave him not only relief from his own sufferings but inward peace such as he had never experienced before. He suddenly felt that the very thing that was the source of his sufferings had become the source of his spiritual joy; that what had appeared insoluble so long as he indulged in censure, recriminations, and hatred had become simple and clear when he forgave and loved.

He forgave his wife and pitied her for her sufferings and remorse. He forgave Vronsky and pitied him, especially after reports reached him of his desperate action. He pitied his son, too, more than before, and reproached himself for having taken too little interest in him. But for the new-born baby-girl he felt a quite peculiar sentiment, not of pity only but of tenderness. At first sheer pity had drawn his attention to the delicate little creature, who was not his child, and who had been cast on one side during her mother's illness, and would certainly have died if he had not troubled about her; and he did not realize how fond he became of her. Several times a day he would go to the nursery, and remain there for so long that the nurses, who were at first a little intimidated by his presence, grew quite used to him. Sometimes he would sit gazing for half an hour at a stretch at the downy, wrinkled, tomato-coloured little face of the sleeping baby, watching the frowning forehead and the chubby little hands with their curled-up fingers, rubbing the tiny eyes and nose with the backs of its fists. At such moments especially Karenin felt quite calm and at peace with himself, and saw nothing abnormal in his position, nothing that need be changed.

But as time went on he saw more and more clearly that, however natural his position might appear to him now, he would not be allowed to remain in it. He felt that besides the blessed spiritual force that guided his soul, there was another force, brutal and as powerful, or more powerful, which controlled his life, and that this second force would not allow him the humble peace he longed for. He felt that everyone was looking at him with curiosity, that he was not understood, and that something was expected from him. Above all, he was aware of the instability and unnaturalness of his relations with his wife.

When her softened mood caused by the near approach of death had passed off, Karenin began to notice that Anna was afraid of him, ill at ease with him, and could not look him straight in the face. She seemed to be wanting to tell him something, yet could not make up her mind to do so; as if she foresaw that their present relations could not continue and also expected something from him.

At the end of February it happened that Anna's baby daughter, also named Anna, fell ill. Karenin had been in the nursery in the morning and, after giving orders to send for the doctor, had left for the Ministry. It was towards four o'clock when he finished his business and returned home. Entering the hall he saw a handsome footman in braided livery and a bear-skin cape, holding a white fur cloak.

'Who is here?' asked Karenin.

'The Princess Elizaveta Fiodorovna Tverskoy,' the footman answered, and it seemed to Karenin that he grinned.

All through this difficult time Karenin had noticed that his worldly acquaintances, especially the women, displayed a peculiar interest in him and his wife. He noticed in all these acquaintances a kind of mirth, which they had difficulty in suppressing, like the mirth he had perceived in the lawyer's eyes, and just now in the eyes of this footman. They all seemed elated, as if they had just come from a wedding.

When they met him, with ill-disguised enjoyment they would ask after his wife's health.

The presence of the Princess Tverskoy, because of the memories associated with her, coupled with the fact that he had never liked her, was disagreeable to Karenin, and he went straight to the nursery. In the day-nursery Seriozha, lying flat on the table, his legs dangling on a chair, was drawing something and chattering away merrily. The English governess, who since Anna's illness had replaced the French one, was sitting near the boy, knitting. She got up hurriedly, curt-seyed, and gave Seriozha a tug.

Karenin stroked his son's hair, answered the governess's inquiries about his wife, and asked what the doctor had said of the baby.

'The doctor said it was nothing serious, and ordered baths, sir.'

'But she's still in pain,' said Karenin, listening to the child's scream-ing in the next room.

'I think it's the wet-nurse, sir,' the Englishwoman said firmly.

'What makes you think that?' he asked, stopping short.

'It was just the same at Countess Paul's, sir. They tried all sorts of treatment on the child, and it turned out that the baby was simply not getting enough nourishment: the nurse had no milk, sir.'

Karenin reflected for a moment and then went into the other room. The baby was lying with its head thrown back, stiffening itself in the nurse's arms, refusing either to take the plump breast offered it or to cease screaming, in spite of the hushes of the wet-nurse and the other nurse who was bending over her.

'Still no better?' said Karenin.

'She is very restless,' replied the nurse in a whisper.

'Miss Edward says that perhaps the wet-nurse has no milk,' he said.

'I think so too, Alexei Alexandrovich.'

'Then why didn't you say so?'

'Who's one to say it to? Anna Arkadyevna is still ill ...' grumbled the old nurse.

The nurse was an old servant of the family. And in those simple words of hers Karenin thought he saw an allusion to his position.

The baby screamed louder than ever, catching its breath and chok-ing. The old nurse, with a gesture of despair, came up and took it from the wet-nurse's arms, and began walking up and down, rocking it.

'The doctor must be asked to examine the wet-nurse,' said Karenin.

The trim, healthy-looking wet-nurse, frightened at the idea of losing her place, muttered something to herself and, covering her large breast, smiled scornfully at the notion of her not having sufficient milk. In that smile, too, Karenin saw a sneer at his position.

'Poor little thing!' said the nurse, hushing the baby and continuing to walk to and fro with it.

Karenin sat down, and with a look of suffering and despondency watched the nurse as she paced the room.

When the child at last grew quiet, and had been laid in a deep cot, and the nurse, after smoothing the little pillow, had left her, Karenin got up and walking awkwardly on tiptoe went over to the baby. For a moment he was still, gazing down at the child with the same despondent look; but all at once a smile spread over his face, wrinkling the skin on his forehead and moving his hair, and he went as softly out of the room.

In the dining-room he rang the bell and told the servant who answered it to send for the doctor again. He felt vexed with his wife for not paying more attention to this sweet baby, and in this vexed frame of mind he had no wish to go to her; he had no wish, either, to see the Princess Betsy. But his wife might wonder why he did not come as usual, and so, mastering his disinclination, he went towards the bedroom. As he walked over the soft carpet to the door, he could not help overhearing a conversation he did not want to hear.

'If he hadn't been going away, I could have understood your refusal and his too. But your husband ought to be above that,' Betsy was saying.

'It is not for my husband's sake, but for my own that I don't wish it. Don't say that!' replied Anna's agitated voice.

'Yes, but you can't help wanting to say good-bye to a man who has tried to shoot himself on your account ...'

'That is the very reason I don't want to.'

Karenin stopped with a dismayed and guilty expression, and would have gone back unobserved. But reflecting that this would be undignified, he turned again and, clearing his throat, went towards the bedroom door. The voices fell silent, and he went in.

Anna, in a grey dressing-gown, with her black hair cropped short and standing out like a brush round her shapely head, was sitting on a settee. As usual, at the sight of her husband all her animation instantly vanished; she bowed her head and looked round uneasily at Betsy. Betsy, dressed in the height of the latest fashion, with a hat soaring somewhere above her head like a shade over a lamp and a dove-coloured gown with very pronounced diagonal stripes slanting one way on the bodice and the other way on the skirt, was sitting beside Anna, her tall flat figure very erect. She nodded her head and greeted Karenin with an ironical smile.

'Ah!' she exclaimed, as if in surprise. 'I am so glad you are at home. You never show yourself anywhere and I haven't seen you since Anna's illness. I have heard all about it – about your devotion. You really are a wonderful husband!' she said with a significant, gracious look, as though she were conferring an order of magnanimity on him for his conduct to his wife.

Karenin bowed coldly, and, kissing his wife's hand, asked how she was.

'Better, I think,' she said, avoiding his eyes.

'But you look feverish,' he said, emphasizing the word 'feverish'.

'We've been talking too much,' said Betsy. 'I know it was selfish of me, and I am going.'

She got up, but Anna, suddenly flushing, quickly seized her hand.

'No, stay a moment, please. I have something to tell you ... you, I mean,' and she turned to Karenin, the colour spreading over her neck and forehead. 'I cannot have any secrets from you, nor do I wish to.'

Karenin cracked his fingers and bent his head.

'Betsy says that Count Vronsky wants to come and say good-bye before his departure for Tashkent.' She did not look at her husband, and spoke rapidly, evidently anxious to get out what she wanted to say at any cost. 'I told her I could not receive him.'

'You said, my dear, that it would depend on Alexei Alexandrovich,' Betsy corrected her.

'Oh no, I can't see him, and no object would be ...' She stopped suddenly, and glanced inquiringly at her husband (he did not look at her). 'In short, I don't want ...'

Karenin advanced and would have taken her hand.

Her first impulse was to jerk back her hand from the damp hand with the thick swollen veins that sought hers, but making an obvious effort to control herself she pressed his hand.

'I am very grateful to you for your confidence, but ...' he began in confusion, feeling vexed that what he could so easily and clearly decide within himself he was unable to discuss in the presence of Princess Tverskoy, who appeared to him the personification of that brute force

448

which must govern the life he led in the eyes of the world and hinder him from giving way to his feeling of love and forgiveness. He stopped, looking at the Princess Tverskoy.

'Well, good-bye, my precious!' said Betsy, getting up. She kissed Anna, and went out. Karenin followed her.

'Alexei Alexandrovich! I know you are a truly magnanimous person,' said Betsy, stopping in the little drawing-room and once again pressing his hand with peculiar warmth. 'I am only an outsider but I am so fond of her and respect you so much that I take the liberty of offering advice. Let him come. Alexei Vronsky is the soul of honour, and he is going away to Tashkent.'

'Thank you for your sympathy and advice, Princess. But the question of whether my wife can or cannot receive anyone she must decide for herself.'

He said this with a dignified raising of his brows, from habit, but immediately reflected that whatever he might say there could be no dignity in his position. And he saw this in the suppressed, malicious, mocking smile with which Betsy regarded him when he had spoken.

20

KARENIN took leave of Betsy in the drawing-room, and returned to his wife. She was lying back, but on hearing his footsteps sat up hastily in her former position, and looked at him nervously. He saw she had been crying.

'I am very grateful for your confidence in me,' he said gently, repeating in Russian the phrase he had used in Betsy's presence in French, and sat down beside her. When he spoke to her in Russian and called her 'thou', it always irritated her. 'And I am very grateful for your decision. I, too, think that since he is going away there is no necessity whatever for Count Vronsky to come here. Besides ...'

'But I've said so already, so why repeat it?' Anna suddenly interrupted him with an irritation she could not repress. 'No necessity whatever,' she thought, 'for a man to come and take leave of the woman he loves, for whose sake he tried to kill himself, and who was ready to ruin himself – to say farewell to the woman who cannot live without him. No necessity whatever!' She pressed her lips together and dropped her burning eyes to his hands with their swollen veins, which he was slowly rubbing together.

'Let us never speak of it,' she added more calmly.

'I have left this question to you to decide, and I am very glad to see ...' began Karenin.

'That my wish coincides with yours,' she finished quickly, exasperated to hear him talking so slowly when she knew in advance all he was going to say.

'Yes,' he affirmed, 'and Princess Tverskoy's intrusion in the most difficult private affairs is entirely uncalled for. She of all people ...'

'I don't believe anything they say about her,' Anna put in quickly. 'I know she is genuinely fond of me.'

Karenin sighed and was silent. She played nervously with the tassels of her dressing-gown, glancing at him with that torturing sense of physical repulsion that she reproached herself for but could not control. Her one desire now was to be rid of his loathsome presence.

'Oh, I have just sent for the doctor,' said Karenin.

'I am quite well – what do I want the doctor for?'

'No, it's the baby. She keeps on crying, and they say the nurse hasn't enough milk.'

'Why didn't you let me nurse her, when I begged to? Anyway,' (Karenin knew what was meant by that 'anyway') 'she's a baby and they will be the death of her.' She rang the bell and asked for the baby to be brought to her. 'I begged to nurse her, I wasn't allowed to, and now I'm blamed for it.'

'I am not blaming you ...'

'Oh yes, you are! Oh God, why didn't I die?' And she broke into sobs. 'Forgive me, I am upset, I am not fair,' she said, controlling herself. 'But leave me ...'

'No, things can't continue like this,' Karenin said to himself decidedly as he left his wife's room.

Never had the impossibility of his position in the world's eyes, and his wife's hatred of him, and altogether the might of that mysterious brutal force that guided his life against his spiritual inclinations, exacting fulfilment of its decrees and a change in his relation to his wife, asserted itself so distinctly to him as now. He saw clearly that the world at large and his wife demanded of him something, but what precisely, he could not make out. But it roused a feeling of rancour in his soul, spoiling his peace of mind and destroying all the good of his achievement. He believed that for Anna herself it would be better to break off all relations with Vronsky, but if they thought this impossible he was even prepared to allow those relations to be resumed, provided the children were not disgraced, that he was not deprived of them or forced to change his attitude. Bad as this would be, it was preferable to a complete rupture, which would place her in a hopeless and shameful position and take from him everything he cared for. But he felt helpless; he knew in advance that everybody was against him and that he would not be allowed to do what seemed to him now so natural and right, but would be compelled to do what was wrong, but seemed the proper thing to them.

21

BEFORE Betsy had time to walk out of the drawing-room, she was met in the doorway by Oblonsky, who had just come from Yeliseyev's, where a consignment of fresh oysters had arrived.

'Ah, Princess, what a delightful meeting!' he began. 'I have just been to your house.'

'We meet only for a moment, as I am on my way out,' said Betsy, smiling and putting on her glove.

'Wait a second, Princess, before putting on your glove; let me kiss your little hand. Hand-kissing is the one thing I am most grateful for in the revival of old customs.' He kissed Betsy's hand. 'When shall we see each other now?'

'You don't deserve it,' replied Betsy, smiling.

'Oh yes, I do! I've become a most serious person. I not only settle my own domestic affairs, but other people's as well,' he said, with a significant expression.

'Oh, I am so glad!' answered Betsy, at once understanding that he was referring to Anna. She went back to the drawing-room with him, and they stood in a corner. 'He will kill her,' said Betsy in a whisper full of meaning. 'It's impossible, impossible ...'

'I am very glad you think so,' said Oblonsky, shaking his head with a solemn expression of woe-begone commiseration on his face. 'That is why I have come to Petersburg.'

'The whole town's talking of it,' she said. 'It is an impossible situation. She is pining away, pining away. He doesn't understand that she is one of those women who can't trifle with their feelings. One of two things must happen: either he must take her away, act with energy, or give her a divorce. But this is suffocating her.'

'Yes, yes ... exactly,' sighed Oblonsky. 'That is why I have come. At least, not solely for that. ... They have made me a chamberlain; of course, one has to come and say thank you. But the main thing is to get this affair settled.'

'Well, God help you!' said Betsy.

Having seen Betsy down to the hall and once more kissed her wrist above her glove, where the pulse beats, and having whispered such unseemly nonsense that she did not know whether to be angry or laugh, Oblonsky went to his sister. He found her in tears.

Though he happened to be bubbling over with good spirits, Oblonsky immediately fell naturally into a sympathetic and romantic mood which harmonized with hers. He asked her how she was and how she had spent the morning.

'Very, very miserably. To-day and this morning and all other days, past and future,' she said.

'I think you give way to melancholy. You must rouse yourself, you must look life in the face. I know it's hard, but ...'

'I have heard it said that women love men even for their vices,' Anna began suddenly, 'but I hate him for his virtues. I can't live with him. Do you understand – the sight of him has a physical effect on me? It puts me beside myself. I can't, I can't live with him. What am I to do? I was unhappy before, and used to think one couldn't be more unhappy, but the awful state of things I am going through now, I could never have conceived. Would you believe it – knowing he is a good, excellent man, that I am not worth his little finger, still I hate him! I hate him for his generosity. And there is nothing left for me but ...'

She was going to say 'death', but Oblonsky would not let her finish.

'You are ill and overwrought,' he said. 'Believe me, you are exaggerating dreadfully. Nothing is so very terrible.'

And Oblonsky smiled. No one else in Oblonsky's place, having to do with such despair, would have ventured to smile (the smile would have seemed callous); but in his smile there was so much kindness and almost feminine tenderness that it did not wound but soothed and calmed her. His gentle, comforting words and smiles were as soothing and softening as almond oil. And Anna soon felt this.

'No, Stiva,' she said, 'I'm lost, lost! Worse than lost! I'm not lost yet – I can't say that all is over: on the contrary, I feel that it's not ended. I'm like an over-strained violin string that must snap. But it's not ended yet ... and the end will be terrible.'

'Oh no, the string can be loosened by degrees. There is no situation from which there is no way out.'

'I have thought and thought. There is only one ...'

Again he knew from her terror-stricken face that this one way of escape in her mind was death, and he would not let her say it.

'Not at all,' he said. 'Listen to me. You can't see your own position as I can. Let me give you my candid opinion.' Again he cautiously smiled his almond-oil smile. 'I'll begin from the beginning. You married a man twenty years older than yourself. You married him without love, or without knowing what love was. That was a mistake, let's admit it.'

'A fearful mistake!' said Anna.

'But I repeat – it's an accomplished fact. Then you had, let us say, the misfortune to fall in love with a man not your husband. That was a misfortune, but that, too, is an accomplished fact. And your husband accepted it and forgave it.' He stopped after each sentence, waiting for her to object, but she said nothing. 'That is how matters stand. Now the question is – can you go on living with your husband? Do you wish it? Does he wish it?'

'I don't know, I don't know at all.'

'But you said yourself that you can't endure him.'

'No, I didn't say so. I take it back. I don't know anything, I can't tell.'

'Yes, but let ...'

'You can't understand. I feel I'm flying headlong over some precipice, but ought not to save myself. And I can't.'

'Never mind, we'll hold something out and catch you. I understand you, understand that you can't take it on yourself to express your wishes, your feelings.'

'There's nothing, nothing I wish ... except for it to be all over.'

'But he sees that and knows it. Do you really suppose it weighs on him any less than on you? You're wretched, he's wretched, and what good can come of it? While a divorce would solve everything,' Oblonsky got out at last, not without difficulty expressing his central idea, and looked at her significantly.

She made no reply, and shook her cropped head in dissent. But from the look on her face, suddenly illuminated with its old beauty, he saw that if she did not desire this it was because it seemed to her unattainable happiness.

'I am dreadfully sorry for you both! And how happy I should be if I could arrange things!' said Oblonsky, now smiling more boldly. 'Don't speak, don't say a word! If only God will help me to speak as I feel. I'm going to him.'

Anna looked at him with dreamy, shining eyes, and said nothing.

22

OBLONSKY walked into Karenin's study with the same somewhat solemn expression with which he was wont to take the chair at council meetings. Karenin, with his arms crossed behind his back, was pacing up and down, meditating on the very subject that his wife and Oblonsky had been discussing.

'I'm not disturbing you?' said Oblonsky, at the sight of his brother-in-law suddenly experiencing a feeling of embarrassment unusual with him. To conceal his embarrassment he drew out a cigarette-case with a new kind of clasp which he had just bought and, sniffing the leather, took out a cigarette.

'No. Do you want anything?' Karenin replied reluctantly.

'Yes, I would like ... I must ... yes, I wanted to talk to you,' said Oblonsky, surprised at his own unaccustomed timidity.

The feeling was so unexpected and strange that Oblonsky did not believe it was the voice of conscience telling him that what he was about to do was wrong. He made an effort and conquered the timidity that had come over him.

'I hope you believe in my love for my sister and my sincere affection and respect for yourself,' he said, flushing.

Karenin stood still and said nothing, but Oblonsky was struck by the expression of resigned self-sacrifice on his face.

'I intended ... I wanted to have a little talk with you about my sister and the position in which you both are,' said Oblonsky, still struggling with his unaccustomed bashfulness.

Karenin smiled sadly, looked at his brother-in-law and, without answering, went over to the table, took up a letter he had begun and handed it to his brother-in-law.

'I think of nothing else. And here is what I had begun to write,

454

thinking I could say it better in a letter, and that my presence irritates her,' he said, holding out the letter.

Oblonsky took the letter, looked with perplexed astonishment at the dull eyes fixed on him, and began to read:

'I can see that my presence is disagreeable to you. Painful as it is for me to recognize this, I see that it is so and cannot be otherwise. I do not reproach you, and God is my witness that when I saw you at the time of your illness I resolved with my whole heart to forget all that had come between us and begin life anew. I do not regret, and shall never regret, what I did; my only desire was for your welfare, the welfare of your soul, and now I see I have not attained that. Tell me yourself what would give you true happiness and peace of mind. I put myself entirely in your hands, and trust to your feeling of what is right.'

Oblonsky handed back the letter and continued looking at his brother-in-law with the same wonder, not knowing what to say. The silence was so oppressive to them both that Oblonsky's lips twitched nervously as he stood speechlessly gazing at Karenin's face.

'That is what I wanted to say to her,' said Karenin, turning away.

'Yes, yes ...' said Oblonsky, tears choking his throat and preventing his utterance. 'Yes, yes, I understand you,' he got out at last.

'I must know what she wants,' said Karenin.

'I am afraid she does not understand her own position. She is no judge,' replied Oblonsky, recovering himself. 'She is crushed – literally crushed by your generosity. If she were to read this letter she would be incapable of saying anything – she would only hang her head lower than ever.'

'Yes, but what is to be done in that case? How explain, how find out her wishes?'

'If you will permit me to give an opinion, I think it is for you to point out plainly the steps you consider should be taken to put an end to the situation.'

'Then you think an end must be put to it?' Karenin interrupted him. 'But how?' he added, moving his hands before his eyes, a gesture not usual with him. 'I see no possible way out.'

'There is a way out of every situation,' said Oblonsky, standing up and becoming more cheerful. 'There was a time when you wanted to break off. ... If you are convinced that you cannot make each other happy ...'

'There are so many conceptions of happiness! But let us suppose I agree to everything, I want nothing. What way out is there, in our situation?'

'If you care to know my opinion,' began Oblonsky with the same soothing smile of almond-oil tenderness with which he had addressed Anna. His kindly smile was so persuasive that Karenin, conscious of his own weakness and yielding to it, was involuntarily prepared to accept what Oblonsky should say. 'She would never say so, but there is one way out, one thing she might desire,' Oblonsky went on, 'and that is to terminate your relations and everything that reminds her of them. To my way of thinking, what's essential in your case is to get on a new basis with each other. And that can only be done by both sides having their freedom.'

'Divorce,' Karenin interrupted with aversion.

'Yes, I imagine that divorce – yes, divorce,' repeated Oblonsky, reddening. 'From every point of view that is the most sensible solution for a couple who find themselves in the position you are in. What else can they do if they find life impossible together? It is a thing that may always happen.'

Karenin sighed heavily and closed his eyes.

'There is only one point to be considered: does either party wish to marry again? If not, it is very simple,' said Oblonsky, by degrees losing his embarrassment.

Karenin, his face drawn with emotion, muttered something to himself and made no reply. What appeared so simple to Oblonsky, he had thought over thousands of times, and, far from being simple, it all seemed to him utterly impossible. An action for divorce, with the details of which he was now acquainted, appeared to him out of the question, because his feelings of self-respect and his regard for religion forbade his pleading guilty to a fictitious act of adultery, and still less could he allow his wife, forgiven and beloved by him, to be exposed and put to shame. Divorce seemed to him impossible also on other still more weighty grounds.

In the event of a divorce, what would become of his son? To leave him with his mother was out of the question. The divorced mother would have her own illegitimate family, in which the position and upbringing of a stepson would in all probability be wretched. Should he keep the child himself? He knew that would be an act of vengeance on his part, and he did not want that. But apart from this, what ruled out divorce more than anything in his eyes was that by consenting to a divorce he would be handing Anna over to destruction. What Dolly had said in Moscow, to the effect that in deciding on a divorce he was thinking of himself and not considering that by this he would be ruining her irrevocably, had made a deep impression on him. And since he had forgiven her and become attached to the children, these words of Dolly's had come to have a special meaning for him. To consent to a divorce, to give her her freedom, would mean, as he saw it, to deprive himself of the last tie that bound him to life – the children he loved; and to take from her the last prop that supported her on the path of virtue, to thrust her to perdition. Once divorced, she would, he knew, join her life with Vronsky's, and their union would be both illegal and sinful because a wife, according to ecclesiastical law, may not marry again so long as her husband is living. 'She will join him and in a year or two he will throw her over, or she will enter into a new liaison,' thought Karenin. 'And I, by consenting to an unlawful divorce, shall be the cause of her ruin.' He had thought it all over hundreds of times, and was convinced that a divorce was not at all simple, as his brother-in-law supposed, but quite impossible. He did not believe a word of what Oblonsky was saying, and had a thousand objections ready, but he listened, feeling that his words were the expression of that mighty brutal force which controlled his life and to which he would have to surrender in the end.

'The only question is how – on what conditions you are prepared to consent to a divorce. She does not want anything, would not dare ask you for anything – she leaves it all to your generosity.'

'Oh God, oh God! How have I deserved this?' thought Karenin, remembering the details of a divorce-suit in which the husband had taken the blame on himself, and with the same gesture with which Vronsky had covered his face in shame he hid his face in his hands.

'You are upset – I can quite understand. But if you think it over ...'

'Whosoever shall smite thee on thy right cheek, turn to him the other also, and if any man will take away thy coat, let him have thy cloak also,' thought Karenin.

'Yes, yes!' he cried in a shrill voice. 'I will take the disgrace on myself, I will even give up my son, but ... but wouldn't it be better to let it alone? However, you may do as you like ...'

And, turning away so that his brother-in-law should not see his face, he sat down on a chair by the window. It was very bitter, there was shame in his heart, but with this bitterness and shame he experienced a sense of joy and emotion at the depth of his own humility.

Oblonsky was touched. For a space he was silent.

'Alexei Alexandrovich, believe me, she will appreciate your generosity,' he said. 'But evidently it was God's will,' he added, and having said it felt that it was a foolish remark and could hardly repress a smile at his own foolishness.

Karenin would have made some reply, but tears prevented him.

'This misfortune is an act of fate and must be accepted as such. I accept the calamity as an accomplished fact, and am doing my best to help both her and you,' Oblonsky went on.

When he left his brother-in-law's study he was genuinely affected, but this did not spoil his contentment at having successfully arranged the matter, for he felt certain that Karenin would not go back on his word. To this contentment was added the thought that when the whole thing was over he would be able to put the following conundrum to his wife and intimate friends: 'What is the difference between me and a chemist? A chemist makes solutions and no one is any the better – but I arranged a solution which made three people happier. … Or, why am I like a chemist?… Where … however, I can improve on it later,' he said to himself with a smile.

23

VRONSKY's wound was a dangerous one, even though it had missed the heart, and for several days he lay between life and death. The first time he was able to speak, Varya, his brother's wife, was alone in the room with him.

'Varya!' he said, looking at her sternly. 'It was an accident. And please never speak of it, and tell everybody else so. Otherwise it would seem too ridiculous!'

Without replying, Varya bent over him and looked into his face with a glad smile. His eyes were bright, not feverish, but their expression was severe.

'Well, thank God!' she said. 'You are not in pain?'

'A little here.' He pointed to his chest.

'Then let me change the dressing.'

His broad jaws set, he watched her silently as she bandaged him. When she had finished he said:

'I am not delirious; do please manage so that people don't say I shot myself on purpose.'

'No one does say so. Only I hope that after this you will give up shooting yourself by accident,' she said, with a questioning smile.

'Yes; but it would have been better ...'

And he smiled gloomily.

In spite of these words and that smile, which greatly perturbed Varya, as soon as the inflammation passed and he began to mend, he felt that he was completely free of one part of his misery. By his action he seemed to have wiped away the shame and humiliation he had previously felt. He could now think with equanimity of Karenin, recognizing his magnanimity without being humiliated by it. Besides that, he got back into the beaten track of his life again. He found he could look people in the face once more and resume his former habits. The one thing he could not tear out of his heart, though he never ceased to struggle against it, was a regret, bordering on despair, at having lost her for ever. That now, having expiated the wrong he had done her husband, he must give her up and never come between the repentant wife and her husband, was firmly resolved in his heart; but he could not tear out of his heart sorrow at the loss of her love, could not erase from his memory the moments of happiness he had known with her, moments he had prized so little at the time and which haunted him now with all their charm.

Serpuhovskoy devised a post for him in Tashkent, and Vronsky accepted the proposition without the slightest hesitation. But the nearer the time approached for his departure, the more cruel seemed to him the sacrifice he was making to what he considered his duty.

His wound had healed, and he was able to drive about making preparations for his journey to Tashkent.

'To see her once more and then to bury myself, to die,' he thought, as he was making a round of farewell visits, and uttered this thought to Betsy. With this mission, Betsy went to Anna and brought back a reply in the negative.

'So much the better,' thought Vronsky, when he heard it. 'It was a weakness which would have shattered what strength I have left.'

The next day Betsy herself came to see him in the morning, and announced that she had heard through Oblonsky the news that Karenin positively consented to a divorce, and that therefore he could see Anna.

Without even troubling to escort Betsy to the door, without asking when he could see her, where her husband was, forgetting all his resolutions, Vronsky drove straight to the Karenins'. He flew up the stairs seeing nothing and no one, and with hurried steps, almost at a run, entered her room. And without thinking or looking round to find out whether they were alone or not, he took her in his arms and began showering kisses on her face, her hands, her neck.

Anna had been preparing herself for this meeting, had thought what she would say to him, but she did not succeed in saying any of it, overwhelmed by his passion. She tried to calm him, to calm herself, but it was too late. His emotion communicated itself to her. Her lips trembled so that for a long time she could not speak.

'Yes, you have taken possession of me, and I am yours,' she got out at last, pressing his hands to her breast.

'So it had to be,' he said. 'As long as we live, so it must be. I know it now.'

'That is true,' she said, growing paler and paler and clasping his head. 'Yet there is something terrible in this after all that has happened.'

'It will pass, it will all pass; we shall be so happy! Our love, if it could grow stronger, would do so because of there being something terrible in it,' he said, raising his head with a smile that showed his fine teeth.

She could not help responding with a smile – not to his words, but to the love in his eyes. She took his hand and stroked her cold cheeks and cropped hair with it.

'I hardly know you with this short hair. You have grown so pretty. A little boy! But how pale you are!'

'Yes, I am still very weak,' she said, smiling. And her lips began trembling again.

'We'll go to Italy; you will soon get well,' he said.

'Is it really possible that we could be like husband and wife, alone together, with our own family?' she said, looking close into his eyes.

'It only seems strange to me that it can ever have been otherwise.'

'Stiva says *he* has agreed to everything, but I can't accept *his* generosity,' she said, pensively gazing past Vronsky's face. 'I don't want a divorce. It's all the same to me now. Only I don't know what he will decide about Seriozha.'

He could not conceive how she could, at this moment of their reunion, remember and think of her son, of divorce. What did it all matter?

'Don't talk about that, don't think of it,' he said, turning her hand over in his and trying to draw her attention to himself; but still she kept her eyes averted from him.

'Oh, why did I not die? It would have been better!' she said, and the tears streamed silently down her cheeks; but she tried to smile, so as not to grieve him.

Once Vronsky would have thought it disgraceful and impossible to decline the flattering offer of a post at Tashkent, which was a dangerous one, but now, without an instant's hesitation, he refused it and, observing disapproval in high quarters at this step, at once resigned his commission.

A month later Karenin was left alone in the house with his son, and Anna went abroad with Vronsky, not having obtained a divorce and having resolutely refused one.

PART FIVE

I

PRINCESS SHCHERBATSKY considered it out of the question for the wedding to take place before Lent, to which only five weeks remained, since half of the trousseau could not be ready by that time; but she could not help agreeing with Levin that to put it off until after Easter might mean waiting too long, as Prince Shcherbatsky's old aunt was very ill and likely to die soon, and then mourning would delay the wedding still further. Therefore, having decided to divide the trousseau into two parts – a larger and a smaller trousseau – the princess consented to have the wedding before Lent. She decided to put the smaller part of the trousseau in hand at once and have the rest sent on later, and was most indignant with Levin because he could not give her a serious answer as to whether he approved of this arrangement or not. The plan was the more suitable as immediately after the wedding the young couple were to go to the country, where the main part of the trousseau would not be wanted.

Levin still continued in the same state of delirium in which it seemed to him that he and his happiness constituted the sole aim of all creation, and that he need not now think or bother about anything, as other people were doing and would do everything for him. He had not even any plans or aims for the future, leaving those also to his friends to decide, sure that everything would be delightful. His brother, Koznyshev, Oblonsky and the princess told him what to do. He agreed absolutely to everything that was proposed. His brother raised money for him, the princess advised him to leave Moscow for the country after the wedding. Oblonsky suggested going abroad. He agreed to everything. 'Do what you like, if it amuses you. I am happy, and my happiness can be no greater and no less for anything you do,' he thought. When he told Kitty of Oblonsky's advice that they should go abroad, he was much surprised that she did not agree and had definite ideas of her own in regard to their future. She knew Levin had work he loved in the country. She did not, as he saw, understand this work, she did not even care to understand it. But that did not prevent her from considering it very important. Besides, she knew their home would be in the country, and she wanted to go – not abroad, where they were not going to live, but to the place where their home would be. This decided expression of purpose astonished Levin. But since it was quite immaterial to him where they went, he at once asked Oblonsky to go down to the country, as though it were Oblonsky's duty to do so, and arrange everything there to his own good taste, of which he had so much.

'By the way,' Oblonsky said to Levin one day after his return from the country, where he had made all the preparations for the young couple's arrival, 'have you got your certificate to show you've been to confession?'

'No. Why?'

'They won't marry you without it.'

'What!' exclaimed Levin. 'It must be about nine years since I went to communion! I never even thought of it.'

'You're a fine one!' said Oblonsky, laughing. 'And you call *me* a Nihilist! But it won't do, you know. You must confess and take the sacrament.'

'But when? There are only four days left.'

Oblonsky arranged this too. And Levin began to prepare himself. To Levin, as to any unbeliever who respects the beliefs of others, it was very irksome to attend and take part in all the church services. At this moment, in his present softened frame of mind, sensitive to everything, this inevitable act of hypocrisy not only oppressed Levin but seemed to him utterly impossible. To be obliged to lie or commit sacrilege – at the very height of his glory, just when his life was bursting into flower! He felt incapable of doing either the one or the other. But no matter how often he interrogated Oblonsky as to the possibility of obtaining a certificate without actually going to communion, Oblonsky maintained that it was out of the question.

'Besides, what does it amount to – a couple of days! And the priest's such a nice, sensible old man. He'll pull the tooth out for you before you know where you are.'

Standing in church at the first service, Levin tried to revive his youthful recollections of the intense religious emotion he had experienced between the ages of sixteen and seventeen. But he was immediately convinced that it was out of his power to do so. He attempted to look on it all as a meaningless, empty custom, like the custom of paying calls, but he felt he could not do that either. Like the majority of his contemporaries, Levin found himself in the vaguest position in regard to religion. Believe he could not, and at the same time he had no firm conviction that it was all untrue. And so, unable either to believe in the significance of what he was doing or to regard it with indifference as an empty formality, all the time he was preparing for the sacrament he was conscious of a feeling of discomfort and shame at taking part in something he did not understand, which was therefore, an inner voice told him, deceitful and wrong of him.

During the service he would sometimes listen to the prayers, trying to invest them with a meaning that would not run counter to his own views, or, finding that he could not understand and must condemn them, he would try not to listen but to occupy his mind with the thoughts, observations and memories which floated with extraordinary vividness through his brain as he stood vacantly in the church.

He stood through the mass, vespers, and compline, and the next morning at eight o'clock, having risen earlier than usual, he went fasting to church for morning prayers and confession.

There was no one in the church except a beggar soldier, two old women and the clergy and sacristan.

A young deacon, his long backbone clearly discernible through his thin under-cassock, met him, and going at once to a small lectern by the wall began reading prayers. As the reading proceeded, especially at the frequent and rapid repetitions of the same words, 'Lord, have mercy upon us!' which sounded like 'Lordavmercpons!', Levin felt that his mind was closed and sealed, and that to open and stir it now would only result in confusion; and so as he stood behind the deacon he continued his own train of thought, without listening or trying to fathom what was being read. 'How wonderfully expressive her hand is,' he thought, remembering how he and Kitty had sat at a corner table the day before. They had nothing to talk about, as was nearly always the case just then, and she had laid her hand on the table and kept opening and shutting it, until she herself began to laugh at its movements. He remembered how he had kissed the hand and afterwards examined the converging lines on the rosy palm. Again 'Lordavmercpons!' thought Levin, crossing himself, bowing and watching the deacon's supple back as he, too, bowed. 'Then she took my hand

and examined the lines – "You've a nice hand," she said.' And he glanced at his own hand and at the deacon's stumpy hand. 'Well, it will soon be over now,' he thought. 'No, I believe he's going back to the beginning again,' he thought, listening to the prayers. 'Yes, it *is* just ending. There he is, bowing to the ground. That's always at the end.'

The deacon discreetly accepted the three-rouble note slipped into his hand under its cuff of plush, promised to put Levin's name down for confession, and went into the chancel, his new boots clattering briskly over the flagstones of the empty church. A moment later he put his head out and beckoned to Levin. Thought, till then sealed up in Levin's brain, began to stir, but he made haste to drive it away. 'It will be all right somehow,' he decided, and walked towards the desk by the altar-screen. He went up the steps and, turning to the right, saw the priest. The priest, a little old man with a scanty, grizzled beard and kind, weary eyes, was standing beside the lectern, turning over the leaves of a missal. With a slight bow to Levin he immediately began chanting the prayers in the usual way. At the end he bowed down to the ground and turned, facing Levin.

'Christ stands invisible before you to receive your confession,' he said, pointing to the crucifix. 'Do you believe in the doctrines of the Holy Apostolic Church?' the priest went on, turning his eyes away from Levin's face and folding his hands under his stole.

'I have doubted, I doubt everything,' replied Levin in a voice that jarred on his own ears, and stopped.

The priest waited a few seconds to see if he would add anything further, and then, closing his eyes, said quickly with a strong provincial accent:

'To doubt is a natural human weakness, but we must pray to our merciful Lord to strengthen us. What are your special sins?' he added without the slightest pause, as though anxious not to waste time.

'My chief sin is doubt. I doubt everything: most of the while I am in doubt.'

'To doubt is a natural human weakness,' repeated the priest. 'What do you doubt in particular?'

'Everything. I sometimes even have doubts of the existence of God,' replied Levin in spite of himself, and was horrified at the unseemliness of what he was saying. But the words appeared to have no effect on the priest.

'What doubt can there be of the existence of God?' he asked hurriedly, with a faint smile.

Levin was silent.

'What doubt can you have of the Creator when you contemplate His works?' continued the priest in the rapid customary jargon. 'Who adorned the celestial vault with stars? Who decked the earth with her beauty? How could these things be without a Creator?' he said, with an inquiring glance at Levin.

Levin felt it would be out of place to enter upon a metaphysical discussion, so he merely replied directly to the question.

'I don't know,' he said.

'You don't know? Then how can you doubt that God created all?' asked the priest with puzzled good humour.

'I don't understand it at all,' said Levin, blushing and feeling the absurdity of his words, which could not be anything but absurd in the circumstances.

'Pray to God and beseech Him. Even the holy fathers had doubts and prayed to God to strengthen their faith. The devil is very powerful, and we must resist him. Pray to God, beseech Him. Pray to God,' he repeated hurriedly.

The priest paused for some time, as though meditating.

'I hear you are about to enter into holy matrimony with the daughter of my parishioner and spiritual son, Prince Shcherbatsky?' he resumed with a smile. 'A fine girl!'

'Yes,' responded Levin, blushing for the priest. 'Why need he ask about that at confession?' he thought.

And, as though in answer to his thought, the priest said to him:

'You are about to enter into holy matrimony, and God may bless you with offspring, is that not so? Well, what sort of upbringing can you give your little ones if you do not conquer in yourself the temptation of the devil enticing you to unbelief?' he said in gentle reproach. 'If you love your child, as a good father you will desire not only wealth, luxury, honour for your infant: you will be anxious for his salvation, his spiritual advancement in the light of truth. Is that not so? What will you say to your innocent babe when he asks, "Papa, who made all the lovely things in the world – the earth, the water, the sun, the flowers, the grass?" Will you really reply, "I don't know"? You cannot help knowing, since the Lord in his infinite mercy has revealed it to you. Or supposing your child asks, "What awaits me in the life beyond the tomb?" What will you tell him if you yourself know nothing? How will you answer him? Will you abandon him to the allurements of the world and the devil? That would be wrong!' said he, stopping and with his head on one side regarding Levin with kindly, gentle eyes.

Levin was silent but this time not because he wanted to avoid a discussion with the priest, but because no one had ever yet asked him such questions, and it would be time enough to consider the answers when his children started asking the questions.

'You are entering upon a time of life,' pursued the priest, 'when a man must choose his path and stick to it. Pray that God in His goodness may help you and have mercy upon you!' he concluded. 'May our Lord God, Jesus Christ, in the grace and bounty of His loving-kindness toward all mankind, pardon this His child ...' and, having pronounced the absolution, the priest blessed him and let him go.

Back home that day, Levin had a delightful feeling of relief at the uncomfortable situation being over and that he had come through it without the necessity of telling a lie. Besides, there remained a vague impression that what the dear, kind old man had said was not at all so stupid as he had fancied at first, and that there was something in it that must be looked into.

'Of course, not immediately,' thought Levin, 'but some day later on.' Levin felt more than ever now that there was something dark and uncertain in his soul, and that his attitude towards religion was exactly the same as the attitude he saw so distinctly and disliked in others, and which he condemned in his friend Sviazhsky.

He spent the evening with his betrothed at Dolly's, and was in particularly gay spirits. To explain to Oblonsky his state of elation, he said he felt as pleased as a dog that was being taught to jump through a hoop and which, having at last caught the idea and done what was required of it, barks and wags its tail, jumping on to the table and window-sills in its delight.

2

ON the day of the wedding, according to custom – the princess and Dolly insisted on all the conventions being strictly observed – Levin did not see his betrothed, and dined at his hotel with three bachelor friends, who happened to drop in. They were his brother, Koznyshev,

Katavasov, an old fellow-student at the university and now professor of natural science, whom Levin had met in the street and insisted on bringing home with him, and Tchirikov, his best man, a Moscow magistrate and a bear-hunting comrade of Levin's. The dinner was a very merry one. Koznyshev was in the best of spirits, and enjoyed Katavasov's originality. Katavasov, feeling that his personality was appreciated and understood, paraded it. Tchirikov always gave a lively and good-humoured support to conversation of any sort.

'There now,' said Katavasov, drawling his words, a habit acquired in the lecture-room, 'what a talented fellow our friend Constantine Dmitrich used to be! I am speaking of one who is not with us, for he is no more. He was fond of science in those days, when he left the university, and took an interest in humanity; but now he employs one half of his talents in deceiving himself and the other in justifying the deceit.'

'A more determined enemy of matrimony than yourself I have never come across,' remarked Koznyshev.

'Oh no, I'm no enemy of matrimony. I'm in favour of division of labour. People who can do nothing else ought to propagate the race, while the rest work for its enlightenment and happiness. That's how I look at it. There are hosts of aspirants ready to mix the two occupations, but I'm not one of them!'

'How delighted I shall be when I hear that you're in love!' said Levin. 'Do invite me to the wedding.'

'I'm in love now.'

'Yes, with a cuttle-fish! You know,' Levin turned to his brother, 'Katavasov is writing a work on the digestive organs of the ...'

'Go on, get it all wrong! It makes no difference what it's about. The point is, I certainly do love my cuttle-fish.'

'But that need not interfere with your loving a wife!'

'The cuttle-fish would not interfere with my wife, but my wife would interfere with the cuttle-fish.'

'Why?'

'Oh, you'll soon find out! Now you like farming, hunting, and shooting – well, you wait and see!'

'Arhip was here to-day. He says there are quantities of elks at Prudno, and two bears,' said Tchirikov.

'Well, you must go and get them without me.'

'There you are!' said Koznyshev. 'It's good-bye to bear-hunting in future – your wife won't allow it.'

Levin smiled. The idea of his wife not letting him go hunting was so delightful that he was ready to forgo the pleasure of ever setting eyes on a bear again.

'All the same, it's a pity to get those two bears without you. Do you remember last time in Hapilovo? What fine sport we had!' said Tchirikov.

Levin had not the heart to disillusion him of the notion that there could be anything anywhere of interest to him without Kitty, so he said nothing.

'The custom of saying good-bye to one's bachelor life is not without sense,' said Koznyshev. 'However happy you may be, you can't help but regret your freedom.'

'Confess now you feel like jumping out of the window, like the bridegroom in Gogol's play?'

'Of course he does, only he won't own up!' said Katavasov, and he broke into loud laughter.

'Well, the window's open. ... Let's start off this instant for Tver. One of them is a she-bear: you can go right up to her lair. Seriously, let's catch the five o'clock train! And here let them do what they like,' said Tchirikov, smiling.

'I am ready to swear,' said Levin with a smile, 'I can't find a trace of regret in my heart for my lost freedom.'

'Ah, but your heart is in such chaos just now that you can't find anything there,' said Katavasov. 'Wait till you've settled down a bit, then you'll find it!'

'No; else I should have had a little feeling of regret, in spite of my ...' (he could not use the word *love* before Katavasov) 'happiness. On the contrary, I rejoice at the very loss of my freedom.'

'Bad! A hopeless case!' said Katavasov. 'Well, let us drink to his recovery, or wish that a hundredth part even of his dreams comes true – and that would be happiness such as never was on this earth!'

Soon after dinner the guests departed to change for the wedding.

Left alone, Levin began thinking over the remarks of his bachelor friends and once more asked himself whether there was in his heart any of that regret for his freedom they had been talking about. 'Freedom?' The question made him smile. 'What is the good of freedom? Happiness consists only in loving and wishing her wishes, thinking her thoughts, which means having no freedom whatever – that is happiness!'

'But do I know her thoughts, her wishes, her feelings?' a voice suddenly whispered. The smile faded from his face, and he grew thoughtful. And all at once a strange sensation came over him. Fear and doubt possessed him, doubt of everything.

'Supposing she does not love me? Supposing she is only marrying me for the sake of getting married? Supposing she does not see herself what she's doing?' he asked himself. 'Supposing she should come to her senses and only when we are being married realize that she does not and never could love me.' And strange, most evil thoughts of her began to come into his mind. He felt as jealous of Vronsky as he had been a year ago, as if that evening that he had seen her with Vronsky had been but yesterday. He suspected she had not told him everything.

He sprang up. 'No, this won't do!' he said to himself in despair. 'I'll go to her; I'll ask her. I will say for the last time: we are free, and wouldn't it be better to stay so? Anything would be better than life-long misery, disgrace, infidelity!' With despair in his heart and hatred for himself, for her, for the whole world, he left the hotel and drove round to her.

He found her in one of the back rooms. She was sitting on a trunk, busy with her maid, sorting piles of dresses of different colours hung on the backs of chairs and lying on the floor.

'Oh!' she cried when she saw him, and her face lit up with joy. 'How are you? How ... Well, this is a surprise! And I am just sorting out my old dresses to give away ...'

'Ah, that is very nice,' he said with a gloomy look towards the maid. 'Run away, Dunyasha. I will call you presently,' said Kitty. 'What is the matter?' she asked as soon as the maid had gone. She noticed his strange, agitated, sombre expression, and was seized with panic.

'Kitty, I am in torment! I can't bear it alone,' he cried with despair in his voice, standing before her and looking beseechingly into her eyes. Already he saw by her loving, truthful face that nothing could come of what he had meant to say, yet he felt an urgent need to hear her reassure him. 'I came to say that there is still time. We can still put a stop to it all – put it right.'

'What? I don't understand. What is the matter?'

'What I have said a thousand times and cannot help thinking ... that I am not worthy of you. You couldn't really consent to marry me. Think it over. You have made a mistake. Think it well over. You can't love me ... If ... better say so,' he said, not looking at her. 'I shall be wretched. Let people say what they like: anything's better than the misery .... Better now, while there's still time ...'

'I don't understand,' she replied, frightened. 'You mean you want to withdraw ... don't want ...'

'Yes, if you don't love me.'

'You're out of your mind!' she cried, flushing with chagrin. But his face was so piteous that she restrained her chagrin and flinging some clothes from an arm-chair sat down closer to him. 'What are you thinking? Tell me everything.'

'I am thinking you can't love me. Why should you love me?'

'Oh God, what can I do?' she cried, and burst into tears.

'Oh, what have I done?' he exclaimed, and kneeling before her began kissing her hands.

When the princess came into the room five minutes later, she found them quite reconciled. Kitty had not only assured him that she loved him but had gone so far, in answer to his question, as to explain why. She told him that she loved him because she understood him perfectly, because she knew what he would like, and everything he liked was good. And this seemed absolutely clear to him. When the princess entered, they were sitting side by side on the trunk, sorting the dresses and disputing because Kitty wanted to give Dunyasha the cinnamon-coloured dress she had been wearing the day Levin proposed to her, while he insisted on her keeping it and giving Dunyasha a blue one instead.

'How is it you don't see? She is dark and it won't suit her ... I've thought it all out.'

Upon hearing what had brought him there, the princess upbraided him half humorously, half in earnest, and sent him home to dress and not delay Kitty, as Charles the hairdresser was expected at any moment to do her hair.

'As it is, she has eaten nothing for days and is losing her looks, and here you come and upset her more still with your nonsense,' she said to him. 'Be off, be off, my dear!'

Guilty and shamefaced, but comforted, Levin went back to his hotel. His brother, Dolly, and Oblonsky, all in evening dress, were waiting to bless him with the icon. There was no time to lose. Dolly had to return home again to fetch her son, who, his hair curled and pomaded, was to drive in the bride's carriage with the icon. Then a carriage had to be sent for the best man, and another was to take Koznyshev back and return again. ... Altogether there were all sorts of complicated arrangements to consider. One thing was certain: there was no time to dawdle, for it was already half-past six.

The blessing with the icon was not particularly solemn. Oblonsky stood in a comically serious pose beside his wife, took the icon, and ordered Levin to bow down to the ground. Then he blessed him, smiling a kindly amused smile, and kissed him three times. Dolly did the same and immediately made haste to be off, and again got into a muddle about the arrangements for the carriages.

'Come, I'll tell you how we'll manage: you go and fetch him in our carriage, and Koznyshev, if he will be so good, can go and then send his carriage back again.'

'Of course; with pleasure.'

'Then I'll come on directly with him. Have your things been sent off?' asked Oblonsky.

'Yes, they've gone,' replied Levin, and he told Kuzma to put out his clothes for him to dress.

3

A CROWD of people, mostly women, stood outside the church lighted up for the wedding. Those who had arrived too late to get into the middle of the crowd pressed round the windows, pushing, wrangling, and peeping through the gratings.

More than twenty carriages had already been ranged along the street by the police. A police officer, regardless of the frost, stood at the entrance, looking gorgeous in his uniform. More carriages kept driving up, and ladies with flowers in their hair got out, holding up their trains; or men, who doffed their helmets or black hats as they entered the church. Inside, the candles in both lustres were already lit, as well as all the candles before the icons. The golden glitter on the crimson background of the iconostasis, the wrought gold of the icons, the silver of the lustres and candlesticks, the flagstones, the mats, the banners above in the choir, the steps up to the chancel, the ancient books black with time, the cassocks and surplices – all were flooded with light. On the right-hand side of the well-heated church a discreet but lively conversation was going on among the swallow-tail coats and white ties, the uniforms, brocades, velvets and satins, the hair, flowers, bare shoulders and arms in long gloves – the sound of which re-echoed strangely in the high cupola above. Every time the door creaked there was a hush and everyone turned round, expecting to see the bride and bridegroom come in. But the door had opened at least ten times to admit some late-comer who joined the circle of invited guests on the right, or a spectator who had managed to elude or get round the police officer, and who joined the crowd on the left. And both relatives and the outside public had by now passed through every phase of anticipation.

At first it was supposed that the bride and bridegroom would arrive at any moment, and no importance was attached to the delay. Then people began looking more and more often towards the door, wondering whether anything could have happened. At length the delay became positively awkward, and relations and friends tried to look as if they were not thinking of the bridegroom and were absorbed in their own conversation.

The head deacon, as if to draw attention to the value of his time, coughed impatiently, making the windows rattle. In the choir the bored choristers could be heard trying their voices and blowing their noses. The priest kept sending first the beadle then a deacon to see if the bridegroom had arrived, and he himself, in his purple vestment and embroidered sash, went with increasing frequency to the side door, in expectation of the bridegroom. At last one of the ladies looked at her watch and said, 'This is really strange, though!' and all the guests became uneasy and began loudly expressing their surprise and displeasure. One of the groomsmen went to find out what had happened.

All this time Kitty, ready and waiting in her white dress, long veil, and wreath of orange blossom, stood in the drawing-room of the Shcherbatskys' house with her nuptial godmother and sister, Princess Lvov. For the last half-hour or so she had been vainly looking out of the window for her best man to come and announce that the bridegroom had reached the church.

Levin meanwhile, in his trousers but without coat or waistcoat, was pacing up and down his room at the hotel, perpetually thrusting his head out at the door and looking along the corridor. But there was no sign in the corridor of the person he was waiting for, and with a gesture of despair he turned to Oblonsky, who was quietly smoking.

'Was ever a man in such a fearfully idiotic position?' he exclaimed.

'Yes, it is silly,' agreed Oblonsky with a soothing smile. 'But don't worry, it will be here in a minute.'

'But how can I help it?' said Levin, with smothered fury. 'And these idiotic open waistcoats! Impossible!' he said, looking at the crumpled front of his shirt. 'And suppose the things have already gone to the station!' he cried in despair.

'Then you'll have to wear mine.'

'I ought to have done that long ago if I was going to.'

'You mustn't look ridiculous ... Wait a bit! It will turn out all right.'

The fact of the matter was that when Levin had told his old servant to get his things ready, Kuzma had brought his dress coat, waistcoat, and what else he considered necessary.

'And the shirt?' Levin cried.

'You've got a shirt on,' Kuzma replied with a placid smile.

It had not occurred to Kuzma to leave out a clean shirt, and having been told to pack and send all the luggage round to the Shcherbatskys' house, whence the young couple were to set out that evening, he had done so, putting everything in but the dress suit. The shirt Levin had worn all day was crumpled and quite unfit to wear with the fashionable low waistcoat. It was a long way to send to the Shcherbatskys'. A servant was despatched to buy a shirt. He returned: the shops were shut – it was Sunday. Someone was sent to Oblonsky's but came back with a shirt that was much too wide and too short. Finally Levin was obliged to send to the Shcherbatskys' to have his things unpacked. So while everyone in the church waited for the bridegroom, here he was pacing up and down like a wild beast in a cage, looking out along the corridor, and with horror and despair recalling what absurd things he had said to Kitty and wondering what she must be thinking now.

At last Kuzma, whose fault it all was, panting and out of breath, rushed in with the shirt.

'Only just in time. They were hoisting the luggage into the cart.'

Three minutes later, not daring to look at the time for fear of aggravating his agony of mind, Levin tore down the corridor.

'You won't help matters like that,' said Oblonsky smiling and following without haste. 'It will turn out all right, it will turn out all right ... I assure you.'

4

'THEY'VE come!' 'Here he is!' 'Which one?' 'Is it the younger one?' 'And look at her, poor little dear – more dead than alive!' people murmured in the crowd as Levin met his bride at the door and entered the church with her.

Oblonsky told his wife why they were late, and the guests smiled and whispered it about themselves. Levin saw nothing and no one: he did not take his eyes off his bride.

Everyone said she had lost her looks the last few days, and on her wedding-day was nothing like so pretty as usual; but Levin did not find it so. He looked at her hair dressed high beneath the long veil and white flowers, at the high, stand-up, scalloped collar that in such a maidenly fashion hid her long neck at the sides and just showed it a little in front, and at her strikingly slender waist, and it seemed to him she was more beautiful than ever – not because those flowers, the veil, or the gown from Paris added anything to her beauty, but because, in spite of the elaborate sumptuousness of her attire, the expression on her sweet face and lips was still that same look of hers of innocent truthfulness.

'I was beginning to think you had made up your mind to run away,' she said, smiling at him.

'It was so silly, what happened to me – I'm ashamed to speak of it!' he said with a blush, and was obliged to turn round to Koznyshev, who came up to him.

'A fine story that, about your shirt!' said Koznyshev, shaking his head and smiling.

'Yes, yes,' Levin replied, with no idea of what they were talking about.

'Now, Kostya,' said Oblonsky with an air of mock dismay, 'you have to settle an important point. You are just in the right state to appreciate all its gravity. I have been asked if they are to light new candles or will you have candles that have been used before? It's a matter of ten roubles,' he added, relaxing his lips into a smile. 'I have decided, but I am afraid you might not agree.'

Levin saw it was a joke, but he could not smile.

'Well, then, what's it to be – fresh candles or old ones? That is the question.'

'Yes, yes, fresh ones.'

'Oh, I'm very glad. The question's settled!' said Oblonsky, smiling. 'How foolish people become in these circumstances!' he remarked to Tchirikov, when Levin, after a bewildered glance at him, moved back to his bride.

'Kitty, mind you're the first to step on the carpet,' said Countess Nordston, coming up. 'You're a nice person!' she added, addressing Levin.

'What, don't you feel frightened?' asked Kitty's old aunt, Marya Dmitrievna.

'You aren't cold, are you? You look pale. Stop a moment, bend your head down,' said Kitty's sister, Princess Lvov, raising her plump, beautiful arms to adjust the flowers on Kitty's head.

Dolly came up, tried to say something, but could not speak and began crying and laughing nervously.

Kitty looked at them all as absent-mindedly as did Levin. To everything that was said she could only reply with the smile of happiness that was now so natural to her.

Meanwhile the clergy had got into their vestments, and the priest and deacon came forward to the lectern that stood near the entrance of the church. The priest turned to Levin and said something. Levin did not hear what the priest said.

'Take the bride's hand and lead her up,' said the best man to Levin.

It was a long while before Levin could make out what was wanted of him. They were a long time trying to set him right. Just as they were about to give it up, because he would either use the wrong arm himself or take her by the wrong one, he at last understood that he must take her right hand in his right hand, without changing his position. When at last he had taken the bride's hand properly, the priest went a few steps ahead of them and stopped at the lectern. The crowd of friends and relations, amid a buzz of talk and a rustle of skirts, moved after them. Someone stooped down to arrange the bride's train. The church became so quiet that the drops of wax could be heard falling from the candles.

The little old priest in his sacerdotal headgear, with his locks of grey hair, glistening like silver, drawn behind his ears, put forth his small old hands from under the heavy silver vestment with the gold cross on the back, and began fumbling with something at the lectern.

Oblonsky approached him cautiously, whispered something and, making a sign to Levin, walked back again.

The priest lit two wax candles wreathed with flowers and, holding them askew in his left hand so that the wax kept slowly dripping, turned, facing the bridal pair. It was the same priest who had heard Levin's confession. He looked with sad, weary eyes at the bride and bridegroom, sighed and, disengaging his right hand from his vestment, held it up in blessing over the bridegroom and afterwards, but with a shade of solicitous tenderness, laid his fingers on Kitty's bowed head. Then he gave them the candles and, taking the censer, moved slowly away from them.

'Can it really be true?' thought Levin, and he glanced round at his bride. He could just get a glimpse of her profile from above, and by the scarcely perceptible quiver of her lips and eyelashes he knew she was aware of his eyes upon her. She did not look round, but the high scalloped collar that reached to her little pink ear moved slightly. He saw that a sigh was suppressed in her breast, and the little hand in the long glove shook as it held the candle.

All the fuss about the shirt, about being late, his conversation with friends and relatives, their displeasure, his ludicrous position – all suddenly vanished, and he was filled with joy and terror.

The tall, handsome head-deacon, wearing an alb of silver cloth, his curly locks sticking out on either side of his head, advanced briskly and, lifting his stole with a practised movement of two fingers, stood opposite the priest.

'Bless us, O Lord!' One after the other the solemn tones slowly vibrated through the air.

'Blessed be our God, now and hereafter, for ever and ever!' meekly chanted the old priest in response, still fingering something at the lectern. And then, filling the whole church from windows to vaulted roof, a full chord sung by the invisible choir rose melodiously, swelled, hung for a moment, and softly died away.

The usual prayers were offered up for peace from on high and for salvation, for the Holy Synod and the Emperor; and then they prayed for the servants of God, Constantine and Ekaterina, now plighting their troth.

'Vouchsafe to them love made perfect, peace and help, O Lord, we beseech thee,' the whole church seemed to breathe with the voice of the head-deacon.

Levin heard the words and was struck by them. 'How did they guess that it is help – that help is exactly what is needed?' he wondered, recalling his recent fears and doubts. 'What do I know? What can I do in this tremendous matter without help?' he thought. 'Yes, it is help I want now.'

When the deacon had finished the litany, the priest turned to the bridal pair with a book in his hand.

'Eternal God, who unitest them that were separated,' he read in his gentle, sing-song voice, 'and hast ordained for them an indissoluble bond of love; thou who didst bless Isaac and Rebecca and show thy mercy to their descendants, according to thy holy Covenant, bless now thy servants Constantine and Ekaterina, and incline their hearts to good. For thou God art merciful and lovingkind. Glory be to the Father, and to the Son, and to the Holy Ghost, now and for ever.'

'Amen!' floated through the air from the invisible choir.

' "Unitest them that were separate" – how profound those words are, and how they correspond with what one feels at this moment,' thought Levin. 'Does she feel the same as I do?'

He looked round, and their eyes met. And by the expression in hers he concluded that she understood the words just as he did. But this was not so. She had scarcely understood a single word of the service and was not even listening to the words of the ceremony. She could not listen to them and take them in, so strong was the one feeling that filled her soul, growing stronger and stronger. It was a feeling of joy at the completion of all that had been going on in her soul for the last month and a half, and had during those six weeks gladdened and tortured her. On the day on which, wearing her cinnamon-coloured dress, she had gone up to him in the drawing-room of the house in Arbat Street and silently plighted herself to him – on that day, at that hour, there took place in her heart a complete severance from her old life, and a quite different, new, utterly strange existence had begun for her, while outwardly in fact she continued to live the old one. Those six weeks had been a time of the utmost bliss and the utmost misery. All her life, all her desires and hopes were centred on this one man, still uncomprehended by her, to whom she was bound by a feeling of alternate attraction and repulsion even less comprehensible than the man himself, and all the while she went on living her former life. Living the old life, she was horrified at herself, at her utter and unconquerable indifference to her past, to the things, the habits, the people she had loved, who loved her – to her mother, who was grieved by her indifference; to her dear, affectionate father, whom she had loved more than anyone else in the world. At one moment she was appalled by this indifference, and at the next she rejoiced at what had brought it about. She could not think of or desire anything apart from life with this man; but this new life was not yet, and she could not even picture it clearly. There was only anticipation – the dread and joy of the new and unknown. And now behold, anticipation and uncertainty, and remorse at repudiating her old life – were all at an end and the new was beginning. This new life could not but hold terrors in its obscurity; but terrible or not, the present moment was only the consummation of what had taken place in her soul six weeks ago.

Turning again to the lectern, the priest with some difficulty picked up Kitty's little ring and, asking Levin for his hand, put the ring on the tip of his finger. 'The servant of God, Constantine, plights his troth to the servant of God, Ekaterina.' And putting the big ring on Kitty's slender, rosy finger, pathetic in its softness, the priest repeated the same words.

Several times the bridal pair tried to guess what they had to do, and blundered each time, the priest correcting them in a whisper. At last, having duly performed the rite, having made the sign of the cross over them with the rings, the priest handed the large one to Kitty and the little one to Levin. Again they were perplexed and twice passed the rings backwards and forwards, still without doing what was required.

Dolly, Tchirikov, and Oblonsky stepped forward to help them. The result was some confusion, whispering and smiles, but the expression of solemn emotion on the faces of the betrothed pair did not change: on the contrary, while they got mixed up over their hands they looked more solemn and serious than before, and the smile with which Oblonsky whispered to put on their rings involuntarily died on his lips. He instinctively felt that any smile would jar on them.

'From the beginning Thou hast created them male and female,' read the priest after they had exchanged rings, 'and hast joined the wife to her husband to be a helpmeet to him and for the procreation of the human race. Do thou, O Lord our God, who hast poured down Thy truth on Thine inheritance and gavest Thy promise to our fathers from generation to generation of Thy chosen people, look down upon

Thy servant Constantine and Thy servant Ekaterina and confirm their union in faith and concord, in truth and love ...'

Levin felt more and more that all his ideas about marriage, all his dreams of how he would order his life, had been mere childishness, and that this was something he had never understood hitherto, and was now still farther from understanding, although it was happening to him. There was a quiver in his breast, a lump rose to his throat and the unruly tears came to his eyes.

5

ALL Moscow was in the church – relatives, friends, and acquaintances. During the ceremony of plighting troth, in the brilliantly lit church, among the throng of elegantly clad women and girls, and men in white ties, frock-coats, or uniforms, conversation in decorously low tones never flagged. It was mostly kept up by the men, for the women were absorbed in watching every detail of the service, which is so close to their hearts.

In the little circle nearest to the bride were her two sisters, Dolly and the eldest one, Princess Lvov, a placid beauty who had arrived from abroad.

'Why is Marie in lilac? It's almost as unsuitable at a wedding as black,' remarked Madame Korsunsky.

'With her complexion it's her only salvation,' replied Princess Drubetskoy. 'I wonder why they are having the wedding in the evening, like shop-people ...'

'It's prettier. I was married in the evening too,' sighed Madame Korsunsky, remembering how sweet she had looked that day, how absurdly in love her husband had been, and how different it all was now.

'They say if you are best man more than ten times you'll never be married yourself. I wanted to be best man for the tenth time, to make myself safe, but I was too late,' Count Sinyavin was saying to the pretty young Princess Tcharsky, who had designs on him.

Princess Tcharsky only answered with a smile. She was looking at Kitty and thinking of the time when she would be standing there beside Count Sinyavin, in the place where Kitty now stood, and of how she would remind him of his present joke.

Young Shcherbatsky was telling the old maid of honour, Madame

Nikolayev, that he intended putting the crown on Kitty's chignon for luck.

'She ought not to have worn a chignon,' replied Madame Nikolayev, having long ago made up her mind that, if the elderly widower at whom she was setting her cap married her, she would have a very simple wedding. 'I don't like all this show.'

Koznyshev was talking to Dolly, jestingly assuring her that the custom of going away after the wedding was becoming common because newly-married couples always felt slightly shamefaced.

'Your brother may well be proud of himself. She is wonderfully sweet. I am sure you envy him, don't you?'

'Oh, I am past all that, Darya Alexandrovna,' he replied, and his face unexpectedly became sad and serious.

Oblonsky was telling his sister-in-law his pun about dissolving marriages.

'Her wreath wants putting straight,' she answered, not hearing him.

'What a pity she has lost her looks so,' remarked Countess Nordston to Princess Lvov. 'Still, he's not worth her little finger. Don't you agree?'

'No, I like him immensely – not just because he's my future brother-in-law,' answered the princess. 'And how well he carries himself! So few men know how to behave on these occasions and not appear ridiculous. And he's not ridiculous, or stiff, and it is obvious that he's moved.'

'You expected it, I suppose?'

'In a way. She always liked him.'

'Well, let us see which of them is the first to step on the mat. I told Kitty to remember.'

'It won't make any difference,' replied Kitty's sister. 'We all make obedient wives – it runs in the family.'

'Well, I stepped on the mat before Vassily on purpose. What about you, Dolly?'

Dolly was standing near them, and she heard but made no reply. She was too much affected. Her eyes were wet and she could not have spoken without bursting into tears. She rejoiced for Kitty and Levin, and her thoughts went back to her own wedding. Her glance kept straying to the beaming Oblonsky and, forgetting the present, she remembered only her young and innocent love. She recalled not herself only, but all her women-friends and acquaintances; thought of them on the one day of their triumph when, like Kitty, they had stood beneath the nuptial crown, with love, hope, and dread in their hearts, renouncing the past and stepping forward into the mysterious future. Among those brides she recalled also her dear Anna, of whose possible divorce she had just been hearing. She, too, had once stood there just as innocent in her veil and orange blossom. And now? 'How strange and dreadful!' she murmured.

The two sisters, the women-friends and relatives were not the only ones to follow every detail of the ceremony: the women spectators, who were quite strangers, looked on breathless with excitement, afraid of missing a single movement or expression of the bride or bridegroom. Annoyed with the men for their indifference, they did not answer and often did not hear their joking or irrelevant observations.

'Why is her face so tear-stained? Is she being married against her will?'

'Against her will to a fine fellow like that? A prince, isn't he?'

'Is that her sister in the white satin? Now hear how the deacon will roar: "Wife, obey thy husband!"'

'Is it the Tchudovsky choir?'

'No, from the Synod.'

'I asked the footman. It seems he's taking her straight to his home in the country. They say he's awfully rich. That's why she's being married to him.'

'Oh no, they make a very well-matched pair.'

'There now, Marya Vassilievna, you would insist those fly-away crinolines were not being worn. Look at that one in puce – an ambassador's wife, they say. See how hers swings ... first one side and then the other!'

'What a dear little creature the bride is – like a lamb decked for the slaughter. Say what you like, one does feel sorry for the girl.'

So chattered the crowd of women who had succeeded in slipping in at the church doors.

6

WHEN the first part of the ceremony was over, the beadle spread a piece of rose-coloured silk in front of the lectern in the centre of the church, while the choir began singing a psalm to some elaborate and complicated setting in which bass and tenor sang responses to each other, and the priest, turning round, motioned the bridal pair to the rose-silk carpet. Often as they had both heard the saying that the one who steps first on the carpet will be the head of the house, neither Levin nor Kitty could think of that as they took those few steps towards it. They did not even hear the loud remarks and disputes that followed, some maintaining that Levin was first and the others insisting that they had both stepped on together.

After the customary questions whether they desired to enter into matrimony and were not pledged to anyone else, and their answers, that sounded strange in their own ears, the second part of the service began. Kitty listened to the words of the prayer, trying to grasp their meaning but unable to do so. Her heart overflowed more and more with triumph and radiant joy as the ceremony proceeded, making it impossible for her to fix her attention.

There were prayers 'that they may be endowed with the gift of continence for the sake of the fruit of the womb, and find joy in their sons and daughters'. They were reminded that God created woman from Adam's rib, and 'for this cause shall a man leave his father and mother, and cleave unto his wife, and they twain shall be one flesh', and that 'this is a great mystery'; they prayed that God would make them fruitful and bless them as he blessed Isaac and Rebecca, Joseph, Moses, and Zipporah, and that they might look upon their children's children. 'It is all very beautiful,' thought Kitty, hearing the words, 'and just as it should be.' And a smile of happiness, which involuntarily infected everyone looking at her, shone on her enchanted face.

'Put it right on!' was the advice heard from all sides when the priest brought forward the crowns and Shcherbatsky, his hand shaking in its three-button glove, held the crown high above Kitty's head.

'Put it on!' she whispered, smiling.

Levin looked round at her and was struck by her beatific expression. He could not help being infected by her feeling and becoming as glad and happy as she was.

With light hearts they listened to the reading of the Epistle and heard the head-deacon thunder out the last verse, awaited with such impatience by the outside public. With light hearts they drank the warm red wine and water from the shallow cup, and their spirits rose still higher when the priest, flinging back his stole and taking their hands in his, led them round the lectern while a bass voice rang out,

'*Rejoice, O Isaiah!*' Shcherbatsky and Tchirikov, who were supporting the crowns and getting entangled in the bride's train, smiled, too, and were inexplicably happy. They either lagged behind or stumbled on the bride and bridegroom every time the priest came to a halt. The spark of joy glowing in Kitty's heart seemed to have spread to everyone in the church. Levin fancied that the priest and deacon wanted to smile as much as he did.

Lifting the crowns from their heads, the priest read the last prayer and congratulated the young couple. Levin glanced at Kitty and thought he had never seen her look like that before, so lovely with the new light of happiness shining in her face. Levin longed to say something to her but did not know whether the ceremony was over yet. The priest came to his aid, saying softly, a smile on his kindly mouth, 'Kiss your wife, and you, kiss your husband,' and took the candles from their hands.

Levin carefully kissed her smiling lips, offered her his arm, and with a strange new sense of closeness led her out of the church. He did not believe, he could not believe that it was all true. Only when their bewildered, timid glances met did he believe in it, because he felt that they were one already.

After supper, the same night, the young people left for the country.

7

VRONSKY and Anna had already been travelling together in Europe for three months. They had visited Venice, Rome, Naples, and had just arrived in a small Italian town where they intended to stay for some time.

A handsome head waiter, his thick, greased hair parted from the nape of his neck upwards, wearing a tail-coat and a broad white cambric shirt-front, a bunch of charms dangling on his round stomach, stood with his hands in his pockets and his eyes contemptuously screwed up curtly answering a gentleman standing by him. Catching the sound of footsteps coming from the other side of the entrance towards the staircase, the waiter turned and recognized the Russian count, who occupied the best rooms in the hotel. He respectfully withdrew his hands from his pockets, bowed, and announced that a courier had been, to say that the business about the palazzo had been arranged. The agent was prepared to sign the agreement.

'Ah! I'm glad to hear it,' said Vronsky. 'And is Madame in or not?'

'Madame went out for a walk but has returned now,' replied the waiter.

Vronsky took off his soft, broad-brimmed hat and passed his hand-kerchief over his perspiring brow and hair, which he allowed to grow half-way down his ears and wore brushed back to hide a bald patch. And, after a casual glance at the gentleman who still stood there earn-estly looking at him, he would have gone on.

'This Russian gentleman has been inquiring after you,' said the head waiter.

With mixed feelings of annoyance at being unable to get away from acquaintances anywhere, and longing to find some sort of diversion from the monotony of his life, Vronsky looked round once more at the gentleman, who had moved away and then halted; and at the same moment the eyes of both lit up.

'Golenishchev!'

'Vronsky!'

It was indeed Golenishchev, a comrade of Vronsky's in the Corps of Pages. In the Corps Golenishchev had belonged to the Liberal Party; he left the corps without entering the army and had never taken office under the Government. The two friends had drifted apart on leaving the corps, and had only met once since.

On that occasion Vronsky gathered that Golenishchev had em-barked on some high-flown liberal activity and was consequently dis-posed to look down upon Vronsky's interests and calling in life. Hence Vronsky had treated him in the cold, haughty manner at which he was an adept, the meaning of which was: 'You may or may not like my way of life. That is a matter of complete indifference to me: if you want to know me, you will have to treat me with respect.' Golenishchev, however, had been contemptuously indifferent to the tone taken by Vronsky. This meeting, one would suppose, should have driven them still farther apart. But now they both beamed and exclaimed with delight when they recognized one another. Vronsky would never have dreamed he could be so pleased to see Golenish-chev: probably he did not realize himself how bored he was. He for-got the disagreeable impression left by their last encounter and with obvious pleasure held out a hand to his old schoolfellow. A similar expression of happiness replaced the former look of uneasiness on Golenishchev's face.

'How pleased I am to see you!' said Vronsky, displaying his fine white teeth in a friendly smile.

'I heard the name Vronsky, but did not know which Vronsky it was. I'm very, very glad!'

'Let's go in. Come, tell me what you're doing.'

'Oh, I have been living here for over a year now. I am working.'

'Ah!' said Vronsky with interest. 'Let's go in.'

And, in the usual way with Russians when they do not wish the servants to understand what they are saying, he began speaking in French.

'You know Madame Karenin? We are travelling together. I am just going to see her now,' he said in French, attentively watching Golenishchev's face.

'Ah! I did not know,' Golenishchev replied casually (though he knew quite well). 'Have you been here long?' he added.

'I? ... Three days,' answered Vronsky, again giving his friend a searching look. 'Yes, he's a decent fellow, and looks at the matter in the right light,' Vronsky said to himself, satisfied with the expression of the other's face and the way he had changed the subject. 'I can introduce him to Anna; his views are all right.'

During the three months he had spent abroad with Anna, every time he made a new acquaintance Vronsky asked himself how that person would view his relations with Anna, and for the most part the men he met understood them in the 'right' way. But had he, and those who understood in the 'right' way, been asked exactly how they did look at it, both he and they would have found it very difficult to say.

In reality, those who in Vronsky's opinion had the 'right' attitude had no sort of attitude at all, but behaved in general as well-bred people do behave in regard to all the complex and insoluble problems with which life is encompassed: they conducted themselves with propriety, avoiding indiscreet allusions and awkward questions. They pretended to understand perfectly the significance and import of the situation, to countenance and even approve of it, but to consider it superfluous and uncalled for to put all this into words.

Vronsky at once divined that Golenishchev was of this kind, and was therefore doubly glad to see him. Indeed, Golenishchev's manner to Madame Karenin, when he was taken to call on her, was all that Vronsky could have desired. Without the smallest effort he seemed to steer clear of all subjects which might lead to embarrassment.

He had never met Anna before and was struck by her beauty, and still more by the simplicity with which she accepted her position. She had blushed when Vronsky brought in Golenishchev, and the child-like blush overspreading her frank and lovely face pleased him exceedingly. But what he liked particularly was the way she at once and apparently intentionally called Vronsky Alexei, so that there might be no misunderstanding with an outsider, and said they were moving into a house they had just taken, what was locally called a palazzo. This straightforward and simple attitude to her own position pleased Golenishchev. As he watched her gay and vivacious manner, and knowing Karenin and Vronsky, it seemed to Golenishchev that he quite understood her. He fancied he understood what she was utterly unable to understand: how it was that, having made her husband wretched, having abandoned him and her son and lost her own good name, she could feel vivacious and happy.

'It's mentioned in the guide-book,' said Golenishchev, referring to the palazzo Vronsky had taken. 'There is a fine Tintoretto there. One of his latest period.'

'I tell you what: it's a glorious day – supposing we go and have another look at the place,' said Vronsky, addressing Anna.

'I should like to very much. I'll go and put on my hat. You say it's hot?' she said, stopping at the door and looking inquiringly at Vronsky. And again the bright colour suffused her face.

Vronsky saw from her eyes that she did not know on what terms he wanted to be with Golenishchev, and so was afraid of not behaving as he would wish.

He looked at her long and tenderly. 'No, not very,' he said.

And it seemed to her that she comprehended everything, most of all, that he was satisfied with her. She gave him a smile and walked out of the room with her rapid step.

The two friends glanced at one another, and a look of hesitation came into both their faces, as though Golenishchev, who obviously admired her, would have liked to say something about her but did not know what, while Vronsky longed for him to do so, yet dreaded it.

'Well, then,' began Vronsky to start a conversation of some sort, 'so you're settled here? I suppose you are still at work on the same thing,' he went on, recollecting that he had heard Golenishchev was writing some book.

'Yes, I'm working on the second part of the *Two Principles*,' said Golenishchev, colouring with pleasure at the question. 'To be exact, I am not writing yet but preparing and collecting material. The book will be of far wider scope, and will deal with almost all questions. We Russians refuse to recognize that we are the heirs of Byzantium,' and he launched into a long and heated dissertation.

At first Vronsky felt uncomfortable because he did not even know the early part of *Two Principles*, of which the author spoke as though it were a classic. But as Golenishchev began expounding his ideas and Vronsky was able to follow him, despite his ignorance of *Two Principles*, he listened with interest, for Golenishchev talked well. But Vronsky was surprised and sorry to see the irritable excitement with which Golenishchev spoke on his subject. The longer he went on, the more his eyes blazed, the more vehemently did he refute imaginary opponents, and the more agitated and injured grew the expression on his face. Remembering him as a thin, lively, good-natured, gentle boy, always at the top of the class, Vronsky was at a loss to understand the reason for his irritability, and did not like it. What particularly displeased him was that Golenishchev, a man of good social standing, should descend to the level of a lot of common scribblers who irritated him and made him angry. Was it worth while? Vronsky did not like it, yet he felt that Golenishchev was not happy, and was sorry for him. Signs of unhappiness, of mental derangement almost, were visible on his mobile, rather handsome face as, without even noticing that Anna had come back into the room, he went on expounding his views in the same hurried, heated manner.

When Anna, in her hat and cloak, came and stood beside him, toying with her parasol with quick movements of her lovely hand, it was with a feeling of relief that Vronsky broke away from Golenishchev's plaintive eyes, which fastened on him persistently, and with a fresh rush of love looked at his charming companion, so full of life and gaiety. Golenishchev, recovering himself with an effort, was at first dejected and morose, but Anna, well disposed to the whole world as she was at that time, soon revived his spirits by her direct, cheerful manner. After trying various topics of conversation she got him on to the subject of painting, about which he talked very well, and listened to him attentively. They walked to the house they had taken, and went over it.

'I am very glad of one thing,' Anna said to Golenishchev when they were on their way back. 'Alexei will have a nice studio. You certainly must take that room, Alexei,' she said to Vronsky, realizing that they were likely to see a good deal of Golenishchev in their isolation, and that there was no need to be reserved in his presence.

'Do you paint?' inquired Golenishchev, turning round quickly to Vronsky.

'Yes, I used to a long time ago, and now I have taken it up again,' said Vronsky, blushing red.

'He has great talent,' said Anna with a happy smile. 'I'm no judge, of course, but people who do know say the same.'

8

ANNA, in that first period of her freedom and rapid return to health, felt unpardonably happy and full of the joy of life. The thought of her husband's misery did not poison her own happiness. On the one hand, that memory was too terrible to dwell on. On the other, what had made her husband unhappy had brought her too much happiness to be the subject of regret. The memory of all that had happened after her illness – the reconciliation with her husband, the breach that followed, the news of Vronsky's wound, his sudden reappearance, the preparations for divorce, the departure from her house, the parting from her son – all seemed like some fevered dream from which she had wakened abroad and alone with Vronsky. The thought of the wrong she had done her husband aroused in her a feeling akin to revulsion, like the feeling a drowning man might have who has shaken off another man clinging to him in the water. That other was drowned. It was wicked, of course, but it had been the only hope of saving oneself, and better not to brood over such horrible details.

One comforting reflection about her conduct had occurred to her at the first moment of the final rupture, and now whenever she thought about the past she recalled that reflection. 'I have inevitably made that man wretched,' she thought, 'but I don't want to profit by his misery. I, too, am suffering, and shall go on suffering: I am losing what I most cherished – my good name and my son. I have done wrong, and so I don't want happiness, I don't want a divorce: I shall go on enduring my shame and the separation from my son.' But no matter how sincere Anna was in her desire to suffer, she did not suffer. She was conscious of no disgrace. With the tact they both possessed to

489

such a high degree, they had succeeded in avoiding Russian ladies abroad, and so had never placed themselves in a false position, and everywhere associated with people who pretended to understand their position far better than they did themselves. Separation from the son she loved – even that did not cause her pain at first. The baby girl – *his* child – was so sweet, and Anna had grown so attached to her since she was all that was left her, that she rarely thought of her son.

The desire for life, waxing stronger with recovered health, was so intense, and the conditions of life were so novel and delightful, that Anna felt unpardonably happy. The more she got to know Vronsky, the more she loved him. She loved him for himself, and for his love for her. To have him entirely to herself was a continual joy, his presence always a delight. All the traits in his character, which she learned to know better and better, were inexpressibly dear. His appearance, altered by civilian clothes, was as attractive to her as though she were a young girl in love for the first time. In everything he said, thought, and did, she saw something peculiarly fine and noble. The rapture he caused her frequently frightened her: she tried in vain to find some imperfection in him. She dared not confess to him her own feeling of inferiority. It seemed to her that if he knew of it he might the sooner cease to love her; and she dreaded nothing now so much as losing his love, though she had no grounds for fearing this. But she could not help being grateful to him for his attitude to her, and showing him how much she appreciated it. He, who in her opinion had such a decided vocation for a public career, in which he would have been conspicuously successful – he had sacrificed his ambition for her sake, and never betrayed the smallest regret. He was more lovingly respectful to her than ever, and care that she should not feel the awkwardness of her position never deserted him for a single instant. He, ordinarily so manly a man, not only never opposed her but where she was concerned seemed to have no will of his own, and to be occupied only in anticipating her every wish. And she could not help appreciating this, even though the very intensity of his solicitude and the atmosphere of care with which she was surrounded sometimes weighed on her.

Vronsky, meanwhile, notwithstanding the complete fulfilment of what he had so long desired, was not entirely happy. He soon began to feel that the realization of his desires brought him no more than a grain of sand out of the mountain of bliss he had expected. It showed him the eternal error men make in imagining that happiness consists in the realization of their desires. For a time after uniting his life with hers, and donning civilian clothes, he had experienced all the charm of freedom in general, of which he had known nothing before, and of freedom to love, and he was content, but not for long. Soon he felt a desire spring up in his heart for desires – *ennui*. Involuntarily he began to clutch at every fleeting caprice, mistaking it for a need and a purpose. Sixteen hours of the day must be filled somehow, living abroad as they were, in complete freedom, cut off from the round of social life that had absorbed so much time in Petersburg. As for any of the bachelor amusements he had enjoyed on previous travels abroad, he dared not even think of them: one attempt in that direction had produced such unexpected depression in Anna, quite out of proportion with the offence of a late supper with some acquaintances. Social intercourse with Russians or local people was likewise out of the question, on account of their irregular position. Sight-seeing, apart from the fact that he had already seen everything, had for him, a Russian and a sensible being, none of that inexplicable importance the English manage to attach to it.

As a hungry animal seizes upon everything it can get hold of in the hope that it may be food, so Vronsky quite unconsciously clutched first at politics, then at new books, then pictures.

In the same way as in his youth he had shown an aptitude for painting and, not knowing what to do with his money, had begun collecting engravings, so now he settled down to work at painting, putting into it all the undefined longings that demanded gratification.

He had a talent for understanding art and probably, with his gift for copying, he imagined he possessed the creative powers essential for an artist. After hesitating for some time which style of painting to take up – religious, historical, *genre*, or realistic – he set to work. He appreciated all the different styles and could find inspiration in any of them, but he could not conceive that it was possible to be ignorant of the different schools of painting and to be inspired directly by what is within the soul, regardless of whether what is painted will belong to any recognized school. Since he did not know this, and drew his inspiration not directly from life but indirectly from other painters' interpretations of life, he found inspiration very readily and easily; and equally readily and easily produced paintings very similar to the particular style he was trying to imitate.

The graceful and effective French school appealed to him more than any other, and in that manner he began painting a portrait of Anna in Italian costume, and he and everyone who saw it considered the portrait a great success.

9

THE old, neglected palazzo with its lofty stucco ceilings and wall frescoes, its mosaic floors and heavy yellow damask hangings at the tall windows, its vases standing on console-tables and mantelshelves, its carved doors and sombre reception-rooms hung with pictures – this palazzo, after they had moved into it, by its very appearance sustained Vronsky in the agreeable illusion that he was not so much a Russian landed proprietor and equerry without a post as an enlightened connoisseur and patron of the arts, and, in his own modest way, a painter himself who had renounced the world, his connexions, and ambitions for the sake of the woman he loved.

The role chosen by Vronsky with their removal to the palazzo was completely successful, and, having through Golenishchev made the acquaintance of several interesting people, he felt satisfied for a while. Under the guidance of an Italian professor he painted studies from nature, and at the same time interested himself in Italian life in the Middle Ages. He grew so fascinated by medieval Italian life that he even took to wearing his hat and flinging his cloak over his shoulder in the medieval fashion – a style that was very becoming to him.

'Here we live and know nothing of what's going on,' Vronsky said to Golenishchev, who had come to see him one morning. 'Have you seen Mihailov's picture?' he asked, handing him a copy of a Russian newspaper which had just arrived and pointing to an article on a Russian artist, living in that very town, who had just finished a picture long talked of and bought before it left the easel. The article was full of condemnation of the Government and the Academy for leaving so remarkable an artist without encouragement or support.

'Yes, I have,' replied Golenishchev. 'Of course he's not without talent, but he's working in the wrong direction. It's all that everlasting Ivanov–Strauss–Renan attitude to Christ and religious painting.'

'What is the subject of the picture?' asked Anna.

'Christ before Pilate. Christ is represented as a Jew with all the realism of the new school.'

And the question regarding the subject of the picture having brought him to one of his favourite theories, Golenishchev launched forth into a disquisition on it.

'I can't understand how they can fall into so gross an error! In the art of the old masters Christ always has his definite embodiment. Therefore, if they want to depict not God but a revolutionary or a sage, let them take some character from history – Socrates, Franklin, Charlotte Corday – anybody they please, but not Christ. They choose the one figure which cannot be taken as a subject for art, and then ...'

'And is it true that this Mihailov is as poor as they make out?' asked Vronsky, thinking that, as a Russian Maecenas, it was his duty to help this artist irrespective of whether his picture were good or bad.

'Hardly. He is a wonderful portrait-painter. Have you ever seen his portrait of Madame Vassilchikov? But I hear he has given up portrait-painting, so he may be in straitened circumstances, for all I know. I maintain that ...'

'Couldn't we ask him to paint a portrait of Anna Arkadyevna?' said Vronsky.

'Why mine?' said Anna. 'After your portrait of me I want no other. Let him do one of Ani' (as she called her baby girl). 'Here she is,' she added, looking out of the window and catching sight of their handsome Italian nurse, who had just taken the child out into the garden, and then immediately glancing round unnoticed at Vronsky. This handsome nurse, whose head Vronsky was painting for his picture, was the one secret shadow in Anna's life. Using her as a model, Vronsky had admired her medieval type of beauty, and Anna dared not confess to herself that she was afraid of becoming jealous of the nurse, and was for that reason particularly gracious and condescending both to her and her little boy.

Vronsky, too, glanced out of the window and into Anna's eyes, and, turning at once to Golenishchev, he said:

'Do you know this Mihailov?'

'I have met him. But he's a queer fish and quite uneducated. You know, one of those uncouth moderns one comes across so often now-adays – freethinkers, who are reared from the first in theories of athe-ism, nihilism, and materialism. At one time,' Golenishchev continued, either not observing or not willing to observe that both Anna and Vronsky wanted to speak, 'at one time a freethinker was a man who had been brought up in the conceptions of religion, law, and morality, who reached freethought only after conflict and difficulty. But now a new type of born freethinkers has appeared, who grow up without so much as hearing that there used to be laws of morality, or religion, that authorities existed. They grow up in ideas of negation in everything – in other words, utter savages. Mihailov is one of them. I believe he was the son of some Moscow valet, and had absolutely no education. When he got into the Academy and won a reputation for himself, he tried, for he's no fool, to educate himself. And he turned to what seemed to him the very source of culture – the magazines. In the old days, you see, if a man – a Frenchman, for instance – wished to get an education, he would have set to work to study the classics, the theologians, the tragedians, historians, and philosophers – and you can realize all the intellectual labour involved. But nowadays he goes straight for the literature of negation, rapidly assimilates the essence of the science of negation, and thinks he's finished. And that is not all. Whereas twenty years ago this same literature bore traces of conflict with authorities, with the conceptions of centuries, whereby he could realize that there was something else, now he comes at once upon a literature in which the old creeds do not even furnish matter for discussion, and which states baldly: "There is nothing else – evolution, natural selection, the struggle for existence – and that's all." In my article I …'

'I tell you what,' said Anna, who for some time had been furtively exchanging looks with Vronsky and could see he was not in the least interested in the education of this artist but merely concerned to help him by commissioning a portrait; 'I tell you what,' she resolutely interrupted Golenishchev, who was in full flow, 'let's go and see him!'

Golenishchev pulled himself up and readily assented. But as the artist lived in a distant quarter of the town, it was decided to take a carriage.

An hour later Anna, with Golenishchev beside her and Vronsky facing them, drove up to an attractive new house in the remote suburb. Informed by the house porter's wife who came out to them that Mihailov saw visitors at his studio, but that he was now at his lodgings a few steps away, they sent in their cards with a request to see his pictures.

10

THE artist Mihailov was at work as usual when the cards of Count Vronsky and Golenishchev were brought to him. He had been working all the morning at his big picture in the studio. Returning home he had lost his temper with his wife because she had not managed to put off the landlady, who had demanded the rent.

'I've told you twenty times not to enter into discussions. You're a fool at the best of times, and when you start arguing in Italian you become a treble fool,' he said at the end of a long dispute.

'Then you shouldn't get behind; it's not my fault! If I had the money ...'

'Leave me alone, for heaven's sake!' cried Mihailov with tears in his voice, and, stopping his ears, he went off into his workroom on the other side of the partition wall, and locked himself in. 'Idiotic woman!' he said to himself as he sat down at the table. Opening a portfolio, he feverishly set to work on a sketch he had begun.

He never worked with such fervour or so well as when things were going badly with him, and in particular after a quarrel with his wife. 'Oh, if only I could get away somewhere!' he thought as he went on working. He was making a study for the figure of a man in a violent rage. He had already made one sketch but had not been satisfied with it. 'No, the other was better ... where is it?' He went back to his wife and, scowling, without looking at her, asked his eldest little girl what she had done with the piece of paper he had given them. The paper with the discarded drawing was found, but it was dirty and spotted with candle-grease. Still, he took the sketch, laid it on his table and, standing back and screwing up his eyes, fell to gazing at it. All at once he smiled and flung up his hands gleefully.

'That's it! That's it!' he cried, and taking up a pencil rapidly began to draw. One of the grease-spots had the effect of giving the figure a new pose.

He was drawing this new pose when he suddenly recalled the powerful face of a tobacconist with a prominent jaw, where he bought cigars, and he gave the man he was drawing just such a face and jaw. He laughed aloud with delight. The lifeless figure of his imagination had come to life and could not be improved upon. The figure was alive, with a sure and vigorous line. The sketch might be corrected to fit in with the requirements of the figure: the legs could, and even must, be spread farther apart, and the position of the left arm should be altered and the hair thrown back. But in making these alterations he was not putting in another figure but simply getting lucidity. He removed the wrappings, as it were, that partially obscured the form, each new stroke bringing out the action and power of the whole figure that had suddenly been revealed to him by the grease spot. He was carefully finishing the sketch when the cards were brought to him.

'One moment, one moment!'

He went out to his wife.

'It's all right, Sasha, don't be cross!' he said, with a timid, affectionate smile. 'You were wrong, and so was I. I'll see to things.'

Having made peace with his wife, he put on an olive-green overcoat with a velvet collar, took his hat and went to the studio. The successful figure was already forgotten. Now he was pleased and excited at the visit to his studio of these grand people, Russians, who had come in a carriage.

Of his picture, the one at present on the easel, he had at the bottom of his heart but one conviction: that no one had ever painted a picture like it. It was not that he considered his picture better than all the Raphaels, but he knew that what he tried to convey, and had conveyed in that picture, no one had ever conveyed. He was sure of that – had known it a long while, ever since he had begun to paint it; but the criticisms of others, whoever they might be, were of great importance to him none the less, and agitated him profoundly. Every little remark, even the most trivial, which showed that his critics saw even a small part of what he himself saw in the picture agitated him to the depths of his soul. He always endowed his critics with a more complete understanding than he had himself, and always expected them to discover something in his work that had escaped his own observation. And often in their criticisms he fancied that he had found this.

With rapid steps he hurried to the studio door and in spite of his excitement he was struck by the soft radiance of Anna's figure as she stood in the shadow of the porch listening to something Golenishchev was vehemently propounding and at the same time obviously wanting to look round at the artist. He did not himself realize how, as he approached them, he seized and stored up the impression, just as he had done with the chin of the shopkeeper who had sold him the cigars, hiding it away ready for some future use. The visitors, already disenchanted by Golenishchev's account of the artist, were still further disillusioned by his personal appearance. Mihailov was a thick-set man of medium height, and his nervous gait, brown hat, olive-green coat and tight trousers (when wide ones had long been the fashion), and most of all his commonplace, broad face expressing a combination of timidity and pretentious dignity created a disagreeable impression.

'Come in, please,' he said, trying to look indifferent, and going into the passage he took a key out of his pocket and opened the door.

II

As they entered the studio, Mihailov once more examined his visitors and made a mental note of Vronsky's face, especially his jaw. Notwithstanding the fact that the artist in him was always at work collecting material, and though he was growing more and more agitated as the moment approached when an opinion would be expressed about his picture, he quickly took accurate observation of the three, from almost imperceptible indications. That fellow (Golenishchev) was the Russian who lived here. Mihailov did not remember his name, or where he had met him, or what they had talked about. He only remembered his face, as he remembered all the faces he had ever seen; but he also remembered that he had classed it in the immense category of faces which lack expression in spite of an apparent air of consequence. A mass of hair and a very open forehead gave a semblance of distinction to the face, which had only one expression – a petty, childish, restless expression concentrated just above the narrow bridge of the nose. Vronsky and Madame Karenin he put down as distinguished and wealthy Russians knowing nothing about art, like all these wealthy Russians, but posing as connoisseurs and lovers of art. 'I suppose they've done the round of old masters and are now visiting the modern studios. No doubt they've been to that German charlatan, and that pre-Raphaelite fool of an Englishman, and have come to me to finish up.' Well, he knew the dilettanti's way (the more intelligent they were the worse it was) of looking at the work of contemporary artists for no other purpose than to be able to say afterwards that art is a thing of the past and the more one sees of the modern stuff the more evident it becomes that the old masters are inimitable. He expected all this: he saw it in their faces, in the careless indifference with which they talked among themselves, stared at the lay figures and busts, and in leisurely fashion wandered about, waiting for him to uncover his picture. But in spite of this, as he turned over his studies, pulled up the blinds and took the sheet down from the canvas, he felt intense excitement – the more so because though all distinguished and wealthy Russians could not help being beasts and fools in his opinion, he had conceived a liking for Vronsky and especially for Anna.

'Here, if you please,' he said, stepping to one side with his agile gait and pointing to his picture. 'It's *Christ before Pilate* – Matthew, chapter xxvii,' he went on, conscious that his lips were beginning to tremble with agitation. He moved away and stood behind them.

During the few seconds that the visitors were silently gazing at the picture Mihailov, too, looked at it with the indifferent eye of a stranger. For those few seconds he was sure in advance that the most profound and equitable of judgements would be pronounced by those very visitors whom he had been so despising a moment ago. He forgot all he had thought about the picture during the three years he had been working on it, forgot all its qualities which he had been so certain of, and saw it with the fresh, indifferent eyes of these strangers, and saw nothing good in it. He saw in the foreground Pilate's irritated face and the serene face of Christ, and in the background the figures of Pilate's retinue and the face of John, watching what was taking place. Each face that, after so much searching, so many blunders and alterations, had grown up within him with its own character, each face that had caused him such torments and such raptures, and all of them so often placed and replaced to make a whole, all the shades of colour and tone obtained with such effort – seen now with their eyes struck him as a series of commonplaces repeated over and over again. Even the face of Christ, which he most prized, the centre of the picture, that had sent him wild with joy as it unfolded itself to him, was lost when he glanced at the picture with their eyes. He saw a well-painted (and not so well-painted in places either – he noticed a multitude of defects) repetition of those innumerable Christs of Titian, Raphael, Rubens, with the same soldiers and the same Pilate. It was all hackneyed, poor, stale, and positively badly painted – weak and unequal. They would be justified in saying a few polite things in his presence and then pitying and laughing at him when they were gone.

The silence (though it lasted no more than a minute) grew too oppressive for him. To break it and to show he was not agitated, he made an effort and addressed Golenishchev.

'I think I've had the pleasure of meeting you somewhere,' he said, with an uneasy look first at Anna and then at Vronsky, eager not to lose a single detail of the expression on their faces.

'To be sure! We met at Rossi's – you remember, that evening the Italian girl, the new Rachel, recited?' Golenishchev began at once, removing his gaze from the picture without the least show of regret, and turning to the artist.

Noticing, however, that Mihailov was expecting to hear his opinion of the picture, he said:

'Your picture has progressed a great deal since I last saw it. And what strikes me particularly now, as it did then, is the figure of Pilate. One knows that man so well: a good-natured, capital fellow, but an official to his very backbone, blind to the meaning of what he is doing. But it seems to me ...'

The whole of Mihailov's mobile face suddenly lighted up; his eyes sparkled. He tried to say something, but he could not speak for excitement, and pretended to cough. No matter what little store he set by Golenishchev's capacity to understand art, nor how insignificant was the remark, though a true one, about the fidelity of the expression on the face of Pilate the official, and hurtful as might have seemed the utterance of so trivial an observation while what was important remained unmentioned, still Mihailov was delighted with it. Golenishchev had expressed the very idea he had intended to convey. That it was only one reflection in a million that might have been made, with equal truth, as Mihailov well knew, did not detract for him from its importance. His heart warmed to Golenishchev for this remark, and his depression suddenly changed to ecstasy. In an instant his whole picture came alive before his eyes with all the indescribable complexity of every living thing. Mihailov again tried to say that that was how he understood Pilate, but his lips would not stop trembling and he could not utter a word. Vronsky and Anna, too, said something in that subdued voice in which – partly to avoid hurting the artist's feelings and partly to avoid saying out loud the stupid remarks it is so easy to make when speaking about art – people generally talk at exhibitions of pictures. It seemed to Mihailov that the picture had made an impression on them, too. He walked over to them.

'How marvellous Christ's expression is!' said Anna. Of all she saw

499

she liked that expression most of all, and she felt that it was the centre of the picture, and so praise of it would be agreeable to the artist. 'One can see he is sorry for Pilate.'

This again was one of the million just observations that might have been made of the picture and of the figure of Christ. She said he was sorry for Pilate. There was bound to be pity in Christ's face, for there had to be love, a peace not of this world, a readiness for death, and a sense of the vanity of words. Of course there was an expression of the official in Pilate and of pity in Christ, seeing that one is the incarnation of the carnal and the other of the spiritual life. All this and much more flashed through Mihailov's mind. And again his face shone with ecstasy.

'Yes, and how well that figure is done – what atmosphere! One can walk round it,' said Golenishchev, plainly betraying by this remark that he did not approve of the content and conception of the figure.

'Yes, its mastery is wonderful!' said Vronsky. 'How those figures in the background stand out! There's technique for you,' he added, turning to Golenishchev and alluding to the conversation they had had about Vronsky's despair of attaining this technique.

'Yes, yes, marvellous!' Golenishchev and Anna agreed.

In spite of his elation, this remark about technique jarred painfully on Mihailov, and he gave Vronsky an angry look, and scowled. He was always hearing that word technique, and could never make out what people understood by it. He knew it meant a mechanical ability to draw and paint, quite apart from the content of the drawing. He had often noticed that even in actual praise technique was opposed to essential quality, as though it were possible to paint a bad picture with talent. He knew that a great deal of attention and care were required in bringing the idea to birth and producing it; but as to the art of painting, the technique, it did not exist. If the things he saw had been revealed to a child, or to his cook, they would have been able to peel off the outer husk of what they saw. And the most experienced and skilful painter could not by mere mechanical facility paint anything if he could not 'see' the lines of his subject first. Besides, he perceived that as far as technique was concerned he did not come off very well. In all he painted and had ever painted he noticed defects that hurt his eyes, due to carelessness in production – defects he could not remedy now without spoiling the work as a whole. And in nearly all the figures and faces he saw traces of imperfect production which spoiled the picture.

'There is one thing I should like to say if I may ...' observed Gole-nishchev.

'Oh, I should be delighted to hear what it is,' said Mihailov with a forced smile.

'It is that you have painted a man made God, and not God made man. However, I know that was your intention.'

'I cannot paint a Christ that is not in my soul,' said Mihailov gloomily.

'Yes, but in that case, if you will allow me to express what I think. ... Your picture is so good that my remark cannot do it any harm, and, besides, it is only my personal opinion. With you it is different. The idea itself is different. Take Ivanov, for example. It seems to me that if he had to reduce Christ to the level of an historical character he would have done better to have chosen a different historical theme, something fresh and untouched.'

'But if this is the greatest theme that presents itself to art?'

'Other themes are to be found if one looks for them. But the point is, art won't stand discussion and argument. And with Ivanov's picture the question arises for believer and unbeliever alike, "Is this God, or not God?" and the unity of impression is destroyed.'

'Why so? I should have thought that for educated people,' said Mihailov, 'the question cannot exist.'

Golenishchev did not agree with this and, sticking to his first contention that unity of impression is essential to art, he routed Mihailov.

Mihailov was perturbed, but could find nothing to say in defence of his own idea.

12

ANNA and Vronsky had long been exchanging glances, regretting their friend's clever loquacity, and at last Vronsky crossed the room, without waiting for the artist, to look at another, smaller picture.

'Oh, how charming! How exquisite! What a gem! How exquisite!' they cried with one voice.

'What has taken their fancy so?' thought Mihailov.

He had completely forgotten that picture, painted three years before, forgotten all the agonies and ecstasies he had gone through with it, when for months on end he had thought of nothing else day and night – forgotten, as he always forgot all his finished pictures. He did not even care to see it, and had only brought it out because he was expecting an Englishman who wanted to buy it.

'Oh, that's only an old study I did long ago,' he said.

'But it's capital!' said Golenishchev, he too, with unmistakable sincerity, falling under the spell of the picture.

Two boys were angling in the shade of a willow-tree. The elder had just cast the line and, all absorbed, was cautiously drawing the float from behind a bush; the younger boy lay in the grass, leaning on his elbows, with his tangled flaxen head in his hands, staring at the water with dreamy blue eyes. What was he thinking about?

Their enthusiasm over this picture brought back to Mihailov some of his former excitement, but he feared and disliked this idle interest in past work, and so, though their praise gave him pleasure, he tried to draw his visitors away to a third picture.

But Vronsky asked if the picture were for sale. To Mihailov at that moment, in his excitement over their visit, this mention of monetary matters was extremely distasteful.

'It is put out for sale,' he replied, with an overcast frown.

After they had gone, Mihailov sat down before his picture of Pilate and Christ, and went over in his mind all that had been said, and what, though not said, had been implied by his visitors. And, strangely enough, what had had such weight with him while they were there and he had looked with their eyes now suddenly lost all importance for him. He examined his picture with his own artistic vision, and reached that mood of conviction that his picture was perfect and consequently of significance which he needed to sustain the intensity of effort – to the exclusion of all other interests – in which alone he could work.

The foreshortening of Christ's foot was not right, though. He took his palette and set to work. While he was correcting the foot he kept glancing at the figure of John in the background, which the visitors had not even noticed but which he knew was beyond perfection. When the foot was finished he wanted to put a few touches to that figure, but felt he was much too agitated. He could no more work under extreme excitement, when he saw everything too distinctly, than he could when he felt indifferent. There was only one stage in the transition from indifference to inspiration. At this moment he was too agitated. He was about to cover the picture, but stopped and, holding up the sheet, stood a long time with a blissful smile on his face gazing at the figure of John. He tore himself away regretfully at last, let the sheet fall and exhausted but happy went home.

Vronsky, Anna, and Golenishchev were in particularly high spirits on their way back. They talked of Mihailov and his pictures. The word *talent*, by which they meant an inborn, almost physical skill, independent of brain and heart, which was their expression for everything an artist gains from life, occurred frequently in their conversation, since they required it to cover something of which they had no conception but wanted to talk about. They said there was no denying his talent, but declared that his talent could not develop for want of education – the common misfortune of our Russian artists. But the picture of the boys fishing had imprinted itself on their memories, and they kept coming back to it.

'What an exquisite thing it is! How well he has hit it off, and so simply! He does not half appreciate how good it is. Yes, I mustn't let it slip: I must buy it,' said Vronsky.

13

MIHAILOV sold Vronsky the picture and agreed to paint a portrait of Anna. On the appointed day he came and began working.

After the fifth sitting the portrait impressed everybody, especially Vronsky, not only by its likeness but also by its peculiar beauty. It was strange how Mihailov had been able to discover that peculiar beauty. 'One needs to know her and love her, as I have loved her, to discover the very sweetest expression of her soul,' thought Vronsky, though it was only through this portrait that he himself learned this sweetest expression of her soul. But the expression was so true that it seemed to him, and to others, too, that they had always known it.

'I have been struggling on for ages without doing anything,' he said one day, referring to his own portrait of her, 'but he just looks at her once and the thing is done! That's the advantage of technique.'

'It will come in time,' Golenishchev consoled him. In his eyes Vronsky had talent and, more important, the education that gives a wider outlook on art. Golenishchev's conviction that Vronsky had talent was supported by his own need of Vronsky's sympathy and encouragement for his articles and ideas, and he felt that the praise and encouragement should be mutual.

In a strange house, and especially in Vronsky's palazzo, Mihailov was a different man from Mihailov in his own studio. He behaved with hostile courtesy, as if fearful of coming too closely in contact with people he did not respect. He addressed Vronsky as 'your excellency', and never stayed to dinner, despite Anna's and Vronsky's repeated invitations, nor would he come except for a sitting. Anna was even more friendly to him than to other people, and was grateful for her portrait. Vronsky was more than polite to him, and was obviously interested to know the artist's opinion of his, Vronsky's, picture. Golenishchev never missed an opportunity of instilling sound ideas about art into Mihailov. Still Mihailov kept his distance. Anna was aware by his eyes that he liked looking at her, but he avoided conversation with her. When Vronsky talked about his painting he remained stubbornly silent, just as when he was shown Vronsky's picture; and he was unmistakably bored by Golenishchev's discourses, to which he made no rejoinder.

Altogether Mihailov, with his reserved, disagreeable, and apparently hostile attitude, did not please them at all when they got to know him better, and they were glad when the sittings were over, the beautiful portrait was theirs, and his visits ceased.

Golenishchev was the first to give expression to the thought that was in all their minds, that Mihailov was simply jealous of Vronsky.

'Not envious, let us say, because he certainly has *talent*; but it makes him furious that a wealthy man of the highest society, and a count into the bargain – you know they all detest a title – can, without any particular difficulty, do as well, if not better, than someone who has devoted his whole life to it. And, above all, you have the education which he has not.'

Vronsky defended Mihailov, but at the bottom of his heart he agreed with what Golenishchev said, because in his view a man of a different, lower status was bound to be envious.

The two portraits of Anna, his own and Mihailov's, ought to have shown Vronsky the difference between him and Mihailov, but he did not see it. He merely left off painting his own portrait of Anna, deciding that it would be superfluous now that Mihailov's was finished. His picture of medieval life he went on with. And he himself, as well as Golenishchev and especially Anna, thought it very good, because it was far more like the old masters than Mihailov's picture.

As for Mihailov, though he had been much interested in Anna's portrait, he was even more glad than they when the sittings came to an end and he was no longer obliged to listen to Golenishchev's disquisitions upon art, and could forget about Vronsky's painting. He knew that Vronsky could not be prevented from amusing himself with painting; he knew that he and every other dilettante had a perfect right to paint what they liked, but it was distasteful to him. A man could not be prevented from making himself a big wax doll, and kissing it. But if the man were to take his doll and go and sit down in the presence of a man in love, and start caressing his doll as the lover caressed his beloved, it would be distasteful to the lover. Mihailov had just such a feeling of distaste at Vronsky's painting: he was amused, irritated, sorry, and affronted.

Vronsky's interest in painting and the Middle Ages was of short duration. He had enough artistic taste to be unable to finish his picture. The picture came to a standstill. He was dimly conscious that its defects, not very noticeable at first, would become glaring if he went on. The same thing happened to him that happened to Golenishchev, who felt that he had nothing to say and went on deceiving himself with the idea that his theories had not yet matured, that he was working them out and collecting material. But while Golenishchev grew bitter and irritable, Vronsky was incapable of self-deception and self-torment, and even more incapable of exasperation. With characteristic decision, without explanation or apology, he left off painting.

But without this occupation his life and that of Anna, who wondered at his sudden disenchantment, struck them as intolerably boring in the little Italian town. The palazzo suddenly seemed so noticeably old and dirty. The spots on the curtains, the cracks in the floors, the stucco falling away from the cornices were constant eyesores. And then there was the everlasting sameness of Golenishchev, and the Italian professor, and the German tourist – yes, a change was absolutely necessary. They decided to go to Russia, to the country. In Petersburg, Vronsky would make arrangements with his brother about the division of their property, and Anna planned to see her son. The summer they intended to spend on Vronsky's large family estate.

14

LEVIN had been married three months. He was happy, but not at all in the way he had expected. At every step he found his former dreams disappointed, and new, unlooked-for enchantments. He was happy; but, having embarked on married life, he saw at every step that it was not at all what he had anticipated. At every turn he felt like a man who, after admiring the smooth, happy motion of a boat on a lake, suddenly finds himself in it. It was not enough to sit still without rocking the boat – he had to be on the look-out and never forget the course he was taking, or that there was water beneath and all around. He must row, although his unaccustomed hands were made sore. It was one thing to look on and another to do the work, and doing it, though very delightful, was very difficult.

As a bachelor he had watched the conjugal life of others, the petty cares, the squabbles, the jealousy, with an inward smile of contempt. In his own future married life, he was convinced, there could be nothing of that sort: even its outward forms would have nothing in common with the life of others. But now, lo and behold, instead of life with his wife having an individual pattern, it was, on the contrary, made up of all those petty trifles, which he had so despised, but which now, against his will, had gained an extraordinary importance that it was useless to contend against. And Levin saw that it was by no means easy to regulate these trifles, as he had formerly supposed. Although Levin believed himself to have the truest conceptions of married life, like all men he had unconsciously pictured married life as the happy enjoyment of love, which nothing should be allowed to hinder and from which no petty cares should distract. He should, he thought, do his work and then rest from his labours in the happiness of love. His wife was to be beloved, and nothing more. But, like all men, he forgot that she, too, needed occupation. And so he was amazed that she, his poetic, exquisite Kitty, could in the very first weeks – in the very first days, even – of their married life think, remember, and fuss about table-cloths, furniture, spare-room mattresses, a tray, the cook, the dinner, and so forth. While they were still engaged he had been struck by the decisive way in which she had rejected a trip abroad and chosen to go to the country, as though she knew of something she wanted, and could still think of something outside her love. This had jarred upon him then, and now more than once her petty cares and worries jarred upon him. But he saw that this was essential for her. And, loving her as he did, though he did not understand what they were all about and laughed at these domestic pursuits, he could not help admiring them. He laughed at the way in which she arranged the furniture they had brought from Moscow, altered the arrangement of their bedroom, hung up curtains, prepared rooms for visitors, got a room ready for Dolly, and one for her new maid, gave orders about dinner to the old cook, came into collision with Agatha Mihalovna, taking the store-keeping into her own hands. He saw how the old cook smiled admiringly as he listened to her inexperienced, impossible orders; saw Agatha Mihalovna shake her head mournfully and tenderly at her young mistress's new arrangements in the store-room; saw that Kitty looked extraordinarily sweet when she came to him, half laughing, half crying, to report that her maid Masha would insist on treating her like a child, and so no one would obey her. It was all very sweet but strange, and he would have preferred to do without it.

He did not realize how great a sense of change she was experiencing after living at home. There she had sometimes wished for cabbage with kvas, or a favourite sweet, and could not have them; now she could order what she liked, buy pounds of sweets, spend as much money as she pleased, and have any puddings she wanted.

She was now looking forward with joy to Dolly's visit with the children, especially because she meant each child to have its favourite pudding, and Dolly would appreciate all her new arrangements. She herself did not know why or wherefore housekeeping had such an irresistible attraction for her. Instinctively feeling the approach of spring, and knowing that there would be wet weather, too, she fashioned her nest as best she could, hastening to build it and learning as she went along.

Kitty's zeal for trifles, so opposed to Levin's early ideal of lofty happiness, was one of his disappointments; and this sweet activity, the meaning of which he could not understand but which he could not help loving, was one of his new enchantments.

Their quarrels, too, afforded both disenchantment and new enchantment. Levin had never dreamt that there could be any relation between himself and his wife other than that of tenderness, esteem, and love, and all at once in the very early days they quarrelled, so that she said he did not care for her, that he cared for no one but himself, burst into tears and wrung her hands.

This first quarrel arose because Levin had ridden over to see a new farm-building and returned half an hour late, having attempted a short cut and lost his way. He rode home thinking only of her, of her love, of his own happiness, and the nearer he came to the house the warmer grew his tenderness for her. He ran into the room feeling as he had – and more strongly so – on the day he had driven to the Shcherbatskys' house to make his offer. And suddenly he was met by a lowering expression he had never seen in her. He tried to kiss her but she pushed him away.

'What is the matter?'

'You go about enjoying yourself,' she began, wanting to say something coldly stinging.

But directly she opened her mouth, a stream of reproach, of senseless jealousy, of everything else that had been torturing her during the half-hour she had spent sitting motionless at the window, burst from her. Then for the first time he clearly understood what he had not understood when he led her out of the church after the wedding: that he was not simply close to her, but that he could not tell where he ended and she began. He realized this from the agonizing sensation of division which he felt at that instant. He was hurt for a moment but immediately knew he could not be offended with her because she was himself. For a second he felt like a man who, suddenly receiving a violent blow from behind, turns round angrily to find and be revenged on his assailant, and discovers that he has accidentally struck himself, that there is no one to be angry with and he must endure and try to still the pain.

Never afterwards did he feel this so strongly, but this first time it was a long while before he could get over it. His natural feelings urged him to justify himself and prove that she was in the wrong; but to prove her in the wrong would mean irritating her still more and widening the breach which was the cause of all the trouble. One habitual impulse drew him to shift the blame from himself and lay it upon her. Another and more powerful one drew him to smooth over the breach as quickly as possible, and not allow it to widen. To remain under so unjust an accusation was wretched, but to hurt her by justifying himself would be still worse. Like a man half-awake and in an agony of pain, he wanted to tear off and cast away the aching part, and found on coming to his senses that the aching part was – himself. He could do nothing but try to help the aching place to bear it, and this he did.

They made it up. Recognizing that she was wrong, though not confessing it, Kitty became tenderer to him, and they experienced new, redoubled happiness in their love. But that did not prevent such collisions from recurring, and quite frequently too, from causes as unexpected as they were trivial. These collisions often occurred because each had yet to learn what was of importance to the other and because both in those early days were often in a bad humour. When one was in a good temper and the other was not, peace was not broken; but if both chanced to be out of humour, quarrels sprang up from causes so trifling as to be incomprehensible, making them wonder afterwards what they had quarrelled about. It was true that when they were both in good spirits their happiness in life was redoubled. Nevertheless this first period of their married life was a trying one.

During all this early time they had a peculiarly vivid sense of tension, as if the chain that bound them were being pulled in opposite directions. Altogether their honeymoon – the month after their wedding – from which tradition gave Levin to expect so much, was not merely not a time of sweetness but remained in the memories of both as the bitterest and most humiliating period of their lives. They both tried in later life to blot from their memories all the ugly, shameful incidents of that morbid period, when both were rarely in a normal frame of mind, rarely quite themselves.

It was only in the third month of their marriage, after their return from Moscow, where they had spent four weeks, that life began to run more smoothly for them.

15

THEY had just come back from Moscow and were glad to be alone. He was sitting in his study writing. She, in the dark lilac dress she had worn during the first days of their married life and which was fraught with such dear and pleasant recollections for him, was sitting with her *broderie anglaise* on the same old-fashioned leather couch which had always stood in the study in his father's and grandfather's day. All the time he thought and wrote he was deliciously conscious of her presence. He had not abandoned his work on the estate, or on the book which was to explain the principles of the new land system; but just as formerly these pursuits and ideas had seemed petty and insignificant in comparison with the darkness that overshadowed all existence, so now they seemed as petty and insignificant in comparison with the brilliant sunshine in which the future was bathed. He went on with his work but now he felt that the centre of gravity of his attention had shifted, making him look at his work quite differently and with greater clarity. Formerly this work had been an escape from life: he used to feel that without it life would be too gloomy. Now he needed it so that life might not be too uniformly bright. Taking up his manuscript, reading through what he had written, he was glad to find that it was worth working at. It was fresh and valuable. Many of his old ideas now appeared superfluous and extreme, but many gaps became clear to him when he went over the whole thing in his mind. He was writing now a new chapter on the causes of the unproductive condition of agriculture in Russia. He argued that the poverty of Russia was due not only to anomalous distribution of landed property and misdirected reforms, but that of late years those evils had been fostered by an alien civilization artificially grafted on to Russia – to facilities of communication, in particular: railways which produced an exaggerated centralization in the cities, a growth of luxury, and the consequent development of new industries, and the credit system with its concomitant Stock Exchange speculation, all to the detriment of agriculture. It seemed to him that with a normal development of a country's wealth all these phenomena would make their appearance only after a considerable amount of labour had been devoted to agriculture and after the latter had been placed in its rightful – or at any rate a definite – position. The wealth of a country ought to increase proportionally and in such a way, especially, that other sources of wealth should not outstrip agriculture. Means of communication ought to correspond to the needs and condition of agriculture. With our wrong methods of using the land, the railways, called into existence not by economic but by political needs, had come prematurely, and instead of promoting agriculture, as had been expected of them, had outstripped it and stimulated the development of industry and the system of credit, so arresting its progress. Just as the one-sided and premature development of one organ in an animal would hinder its general development, so credit, facilities of communication, and the forced growth of industry – though undoubtedly necessary in Europe, where they had arisen in their proper time – had only harmed the general development of wealth in Russia by thrusting aside the chief and most pressing question of the organization of agriculture.

While he was writing out his ideas, she was thinking how unnaturally cordial her husband had been to the young Prince Tcharsky, who had, with great want of tact, paid court to her the evening before they left Moscow. 'He must be jealous,' she thought. 'Goodness, how sweet and silly he is – jealous of me! If he knew that the whole lot of them are no more to me than Piotr the cook,' she thought, looking at his head and ruddy neck with a strange feeling of proprietorship. 'Though it's a pity to take him from his work (but he's got plenty of time!), I must see his face. Will he feel I'm looking at him? I wish he'd turn round. ... I'll *will* him to!' and she opened her eyes wide, trying thereby to concentrate more force into her gaze.

'Yes, they attract all the sap and give a false appearance of prosperity,' he muttered, putting down his pen and, feeling that she was looking at him and smiling, he turned round.

'Well?' he queried with a smile, and got up.

'He did turn round,' she thought.

'Nothing; I only wanted you to look round,' she said, watching him and trying to discern whether he was vexed at being interrupted.

'How happy we are alone together! I am, that is,' he said, going up to her with a radiant smile of happiness.

'I'm just as happy! I'll never go anywhere, least of all to Moscow.'

'And what were you thinking about?'

'I? I was thinking ... But never mind, go back to your writing, don't be distracted,' she said, puckering her lips. 'And I must cut out these little holes, do you see?'

She took up her scissors and began cutting.

'No, tell me what it was,' he said, sitting down beside her and following the circular movement of the tiny scissors.

'Oh, what was I thinking about? I was thinking about Moscow, and about the back of your neck.'

'What have I done to deserve such happiness? It's not natural – too good to be true,' he said, kissing her hand.

'With me, on the contrary, the better things are, the more natural I find it.'

'You've got a little stray curl,' he said, carefully turning her head round. 'Here it is, see? But enough – we are engaged on serious matters!'

But their serious matters were left to take care of themselves, and they jumped apart guiltily when Kuzma came in to announce that tea was ready.

'And have they returned from town?' Levin inquired of Kuzma.

'They've just got back and are unpacking the things.'

'Be quick and come,' she said as she left the study, 'or I shall read the letters without you. And after that let's play duets.'

Left alone, after putting away his papers in a new portfolio she had bought, he washed his hands at the new washstand with its elegant fittings that had all made their appearance with her. Levin smiled at his thoughts and shook his head disapprovingly at them. A feeling akin to remorse fretted him. There was something shameful, effeminate about his present mode of life – Capuan, as he called it to himself. 'It's not right to go on like this,' he thought. 'It'll soon be three months, and I'm doing next to nothing. To-day is almost the first time I set to work seriously, and what happened? I hardly begin before I stop. Even my ordinary occupations are practically all abandoned. The farm-work – why, I hardly ever go and see about it. Either I am loath to leave her, or I see she's lonely by herself. And I used to think that life before marriage did not count, was nothing much, but that after marriage life began in earnest. And now it will soon be three months and I have never spent my days more idly and unprofitably. No, this won't do; I must turn over a new leaf. Of course, it's not her fault. There is nothing to reproach her with. I ought to have been firmer and asserted my masculine independence. This way I shall get into bad habits, and encourage her to ... Of course it's not her fault,' he said to himself.

But it is difficult for anyone who is dissatisfied not to blame someone else, especially the person nearest, for his discontent, and the vague idea came into Levin's head that though she herself was not to blame (she could never be to blame for anything), it was the fault of her frivolous, shallow upbringing. 'Take that fool Tcharsky, for instance! She wanted, I know, to stop him, but did not know how. Yes, except for her interest in the house (that she has), except for her clothes and her embroidery, she has no real interests. She does not care about my work, or the estate, or the peasants, or music, though she's rather good at it, or reading. She does nothing and is quite content.' In his heart

Levin criticized this, and did not as yet understand that she was preparing herself for the period of activity which was to come to her
when she would be wife to her husband and mistress of the house, at
the same time bearing, nursing, and bringing up her children. He did
not realize that she was instinctively aware of this and, preparing herself for her gigantic task, did not reproach herself for the moments of
idleness and happy love that she enjoyed now while gaily building her
nest for the future.

16

WHEN Levin went upstairs, his wife was sitting near the new silver
samovar behind the new tea service, reading a letter from Dolly, with
whom she kept up a brisk and regular correspondence. She had made
old Agatha Mihalovna sit at a little table with a cup of tea she had
poured out for her.

'You see, your lady's settled me here, told me to sit a little with her,'
said Agatha Mihalovna, with an affectionate smile in Kitty's direction.

In these words of Agatha Mihalovna, Levin read the final act of the
drama which had been enacted of late between her and Kitty. He saw
that, in spite of Agatha Mihalovna's feelings being hurt by a new mistress taking the reins of government out of her hands, Kitty had conquered and made her love her.

'Here, I opened your letter too,' said Kitty, handing him an illiter-
ate-looking letter. 'I think it's from that woman, your brother's ...
I did not read it through. And this is from home, and from Dolly.
What do you think? Dolly took Grisha and Tanya to a children's
party at the Sarmatskys'. Tanya went as a French marquise.'

But Levin was not listening. Flushing, he took Maria Nikolayevna's
letter and began to read it. This was the second letter he had received
from his brother's former mistress. In the first she had written that his
brother had driven her away for no fault of hers, adding with touching simplicity that though she was in want again she did not ask for
anything, or wish for anything, but that the thought that Nikolai
Dmitrich would come to grief without her, his health being so bad,
was killing her, and she begged his brother to look after him. This time
she wrote differently. She had found Nikolai Dmitrich in Moscow,
gone to live with him again, and together they had left for a provincial

town, where he had received a post in the Government service. But that he had quarrelled with his chief, and was on his way back to Moscow, only he had been taken so ill on the way that it was doubtful if he would ever leave his bed again, she wrote. 'He has always talked of you, and, besides, there is no more money left.'

'Read this; Dolly writes about you,' Kitty began with a smile, but she stopped suddenly, noticing the changed expression on her husband's face.

'What is it? What is the matter?'

'She writes that my brother Nikolai is at death's door. I shall go to him.'

Kitty's face changed at once. Thoughts of Tanya as a marquise, of Dolly, all vanished.

'When will you go?' she said.

'To-morrow.'

'And I'll come with you, may I?'

'Kitty! Really! What an idea!' he said reproachfully.

'What do you mean?' she asked, hurt that he should seem to take her suggestion unwillingly and be vexed with it. 'Why shouldn't I go? I shan't be in your way. I ...'

'I have to go because my brother is dying,' said Levin. 'But why should you ...'

'Why? For the same reason as you.'

'Even at a moment of such gravity for me she only thinks of how dull it will be for her alone here,' reflected Levin. And this subterfuge in connexion with something so important infuriated him.

'It's out of the question,' he said sternly.

Agatha Mihalovna, seeing that it was coming to a quarrel, quietly put down her cup and went out. Kitty did not even notice her. The tone in which her husband had spoken the last words wounded her, particularly because he evidently did not believe what she had said.

'And I tell you that if you go, I shall go with you. Most certainly!' she said with angry haste. 'Why is it out of the question? What makes you say it's out of the question?'

'Because the Lord knows how I shall get there, and what sort of inns I shall have to put up at. You would be a hindrance to me,' said Levin, endeavouring to be cool.

'Not at all. I don't want anything. Where you can go, I can ...'

'Well, if only because that woman is there, with whom you can't associate.'

'I don't know and don't care to know who's there and what. I know that my husband's brother is dying, and that my husband is going to him, and that I am going with my husband to …'

'Kitty! Don't be angry! But just think a little – this is such a serious time that I can't bear to think that you should bring your weakness into it, your dislike of being left alone. If you are afraid of feeling lonely, well, go to Moscow for a while!'

'There, you *always* ascribe mean, contemptible motives to me!' she burst out with tears of resentment and fury. 'I didn't mean – it wasn't weakness, it wasn't … I feel it's my duty to be with my husband when he is in trouble, but you want to hurt me on purpose, you just don't want to understand …'

'No, this is dreadful! To be such a slave!' cried Levin getting up, unable to restrain his annoyance any longer. But in the same second he was conscious that he was beating himself.

'Then why did you marry? You could have been free. Why did you, if you regret it?' she said, jumping up and running away into the drawing-room.

When he went after her, he found her sobbing.

He began to speak, striving to find words not to dissuade her but simply to pacify her. But she would not listen and would not agree to any of his arguments. He bent over her and took her hand, which resisted him. He kissed her hand, kissed her hair, kissed her hand again – still she was silent. At last, when he took her face in both his hands and said 'Kitty!' she suddenly recovered herself, and, after she had shed a few more tears, they made it up.

It was settled that they should start together on the following day. Levin told his wife that he believed she wanted to go simply in order to be of use, agreed that there would be no harm in her seeing Maria Nikolayevna at his brother's bedside, but he went dissatisfied at the bottom of his heart with her and with himself. He was dissatisfied with her because she could not bring herself to let him go when it was necessary (and how strange to think that he, who such a short time ago had hardly dared to believe in the happiness of her loving him, now was unhappy because she loved him too much!); and dissatisfied with himself for not having stood his ground. Still less could he with the least conviction agree that it did not matter if she came in contact with the woman who lived with his brother, and he was appalled to think of all the encounters that might take place. The mere idea of his wife, his Kitty, in the same room with a common wench set him shuddering with repulsion and horror.

17

THE inn in the country town where Nikolai Levin lay ill was one of those provincial establishments that are constructed on the latest improved model, with the best of intentions of cleanliness, comfort, and even elegance, but which are speedily converted by the public that patronizes them into filthy pot-houses with pretensions to modern improvements, these very pretensions making them worse than the old-fashioned kind that were frankly dirty. The hotel in question had already reached this stage: everything – the soldier in a filthy uniform smoking at the front door and supposed to be a hall-porter, the dismal and unpleasant ornamental iron staircase, the free-and-easy waiter in a dirty frockcoat, the common dining-room with a dusty bouquet of wax flowers adorning the table, the dirt, dust, and slovenliness everywhere, together with a sort of up-to-date, self-complacent railway bustle all produced a most depressing effect on the Levins after their fresh home life, especially as the air of artificiality about the hotel was so out of keeping with what awaited them.

As is invariably the case, after they had been asked what they wanted to pay for rooms, it appeared that there was not a single decent one to be had: one good room was occupied by a railway inspector, another by a lawyer from Moscow, a third by Princess Astafyev from the country. There was just one dirty room vacant, but they were promised that the one adjoining it would be free by the evening. Annoyed with his wife because his expectations were being realized – that, at the moment of arrival, when his heart throbbed with anxiety to know his brother's condition, he should have to be seeing after her, instead of rushing straight to his brother – Levin conducted her to the room assigned to them.

'Go along, go along!' she said, giving him a timid, guilty look.

He went out without a word, and at once stumbled over Maria Nikolayevna, who had heard of his arrival and had not dared to go in to see him. She was just the same as when he saw her in Moscow – the same woollen dress with no cuffs or collar, and the same good-naturedly stupid expression on her pock-marked face that had grown a little fuller.

'Well? How is he? What is it?'

'Very bad. He can't get up. He has been expecting you all the time. He ... You ... Are you with your wife?'

For a moment Levin did not understand the cause of her embarrassment, but she immediately enlightened him.

'I'll go away – I'll go down to the kitchen,' she got out. 'He will be pleased. He heard about it, and knows your lady, and remembers her abroad.'

Levin realized that she was referring to his wife, and did not know what to say.

'Come along, let us go!' he said.

But he had hardly gone a step before the door opened and Kitty peeped out. Levin crimsoned with shame and vexation that his wife should put herself and him in such an awkward situation; but Maria Nikolayevna crimsoned still more. She shrank into herself and flushed till her eyes filled with tears, and clutching the ends of her kerchief in both hands began twisting them in her red fingers, not knowing what to say or do.

Levin caught an expression of eager curiosity in Kitty's eyes as she looked at this woman, so terrible and incomprehensible to her; but it did not last a moment.

'Well, how is he? How is he?' she said, turning first to her husband and then to Maria Nikolayevna.

'But we can't stand talking here in the corridor!' Levin said with an angry look at a gentleman who was walking jauntily down the passage, ostensibly on business of his own.

'Well, then, come in,' said Kitty to Maria Nikolayevna, who had recovered herself; but observing the look of dismay on her husband's face she added quickly, 'or go on – you go, and send for me afterwards.' She turned back into her room, and Levin went to his brother.

He had not in the least expected what he saw and felt when he reached his brother's side. He had imagined he would find him in that state of self-deception so common with consumptives and which had struck him so much at the time of his brother's visit in the autumn. He had expected to find the physical signs of the approach of death more marked – that his brother would be weaker and more emaciated even, but still in the same sort of condition generally. He had expected to experience the same distress at the loss of a beloved brother and the same horror in the presence of death as he had felt then, only in a greater degree. And he had prepared himself for this; but what he found was utterly different.

In the dirty little room, the painted dado round the walls filthy with spittle, separated by a thin partition from the next room from which issued the sound of voices, the atmosphere evil-smelling and stifling, on a bed drawn away from the wall lay a body covered with a quilt. This body had one arm outside the quilt, and the huge wrist, like a rake, seemed in some incomprehensible way to be attached to a long, thin spindle of an arm smooth from the wrist to the elbow. The head lay sideways on the pillow. Levin could see the thin hair wet with perspiration on the temples, and the drawn, transparent forehead.

'It can't be that this awful body is my brother Nikolai?' thought Levin. But he went closer, saw the face, and doubt became impossible. In spite of the dreadful change in the face, Levin had only to glance at those eager eyes lifted at his approach, to notice the slight twitching of the mouth under the clammy moustache, to realize the frightful truth that this apparent corpse was his living brother.

The glittering eyes looked severely and reproachfully at the brother as he drew near. And immediately this glance established a living relationship between living beings. Levin at once felt the reproach in the eyes directed on him, and remorse at his own happiness.

When Constantine took his hand, Nikolai smiled. It was a faint, scarcely perceptible smile, and the stern expression of the eyes did not change.

'You did not expect to find me like this,' he said, speaking with difficulty.

'Yes ... No,' said Levin, hesitating over his words. 'Why didn't you let me know sooner, I mean at the time of my wedding? I made inquiries everywhere.'

He was obliged to talk so as not to be silent, but he did not know what to say, especially as his brother made no reply, and simply stared without dropping his eyes, and evidently weighed the meaning of each word. Levin told his brother that his wife had come with him. Nikolai expressed pleasure, but said he was afraid of frightening her by his condition. A silence followed. Suddenly Nikolai stirred, and began to speak. From the expression of his face, Levin expected something of peculiar gravity and importance, but Nikolai began speaking of his health. He found fault with the doctor, regretted that he could not have a celebrated Moscow doctor, and Levin saw that he still had hopes of recovery.

Taking advantage of the first moment of silence, Levin got up, anxious to escape, if only for a minute, from his painful emotion, and said that he would go and fetch his wife.

'All right, and I'll have things cleaned up a bit here. It's dirty and stinking, I should think. Masha, tidy up the room,' the sick man said with an effort. 'And when you have finished, go away,' he added, with an inquiring look at his brother.

Levin made no answer. Going out into the corridor, he stopped. He had said he would fetch his wife, but now, taking stock of his own impressions, he decided that on the contrary he would do all he could to persuade her not to go in and see the sick man. 'Why should she suffer as well?' he thought.

'Well, how is he?' Kitty asked with a frightened face.

'Oh, it's awful, awful! What did you come for?' said Levin.

Kitty was silent for a few seconds, looking timidly and ruefully at her husband. Then she went up and took him by the elbow with both hands.

'Kostya, take me to him! It will be easier for us to bear it together. Just take me to him, take me, please, and then go away,' she began. 'Can't you understand that to see you, and not to see him, is much more painful for me. There I might be a help to you and to him. Please let me!' she besought her husband, as though her whole happiness depended on it.

Levin had to give in and, regaining his composure and quite forgetting about Maria Nikolayevna, he returned with Kitty to his brother.

Stepping lightly, and with repeated glances at her husband, showing him a brave face full of compassion, she entered the sick-room and, turning without haste, noiselessly closed the door. With inaudible steps she went quickly to the sick man's bedside and, approaching so that he had not to turn his head, she immediately clasped in her fresh, youthful hand his huge skeleton of a hand, pressed it, and began speaking to him in that unoffending, sympathetic, gently animated way natural to women.

'I remember you at Soden, though we were not acquainted,' she said. 'You little thought I was to be your sister?'

'I don't suppose you would have recognized me?' he asked with a smile that had lighted up his face at her entrance.

'Oh yes, I should. What a good thing you sent us word! Not a day has passed without Kostya's mentioning you and being anxious about you.'

But the sick man's interest did not last long.

Before she had finished speaking the stern, reproachful look of envy felt by the dying man for the living settled on his face again.

'I am afraid you are not very comfortable here,' she said, turning away from his steady gaze and looking about the room. 'We must ask for another room,' she said to her husband. 'He must be nearer us.'

18

LEVIN could not look calmly at his brother, could not be natural and calm in his presence. When he entered the sick-room, his eyes and his attention were unconsciously dimmed, and he could not see or distinguish the details of his brother's condition. He smelt the awful foul air, saw the dirt and disorder, the twisted way his brother lay, and heard the groans, and felt powerless to do anything to help. It never occurred to him to analyse the details of the sick man's situation, to consider how the body was lying under the quilt, how the emaciated legs and loins and spine were doubled up, and see if they could not be made more comfortable, whether something could not be done to make things, if not easier, at least less wretched. A cold shudder would creep down his back when he began to think of all these details. He was convinced beyond doubt that nothing could be done to prolong his brother's life or to alleviate his suffering, and the sick man was conscious of his brother's conviction that there was no help for him, and was exasperated. And this made Levin's lot still more painful. To be in the sick-room was torture to him, not to be there still worse. He went in and out on all sorts of pretexts, incapable of remaining alone.

But Kitty thought and felt and acted quite differently. On seeing the sick man, she was filled with pity for him. And pity in her womanly heart produced not the horror and loathing that it did in her husband but a need for action, a need to find out all the details of his condition and to remedy them. And since she had not the slightest doubt that it was her duty to help him, she had no doubt either that she could help him, and so she set to work without delay. The very details, the mere thought of which was enough to reduce her husband to terror, at once engaged her attention. She sent for the doctor, sent to the chemist's, set the maid who had come with her to help Maria Nikolayevna sweep and dust and scrub, and she herself washed and rinsed and spread something under the quilt. She ordered various things to be brought into the sick-room and others taken away. She herself went several times to and fro to her room, paying no heed to the people she met in the corridor, bringing back clean sheets, pillow-cases, towels, and shirts.

The waiter, who was busy serving a meal to a party of engineers in the dining-room, came several times at her summons with a surly ex-pression on his face, but she gave her orders with such gentle insist-ence that he could not help obeying them. Levin did not approve of all this: he did not believe that any good would come of it for the patient. Above all, he was afraid of the patient being irritated. But the sick man, though apparently indifferent to it all, was not angry but only abashed, and on the whole seemed rather interested in what was being done around him. Returning from the doctor, to whom Kitty had sent him, Levin opened the door and came upon the sick man, at Kitty's orders, having his nightshirt changed. The long white ridge of his spine with the enormous, prominent shoulder-blades and protrud-ing ribs and vertebrae was bare, and Maria Nikolayevna and the waiter were struggling with the sleeve of the nightshirt and could not get the long, limp arm into it. Kitty, who had quickly closed the door after Levin, was not looking that way; but the sick man groaned and she hurried over to him.

'Make haste!' she said.

'Don't come here,' muttered the sick man angrily. 'I can do it my-self ...'

'What say?' asked Maria Nikolayevna.

But Kitty had heard and understood that he felt embarrassed and uncomfortable that she should see him undressed.

'I'm not looking, I'm not looking!' she said, helping his arm in. 'Maria Nikolayevna, you come round this side; you do it,' she added.

'Please go and look in my handbag,' she went on, turning to her husband. 'You'll find a little bottle – you know, in the side pocket. Bring it, please. They'll be quite finished here by the time you come back.'

Returning with the bottle, Levin found the invalid lying back on his pillows and everything around him completely changed. The stuffy air was replaced by the smell of aromatic vinegar, which Kitty, pouting her lips and puffing out her rosy cheeks, was blowing through a little glass tube. There was not a speck of dust anywhere, and a mat had been put beside the bed. The medicine bottles and a carafe of water were neatly arranged on the table, on which was lying a pile of folded linen and Kitty's embroidery. On the other table by the patient's bed stood some kind of drink, powders, and a candle. The sick man himself, washed and combed, lying between clean sheets and propped up by high raised pillows, had on a clean nightshirt, its white collar fastened round his unnaturally thin neck. There was a new expression of hope on his face as he gazed steadily at Kitty, not taking his eyes off her.

The doctor Levin had fetched, and whom he had found at a club, was not the one who had been attending Nikolai, with whom the patient was dissatisfied. The new doctor took out a stethoscope and sounded the patient, shook his head, wrote a prescription, and left minute instructions about taking the medicine and about diet. He ordered raw or very lightly boiled eggs and seltzer water with warm milk at a certain temperature. After the doctor had gone, the sick man said something to his brother, of which Levin made out only the last words: '... your Katya', but by the way he looked at her Levin saw that he was praising her. He signed to Katya, as he called her, to come nearer.

'I feel much better already,' he said. 'Why, with you I should have got well long ago. How nice it feels!' He took her hand and raised it to his lips, but as though afraid she might not like it changed his mind, let it drop and only stroked it. Kitty took his hand in both hers and pressed it.

'Now turn me over on my left side and go to bed,' he murmured.

No one heard what he said, but Kitty understood. She understood because she was all the while on the watch for his needs.

'On the other side,' she said to her husband. 'He always sleeps on that side. Turn him over. I don't like calling the servants, and I can't lift him alone. Can you?' she asked Maria Nikolayevna.

'I'm afraid to,' answered Maria Nikolayevna.

Dreadful as it was to Levin to put his arms round that terrible body and grasp under the quilt the limbs he did not wish to remember, he submitted to his wife's influence, set his face into the determined expression she knew so well, and thrust his arms under the blanket. Despite his great strength he was amazed at the strange weight of those enfeebled limbs. While he was turning him over, conscious of the huge, emaciated arm round his neck, Kitty swiftly and quietly turned and beat the pillow, arranged the invalid's head and smoothed the thin hair that again clung to his temples.

The sick man kept his brother's hand in his own. Levin felt that he wanted to do something with his hand and was pulling it in some direction. Levin yielded with a sinking heart. Yes, he drew it to his lips and kissed it. Levin, shaking with sobs and unable to articulate a word, left the room.

19

'THOU hast hid these things from the wise and prudent, and hast revealed them unto babes.' So Levin thought about his wife as he talked with her that evening.

Levin thought of the Gospel text, not because he considered himself 'wise and prudent'. On the contrary, he did not, but he could not help knowing that he had more intellect than his wife and Agatha Mihalovna, and he could not help knowing that when he thought of death he thought with all the force of his intellect. He knew, too, that many great and virile minds, whose thoughts on death he had read, had brooded over it and yet did not know one hundredth part of what his wife and Agatha Mihalovna knew. Different as those two women were, Agatha Mihalovna and Katya, as his brother Nikolai called her and as Levin particularly liked to call her now, in this respect they were absolutely alike. Both knew, without a shadow of doubt, what sort of a thing was life and what death was, and though neither of them could have answered, or even have comprehended, the questions that presented themselves to Levin, they had no doubt of the significance of this event, and were precisely alike in their way of looking at it – a way they shared not only with each other but with millions of other people. The proof that they knew for a certainty the nature of death lay in the fact that they were never under an instant's uncertainty as to how to deal with the dying, and felt no fear. But Levin and others like him, though they might be able to say a good many things about death, obviously did not know anything about it since they were afraid of death and had no notion what to do in the presence of death.

Had Levin been alone now with his brother Nikolai, he would have looked at him with terror, and would have sat waiting in still greater terror, unable to think of anything else to do.

More than that, he did not know what to say, how to look, how to move. To talk of irrelevant things seemed to him shocking, impossible. To talk of death and depressing subjects was likewise impossible. To keep silent, equally so. 'I am afraid to look at him in case he thinks I am watching him. If I don't look, he will imagine my thoughts are elsewhere. If I walk on tiptoe, he won't like it: to tread firmly seems wrong.' But Kitty evidently did not think, and had no time to think, about herself. Occupied with the patient, she seemed to have a clear idea of something, and so all went well. She would even talk to him about herself and about her wedding, smile, sympathize, and pet him, cite cases of recovery, and all went well; so then she must know what she was about. The surest sign that her behaviour and Agatha Mihalovna's was not instinctive, animal, irrational, was that neither was satisfied simply with nursing the patient and attending to his physical comfort, but both demanded something more important for him that had nothing in common with bodily conditions. Agatha Mihalovna, speaking of the old man that had died, had said: 'Well, God be praised! He took the sacrament and received the last unction. God grant each one of us to die like him!' In the same way Kitty, besides all her care about linen, bedsores, cooling drink, found time the very first day to persuade the sick man of the necessity of taking the sacrament and receiving the last unction.

On returning to their two rooms for the night, Levin sat with bowed head, not knowing what to do. He could not think of supper, of getting ready for bed, of considering what they were to do – he could not even talk to his wife: it seemed to him like sacrilege. Kitty, on the contrary, was more active than usual. She was even more animated than usual. She ordered supper to be brought, unpacked their things herself, helped the maid to make the beds, and did not even forget to sprinkle them with insect powder. She was in the same state of excitement, when the reasoning powers act quickly, as a man before battle, in conflict, in the dangerous and decisive moments of life – those moments when a man proves once and for all his mettle, and shows that his past life has not been lived in vain but has been a preparation for these moments.

She worked swiftly and well, and before midnight everything was arranged, tidy and neat, so that the hotel rooms began to look like home and her own room: the beds were made, brushes, combs, and mirrors spread out, table-napkins put ready.

Levin felt that it would be unpardonable to eat, to sleep, or even talk, and that every movement he made was unseemly. Kitty, however, arranged the brushes, and did it all in such a way that nothing jarred. But neither of them could eat, and it was a long time before they got to sleep – it was a long time even before they went to bed.

'I am very glad I persuaded him to receive extreme unction tomorrow,' she said, sitting in her dressing-jacket before her folding looking-glass, combing her soft, fragrant hair with a fine comb. 'I have never been present before, but Mama told me prayers are said for recovery.'

'Do you really think he can recover?' asked Levin, watching the narrow parting at the back of her round little head which disappeared every time she drew the comb forward.

'I asked the doctor. He says he cannot last more than three days. But how can they be sure? I'm very glad, anyway, that I persuaded him,' she said, peering at her husband through her hair. 'Everything is possible,' she added with the peculiar, rather sly expression that came over her face whenever she spoke of religion.

Since their conversation about religion during their engagement neither had ever started a discussion on the subject, but she regularly went to church, said her prayers and so on, always with the unvarying conviction that it was the necessary thing to do. In spite of his assertion to the contrary, she was firmly persuaded that he was as much a Christian as herself, and indeed a far better one; and that all that he said about it was just one of his funny masculine freaks, like his jest about her *broderie anglaise* when he said that respectable people mend holes but she made them on purpose, and so on.

'Yes, you see, that woman, Maria Nikolayevna, did not know how to manage all this,' said Levin. 'And ... I must own I'm very, very glad you came. You are purity itself, and ...' He took her hand and did not kiss it (to kiss her hand with death so near seemed to him improper); he merely squeezed it with a penitent air, looking at her brightening eyes.

'It would have been wretched for you alone,' she said and, raising her arms high to hide the flush of pleasure on her cheeks, she twisted her braided hair and pinned it on the nape of her neck. 'No,' she went on, 'she not did know how. ... Fortunately I learned a lot at Soden.'

'Surely there are not people there as ill as he is?'

'Some were worse.'

'What is so awful to me is that I can't help seeing him as he was when he was young. ... You would not believe what a charming lad he was, but I did not understand him then.'

'I can quite, quite believe it. I feel so strongly how we *might have been* friends,' and she looked round at her husband, distressed at what she had said, and the tears came into her eyes.

'Yes, *might have been*,' he said sadly. 'He is the kind of man of whom people say they were not born for this world.'

'But we have a difficult time before us – we must go to bed,' said Kitty, glancing at her tiny watch.

20

DEATH

THE next day the sacrament and extreme unction were administered to the sick man. Nikolai prayed fervently during the ceremony. In his large eyes, fastened upon the icon which was set out on a card-table covered with a coloured napkin, there was such passionate entreaty and hope that Levin could not bear to look at them. Levin knew that this passionate entreaty and hope would only make the parting from life, which he so loved, more difficult in the end. Levin knew his brother and the workings of his mind: he knew that his scepticism came not because life was easier for him without faith. His religious beliefs had been shaken step by step by the theories of modern science concerning the phenomena of the universe; and so Levin knew that this present return was not a valid, reasoned one but simply a temporary, interested return to faith in a desperate hope of recovery. Levin knew, too, that Kitty had strengthened this hope by accounts of the marvellous recoveries she had heard of. All this Levin knew, and it was agonizingly painful to him to behold the imploring, hopeful eyes, and the emaciated wrist of the hand lifted with difficulty to touch the drawn skin of the forehead in the sign of the cross, to behold the protruding shoulder-blades and the hollow, rattling chest, which could no longer hold the life for which the sick man was praying. During the sacrament Levin prayed, too, and did what he had done a thousand times before, unbeliever that he was. Addressing himself to God, he said: 'If Thou dost exist, heal this man (it would not be the first time such a thing has happened), and Thou wilt save him and me.'

After the anointing the sick man suddenly felt much better. He did not cough once in the course of an hour, smiled and kissed Kitty's hand, thanking her with tears in his eyes, and saying he was comfortable, had no pain anywhere, and that already his appetite and strength were returning. He even raised himself when his soup was brought, and asked for a cutlet as well. Hopelessly ill as he was, obvious as it was at a glance that he could not recover, Levin and Kitty were for that hour both in the same state of excitement, happy yet fearful of being mistaken.

'Is he better?'

'Yes, much.'

'Wonderful, isn't it?'

'Why wonderful?'

'Anyway, he's better,' they said in a whisper, smiling to one another.

The illusion did not last long. The sick man fell into a quiet sleep, but half an hour later was awakened by his cough. And immediately every hope fled from those about him and from the sick man himself. The reality of his suffering crushed the last glimmer or even recollection of hope in Levin and Kitty, and in the sick man himself.

Ignoring what he had believed in half an hour before, as though ashamed even to recall it, he asked for iodine to inhale in a bottle covered with perforated paper. Levin handed him the bottle, and his brother at once fixed him with the same look of passionate hope with which he had received extreme unction, as though demanding him to confirm the doctor's words that inhaling iodine worked wonders.

'Katya isn't here?' he asked in a hoarse whisper, glancing round while Levin reluctantly assented to the doctor's words. 'No, then I can say it ... I went through that farce for her sake. She is so sweet; but you and I can't deceive ourselves. This is what I pin my faith to,' he said and, squeezing the bottle in his bony hand, he began breathing over it.

Towards eight o'clock that evening Levin and his wife were drinking tea in their room when Maria Nikolayevna rushed in breathless. She was pale and her lips were trembling.

'He is dying!' she gasped. 'I'm afraid he will die this minute.'

They both ran to him. He had raised himself and was leaning with one elbow on the bed, his long back bent and his head hanging low.

'How do you feel?' Levin asked in a whisper, after a moment of silence.

'I feel I'm going,' Nikolai said, speaking with an effort but extremely distinctly, screwing the words out of himself. He did not raise his head, but only looked up, his eyes trying unsuccessfully to reach his brother's face. 'Katya, go away!' he added.

Levin jumped up, and with a peremptory whisper made her leave the room.

'I'm going,' he said again.

'What makes you think so?' asked Levin, for something to say.

'Because I'm going,' he repeated, as if he had taken a liking for the phrase. 'It's the end.'

Maria Nikolayevna approached the bed.

'You had better lie down: you'd be easier,' she said.

'I shall lie down soon enough,' he pronounced slowly, 'when I'm dead,' he added derisively, wrathfully. 'Well, lay me down if you like.'

Levin laid his brother on his back, sat down beside him and, hardly daring to breathe, gazed at his face. The dying man lay with closed eyes but the muscles of his forehead twitched every now and then, as with one thinking deeply and intently. Levin involuntarily meditated with him on what was taking place now in his brother but in spite of all his efforts of mind to follow he saw by the expression of that calm, stern face and the play of the muscle above one eyebrow that something was becoming clearer and clearer to the dying man which for Levin remained as obscure as ever.

'Yes, yes, that is so!' slowly murmured the dying man, pausing between the words. 'Wait a moment.' Again he was silent. 'Right!' he suddenly said in a slow tone of relief, as if all had become clear to him. 'Oh God!' he muttered with a heavy sigh.

Maria Nikolayevna felt his feet. 'Growing cold,' she whispered.

For a long while – a very long while, it seemed to Levin – the sick man lay motionless. But he was still alive, and from time to time he sighed. Levin was already exhausted from mental strain. He felt that with all his efforts of mind he could not understand what it was that was *right*. It seemed to him that he was already lagging far behind his dying brother. He could no longer even think of the problem of death itself: involuntarily thoughts of what he would have to do directly floated through his brain – soon he would be closing the dead man's eyes, dressing him, ordering the coffin. And, strange to say, he felt quite indifferent, and experienced neither sorrow nor a sense of loss, still less of pity for his brother. If he had any feeling for his brother at that moment, it was rather one of envy for the knowledge the dying man now possessed that was denied to him.

For a long time he sat on, leaning over Nikolai and expecting the end. But the end did not come. The door opened and Kitty appeared. Levin got up to stop her. But at that moment he heard the dying man move.

'Don't go away,' said Nikolai, and stretched out his hand. Levin took it in his own, and with his other hand impatiently motioned his wife away.

With the dying man's hand in his, he sat for half an hour, an hour, then another hour. He had left off thinking of death. He wondered what Kitty was doing, who occupied the next room, whether the house the doctor lived in was his own. He longed for food and sleep. Carefully disengaging his hand, he felt his brother's feet. They were cold, but the sick man was still breathing. Levin tried again to go out on tiptoe, but the sick man stirred again and said, 'Don't go away.'

Day began to dawn: the sick man's condition was unchanged. Levin gently withdrew his hand and, without looking at the dying man, went to his own room and fell asleep. When he awoke, instead of the news he expected, that his brother was dead, he heard that the sick man had returned to his earlier condition. Nikolai was again able to sit up, and coughed, ate, and talked, no longer of death, but of his hopes of recovery; and he was even more irritable and morose than before. No one, neither his brother nor Kitty, could soothe him. He was angry with everybody, and abused them all, blaming them for his sufferings and demanding that they should get a celebrated doctor from Moscow. Whenever he was asked how he felt, he replied with the same expression of malice and reproach:

'I'm suffering terrible, intolerable agony!'

The sick man suffered more and more, especially from bedsores, which would no longer heal. His irritability with those about him increased, and he kept on reproaching them for everything, and particularly because they did not bring the doctor from Moscow. Kitty tried her best to make him more comfortable, to pacify him, but in vain, and Levin could see that she was worn out physically and mentally, though she would not admit it. The sense of death they had all felt on the night Levin had been sent for and Nikolai had taken leave of life had given way to something else. They all knew that he must inevitably die soon, that he was half dead already, and they had but one desire – that the end might come as soon as possible; but this they concealed and went on handing him medicines and trying to discover new ones, calling doctors, and deceiving him and themselves and one another. It was all a lie, a repulsive, outrageous, blasphemous lie. And Levin, both because of his nature and because he loved the dying man more than the others did, felt it the most painfully.

Levin, who had long wished to reconcile his two brothers, if only in face of death, had written to Sergei Ivanovich and, on receiving an answer from him, read his letter to the sick man. Koznyshev wrote that he could not come himself, and in touching terms he begged his brother's forgiveness.

The sick man made no comment.

'What shall I write him?' asked Levin. 'You are not angry with him, I hope?'

'No, not in the least,' Nikolai answered, irritated at the question. 'Write and tell him to send me a doctor.'

Three more days of agony followed, the sick man's condition remaining unchanged. A longing for his death was now felt by everyone who saw him – by the hotel servants, the proprietor, all the people staying in the hotel, and the doctor and Maria Nikolayevna and Kitty and Levin. The sick man alone did not express this feeling, but on the contrary he grumbled because the doctor had not been fetched, and continued taking medicines and talking of life. Only in rare moments, when opium made him forget the incessant pain for an instant, he would drowsily utter what was even more intense in his heart than in all the others, 'Oh, if only it were over!' or 'When will this end?'

His sufferings, growing more and more severe, did their work and prepared him for death. He could not lie comfortably in any position, could not for a moment forget himself. There was no part of his body, no limb, that did not ache and cause him agony. Even the memories, the impressions, the thoughts within this body aroused in him now the same aversion as the body itself. The sight of other people, their remarks, his own reminiscences – it was all a torture to him. Those about him felt this and instinctively did not allow themselves to move about or speak freely, or express a wish of their own in his presence. All his life was merged in the one feeling of suffering and desire to be rid of it.

It was evident that that transformation was happening to him that would make him look upon death as the fulfilment of his desires, as happiness. Hitherto each individual desire aroused by suffering or privation, such as hunger, fatigue, thirst, had brought enjoyment when gratified. But now privation and suffering were not followed by relief, and the effort to obtain relief only occasioned fresh suffering. And so all desires were merged in one – the desire to be rid of all this pain and from its source, the body. But he had no words to express this desire for deliverance, and so he did not speak of it, but from force of habit asked for the things that had once given him comfort. 'Turn me over on the other side,' he would say, and immediately after ask to be put back again. 'Give me some beef tea. Take away the beef tea. Talk of something: why are you all silent?' And directly they began to talk, he would close his eyes, and would show weariness, indifference, and loathing.

On the tenth day after their arrival in the town, Kitty was unwell. She had a headache, vomited, and could not leave her bed all the morning.

The doctor opined that she was tired and run down with the strain, and prescribed rest and quiet.

After dinner, however, Kitty got up and went to the sick man's room as usual, taking her embroidery. He looked at her sternly when she entered, and smiled scornfully when she said she had been unwell. That day he was continually blowing his nose, and moaning piteously.

'How do you feel?' she asked him.

'Worse,' he articulated with difficulty. 'The pain is bad.'

'The pain where?'

'All over.'

'The end will come to-day, you see,' said Maria Nikolayevna. Though it was said in a whisper, the sick man, whose hearing as Levin had noticed was very acute, must have heard. Levin said 'Hush!', and looked round at the sick man. Nikolai had heard, but the words produced no impression on him. His eyes had still the same intense, reproachful look.

'What makes you think so?' Levin asked her, when she followed him out into the corridor.

'He has begun picking at himself,' said Maria Nikolayevna.

'How do you mean?'

'Like this,' she said, pulling at the folds of her woollen dress.

Levin had noticed, indeed, how all that day the patient kept clutching at himself as if trying to tear something away.

Maria Nikolayevna's predictions came true. By the evening Nikolai could no longer lift his hands, and lay staring in front of him with a fixed, concentrated gaze. Even when his brother or Kitty bent over him, so that he could see them, he took no notice but continued looking in the same direction. Kitty sent for the priest to read the prayers for the dying.

While the priest was reading the prayers, the dying man showed no sign of life. His eyes were closed. Levin, Kitty, and Maria Nikolayevna stood at the bedside. Before the priest had finished, the dying man stretched, sighed, and opened his eyes. When he had come to the end of the prayer, the priest put the cross to the cold forehead, then slowly wrapped it in his stole and, after standing in silence for a minute or two, touched the huge, bloodless hand that was turning cold.

'He is gone,' said the priest, and made to move away; but suddenly there was a faint stir in the clammy moustaches of the dying man, and from the depths of his chest came the words, sharp and distinct in the stillness:

'Not quite ... Soon.'

A moment later the face brightened, a smile appeared under the moustaches, and the women who had gathered round began carefully laying out the corpse.

The sight of his brother, and the presence of death, revived in Levin that sense of horror in face of the enigma, together with the nearness and inevitability of death, which had seized him that autumn evening when his brother had arrived in the country. Only now the feeling was still stronger than before – he felt even more incapable of apprehending the meaning of death, and its inevitability rose up before him more terrible than ever. But now, thanks to his wife's presence, that feeling did not reduce him to despair. In spite of death he felt the need of life and love. Love saved him from despair, and this love, under the menace of despair, had become still stronger and purer.

Scarcely had the one mystery of death enacted itself before his eyes, when another mystery, equally unfathomable, had arisen, calling him to love and to life.

The doctor confirmed his surmise about Kitty. Her indisposition was due to pregnancy.

21

FROM the moment Karenin understood from his interviews with Betsy and with Oblonsky that nothing was demanded of him except that he should leave his wife alone, without burdening her with his presence, and that his wife herself desired this, he felt so distraught that he was unable to arrive at any decision of himself. He did not know what he wanted now, and, putting himself in the hands of those who took so much pleasure in arranging his affairs, he met everything with unqualified assent. It was only after Anna had left the house and the English governess sent to ask whether she should dine with him or separately by herself that he realized his position for the first time, and was appalled by it.

The most painful part of it was his inability to connect and reconcile the past with what was now. It was not the past when he had lived happily with his wife that troubled him. The transition from that past to a knowledge of his wife's infidelity he had lived through miserably already: it had been a difficult time, but a comprehensible one. Had his wife left him then, after informing him of her unfaithfulness, he would have been wounded, unhappy, but he would not have felt himself in such a hopeless, unintelligible impasse. He could not now at all reconcile his recent act of forgiveness, his emotion, his love for his sick wife and for the other man's child with the present position – that is, with the fact that, as if in return for all this, he now found himself alone, put to shame, a laughing-stock, unwanted and despised by all.

For the first two days after his wife's departure Karenin received applicants for assistance, saw his private secretary, drove to the committee and took his dinner in the dining-room as usual. He did not explain to himself why he was doing it, but during those two days he strained every nerve to appear composed and even indifferent. Answering the servants' inquiries as to what should be done with Anna's rooms and belongings, he had made the greatest efforts to behave as though he had been prepared for what had taken place and saw nothing out of the ordinary in it, and in this he succeeded: no one could

533

have detected any signs of despair. But on the third day of her departure, when Korney brought him a fashionable milliner's bill which Anna had forgotten to pay, and informed him that the shopman had come in person, Karenin had him shown up.

'Excuse me, your excellency, for taking the liberty of troubling you. But if you wish us to address ourselves to her excellency would you kindly oblige us with her address?'

Karenin pondered, as it seemed to the man, and all at once turned away and sat down at the table. Letting his head sink into his hands, he sat thus for a long while, made several attempts to speak, and stopped short.

Feeling for his master, Korney asked the man to call again another time. Left alone, Karenin recognized that he had not the strength to keep up the semblance of firmness and composure any longer. He gave orders for the carriage that was awaiting him to be sent away, said he would receive no one, and did not appear for dinner.

He felt that he could not endure the general shock of contempt and exasperation which he had distinctly read on the face of the man from the shop and of Korney, and of everyone, without exception, whom he had met during the last two days. He felt that he could not divert people's hate from himself, because that hate was not caused by something fundamentally wrong in himself (in that case he could have tried to do better), but because he was disgracefully and odiously unhappy. He knew that people would be merciless for the very reason that his heart was lacerated. He felt that his fellow-men would destroy him, as dogs kill some poor cur maimed and howling with pain. He knew that his only salvation lay in hiding his wounds, and he had instinctively tried to do this for two days, but now he no longer had the strength to keep up the unequal struggle.

His despair was intensified by the consciousness that he was utterly alone in his misery. Not only in Petersburg but in the whole world there was not a single person to whom he might unburden himself, who would feel for him, not as a high official, not as a member of society, but simply as a suffering human being.

Karenin had grown up an orphan. There were two brothers. They did not remember their father, and their mother died when Alexei Alexandrovich was ten years old. Their means were small. Their uncle, Karenin, a distinguished Government official and at one time a favourite of the late Emperor, had brought them up.

Having finished with honours both at school and university, Karenin had, with his uncle's help, at once made a conspicuous start in the service, and from that time forward he had devoted himself exclusively to political ambition. Neither at school nor at the university, nor afterwards with his colleagues, did he make any close friends. His brother had been his only intimate, but he had been in the Foreign Service and had always lived abroad, where he died shortly after Alexei Alexandrovich's marriage.

At the time when Karenin was governor of a province, Anna's aunt, a wealthy provincial lady, had thrown him into the society of her niece – though he was not young in years, he was young to be a governor – and placed him in such a position that he had either to declare himself or leave the town. For a long while Karenin hesitated. There were then as many arguments for the step as against it, and no overwhelming consideration to outweigh his invariable rule of abstaining when in doubt. Anna's aunt, however, managed to insinuate, through a common acquaintance, that he had already compromised the girl and was in honour bound to make her an offer. He made the offer, and bestowed on his betrothed and wife all the feeling of which he was capable.

His attachment to Anna took away the last need he might have felt for any other intimacy. And now among all his acquaintances he had not one friend. He had plenty of so-called connexions, but no friendships. Karenin had plenty of people whom he could invite to dinner, interest in any of his projects, whose influence he could reckon upon for anyone he wished to help, with whom he could freely discuss other people's business and affairs of state; but his relations with these people were confined to this official domain, from which habit made it impossible to depart. There was one man, a fellow student at the university, with whom he had subsequently become friendly and to whom he might have talked about his personal trouble; but this friend had a teaching post in a remote part of the country. Of the people in Petersburg the nearest to him and most likely were his chief secretary and his doctor.

Sludin, his secretary, was an unaffected, intelligent, good-hearted, upright man, and Karenin was aware that he was kindly disposed towards him personally. But the five years of their official relationship had put a barrier in the way of any intimate talk between them.

After signing the papers brought to him, Karenin had sat for a long while in silence, glancing at Sludin. He made several attempts to speak, but could not get started. He had rehearsed the opening: 'You have heard of my misfortune?' But he ended by saying, as usual: 'Then you'll get this ready for me?', and letting him go.

The other person, the doctor, was also well-inclined towards him; but it had long been agreed between them, though they had not expressed it in words, that they were both overwhelmed with work and always in a hurry.

Of his women friends, including the foremost among them, the Countess Lydia Ivanovna, Karenin never thought. All women, simply as women, were dreadful and distasteful to him now.

22

KARENIN had forgotten the Countess Lydia Ivanovna, but she had not forgotten him. At the bitterest moment of his lonely despair she arrived at the house and, without waiting to be announced, walked straight into his study. She found him as he was sitting with his head in both hands.

'*J'ai forcé la consigne* – I've forced my way in!' she said, entering rapidly and breathing hard with excitement and haste. 'I have heard it all, Alexei Alexandrovich! My dear friend!' she went on, warmly clasping his hand in both hers and gazing with her fine pensive eyes into his.

Karenin, frowning, got up and, disengaging his hand, pushed a chair forward for her.

'Won't you sit down, Countess? I am not "at home" because I am not well,' he said, and his lips twitched.

'My dear friend!' the Countess Lydia Ivanovna repeated, never taking her eyes off him, and suddenly the inner corners of her eyebrows rose, describing a triangle on her forehead, and her plain sallow face became plainer still; but Karenin felt that she was sorry for him and on the point of tears. And he, too, was moved: he seized her plump hand and proceeded to kiss it.

'My dear friend!' she said in an unsteady voice. 'You must not give way to your grief. Your sorrow is great, but you must find consolation.'

'I am broken, crushed, completely unmanned!' said Karenin, letting go her hand but still gazing into her eyes that were full of tears.

536

'And the worst of it is that I can find no support anywhere, not even in myself.'

'You will find support,' she said with a sigh. 'Seek it – not in me, though I beg you to believe in my friendship. Our support is love, that love that He has vouchsafed us. His yoke is light,' she went on, with the ecstatic look Karenin knew so well. 'He will be your support and succour.'

Though it was evident that she was touched by her own lofty sentiments, which had a flavour of that new, ecstatic, mystical exaltation which had recently spread in Petersburg, and which Karenin considered excessive, still it was pleasant to him to hear this now.

'I am weak. I am crushed. I foresaw none of this, and now I don't understand it.'

'My dear friend,' said Lydia Ivanovna once more.

'It's not the loss of what no longer exists – it is not that,' pursued Karenin. 'I do not grieve for that. But I cannot help feeling humiliated before other people at the position I am in. It is wrong, but I can't help it, I can't help it.'

'Not you it was who performed that high act of forgiveness, at which I was filled with rapture, and everyone else too, but He who dwells within your heart,' said the Countess Lydia Ivanovna, turning up her eyes ecstatically, 'and so you cannot be ashamed of your act.'

Karenin frowned and, crooking his hands, began cracking the joints of his fingers.

'One must know all the facts,' he said in his thin voice. 'There are limits to a man's strength, Countess, and I have reached the limits of mine. The whole day I have had to spend making arrangements, arrangements about household matters arising –' (he laid special stress on the word *arising*) 'from my new, solitary situation. The servants, the governess, bills. ... These petty flames have devoured me, I have not the strength to endure it. At dinner ... yesterday I very nearly got up from the table. I could not bear the way my son looked at me. He did not ask the meaning of it all, but he wanted to, and I could not bear the look in his eyes. He was afraid to look at me, but that is not all ...' Karenin wanted to refer to the milliner's bill that had been brought to him, but his voice shook and he stopped. That bill on blue paper, for a bonnet and some ribbons, he could not recall without a rush of self-pity.

'I understand, my dear friend,' said the Countess Lydia Ivanovna. 'I understand it all. Succour and consolation you will find not in me, though I have come expressly to help you if I can. If I could take all these petty, humiliating cares off your shoulders ... I see a woman's word, a woman's guiding hand are needed. Will you entrust it to me?'

Silently and gratefully Karenin pressed her hand.

'We will take care of Seriozha together. Practical affairs are not my strong point. But I will set to work – I will be your housekeeper. Don't thank me. I do it not of myself ...'

'I cannot help thanking you.'

'But, my dear friend, do not give way to the feeling you were speaking about – of being ashamed of what is the highest degree of perfection in a Christian: "*he that humbleth himself shall be exalted*". And you cannot thank me. You must thank Him, and ask His help. In Him alone we find peace, comfort, salvation, and love,' she said, and, raising her eyes to heaven, she began praying, as Karenin gathered from her silence.

Karenin listened to her now, and those very expressions which had formerly seemed to him, if not distasteful, at least excessive, now seemed natural and consoling. Karenin had disliked this new ecstatic fervour. He was a sincere believer, interested in religion primarily in its political aspect, and this new teaching which ventured upon several novel interpretations, just because it paved the way for argument and analysis, was disagreeable to him on principle. He had hitherto adopted a cold and even antagonistic attitude towards this new teaching, and had never discussed it with the Countess Lydia Ivanovna (who had been carried away by it), but had assiduously and silently evaded her challenges. Now for the first time he listened to her words with pleasure, and did not inwardly oppose them.

'I am very, very grateful to you, both for your deeds and for your words,' he said, when she had finished praying.

Countess Lydia Ivanovna once more pressed both her friend's hands.

'Now I must set to work,' she said with a smile after a pause, as she wiped away the traces of tears. 'I am going to Seriozha. I shall only apply to you in the last extremity.' And she got up and went out.

The Countess Lydia Ivanovna went to Seriozha's part of the house and there, wetting the scared boy's cheeks with her tears, she told him that his father was a saint and his mother was dead.

The countess kept her word. She did actually take upon herself the care of the organization and management of Karenin's household. But she had not exaggerated when she said that practical affairs were not her strong point. Her orders were impossible as she gave them, and had to be amended by Korney, Karenin's valet, who, though no one was aware of the fact, now ran the whole establishment. Quietly and tactfully, while helping his master to dress, he would inform him of anything that it was necessary for him to know. But Lydia Ivanovna's help was none the less valuable: she gave Karenin moral support in the consciousness of her affection and esteem for him, and still more (as it consoled her to believe) in that she almost succeeded in turning him to Christianity – that is, from a lukewarm and apathetic believer into a fervent and steadfast adherent of the new interpretation of Christian doctrine, which had been gaining ground of late in Petersburg. Karenin did not find the conversion difficult. Like Lydia Ivanovna and others who shared her views, he was quite devoid of that deep imaginative spiritual faculty in virtue of which conceptions springing from the imagination become so vivid that they must needs be given harmony with other conceptions and with actual fact. He saw nothing impossible and incongruous in the notion that death, though existing for unbelievers, did not exist for him, and that being in possession of the most perfect faith – of the measure of which he was himself the judge – his soul was free from sin, and he was already experiencing complete salvation here on earth.

It is true that the shallowness and error of this conception of his faith were dimly felt by Karenin, and he knew that when, without the slightest thought that his forgiveness was the action of a Higher Power, he had surrendered directly to the feeling of forgiveness, he had known more happiness than now, when he was perpetually thinking about Christ dwelling in his heart, and that in signing official documents he was doing His will. But for Karenin it was a necessity to think thus: it was so essential to him in his humiliation to have some elevated standpoint, however imaginary, from which, looked down upon by all, he could look down on others, that he clung to this delusion of salvation as if it were the real thing.

23

THE Countess Lydia Ivanovna, when quite a young girl, and highly romantic, had been married to a wealthy, distinguished, very good-natured *bon vivant*, who was extremely dissipated. Less than two months after the wedding her husband left her, and her impassioned protestations of affection he met with a sarcasm and even hostility which those who knew the count's kindliness and saw no fault in the effusive Lydia were at a loss to explain. Since then, though not divorced, they lived apart, and whenever the husband met his wife he invariably treated her with the same malignant irony, the cause of which was incomprehensible.

The Countess Lydia had long given up being in love with her husband, but she had never ceased being in love with someone or other. She was in love with several people at once, both men and women; she had been in love with almost every person of note. She had lost her heart to each of the new princes and princesses who married into the Imperial family; she had been in love with a high dignitary of the Church, a vicar, and a parish priest; with a journalist, three slavophiles, with Komisarov, with a minister, a doctor, an English missionary, and Karenin. All these passions, ever waxing or waning, did not prevent her from keeping up the most extended and complicated relations with the Court and society. But from the day she took Karenin in his misfortune under her special protection, from the time when she began to busy herself in Karenin's household looking after his welfare, she had come to feel that all her other attachments were not the real thing, and that she was now genuinely in love, and with no one but Karenin. The feeling she now experienced for him seemed to her stronger than any she had ever had before. Analysing and comparing it with her previous loves, she saw clearly that she would never have been in love with Komisarov had he not saved the life of the Tsar, that she would never have been in love with Ristich-Kudzhitsky if there had been no Slavonic question; but that she loved Karenin for himself, for his lofty, uncomprehended soul, for the sweet – to her – high-pitched sound of his voice, for his drawling intonation, his weary eyes, his character, and his soft white hands with their swollen veins. She was not only overjoyed when they met, but she was always studying his face for signs of the impression she was making on him. She was anxious to please him, not merely by her conversation but by her whole person. For his sake she now lavished more pains on her dress than before. She caught herself day-dreaming as to what might have been, had she not been married and he been free. She blushed with excitement when he entered the room, she could not repress a smile of rapture when he happened to say something amiable to her.

For several days now the Countess Lydia Ivanovna had been in the greatest state of agitation. She had heard that Anna and Vronsky were in Petersburg. Karenin must be saved from seeing her: he must be spared even the painful knowledge that that dreadful woman was in the same town with him, and that he might come across her any minute.

Lydia Ivanovna set inquiries on foot among her acquaintances to find out what those *infamous people*, as she called Anna and Vronsky, intended doing, and endeavoured so to guide every movement of her friend during those days that he should not meet them. The young adjutant, a friend of Vronsky's, through whom she obtained her information and who was hoping that she would use her influence for him, told her that they had finished their business and were going away the following day. Lydia Ivanovna was beginning to breathe freely again when the next morning she received a note and with horror recognized the handwriting. It was the handwriting of Anna Karenin. The envelope was of thick, stiff paper; there was a huge monogram on the oblong yellow sheet inside, and the letter exhaled a delicious scent.

'Who brought it?'

'A commissionaire from the hotel.'

It was some time before the Countess Lydia Ivanovna could sit down to read the letter. Her agitation brought on an attack of asthma, to which she was subject. When she had recovered her composure, she read the following, written in French:

Madame la Comtesse,

The Christian sentiments with which your heart is filled encourage me to the, I feel, unpardonable boldness of writing to you. I am unhappy at being parted from my son. I beg to be allowed to see him once before my departure. Forgive me for reminding you of myself. I address myself to you and not to Alexei Alexandrovich simply because I do not wish to make that great-hearted man suffer in remembering me. Knowing your friendship for him, I know you will understand me. Will you send Seriozha to me, or should I come to the house at some fixed hour?

Or will you let me know when and where I could see him away from home? I do not anticipate a refusal, as I know the magnanimity of him with whom it rests. You cannot conceive the yearning I have to see him, and so cannot conceive the gratitude your help will arouse in me.

Anna

Everything about the letter irritated the Countess Lydia Ivanovna – its contents, and the allusion to magnanimity, and especially what she considered its free-and-easy tone.

'Say there is no answer,' said the Countess Lydia Ivanovna, and immediately opening her blotting-book she wrote to Karenin that she hoped to see him around one o'clock at the Palace, at the levée.

'I must consult with you on a grave and painful matter. There we can arrange where to meet. Best of all at my house, where I will order tea as *you* like it. It is urgent. He sends the cross, but He also sends the strength to bear it,' she added, to prepare him somewhat.

The Countess Lydia Ivanovna generally wrote two or three notes a day to Karenin. She enjoyed this form of communication with him: it had an elegant secrecy about it that was lacking in their personal interviews.

24

THE levée was drawing to a close. As they were going away, people met and chatted about the latest news, the honours awarded that day and the changes among high officials.

'How would it be to appoint Countess Maria Borisovna Minister of War, and make Princess Vatkovsky Chief of Staff?' said a grey-haired old man in a gold-laced uniform, addressing a tall, handsome maid of honour, who had been asking him about the new appointments.

'And me among the adjutants,' replied the maid of honour, smiling.

'You have an appointment already – in the ecclesiastical department. And your assistant's Madame Karenin.'

'Good day, Prince!' said the little old man, shaking hands with a man who came up to him.

'What was that you were saying about Karenin?' inquired the prince.

'He and Putyatov have received the Order of Alexander Nevsky.'

'I thought he had it already.'

'No. Just look at him,' said the little old man, pointing with his gold-laced hat to Karenin, who was standing in the doorway of the hall in his court uniform with the new red ribbon across his shoulder, talking to an influential member of the Imperial Council. 'Happy and contented as a brass farthing,' he added, pausing to shake hands with a handsome gentleman of the bedchamber of strapping proportions.

'No, he's aged,' said the gentleman of the bedchamber.

'From overwork. He spends his days writing projects. He won't let that poor devil go now until he has expounded the business, point by point.'

'Aged indeed! *Il fait des passions*. I hear Countess Lydia Ivanovna's jealous now of his wife.'

'Oh come, I beg you not to speak ill of the Countess Lydia Ivanovna.'

'Why, is there any harm in her being in love with Karenin?'

'But is it true Madame Karenin's here?'

'Well, not here at the palace, but in Petersburg. I met her yesterday with Alexei Vronsky, *bras dessus, bras dessous*, in the Morsky.'

'There's a man who has no ...' the gentleman of the bedchamber was beginning, but he stopped to make room, bowing, for a member of the Imperial family to pass.

While they were thus discussing Karenin, finding fault with him and laughing at him, he was barring the way of the member of the Imperial Council he had buttonholed, expounding item by item his new financial project, never interrupting his discourse for an instant, for fear he should escape.

Almost at the same time that his wife left Karenin there had come to him that bitterest moment in the life of an official – the moment when his upward career comes to a full stop. This full stop had arrived and everyone perceived it, but Karenin himself had not yet realized that his career was over. Whether it was due to his feud with Stremov, or his misfortune with his wife, or simply that he had reached his destined limits, it had become obvious to everyone in the course of that year that his official race was run. He still held a position of consequence, he sat on many commissions and committees, but his day was over and nothing more was expected from him. Whatever he might say, whatever he proposed, was listened to as if it were something long familiar and the very thing that was not needed. But Karenin was not aware of this and, on the contrary, being cut off from direct participation in the work of the Government, he saw more clearly than ever the defects and blunders of others, and considered it his duty to point out means for their correction. Shortly after the separation from his wife, he began his first memorandum on the new judicial procedure, the first of an endless series of unwanted notes that he was to write on every branch of the administration.

Karenin did not merely fail to observe his hopeless position in the official world, he was not merely free from anxiety on that score, but he was more than ever satisfied with his own activity.

'He that is married careth for the things of the world, how he may please his wife ... he that is unmarried careth for the things that belong to the Lord, how he may please the Lord,' says the Apostle Paul, and Karenin, who was now guided in every action by Scripture, often recalled this text. It seemed to him that ever since he had been left without a wife he had in these very projects of reform been serving the Lord more zealously than before.

The manifest impatience of the member of the Council who wanted to get away from him did not disconcert Karenin; he gave up his exposition only when the member of the Council, seizing his chance when one of the Imperial family was passing, slipped away from him.

Left alone, Karenin looked down, collecting his thoughts, then glanced casually about him and walked towards the door, where he hoped to meet the Countess Lydia Ivanovna.

'And how strong they all are, how physically sound,' he said to himself, looking at the powerfully-built gentleman of the bedchamber with his well-groomed, perfumed whiskers, and at the red neck of the prince in a tight-fitting uniform, whom he had to pass on his way out. 'It is truly said that all is evil in the world,' he thought, with another sidelong glance at the calves of the gentleman of the bedchamber.

Moving forward unhurriedly, Karenin bowed with his customary air of weariness and dignity to the gentlemen who had been talking about him, and looking towards the door his eyes sought the Countess Lydia Ivanovna.

'Ah, Alexei Alexandrovich!' said the little old man, with a malicious gleam in his eye, as Karenin drew level and was nodding frigidly. 'I haven't congratulated you yet,' and he pointed to the new ribbon.

'Thank you,' replied Karenin. 'What an *exquisite* day we are having,' he added, laying emphasis in his peculiar way on the word *exquisite*.

That they laughed at him he was well aware, but he did not expect anything but hostility from them: he was used to that by now.

Catching sight, just as she entered, of the Countess Lydia Ivanovna's sallow shoulders soaring from her *décolleté*, and her fine dreamy eyes summoning him, Karenin smiled, revealing impeccable white teeth, and went up to her.

Lydia Ivanovna's toilette had cost her great pains, like all her recent efforts in this direction. She was pursuing a very different aim in her dress now from that which she had set herself thirty years before. Then her desire had been to adorn herself with something, and the more adorned the better. Now, on the contrary, she was decked out in a way so inconsistent with her age and figure that her one anxiety was to dress so that the contrast between her finery and her looks should not be too appalling. And as far as Karenin was concerned she succeeded, and was in his eyes attractive. For him she was the one islet not of kindly feeling only but of affection in the ocean of hostility and ridicule that surrounded him.

As he ran the gauntlet of those mocking eyes, he was drawn as naturally to her enamoured look as a plant is attracted to the light.

'I congratulate you,' she said, indicating his ribbon with her eyes.

Suppressing a complacent smile, he shrugged his shoulders and closed his eyes, as if to say that this could not be a source of joy to him. The Countess Lydia Ivanovna knew very well that it was one of his chief sources of satisfaction, though he would never admit it.

'How is our angel?' she asked, meaning Seriozha.

'I can't say I am altogether satisfied with him,' replied Karenin, raising his eyebrows and opening his eyes. 'Sitnikov is not pleased with him either.' (Sitnikov was the tutor to whom Seriozha's secular education had been entrusted.) 'As I have mentioned to you, he displays a certain indifference towards the essential questions which ought to touch the heart of every man and every child.' Karenin began expounding his views on the sole subject that interested him outside the service – the education of his son.

When Karenin with Lydia Ivanovna's help had been brought back to life and activity, he had felt it his duty to see to the education of the son left on his hands. Having never taken any interest in educational matters before, he devoted some time to theoretical study of the question. After reading several books on anthropology, pedagogics, and didactics, he drew up a plan of education and, engaging the best tutor in Petersburg to superintend it, he set to work. And this work occupied him continually.

'Yes, but his heart! I see in him his father's heart, and with such a heart a child cannot go far wrong,' said the Countess Lydia Ivanovna enthusiastically.

'Yes, perhaps. ... As for me, I perform my duty. It's all I can do.'

'You're coming to me,' said the countess after a pause. 'We have to talk over something painful to you. I would have given anything to spare you certain memories, but others are not of the same mind. I have received a letter from *her*. *She* is here in Petersburg.'

Karenin started at the allusion to his wife, but immediately his face assumed that death-like immobility which expressed his utter help-lessness in the matter.

'I was expecting it,' he said.

Countess Lydia Ivanovna looked at him ecstatically, and tears of rapture filled her eyes at the greatness of his soul.

25

WHEN Karenin entered the Countess Lydia Ivanovna's cosy little bou-doir, which was full of old china and hung with portraits, the hostess herself had not yet made her appearance. She was changing her dress.

A cloth was laid on a round table, and on it stood a Chinese tea service and a silver spirit-lamp and tea-kettle. Karenin glanced idly at the endless familiar portraits which adorned the room and, seating himself by the table, opened a New Testament lying upon it. The rustle of the countess's silk skirt diverted his attention.

'Well now, we can sit quietly,' said the Countess Lydia Ivanovna, with an agitated smile on her lips as she hurriedly squeezed herself in between the table and the sofa, 'and talk over our tea.'

After a few words of preparation, the countess, breathing hard and flushing, handed him the letter she had received.

After reading the letter, he sat for a long while in silence.

'I don't think I have the right to refuse her,' he said timidly, lifting his eyes.

'My dear friend, you never see evil in anyone!'

'On the contrary, I see that all is evil. But is it fair to ...?'

His face showed irresolution, and a seeking for counsel, support, and guidance in a matter he did not understand.

'No,' the countess interrupted him, 'there are limits to everything. I can understand immorality,' she said, not altogether truthfully, since she never had been able to understand what it was that led women astray; 'but I don't understand cruelty, and to whom? To you! How can she stay in the town where you are? No, the longer one lives the more one learns. And I'm learning to understand your loftiness and her baseness.'

'And who shall cast the stone?' said Karenin, unmistakably pleased with the part he had to play. 'I have forgiven all, and so I cannot refuse her what her love – her love for her son – exacts ...'

'But is it love, my friend? Is it sincere? Admitting that you have forgiven – that you forgive – but have we the right to work on the feelings of that little angel? He thinks she is dead. He prays for her, and beseeches God to have mercy on her sins. ... And it is better so. But what will he think if he sees her?'

'I had not thought of that,' said Karenin, evidently agreeing.

The Countess Lydia Ivanovna hid her face in her hands and was silent. She was praying.

'If you ask my advice,' she said, having finished her prayer and uncovered her face, 'I do not advise you to do it. Do I not see how you are suffering, how this has re-opened your wounds? But supposing that, as usual, you don't think of yourself, what can it possibly lead to? Further suffering for yourself and torture for the child! If she had a grain of humanity left in her, she ought not to wish for it herself. No, I have no hesitation in advising you not to allow it, and with your permission I will write to her.'

Karenin consented, and the Countess Lydia Ivanovna sent the following letter in French:

Madame, To remind your son of you might lead to questions on his part which it would be impossible to answer without implanting in the child's soul a spirit of condemnation towards what should be sacred for him; and in the circumstances I beg you to interpret your husband's refusal in the spirit of Christian love. I pray to Almighty God to have mercy on you.

COUNTESS LYDIA

This letter achieved the secret purpose which the countess hid even from herself. It wounded Anna to the quick.

For his part, Karenin, on returning home from Lydia Ivanovna's, all that day could not concentrate on his usual pursuits, or find that spiritual peace he had of late felt in the consciousness of his own salvation.

The thought of his wife, who had so greatly sinned against him and towards whom he had been so saintly, as the Countess Lydia Ivanovna had so justly told him, ought not to have upset him; but he was not easy. He could not comprehend a word of the book he was reading; he could not drive away painful memories of his relations with her, of the mistakes which, as it now seemed, he had made in regard to her. The recollection of how he had received her confession of unfaithfulness on their way home from the races (especially that he had insisted only on the observance of the proprieties, and had not sent a challenge) tortured him like remorse. The letter he had written her tormented him too; and, most of all, his forgiveness, which nobody wanted, and his care of the other man's child made his heart burn with bitter shame.

With the same sense of shame and regret he reviewed all his past with her, recalling the awkward way in which, after months of wavering, he had made her an offer.

'But how have I been to blame?' he said to himself. And as usual this question set him wondering whether all those other men – the Vronskys and Oblonskys and those gentlemen of the bedchamber with their fine calves – felt differently, did their loving and marrying differently. And there arose before his mind's eye a whole row of those dashing, vigorous, self-confident men, who always and everywhere drew his inquisitive attention in spite of himself. He tried to dispel these thoughts, he tried to persuade himself that he was not living for this transient life but for the life eternal, and that there was peace and love in his heart. But the fact that he had in this transient, trivial life made, as it seemed to him, a few trivial mistakes tortured him as though the eternal salvation in which he believed did not exist. But this trial did not last long, and soon he felt a return of that tranquil elevation which allowed him to forget what he did not want to remember.

26

'WELL, Kapitonich?' said Seriozha, coming back rosy and bright from his walk the day before his birthday and giving his overcoat to the tall old hall-porter, who smiled down at the little fellow. 'Has that muffled-up man been to-day? Did Papa see him?'

'Yes, he did. The minute the secretary came out, I announced him,' said the hall-porter with a good-humoured wink. 'Here, I'll take it off, shall I?'

'Seriozha!' called the tutor, stopping in the doorway leading to the inner apartments. 'Take it off yourself.'

But Seriozha, though he heard his tutor's feeble voice, paid no heed to it. He stood holding on to the hall-porter's belt and looking up into his face.

'Well, and did Papa do what he wanted him to?'

The hall-porter nodded affirmatively.

The man with his face muffled up, who had already been seven times to ask some favour of Karenin, interested both Seriozha and the hall-porter. Seriozha had come upon him in the hall one day and heard him plaintively begging the hall-porter to be announced, saying that death was staring him and his children in the face. Since then, having met him a second time in the hall, Seriozha took great interest in him.

'Well, was he awfully pleased?'

'I should say so! Almost jumping for joy as he walked away.'

'And has anything come for me?' asked Seriozha, after a pause.

'Well, sir,' the hall-porter replied in a whisper, with a shake of his head, 'there is something from the countess.'

Seriozha understood at once that the hall-porter was speaking of a present from the Countess Lydia Ivanovna for his birthday.

'What do you say? Where is it?'

'Korney took it to your Papa. Something fine it must be too!'

'How big is it? Like this?'

'Not quite, but something good.'

'Is it a book?'

'No, something else. You had better run along now, Vassily Lukich is calling,' said the hall-porter, hearing the tutor's steps approaching, and gently disengaging the little hand in the half pulled off glove which was holding on to his belt he signed with his head towards the tutor.

'Just coming, Vassily Lukich!' answered Seriozha with that merry affectionate smile which always won the conscientious Vassily Lukich.

Seriozha was in too high spirits, he felt too happy not to share with his friend the hall-porter the piece of family good fortune of which he had heard from the Countess Lydia Ivanovna's niece during his walk in the public gardens. This good news seemed all the more important because it coincided with the happiness of the muffled-up man and his own happiness at having toys come for him. To Seriozha it seemed that this was a day on which everyone ought to be glad and happy.

'Do you know, Papa has received the Order of Alexander Nevsky?'

'I should say I do! People have already started calling to congratulate him.'

'Well, and is he pleased?'

'How could he help being pleased at the Tsar's gracious favour? It shows he's deserved it,' said the hall-porter, solemnly severe.

Seriozha reflected for a moment as he peered into the hall-porter's face, which he had studied down to the minutest detail, especially the chin between the grey whiskers, never seen by anyone but Seriozha, who always looked at him from below.

'Well, and has your daughter been to see you lately?'

The porter's daughter was a ballet-dancer.

'How could she come on week-days? They have to study too. And so must you, sir; run along.'

When Seriozha reached his room, instead of sitting down to his lessons, he began talking to his tutor about the parcel that had come for him, saying that it must be a locomotive engine. 'What do you think?' he inquired.

But Vassily Lukich was only thinking that Seriozha ought to be preparing his grammar lesson for the master, who was due at two o'clock.

'Tell me just one thing, Vassily Lukich,' asked Seriozha suddenly, when he was seated at his desk with his book in his hand. 'What is higher than the Alexander Nevsky? You know Papa's received the Order of Alexander Nevsky?'

The tutor replied that the Order of Vladimir was higher than the Alexander Nevsky.

'And higher than that?'

'Well, highest of all is the St Andrew.'

'And higher than that?'

'I don't know.'

'What, you don't know?' And Seriozha, leaning his elbows on the table, sank into deep meditation.

His meditations were of the most complex and diverse character.

He imagined his father having suddenly been presented with both the Vladimir and St Andrew to-day, and in consequence being much more lenient at lesson-time, and dreamed how, when he was grown up, he himself would receive all the Orders, and that they would invent one higher than the St Andrew. Directly they invented it, he would win it. They would make a higher one still, and he would immediately get that too.

With such thoughts as these the moments soon slid by, and when the teacher came the lesson about the adverbs of time and place and manner of action was not ready, and the teacher was not only displeased but hurt. This touched Seriozha. He felt he was not to blame for not having learned the lesson: try as he would, he positively could not manage it. While the teacher was explaining, he believed that he understood, but as soon as he was left alone he positively could not remember or understand how the short and familiar word 'suddenly' could be an *adverb of manner of action*. Still, he was sorry he had disappointed the teacher, and wanted to cheer him up.

He chose a moment when the teacher was silently looking at the book.

'Mihail Ivanich, when is your birthday?' he asked all of a sudden.

'You would do better to think of your work. Birthdays are of no importance to a rational being. It's a day like any other, on which one has to do one's work.'

Seriozha looked attentively at the teacher, at his scanty beard, at the spectacles which had slipped down below the ridge on his nose, and fell into such a deep reverie that he heard nothing of what the teacher was explaining to him. He knew that the teacher did not believe what he said, he felt it from the tone in which it had been spoken. 'But why have they all agreed to talk in the same way this most tiresome and useless stuff? Why does he hold me off? Why doesn't he love me?' he asked himself mournfully, and could not think of any answer.

27

AFTER the lesson with the grammar teacher came his father's lesson. While waiting for his father, Seriozha sat at the table playing with a pen-knife and thinking. One of his favourite occupations was to keep a look-out for his mother during his walks. He did not believe in death generally, and in her death in particular, in spite of what Lydia

Ivanovna had told him and his father had confirmed, and it was just because of that, and after he had been told she was dead, that he had begun looking for her when he was having his walk. Every comely, graceful woman with dark hair was his mother. At the sight of every such woman his heart would swell with tenderness until his breath failed him and the tears came into his eyes. And he was on tiptoe with expectation that she would come up to him, would lift her veil. All her face would be visible, she would smile, she would take him in her arms, he would sniff her fragrance, feel the tender clasp of her hand, and cry with happiness, just as he had done one evening when he had rolled at her feet and she had tickled him, while he shook with laughter and bit her white hand with the rings on the fingers. Later, when he accidentally learned from his old nurse that his mother was not dead, and his father and Lydia Ivanovna had explained that to him she was dead because she was a wicked woman (which he could not possibly believe, because he loved her), he went on looking for her and expecting her in the same way. That day in the public gardens there had been a lady in a lilac veil, whom he had watched with throbbing heart, believing it to be her as she came towards them along the path. The lady had not come up to them, but had disappeared somewhere. To-day Seriozha felt a rush of love for her, stronger than ever, and now as he sat waiting for his father he forgot everything, and notched all round the edge of the table with his knife, staring before him with shining eyes and dreaming of her.

'Here comes your Papa!' said Vassily Lukich, rousing him.

Seriozha jumped up and went to kiss his father's hand, looking at him searchingly, trying to discover signs of his joy at receiving the Alexander Nevsky.

'Did you have a nice walk?' asked Karenin, sitting down in his easy-chair, pulling towards him the volume of the Old Testament and opening it. Although Karenin had more than once impressed upon Seriozha that every Christian ought to have a thorough knowledge of Bible history, he himself often referred to the Old Testament during the lesson, and Seriozha observed this.

'Yes, it was very nice indeed, Papa,' said Seriozha, sitting sideways on his chair and rocking it, which he had been told not to do. 'I saw Nadinka' (Nadinka was Lydia Ivanovna's niece, who was being brought up by her aunt). 'She told me you've been given a new decoration. Are you glad, Papa?'

'First of all, don't rock your chair, please,' said Karenin. 'And secondly, it is not the reward that is precious, but the work itself. And I could wish you understood that. You see, if you are going to take pains and learn your lessons in order to win a reward, the work will seem hard; but when you work' (Karenin said this, remembering how he had been sustained by a sense of duty that morning in the monotonous task of signing one hundred and eighteen documents), 'loving your work, you will find your reward in the work itself.'

The sparkling, affectionate light in Seriozha's eyes faltered and died under his father's gaze. This was the same old tone his father always took with him, and Seriozha had learned by now to fall in with it. His father always talked to him, Seriozha felt, as if he were addressing some imaginary boy out of a book, utterly unlike himself. And when he was with his father Seriozha always tried to be that boy out of a book.

'You understand that, I hope?' said his father.

'Yes, Papa,' answered Seriozha, acting the part of the imaginary boy.

The lesson consisted in learning by heart some verses from the Gospel and repeating the beginning of the Old Testament. The verses from the Gospel Seriozha knew fairly well, but just as he was reciting them he became so absorbed in watching a bone in his father's forehead, which turned so abruptly at the temples, that he got mixed up and put the end of one verse on to the beginning of another where the same word occurred. Karenin concluded that he did not understand what he was saying, and this irritated him.

He frowned, and began explaining what Seriozha had heard dozens of times before and never could remember, because he understood it too well, just as he could not remember that 'suddenly' is an adverb of manner of action. Seriozha looked at his father with scared eyes, and could think of nothing but whether his father would make him repeat what he had just said, as he sometimes did. He was so terrified at the thought that he no longer understood anything. However, his father did not make him repeat it, and passed on to the lesson from the Old Testament. Seriozha related the events themselves well enough, but when it came to answering questions as to what some of the events foretold, he knew nothing, though he had been punished before over this lesson. The passage about which he could not say anything at all, and at which he began floundering and cutting the table and rocking his chair, was where he had to repeat the patriarchs before the Flood. He did not know one of them, except Enoch, who had been taken up to heaven alive. Last time he had remembered their names, but now he could only think of Enoch, chiefly because Enoch was his favourite character in the whole of the Old Testament, and attached to Enoch's being taken up alive to heaven there was a whole train of thought to which he surrendered himself now while he stared at his father's watch-chain and a half-unfastened button on his waistcoat.

In death, of which they had told him so many times, Seriozha disbelieved entirely. He did not believe that the people he loved could die, above all that he himself would die. That was to him something quite inconceivable and impossible. But he had been told that everyone dies: he had gone so far as to ask people whom he trusted, and found that they, too, believed in death – even his old nurse said the same, though reluctantly. But Enoch had not died, so not everybody died. 'And why shouldn't anyone else deserve the same in God's sight and be taken up to heaven alive?' thought Seriozha. Bad people – that is, those whom Seriozha did not like – they might die, but all the good ones might be like Enoch.

'Well, what are the names of the patriarchs?'

'Enoch, Enos ...'

'Yes, you have already said them. This is bad, Seriozha, very bad. If you don't try to learn the things that are more necessary than anything for a Christian,' said his father, getting up, 'whatever can interest you? I am not pleased with you, and Piotr Ignatich' (this was the most important of his teachers) 'is not pleased with you. ... I shall have to punish you.'

His father and his teacher were both dissatisfied with Seriozha, and he certainly did learn his lessons very badly. Yet it could not be said that he was a stupid boy. On the contrary, he was far cleverer than the boys his teacher held up as examples to Seriozha. In his father's opinion, he did not try to learn what he was taught. As a matter of fact, he could not learn it. He could not, because his soul was full of other more urgent claims than those his father and the teacher made upon him. Those claims were in opposition, and he was in direct conflict with his instructors.

He was nine years old; he was a child; but he knew his own soul and treasured it, guarding it as the eyelid guards the eye, and without the key of love he let no one into his heart. His teachers complained that he would not learn, while his soul was thirsting for knowledge. So he learned from Kapitonich, from his nurse, from Nadinka, from Vassily Lukich, but not from his teachers. The water which his father and his teacher hoped would turn their mill-wheels had long since leaked away and was doing its work in another channel.

His father punished Seriozha by not letting him go and see Nadinka, Lydia Ivanovna's niece; but this punishment turned out happily for Seriozha. Vassily Lukich was in a good humour, and showed him how to make windmills. He spent the whole evening trying to make one and dreaming of a windmill you could turn round on, either by catching hold of the sails or tying yourself on and spinning round. Seriozha did not think of his mother all the evening, but when he was in bed he suddenly remembered her and prayed in his own words that tomorrow, for his birthday, his mother might leave off hiding herself and come to him.

'Vassily Lukich, do you know what I have been saying an extra special prayer for?'

'To learn your lessons better?'

'No.'

'For toys?'

'No. You'll never guess. It's a lovely secret! When it comes true I'll tell you. Can't you guess?'

'No, I can't guess. You will have to tell me,' said Vassily Lukich with a smile, which was rare with him. 'Now lie down; I'm going to blow out the candle.'

'The thing I've been praying for I can see better without the candle. There! I nearly told you the secret!' said Seriozha, laughing merrily.

When the candle was taken away, Seriozha heard and felt his mother. She stood over him and caressed him with a loving look. But then windmills appeared, and a pen-knife, and everything began to be mixed up, and he fell asleep.

28

WHEN Vronsky and Anna reached Petersburg they put up at one of the best hotels: Vronsky separately on the lower floor, and Anna with the baby, the nurse, and a maid, upstairs in a large suite of four rooms.

On the day they arrived Vronsky went to see his brother. There he found his mother, who had come from Moscow on business. His mother and sister-in-law greeted him as usual, asked him about his trip abroad and spoke of mutual acquaintances, but did not let drop a single word about his union with Anna. His brother, however, who came to see him the following morning, of his own accord asked about her, and Alexei Vronsky told him frankly that he looked upon his union with Madame Karenin as marriage, that he hoped a divorce would be arranged, and then he would marry her, and meanwhile he considered her as much a wife as any other wife, and he begged him to tell their mother and his wife so.

'The world may not approve, but I don't care,' said Vronsky. 'But if my relations want to be on good terms with me they will have to be on the same terms with my wife.'

The elder brother, who had always had a respect for his younger brother's judgement, could not tell whether he was right or not till the world had decided the question; for his part he had nothing against it, and with Alexei he went up to see Anna.

Before his brother, as he always did in the presence of a third party, Vronsky addressed Anna with a certain formality, treating her as he might a close friend, but it was understood that his brother knew their real relations, and they talked of Anna's going to Vronsky's estate.

For all his experience of the world Vronsky, in the new position in which he was placed, had fallen into a strange misapprehension. He ought to have known that society would shut its doors upon him and Anna; but some vague notion got into his head that public opinion had progressed beyond its ancient prejudices (without noticing it, he had become the partisan of every kind of progress), the views of society had changed, and that the question whether they would be received in society was not a foregone conclusion. 'Of course,' he said to himself, 'they will hardly receive her at Court, but our intimate friends can and must look at it in the proper light.'

A man may sit in one position with his legs doubled under him for several hours at a time, provided he knows there is nothing to prevent him moving if he wishes to; but if he thinks he is compelled to stay with his legs doubled up, he will get cramp and his legs will begin to twitch and strain in the direction in which he would like to stretch them. This was what Vronsky was experiencing in regard to the world. Though at the bottom of his heart he knew that the world was closed to them, he kept on trying to see whether it might not have changed by now and receive them. But he very soon perceived that though society was prepared to welcome him personally, it was closed to Anna. As in the game of cat and mouse, the arms that were raised to allow him to get inside the circle were immediately lowered to bar the way for Anna.

One of the first Petersburg ladies Vronsky happened to meet was his cousin Betsy.

'At last!' she greeted him joyfully. 'And Anna? I am so glad you're back! Where are you staying? I can imagine how horrible our Petersburg must seem to you after your delightful travels. I can imagine your honeymoon in Rome. How about the divorce? Is that all settled?'

Vronsky noticed that Betsy's enthusiasm waned when she learned that no divorce had as yet taken place.

'People will throw stones at me, I know,' she said, 'but I shall come and see Anna. I really must. You won't be here long, I suppose?'

She did, in fact, call on Anna that very day; but her manner was very different from what it used to be. She was evidently proud of her courage, and wanted Anna to appreciate the fidelity of her friendship. She did not stay more than ten minutes, chattering society gossip, and on leaving she said:

'You have not told me when the divorce is to be. Of course I have ignored the conventions but other starchy people will give you the cold shoulder until you are married. And that's so simple nowadays. *Ça se fait.* So you are going on Friday? A pity we shan't see each other again.'

From Betsy's tone Vronsky might have gathered what he had to expect from society; but he made another attempt in his own family. Of his mother he had no hopes. He knew that his mother, who had been so enthusiastic over Anna at their first meeting, would have no mercy on her now for having ruined her son's career. But he placed great hopes on Varya, his brother's wife. He fancied she would cast no stones, but in that simple and determined way of hers would come and see Anna, and receive her in her own house.

The day after his arrival Vronsky called on her and finding her alone told her plainly what he wanted.

'You know how fond I am of you, Alexei,' she said when she had heard what he had to say, 'and how ready I am to do anything for

557

you; but I have held back because I knew I could be of no use to you and Anna Arkadyevna.' She articulated the formal 'Anna Arkadyevna' with particular care. 'Please don't think I am criticizing her. Not at all! Perhaps in her place I should have done the same. I don't and can't enter into that,' she continued, looking timidly into his gloomy face. 'But one must call things by their names. You want me to go and see her, to ask her here, and to rehabilitate her in society; but do understand – I *cannot* do so. I have daughters growing up, and I must mix in society for my husband's sake. Well, I'm ready to come and see Anna Arkadyevna: she will understand that I can't ask her here, or at any rate not when she would be likely to meet people who look at things differently. That would wound her. I can't raise her ...'

'Oh, I don't consider she has fallen any more than hundreds of other women whom you do receive!' Vronsky interrupted still more gloomily, and he got up in silence, realizing that his sister-in-law's decision was not to be shaken.

'Alexei, don't be angry with me. Please try to understand that it's not my fault,' began Varya, looking at him with a timid smile.

'I'm not angry with you,' he said, still as gloomily; 'but I'm sorry in two ways. I'm sorry because this means breaking up our friendship – if not breaking it, at least impairing it. You understand that for me, too, there can be no other course.'

And with that he left her.

Vronsky saw that further efforts were futile, and that he would have to spend these few days in Petersburg as though in a strange town, avoiding every sort of contact with his former world, in order not to be exposed to the unpleasantness and humiliations which were so intolerable to him. One of the most disagreeable features of his position in Petersburg was that Karenin seemed to be everywhere and his name on everyone's lips. It was impossible to start any conversation without its turning on Karenin, impossible to go anywhere without risk of meeting him. So at least it seemed to Vronsky, just as it seems to a man with a sore finger that he is fated to keep knocking it against something.

Their stay in Petersburg was the more painful to Vronsky in that he noticed all the time a sort of new mood in Anna that he could not understand. One moment she would seem in love with him, the next she would become cold, irritable and distant. She was worrying over something, and keeping something back from him, and appeared not to see the slights which poisoned his existence and which with her sensitiveness must have been still more unendurable.

29

ONE of Anna's objects in coming back to Russia had been to see her son. From the day she left Italy the thought of seeing him had never ceased to agitate her. And the nearer she drew to Petersburg, the greater did the delight and importance of this meeting appear in her imagination. She did not even stop to ask herself how it could be arranged. It seemed such a simple and natural thing to see her son when she should be in the same town with him. But as soon as she arrived in Petersburg she suddenly realized her present position in society, and grasped the fact that it would be no easy matter to arrange this meeting.

She had been two days now in Petersburg. The thought of her son never left her for a single instant, but she had not yet seen him. She felt she had no right to go straight to the house, where she ran the risk of encountering Karenin. Besides, they might insult her and refuse to let her in. The thought of writing to her husband, and so enter into relations with him, was too painful to entertain: she could be at peace only when she did not think of her husband. To get a glimpse of her son out walking, finding out where and when he went out, was not enough for her: she had so long been looking forward to this meeting, had so much to say to him and so many hugs and kisses to give him. Seriozha's old nurse might have helped and advised her, but she was no longer in Karenin's house. Thus two days went by in this uncertainty and in efforts to find the old nurse.

Hearing of the close friendship between Karenin and the Countess Lydia Ivanovna, Anna decided on the third day to write her a letter, which cost her great pains, in which she purposely mentioned that permission to see her son must depend on her husband's generosity. She knew that if the letter were shown to her husband, he would keep up his role of the magnanimous husband, and would not refuse her request.

The commissionaire who took the letter brought back the cruellest and most unexpected of answers, that there was no answer. She had never felt so humiliated as when, sending for the commissionaire, she heard from him a detailed account of how he had waited, and how afterwards he had been told there was no answer. Anna felt humiliated, insulted, but she saw that from her own point of view the Countess Lydia Ivanovna was right. Her suffering was the more poignant that she had to bear it in solitude. She could not and would not share it with Vronsky. She knew that to him, though he was the primary cause of her distress, the question of seeing her son would seem a matter of very little account. She knew that he would never be capable of appreciating all the depth of her anguish, and that his cool tone if the subject were mentioned would make her hate him. And she dreaded that more than anything else in the world, and so she concealed from him everything that related to her son.

She remained in the hotel all that day, trying to think out ways of seeing the boy, and finally resolved to write to her husband. She was just composing the letter in her mind when Lydia Ivanovna's letter was brought to her. The countess's silence had subdued and humbled her, but the letter and what she read between its lines so infuriated her, this malice seemed so shocking beside her passionate, legitimate love for her son, that she was filled with anger against other people and left off blaming herself.

'That coldness, that pretence of feeling!' she said to herself. 'They are only out to wound me and torture the child, and I am to submit! Not on any account! She is worse than I am: at least I don't lie!' And there and then she decided that the very next day, Seriozha's birthday, she would go straight to her husband's house, bribe the servants – do anything – but at all costs see her son and destroy the monstrous web of falsehood with which they had surrounded the unfortunate child.

She drove to a toyshop, bought a whole lot of toys, and thought over a plan of action. She would go early in the morning, about eight o'clock, when Karenin would be certain not to be up. She would have money in her hand to give the hall-porter and the footman, so that they should let her in. Without raising her veil, she would say she had come from Seriozha's godfather to wish him many happy returns, and that she had been charged to leave the toys at his bedside. The only thing she did not prepare was what she would say to her son. Often as she thought about it, she could not form the least idea.

At eight o'clock the next morning Anna got out of a hired sledge and rang the bell at the front entrance of her former home.

'Go and see what's wanted. It's a lady,' said Kapitonich, who, not yet dressed, in his overcoat and goloshes, had peeped out of a window and caught sight of a lady in a veil standing close up to the door. His assistant, a lad Anna did not know, had no sooner opened the door than she stepped in and, pulling a three-rouble note from her muff, hastily thrust it into his hand.

'Seriozha – Sergei Alexeich,' she said, and walked past. Scrutinizing the note, the lad rushed after her and stopped her at the other glass door.

'Whom do you want?' he asked.

She did not hear, and made no answer.

Observing the embarrassment of the unknown lady, Kapitonich himself came out, opened the second door for her, and inquired what she was pleased to want.

'I come from Prince Skorodumov to see Sergei Alexeich,' she said.

'His honour's not up yet,' said the hall-porter, looking at her attentively.

Anna had not anticipated that the totally unaltered appearance of the hall of the house which had been her home for nine years would affect her so powerfully. Memories sweet and painful rose one after another in her heart, and for a moment she forgot why she was there.

'Will you be so kind as to wait a little?' said Kapitonich, helping her off with her fur cloak.

When he had done so, Kapitonich glanced at her face and, recognizing her in silence, made her a low bow.

'Come in, your excellency,' he said.

She tried to speak, but her voice refused to utter a sound. With a guilty and imploring look at the old man she went with light, swift steps up the staircase. Bent double, his goloshes catching on the stairs, Kapitonich ran after her, trying to overtake her.

'The tutor's there – maybe he's not dressed. I'll let him know.'

Anna continued up the familiar staircase, not understanding what the old man was saying.

'This way, to the left, please. Excuse its not being tidy. His honour's been moved into the old parlour now,' said the hall-porter, panting. 'Allow me! Please wait a moment, your excellency. I'll just have a look.' He got in front of her, half opened the big door and disappeared behind it. Anna stood still waiting. 'He's only just awake,' said the hall-porter, coming out again.

As he spoke, Anna heard the sound of a childish yawn. By this sound alone she recognized her son and seemed to see him before her eyes.

'Let me in, let me in – go away!' she said, and went in through the high doorway. To the right of the door stood a bed, and sitting up in the bed was the boy. His nightshirt unbuttoned, his little body bent forward, he was stretching and finishing his yawn. The instant his lips came together they curved into a blissful sleepy smile, and he rolled slowly and deliciously back again, still smiling.

'Seriozha!' she whispered, walking softly up to the bed.

When she was parted from him, and all this latter time when she had been feeling an access of love and longing for him, she had pictured him as he was at four years old, the age at which she had loved him most. Now he was not even the same as when she had left. He was still further from the four-year-old baby: he had grown taller and was thinner. Oh, and how thin his face looked, and how short his hair was! How long his arms seemed! How much he had changed since she left him! But it was still Seriozha – there was the shape of his head, his lips, his soft neck and broad little shoulders.

'Seriozha!' she repeated almost in the child's ear.

He raised himself again on his elbow, turned his tousled head from side to side as though seeking something, and opened his eyes. Slowly and inquiringly he gazed for several seconds at his mother standing motionless before him; then all at once he smiled blissfully and closing his sleepy eyelids toppled not backwards but forward into her arms.

'Seriozha, my darling boy!' she murmured, catching her breath and putting her arms round his chubby little body.

'Mama!' he whispered, wriggling about in her arms so as to touch them with different parts of him.

Smiling sleepily, with his eyes still shut, he moved his plump little hands from behind him, flinging his arms round her shoulders and leaning against her, enveloping her with that sweet fragrance of warmth and sleepiness peculiar to children, and began rubbing his face against her neck and shoulder.

'I knew,' he said, opening his eyes. 'To-day is my birthday. I knew you'd come. I'll get up now ...' And as he spoke he began to doze off again.

Anna watched him with hungry eyes. She noticed how he had grown and changed in her absence. She recognized and did not recognize the bare legs so long now, which he had freed from the quilt, the cheeks that had grown thinner, and those short-cropped curls on his neck, where she so often used to kiss him. She passed her hand over it all and could not speak: tears choked her.

'Why are you crying, Mama?' he said, completely awake now. 'Mama, what are you crying for?' he asked in a tearful voice.

'I won't cry … I'm crying for joy! It's such a long time since I've seen you. But I won't cry any more,' she said, gulping down her tears and turning away. 'Come, it's time for you to get dressed,' she added, after a pause, when she had recovered; and, never letting go his hands, she sat down on the chair beside the bed where his clothes were lying ready for him.

'How do you dress without me? How …' She wanted to talk to him naturally and cheerfully, but could not, and again she had to turn away.

'I don't have a cold bath. Papa won't let me. And you haven't seen Vassily Lukich, have you? He'll come in presently. Why, you're sitting on my clothes!'

And Seriozha went off into a peal of laughter. She looked at him and smiled.

'Mama! Dearest, darling!' he cried, flinging himself on her again and hugging her, as though seeing her smile had made him realize for the first time what had happened. 'You don't want that on,' he said, taking off her hat. And seeing her afresh, as it were, without her hat, he fell to kissing her again.

'But what did you think about me? You didn't think I was dead, did you?'

'I never believed it.'

'You didn't believe it, my precious?'

'I knew, I knew!' he said, repeating his favourite phrase, and seizing the hand that was stroking his hair, he pressed the palm to his mouth and covered it with kisses.

30

MEANWHILE Vassily Lukich, who had not at first understood who this lady was, having come to the house only after her departure, realized from the conversation that it was no other person than the mother who had left her husband, and could not make up his mind whether

563

to go in or to inform Karenin. Reflecting finally that it was his duty to get Seriozha up at the hour fixed, and that it was therefore not his business to consider who was sitting there – the boy's mother or anyone else – but that he must do his duty, he finished dressing, walked over to the door and opened it.

But the embraces of mother and child, the sound of their voices and what they were saying, made him change his mind. He shook his head, and with a sigh closed the door again. 'I'll wait another ten minutes,' he said to himself, clearing his throat and wiping away tears.

In the meantime a great commotion was going on in the servants' quarters. They all knew that the mistress had come, that Kapitonich had let her in, and that she was now in the nursery. But the master was in the habit of going to the nursery before nine, and they all realized that a meeting between husband and wife was inconceivable and must be prevented. Korney, the valet, went down to the hall-porter's room to find out who had let her in, and why, and hearing that it was Kapitonich who had done so he gave the old man a talking-to. The hall-porter maintained a dogged silence but when Korney told him he deserved to be dismissed Kapitonich darted up to him and waving his hands in Korney's face burst out:

'Oh no, you'd never have let her in! Ten years' service, and nothing but kindness from her, and you'd have gone up and shown her the door! You know which side your bread's buttered on, don't you? Why not mind your own business instead of robbing master of his fur coats!'

'Old fool!' said Korney contemptuously, and he turned to the nurse who was just coming in . 'What do you think, Maria Yefimovna? He lets her in without a word to anyone,' Korney said, addressing her. 'Alexei Alexandrovich will be up directly – and go into the nursery.'

'Oh dear, oh dear, a fine how-d'you-do!' exclaimed the nurse. 'You must detain the master somehow or other, Korney Vassilich, while I run and get her out of the way. A fine how-d'you-do!'

When the nurse entered, Seriozha was telling his mother how he and Nadinka had fallen down a hill and rolled over and over, turning three somersaults. She was listening to the sound of his voice, watching his face and the play of his features, touching his hand, but she did not follow what he was saying. She must go, she must leave him – that was the only thought that possessed her heart and mind. She heard Vassily Lukich's step as he came to the door and coughed; then the footsteps of the nurse coming into the room; but she sat as though turned to stone, unable to speak or rise.

'Madam, dear!' began the nurse, going up to Anna and kissing her hands and shoulders. 'The Lord has brought joy indeed to our boy on his birthday! And you haven't changed one bit.'

'Why, nurse darling, I did not know you were in the house,' said Anna, rousing herself for a moment.

'I don't live here. I am living with my daughter. I came to wish him many happy returns, Anna Arkadyevna, dear!'

The nurse suddenly burst into tears, and began kissing her hand again.

Seriozha, beaming and smiling, holding his mother by one hand and his nurse by the other, began to stamp his little bare feet on the rug, in ecstasy at his beloved nurse's tenderness for his mother.

'Mama! She often comes to see me, and when she comes ...' he was beginning, but he stopped short, noticing that the nurse was saying something in a whisper to his mother, and that in his mother's face there was a look of dread and something like shame, which was so strangely unbecoming to her.

She went up to him.

'My darling!' she said.

She could not say *good-bye*, but the expression on her face said it, and he understood. 'My precious little Kootik!' she murmured, calling him by the pet name she had used when he was a baby, 'you won't forget me? You ...' but she could say no more.

How many times afterwards did she think of all the things she might have said! But now she did not know what to say, and was unable to speak. But Seriozha understood all she wanted to say to him. He understood that she was unhappy, and that she loved him. He even understood what it was the nurse had whispered. He had caught the words 'regularly at nine o'clock', and he understood that they referred to his father, and that his mother and father must not meet. All this he understood, but one thing he could not understand: why there should be a look of dread and shame in her face. She could not have done anything wrong, but she was afraid and ashamed of something. He wanted to ask a question that would set his doubts at rest, but he did not dare: he saw that she was suffering, and he felt for her. He clung to her in silence and whispered, 'Don't go away. He won't come just yet.'

His mother held him away from her a little, to look into his face and see whether he understood the meaning of what he was saying, and by his frightened expression she read not only that he was speaking of his father but was, as it were, asking her what he ought to think about his father.

'Seriozha, my darling,' she said. 'You must love him. He's better and kinder than I am, and I have been wicked to him. When you are grown up you will understand.'

'No one is better than you!' he cried in despair through his tears, and, clutching her by the shoulders, he hugged her with all his might, his arms trembling with the effort.

'My precious, my little one!' murmured Anna and burst into tears, crying in the same thin childlike way as he did.

At that moment the door opened, and Vassily Lukich entered. Steps were heard approaching the other door, and in a scared whisper the nurse exclaimed, 'He's coming!' and handed Anna her hat.

Seriozha sank back on the bed and began to sob, hiding his face in his hands. Anna moved his hands, once more kissed his wet face, and then walked rapidly towards the door. Karenin was just coming in. Seeing her, he stopped short and bowed his head.

Though she had declared but a moment ago that he was better and kinder than she, after a swift glance which took in his whole figure down to the minutest detail, she was seized by a feeling of loathing and hatred for him and jealousy over her son. She hurriedly put down her veil and, quickening her steps, almost ran out of the room.

She had not had time to undo, and so carried back with her, the parcel of toys she had chosen so sadly and with so much love the day before.

31

INTENSELY as Anna had longed to see her son, and much as she had thought of the meeting beforehand, preparing herself for it, she had never imagined that seeing him would affect her so violently. When she returned to her lonely suite at the hotel, it was a long time before she could remember why she was there. 'Yes, it's all over, and I am alone again,' she said to herself, and without taking off her hat she dropped into a low chair by the hearth. Fixing her eyes on a bronze clock standing on a table between the windows, she tried to think.

The French maid, whom she had brought from abroad, came in to suggest she should dress. She gazed at her wonderingly and said, 'Presently.' A footman offered her coffee. 'Presently,' she said again.

The Italian nurse came in with the baby, whom she had just dressed, and held her out to Anna. As she always did when she saw her mother, the chubby, well-nourished little baby turned her little hands – so fat that they looked as if the wrists had threads tightly tied around them – palms downward and smiling with her toothless mouth began beating the air like a fish waving its fins, making the starched folds of her embroidered frock rustle. It was impossible not to smile, not to kiss the little thing; impossible not to hold out a finger for her to clutch, crowing with delight and wriggling from top to toe; impossible not to pout one's lip which she sucked into her little mouth by way of a kiss. And all this Anna did, and took her in her arms, danced her up and down on her knee, and kissed the fresh little cheek and bare elbows; but the sight of this child made it plainer than ever that the feeling she had for her could not even be called love in comparison with what she felt for Seriozha. Everything about the baby was sweet, but for some reason she did not grip the heart. On her first-born, although he was the child of a man whom she did not love, had been concentrated all the love that had never found satisfaction. The little girl had been born in the most painful circumstances and had not had a hundredth part of the care and thought bestowed on the first child. Besides, in the little girl everything was still in the future, while Seriozha was now almost a personality, and a beloved one, already struggling with thoughts and feelings of his own; he understood her, he loved her, he judged her, she thought, recalling his words and his eyes. And she was for ever separated from him, not physically only but spiritually, and there was no help for it.

She gave the baby back to the nurse, let her go, and opened the locket containing a portrait of Seriozha at about the same age as the little girl. She got up and, removing her hat, took from the table an album in which there were photographs of her son at different ages. She wanted to compare the likenesses, and began taking them out of the album. She got them all out except one, the latest and best photograph. It showed him in a white smock, sitting astride a chair, with knitted brow and smiling lips. This was his most characteristic, his best expression. Her deft little hands, whose slender white fingers moved with a peculiar nervous energy that day, pulled at a corner of the photograph, but the photograph had caught somewhere, and she could not get it out. There was no paper-knife on the table, and so, pulling out the photograph that was next to it (it was one of Vronsky taken in Rome in a round hat and long hair), she used it to push out her son's photograph. 'Yes, there he is!' she said, glancing at the portrait of Vronsky and suddenly remembering that he was the cause of her present misery. She had not once thought of him all the morning. But now, coming all at once upon that manly, noble face, so familiar and so dear to her, she felt an unexpected surge of love for him.

'But where is he? How is it he leaves me alone in my misery?' she thought suddenly with a feeling of reproach, forgetting that she herself had kept from him everything concerning her son. She sent a message asking him to come to her immediately, and sat waiting with beating heart, rehearsing to herself the words in which she would tell him all about it, and the expressions of love with which he would comfort her. The servant returned with the answer that he had a visitor with him but that he would come immediately, and that he asked whether he might bring Prince Yashvin, who had just arrived in Petersburg. 'He's not coming alone, and he hasn't seen me since dinner yesterday,' she thought. 'He'll be coming with Yashvin, so that I shan't be able to tell him everything.' And all at once a strange idea crossed her mind: what if he had ceased to love her?

Going over the incidents of the last few days, it seemed to her that they all confirmed this dreadful thought: yesterday he had not dined at home; he had insisted on their taking separate apartments in Petersburg; and even now he was not coming alone but bringing someone with him, as though he were trying to avoid a *tête-à-tête* with her.

'But he ought to tell me so. I must be told! If I know the truth, then I shall know how to act,' she said to herself, quite powerless to imagine the position she would be in if she were convinced of his indifference. She thought he had ceased to love her, felt on the verge of despair, and this galvanized her. She rang for her maid and went to the dressing-room. She took more pains over her toilet than she had of late, as though he might, if he had fallen out of love with her, love her again because she had dressed and arranged her hair in the style that was most becoming.

She heard the bell ring before she was ready.

When she went into the drawing-room, it was not he, but Yashvin, who met her eyes. Vronsky was looking through the photographs of her son, which she had forgotten on the table, and did not hurry to turn round.

'We have met before,' she said, placing her little hand in the huge hand of Yashvin (whose bashfulness was so oddly out of keeping with his powerful figure and coarse face). 'We met last year at the races. Give them to me,' she said, almost snatching from Vronsky the photographs he was looking at, and her eyes flashed at him significantly. 'Were the races a success this year? I saw the races on the Corso in Rome instead. But you don't care for life abroad, do you?' she went on with a cordial smile. 'You see, I know all your tastes, though we have met so seldom.'

'I'm awfully sorry for that, for my tastes are mostly bad,' said Yashvin, gnawing at the left side of his moustache.

After they had talked for a few minutes, Yashvin, seeing Vronsky glance at the clock, asked her whether she would be staying much longer in Petersburg, and straightening his huge back reached for his képi.

'Not long, I think,' she said in confusion, with a look at Vronsky.

'Then I shall not see you again?' said Yashvin, rising and turning to Vronsky. 'Where are you dining?'

'Come and dine with me,' said Anna resolutely, angry with herself it seemed for her embarrassment, but flushing as she always did whenever she had to define her position before a fresh person. 'The food here is not good, but at least you will see each other. Of all his regimental friends, Alexei is fondest of you.'

'Delighted,' said Yashvin with a smile, from which Vronsky could see that he was much taken with Anna.

Yashvin took his leave and went away. Vronsky stayed behind.

'Are you going too?' she asked him.

'I'm late as it is,' he replied. 'You go on – I'll catch you up in a minute,' he called after Yashvin.

She took his hand and, without removing her eyes from him, gazed at him while she cast about her mind for words that would keep him.

'Wait a minute; there's something I want to say to you.' And raising his broad hand, she pressed it to her neck. 'Did it matter asking him to dinner?'

'You did quite right,' he said with a serene smile that showed his even teeth, and he kissed her hand.

'Alexei, you have not changed towards me?' she said, pressing his hand in both of hers. 'Alexei, I am miserable here. When are we going?'

'Soon, soon. You wouldn't believe how disagreeable our way of living here is for me too,' he said, drawing away his hand.

'All right, go, go!' she said in a hurt tone, and walked away from him quickly.

32

WHEN Vronsky returned, Anna was not there. Soon after he had left, some lady, so they told him, had come to see her, and she had gone out with her. That she had gone out without leaving word where she was going, that she was not yet back, and that she had been away somewhere in the morning without telling him about it – all this, added to her strange look of excitement that day, and the hostile fashion in which when Yashvin was there she had snatched her son's photographs out of his hands, set him thinking. He decided it was essential to have things out with her, and sat down to wait in the drawing-room. But Anna did not return alone: she brought with her her old maiden aunt, Princess Oblonsky. This was the lady who had called in the morning, and with whom Anna had gone out shopping. Anna appeared not to notice Vronsky's worried, inquiring expression, and began a lively account of the purchases she had made. He saw that something unusual was taking place within her: her eyes glittered with strained attention when they rested on him for a moment, and there was that nervous rapidity and grace in her speech and movements which had so fascinated him in the early days of their intimacy, but which now disturbed and alarmed him.

Dinner was laid for four. They were all assembled and about to go into the little dining-room when Tushkevich arrived with a message from the Princess Betsy. The princess begged to be excused for not having come to say good-bye; she was indisposed, but asked Anna to come and see her between half-past six and nine o'clock. At this mention of a specified time, showing care had been taken that she should meet no one, Vronsky glanced at Anna; but Anna did not appear to notice it.

'I am very sorry but between half-past six and nine is just the time when I cannot come,' she said with a faint smile.

'The princess will be very disappointed.'

'And so am I.'

'I suppose you are going to hear Patti?' asked Tushkevich.

'Patti! That's an idea! I would go if it were possible to get a box.'

'I could get you one,' offered Tushkevich.

'I should be very grateful indeed,' said Anna. 'But won't you stay and dine with us?'

Vronsky gave a slight shrug. He simply did not know what to make of Anna. What had she brought the old Princess Oblonsky back for? Why did she ask Tushkevich to stay to dinner? And, most amazing of all, why was she sending him for a box? Did she really think in her position of going to Patti's benefit, where she would meet all her circle of acquaintances? He gave her a searching glance but she responded with that same defiant look of high spirits or despair, the meaning of which he could not fathom. All through dinner Anna was aggressively gay – she almost flirted both with Tushkevich and with Yashvin. When they rose from table Tushkevich went to see about the box, while Yashvin retired to have a smoke. Vronsky accompanied him but after sitting with him for a while ran upstairs. Anna was already dressed for the opera in a low-necked gown of light silk and velvet that she had had made in Paris. The rich white lace on her head framed her face and set off her dazzling beauty to great advantage.

'Are you really going to the theatre?' he said, trying not to look at her.

'Why do you ask with such alarm?' she said, again hurt that he did not look at her. 'Why shouldn't I go?'

She appeared not to understand the motive of his words.

'Oh, of course there's no reason whatever,' he replied with a frown.

'That's exactly what I say,' she answered, wilfully ignoring the irony of his tone and calmly turning back her long, perfumed glove.

'Anna, for heaven's sake, what has come over you?' he said, appealing to her as once her husband had done.

'I don't understand what you mean.'

'You know you can't go.'

'Why not? I'm not going alone. Princess Varvara has gone to dress. She is coming with me.'

He shrugged his shoulders with a bewildered air of despair.

'But don't you know ...?' he began.

'I don't care to know!' she almost shrieked. 'I don't care to. Do I regret what I have done? No, no, no! If it were all to do again, from the beginning, I should do just the same. For us, for you and me, there is only one thing that matters, whether we love each other. Other people we need not consider. Why are we living apart here and not seeing each other? Why can't I go out? I love you, and nothing else matters to me so long as you have not changed,' she said in Russian, glancing at him with a strange glitter in her eyes which he could not understand. 'Why don't you look at me?'

He looked at her. He saw all the beauty of her face and full evening dress, always so becoming to her. But now her beauty and elegance were just what irritated him.

'My feelings cannot change, you know that; but I entreat you, I beseech you not to go,' he said, speaking again in French, with a note of tender supplication in his voice, but with coldness in his eyes.

She did not hear his words, but she saw the coldness of his eyes.

'And I beg you to explain why I should not go,' she answered irritably.

'Because it might cause you ...' He hesitated.

'I don't understand you at all. Yashvin *n'est pas compromettant*, and Princess Varvara is no worse than others. Ah, here she is!'

33

FOR the first time Vronsky experienced a feeling of anger, almost hate, for Anna for her refusal to realize her position. This feeling was aggravated because he could not tell her plainly the reason for his anger. Had he been able to tell her frankly what he thought, he would have said:

'For you to appear at the theatre in that dress, accompanied by the princess who is only too well known to everyone is equivalent not merely to acknowledging yourself a fallen woman but to throwing down the gauntlet to society, that is to say, cutting yourself off from it for ever.'

He could not say that. 'But how can she fail to see it? What is going on in her?' he said to himself, feeling that his regard for her was diminishing while his consciousness of her beauty was intensified.

Frowning, he went back to his rooms, where he took a seat beside

Yashvin, who with his long legs stretched out on a chair was drinking brandy and seltzer water. He ordered the same for himself.

'You were talking of Lankovsky's Powerful. A fine horse, that, and I should advise you to buy,' said Yashvin, glancing at his comrade's gloomy face. 'True, the hind-quarters aren't perfect, but the legs and head leave nothing to be desired.'

'I think I'll take him,' answered Vronsky.

The conversation about horses interested him, but he did not for a moment forget Anna, and could not help listening to the sound of steps in the corridor and looking at the clock on the chimney-piece.

'Anna Arkadyevna sent me to say that she has gone to the theatre,' a servant came to announce.

Yashvin, tipping another glass of brandy into the sparkling water, drank it and got up, buttoning his coat.

'Well, shall we go?' he said, faintly smiling under cover of his moustache and showing thereby that he understood the cause of Vronsky's gloominess, and did not attach any importance to it.

'I'm not going,' Vronsky replied darkly.

'Well, I must – I promised to. Good-bye, then. If you do come, come to the stalls: you can take Krasinsky's stall,' Yashvin added as he went out.

'No, I've some work to do.'

'A wife is a worry, but it's worse when she's not a wife,' thought Yashvin, as he walked from the hotel.

Left alone, Vronsky got up from his chair and began pacing the room.

'What are they doing this evening? It's the fourth subscription night … Yegor and his wife are there, and my mother, most likely. That's to say, all Petersburg will be there. Now she's gone in, taken off her cloak and stepped forward into the light. Tushkevich, Yashvin, the Princess Varvara.' He pictured the scene to himself. 'But what about me? Am I afraid, or have I turned her over to Tushkevich for protection? Whichever way one looks at it, it's stupid, stupid! … Why on earth is she putting me in such a position?' he asked himself with a gesture of despair.

With the gesture he knocked against the table on which the seltzer water and decanter of brandy were standing, and almost upset it. In trying to steady it, he did upset it, and angrily kicked the table over, and rang the bell.

'If you care to be in my service,' he said to the valet who entered, 'you had better remember your duties. Mind this doesn't happen again. You ought to have cleared away.'

Conscious that he was not to blame, the valet was about to defend himself, but a glance at his master's face told him that he had better keep quiet; so hurriedly picking his way he got down on his hands and knees on the carpet and began gathering up pieces of broken glass and the whole glasses and bottles.

'That is not your work. Send the waiter to clear away, and put out my dress-suit.'

Vronsky got to the theatre at half-past eight. The performance was in full swing. The little old box-attendant recognized Vronsky as he helped him off with his fur coat and called him 'Your Excellency', suggesting he need not take a number but should simply call 'Fiodor' when he wanted his coat. The brilliantly lighted corridor was empty save for the box-attendant and two footmen with fur cloaks over their arms listening at the doors. Through a slightly open door came the sounds of the discreet *staccato* accompaniment of the orchestra, and a solo woman's voice rendering a musical phrase with precision. The door opened to let an attendant slip through, and the phrase drawing to the end reached Vronsky's ears distinctly. But the door immediately closed again, and Vronsky did not hear the end of the phrase and the cadenza after it, but he knew from the thunder of applause behind the door that the aria was finished. When he entered the auditorium, brilliantly lighted by chandeliers and bronze gas-brackets, the noise was still going on. On the stage the prima donna, bare shoulders and diamonds glittering, was bowing and smiling, as, with the help of the tenor who had given her his hand, she gathered up the bouquets that came flying clumsily across the footlights. She walked over to a gentleman with glossy, pomaded hair parted down the centre, who was stretching his long arms to hand her something across the footlights, and all the audience in the stalls as well as in the boxes stirred excitedly, craning forward, shouting and clapping. The conductor in his high chair assisted in passing the offering, and straightened his white tie. Vronsky advanced into the middle of the stalls, then stood still and looked about him. To-day he paid less attention than ever to the familiar surroundings: the stage, the noise, all the well-known, uninteresting, parti-coloured herd of spectators in the packed theatre.

There were the same ladies in the boxes, with the same officers in the background; the same gaily-dressed women – heaven alone knew who – the same uniforms and black coats; the same dirty crowd in the gallery; and in the whole of that throng, in the boxes and the front rows, were some forty men and women who represented *society*. To these oases Vronsky at once directed his attention, and with them he entered at once into relation.

The act was over when he went in, and so he did not go straight to his brother's box but walked down to the front row of the stalls and stopped beside Serpuhovskoy, who was standing by the footlights with one knee raised tapping the wall of the orchestra with his heel. He had caught sight of Vronsky in the distance and beckoned him with a smile.

Vronsky had not yet seen Anna. He purposely avoided looking her way. But from the direction in which all eyes were turned he knew where she was. He glanced round unobtrusively, but he did not look for her. Prepared for the worst, his eyes sought for Karenin. To his relief, Karenin was not in the theatre that evening.

'How little of the military man there is left in you!' remarked Serpuhovskoy. 'You might be a diplomat, an artist, something of that sort.'

'Yes, as soon as I got home I put on a black coat,' replied Vronsky with a smile, slowly taking out his opera-glasses.

'Well, I'll confess I envy you there. When I came back from abroad and put on these' (he touched his epaulets), 'I regretted my lost liberty.'

Serpuhovskoy had long washed his hands of Vronsky's career, but he was as fond of him as ever, and was now particularly cordial.

'A pity you were not in time for the first act!'

Vronsky, listening with one ear, moved his opera-glass from the stalls and scanned the boxes. Near a lady in a turban and a bald-headed old man who blinked angrily just as Vronsky's moving glass reached him, he suddenly caught sight of Anna's proud head, strikingly beautiful, and smiling in its frame of lace. She was in the fifth box in the lower tier, not more than twenty paces away. She sat in the front of the box and, half leaning round, was saying something to Yashvin. The poise of her head on her lovely, broad shoulders and the restrained excitement and brilliance of her eyes and her whole face reminded him of her just as he had seen her at the ball in Moscow. But he felt utterly different towards her beauty now. In his feeling for her now there was no element of mystery, and so her beauty, though it attracted him even more than before, gave him now a sense of injury. She was not looking in his direction, but Vronsky felt that she had already seen him.

When Vronsky directed his opera-glass that way again, he noticed that the Princess Varvara was unusually red in the face, and kept laughing unnaturally and glancing round at the next box. Anna, tapping with her folded fan on the red plush edge of the box, was gazing fixedly somewhere else, not seeing and obviously not wishing to see what was taking place in the next box. Yashvin's face wore the expression which was common when he was losing at cards. He sat scowling and sucking the left end of his moustache farther and farther into his mouth, and cast sidelong glances towards the neighbouring box.

In that box on the left were the Kartasovs. Vronsky knew them, and knew that Anna was acquainted with them. Madame Kartasov, a thin little woman, was standing up in her box and, her back turned upon Anna, she was putting on an opera-cloak that her husband was holding out for her. Her face looked pale and angry, and she was speaking excitedly. Kartasov, a stout, bald-headed man, kept glancing round at Anna, while he endeavoured to pacify his wife. When his wife had left the box, he loitered behind, trying to catch Anna's eye, obviously anxious to bow to her. But Anna, with unmistakable intention, avoided noticing him, and talked to Yashvin, whose closely cropped head was bent over her. Kartasov eventually went without making his salutation, and the box was left empty.

Vronsky could not discern exactly what had passed between the Kartasovs and Anna, but he saw that something humiliating for Anna had happened. He realized this both from what he had seen and, more especially, from Anna's face. He could see she was taxing every nerve to sustain the role she had taken up. And she was entirely successful in appearing outwardly tranquil. Anyone who did not know her and her circle, who had heard none of the utterances of commiseration, indignation, and amazement that she should show herself in society – and show herself so ostentatiously with her lace and her beauty – would have admired the serenity and loveliness of this woman, without a suspicion that she was undergoing the sensations of a man in the stocks.

Knowing that something had happened, but not knowing precisely what, Vronsky felt painfully agitated, and decided to go to his brother's box in the hope of finding out. Purposely leaving the auditorium at the opposite side from where Anna was, he ran into the colonel of his old regiment talking to two acquaintances. Vronsky caught the name Karenin, and noticed how the colonel hastened to address him loudly by name, with a meaning glance at his two companions.

'Ah, Vronsky! When are you coming to see us at the regiment? We can't let you off without a supper. You're one of the old set,' said the colonel.

'I can't stop; awfully sorry, another time,' said Vronsky, and he ran upstairs to his brother's box.

The old countess, Vronsky's mother, with her steel-grey curls, was in his brother's box. Varya with the young Princess Sorokin met him in the corridor.

Having conducted the Princess Sorokin back to her mother, Varya held out her hand to her brother-in-law, and instantly began talking of what interested him. He had rarely seen her so excited.

'I think it's mean and hateful, and Madame Kartasov had no right to behave as she did! Madame Karenin ...' she began.

'But what happened? I don't know.'

'What, haven't you heard?'

'You realize I should be the last to hear.'

'There isn't a more spiteful creature than that Kartasov woman!'

'But what has she done?'

'My husband told me. ... She insulted Madame Karenin. Her husband began talking to her across the box, and Madame Kartasov made a scene. She said something offensive in a loud voice, he says, and went out.'

'Count, your *maman* is asking for you,' said the young Princess Sorokin, peeping out of the door of the box.

'I have been expecting you all the while,' said his mother, smiling sarcastically. 'You were nowhere to be seen.'

Her son saw that she could hardly contain her delight.

'Good evening, *maman*. I was coming to you,' he said coldly.

'Why don't you go and *faire la cour à Madame Karénin*?' she went on, when Princess Sorokin had moved away. '*Elle fait sensation. On oublie Patti pour elle.*'

'*Maman*, I have asked you not to speak to me of that subject,' he answered, scowling.

'I am only saying what everyone is saying.'

Vronsky made no reply, and after addressing a few words to the Princess Sorokin he left the box. In the doorway he met his brother.

'Ah, Alexei!' his brother greeted him. 'How abominable! The woman is nothing but an idiot ... I was just going to her. Let's go together.'

Vronsky did not hear him. He hurried downstairs, feeling that he must do something but he did not know what. He was moved by indignation with her for having put herself and him in such a false position, together with pity for her suffering. He descended to the stalls and made straight for Anna's box. At her box stood Stremov talking to her.

'There are no more tenors. *Le moule en est brisé.*'

Vronsky bowed to her and stopped to exchange greetings with Stremov.

'You got here late, I think, and missed the best aria,' Anna said to Vronsky, with what seemed to him a mocking glance.

'I am a poor judge of music,' he said, returning her gaze sternly.

'Like Prince Yashvin, who considers that Patti sings too loud,' she said with a smile. 'Thank you,' she added, taking in her little hand in its long glove the playbill Vronsky picked up, and suddenly at that instant her lovely face quivered. She rose and went to the back of the box.

Noticing in the next act that her box was empty, Vronsky, rousing murmurs of 'hush' from the silent audience who had settled quietly to listen to a *cavatina*, went out and drove back to the hotel.

Anna was already there. When Vronsky entered, she was still in the same dress as she had worn at the theatre. She was sitting in the first arm-chair against the wall, staring straight before her. She glanced up at him, and immediately resumed her former position.

'Anna,' he said.

'It's all your fault, all your fault!' she cried, tears of despair and anger in her voice, and rose.

'But I begged, I implored you not to go. I knew it would be unpleasant ...'

'Unpleasant!' she cried. 'It was awful! As long as I live I shall never forget it. She said it was a disgrace to sit beside me.'

'A silly woman's chatter,' he said. 'But why risk it, why provoke ...?'

'I hate that self-possession of yours. You ought not to have brought me to this. If you had loved me ...'

'Anna! What has my love to do with it?'

'Yes, if you loved me, as I love you, if you were tortured as I am! ...' she said, looking at him with an expression of terror.

He was sorry for her, but angry all the same. He assured her of his love because he saw that this was the only means of soothing her, and he did not reproach her in words, but in his heart he reproached her.

And those assurances of his love, which seemed to him so hackneyed and commonplace that he was ashamed to utter them, she drank in eagerly, and gradually became calmer. The next day, fully at peace with one another, they left for the country.

PART SIX

I

DOLLY and her children were spending the summer at Pokrovskoe, at her sister Kitty Levin's. The house on her own estate was quite dilapidated, and Levin and his wife had persuaded her to spend the summer with them. Oblonsky heartily approved of the arrangement. He said he was very sorry his official duties prevented him from passing the summer in the country with his family, which would have been the greatest happiness for him. He remained in Moscow, from time to time visiting them in the country for a day or two. Besides the Oblonskys, with all their children and the governess, the Levins had with them the old princess, who considered it her duty to watch over her inexperienced daughter in her *interesting condition*. They also had Varenka, Kitty's friend abroad, who was fulfilling her promise to visit Kitty when she was married. All these people were friends or relations of Levin's wife, and though he liked them all he regretted a little his own Levin world and order of things, which was being smothered by this influx of the 'Shcherbatsky element', as he called it to himself. Sergei Ivanich was their only guest from his side of the family, but even he was a Koznyshev and not a Levin, so that the Levin spirit was completely suppressed.

In the Levin house, so long deserted, there were now so many people that almost all the rooms were occupied, and nearly every day the old princess would count those present before sitting down to a meal, and put the thirteenth grandson or granddaughter at a separate table. And Kitty, who conducted her household with unfailing care, had no little trouble in getting the chickens, turkeys, and ducks to satisfy the summer appetites of the visitors and children.

The whole family were at dinner. Dolly's children, with their governess and Varenka, were making plans to go and look for mushrooms. Koznyshev, who commanded from all the party a respect almost amounting to awe for his intellect and learning, surprised every-one by joining in the conversation about mushrooms.

'Take me with you. I am very fond of picking mushrooms,' he said, with a glance at Varenka. 'I think it is an excellent occupation.'

'Why, certainly! We should be delighted to,' replied Varenka with a blush.

Kitty and Dolly exchanged looks. That the learned and intellectual Koznyshev should suggest going to gather mushrooms with Varenka confirmed certain suppositions that had engrossed Kitty's mind of late. She hastened to make some remark to her mother, so that her glance should not be noticed.

After dinner Koznyshev sat with his cup of coffee at the drawing-room window, and while he took part in a conversation he had begun with his brother he watched the door through which the children would have to come out on their way to pick mushrooms. Levin sat down in the window near his brother.

Kitty stood beside her husband, evidently awaiting the end of a conversation that had no interest for her, in order to tell him some-thing.

'You have changed in many respects since your marriage, and for the better,' said Koznyshev, smiling to Kitty and apparently little interested in the conversation with his brother; 'but you have re-mained true to your passion for defending the most paradoxical theories.'

'Katya, it is not good for you to be standing,' said her husband, with a meaning look, moving a chair towards her.

'However, there's no time to talk now,' added Koznyshev, seeing the children come running out.

At the head of them all galloped Tanya sideways, her stockings tightly dragged up, flourishing a basket and Koznyshev's hat in her hand. She ran right up to him, boldly, with shining eyes so like her father's fine eyes, and handed him his hat, and made as though she would put it on for him, softening her daring by a shy and friendly smile.

'Varenka's waiting,' she said, carefully putting the hat on his head when she saw from Koznyshev's smile that she might do so.

Varenka was standing at the door, having changed into a yellow print dress, with a white kerchief on her head.

'I'm coming, I'm coming, Mademoiselle Varenka,' said Koznyshev, finishing his cup of coffee and putting his handkerchief and cigar-case into their separate pockets.

'What a darling my Varenka is, don't you think?' said Kitty to her husband the moment Koznyshev had risen. She spoke so that Koznyshev could hear, and it was clear that she meant him to do so. 'And how lovely – what a refined type of beauty! Varenka!' Kitty called. 'Will you be in the copse by the mill? We'll drive out to you there.'

'You quite forget your condition, Kitty,' said the old princess, hurriedly coming in at the door. 'You ought not to shout like that.'

Hearing Kitty's voice and her mother's reprimand, Varenka ran up to Kitty with her light step. The rapidity of her movements, her flushed and eager face all betrayed that something out of the ordinary was going on in her. Kitty knew what this was, and had been observing her closely. She called Varenka at that moment merely to bestow on her a silent blessing for the important event which, Kitty fancied, was bound to come to pass in the woods that day after dinner.

'Varenka, I should be very happy if a certain something were to happen,' she whispered, kissing her.

'And are you coming, too?' Varenka said to Levin in confusion, pretending not to have heard what had been said.

'Yes, but only as far as the threshing-floor. I shall stop there.'

'Why, what do you want to do there?' said Kitty.

'I must go and have a look at the new wagons, and check the invoice,' said Levin. 'And where will you be?'

'On the terrace.'

2

ALL the ladies of the party were assembled on the terrace. They always liked sitting there after dinner, but that day they had special reason for doing so. Besides the sewing of baby garments and the knitting of swaddling bands, on which all of them were engaged, jam was being made on the terrace that afternoon after a recipe new to Agatha Mihalovna, without the addition of water to the fruit. Kitty had introduced this new method, which had been in use in her mother's home. Agatha Mihalovna, to whom the task of jam-making had always been entrusted, and who considered that nothing that had been done in the Levin household could be amiss, had gone against her instructions and put water with the strawberries, insisting that the jam could not be made without it. She had been caught in the act, and now the rasp-berry jam was to be made in the presence of all, and it was to be proved to her conclusively that jam could turn out very well without water.

Agatha Mihalovna, with a flushed face and aggrieved expression, her hair ruffled and her thin arms bared to the elbow, was moving the preserving-pan over the brazier with a circular movement, looking darkly at the raspberries and devoutly praying that the jam would thicken before the raspberries were done. The princess, conscious that Agatha Mihalovna's wrath must be chiefly directed against her, as principal adviser in the matter of jam-making, was trying to look as if she were absorbed in other things and not interested in raspberries. She talked of other matters, but watched the brazier out of the corner of her eye.

'I always buy my maids ready-made dresses from the market,' the princess said, continuing the conversation. 'Isn't it time to skim it, my dear?' she added, turning to Agatha Mihalovna. 'There's not the slightest need for you to do it, and it's too hot for you,' she said, stop-ping Kitty.

'I'll do it,' said Dolly, and getting up she began carefully sliding the spoon over the bubbling syrup, and from time to time shook off the clinging jam from the spoon by knocking it on a plate that was already covered with yellowish pink scum and blood-red streaks of syrup. 'How the children will lick this up with their tea,' she thought, re-membering how she herself as a child had marvelled that grown-ups did not eat the scum – the nicest part of the jam.

'Stiva says it's much better to give money,' Dolly remarked, re-turning to the weighty topic under discussion – the kind of presents to give the servants. 'But ...'

'Money's out of the question!' the princess and Kitty exclaimed with one voice. 'They do so appreciate a present.'

'Well, last year, for instance, I bought our Matriona Semeonovna, not exactly a poplin, but something of the sort,' said the princess.

'I remember, she was wearing it on your name day.'

'It was a dear little pattern, so simple and nice. I should have liked it myself, if she hadn't had it. It was something like Varenka's. So pretty and inexpensive.'

'Well, I think it's done now,' said Dolly, letting the syrup drop off the spoon.

'When it begins to set, it's ready. Boil it up a little longer, Agatha Mihalovna.'

'These flies!' said Agatha Mihalovna crossly. 'It'll be just the same,' she added.

'Look, how sweet! Don't frighten it!' Kitty said suddenly, watching a sparrow that had alighted on the balustrade, turned over a raspberry, and started pecking at the centre of it.

'Yes, but you keep away from the brazier,' said her mother.

'*A propos de Varenka*,' said Kitty in French, which they had been talking all the time so that Agatha Mihalovna should not understand, 'you know, *maman*, I am somehow expecting things to be settled to-day. You know what I mean. How splendid it would be!'

'Dear me! Quite a match-maker!' said Dolly. 'How carefully and cleverly she throws them together!'

'No, tell us, *maman*, what you think?'

'What is there to think? He' (*he* meant Koznyshev) 'could have made the best match in Russia at any time; now, of course, he's not so young as he was, still I know ever so many girls would be glad to marry him even now. ... She's very nice, but he might ...'

'Oh, but think, Mama; why, nothing better could be imagined, for him or for her. First of all, she's simply charming!' expostulated Kitty, folding one finger.

'He certainly likes her very much,' Dolly assented.

'Then his standing in society is such that he has no need to look for either fortune or position in his wife. All he needs is a good, sweet, quiet girl ...'

'Yes, she is certainly quiet enough,' put in Dolly again.

'Thirdly, and a girl that loves him, as I'm sure Varenka does. ... In a word, it would be splendid! I look forward to seeing them come back from the wood – and everything settled. I shall be able to tell at once by their eyes. I should be so delighted! What do you think, Dolly?'

'Don't get so excited. It's not at all the thing for you to be excited,' said her mother.

'I'm not excited, Mama. I fancy he will make her an offer to-day.'

'Ah, that's so strange, how and when a man makes an offer! ... There is a sort of barrier, and all at once down it goes,' said Dolly with a dreamy smile, recalling her past with Oblonsky.

'Mama, how did Papa make you an offer?' Kitty asked suddenly.

'There was nothing out of the ordinary, it was very simple,' answered the princess, but her face lighted up at the memory.

'Oh, but how was it? You loved him, anyway, before you were allowed to speak?'

Kitty felt a peculiar pleasure in being able now to talk to her mother on equal terms about questions of such paramount importance in a woman's life.

'Of course I did. He used to come and stay with us in the country.'

'But how was it settled between you, Mama?'

'I suppose you think you invented something quite new? I assure you, it's always the same: it was settled by looks and smiles ...'

'How well you put it, Mama! Looks and smiles – that's exactly it,' Dolly agreed.

'But what were the words he used?'

'What words did Kostya say to you?'

'He wrote it down with a piece of chalk. It was wonderful. ... What a long time ago it seems!' she said.

And the three women fell to musing on the same thing. Kitty was the first to break the silence. She had been remembering all that last winter before her marriage, and her infatuation for Vronsky.

'There's one thing ... that old love affair of Varenka's,' she said, a natural chain of ideas bringing her to this point. 'I should have liked to say something to Sergei Ivanich, to prepare him. They're all – men, I mean – terribly jealous of our pasts.'

'Not all,' said Dolly. 'You are judging by your own husband. The thought of Vronsky still makes him miserable, doesn't it? I'm right, aren't I?'

'Yes,' Kitty answered, a pensive smile in her eyes.

'But I really don't know,' interposed the princess in defence of her maternal care of her daughter, 'what there is in your past that could worry him? That Vronsky paid you attentions? That happens to every girl.'

'Oh yes, but we didn't mean that,' Kitty said, flushing.

'No, let me speak,' her mother went on. 'Why, when I wanted to have a talk to Vronsky, you yourself would not let me. Don't you remember?'

'Oh, Mama!' Kitty implored, a look of pain on her face.

'Nowadays there's no holding you girls in ... Your friendship could never have gone beyond what was suitable. I should myself have called upon him to explain himself. However, my love, it won't do for you to get agitated. Please remember that, and calm yourself.'

'I'm perfectly calm, *maman*.'

'What a good thing it was for Kitty that Anna arrived on the scene,' observed Dolly, 'and how unfortunately it turned out for her. The tables have turned,' she added, struck by the thought. 'Then Anna was so happy, and Kitty believed herself unhappy. Now it is exactly the opposite. I often think of her.'

'A nice person to think of! Horrid, disgusting woman – no heart,' said her mother, who was not resigned to having Levin for her son-in-law instead of Vronsky.

'What is the use of talking about that?' Kitty asked with annoyance. 'I never think about it, and I don't want to. ... And I don't want to think about it,' she said, catching the well-known sound of her husband's step coming up to the terrace.

'What's that you don't want to think about?' inquired Levin, coming on to the terrace.

But no one offered a reply, and he did not repeat the question.

'I'm sorry to have broken in on your feminine parliament,' he said, glancing round at them all with vexation, perceiving that they had been discussing something which they would not talk about before him.

For a second he found himself sharing Agatha Mihalovna's discontent at having to boil the jam without water, and with the alien Shcherbatsky element in general. He smiled, however, and went up to Kitty.

'Well, how do you feel?' he asked, looking at her with the expression with which everyone looked at her now.

'Oh, very well,' said Kitty, smiling. 'And how did you get on?'

'The wagons hold three times as much as the old carts did. Well, are we going for the children? I've ordered the horses to be put in.'

'What! you want to take Kitty in the wagonette?' said her mother reproachfully.

'Only at a walking-pace, Princess.'

Levin never called the princess '*maman*', as sons-in-law often do, and this annoyed her. But though he liked and respected the princess, Levin could not address her so without a sense of profaning his feeling for his dead mother.

'Come with us, *maman*,' said Kitty.

'I don't want to be a witness to such folly.'

'Well, I'll walk, then. Walking's good for me.' Kitty got up and went to her husband and took his arm.

'It may be good for you, but everything in moderation,' said the princess.

'Well, Agatha Mihalovna, is the jam done?' asked Levin, smiling to Agatha Mihalovna and trying to cheer her up. 'Has it turned out well the new way?'

'I suppose it's all right. For our notions it's boiled too long.'

'It'll keep all the better, Agatha Mihalovna; it won't mildew, even though our ice has begun to thaw already, so that we've no cool place to store it,' said Kitty, at once divining her husband's intention and addressing the old woman in the same spirit. 'Your pickling, now, it's so good that Mama says she never tasted better,' she added, smiling and putting the old woman's kerchief straight.

Agatha Mihalovna looked at Kitty crossly.

'You needn't try to console me, ma'am. I've only to look at you and him together, and I feel happy,' she said, and the rough familiarity of that *him* touched Kitty.

'Come and help us look for mushrooms. You can show us all the good places.'

Agatha Mihalovna smiled and shook her head, as much as to say, 'I should like to be angry with you too, but I can't.'

'Please take my advice,' said the princess, 'cover the jam with paper soaked in rum, and it will keep perfectly, even without ice.'

3

KITTY was particularly glad of a chance of being alone with her husband, for she had noticed the shade of mortification that had flitted over his face – which always so vividly reflected what he was feeling – when he had come on to the terrace and asked what they were talking about, and had got no answer.

When they started off on foot, ahead of the others, and were out of sight of the house, on the hard dusty road, strewn with rye-ears and grain, she leaned more heavily on his arm and pressed it to her side. He had quite forgotten the momentary unpleasant impression, and alone with her experienced, now that the thought of her approaching motherhood was never for a moment absent from his mind, a new and delicious bliss, quite pure from all alloy of the senses, in being near to the woman he loved. He had nothing especial to say to her but he longed to hear the sound of her voice, which like her eyes had changed since she had been with child. There was a gentle gravity in her voice, as in her eyes: the gravity found in people continually intent upon one cherished purpose.

'You are sure you won't get tired? Lean more on me,' he said.

'No, I'm so glad of a chance to be alone with you. Nice as it is to have them all, I must confess I miss the winter evenings we had to ourselves.'

'They were pleasant, but this is still better. ... Both are better,' he he said, squeezing her hand.

'Do you know what we were talking about when you came in?'

'About the jam?'

'Oh yes, about jam too; but afterwards about how men propose.'

'Ah!' said Levin, listening more to the sound of her voice than to the words she was saying, and all the while paying attention to the road, which now passed through the wood, and avoiding places where she might stumble.

'And about Sergei Ivanich and Varenka. Have you noticed? ... I want it to happen so much,' she went on. 'What do you think about it?' And she looked into his face.

'I really don't know,' Levin replied, smiling. 'I don't understand Sergei in that respect. I told you about ...'

'Oh yes, that he was in love with that girl who died. ...'

'It happened when I was still a child. I know about it from hearsay. I remember him in those days. He was wonderfully charming. But I've observed him since with women: he is friendly and some of them he likes, but you feel that to him they're simply people, not women.'

'Yes, but now with Varenka ... I fancy there's something ...'

'Perhaps there is. ... But one has to know him. ... He's a peculiar, wonderful person. He's bound up in the spiritual life. He is a man of too pure, too exalted a nature.'

'What, you mean this would lower him?'

'No, but he's so used to living a purely spiritual life that he can't. reconcile himself with actual fact, and Varenka is, after all, fact.'

Levin had grown used by now to uttering his thought boldly, without taking the trouble to clothe it in exact language; he knew that his wife, in such moments of loving tenderness as now, from a hint would understand what he meant to say, and she did understand him.

'Yes, but there's not so much of that actual fact about her as about me. I can see that he would never have cared for me. She is all spirit ...'

'Oh no, he is so fond of you, and it is always such a joy to me that my people like you.'

'Yes, he's very nice to me, but ...'

'But it's not the same as it was with poor Nikolai though ... you and he took a liking to each other at first sight,' Levin finished. 'Why don't we speak of him?' he added. 'Sometimes I reproach myself for not doing so: it will end by our forgetting him. Oh, what a tragic, charming man he was! ... Yes, what were we talking about?' Levin asked, after a pause.

'You think then that Sergei Ivanich can't fall in love,' said Kitty, translating his thoughts into her own words.

'It's not so much that he can't fall in love,' Levin said, smiling, 'but he has not that soft side which is necessary. ... I've always envied him, and even now, when I'm so happy, I still envy him.'

'You envy him for not being able to fall in love?'

'I envy him because he is better than I am,' replied Levin with a smile. 'He does not live for himself. His whole life is subordinated to duty. And that's why he can be serene and contented.'

'And you?' Kitty asked with a mocking, affectionate smile.

She could never have explained the chain of thought that made her smile; but the last link in it was that her husband in exalting his brother and depreciating himself was not altogether sincere. Kitty knew that this insincerity came from his love for his brother, from his sense of guilt at being too happy, and above all from his persistent craving to be better – she loved this in him, and so she smiled.

'And you? What are you dissatisfied with?' she asked, with the same smile.

Her disbelief in his dissatisfaction with himself rejoiced him, and unconsciously he tried to draw her to express her reasons for it.

'I am happy, but dissatisfied with myself ...' he said.

'Why, how can you be dissatisfied with yourself if you are happy?'

'I mean – how shall I say? ... In my heart I really care for nothing whatever but that you should not stumble – see? Oh dear, you mustn't jump about like that!' he cried, breaking off to scold her for too agile a movement over a branch that lay in the path. 'But when I examine myself, and begin comparing myself with others, especially with my brother, I feel I'm a poor creature.'

'But in what way?' Kitty persisted, still smiling. 'Don't you, too, do things for others? What about your small-holdings arrangement, and your work on the estate, and your book?'

'Oh, but I feel, and particularly just now – it's your fault – that all that doesn't count,' he said, pressing her arm. 'I don't take it seriously enough. Now, if I could care for my work as I care for you ... but lately I've been doing it as a sort of task set me.'

'Well, then, what do you say to Papa?' asked Kitty. 'Is he a poor creature, too, as he does nothing for the common good?'

'He? Oh no! But then one ought to have the simplicity, the straightforwardness, the goodness of your father: and have I got that? I do nothing, and I fret about it. It's all your fault. Before I had you – and *this* too' (he gave a glance at her figure which she understood), 'I put all my energies into my work; but now I can't, and I'm conscience-stricken. I do it just like a task that has been set me. I pretend ...'

'Then would you like to change places with Sergei Ivanich?' asked Kitty. 'Would you prefer to be working for the general good, and to love the task set you, as he does, and nothing more?'

'Of course not,' said Levin. 'The fact is, I am too happy to reason clearly. So you think he'll make her an offer to-day?' he added after a brief silence.

'I do and I don't. But I'm awfully anxious for him to! Stop a moment.' She stooped down and picked a wild camomile at the edge of the path. 'Come, count: he will propose, he won't ...' and she handed him the flower.

'He will, he won't,' Levin began, pulling off the little white petals one by one.

'No, no!' Snatching at his hand, Kitty stopped him. She had been watching his fingers with excitement. 'You picked off two at once.'

'Well then, we won't count this tiny one,' said Levin, tearing off a short half-grown petal. 'But here's the wagonette overtaking us.'

'You haven't tired yourself, Kitty?' called the princess.

'Not a bit.'

'Otherwise you had better get in, if the horses are quiet and we drive slowly.'

But it was not worth while getting in. They were quite near the place, and all walked the rest of the way on foot.

4

Varenka, with her white kerchief over her black hair, surrounded by the children and gaily and good-humouredly busy with them, and at the same time visibly excited at the possibility of an offer of marriage from a man she cared for, looked very attractive. Koznyshev walked by her side and kept casting admiring glances at her. Looking at her, he recalled all the delightful things he had heard from her lips, all the good he knew about her, and became more and more conscious that the feeling he had for her was something rare, something he had felt but once before, long, long ago, in his early youth. The joy of being near her increased step by step, and at last reached such a point that, as he put a huge birch mushroom with a slender stalk and up-curling top into her basket, he looked into her eyes and, noting the flush of glad and frightened agitation that suffused her face, he was confused himself, and in silence gave her a smile that said too much.

'If this is the case,' he said to himself, 'I ought to think it over and make up my mind, and not let myself be carried away like a boy by the impulse of the moment.'

'I'm going off to pick mushrooms by myself,' he said, 'otherwise my contributions will not be noticed.' And he moved away from the edge of the wood where they were walking on the short silky grass in the long stretches between the old birches and penetrated deep into the wood, where among the white birch trunks grew grey-stemmed aspens and dark hazel bushes. After he had gone a dozen yards, knowing he was out of sight, he stood still behind a spindle bush in full flower with pinky red catkins. Around him everything was quiet. Only the hum of flies, like a swarm of bees, sounded continually high over the tops of the birch trees beneath which he was standing, and now and again the children's voices floated across to him. All at once he heard, not far from the skirts of the wood, Varenka's contralto voice calling Grisha, and a joyous smile lit up his face. Conscious of the smile, Koznyshev shook his head disapprovingly at his own condition, and taking out a cigar began to light it. For a long while he could not get the match to strike against the trunk of a birch. The soft scales of the white bark stuck to the phosphorus, and the light went out. At last one match did burn, and the fragrant cigar smoke, wavering like a broad sheet, stretched forward and up over the bush under the drooping branches of the birch-tree. Watching the streak of smoke, he strolled on gently, deliberating on his position.

'And why not?' he thought. 'If it were only a passing fancy or a sudden infatuation – if it were only this attraction, this mutual attraction (I can call it a *mutual* attraction), but I felt that it was contrary to the whole tenor of my life, if I felt that in giving way to this attraction I should be false to my vocation and my duty ... but it's not so. The only thing I can find against it is that when I lost Marie I vowed to myself I would remain true to her memory. That is the only thing I can say against my feeling ... it's an important factor,' he said to himself, aware nevertheless that this consideration had not the slightest importance for him personally, except that it might detract from the romantic role he played in the eyes of others. 'But apart from that, however much I searched, I should find nothing to say against my sentiment. Had reason alone guided my choice, I could not have found anything better.'

Of all the women and girls of his acquaintance he could not think of a single one who united in herself to such a degree all, literally all, the qualities which, considering the matter in cold blood, he would wish to see in his wife. She had all the charm and freshness of youth but she was not a child, and if she loved him she loved him consciously as a woman ought to love. That was one point. Another point: she was not only far from being worldly – she had an unmistakable distaste for worldly society, and at the same time she knew the world and had all the ways of a woman of the best society, the absence of which in a life-companion would be unthinkable for him. Thirdly, she was religious, and not unwittingly religious and good like a child – like Kitty, for example – but her life was based on religious principles. Even down to small details Koznyshev found in her all that he desired in a wife: she was poor and without family, so she would not bring into her husband's house a mass of relations with their influence, as he saw Kitty doing. She would be indebted to her husband for everything, which, too, was what he had always desired for his future married life. And this girl, who combined all these qualities, loved him. He was a modest man, but he could not help seeing it. And he loved her. The one argument against it was his age. But he came of long-lived stock, he had not a single grey hair in his head, and nobody would have taken him for forty. He remembered Varenka's saying that it was only in Russia that men regarded themselves as old at fifty, and that in France a man of fifty considers himself *dans la force de l'âge* – in the prime of life – while a man of forty is *un jeune homme*. And what did the mere reckoning of years matter when he felt as young at heart as he had been twenty years ago? Was it not youth to feel as he felt now, as he came out again to the edge of the wood and saw, in the bright slanting sunbeams, the graceful figure of Varenka in her yellow dress with her basket on her arm, stepping lightly past the trunk of an old birch-tree? Was it not youth that made the sight of her blend so harmoniously with the beauty of the view: the view of the field of ripening oats bathed in the slanting rays of the sun, and the old forest beyond, flecked with yellow and fading away into the bluish distance? His heart contracted with happiness, and melted within him. He felt that he had made up his mind. Varenka, who had just crouched down to pick a mushroom, rose buoyantly and looked round. Throwing away his cigar, Koznyshev advanced towards her with a determined step.

<h1 style="text-align:center">5</h1>

'MADEMOISELLE VARENKA, when I was a very young man I formed for myself my ideal of the woman I should love and whom I should be happy to call my wife. Many years have gone by, and now for the first time I have met what I sought – in you. I love you, and offer you my hand.'

Koznyshev was saying this to himself until he came within ten paces of Varenka. She was down on her knees, her hands trying to defend a mushroom from Grisha, while she called little Masha.

'Come this way, little ones! There are lots here,' she cried in her sweet, deep voice.

She did not get up or change her position when she saw Koznyshev approaching, but everything told him that she felt his presence and was glad of it.

'Well, did you find any?' she asked from under the white kerchief, turning her beautiful face to him with a gentle smile.

'Not one,' said Koznyshev. 'Did you?'

She did not answer, busy with the children who surrounded her.

'There's another one there, next to that twig,' she said to little Masha, pointing to a small mushroom, its rubbery pinkish crown cut across by a dry blade of grass from beneath which it had thrust itself.

Varenka got up while Masha picked it, breaking it into two white halves. 'This brings back my childhood,' she added, as she moved away from the children by Koznyshev's side.

They walked a few steps in silence. Varenka saw that he wanted to speak; she divined what it was that he wished to say, and her heart grew faint with joy and panic. They were already out of earshot but still he did not speak. Varenka would have done better to remain silent. It would have been easier for them to say what they wanted to say after a silence than after talking about mushrooms. But against her will, and as if by accident, Varenka said:

'So you did not find any? But of course there are always fewer in the middle of the wood.'

Koznyshev sighed and made no answer. He was vexed that she had spoken about the mushrooms. He wanted to bring her back to her first remark about her childhood; but after a pause of some length, as though against his own will, he made an observation in reply to her last words.

'I've only heard that the white edible funguses are found chiefly at the edge of the wood, though I can't tell a white boletus when I see one.'

A few more minutes passed. They had gone still farther away from the children, and were quite alone. Varenka could hear the beating of her own heart and felt herself turning red, then pale and red again.

To be the wife of a man like Koznyshev, after her position with Madame Stahl, seemed to her the height of happiness. Besides, she was almost sure she was in love with him. And now in a moment her fate was to be decided. She was mortally afraid – afraid both of his speaking and not speaking.

Now or never was the moment for his declaration – Koznyshev felt that, too. Everything about Varenka, her expression, the flushed cheeks and downcast eyes, betrayed painful suspense. He saw it and felt sorry for her. He even felt that to keep silent now would be to wrong her. He quickly ran over in his mind all the arguments in support of his decision. He even repeated to himself the words in which he had intended to put his offer, but instead of those words some perverse reflection caused him to ask:

'What is the difference between a white boletus and a birch mushroom?'

Varenka's lips trembled with agitation as she replied:

'There is hardly any difference in the top part, but the stalks are different.'

And as soon as these words were out of her mouth, both he and she understood that it was over, that what was to have been said would not be said; and their excitation, having reached its climax, began to subside.

'The stalk of a birch mushroom makes one think of the beard on a dark man's face who has not shaved for a couple of days,' Koznyshev remarked, speaking quite calmly now.

'Yes, that's true,' answered Varenka with a smile, and instinctively they changed their course and began walking towards the children. Varenka felt sore and ashamed, but at the same time was conscious of a sense of relief.

When Koznyshev got home and reviewed all his arguments, he found that his first decision had been a mistaken one. He could not be untrue to the memory of Marie.

'Gently, children, gently!' Levin shouted quite angrily, stepping in front of his wife to protect her when the children came rushing at them with shrieks of delight.

Koznyshev and Varenka followed the children out of the wood. Kitty had no need to question Varenka: she saw by the calm and somewhat abashed faces of both that her plans had not come off.

'Well?' inquired her husband on their way back.

'It didn't take,' said Kitty, her smile and manner of speaking like her father's, a similarity Levin often observed with pleasure.

'Didn't take? How do you mean?'

'I'll show you,' she said, taking her husband's hand, lifting it to her mouth and just touching it with closed lips. 'The way one kisses the bishop's hand.'

'Whose fault was it?' he said, laughing.

'Both their faults. But it should have been like this ...'

'Here are some peasants coming ...'

'Oh, they didn't see!'

6

DURING the children's tea the grown-up people sat on the balcony and talked as if nothing had happened, though they all, especially Koznyshev and Varenka, knew very well that something had happened which, though negative, was of very great importance. The pair of them felt like children who had failed in their examinations and would have to remain on in the same class or leave the school for ever. Everyone present, feeling, too, that something had happened, joined in an animated conversation about extraneous subjects. Levin and Kitty felt particularly happy and in love with one another that evening. And their happiness in their love seemed like an unpleasant comment on those who would have liked to feel the same and could not – and they felt a prick of conscience.

'Mark my words, Alexandre will not come,' said the old princess.

They were expecting Oblonsky by the evening train, and the old prince had written to say that he might come too.

'And I know why,' the princess went on. 'He says a young couple should be left alone at first.'

'But Papa has left us alone. We've never seen him,' said Kitty. 'Besides, we're not a young couple any longer – we're quite old married people now.'

'Only if he doesn't come, I shall have to say good-bye to you, my dears,' said the princess with a mournful sigh.

'Oh, Mama, what an idea!' both daughters fell on her at once.

'But think of him all alone! You see, now ...'

And suddenly there was an unexpected quaver in the princess's voice. Her daughters were silent, and looked at one another. 'Mama will always find something to be miserable about,' was what that look meant. They did not know that though the princess liked staying in her daughter's house, and useful as she felt herself to be there, she had not ceased grieving both on her own account and her husband's ever since they had married their last and favourite daughter, leaving the family nest empty.

'What is it, Agatha Mihalovna?' Kitty asked suddenly of Agatha Mihalovna, who was standing with a mysterious air and a face full of meaning.

'About supper.'

'Very well,' said Dolly. 'You go and see about supper, and I'll hear Grisha his lesson. Otherwise he will have done nothing to-day.'

'That is a lesson to me! No, Dolly, I'll go,' exclaimed Levin, jumping up.

Grisha, who already went to a high school, had some homework to do during the summer holidays. Dolly had begun learning Latin with him when they were still in Moscow, and had made it a rule on coming to the Levins' to go over with him, at least once a day, the most difficult lessons, Latin and arithmetic. Levin had offered to take her place, but the mother, having once heard Levin give the lesson and noticing that his method was not the same as the master's in Moscow, said resolutely, though she was embarrassed and anxious not to offend Levin, that they must keep to the text-book as the teacher had done, and that she had better attend to it again herself. Levin was indignant with Oblonsky for not supervising the boy's education himself instead of unconcernedly leaving it to the child's mother who knew nothing about it, and equally indignant with the masters for teaching so badly. But he promised his sister-in-law to conduct the lessons exactly as she wished. And so he continued to work with Grisha, not in his own way, but according to the book, but did so reluctantly and therefore often forgot the hour of the lesson. That is what had happened now.

'No, I will go, Dolly; you sit still,' he said. 'We'll do everything properly, according to the book. Only when Stiva comes and we go shooting, then we shall have to miss the lessons.'

And Levin went to Grisha.

Varenka was saying something similar to Kitty. Even in the Levins' happy, well-ordered household Varenka had succeeded in making herself useful.

'I'll see to the supper; you sit still,' she said, and got up to go to Agatha Mihalovna.

'Yes, yes, most likely they've not been able to get any chickens. If so, ours ...' Kitty began.

'Agatha Mihalovna and I will see about it.' And Varenka disappeared with the old woman.

'What a nice girl she is!' said the princess.

'Not nice, *maman*; she's sweet, and there's no one like her.'

'So you are expecting Oblonsky to-day?' said Koznyshev, evidently disinclined to pursue the conversation about Varenka. 'It would be difficult to find brothers-in-law less like each other,' he said with a subtle smile. 'The one always on the move, only at home in society, like a fish in water; the other, our Kostya, lively, alert, sensitive, but when it comes to society either hasn't a word to say for himself or flounders about like a fish on dry land!'

'Yes, he's very remiss,' said the princess, addressing Koznyshev. 'I've been meaning to ask you to tell him that it's out of the question for her' (she indicated Kitty) 'to remain here. She positively must come to Moscow. He talks of getting a doctor down ...'

'*Maman*, he'll do all that's necessary; he has agreed to everything,' Kitty put in, annoyed with her mother for appealing to Koznyshev on such a matter.

In the midst of their conversation they heard the snorting of horses and the scraping of wheels along the gravel.

Dolly had not time to get up and go and meet her husband before Levin leaped out of the window of the room below, where Grisha was having his lesson, and helped the boy out after him.

'It's Stiva!' Levin shouted from under the balcony. 'We've finished, Dolly, don't worry!' he added, and started running like a boy to meet the carriage.

'*Is, ea, id, ejus, ejus, ejus!*' shouted Grisha, skipping along the avenue.

'And there is someone with him! It must be Papa!' cried Levin, stopping at the entrance of the avenue. 'Kitty, don't come down those steep steps; go round.'

But Levin was mistaken in taking the other person in the carriage for the old prince. When he drew nearer he saw sitting beside Oblonsky not the prince but a handsome, stout young man in a Scotch cap with long streamers behind. It was Vasenka Veslovsky, a distant cousin of the Shcherbatskys, a dashing young ornament of Petersburg and Moscow society – 'a capital fellow and a keen sportsman,' as Oblonsky said, introducing him.

Not in the least disconcerted by the disappointment he caused by appearing instead of the old prince, Veslovsky greeted Levin gaily, reminding him that they had met before, and picking up Grisha lifted him into the carriage over the head of the pointer Oblonsky had brought with him.

Levin did not get into the carriage, but followed on foot. He was a little put out at the non-arrival of the old prince, whom the more he knew the better he liked, and at the arrival of this Vasenka Veslovsky, a quite uncongenial and superfluous person. And his annoyance increased still further when he got to the steps, where the whole excited party of children and grown-ups had gathered, and saw Vasenka Veslovsky kissing Kitty's hand with a most cordial and gallant air.

'Your wife and I are cousins and very old friends,' said Vasenka Veslovsky, once more giving Levin's hand a vigorous shake.

'Well, is there any game?' Oblonsky asked, turning to Levin almost before everyone had had time to voice their greetings. 'We've come with the most savage intentions. ... Why, *maman*, they've not been in Moscow since! ... Tanya, I've got something for you! ... Get it, please; it's in the carriage, at the back!' He talked in all directions at once. 'How much better you look, Dolly dear,' he said to his wife, once more kissing her hand, holding it in one of his and patting it with the other.

Levin, who a minute before had been in the happiest frame of mind, now looked darkly at everyone, feeling out of temper with everything.

'Who was it he kissed yesterday with those lips?' he thought, looking at Oblonsky's tender demonstrations to his wife. He glanced at Dolly, and did not like her either.

'She doesn't believe in his love. So what is she so pleased about? Revolting!' thought Levin.

He looked at the princess, who had been so dear to him a minute ago, and he did not like the manner in which she welcomed this Vasenka with his streamers, just as though she were in her own house.

Even his brother, Koznyshev, who had also come out on to the steps, irritated him with the show of cordiality with which he greeted Oblonsky, for whom, as Levin knew, he had neither liking nor esteem.

And Varenka, too, was hateful as she shook hands with the fellow, with her air of being too holy for words, when all she thought about was getting married.

And most hateful of all was Kitty for falling in with the cheerful satisfaction of this gentleman who appeared to consider his visit in the country a piece of good fortune for himself and all concerned; and particularly objectionable was that special smile of hers with which she responded to his smiles.

Chattering noisily, they went into the house; but as soon as they were all seated Levin turned and left the room.

Kitty saw something was wrong with her husband. She tried to seize a moment to speak to him alone, but he hurried away from her, saying he had business to attend to in the office. It was a long time since his farm affairs had seemed to him so important as at that moment. 'It's all holiday for them,' he thought, 'but these are no holiday matters. They won't wait, and life can't go on without them.'

7

LEVIN came back to the house only when they sent to summon him to supper. Kitty and Agatha Mihalovna were standing on the stairs, deliberating what wines to serve.

'Why all this fuss? Have what we usually do.'

'No, Stiva doesn't drink. ... Kostya, stop – what's the matter?' Kitty began, hurrying after him, but he strode ruthlessly away to the dining-room without waiting for her, and at once joined in the animated general conversation which was being maintained there by Vasenka Veslovsky and Oblonsky.

'Well, what do you say, are we going shooting to-morrow?' inquired Oblonsky.

'Yes, please let's go,' said Veslovsky, moving to another chair, where he sat down sideways, with one fat leg doubled under him.

'All right, if you like. And have you had any shooting yet this year?' Levin asked Veslovsky, staring at his leg but speaking with that forced amiability that Kitty knew so well and which suited him so ill. 'I doubt if we shall find any snipe, but there are plenty of woodcock. Only we ought to start early. You won't be tired? What about you, Stiva – you're not tired?'

'Me tired? I've never been tired yet. I don't mind if we stay up all night. Let's go for a walk!'

'Yes, don't let's go to bed at all! Capital!' Veslovsky chimed in.

'Oh, we all know you can do without sleep, and keep other people up too,' Dolly said to her husband in the faintly ironical tone which she now almost always adopted towards him. 'But I think it's time we all went to bed. ... I'm going, I don't want any supper.'

'No, stay here, Dolly dear,' said Oblonsky, going round to her side of the long supper-table. 'I've still got a lot to tell you.'

'I don't expect you've any real news.'

'Do you know, Veslovsky has been to Anna's, and he's going again?

They're not fifty miles from here. I, too, must certainly go over. Veslovsky, come here!'

Vasenka came over to the ladies, and sat down beside Kitty.

'Oh, do tell us! You have been to see her? How was she?' asked Dolly.

Levin was left at the other end of the table and, though never pausing in his conversation with the princess and Varenka, he noticed the eager and mysterious conversation going on between Oblonsky, Dolly, Kitty, and Veslovsky. And that was not all. He saw on his wife's face an expression of deep emotion as she gazed with fixed eyes into the handsome face of Vasenka, who was telling her something with great animation.

'It's awfully nice at their place,' Vasenka was saying, speaking of Vronsky and Anna. 'Of course, I can't take it upon myself to judge, but in their house there's a real feeling of home.'

'What do they intend doing?'

'I believe they think of going to Moscow for the winter.'

'How jolly it would be for us all to go over and see them together! When are you going?' Oblonsky asked Vasenka.

'I'm spending July there.'

'Would you come?' Oblonsky asked his wife.

'I've been wanting to for a long while, and I certainly shall,' replied Dolly. 'I am sorry for her, and I know her. She is a fine woman. I shall go alone, when you go back, and then I shall be in no one's way. I shall even prefer it without you.'

'Very well,' said Oblonsky. 'What about you, Kitty?'

'I? Why should I go?' Kitty said, flushing deeply and glancing round at her husband.

'Do you know Anna Arkadyevna, then?' Veslovsky asked her. 'She's a very fascinating woman.'

'Yes,' she answered Veslovsky, crimsoning still more, and she rose and went over to her husband.

'So you are off shooting to-morrow?' she said.

Levin's jealousy had in those few moments, especially after the flush that had suffused her cheeks while she was talking to Veslovsky, gone far indeed. Now as he listened to her he construed her words in his own fashion. Strange as it was to him when he recalled it later, it seemed at the moment clear that she asked whether he was going shooting only because she wanted to know whether he would give that pleasure to Vasenka Veslovsky, with whom, as he fancied, she was already in love.

'Yes, I am,' he replied in an unnatural voice that grated on his own ear.

'Why not stay at home to-morrow, or Dolly won't have seen any-thing of her husband? You could go the day after to-morrow,' said Kitty.

This time Levin now interpreted her thus: 'Don't part me from *him*. I don't mind if *you* go – but do let me enjoy the society of this delightful young man.'

'Oh, we can stay at home to-morrow, if you wish,' he replied with pronounced amiability.

Vasenka meanwhile, utterly unsuspecting the misery his presence occasioned, got up from the table after Kitty, watching her with an affectionate smile in his eyes.

Levin saw that look. He turned pale, and for a minute he could hardly breathe. 'How dare he look at my wife like that!' he thought, boiling with rage.

'To-morrow, then? Do let us!' said Vasenka, dropping into a chair and again doubling a leg under him in his habitual fashion.

Levin's jealousy increased still further. He already saw himself as the deceived husband, necessary to his wife and her lover simply in order to provide them with the conveniences and pleasures of life. ... But in spite of this he made polite and hospitable inquiries of Vasenka about his shooting, his gun, his boots, and agreed to go shooting next day.

Happily for Levin, the old princess cut short his agonies by getting up herself and advising Kitty to go to bed. But even here there was another pang in store for him. Bidding his hostess good-night, Vasen-ka would again have kissed her hand, but Kitty, reddening and with a naïve rudeness for which she was afterwards scolded by her mother, drew her hand back and said:

'That is not customary in our house.'

In Levin's eyes Kitty was to blame for having laid herself open to such behaviour, and still more to blame for showing so awkwardly that she did not like it.

'What a pity to go to bed now!' said Oblonsky, who after several glasses of wine at supper was in his most charming and romantic mood. 'Look, Kitty,' he went on, pointing to the moon rising behind the lime-trees. 'How exquisite! Veslovsky, now's the time for a serenade. You know, he has a splendid voice: we practised songs together on the way here. He has brought some lovely songs with him, two new ones. He and Mademoiselle Varenka must sing duets together.'

Oblonsky and Veslovsky walked up and down the avenue long after the others had retired, and their voices could be heard singing one of the new songs.

Levin sat scowling in an easy-chair in his wife's bedroom, listening to them, and maintaining an obstinate silence when Kitty asked him what was the matter. But when at last with a timid smile she hazarded the question: 'Is it something you don't like about Veslovsky?' it all burst out and he told her everything that was on his mind. He felt humiliated himself at what he was saying, and that exasperated him still further.

He stood facing her, his eyes flashing menacingly under his scowling brows, and he pressed his strong arms against his chest, as though trying with all his might to hold himself in. The expression of his face would have been harsh, and even cruel, but for a look of suffering which touched her. His jaws were twitching, and his voice kept breaking.

'You understand that I'm not jealous, that's a horrible word. I can't be jealous, and believe that … I can't say what I feel, but it is dreadful … I'm not jealous, but I'm affronted, humiliated that anyone should dare to think – should dare to look at you with eyes like that …'

'Eyes like what?' said Kitty, trying to remember as honestly as she could every word and gesture of that evening and every shade of meaning implied in them.

In the depths of her heart she did think that there had been something just at the moment when Veslovsky had followed her to the other end of the table; but she dared not acknowledge it even to herself, much less bring herself to say so to him, and so increase his suffering.

'And what attraction could I possibly have in my condition?'

'Ah!' he cried, clutching his head. 'You had better be silent! … I suppose if you had been attractive then …'

'Oh no, Kostya! Wait – listen!' she implored, looking at him in compassionate pain. 'Why, what can you be thinking about! When you know men simply do not exist for me! ... Would you like me never to see anyone?'

For the first minute she had been wounded by this jealousy of his; she was angry to think that the slightest distraction, even the most innocent, should be forbidden her; but now she would gladly have sacrificed, not only mere trifles like that, but everything, for his peace of mind, to save him from the agony he was suffering.

'Try and understand the horror and absurdity of my position,' he went on in a desperate whisper. 'He's my guest, strictly speaking he has done nothing improper, except that I don't like his free-and-easy airs and the way he has of tucking his leg under him. He thinks it's the best possible form, and I am obliged to be civil to him.'

'But Kostya, you're exaggerating,' said Kitty, at bottom rejoicing at the strength of his love for her, shown now in his jealousy.

'The most awful part of it all is that you're just as you always are – and now when you are my holy of holies, and we're so happy, so particularly happy, all of a sudden this trash comes along ... No, he's not trash. Why should I abuse him? He's not my business. But why should my, your happiness ...?'

'Do you know, I think I see how it all started?' Kitty was beginning.

'How? How?'

'I saw you looking at us when we were talking at supper!'

'Yes, well?' Levin said in dismay.

She told him what they had been talking about. And as she told him she was breathless with agitation. Levin was silent for a space, then he scanned her pale distressed face, and suddenly seized his head in his hands.

'Katya, I have worn you out. My darling, forgive me! It was madness! Katya, I'm a criminal. How could I torture you over such nonsense?'

'Oh, I was sorry for you.'

'For me? For me? I'm an utter madman! ... But why make you wretched? It's terrible to think that any outsider can come along and upset our happiness.'

'It's humiliating too, of course.'

'No, I shall make him stay the whole summer, and lavish attentions on him,' said Levin, kissing her hands. 'You shall see. To-morrow. ... Oh yes, but we are going out shooting to-morrow.'

8

NEXT day, before the ladies were up, a shooting-brake and a wagonette stood at the door waiting for the guns, and Laska, aware since early morning that they were going shooting, after much whining and darting to and fro had seated herself beside the coachman and, disapproving of the delay, was excitedly watching the door whence the sportsmen still had not appeared. The first to come was Vasenka Veslovsky, in new high boots that reached half-way up his fat thighs, a green blouse girdled with a new cartridge-belt smelling of leather, and on his head the Scotch cap with the streamers. He carried a brandnew English hammerless gun without a sling. Laska made one bound to greet him, jumping up and asking in her own way how soon the others were coming, but getting no answer from him she returned to her post of observation and sat motionless, her head on one side, and one ear pricked up to listen. At last the door opened with a creak, and out flew Oblonsky's spotted tan pointer, Krak, spinning and twisting round in the air, followed by Oblonsky himself, a gun in his hand and a cigar in his mouth.

'Good dog, Krak, good dog!' he exclaimed affectionately to the dog, who put his paws up on his chest, catching at his game-bag. Oblonsky was wearing rough leggings and raw-hide shoes, a pair of torn trousers and a short coat. On his head was a wreck of a hat of indefinite shape, but his gun was a beauty, the latest thing in guns, and his game-bag and cartridge-belt, though much worn, were of the very best quality.

Vasenka Veslovsky had not realized till then that good form in a sportsman consisted in being dressed in old clothes but having the finest possible appurtenances for shooting. He saw it now as he looked at Oblonsky, beaming with elegance and well-fed *bonhomie* in his shabby clothes, a typical gentleman; and he resolved to follow his example next time he went shooting.

'Well, and what about our host?' he asked.

'He has a young wife,' answered Oblonsky, smiling.

'Yes, and such a charming one too!'

'He was quite ready. I suppose he has run up to her again.'

Oblonsky had guessed right. Levin had run back to ask his wife once more if she forgave him for his foolishness yesterday, and also to entreat her for heaven's sake to be more careful of herself; and especially to keep away from the children, who at any moment might push against her. Then he had to be assured all over again that she was not angry with him for going away for a couple of days, and to beg her to be certain to send him a note next morning by a servant on horseback – a word or two would do – to let him know that all was well with her.

As always, it was hard for Kitty to be parted from her husband for two days; but when she saw his eager figure, looking so big and strong in his shooting-boots and his white blouse, and his radiant excitement, so incomprehensible to her, at the prospect of the shoot, she forgot herself in his happiness and said good-bye to him cheerfully.

'Sorry, gentlemen!' he said, running out on to the steps. 'Have they put the lunch in? Why is the chestnut on the right? Never mind, though. Laska, down! Back to your place!

'Turn them in with the heifers,' he said to the herdsman, who had come up to ask about some young bullocks. 'Sorry, here comes another wretch.'

Levin jumped down from the brake, in which he had already taken his seat, to meet the carpenter, who was approaching with a foot-rule in his hand.

'There, you see, you didn't come to the office last night, and now you're detaining me. Well, what is it?'

'Would your honour let me make another turning? It'll only mean three more steps to add. And we make it just fit at the same time. It will be much more convenient.'

'You should have listened to me,' said Levin in annoyance. 'I told you to fix the string-boards first, and then fit the treads. You can't alter it now. Do as I tell you, and make a new staircase.'

The facts of the matter were that in the new wing that was being built the carpenter had spoilt the staircase, having constructed it without calculating the elevation, so that when it was put in position the stairs all sloped. Now the man wanted to keep the same staircase, adding another three steps.

'It would be much better, sir.'

'But where would your staircase reach to with its three extra steps?'

'Excuse me, sir,' the carpenter said with a disdainful smile. 'It will be just right. It will start at the bottom, you see,' he continued with a persuasive gesture, 'and go up and up until it gets there.'

'But three steps will add to the length too ... where is it to come out?'

'Why, to be sure, if it begins from the bottom it must get there,' the carpenter repeated obstinately and persuasively.

'Yes, go up the wall and get to the ceiling.'

'Excuse me, sir! Why, it'll start from the bottom, and go on and on until it gets there.'

Levin pulled out his ramrod and began drawing a plan of the staircase in the dust.

'There, do you see what I mean?'

'As your honour pleases,' said the carpenter, his eyes suddenly brightening. He had obviously understood at last. 'It seems we shall have to make a new one.'

'Well, then, do as you're told,' Levin called to him, seating himself in the brake. 'Now we're off! Hold the dogs, Philip!'

Leaving the cares of home and estate behind him, Levin had such a strong feeling of anticipation and joy in life that he was disinclined for talk. Besides, he was full of the suppressed excitement that every sportsman knows as he approaches the scene of action. He had no thought for anything just then but whether they would find any game in the Kolpensky marsh, how Laska would compare with Krak, and what sort of shot he himself would make that day. 'If only I don't disgrace myself before this Veslovsky! If only Oblonsky does not outdo me!' he said to himself.

Oblonsky was occupied with similar thoughts, and was likewise not disposed to talk. Vasenka Veslovsky alone kept up a ceaseless flow of cheerful chatter. Listening to him now, Levin felt ashamed to think how unjust he had been to him the night before. Vasenka was really a good sort, simple, kind-hearted, and very jolly. Had Levin met him before his marriage, he would have made a friend of him. Levin did not quite like Vasenka's way of treating life as a perpetual holiday, or his rather free-and-easy elegance. He seemed to assume that long nails, a stylish cap, and all the rest were incontestable proofs of superiority; but this could be forgiven for the sake of his open-heartedness and good form. Levin was attracted by his breeding, his excellent French and English, and by the fact that he was a man of his own class.

Vasenka greatly admired the Cossack horse from the Don harnessed alongside on the left. He went into raptures over it. 'Wouldn't it be fine to gallop over the steppes on a Cossack horse, eh? Don't you think so?' he said.

He appeared to see something wild and romantic in a gallop on a Cossack horse; he could not have explained why he thought so, but his naïveté, especially in conjunction with his good looks, charming smile, and graceful movements, was very attractive. Either Levin found Vasenka congenial, or he was trying to atone for his sins of the previous evening and see nothing but good in him – anyway, he took pleasure in his company.

They had gone about two miles when Veslovsky suddenly missed his cigars and pocket-book, and did not know whether he had lost them or left them behind on the table. There were three hundred and seventy roubles in the pocket-book, so the matter could not be ignored.

'I say, Levin, let me gallop back on that left trace-horse. That will be fine, eh?' he said, preparing to mount.

'No, why should you go?' answered Levin, calculating that Vasenka could hardly weigh less than fifteen stone. 'I'll send the coachman.'

So the coachman rode back on the trace-horse, and Levin drove the remaining pair himself.

9

'WELL, now, what is our plan of campaign? Tell us all about it,' said Oblonsky.

'The plan is this. I thought we'd go as far as Gvozdev. On this side of Gvozdev there is a snipe marsh, and beyond Gvozdev some magnificent marshes, where there are great snipe too. It's hot now, but we shall get there towards evening – it's about thirteen or fourteen miles. We can have some shooting, spend the night there, and attack the bigger marshes to-morrow.'

'And is there nothing on the way?'

'Yes, there is, but we should lose time, and it's too hot. There are two nice little spots but nothing much there.'

Levin himself would have liked to stop at these two little places, but they were near home: he could take them any time, and they were not large enough for three guns. So he stretched a point and said that they would hardly find anything there. When they came to one of

608

the small marshes he wanted to drive past, but Oblonsky's experienced eye at once detected the place from the road.

'Shall we not try this?' he said, pointing to the little marsh.

'Oh yes, do let us! How splendid!' implored Vasenka Veslovsky, and Levin had to give in.

They had barely time to pull up before the dogs flew towards the marsh, racing one another.

'Krak! Laska! ...'

The dogs came back.

'There won't be room for three: I'll wait here,' said Levin, hoping they would find nothing but peewits, who had been startled by the dogs and turning over in their flight were plaintively wailing above the marsh.

'No, come along, Levin! Let's all go together!' Veslovsky called.

'Really, there's not room. Back, Laska! You don't want the two dogs, do you?'

Levin remained by the brake, looking enviously at the others. They went over the whole marsh, but found nothing except a moorhen and some peewits, of which Veslovsky got one.

'There, you see, I was not grudging you the marsh,' said Levin. 'It was only a waste of time.'

'It was jolly all the same. Did you see?' said Vasenka Veslovsky, clambering awkwardly into the brake with his gun in one hand and the peewit in the other. 'I got this one all right, didn't I? Well, how soon shall we be at the real place?'

Suddenly the horses plunged forward, Levin knocked his head against the barrel of someone's gun, and there was a report. Actually the report came first, but it seemed the other way round to Levin. What had happened was that Vasenka Veslovsky, while uncocking one trigger, had discharged the other. The shot buried itself in the ground without hurting anybody. Oblonsky shook his head and laughed reproachfully at Veslovsky. But Levin had not the heart to reprove him: in the first place, any comment from him would have looked as though it were provoked by the danger he had just escaped and the bump which had come up on his forehead; and secondly, Veslovsky was at first so naïvely distressed, and then laughed so good-humouredly and infectiously at their general dismay, that Levin could not help laughing himself.

When they reached the second marsh, which was fairly large and would take some time to shoot over, Levin tried to dissuade them from getting out. But Veslovsky again persuaded him, and again, the marsh being narrow, Levin, like a good host, remained with the vehicles.

Krak made straight for some hummocks. Vasenka Veslovsky was the first to run after the dog, and before Oblonsky had time to come up a snipe flew out. Veslovsky fired and missed, and the snipe alighted in an unmown meadow. The bird was left to Veslovsky to follow up. Krak found it again, pointed, and Veslovsky shot it and went back to the carriages.

'Now you go, and I'll stay with the horses,' he said.

The sportsman in Levin had begun to feel the pangs of envy. He handed the reins to Veslovsky and walked into the marsh.

Laska, who had long been whining plaintively and fretting against the injustice of being kept back, bounded straight ahead to a promising spot covered with hummocks that Levin knew well, and that Krak had not yet come upon.

'Why don't you stop her?' shouted Oblonsky.

'She won't spring them,' answered Levin, pleased with his dog and hastening after her.

The nearer Laska drew to the familiar hummocks, the more intent did she become in her pursuit. A little marsh bird did not distract her attention for more than an instant. She circled once in front of the hummocks, started again, and then suddenly quivered with excitement and stopped dead.

'Here, Stiva, here!' shouted Levin, feeling his heart beginning to beat more violently; and all at once, as though some sort of shutter had been lifted from his straining ears, which had lost all sense of distance, he could not distinguish the sounds that came to him, confused but clear. He heard Oblonsky's steps and took them for the distant tramp of horses; he heard the crumbling of earth when he stepped on the edge of a hummock, which broke off, pulling the grass out by the roots, and he took it for the noise of a snipe on the wing. He heard, too, not far behind him, a sound of splashing for which he could not account.

Picking his way, he approached the dog.

'Fetch it!'

It was not a great snipe but a woodcock that flew up from beside the dog. Levin lifted his gun, but just as he was taking aim the sound of splashing grew louder, came nearer and was mingled with Veslovsky's voice shouting something in a strange loud manner. Levin saw that his aim was behind the snipe, but still he fired.

When he was sure he had missed, Levin looked round and saw that the horses and the brake were not on the road but in the marsh.

Eager to watch the shooting, Veslovsky had driven into the marsh, and got the horses stuck in the mud.

'Damn the fellow!' muttered Levin to himself, as he went back to the carriage that had sunk in the mire. 'Why did you leave the road?' he asked drily, and, calling the coachman, he set to work to get the horses out.

Levin was vexed both at having been put off his shot and at his horses being led into the bog and, above all, that neither Oblonsky nor Veslovsky gave him and the coachman a hand with unharnessing the horses and getting them out, since neither of them understood the first thing about harness. Disregarding Vasenka's protestations that the ground had been quite dry there, Levin worked in silence with the coachman to extricate the horses. But soon, beginning to get warm at what he was doing and seeing Veslovsky tug at one of the splashboards so strenuously that in his zeal he actually wrenched it off, Levin reproached himself with being influenced by his sentiments of the previous day and so treating Veslovsky too coldly, and he tried to efface his brusqueness by being particularly genial. When everything was in order again and the vehicles back on the road, Levin directed lunch to be got out.

'Bon appétit – bonne conscience! Ce poulet va tomber jusqu'au fond de mes bottes,' remarked Vasenka, quoting the French saying as he finished his second chicken. 'Now our troubles are over; now everything will go right. Only for my sins I must sit on the box. Isn't that so? No, no! I'm a perfect Automedon – you wait and see how I get you there!' he said, keeping hold of the reins when Levin begged him to let the coachman drive. 'No, I must atone for my sins, and I'm quite comfortable on the box.' And he drove off.

Levin was rather afraid that Veslovsky would wear the horses out, especially the chestnut on the left, whom he did not know how to handle; but he could not resist Veslovsky's high spirits, the songs he sang all the way on the box, the stories he told and his imitation of driving four-in-hand in the English fashion. And it was in the very best of spirits that after lunch they drove to the Gvozdev marsh.

10

VASENKA had driven so fast that they reached the marsh too early, before the cool of the evening.

When they got to the real marsh, the main object of their expedition, Levin involuntarily began considering how he could get rid of Vasenka so as to go about unhampered. Oblonsky was evidently possessed with the same desire, and Levin read on his face the preoccupation felt by every true sportsman before a shoot begins, together with a certain good-humoured slyness characteristic of him.

'Well, how shall we go? It's a splendid marsh, I see, and there are hawks,' said Oblonsky, pointing to two large birds circling over the reeds. 'Where there are hawks, there is sure to be game.'

'Now, gentlemen,' said Levin, pulling up his boots and examining the caps of his gun with a somewhat gloomy expression, 'you see those reeds?' He pointed to a little island of blackish green in the huge half-mown wet meadow stretching along the right bank of the river. 'The marsh begins here, straight in front of us, do you see – where it looks greener? From here it runs to the right, where those horses are. There are hummocks, and great snipe; and it goes all round those reeds as far as that alder grove and right down to the mill. Over there look, where the pools are! That's the best place. I once shot seventeen snipe there. We can separate, going in different directions with the dogs, and meet again at the mill.'

'Well, who goes to the right, and who left?' asked Oblonsky. 'It's broader on the right, so you two go that way, and I'll take the left,' he added with affected indifference.

'Right! We'll get the best bag! Come along, come along!' Vasenka exclaimed.

Levin was obliged to accept this arrangement, and they divided.

The moment they entered the marsh, the two dogs began hunting about together and made towards the green, slimy-looking pool. Levin knew what that cautious, seemingly vague search of Laska's meant; he knew the place, too, and expected a whole wisp of snipe.

'Veslovsky, beside me, walk beside me!' he whispered with bated breath to his companion splashing along in the water behind him.

Levin could not escape feeling an interest in the direction Vasenka's gun was pointed, after that casual shot by the Kolpensky marsh.

'No, I don't want to get in your way. Don't bother about me.'

But Levin could not help remembering Kitty's parting words: 'Mind you don't shoot one another!' Nearer and nearer drew the dogs, keeping out of each other's way, each pursuing a different scent. The expectation of snipe was so intense that the squelching sound of his own heel, as he drew it out of the rusty mud, sounded to Levin like the call of a bird, and he grasped the butt of his gun firmly.

Bang! bang! he heard just above his ear. Vasenka had fired at a flight of ducks circling over the marsh and flying at that moment towards the sportsmen, far out of range. Before Levin had time to look round, he heard the whirr of a snipe, and first one, then another, and a third, followed by about eight more, rose from the ground. Oblonsky got one just as it was beginning to zigzag in the air, and the bird fell with a thud into the bog. He turned his gun leisurely to another, still flying low in the reeds, and as the shot rang out the snipe dropped down and could be seen fluttering out of the cut sedges, flapping its unhurt wing that showed white underneath.

Levin was not so lucky. He aimed at his first bird too low, and missed; he aimed at it again, just as it was rising, but at that instant another flew up from beneath his feet, distracting his attention, so he missed again.

While they were loading their guns, another snipe rose, and Veslovsky, who had finished reloading, sent two charges of small-shot into the water. Oblonsky picked up his game, and with sparkling eyes looked at Levin.

'Well, now let's separate,' he said and, limping with his left leg and holding his gun ready, he whistled to his dog and walked off to one side. Levin and Veslovsky took the other.

Whenever Levin made a bad start, he invariably got worked up and out of temper, and shot badly for the rest of the day. So it was this time. There were snipe in plenty: they kept rising from under the dogs, from under the sportsmen's feet, and Levin might have recovered himself; but the more he fired the more he disgraced himself before Veslovsky, who kept blazing away merrily, in and out of range, never hitting anything and not in the least abashed thereby. Levin was too hasty. He grew impatient, and got more and more flurried, until at last he was shooting almost without hope of hitting. Even Laska seemed to feel this. She scented less eagerly, looking round at the sportsmen in perplexity and reproach. Shot followed shot.

Powder-smoke hung about the sportsmen, but in the great roomy net of the game-bag there were only three light little birds, and one even of these had been shot by Veslovsky and another belonged to them both. Meanwhile from the other side of the marsh came not frequent but, as Levin fancied, telling reports from Oblonsky's gun, followed almost every time by a shout to 'Fetch it, Krak!'

This excited Levin still more. The snipe kept floating in the air over the reeds. From every side came the incessant sound of whirring wings close to the ground, and harsh cries high in the air. The snipe that had risen previously and been flying about now descended in front of the guns. Instead of two, dozens of hawks now screeched overhead.

Having tramped more than half the marsh, Levin and Veslovsky came to a spot where the peasants' meadow-land was divided into long strips reaching to the reeds, marked off either by the grass having been trodden down or by a path cut through. Half of these strips were already mown.

Though there was little hope of finding as many birds in the unmown strips as on the mown part, Levin, having promised to meet Oblonsky, trudged on with his companion through mown and unmown strips alike.

'Hi, there, sportsmen!' shouted a peasant who was sitting with some others near a cart without a horse. 'Come and have some dinner with us! Have a drop of wine!'

Levin looked round.

'Come along; it's all right!' shouted a jolly-looking bearded peasant with a red face, displaying his white teeth in a grin, and holding aloft a greenish bottle that glittered in the sun.

'*Qu'est-ce qu'ils disent ?*' asked Veslovsky.

'They invite us to go and have a drink of vodka with them. They've probably been dividing the meadow into lots. Why don't you go?' said Levin, not quite disinterestedly, hoping the vodka would tempt Veslovsky and lure him away.

'Why do they invite us?'

'Oh, they're merry-making. Go along. You'd find it interesting.'

'*Allons, c'est curieux.*'

'You go, you go – you can find your way to the mill!' cried Levin, and, looking round, was delighted to see that Veslovsky, bent and stumbling with weariness, holding his gun at arm's length, was making his way out of the marsh towards the peasants.

'You come too!' the peasant shouted to Levin. 'Never fear! You taste our pie!'

Levin badly wanted a drink of vodka and a slice of bread. He was exhausted and could hardly drag his faltering legs out of the bog, and for a moment he hesitated. But the dog was setting. Immediately all his weariness vanished, and he walked lightly through the swamp towards Laska. A snipe rose from under his feet: he fired and got it. The dog still pointed. 'Fetch it!' Another bird flew up close to her. Levin fired. But that day he had no luck: he missed, and when he went to look for the one he had shot he could not find it either. He crawled among the reeds, but Laska would not believe he had shot anything, and when he sent her to find it she only pretended to hunt and did not really search.

Even without Vasenka, on whom Levin threw the blame for his want of success, matters did not improve. There were plenty of birds here too, but Levin made one miss after another.

The slanting rays of the sun were still hot; his clothes, soaked through with perspiration, stuck to his body; his left boot full of water was heavy and made a squelching sound as he walked; drops of sweat ran down his powder-grimed face; there was a bitter taste in his mouth, and in his nose the smell of gunpowder and stagnant water; the perpetual whirr of wings rang in his ears; he could not touch the barrels of his gun, they were so hot; his heart thumped with quick, short beats; his hands shook agitatedly and his weary legs stumbled as he dragged them over the hummocks and through the swamp; but still he went on and still he shot. Finally, after a disgraceful miss, he flung his gun and his hat on the ground.

'No, I must pull myself together,' he said to himself.

Picking up the gun and his hat, he called Laska, and got out of the swamp. Reaching a dry place he sat down, took off his boot and emptied it, and then went back to the marsh, drank a little of the rusty-tasting water, wetted the heated barrels of his gun, and bathed his face and hands. Feeling refreshed, he returned to the spot where a snipe had settled, firmly resolved not to get flurried.

He tried to keep calm but again it was the same. His finger pressed the trigger before he had taken good aim. Things went from bad to worse.

There were only five birds in his game-bag when he came out of the marsh and walked towards the alder grove to rejoin Oblonsky.

Before he caught sight of Oblonsky, he saw his dog. Krak, black all over with the stinking marsh slime, darted out from behind the twisted root of an alder and started sniffing Laska with the air of a conqueror. Behind Krak, in the shade of the alders, appeared Oblonsky's dignified figure. He came towards Levin, red and perspiring, his collar unbuttoned, and limping a little as before.

'Well? You were shooting a lot!' he said, smiling merrily.

'How have you got on?' queried Levin. But there was no need to ask – he had already seen the full game-bag.

'Oh, pretty fair.'

He had fourteen birds.

'A grand marsh! Veslovsky must have got in your way, I'm afraid. It's awkward for two guns with one dog,' said Oblonsky, to soften his triumph.

11

WHEN Levin and Oblonsky reached the peasant's hut where Levin always put up, Veslovsky was already there. He was sitting on a bench in the middle of the hut, holding on with both hands and laughing his gay infectious laugh, while a soldier, the brother of the peasant's wife, was tugging at his mud-covered boots.

'I've only just come. *Ils ont été charmants!* Just fancy – they gave me drink, fed me! Such bread, it was marvellous! *Délicieux!* And the vodka … I never tasted better. And they positively wouldn't take a penny for anything. And they kept on saying "No offence meant!" or something of the sort.'

'Why should they take anything? They were entertaining you, you see. Do you suppose they keep vodka to sell?' said the soldier, who had at last succeeded in dragging off one wet boot together with a blackened stocking.

In spite of the dirtiness of the hut, which was all muddied by the sportsmen's boots and the filthy dogs trying to lick themselves clean, and the smell of bog and gunpowder that filled the room, and the absence of knives and forks, the party drank their tea and ate their supper with a relish only a day's shooting can produce. Washed and clean, they betook themselves to the newly-swept hay-barn, where the coachman had been making up beds for the gentlemen.

Though it was already dark, none of the three felt like sleep. They lay talking reminiscences and anecdotes of guns, of dogs, of other shooting parties, until the conversation came to rest on a topic that interested all of them. Inspired by Vasenka's repeated expressions of delight at the charm of their arrangements for the night and the scent of the hay, of a broken cart (he thought it was broken because the shafts had been taken out), of the good-nature of the peasants who had treated him to vodka, and of the dogs, each stretched out at its master's feet, Oblonsky began telling them of the attractions of a shoot last summer over the estates of a man called Malthus. Malthus was a well-known railway magnate. Oblonsky described the moors which Malthus had leased in the province of Tver, and how they were preserved, and spoke of the carriages and dog-carts that had driven the party to the shoot, and of the great lunch-tent that had been pitched beside the marsh.

'I don't understand you,' said Levin, sitting up in the hay. 'How is it these people don't disgust you? I know lunch with Lafitte is all very nice, but doesn't the very sumptuousness of it revolt you? All these people, just like our spirit monopolists in the old days, make their money in ways that earn everyone's contempt. They ignore that contempt, and then afterwards use their dishonest gains to live it down.'

'Perfectly true!' chimed in Vasenka Veslovsky. 'Perfectly true! Of course we know that Oblonsky accepts their invitations out of *bonhomie*, but other people say, "Well, Oblonsky goes and stays with them ..."'

'Not a bit of it!' Levin could hear that Oblonsky was smiling as he spoke. 'I simply consider him no more dishonest than any other wealthy merchant or nobleman: they've all made their money alike – by their work and their intelligence.'

'Oh, by what work? Do you call it work to get hold of a concession and then speculate with it?'

'Of course it is. Work in this sense, that if it were not for him and others like him, we should have no railways.'

'But it's not work in the sense in which a peasant or a professional man understands it.'

'I dare say; but it is work in that his activity produces a result – the railways. But I forgot, you don't approve of railways anyhow.'

'That's quite another question. I am prepared to admit that they're useful. But all profit that is out of proportion to the labour expended is dishonest.'

'But who is to determine what is proportionate?'

'Making profit by dishonest means, by sharp practice' – began Levin, conscious that he could not draw a distinct line between honesty and dishonesty – 'like the profits made by banks,' he went on, 'is wrong. The amassing of enormous fortunes without labour is an evil, the same as it was with the spirit monopolists: the form has changed, that's all. *Le roi est mort, vive le roi!* No sooner were the spirit monopolies abolished than railways and banking houses appeared: other means of acquiring wealth without work.'

'All you say may be quite true and ingenious. ... Lie down, Krak!' exclaimed Oblonsky to the dog that was scratching itself and turning round in the hay. He was obviously so convinced of the righteousness of his case that he spoke urbanely and without haste. 'But you have not drawn the line between honest and dishonest work. That I draw a bigger salary than my chief clerk, though he knows the business better than I do – is that dishonest?'

'I can't say.'

'Well, but I can tell you: your getting, let's say, five thousand for the labour you put in on your estate, while our peasant host here, work as he may, can never get more than about fifty is just as dishonest as my earning more than my chief clerk, and Malthus more than a railway mechanic. In fact it seems to me that the quite unjustified hostility towards men like Malthus that I notice on the part of society is probably due to envy ...'

'No, that's not fair!' objected Veslovsky. 'Envy has nothing to do with it. There is something not nice about that sort of business.'

'Let me continue,' Levin went on. 'You say it is not right for me to get five thousand while a peasant gets only fifty. That's true. It is unfair, and I feel it, but ...'

'It is, when you think of it. Why should we spend our time eating, drinking, shooting, doing nothing, while the peasant is at work from morning to night?' said Vasenka Veslovsky, speaking quite sincerely, the thought having evidently just occurred to him for the first time in his life.

'Yes, you feel it, but you don't give him your property,' said Oblonsky, as if purposely to sting Levin.

Of late a sort of covert antagonism had arisen between the brothers-in-law, as if the fact of their being married to sisters had provoked rivalry between them as to who had ordered his life best, and now this hostility showed itself in the personal tone the discussion was beginning to assume.

'I don't give it away because no one demands that of me, and if I wanted to, I couldn't,' replied Levin. 'And there's no one to give it to.'

'Try this peasant here: he wouldn't refuse it.'

'Yes, but how can I give it to him? Go with him and make out a deed of conveyance?'

'I don't know; but if you are convinced that you have no right ...'

'I'm not at all convinced. On the contrary, I feel I have no right to give it up, that I owe certain duties both to the land and to my family.'

'No, excuse me, if you look upon this inequality as unjust, I can't see why you don't act accordingly. ...'

'I do, only in a negative way, in the sense that I don't try to increase the difference that exists between my position and his.'

'Come, now, that's a paradox.'

'Yes, that does savour of sophistry,' Veslovsky agreed. 'Ah, our host!' he said, as the barn door creaked and the peasant came in. 'How is it you're not asleep?'

'Sleep indeed! I thought you gentlemen would be asleep, but I heard you chattering. I've come for a crook. The dog won't bite?' he asked, stepping cautiously with his bare feet.

'And where will you sleep?'

'We are going to take the horses to grass to-night.'

'Oh, what a night!' said Veslovsky, gazing through the great frame of the now open barn door at a corner of the hut and the unharnessed wagonette, visible in the faint after-glow. 'But listen! Women's voices singing, and not at all badly either. Who's that singing?' he asked of the peasant.

'The maid-servants from close by.'

'Let's go for a walk! We shan't sleep, you know. Oblonsky, come along!'

'If only I could do both – lie here and go at the same time,' answered Oblonsky, stretching. 'It's very comfortable here.'

'All right, I shall go by myself,' said Veslovsky, starting up and putting on his shoes and stockings. 'Good-bye, gentlemen. If it's fun, I'll call you. You've given me my shooting, and I won't forget you.'

'He's a good fellow, isn't he?' said Oblonsky, when Veslovsky had gone and the peasant had shut the door after him.

'Yes, rather,' Levin replied, still thinking of the matter they had been discussing. It seemed to him that he had expressed his ideas and feelings as clearly as he knew how, and yet both the others – sincere and intelligent men – had declared with one voice that he was comforting himself with sophistries. This disconcerted him.

'It comes to this, my dear boy: one must do one of two things – either accept the existing social order as a just one, and then stick up for your rights; or acknowledge that you are enjoying unfair privileges, as I do, and get all the pleasure out of them you can.'

'No, if one had no right to them one could not enjoy these advantages – at least I could not. The great thing for me is not to feel that I am in the wrong.'

'What do you say – why don't we go out for a turn after all?' said Oblonsky, evidently weary of mental strain. 'We shan't sleep, you know. Come on, let's go!'

Levin did not reply. The remark made during the conversation about his acting justly only in a negative sense absorbed his attention. 'Is it possible that one can be just only negatively?' he was asking himself.

'How strong the smell of the fresh hay is!' remarked Oblonsky, sitting up. 'Nothing will make me sleep. Vasenka is up to something out there. Do you hear the laughter and his voice? Hadn't we better go too? Come along!'

'No, I'm not coming,' answered Levin.

'Is that also on a point of principle?' said Oblonsky with a smile, searching round in the dark for his cap.

'No, not on principle, but why should I go?'

'You know, you are preparing trouble for yourself,' said Oblonsky, having found his cap and getting up.

'How?'

'Do you suppose I don't see the way you have got into with your wife? I heard you making it a matter of first importance whether or not you should go off for a couple of days' shooting. That's all very well for the honeymoon period but not for a whole lifetime. A man must be independent – he has his own masculine interests. A man has to be manly,' said Oblonsky, opening the door.

'What does that mean? Running after servant-girls?' asked Levin.

'Why not, if it amuses him? *Ça ne tire pas à conséquence.* My wife won't be any the worse off, and I shall enjoy myself. The main thing is to respect the sanctity of the home. Nothing of that kind at home. But you needn't tie your own hands.'

'Perhaps so,' said Levin drily, and he turned on his side. 'We must make an early start to-morrow, and I won't wake anyone, but go off at daybreak.'

'*Messieurs, venez vite!*' called Vasenka, coming back. '*Charmante!* I've made such a discovery. *Charmante!* A perfect Gretchen, and we're friends already. She's really awfully pretty,' he declared in a tone of approval, as though she had been made pretty entirely for his benefit, and he were expressing his satisfaction with the maker.

Levin pretended to be asleep, but Oblonsky put on his slippers, lit a cigar, and left the barn. Soon their voices died away.

Levin lay awake for a long while. He heard his horses munching hay, then the peasant setting out with his eldest son to grass their horses. He could hear the soldier settling down to sleep on the other side of the barn with his nephew, the peasant's youngest boy, and the child's treble voice telling his uncle what he thought of the dogs, who seemed to him huge, terrible creatures. Then the boy asked what those dogs were going to hunt, and the soldier in a hoarse, sleepy voice explained that the gentlemen would go off to the marshes in the morning, where they would fire their guns, adding, to stop the boy's questions: 'Go to sleep, Vaska, go to sleep, or you'll catch it.' Soon after that the soldier began snoring himself, and all was still, except for the neighing of the horses and the cry of snipe. 'Can it really only be done negatively?' Levin repeated to himself. 'Well, what of it? It's not my fault.' And he began thinking about the next day.

'To-morrow I'll turn out early, and make up my mind to keep cool. There are quantities of snipe, and great snipe too. And when I come back there'll be the note from Kitty. Yes, maybe Stiva is right: I'm not manly enough with her, I'm tied to her apron-strings. ... Well, it can't be helped! The negative answer again!'

As he was dropping off to sleep he could hear laughter and the merry voices of Veslovsky and Oblonsky. For an instant he opened his eyes: the moon was up and in the open doorway, in the moonlight, the two were standing chatting. Oblonsky was saying something about the freshness of a girl and comparing her to a newly-opened hazel-nut, while Veslovsky was laughing his infectious laugh and repeating what a peasant had no doubt said to him: 'Ah, you'd better look out for a wife of your own!'

'Gentlemen, to-morrow at dawn!' Levin mumbled drowsily, and fell asleep.

12

WAKING at daybreak Levin tried to rouse his companions. Vasenka was lying face downwards, one stockinged leg outstretched, and sleeping so soundly that he could not wake him. Oblonsky sleepily declined to budge so early. Even Laska, who had slept curled round in the hay, got up reluctantly, and lazily stretched and settled one hind leg and then the other. Levin put on his boots and stockings, took his gun, cautiously opened the creaking door of the barn, and went out into the open air. The coachmen were asleep beside the vehicles, the horses were dozing. Only one was lazily eating oats, scattering and blowing them about in the trough. The outside world was still grey.

'Why are you up so early, my dear?' the old woman of the hut asked from the doorway, addressing him in a friendly tone as a good acquaintance of long standing.

'I'm off shooting, Granny. Can I get to the marsh this way?'

'Straight along at the back; past our threshing-floors, my dear, and then by the hemp-patches. You'll find the footpath.'

Treading carefully with her bare, sunburnt feet, the old woman conducted him to the threshing-floor and moved back the fence for him.

'Go straight on and you'll come upon the marsh. Our lads took the horses that way last night.'

Laska bounded gaily ahead along the footpath. Levin followed with a light, brisk step, continually glancing up at the sky. He was anxious to get to the marsh before sunrise. But the sun would not wait. The moon, which had been bright when he first came out, now only gleamed like quicksilver. The pink flush of dawn, which one could not help seeing before, now had to be sought to be discerned at all. What had been vague smudges in the distant countryside were now quite distinct. They were shocks of rye. The dew, not visible till the sun was up, on the tall fragrant hemp which had already shed its pollen, drenched Levin's legs and his blouse even above the belt. In the translucent stillness of the morning the minutest sounds were audible.

A bee flew past Levin's ear like the whizz of a bullet. He looked close, and saw another, and then a third. They all came from behind the wattle-fence of an apiary, and disappeared over the hemp-field in the direction of the marsh. The path led straight to the marsh, which was recognizable by the vapours rising from it, thicker in one place and thinner in another, so that the reeds and willow-bushes swayed like little islands in the mist. At the edge of the marsh by the road the peasant boys and men, who had pastured their horses in the night, were lying under their coats, having fallen asleep at daybreak. Near by three hobbled horses were moving about, one of them clattering its chain. Laska trotted beside her master, beseeching to be allowed to run forward, and looking around. Passing the sleeping peasants and reaching the first bog, Levin examined his percussion caps and let the dog go. One of the horses, a sleek, chestnut three-year-old, shied at the sight of Laska, switched its tail and snorted. The other horses were also startled, and splashed through the water with their hobbled feet, making a sucking sound as they drew their hooves out of the thick, clayey mud and began floundering their way out of the marsh. Laska stopped, looking derisively at the horses and inquiringly at Levin. Levin patted her, and gave a whistle to tell her she might begin.

Joyful and intent, Laska started through the bog, which gave beneath her feet.

Running into the marsh, Laska at once detected all over the place, mingled with the familiar smells of roots, marsh grass, slime, and the extraneous odour of horse dung, the scent of birds – of that strong-smelling bird that always excited her more than any other. Here and there among the moss and swamp-sage this scent was very strong, but it was impossible to be sure in which direction it grew stronger or fainter. To find this out it was necessary to get farther to the lee of the wind. Scarcely aware of her legs under her, Laska bounded on with a stiff gallop, so that at each bound she could stop short, going to the right, away from the morning breeze blowing from the east, and turned to face the wind. Sniffing in the air with dilated nostrils, she knew at once that not their scent only but they themselves were here before her, and not only one but a great many of them. Laska slackened her pace. They were here, but precisely where she could not yet decide. To find the exact spot, she began circling round, when suddenly her master's voice drew her off. 'Laska! Here!' he called, pointing to the other side. She stood still, asking him if it would not be better to let her go on as she had begun. But he repeated his command in an angry voice, pointing to a tufty place under water, where there could not be anything. She obeyed, pretending to search, and to please him went over the whole place and then returned to the first spot, and was at once on the scent again. Now, when he was not hindering her, she knew what to do, and without looking where she was stepping, stumbling impatiently over hummocks and falling into water, but righting herself with her strong, supple legs, she began the circle that was to make everything clear. *Their* scent came to her more and more pungently, more and more distinctly, until all at once it became quite plain that one of them was here, on the other side of this tuft of reeds, five paces in front of her. She stopped and her whole body grew rigid. Her short legs prevented her from seeing ahead, but by the scent she was certain it was there, not five paces off. More and more conscious of its presence, she stood still, in the joy of anticipation. Her tail was stretched straight and tense, only the very tip twitching. Her mouth was slightly open, her ears pricked. One ear had got folded back when she was running. She breathed heavily but warily, and still more warily looked round, more with her eyes than her head, to her master. He was coming along, with his familiar face but ever terrible eyes, stumbling over the hummocks and taking to her an unusually long time. She thought he came slowly but in reality he was running.

From Laska's peculiar posture – her mouth half open and her body crouched down as if dragging her hind legs along the ground – Levin knew she was pointing at snipe, and with an inward prayer for success, especially with his first bird, he ran towards her. When he came up close to her and looked beyond, he saw from his height what she had perceived with her nose. In a little space between two hummocks he caught sight of a snipe. It had turned its head and was listening. Then lightly preening and folding its wings, it disappeared round a corner with an awkward jerk of its tail.

'Go, Laska, go!' shouted Levin, giving her a shove from behind.

'But I can't go,' thought Laska. 'Where am I to go? I can scent them from here, but if I move I shan't know where they are or what they are.' But now he pushed her with his knee, and in an excited whisper said, 'Go, Laska, good dog, go!'

'All right, if that's what he wants, but I can't answer for myself now,' thought Laska, and rushed forward at full tilt between the hummocks. She was no longer on the scent, but only saw and heard, without understanding anything.

Ten paces from her former place a snipe rose with a guttural cry, its wings making the hollow sound peculiar to snipe. And immediately following the report it fell heavily on its white breast in the wet bog. Another rose behind Levin, without waiting to be put up by the dog. By the time Levin had turned towards it, it was already some way off. But his shot caught it. It flew on about twenty feet, rose sharply, and then, turning over and over like a ball, dropped heavily to the ground, on a dry spot.

'This looks like business!' thought Levin, stowing the warm fat snipe into his game-bag. 'Eh, Laska, what do you think?'

When Levin had reloaded his gun and moved on, the sun, though still invisible behind the clouds, had already risen. The moon had lost all her splendour, and gleamed pale in the sky like a small cloud. There was no longer a single star to be seen. The sedge, silvery with dew before, now glistened like gold. The patches of rust were now amber. The bluish grass had turned a yellowy-green. Marsh-birds bustled about in the bushes that sparkled with dew and cast long shadows beside the brook. A hawk woke up and settled on a haycock, turning its head from side to side and surveying the marsh with an air of discontent. Crows were flying about the field, and a barefooted boy was already driving the horses towards an old man, who had raised himself from under his coat and was scratching different parts of his body. The smoke from the gun stretched white as milk over the green grass.

One of the boys ran up to Levin.

'There were wild ducks here yesterday!' he shouted, following Levin at a distance.

And Levin knew a double pleasure in killing three more snipe, one after another, in sight of the boy, who expressed his approval.

13

THE saying that if the first shot brings down bird or beast the sport will be good was justified.

Tired, hungry, and happy, Levin returned towards ten o'clock, having tramped some twenty miles and brought down nineteen fine head of game and one duck, which he hung at his belt, there being no room left in the game-bag. His companions had long been awake, and had had time to get hungry and have breakfast.

'Hold on, hold on, I know there are nineteen,' said Levin, counting his snipe and great snipe for the second time. They were twisted and dried up and bloodstained, their heads drooping, and did not look so inspiring as they had done when on the wing.

The count was correct, and Oblonsky's envy gratified Levin. He was pleased, too, to find the man sent by Kitty already there waiting for him with a note.

'I am perfectly well and happy. If you were worried about me, you can feel easier than ever about me now. I've a new bodyguard, Maria Vlasyevna' (this was the midwife, a new and important addition to Levin's household). 'She came to have a look at me. She finds me perfectly all right, and we are making her stay until your return. Everyone is happy and well, and if you are having good sport, please don't hurry back, but stay another day.'

These two delights – his successful shooting and the note from his wife – were so great that two slightly disagreeable incidents that occurred later passed lightly over Levin. One was that the chestnut trace-horse, having evidently been overworked the day before, was off his feed and out of sorts. The coachman said the horse had been strained.

'Over-driven yesterday, Constantine Dmitrich,' he said. 'The idea! Seven miles like that, driving with no sense!'

The other piece of unpleasantness, which for a moment impaired his good humour though afterwards he laughed heartily at it, was that, of all the provisions Kitty had provided in such abundance that one would have thought they had enough for a week, absolutely nothing was left. On his way back from the marsh, tired and hungry, Levin looked forward so vividly to meat-pies that as he approached the hut he seemed to smell and taste them in his mouth, in the way Laska scented game, and he immediately told Philip to serve them. It appeared that there were no pies left, nor even any chicken.

'This fellow's appetite!' said Oblonsky, laughing and nodding at Vasenka Veslovsky. 'I don't suffer from lack of appetite myself, but he's really astonishing ...'

'Well, it can't be helped,' said Levin, looking gloomily at Veslovsky. 'Philip, bring me some beef, then.'

'The beef's all gone, sir, and the dogs have got the bone,' answered Philip.

Levin was so annoyed that he said crossly:

'You might have left me something!' He felt ready to cry.

'Well, then, draw some game,' he told Philip in a trembling voice, trying not to look at Vasenka, 'and stuff them with nettles. And ask them to let me have some milk.'

It was only later, when he had appeased his hunger with milk, that he felt ashamed of having shown his annoyance before a stranger, and he began to laugh at his hungry mortification.

In the evening they went out shooting again, and Veslovsky also got several birds, and at night they set off for home.

Their homeward journey was as lively as the drive out had been. Veslovsky sang songs and recalled with gusto his adventures with the peasants who had regaled him with vodka and said 'No offence meant!' He related his night exploits – the games – 'Here we go gathering nuts and may' – and the servant-girl and the peasant, who had asked him whether he was married and on learning that he was a bachelor had said: 'Don't you ogle other men's wives – try and get one of your own!' This amused Veslovsky more than anything.

'Altogether, I've enjoyed our outing awfully. Haven't you, Levin?'

'Yes, very much,' Levin replied quite sincerely. He was particularly happy to have got rid of the animosity he had felt for Vasenka Veslovsky at home and, on the contrary, to be very friendlily disposed to him.

14

NEXT morning at ten o'clock Levin, having already made the round of the farm, knocked at the door of Vasenka's room.

'Entrez!' called Veslovsky. 'Excuse me, I've only just finished my ablutions,' he said with a smile, standing before Levin only in his underclothes.

'Please don't mind me,' and Levin sat down by the window. 'Did you sleep well?'

'Like the dead. What sort of day is it for shooting?'

'What do you take, tea or coffee?'

'Neither, thanks. I'll wait for lunch. I really feel ashamed of myself. The ladies, I suppose, are already up? A walk now would be first-rate. You show me your horses.'

After they had walked round the garden, visited the stables, and even done some gymnastics together on the parallel bars, Levin brought his guest back to the house, and entered the drawing-room with him.

'The shooting was splendid, and so was everything else,' said Veslovsky, going up to Kitty, who was sitting at the samovar. 'What a pity it is ladies are cut off from these delights!'

'Well, I suppose he must say something to the lady of the house,' Levin told himself, again fancying he detected something in the smile, in the all-conquering air with which their guest addressed Kitty ...

The princess, sitting at the other side of the table with the midwife and Oblonsky, called Levin to her and began talking about moving to Moscow for Kitty's confinement, and getting rooms ready for them. Just as Levin had disliked all the trivial wedding preparations for detracting from the majesty of the event, so now he felt even more of an affront the preparations for the coming birth, the date of which they seemed to be reckoning on their fingers. For weeks past he had been trying to turn a deaf ear to these discussions on the proper way of swaddling the new baby; trying to turn away and not see those mysterious endless strips of knitting, the triangles of linen, and so on, to which Dolly attached special importance. The birth of a son (he was certain it would be a son) which they promised him, but which he still could not believe in – so marvellous did it seem – appeared to him on the one hand such an immense and therefore incredible happiness; on the other, an event so mysterious that this assumption of knowledge of what would be, and consequent preparation for it as for something ordinary, something brought about by human beings, shocked and humiliated him.

But the princess did not understand his feelings, and gave him no peace, attributing his reluctance to think and talk about it to thoughtlessness and indifference. She had commissioned Oblonsky to look at a flat, and now she called Levin to her.

'I don't know at all, princess. Do as you think fit,' he said.

'You must decide when you will move.'

'I really don't know. I know that millions of babies are born away from Moscow, without doctors ... so why ...'

'Well in that case ...'

'No, let Kitty decide ...'

'We can't talk to Kitty about it! Do you want me to frighten her?

Why, only this spring Natalie Golitzin died in child-birth because she did not have proper attention.'

'I will do just what you say,' he replied morosely.

The princess began talking to him, but he did not listen to her. Though the conversation with the princess had indeed upset him, it was not that but what he saw by the samovar that made him morose.

'No, this can't go on,' he thought, every now and again casting a look at Vasenka bending over Kitty and telling her something with his handsome smile, and at Kitty herself, flushed and disturbed.

There was something not nice about Vasenka's attitude, about his eyes and his smile. Levin even saw something not nice in Kitty's attitude and look. And as before, the light died out of his eyes. Again, as on the previous occasion, without the slightest warning, he felt himself cast down from a pinnacle of happiness, peace, and dignity into an abyss of despair, rancour, and humiliation. Again he hated everything and everybody.

'You do just as you think best, Princess,' he said, looking round again.

' "Heavy is the Autocrat's crown!" ' quoted Oblonsky jestingly, evidently referring not only to the princess's conversation but to the cause of Levin's agitation, which he had noticed. 'How late you are to-day, Dolly!'

Everyone rose to greet Dolly. Vasenka got up for an instant and, with the absence of courtesy to ladies typical of the modern young man, he scarcely bowed before resuming his conversation, laughing at something.

'I feel worn out with Masha. She was very restless during the night, and is dreadfully capricious this morning,' said Dolly.

The conversation Vasenka had started with Kitty was running on the same lines as on the previous evening, turning upon Anna and whether love is to be put higher than social conventions. Kitty disliked the conversation, which she found upsetting both in its subject and the tone in which it was conducted, and especially because she already knew the effect it would have on her husband. But she was too simple and guileless to know how to cut it short, or even how to conceal the superficial pleasure afforded her by the young man's very obvious admiration. She wanted to put an end to the conversation, but did not know what to do. Whatever she did she knew would be observed by her husband and have a wrong construction put on it. And indeed when she asked Dolly what was the matter with Masha, and Vasenka, waiting for this uninteresting conversation to finish, began to gaze indifferently at Dolly, the question struck Levin as an unnatural and disgusting piece of hypocrisy.

'Well, shall we go mushroom picking to-day?' said Dolly.

'Yes, do, and I will come too,' said Kitty, and blushed. She wanted to ask Vasenka out of politeness if he would go with them, but refrained. 'Where are you off to, Kostya?' she asked with a guilty look as her husband walked past her with resolute steps. This guilty air confirmed all his suspicions.

'The mechanic came while I was away; I haven't seen him yet,' he said, not looking at her.

He went downstairs and was just leaving his study when he heard his wife's familiar footsteps hurrying after him with reckless speed.

'What is it?' he asked her shortly. 'We are busy.'

'I beg your pardon,' she said to the German mechanic. 'I should like a few words with my husband.'

The German turned to go, but Levin said to him:

'Don't bother.'

'The train is at three?' queried the German. 'I must not miss it.'

Levin did not answer him but went out with his wife.

'Well, what have you to say to me?' he asked in French.

He did not look her in the face, and refused to see how she in her condition stood with her whole face twitching, looking piteous and crushed.

'I ... I wanted to say that we can't go on like this: it's torture,' she blurted out.

'The servants are there in the pantry,' he said angrily; 'don't make a scene.'

'Well, let's go in here!'

They were standing in the passage. Kitty would have gone into the next room but the English governess was there, giving Tanya her lessons.

'All right, come into the garden.'

In the garden they came upon a man weeding the path. And, without stopping to consider that the man could see her tear-stained face and Levin's agitated one, that they looked like people fleeing from some disaster, they hurried on with rapid steps, feeling that they must say their minds and clear up misunderstandings, must be alone together, and together free themselves from the misery both were suffering.

'We can't go on like this! It is torture! I am wretched; you are wretched. And what for?' she said, when they had at last reached a solitary garden-seat at a turn in the lime walk.

'But tell me one thing: was there anything unseemly, not nice, degradingly horrible in his tone?' he said, standing before her with his fists pressing his chest, as he had stood before her the night of Vasenka's arrival.

'Yes, there was,' she said in a shaking voice. 'But, Kostya, can't you see I'm not to blame? Ever since I came down this morning I've tried to adopt a tone ... but people like that ... Why did he come? We were so happy!' she said, choking with sobs that shook her now heavy body.

The gardener saw with astonishment that, though nothing had been pursuing them and there had been nothing for them to run away from – nor could they possibly have found anything particularly blissful about that garden-seat – they passed him on their way back to the house with comforted and radiant faces.

15

AFTER escorting his wife upstairs, Levin went to Dolly's part of the house. She, too, was in great distress that day. She was walking up and down the room, scolding a little girl who stood howling in a corner.

'And you'll stand in that corner all day, and have your dinner by yourself, and not see a single doll, and there'll be no new frock,' she was saying, trying to think of punishments for the child.

'Oh, she is a wicked girl!' she cried, turning to Levin. 'I don't know where she gets her nasty habits from.'

'Why, what has she done?' asked Levin without much interest, for he wanted to consult her about his own affairs and was annoyed to have come at an inopportune moment.

'She and Grisha went among the raspberry canes, and there ... I can't even tell you what she did. It's a thousand pities Miss Elliot's not with us. This one sees to nothing – she's just a machine. ... *Figurez-vous que la petite ...*'

And Dolly related Masha's crime.

'That doesn't prove a thing. It's not a question of evil propensities at all; it's simply mischief,' Levin assured her.

'But you look upset about something? Why have you come?' asked Dolly. 'What's going on there?'

And by the tone of her question Levin knew that it would not be difficult for him to tell her what it was he had come to say.

'I've not been in there. I was alone in the garden with Kitty. We had a quarrel for the second time since ... Stiva came.'

Dolly looked at him with her shrewd, comprehending eyes.

'Now tell me, hand on your heart, has there been ... not in Kitty, but in the manner of that young gentleman, something which might be unpleasant – not unpleasant, but horrible, offensive to a husband?'

'You mean, how shall I say ... Masha, stay in the corner!' she said to the child who, detecting a faint smile on her mother's face, had been turning round. 'Most people would say he is behaving like any other young man. *Il fait la cour à une jeune et jolie femme*, and a husband who's a man of the world should only feel flattered by it.'

'Yes, yes,' said Levin gloomily; 'but you noticed it?'

'Not only I, but Stiva too. After breakfast this morning he said to me in so many words: " *Je crois que Veslovsky fait un petit brin de cour à Kitty.* "'

'Very well; now I'm satisfied. Now I can tell him to go,' said Levin.

'What do you mean? Have you gone out of your mind?' Dolly exclaimed aghast. 'Really, Kostya, think!' she said, laughing. 'You can run away to Fanny now,' she said to Masha. 'No, if you like, I'll speak to Stiva. He'll take him away. We can say you are expecting visitors. Anyway, I don't think he quite fits in with us here.'

'No, no, I'll do it myself.'

'But you'll quarrel with him?'

'Not a bit of it. I shall quite enjoy it,' said Levin, his eyes lighting up with real enjoyment. 'Come, forgive her, Dolly! She won't do it again,' he pleaded for the little culprit, who had not gone to Fanny but was standing irresolutely before her mother, waiting and looking up from under her brows to catch her mother's eye.

The mother looked down at her. The child broke into sobs and buried her face in her mother's lap, and Dolly laid her thin hand tenderly on the little head.

'And what have we and he in common?' thought Levin, as he went in search of Veslovsky.

Passing through the hall he gave orders for the carriage to be made ready to drive to the station.

'One of the springs got broken yesterday,' said the footman.

'Well, the covered trap, then, and be quick about it. Where is the visitor?'

'The gentleman's gone to his room.'

Levin came upon Veslovsky just as the latter, having pulled his things out of his portmanteau and spread out some new songs, was trying on a pair of leather gaiters in preparation to go riding.

Whether there was something unusual in Levin's face or whether Vasenka himself was conscious that *ce petit brin de cour* which he had embarked upon was out of place in this family, at all events he was somewhat disconcerted (as far as a man of the world can be disconcerted) at Levin's entry.

'You wear gaiters for riding?'

'Yes, it's much cleaner,' Vasenka replied, putting his fat leg on a chair, and fastened the bottom hook, smiling with simple-hearted good humour.

He was undoubtedly a good sort, and Levin began to feel sorry for him and ashamed of himself as his host when he saw the abashed look on Vasenka's face.

On the table lay part of a stick which they had broken that morning doing gymnastics together and trying to straighten the warped parallel bars. Levin picked up the broken fragment and started pulling off the splintered bits at the end, not knowing how to begin.

'I wanted ...' He paused, but suddenly thought of Kitty and everything that had happened. 'I have ordered the carriage for you,' he went on, looking him resolutely in the face.

'I don't understand!' began Vasenka in surprise. 'Where are we going?'

'You are going to the station,' Levin said gloomily.

'Why, are you off anywhere, or has something happened?'

'I happen to be expecting visitors,' said Levin, his strong fingers attacking the splintered ends of the stick more and more energetically. 'And I'm not expecting visitors, and nothing has happened, but I ask you to leave. You can explain my incivility as you please.'

Vasenka drew himself up.

'I ask *you* to explain ...' he said with dignity, understanding at last.

'That I cannot do,' said Levin quietly and deliberately, trying to control the trembling of his jaw. 'And it would be better for you not to insist.'

And as the split ends were now all broken off, Levin took hold of the thick end in his fingers, snapped the stick in two, and carefully caught one piece as it fell.

Probably the sight of those tense hands, of the muscles he had proved that morning at gymnastics, together with the gleam in Levin's eye, his low voice, and quivering jaw convinced Vasenka better than any words. He shrugged his shoulders, smiled scornfully and bowed.

'I suppose I can see Oblonsky?'

The shrug and the smile did not irritate Levin. 'What else could he do?' he thought.

'I will send him to you.'

'What is this nonsense I hear?' Oblonsky said when, after learning from his friend that he was being turned out of the house, he found Levin walking about in the garden, waiting for the departure of his guest. '*Mais c'est ridicule!* What fly's bitten you? *Mais c'est du dernier ridicule!* Do you suppose, just because a young man …'

But the place where Levin had been bitten was evidently still sore, for he went pale again and abruptly cut Oblonsky short when the latter would have enlarged on his argument.

'Please don't go into it! I can't help it. I feel ashamed of myself before you and him. But I don't imagine it will be a great grief to him to go, and my wife and I don't care for his presence here.'

'But it's insulting to him! *Et puis c'est ridicule.*'

'It was also insulting to me, and very painful too! It was not my fault, and I don't see why I should suffer.'

'Well, I should never have expected it of you! *On peut être jaloux, mais à ce point, c'est du dernier ridicule!*'

Levin turned quickly and walked away from him to the far end of the avenue, where he paced up and down alone. Soon he heard the rattle of the trap, and through the trees saw Vasenka in his Scotch cap sitting in it on some straw (unfortunately there was no seat), jolting over the ruts as he was driven along the avenue.

'Now what does that mean?' wondered Levin, when a footman ran out of the house and stopped the trap. It was for the mechanician, whom Levin had totally forgotten. The German bowed and said something to Veslovsky, then climbed in, and they drove off together.

Oblonsky and the princess were indignant at Levin's conduct. And he himself felt not only extremely ridiculous but thoroughly shamed and in the wrong. But when he remembered what he and his wife had suffered, and asked himself how he would act another time, his answer was that he would do just the same again.

In spite of all this, towards the end of that day, everyone except the princess, who could not pardon Levin's conduct, became extraordinarily gay and lively, like children after a punishment or grownup people after a tiresome official reception, so that by the evening, after the princess had retired, Vasenka's expulsion was talked of as though it were some remote event. And Dolly, who had her father's gift of putting things humorously, made Varenka helpless with laughter as she related for the third and fourth time, always with humorous little additions, how she had only just put on a fresh knot of ribbons in the visitor's honour, and was about to go to the drawing-room, when suddenly she heard the clatter of the ramshackle trap. And who should be in the trap but Vasenka himself, Scotch cap, songs, gaiters and all, sitting on the straw!

'At least you might have let him have the brougham! But no; and then I hear a shout: "Stop!" Aha, they've relented, I think. Not at all. I look out and behold them put a fat German in beside him, and the pair are driven off together. ... And my new ribbons all for nothing!'

16

DOLLY carried out her intention and went to see Anna. She was sorry to chagrin her sister and displease Levin. She quite understood how right the Levins were in not wishing to have anything to do with Vronsky; but felt she must go and see Anna, and show her that the altered circumstances could not change her feelings towards her.

To be independent of the Levins, Dolly sent to the village to hire horses for this expedition; but Levin heard of it and came to her in protest.

'What makes you suppose I disapprove of your going? And if I did I should find it still less pleasant if you would not use my horses,' he said. 'You never told me definitely that you were going. In the first place, it is not very nice for me to have you hiring horses in the village, and, what's of more importance, they'll undertake the job and never get you there. I have horses. And if you don't wish to hurt my feelings you will make use of them.'

Dolly had to consent, and on the appointed day Levin had a team of four ready for his sister-in-law, as well as a change of horses waiting for her at the post-house for the second part of the journey. They were not at all a smart-looking lot, being made up of farm and saddle-horses, but they would get Dolly to her destination in a single day. It was awkward for Levin, as he needed horses for the princess, who was leaving, and for the midwife, but by the laws of hospitality he could not allow Dolly to hire horses when she was staying in his house. Moreover, he was well aware that the twenty roubles it would have cost were a serious matter for her; Dolly's pecuniary affairs, which were in a very unsatisfactory state, were taken to heart by Levin as if they were his own.

Acting on Levin's advice, Dolly started before daybreak. The road was good, the carriage comfortable, the horses trotted briskly, and on the box, in addition to the coachman, sat the clerk from the estate office, whom Levin was sending for greater security instead of a groom. Dolly dozed, and only woke when they drew up at the inn where the horses were to be changed.

After drinking tea at the same well-to-do peasant's where Levin had put up on his way to Sviazhsky's, and chatting with the women about their children, and with the old man about Count Vronsky, of whom he spoke highly, Dolly, at ten o'clock, continued her journey. At home, looking after the children left her no leisure for reflection. So now, during this four-hour drive, all the thoughts she had suppressed before rushed swarming into her brain, and she reviewed her whole life, from every aspect, as she had never done before. Even to herself her thoughts seemed strange. At first she thought about the children, worrying about them, although the princess and Kitty (she had greater faith in Kitty) had promised to look after them. 'If only Masha doesn't fall into mischief, or Grisha get kicked by a horse, or Lily's stomach get out of order again!' But soon present difficulties gave way to questions of the immediate future. They would have to move into another flat in Moscow for the winter, the drawing-room furniture needed re-upholstering, and the eldest girl must have a new winter coat. Then she looked still farther ahead, to problems of a more remote future: how she was to launch her children in the world. 'The girls are all right,' she thought, 'but what about the boys?'

'Fortunately I am free to devote myself to Grisha just now, but supposing I were to have another baby? Stiva, of course, there's no counting on. With the help of good-natured friends I can bring them up ... but if another baby comes ...' And it occurred to her how untrue was the saying that woman's curse was to bring forth children in travail.

'The birth itself, that's nothing – it's the period of pregnancy that is torture,' she thought, recalling her last pregnancy and the death of the baby. This brought back to her mind the conversation she had just had with the young woman at the inn, where they had changed horses. She had asked the good-looking young peasant whether she had any children, and the girl had answered cheerfully:

'I had a baby girl, but God set me free. I buried her last Lent.'

'Did you grieve for her dreadfully?' asked Dolly.

'Why grieve? The old man has grandchildren enough as it is. They are only a trouble. You can't work or do anything. They tie you hand and foot.'

Dolly had been shocked at such words coming from the mouth of a young woman who looked good-natured and kind; but now she could not help recalling them. It was cynical but there was some truth in what the girl had said.

'Yes, it comes to this,' she thought, looking back over her fifteen years of married life, 'nothing but pregnancy, sickness, mind dulled and indifferent to everything and, most of all – the disfigurement. Even Kitty, young and pretty as she is, has lost her looks; and when I'm with child I become hideous, I know. The birth, the agony, the hideous agonies, that last moment ... then nursing the baby, the sleepless nights, the fearful pains ...'

Dolly shuddered at the mere recollection of the pain she had endured from sore nipples which she had suffered with almost every baby. 'Then the children's illnesses, and the everlasting anxiety; then bringing them up, their nasty tendencies' (she thought of little Masha's delinquency among the raspberry canes), 'lessons, Latin – it's all so incomprehensible and difficult. And on top of it all, the death of these children.' And the cruel memory that never ceased to tear her mother's heart rose up of the death of her last born, who had died of croup. She recalled the funeral, the general indifference round the little pink coffin, and her own heart-rending, lonely anguish as she gazed at the pale little forehead fringed with curls and the half-open wondering little mouth – the last thing she had seen as the pink lid with the embroidered cross was closed over him.

'And what is it all for? What will come of it all? Here am I, with never a moment's peace, either with child or nursing a child, always irritable and bad-tempered, a nuisance to myself and everyone else, and unbearable to my husband. So I shall go on for the rest of my life, producing a lot of unfortunate, badly-brought up, penniless children. Even now, I don't know what we should have done if Kitty and Kostya had not invited us to spend the summer with them. Of course they are so considerate and have so much tact that we don't feel uncomfortable about it, but it can't go on for ever. They'll have children of their own and won't be able to help us. It's a drag on them as it is. How is papa to help us – he has already almost ruined himself for us? So it comes to this: I can't give the children a start myself, except with other people's assistance at the cost of humiliation. At best, supposing I have the good fortune not to lose any more of them and manage to bring them up somehow – the very best that can happen is that they won't turn out badly. That is as much as I can hope for. And what agonies, what toil, just for that – my whole life ruined!' Again she recalled the words of the young peasant woman, and again they were abhorrent to her; but she could not help admitting that there was a measure of brutal truth at the back of them.

'Is it far now, Mihail?' she asked the estate-office clerk, to divert her mind from the thoughts that frightened her.

'They say it's less than five miles from this village.'

The carriage drove down the village street to a small bridge. A crowd of cheerful peasant women, with ready-twisted sheaf-binders hanging from their shoulders, were crossing the bridge, chattering noisily and merrily. They stopped and stared inquisitively at the carriage as it passed them on the bridge. All the faces turned to her seemed to Dolly healthy and bright, mocking her with their joy in life. 'Everyone else seems to be alive and enjoying the world,' she mused, continuing her reflections as they left the peasant women behind and reached the top of the hill, the old carriage, which the horses were drawing at a trot again, swaying comfortably on its soft springs. 'But I am like a prisoner let out from the world of worries that fret me to death, to look about me for a moment. Everyone enjoys life: those peasant women, and my sister Natalie, and Varenka, and Anna, whom I'm on my way to now – all of them, but not I.

'And they are all down on Anna! What for? Am I any better than she is? I at least have a husband I love – not as I should like to love him, but still I do love him, while Anna never loved hers. How is she to blame? She wants to live. We were born with that need in our hearts. Very likely I should have done the same. To this day I don't know whether I did well to listen to her that terrible time when she came to me in Moscow. I ought to have left my husband then, and started life afresh. Then I might have loved and been loved the real way. Is what I am doing now any better? I don't respect him. He's necessary to me,' she went on, thinking of her husband, 'and I put up with him. Is that any better? At that time I was still attractive and had not lost my looks,' and she was seized with a desire to see herself in a glass. She had a little travelling mirror in her handbag and wanted to get it out; but a glance at the backs of the coachman and the clerk, who sat swaying beside him, told her she would feel embarrassed if either of them chanced to look round, so she forbore.

But even without looking at herself in the glass, it occurred to her that it might not be too late: she thought of Koznyshev, who was always particularly attentive to her, of Stiva's friend, the good-hearted Turovtsyn, who had helped her nurse the children through scarlet-fever, and was in love with her. Then there was another man – quite young – who declared, so Stiva teased her, that she was the handsomest of the three sisters. And all sorts of passionate, impossible romances presented themselves to her fancy. 'Anna did quite right, and I certainly shall have no reproaches for her. She is happy, and she's making another person happy. She is not crushed as I am, but most likely as bright, clever and interested in everything as she always was.' A mischievous smile curved her lips, chiefly because, as she pondered on Anna's love affair, she invented on parallel lines an almost identical romance for herself with an imaginary composite figure, the ideal man who was in love with her. She saw herself like Anna, making a clean breast of it to her husband, and Oblonsky's amazement and perplexity at this avowal made her smile.

With Dolly day-dreaming thus, they reached the turning leading from the high-road to Vozdvizhenskoe.

17

THE coachman pulled up and looked round to a field of rye on the right, where some peasants were sitting beside a cart. The estate-office clerk was on the point of jumping down but changed his mind and shouted peremptorily to one of the peasants instead, beckoning him to come up. The breeze which they had felt while driving fell as soon as the carriage came to a standstill; gad-flies settled on the steaming horses, which angrily tried to switch them off. The metallic sound of a scythe being hammered beside the cart ceased, and one of the peasants got up and came towards the carriage.

'Hi, make haste!' the clerk shouted impatiently to the peasant stepping slowly with his bare feet over the ruts in the dry uneven ground. 'Come along, do!'

The old man, his curly hair tied round with a bit of bast, his bent back dark with perspiration, quickened his steps, and coming up to the carriage put his sunburnt arm on the splash-board.

'Vozdvizhenskoe, the manor-house? The count's?' he repeated. 'Go on to the end of this track. Then turn to the left. Drive right down the avenue, and you can't miss it. But who do you want? The count himself?'

'Are they at home?' Dolly asked vaguely, not knowing how to inquire about Anna, even of this peasant.

'I should think so,' said the peasant, shifting from one bare foot to the other, and leaving a distinct imprint in the dust of the ball of his foot and his five toes. 'I should think so,' he repeated, evidently eager to talk. 'More visitors arrived yesterday. They have a terrible lot of company. ... What do you want?' he asked, turning round to a lad who was shouting something from the cart. 'Quite right – a while ago they passed by here on horseback, going to look at the reaper. They must be home again by now. And who may you be?'

'We come from a distance,' said the coachman, climbing on to the box. 'So you say it's not far?'

'I tell you, it's just here. As soon as you get past the hollow ...' he replied, rubbing his arm along the splash-board of the carriage.

Just then a fresh-looking, broad-shouldered youth came up.

'What, is there a job to be had harvesting?' he asked.

'I don't know, my boy.'

'So you see, you keep to the left and you knock right up against it,' said the peasant, unmistakably reluctant to let the travellers go, and anxious to talk.

The coachman started the horses, but hardly had they gone round the bend when the peasant shouted.

'Stop! Hi, friend, stop!' called the two voices.

The coachman pulled up.

'There they are! Look!' shouted the old man. 'See, what a turnout!' he said, pointing to four riders on horseback, and two people in a *char-à-banc*, coming along the road.

It was Vronsky with a jockey, Veslovsky and Anna, all on horseback, and the Princess Varvara and Sviazhsky in the *char-à-banc*. They had been out to inspect some newly-arrived reaping machines in operation.

When the carriage stopped, the party on horseback were advancing at a walking pace. Anna was in front with Veslovsky. She rode quietly on a small, sturdy English cob with cropped mane and short tail. Dolly was struck by Anna's beautiful head with the black curls escaping from under her top hat, her full shoulders, her slender waist in the black riding-habit, and all the ease and grace of her bearing.

For a moment it had seemed to her unsuitable for Anna to be on horseback. The notion of horseback riding for a lady was associated in Dolly's mind with ideas of youthful flirtation and frivolity, ill-becoming, in her opinion, to a woman in Anna's position. But when she saw her closer, she was at once reconciled to her riding. For all her elegance, she looked so simple, quiet, and dignified in her poise, clothes, and movements that nothing could have been more natural.

At Anna's side, on a grey cavalry horse that looked hot, rode Vasenka Veslovsky in his Scotch cap with the fluttering streamers, his stout legs stretched out, unmistakably pleased with his own appearance. Dolly could not repress an amused smile when she recognized him. Behind them came Vronsky on a dark bay thoroughbred, obviously heated from galloping. He was pulling on the reins to hold the mare in.

After Vronsky rode a little man in the dress of a jockey. Sviazhsky and the Princess Varvara in a new *char-à-banc*, to which was harnessed a big, raven-black trotter, brought up the rear.

Anna's face suddenly lighted up with joy as she recognized Dolly in the small figure huddled back in a corner of the old carriage. She gave an exclamation, started in the saddle, and touched her horse to a gallop. When she reached the carriage she jumped down unaided, and, holding up her riding-habit, ran to greet Dolly.

'I thought it was you but didn't dare believe it! How delightful! You can't imagine how glad I am!' she cried, one moment pressing her face to Dolly's and kissing her, at the next standing back and surveying her with a smile.

'Here's a lovely surprise, Alexei!' she said, turning to Vronsky, who had dismounted and was walking towards them. He took off his grey top hat and came up to Dolly.

'You have no idea how pleased we are to see you,' he said, giving peculiar emphasis to the words, and showing his strong white teeth in a smile.

Vasenka Veslovsky, without getting off his horse, raised his cap and greeted the visitor by gleefully waving the streamers over his head.

'You know the Princess Varvara,' Anna said in reply to a glance of inquiry from Dolly as the *char-à-banc* drove up.

'Oh!' said Dolly, and unconsciously her face betrayed her dissatisfaction.

The Princess Varvara was an aunt of her husband's. Dolly had long known her and did not respect her. She knew that the Princess Varvara passed her whole life toadying to her rich relations, but that she should now be sponging on Vronsky, who was no connexion, mortified Dolly on her husband's account. Anna noticed Dolly's expression and was disconcerted by it. She blushed, let her riding-habit slip out of her hands and stumbled over it.

Dolly walked up to the *char-à-banc* and coldly greeted the Princess Varvara. She was acquainted with Sviazhsky too. He inquired how his eccentric friend was with his young wife, and running his eyes over the ill-matched horses and the patched splash-boards of the carriage proposed that the ladies should get into the *char-à-banc*.

'I'll go in that vehicle,' he said. 'You need not be afraid – the horse is quiet, and the princess drives splendidly.'

'No, stay as you are,' said Anna, coming up. 'We'll go in the carriage,' and taking Dolly's arm she led her away.

Dolly was dazzled by the elegant *char-à-banc* – she had seen nothing like it before – by the fine horses and the elegant, brilliant people about her. But what struck her most of all was the change that had taken place in her beloved Anna. Any other woman who was less observant, who had not known Anna before, or who had not thought the thoughts Dolly had been thinking on the road, would not have noticed anything special in Anna. But now Dolly was struck by that fleeting beauty which comes to women when they are in love, and which she saw now on Anna's face. Everything about her: the pronounced dimples in her cheeks and chin, the curve of her lips, the smile that seemed to hover about her face, the light in her eyes, the grace and swiftness of her movements, her ringing voice, even the manner in which she replied, half-crossly, half-fondly, to Veslovsky when he asked permission to ride her cob, so as to teach it to lead from the right leg when starting to gallop – it was all peculiarly fascinating, and it seemed as if she herself were deliciously aware of it.

Seated in the carriage, the two women were suddenly seized with shyness. Anna was embarrassed by the intent look of inquiry Dolly fixed on her, while Dolly felt ill at ease after Sviazhsky's remark about 'that vehicle' and ashamed of the shabby old carriage as Anna sat down beside her. Philip the coachman and the estate-office clerk were experiencing the same sensation. To conceal his embarrassment, the clerk bustled about, helping the ladies to get in, but Philip the coachman became sullen, and was bracing himself not to be over-awed in future by this show of superiority. He smiled ironically as he glanced at the raven horse, and was already deciding in his own mind that this smart trotter in the *char-à-banc* was only good for *promenage* and could never do thirty miles at a stretch on a hot day.

The peasants had all got up from beside the cart, and were inquisitively and mirthfully staring at the meeting of the friends, making their comments on it.

'The others seem pleased, too; haven't seen each other for a long while,' said the curly-headed old man with the piece of bast tied round his hair.

'Hey, Granddad Gerasim, if we could have that raven gelding to cart the sheaves now, we'd be done in no time!'

'I say, is that a woman in breeches there?' cried a third, pointing to Vasenka Veslovsky sitting side-saddle.

'Nay, a man! See how easy he jumped up!'

'Look, lads, aren't we having our nap to-day?'

'No chance of a nap now,' said the old man, blinking up at the sun. 'It's getting late, look. Get your hooks and come along!'

18

ANNA looked at Dolly's thin, careworn, travel-stained face, and was on the point of saying what she was thinking – that Dolly had got thinner; but remembering that her own looks had improved, and that Dolly's eyes were telling her so, she sighed and began to speak about herself.

'You look at me,' she said, 'and wonder how I can be happy in my position? Well, I'm ashamed to confess it, but I ... I am inexcusably happy. Something magical has happened to me; like suddenly waking up after a horrible, frightening dream and finding that your terrors are no more. I have waked up! I have lived through the agony and misery, and now for a long while past, especially since we came here, I've been so happy! ...' she said, looking at Dolly with a timid, questioning smile.

'I am so glad!' said Dolly, returning her smile but speaking more coldly than she intended. 'I'm very glad for you. Why haven't you written to me?'

'Why? ... Because I hadn't the courage. .... You forget my position.'

'To me? Hadn't the courage to write to me? If you knew how I ... I consider ...'

Dolly wanted to tell Anna her thoughts of the morning but now for some reason they seemed inappropriate.

'However, we can talk about that later. What are all those buildings?' she asked, wanting to change the subject, and pointing to some red and green roofs that could be seen through a quickset hedgerow of acacia and lilac. 'It looks quite a little town.'

But Anna did not answer her.

'No, no, tell me how you look at my position? What do you think of it, tell me?' she asked.

'I consider ...' Dolly was beginning, but at that instant Vasenka Veslovsky, who had got the cob to lead with the right leg, galloped past in his short jacket, bumping heavily up and down on the chamois leather of the side-saddle. 'I've got him to do it, Anna Arkadyevna!' he shouted.

Anna did not even glance at him; but again it seemed to Dolly that the carriage was hardly the place to enter upon a long conversation, and so she cut short her thought.

'I don't think anything,' she said. 'I've always loved you, and if one loves anyone, one loves the whole person, just as they are and not as one would like them to be ...'

Anna turned her eyes away from her friend's face and screwing them up (a new habit Dolly had not seen in her before) pondered, trying to penetrate the full significance of the remark. Having evidently interpreted it in her own way, she glanced at Dolly.

'All your sins, if you had any,' she said, 'would be forgiven you for this visit and what you have just said.'

And Dolly saw that tears stood in her eyes. She pressed Anna's hand in silence.

'Well, what are those buildings? What a lot of them there are!' she said, after a moment's silence, repeating her question.

'They are the servants' cottages, the stud farm, and the stables,' answered Anna. 'And the park begins here. Everything had been neglected, but Alexei has had it all done up. He is very fond of this place and, what I never expected, he has become terribly enthusiastic about looking after it. But of course he's so full of ideas – he can do anything he sets his mind to. So far from being bored, he works with passionate interest. I can see that he has turned into a careful, first-rate landlord, positively reckoning every penny in his management of the place. But only in that. When it's a question of tens of thousands, he doesn't think of money.' She spoke with that gleeful knowing smile with which women often talk of the secret characteristics, known only to them, of the man they love. 'Do you see that big building over there? It is the new hospital. I think it's going to cost more than a hundred thousand. That's his special hobby just now. And do you know what started it? Apparently the peasants asked him to let them have some meadow-land at a lower rent and he refused, and I accused him of meanness. Of course it was not just that only, but everything together started him building this hospital to prove, do you see, that he was not mean. *C'est une petitesse*, if you like, but I love him all the more for it. Now in a moment you will see the house. It was his grandfather's house, and the outside has not been altered at all.'

'How lovely!' Dolly exclaimed, looking with involuntary admiration at the beautiful house with columns, standing out among the different-coloured greens of the old trees in the garden.

'Isn't it? And we get a wonderful view from upstairs.'

They drove into a gravelled courtyard bright with flowers, where two workmen were making a border of rough porous stones round a well-forked flower-bed, and drew up beneath a covered portico.

'Ah, they've got here before us!' said Anna, looking at the saddle-horses being led away from the steps. 'Isn't she a pretty creature? It's my cob, my favourite. Bring her here, and get me some sugar. Where is the count?' she inquired of two footmen in faultless livery who darted out. 'Ah, here he is!' she said, seeing Vronsky coming out to meet her with Veslovsky.

'Where are you putting the princess?' Vronsky asked Anna in French, and without waiting for a reply he turned to Dolly, welcomed her again and this time kissed her hand. 'The big balcony room, I should think.'

'Oh no, that's much too far off! She will be better in the corner room – we shall see each other more. Come along,' said Anna, who had been giving her favourite horse the sugar the footman had brought her.

'*Et vous oubliez votre devoir,*' she said to Veslovsky, who had also come out on the porch.

'*Pardon, j'en ai tout plein les poches,*' he answered with a smile, his fingers feeling in his waistcoat pocket.

'*Mais vous venez trop tard,*' she said, wiping with her handkerchief the hand the horse had licked in taking the sugar.

Anna turned to Dolly. 'You can stay some time? Only one day? That's impossible!'

'I promised to be back, and the children ...' said Dolly, feeling embarrassed because she had to get her shabby little bag out of the carriage, and because she knew her face must be covered with dust.

'No, Dolly, darling! ... Well, we'll see. Come! Come along!' and Anna led the way to Dolly's room.

It was not the grand guest-room Vronsky had suggested but one for which Anna was apologetic. But even this room, for which apologies were needed, was furnished with more luxury than Dolly had ever known, luxury which reminded her of the best hotels abroad.

'Well, dearest, how happy I am!' Anna said, sitting down in her riding-habit for a moment beside Dolly. 'Tell me all about everyone. Stiva I only had a glimpse of, and he can never tell one about the children. How is my pet, Tanya? She must be quite a big girl now, I expect?'

'Yes, she's very tall,' replied Dolly shortly, surprised herself that she could respond so coldly about her children. 'We are having a delightful time at the Levins',' she added.

'There now, if I had only known that you don't despise me ... you might all have come to us. Stiva's an old and good friend of Alexei's, you know,' she added, and suddenly blushed.

'Yes, but we are all ...' replied Dolly in confusion.

'However, I'm so happy I'm talking nonsense. The one thing, dearest, is that I am so glad to have you,' said Anna, kissing her again. 'You haven't told me yet how and what you think about me, and I keep wanting to know. But I am glad you will see me as I am. Above all I don't want anyone to think I'm trying to prove anything. I don't want to prove anything: I merely want to live, doing no harm to anyone but myself. I have the right to that, haven't I? But it is a big subject, and we'll talk over everything properly later. I will go and dress now, and send a maid to help you.'

19

Left alone, Dolly surveyed the room with the expert eye of a housewife. Everything she had seen both inside and outside the house, and all she saw now in her room, gave her an impression of wealth and sumptuousness, of the new European kind of luxury which she had only read about in English novels but had never seen in Russia and in the country before. Everything was new, from the new French wallpaper to the carpet which covered the whole floor. The bed had a spring mattress, and a special sort of bolster, while the little pillows had silk slips. The marble washstand and the dressing-table, the couch, the tables, the bronze clock on the chimney-piece, the window-curtains and door-hangings were all costly and new.

The smart maid who came in to offer her services was more fashionably dressed and had her hair arranged more stylishly than Dolly, and was as new and expensive as everything else in the room. Dolly liked her polite manners, neatness, and obligingness, but she felt ill at ease with her. She was ashamed to let her see the patched dressing-jacket, which, as ill-luck would have it, had been packed for her by mistake. The very patches and darns of which she had been so proud at home now made her feel uncomfortable. At home everyone knew that six jackets took over eighteen yards of nainsook at one-and-three a yard, which was a matter of thirty shillings, besides the trimmings and making, and she had saved all that. But before the maid she felt, if not exactly ashamed, at least uncomfortable.

Dolly was immensely relieved when Annushka, whom she had known for years, came in to take the place of the smart lady's-maid who was wanted by her mistress.

Annushka was obviously very pleased to see her, and began to chatter away without pause. Dolly noticed that she was longing to express her opinion in regard to her mistress's position, especially as to the count's love and devotion towards Anna, but Dolly was careful to stop her whenever she began on the subject.

'I grew up with Anna Arkadyevna; my lady's dearer to me than all the world. Well, it's not for us to judge. And, to be sure, the love ...'

'So will you get this washed for me, if you can, please,' Dolly interrupted her.

'Yes, ma'am. There are two women specially kept for washing small things, but the big laundry's done by machine. The count goes into everything himself. Ah, what a husband ...'

Dolly was glad when Anna came in, thereby putting a stop to Annushka's gossip.

Anna had changed into a very simple muslin gown. Dolly looked particularly at this simple dress. She knew what such simplicity meant, and what it cost.

'An old friend,' said Anna, of Annushka.

Anna was no longer embarrassed. She was perfectly self-possessed and at ease. Dolly saw that she had quite got over the excitement her arrival had produced in her, and had assumed a superficial, careless tone which closed the door, as it were, on that compartment where her innermost thoughts and feelings were kept.

'Well, Anna, and how is your little girl?' asked Dolly.

'Ani?' (this was what she called her little daughter Anna). 'Very well. She has got on wonderfully. Would you like to see her? Come along, I'll show her to you. We've had awful difficulty over nurses,' she began telling her. 'We engaged an Italian wet-nurse. A nice creature, but so stupid! We wanted to get rid of her but the child is so used to her that we've gone on keeping her.'

'But how did you manage ...?' Dolly stopped. She had meant to ask what surname the little girl would have; but observing the sudden frown on Anna's face she changed the drift of her question, and said: 'How did you manage – have you weaned her yet?'

But Anna had understood.

'That wasn't what you were going to ask? You wanted to know about her surname, isn't that so? That worries Alexei. She has no name – that is, she's a Karenin,' said Anna, screwing up her eyes until the lashes met. 'But we'll talk about all that later,' she added, her face suddenly brightening. 'Come and see her. *Elle est très gentille.* She can crawl now.'

The luxuriousness of the nursery impressed Dolly even more than the luxury she had noticed in the rest of the house. There were little go-carts ordered from England, an appliance for teaching babies to walk, a specially constructed piece of furniture after the fashion of a billiard table for the child to crawl on, and swings and novel kinds of baths. Everything was of English make, solid, of good quality, and obviously very expensive. The room itself was large, light, and airy.

When they entered, the baby was sitting in a tiny arm-chair at the table, with nothing on but a little chemise, having her dinner of broth, which she was spilling all down her front. A Russian nursemaid was feeding the child and evidently herself eating at the same time. Neither the wet-nurse nor the head-nurse was to be seen: they were in the next room, where they could be heard carrying on a conversation in the queer French which was their only means of communication.

Hearing Anna's voice, a tall, smart English nurse with a disagreeable, wanton face came into the room, giving her fair curls a quick shake, and at once began excusing herself, though Anna had not found fault with her. To every word of Anna's the woman kept saying hurriedly, 'Yes, my lady.'

The rosy-faced little girl with her black hair and eyebrows, her sturdy little body all over gooseflesh, won Dolly's heart in spite of the severe way she stared at the stranger. Dolly even felt envious of the child's healthy appearance. She was also particularly taken by the way the baby crawled: not one of her own children had crawled like that. When the baby was put on the carpet and its little dress tucked up behind, it looked wonderfully sweet. Peeping round at them with her bright black eyes, like some little wild animal, she smiled, unmistakably delighted to be admired, and keeping her legs out sideways she energetically supported herself on her hands, drew her little seat forward and again advanced on her hands.

But the general atmosphere of the nursery, and especially the English nurse, Dolly did not like at all. How could Anna, with her insight into people, have engaged such an unprepossessing fast-looking woman as nurse to her child? The only explanation Dolly could think of was that no respectable nurse would have taken service in so irregular a household as Anna's. Moreover, from a few words that were dropped, Dolly immediately realized that Anna, the two nurses and the baby were not used to each other, and that the mother's visit was an uncommon event. Anna wanted to get the baby one of her toys, but did not know where to look for it.

Most astonishing of all, when Dolly asked her how many teeth the child had, Anna made a mistake and knew nothing whatever of the two latest teeth.

'It is often a grief to me that I'm so useless here,' said Anna, lifting her skirt to avoid the playthings lying in the doorway, as they left the nursery. 'It was not like that with my first.'

'I should have expected it to be the other way round,' said Dolly timidly.

'Oh no! By the way, I have seen Seriozha, did you know?' said Anna, screwing up her eyes as though peering at something far away. 'But I'll tell you about that later. You wouldn't believe it – I feel like some starved beggar-woman who suddenly has a full dinner set before her, and she doesn't know what to start on first. The dinner is you and the talks we're going to have together, which I could never have with anyone else; and I don't know what to begin on first. *Mais je ne vous ferai grâce de rien!* We must talk about everything. Oh, I suppose I ought to give you an idea of the company you will find here,' she went on. 'I will begin with the lady: Princess Varvara – you know her, and I know your and Stiva's opinion about her. Stiva says her one aim in life is to prove her superiority over Aunt Katerina Pavlovna. That's quite true; but she is a good soul, and I am very grateful to her. There was a moment in Petersburg when I needed a chaperon. Then she turned up. She really is a good-natured creature. She made my position much easier. I can see you don't realize all the difficulty of my position ... there in Petersburg,' she added. 'Here I'm perfectly at ease and happy. Well, of that later on, though. I must continue the list. There is Sviazhsky – he's the marshal of the district, and a very decent fellow, but he wants to get something out of Alexei. You see, now that we have settled in the country, with his means Alexei can exercise a great deal of influence. Next there's Tushkevich: you have met him – Betsy's admirer. Now he's been thrown over and come to see us. As Alexei says, he is one of those people who are very pleasant if one accepts them for what they try to appear, *et puis, il est comme il faut*, as Princess Varvara says. Then Veslovsky … you know him. He is a nice boy,' she said, and a mischievous smile puckered her lips. 'What is this wild story about him and Levin? Veslovsky told Alexei about it and we couldn't believe it. *Il est très gentil et naif*,' she added with the same smile. 'Men need recreation and Alexei needs an audience. That is why I like all this company. We must make it lively and gay here or Alexei will long for something fresh. Then you'll see our steward. He is a German, an excellent person, who knows his business. Alexei thinks highly of him. After that, there's the doctor, a young man, not exactly a Nihilist, but eats with his knife, you know … but a very good doctor. Lastly, the architect … Quite *une petite cour*!'

20

'WELL, here's Dolly for you, Princess. You were so anxious to see her,' said Anna as she and Dolly came out on to the large stone terrace, where the Princess Varvara was sitting in the shade before an embroidery frame, working at a chair-cover for Count Vronsky's easy-chair. 'She declares she doesn't want anything before dinner, but will you see that she gets some lunch, while I go and find Alexei and fetch them all in?'

The Princess Varvara gave Dolly a cordial and rather patronizing reception, and at once began explaining that she was living with Anna because she had always been fonder of her than was her sister Katerina Pavlovna, the aunt who had brought Anna up; and that now, when everyone else had thrown Anna over, she considered it her duty to help her in this most trying period of transition.

'When her husband divorces her, I shall return to my solitude; but at present I can be of use, and I am doing my duty, however difficult it may be for me – not like some people. And how kind and good it was of you to come! They live like the best of married couples: it's for God to judge them, not for us. Remember Biryuzovsky and Madame Avenyev … and even Nikandrov! And how about Vasilyev with Madame Mamonov, or Liza Neptunov? … No one said anything against them! And in the end they were all received back in society. And then, *c'est un intérieur si joli, si comme il faut. Tout-à-fait à l'anglaise. On se réunit le matin au breakfast et puis on se sépare.* Everyone does as he pleases until dinner. Dinner is at seven. Stiva did very rightly to send you. He must keep in with them. You know, through his mother and brother the count can do anything. And then they do so much good. Has he told you about his hospital? *Ce sera admirable –* everything straight from Paris.'

Their conversation was interrupted by Anna, who had discovered the men of the party in the billiard-room and brought them back with her to the terrace. There was still plenty of time before dinner, the weather was exquisite, and so several different ways of passing the next two hours were proposed. There were a great many ways of spending time at Vozdvizhenskoe, such as were never dreamed of at Pokrovskoe.

'*Une partie de lawn-tennis,*' Veslovsky suggested with his pleasing smile. 'You and I will be partners again, Anna Arkadyevna.'

'No, it's too hot for tennis. Let us stroll round the garden and go for a row in the boat, to show Darya Alexandrovna the river-banks,' proposed Vronsky.

'I am ready for anything,' said Sviazhsky.

'I imagine Dolly would like a walk best, wouldn't you? We can go in the boat afterwards, perhaps,' said Anna.

So it was decided. Veslovsky and Tushkevich went off to the bathing-place, promising to get the boat ready and wait there for the others, who started off down the garden path in pairs – Anna with Sviazhsky, and Dolly with Vronsky.

Dolly was somewhat embarrassed and anxious in the entirely novel environment in which she found herself. In the abstract, theoretically, she not only justified but positively approved of Anna's conduct. As is not infrequently the case with women of unimpeachable virtue, weary of the monotony of respectable existence, at a distance she not only condoned an illicit love, but even envied it. Besides, she loved Anna with her whole heart. But when she actually saw Anna among all these strange people with their *bon ton*, which was quite new to her, Dolly felt ill at ease. What she disliked particularly was seeing the Princess Varvara ready to overlook everything for the sake of the comforts she enjoyed.

As a general principle, in the abstract, Dolly approved of the step

Anna had taken; but the sight of the man on whose account the step had been taken was disagreeable. Moreover, she had never found Vronsky congenial. She thought him proud, and saw nothing in him of which he could be proud except his wealth. But here in his own house he impressed her in spite of herself, and she could not be at ease with him. He made her feel the same way the maid had made her feel over the dressing-jacket. Just as with the maid she had felt not so much ashamed as uncomfortable at the patches, so now with him she felt not exactly ashamed, but embarrassed at herself.

Ill at ease, she tried to think of something to talk about. She supposed that, with his pride, he would not like to hear her praise his house and garden, yet, not finding any other subject of conversation, she told him, all the same, how much she admired his house.

'Yes, it is a handsome building, in the good old style,' he said.

'I like the courtyard in front of the steps very much. Was it like that before?'

'Oh no!' he replied, and his face lit up with pleasure. 'You should have seen that courtyard in the spring!'

And by degrees, rather diffidently at first and then more and more carried away by his subject, he began pointing out to her the various improvements in the house and garden. It was clear that, having devoted a great deal of trouble to restore and improve his home, Vronsky felt a need to show off his efforts to a fresh person, and Dolly's praises were music in his ears.

'If you would care to have a look at the hospital, and are not too tired, it is quite near. Shall we go?' he suggested, glancing into her face to make sure that she really was not bored.

'Will you come, Anna?' he asked, turning to her.

'Yes, shall we?' she said, addressing Sviazhsky. *'Mais il ne faut pas laisser le pauvre Veslovsky et Tushkevich se morfondre là dans le bateau.* We must let them know. Yes, it's a monument he will leave behind him,' Anna said to Dolly with the same artful, knowing smile with which she had spoken about the hospital before.

'Oh, it's a grand undertaking!' said Sviazhsky. But, to show he was not trying to make up to Vronsky, he promptly added a slightly critical remark. 'I wonder, though, Count, that while you do so much for the health of the peasants, you take so little interest in schools for them.'

'C'est devenu tellement commun, les écoles,' said Vronsky. 'Of course

653

that's not the reason. I simply became carried away. We go this way to the hospital,' he said, turning to Dolly and indicating a side-path that led out of the avenue.

The ladies opened their parasols and entered the sidewalk. After going down several turnings and through a little gate, Dolly saw on rising ground before her a large red, nearly completed building of fanciful design. The iron roof, not yet painted, shone with dazzling brightness in the sunshine. At the side of the almost finished building another had been begun, surrounded by scaffold-poles. Workmen in aprons stood on the scaffolding laying bricks, pouring mortar from wooden tubs and smoothing it with trowels.

'How quickly they've got on!' said Sviazhsky. 'The last time I was here there was no sign of the roof.'

'By the autumn it will all be ready. Inside they've nearly finished,' remarked Anna.

'And what is this new building?'

'That will be the doctor's quarters and the dispensary,' answered Vronsky; and, seeing the architect in his short jacket coming towards them, he excused himself to the ladies, and went to meet him.

Going round the pit where the workmen were slaking lime, he stopped and began a heated discussion with the architect.

'The pediment is still too low,' he said to Anna, when she asked him what the trouble was.

'I said all along that the foundation ought to be raised,' remarked Anna.

'Yes, to be sure, it would have been better, Anna Arkadyevna,' said the architect, 'but it's done now.'

'Yes, I am very much interested in architecture,' Anna said to Sviazhsky, who was expressing his surprise at her knowledge of the subject. 'This new building ought to have been in keeping with the hospital. But it was an afterthought, and begun without a plan.'

Having disposed of the architect, Vronsky rejoined the ladies and led them inside the hospital.

Although men were still busy on the cornices outside and at work painting inside on the ground floor, the upper storey was nearly finished. Going up the broad iron staircase to the landing, they entered the first large room. The walls were stuccoed to look like marble, the enormous plate-glass windows were already in, only the parquet floor was not yet finished, and the carpenters, who were planing a square of parquet, stopped their work, taking off the tapes that kept their hair out of the way, to greet the gentry.

'This is the reception-room,' said Vronsky. 'There will be nothing but a desk, a table, and a cupboard in here, that's all.'

'This way – come this way, but don't go near the window,' said Anna, feeling to see if the paint were still wet. 'Alexei, the paint's dry already,' she added.

From the reception-room they passed into the corridor. Here Vronsky pointed out the new system of ventilation he had installed. Then he showed them the marble baths and the specially-sprung beds. Next they visited the wards, one after another, the store-room, the linen-room. He showed them the up-to-date stoves, the silent trolleys for carrying things along the corridors, and much besides. Sviazhsky, a connoisseur where the latest modern improvements were concerned, was full of appreciation. Dolly simply wondered at everything she saw, which was all new to her, and, anxious to understand, made minute inquiries about everything, to Vronsky's evident gratification.

'Yes, I imagine this will be the unique example of a perfectly-planned hospital in Russia,' remarked Sviazhsky.

'And won't you have a maternity ward?' asked Dolly. 'It is so necessary in the country. I've often thought …'

Contrary to his usual courtesy, Vronsky interrupted her. 'This is not a lying-in home, but a hospital intended for all kinds of diseases, except infectious complaints,' he said. 'But have a look at this …' and he rolled up to Dolly an invalid-chair that had just been ordered for convalescents. 'Look.' He seated himself in the chair and began propelling it along. 'The patient can't walk – still too weak, perhaps, or there's something wrong with his legs, but he needs fresh air, so he just sits in this and takes himself out for a ride …'

Dolly was interested and charmed by everything, and especially by Vronsky himself, with his natural, naïve enthusiasm. 'Yes, he's a very nice, kind man,' she thought time and again, not listening to what he was saying but watching him, trying to fathom his expression, while she mentally put herself in Anna's place. He was so eager and she liked him so much now that she began to understand how Anna could be in love with him.

21

'No, I think the princess is tired, and horses don't interest her,' Vronsky said to Anna, who had proposed they should go on to the stud farm, where Sviazhsky wanted to see the new stallion. 'You go, while I escort the princess back to the house, and we'll have a talk together – that is, if you would like to?' he added, turning to Dolly.

'I should be delighted – I don't understand a thing about horses,' answered Dolly, rather taken aback.

She saw by Vronsky's face that there was something he wanted of her. She was not mistaken. As soon as they had passed back through the little gate into the garden, he glanced in the direction Anna had taken, and, having made sure that she could neither hear nor see them, he began:

'You guess that I have something I want to say to you?' he said, looking at her with laughing eyes. 'I am not wrong in believing you to be Anna's friend.' He took off his hat, and with his handkerchief wiped his head, which was beginning to go bald.

Dolly made no answer, and merely stared at him in dismay. Now that she was left alone with him, she suddenly felt afraid: his laughing eyes and stern expression scared her.

The most diverse speculations as to what he was about to say flashed through her mind. 'He is going to ask me to bring the children to stay with them, and I shall have to refuse; or maybe he wants me to find a circle of friends for Anna in Moscow. Or talk about Vasenka Veslovsky and his attitude to Anna? Or perhaps it is about Kitty, and he is going to tell me he feels guilty?' All her surmises were unpleasant ones, but she did not hit upon what he actually did want to talk to her about.

'You have so much influence with Anna; she is so fond of you,' he said. 'I wish you would help me.'

Dolly looked with timid inquiry into his energetic face, which was now wholly, now partly in the sunlight that fell between the lime trees, and then passed into complete shadow again. She waited for him to say more, but he walked by her side in silence, prodding the gravel with his cane as he went.

'You are the only one of Anna's women friends to come and see us – I don't count the Princess Varvara. Of course I know that you have done so not because you regard our position as normal, but because, understanding all the difficulty of the position, you still love and want to help her. Am I right?' he asked, looking round at her.

'Oh, yes,' answered Dolly, shutting up her parasol, 'but ...'

'No,' he broke in, and unconsciously, oblivious of the awkward situation in which he was placing his companion, he stopped abruptly, so that she had to stop short too. 'No one feels the burden of Anna's position more deeply and intensely than I do; and that is understandable, if you do me the honour of believing I am not heartless. I am to blame for that position, and that is why I feel it.'

'I understand,' said Dolly, involuntarily admiring the sincerity and firmness with which he said this. 'But just because you feel yourself responsible, you exaggerate it, I am afraid. Her position in the world is a hard one, I can well understand.'

'In the world it is hell!' he said quickly, with a dark frown. 'You can't conceive moral torture worse than what she went through in Petersburg that fortnight ... and I beg you to believe me.'

'Yes, but here, so long as neither Anna ... nor you miss society ...'

'Society!' he exclaimed contemptuously. 'What need can I have of society?'

'So long as you feel like that – and perhaps you always will – you are happy and at peace. I can see that Anna is happy, perfectly happy; she has already told me so,' said Dolly, smiling; and involuntarily, as she said this, a doubt entered her mind as to whether Anna really was happy.

But Vronsky, it appeared, had no doubts on that score.

'Yes, yes,' he said, 'I know that she has recovered after all her sufferings; she is happy. She is happy in the present. But I? ... I fear for what the future has in store for us. ... I beg your pardon, you would like to walk on?'

'No, it is all right.'

'Well, then, let us sit here.'

Dolly sat down on a garden-seat in a corner of the avenue. He stood facing her.

'I see that she is happy,' he repeated, and the doubt whether Anna was happy struck Dolly more forcibly than before. 'But can it last? Whether we have acted rightly or wrongly is another question; but the die is cast,' he said, passing from Russian to French, 'and we are bound together for life. We are united by all the ties of love that we hold most sacred. We have a child, we may have other children. Yet the law and all the circumstances of our situation are such that thousands of complications arise which she, resting now after all her trials and sufferings, neither sees nor wants to see. And that one can well understand. But I can't help seeing them. My daughter is by law not my daughter, but Karenin's. I cannot bear the falsity of it!' he said, with a vigorous gesture of protest, and he looked with gloomy inquiry towards Dolly.

She made no answer but simply gazed at him.

'Some day we may have a son,' he went on, 'my son, and by law he would be a Karenin. He would not be heir to my name or my property; and no matter how happy we may be in our home life nor how ever many children we may have, there will be no legal bond between us. They would be Karenins. Think of the bitterness and horror of such a position! I have tried to talk to Anna about it but it only irritates her. She does not understand, and to *her* I cannot speak plainly of all this. Now look at another side. I am happy in her love, but I must have occupation. I have found occupation and am proud of what I am doing – I consider it far more creditable than the pursuits of my former comrades at Court and in the army. And I certainly wouldn't exchange with any of them. I work here, I live here, and I am happy and contented, and we need nothing more to make us happy. I love my work here. *Cela n'est pas un pis-aller*, on the contrary ...'

Dolly observed that at this point he wandered away from his argument, and she was at a loss to understand this digression, but she felt that having once begun to speak of matters near his heart, of which he could not speak to Anna, he was now making an effort to tell her everything, and that the question of his pursuits in the country fell into the same category of matters near his heart as the question of his relations with Anna.

'Well, to continue,' he said, recovering himself. 'The great thing is that, as I am working, I want to know that what I am doing will not die with me, that I shall have heirs to come after me – and this I have not. Conceive the feelings of a man who knows that his children, the children of the woman he loves, will not be his, but will belong to someone who hates them and will have nothing to do with them! It is horrible!'

He paused, evidently profoundly moved.

'Yes, indeed, I see that. But what can Anna do?' queried Dolly.

'Yes, that brings me to my point,' he said, mastering himself with an effort. 'Anna could ... it depends on her. ... Even to petition the Emperor for permission to adopt, a divorce is essential. And that depends on Anna. Karenin agreed to a divorce – at that time your husband had practically arranged it – and I feel certain he would not refuse now. It is only a matter of writing to him. He said plainly enough then that if she expressed the desire he would not refuse. Of course,' he added gloomily, 'it is one of those Pharisaical cruelties of which only heartless men like him are capable. He knows what torture it is for her even to think of him, and, knowing her, he must have a letter from her. I know how painful it would be for her to write. But the affair is of such importance that one must *passer par-dessus toutes ces finesses de sentiment. Il y va du bonheur et de l'existence d'Anne et de ses enfants.* I won't speak of myself, though it's hard for me – very hard,' he said, with a menacing look for someone for making it hard. 'And so it is, Princess, that I am shamelessly clutching at you as an anchor of salvation. Help me to persuade her to write to him and ask for a divorce.'

'Of course I will,' said Dolly thoughtfully, recalling vividly her last meeting with Karenin. 'Of course I will,' she repeated resolutely, thinking of Anna.

'Use your influence with her, make her write. I don't like – and it is almost impossible for me – to speak to her about this myself.'

'Very well, I will talk to her. But how is it she does not think of it herself?' asked Dolly, for some reason suddenly recalling Anna's strange new habit of half-closing her eyes. And she remembered that it was just when her inner feelings were touched upon that Anna drooped her eyelids. 'As if she half-shut her eyes to her own life, so as not to see everything,' thought Dolly. 'Yes, indeed, for my own sake as for hers I will talk to her,' Dolly said in response to his look of gratitude.

They got up and walked back to the house.

22

FINDING Dolly home before her, Anna looked intently at her, her eyes seeming to question Dolly about the talk she had had with Vronsky, but she did not ask about it.

'It must be nearly dinner-time,' she said. 'We've not seen anything of each other yet. I am counting on this evening. Now I must go and change. I expect you want to, too. We got all dirty in the new building.'

Dolly went to her room and felt like laughing. She had nothing to change into for she was already wearing her best dress; but in order to show in some way that she had prepared for dinner she asked the maid to brush her gown, and she put on clean cuffs and a fresh ribbon, and arranged some lace on her head.

'This is all I could do,' she laughed to Anna, who came in wearing another extremely simple gown, the third Dolly had seen her in that day.

'Yes, we are too formal here,' Anna remarked, as though in apology for her own elegance. 'I have seldom seen Alexei so pleased with anything as he is with your visit. He has completely lost his heart to you,' she added. 'You're sure you're not tired?'

There was no time to talk before dinner. When they entered the drawing-room, they found the Princess Varvara and the gentlemen of the party already there, the latter in black frock-coats, except for the architect who was wearing a swallow-tail. Vronsky introduced the doctor and the steward to the visitor. The architect she had already met at the hospital.

A portly butler, his round, clean-shaven face beaming, his starched white necktie resplendent, announced that dinner was served, and the ladies got up. Vronsky asked Sviazhsky to take in Anna, and himself went up to Dolly. Veslovsky offered his arm to the Princess Varvara before Tushkevich could do so, so Tushkevich, the steward, and the doctor went in by themselves.

The dinner, the dining-room, the dinner-service, the waiting at table, the wine, and the food were not only in keeping with the general air of up-to-date luxury throughout the house, but were, if anything, even more sumptuous and modern. Dolly observed all this luxury, which was novel to her, and, being herself the mistress of a house, she instinctively noted every detail (though she had no hope of introducing anything she saw to her own household – such luxury was far above her means and manner of life), and wondered how it was all done and by whom. Vasenka Veslovsky, her own husband and even Sviazhsky, and a great many other people she knew, would never have stopped to consider this question but were quite ready to believe what every well-bred host wishes his guests to feel – that everything that is so well ordered in his house has cost him, the host, no trouble whatever, but comes about of itself. Dolly, however, was well aware that not even porridge for the children's breakfast comes of itself, and therefore, where so complicated and magnificent an establishment was maintained, someone must give earnest attention to its organization. And from the glance with which Vronsky scanned the table, from the way he nodded to the butler, and offered Dolly her choice of cold soup or hot, she concluded that it was all organized and maintained by the care of the master of the house himself. Anna had no more to do with it than had Veslovsky. She was as much a guest as Sviazhsky, the princess, and Veslovsky, and, like them, gaily enjoying what had been arranged for them.

Only as far as conducting the conversation was Anna the hostess. And that most difficult task for the hostess of a small dinner-party which includes such guests as the steward and the architect – people of quite a different world, struggling not to be overawed by an elegance to which they were unaccustomed, and unable to sustain a large share in the general conversation – Anna managed with her usual tact, naturally, and even taking pleasure in it herself, as Dolly observed.

The conversation began about the row Tushkevich and Veslovsky had taken alone together in the boat, and Tushkevich started describing the last races at the Petersburg Yacht Club. But at the first opportunity Anna turned to the architect, to draw him out of his silence.

'Nikolai Ivanich was struck,' she said (referring to Sviazhsky), 'at the progress made by the new building since he was here last. It amazes me, too, though I am there and see it every day.'

'It is a pleasure to work with his excellency,' the architect replied with a smile. He was a quiet, respectful man, though conscious of his own dignity. 'It's not like having to do with local authorities. A matter they would use reams of paper writing about, I merely report to the count, we talk it over and in three words we settle the whole business.'

'American fashion!' said Sviazhsky, with a smile.

'Yes, there they build in a rational manner ...'

The conversation passed to the misuse of political power in the United States, but Anna quickly brought it round to another topic that would be of interest to the steward.

'Have you ever seen a reaping-machine?' she said, addressing Dolly.

'We had just ridden over to have a look at one when we met you. It's the first time I ever saw one.'

'How do they work?' asked Dolly.

'Exactly like a pair of scissors. A plank and a lot of little scissors. Like this …'

Anna took a knife and fork in her beautiful white hands, sparkling with rings, and began to demonstrate. She saw that she was not making herself very clear, but aware that her voice sounded pleasant and her hands were beautiful she persevered.

'More like little pen-knives,' remarked Veslovsky playfully, never taking his eyes off her.

Anna gave a faint smile but made no answer.

'Am I not right, Karl Fedorich – they are like scissors?' she asked, turning to the steward.

'*O, ja,*' replied the German. '*Es ist ein ganz einfaches Ding,*' and he began to explain the construction of the machine.

'What a pity it does not bind too! I saw one at the Vienna exhibition that bound the sheaves with twine,' said Sviazhsky. 'It would be far more profitable.'

'*Es kommt drauf an. … Der Preis vom Draht muss ausgerechnet werden.*' And the German, drawn from his silence, turned to Vronsky. '*Das lässt sich ausrechnen, Erlaucht.*' The German was just feeling in the pocket where he kept his pencil and the notebook in which he made all his calculations but, recollecting that he was at dinner and observing Vronsky's chilly glance, he checked himself. '*Zu kompliziert, macht zu viel Klopot,*' he concluded.

'*Wünscht man Dorhots, so hat man auch Klopots,*' said Vasenka Veslovsky, mimicking the German. '*J'adore l'allemand,*' he said, turning to Anna again with the same smile.

'*Cessez!*' she said with mock severity.

'We expected to find you in the fields, Vasily Semeonich,' she remarked to the doctor, a sickly-looking man. 'Were you?'

'Yes, but I vanished,' the doctor replied with dismal jocularity.

'Then you got some good exercise?'

'First-rate!'

'Well, and how was the old woman? I hope it's not typhus?'

'Typhus or not, she's in a bad way.'

'Poor thing!' said Anna, and, having thus done her duty by the members of the household, she turned her attention to her own friends.

'All the same, it wouldn't be easy to construct a machine from your description, Anna Arkadyevna,' Sviazhsky chaffed her.

'Oh, why?' said Anna, with a smile which showed that she knew there had been something engaging in her descriptions of the reaper that had been noticed by Sviazhsky. This new trait of youthful coquetry jarred on Dolly.

'Anna Arkadyevna's knowledge of architecture, though, is marvellous,' put in Tushkevich.

'Oh yes! Only last night I heard Anna Arkadyevna talking about damp-courses and plinths,' said Veslovsky. 'Have I got it right?'

'There's nothing marvellous about it, considering how much I see and hear of it,' said Anna. 'But I dare say you don't even know what houses are made of?'

Dolly saw that Anna disliked the playful tone that existed between her and Veslovsky, but fell in with it against her will.

Vronsky reacted in this matter quite differently from Levin. He obviously attached no significance to Veslovsky's chatter; on the contrary, he encouraged his jests.

'Come, tell us, Veslovsky, what keeps the bricks together?'

'Cement, of course.'

'Bravo! And what is cement?'

'Oh, some sort of paste ... no, putty,' Veslovsky replied, making them all laugh.

The company at dinner, with the exception of the doctor, the architect, and the steward, who sat in gloomy silence, never stopped talking, the conversation glancing off one subject, fastening on another, and at times touching one or other of the party to the quick. Once Dolly was provoked and felt so angry that she positively flushed, and wondered afterwards whether she had said too much or been rude. Sviazhsky had begun talking of Levin and his strange idea that machinery only did harm to Russian agriculture.

'I have not the pleasure of knowing the gentleman,' said Vronsky, with a smile, 'but probably he has never seen the machines he condemns. Or if he has seen and tried them, they must have been some home-produced Russian imitation, not a machine imported from abroad. What ideas can he have of the subject?'

'Turkish ones, in general,' said Veslovsky, turning to Anna with a smile.

'I can't defend his opinions,' Dolly said, flaring up, 'but I can say that he's a very well-informed man, and if he were here he would be able to give you the answer, though I am not capable of doing so.'

'I am very fond of him, and we are great friends,' said Sviazhsky, smiling good-naturedly. '*Mais pardon, il est un petit peu toqué.* For instance, he maintains that district councils and arbitration boards are all quite unnecessary, and he won't have anything to do with them.'

'There's our usual Russian apathy,' said Vronsky, pouring iced water from a decanter into a glass with a slender stem. 'We've no sense of the duties our privileges impose upon us, and so deny their very existence.'

'I know no man more strict in the performance of his duties,' said Dolly, irritated by Vronsky's tone of superiority.

'For my part,' pursued Vronsky, evidently for some reason stung by this conversation, 'I, on the contrary, such as I am, feel extremely grateful for the honour they have done me, thanks to Nikolai Ivanich here,' (he indicated Sviazhsky) 'in electing me a justice of the peace. I consider the duty of attending the sessions, of deliberating on the case of some peasant's horse, as important as anything I can do. And I should regard it an honour to be elected to the district council. It is my only way of making a return for the advantages I enjoy as a landowner. Unfortunately people do not understand the important part the big landowners ought to take in the affairs of the country.'

His calm assurance of righteousness, here at his own table, sounded strange to Dolly. She remembered how Levin, who held views diametrically opposed, was equally positive in his opinions at his own table. But she was very fond of Levin, and therefore on his side.

'So we can reckon on you, Count, for the coming elections?' said Sviazhsky. 'But you must leave in good time, so as to be on the spot by the eighth. If you would do me the honour of staying with me ...'

'I rather agree with your *beau-frère*,' said Anna, 'though I do not go to his lengths,' she added with a smile. 'To my mind too many of these public duties have sprung up of late. Just as in the old days there were so many government officials that we had an official for everything, so now everyone's performing some sort of public function! Alexei has been here barely six months, and I do believe he's already a member of half a dozen different public bodies. He is a guardian of the poor, a justice of the peace, a county councillor, a juryman, and a member of some commission on horses. *Du train que cela va,* his whole time will be taken up. And I fear that with such a multiplicity of these bodies, they'll end up by being a mere form. How many are you a member of, Nikolai Ivanich?' she asked, addressing Sviazhsky. 'Over twenty, isn't it?'

Though Anna spoke lightly, a note of irritation could be discerned in her tone. Dolly, watching Anna and Vronsky attentively, detected it instantly. She noticed, too, that at this conversation Vronsky's face had immediately assumed a set, obstinate expression. Coupling these observations with the fact that the Princess Varvara hastened to change the subject by talking of Petersburg acquaintances, and remembering the way Vronsky had dragged in the problem of his work in the country when they were in the garden together, Dolly surmised that this question of public activity must be connected with some deep private disagreement between Anna and Vronsky.

The dinner, the wines, the service were all excellent; but it all seemed to Dolly, though she had grown out of the habit of them, too much like a formal dinner-party or a ball: there was the same impersonal atmosphere and strain, and so on an everyday occasion and in a small gathering they produced a disagreeable impression on her.

After dinner they sat out on the terrace for a while, and then proceeded to play lawn-tennis. The players, having chosen their partners, took their places on the carefully levelled and rolled croquet-lawn, on either side of a net stretched between two gilt posts. Dolly made an attempt to play, but it was a long while before she could understand the game, and by the time she did understand it she felt so tired that she gave up and sat down to watch by the Princess Varvara. Her partner Tushkevich also gave up, but the others continued for a long time. Sviazhsky and Vronsky both played very well and earnestly. They kept their eyes on the balls served to them, and without haste or getting in each other's way ran adroitly up, waited for the ball to bounce, and then, striking well and truly with the racquet, returned it across the net. Veslovsky was a poor player. He got too excited, but, to make up for that, his high spirits inspired the others. His laughter and outcries were never silent. With the ladies' permission the men had taken off their coats, and he made an impressive picture with his fine, handsome figure in white shirt-sleeves, his red perspiring face and impetuous movements. When Dolly lay in bed that night, as soon as she closed her eyes, she saw Vasenka Veslovsky flying about the croquet-lawn.

Dolly did not feel happy while they were playing. She did not like the bantering tone that Vasenka Veslovsky and Anna kept up all through the game, nor the unnaturalness altogether of grown-up people playing a child's game in the absence of children. But not to break up the party, and to while away the time, after a rest she rejoined the players and pretended to be enjoying herself. It seemed to her that she had been play-acting all day with better actors than herself, and that her bad performance was spoiling the show.

She had come with the intention of staying a couple of days, if all went well. But in the evening, during the game, she made up her mind to leave next morning. The maternal cares and worries, which she had so hated on the way, now, after a day spent without them, struck her in quite another light, and drew her back to them.

When, after evening tea and a night row in the boat, Dolly retired to her room alone, took off her dress and sat down to pin up her thin hair for the night, she felt a great sense of relief. She did not even like the idea that in a moment Anna would be coming in to talk to her. She longed to be alone with her thoughts.

23

DOLLY was ready to get into bed when Anna came in in her dressing-gown.

In the course of the day Anna had several times been on the point of speaking of matters near her heart, and every time after a few words she had always stopped, saying, 'We'll talk about everything later, when we are by ourselves. I've so much I want to tell you.'

Now they were by themselves, and Anna did not know what to talk about. She sat in the window looking at Dolly, and reviewing in her mind all the store of intimate topics which had seemed so inexhaustible, and could find nothing to say. She felt at that moment as if everything had already been said.

'Well, and how's Kitty?' she asked with a heavy sigh and a guilty glance at Dolly. 'Tell me the truth, Dolly: is she angry with me?'

'Angry? Oh no!' replied Dolly, smiling.

'Then she probably hates and despises me?'

'Oh no! But you know there are things one does not forgive.'

'I know,' said Anna, turning away and looking out of the open window. 'But I was not to blame. And who is to blame? What does being to blame mean? Could things have been otherwise? Tell me what you think? Could it possibly have happened that you didn't become the wife of Stiva?'

'I really don't know. But tell me ...'

'Yes, but we haven't finished about Kitty. Is she happy? Levin's a very nice man, they say.'

'He's much more than very nice. I don't know a better man.'

'Oh, I am so glad! I am so glad! Much more than very nice,' she repeated.

Dolly smiled.

'But tell me about yourself. There is such a lot I want to know. And I've had a talk with ...' Dolly did not know what to call Vronsky. She felt it would be awkward to say 'the count' or 'Alexei Kirillich'.

'With Alexei,' said Anna. 'I know you have. But I wanted to ask you frankly what you think of me, of my life?'

'How can I say all at once? I really don't know.'

'No, but you must tell me. ... You see the life I am leading. But you mustn't forget, you're seeing us in summer, when you have come and we are not alone. ... But we arrived here early in the spring and lived quite alone, and we shall be alone again. I can wish for nothing better. But imagine me living alone without him, alone, and that will happen. ... Everything goes to show that it will often happen – that he will spend half his time away from home,' she said, getting up and seating herself closer to Dolly.

'Of course,' she interrupted Dolly, who was about to answer, 'of course, I won't try to keep him by force. I don't hold him back as it is. Soon the races will be on, his horses are running and he will go. I don't grudge it. But think of me, imagine my position. ... What is the use of talking about it, though?' She smiled. 'Well, what did he say to you?'

'He spoke of something I wanted to ask you myself, so it is easy for me to be his mouthpiece: of whether ... it isn't possible ... whether you could not ...' (Dolly hesitated) 'put things right and improve your position. ... You know how I look at it. ... But all the same, if it's possible, I think you ought to get married. ...'

'You mean a divorce?' said Anna. 'Do you know, the only woman who called on me in Petersburg was Betsy Tverskoy? You know her, of course? *Au fond c'est la femme la plus dépravée qui existe.* She was Tushkevich's mistress, deceiving her husband in the most disgraceful way. And she told me that she did not care to know me so long as my position was irregular. Don't think I am making comparisons. ... I know you, my darling. But I could not help remembering. ... Well, and what did Alexei say?' she repeated.

'He said that he suffers on your account and on his own. You can call it egoism if you like, but what a justifiable noble egoism! He wants first of all to make his daughter legitimate, and to be your husband, to have a legal right to you.'

'What wife, what slave could be more of a slave than I am in my position?' Anna interrupted sullenly.

'But the chief thing he desires ... he desires that you should not suffer.'

'That's impossible! Well?'

'Well, and his most proper wish is that your children should have a name.'

'What children?' asked Anna, half closing her eyes and not looking at Dolly.

'Ani, and others that will come ...'

'He can be at ease on that score: I shall have no more children.'

'How can you say that – how can you tell that you won't?'

'I shan't, because I don't wish it.'

And, in spite of her agitation, Anna could not help smiling as she caught the naïve expression of curiosity, wonder, and horror on Dolly's face.

'The doctor told me after my illness ...'

. . . . . .

'Impossible!' exclaimed Dolly, opening her eyes wide.

For her this was one of those discoveries the consequences and inferences of which are too vast to take in at a moment's notice. She would have to reflect a great, great deal upon it.

This discovery, suddenly throwing light on all those families of one or two children, which had hitherto been so incomprehensible to her, aroused so many ideas, reflections, and contradictory emotions that she was unable to say anything, and could only stare at Anna wide-eyed with amazement. This was precisely what she had been dreaming of on the way to Anna's that morning, but now that she learned that it was a possibility she was horrified. It seemed to her too simple a solution for too complicated a problem.

'N'est-ce pas immoral ?' was all she said, after a brief pause.

668

'Why? Do not forget, I have a choice of two alternatives: either to be with child, that is, an invalid, or to be the friend and companion of my husband – practically my husband,' said Anna in a tone intentionally superficial and frivolous.

'You may be right,' said Dolly, hearing the very arguments she had used to herself and not finding them so convincing as before.

'For you, for other people,' said Anna, as though divining her thoughts, 'there may be reason to hesitate; but for me. ... Remember, I am not his wife: he loves me as long as he loves me. And how am I to keep his love? Like this?'

She curved her white arms in front of her stomach.

All sorts of ideas and memories crowded into Dolly's brain with extraordinary rapidity, as happens at moments of great agitation. 'I,' she thought, 'lost my attraction for Stiva; he left me for others, and the first woman for whom he betrayed me did not keep him by being always pretty and gay. He threw her over and took up a third. And can Anna attract and hold Count Vronsky in that way? If that is all he looks for, he will find dresses and manners still more attractive and charming. And however white and shapely her bare arms, however beautiful her stately figure and her eager face under that black hair, he will find others still lovelier, just as my poor dear reprobate of a husband does.'

Dolly made no answer and merely sighed. Anna noticed this sigh, indicating disagreement, and went on. She had a store of arguments so powerful that they were unanswerable.

'You say it is not right? But you must consider,' she insisted. 'You forget my position. How can I wish for children? It's not the suffering I'm afraid of. No. But think what my children would be. Ill-fated creatures bearing a stranger's name. By the very fact of their birth forced to be ashamed of their mother, their father, their very existence.'

'That's just why you should get a divorce.'

But Anna did not hear. She was anxious to give voice to all the arguments with which she had so often tried to convince herself.

'What was my reason given me for, if I am not to use it to avoid bringing unhappy beings into the world?'

She looked at Dolly but continued without waiting for a reply.

'I should always feel I had wronged these unhappy children,' she said. 'If they do not exist, at any rate they are not unhappy; while if they are unhappy, I alone should be to blame for it.'

These were the very arguments Dolly had used to herself; but now as she listened they made no impression. 'How can one wrong creatures that don't exist?' she thought. 'Would her darling Grisha have been better off if he had never existed?' she suddenly wondered. This idea appeared to her so wild and strange that she shook her head to drive away the insane tangle that whirled in her brain.

'No, I don't know; it's not right,' was all she said, with an expression of disgust on her face.

'Yes, but think what you are and what I am. ... And besides,' added Anna, seeming in spite of the wealth of her arguments and the poverty of Dolly's objections to admit all the same that it was not right, 'don't forget the chief point, that I am not now in the same position as you. For you the question is whether you do not want to have any more children; while for me it is a question of whether I wish to have them at all. And there is a big difference. Don't you see that I could not possibly want children in my position?'

Dolly was silent. She suddenly felt an immense gulf between her and Anna. She saw that there lay between them a barrier of questions on which they could never agree, and about which it was best not to speak.

24

'THEN all the more reason why you should regularize your position, if it is possible,' said Dolly.

'Yes, if it is possible,' Anna said in a voice that was suddenly entirely different, subdued and sad.

'Surely a divorce is not out of the question? I was told your husband had consented ...'

'Dolly, I don't want to talk about that.'

'Very well, we won't,' Dolly hastened to say, noticing the expression of suffering on Anna's face. 'All I think is that you look at things too much on the dark side.'

'I? Not at all! I'm always happy and contented. You saw, *je fais des passions*. Veslovsky ...'

'To tell you the truth, Anna, I don't like Veslovsky's manner,' said Dolly, anxious to change the subject.

'Oh, that's nonsense! It only amuses Alexei! He is just a boy, and like wax in my hands. You know, I can do what I like with him. He's only a child, like your Grisha ... Dolly!' – she suddenly changed her tone – 'you say I look on the dark side. You cannot understand. It is too awful. I try not to look at all.'

'But I think you ought to. You ought to do all you can.'

'But what can I do? Nothing. You tell me to marry Alexei, and say I don't think about it. I not think about that!' she repeated, and the colour flew to her cheeks. She rose, drew herself up, sighed deeply and began pacing the room with her light step, halting now and then. 'I not think about that? Not a day, not an hour passes without my thinking of it, and upbraiding myself for doing so ... because thinking of it may drive me mad. Drive me mad!' she repeated. 'When I think of it, I can never get to sleep without morphine. But never mind. Let us discuss it calmly. People talk about a divorce. In the first place, *he* would not agree now. He's under the influence of the Countess Lydia Ivanovna.'

Dolly, sitting bolt upright in her chair, sympathy marking her face with a look of suffering, turned her head to follow Anna as she walked backwards and forwards.

'You can but try,' she said gently.

'Supposing I do. What would it mean?' said Anna, evidently expressing a thought she had considered a thousand times and knew by heart. 'It means that I, hating him, but still recognizing that I have wronged him – and I believe in his magnanimity – must humiliate myself to write to him. ... Well, suppose I make the effort: I do it. I shall either receive an insulting refusal or his consent. Good, I get his consent ...' She had reached the other end of the room and stopped to arrange one of the window curtains. ... 'I receive his consent, but my ... my son? They will never let me have him. And so he will grow up despising me, in the house of his father, whom I have abandoned. Do you see, I love ... equally, I think, but both more than myself, two beings – Seriozha and Alexei.'

She came out into the middle of the room and stood facing Dolly, pressing her hands to her breast. In her white dressing-gown she looked unusually tall and large. She bent her head and with eyes glistening with tears looked from under her brows at Dolly, a thin, pitiful little figure in her patched dressing-jacket and night-cap, trembling all over with emotion.

'I love these two beings only, and the one excludes the other. I cannot have them both; yet that is my one need. And since I can't have that, I don't care about the rest. Nothing matters; nothing, nothing! And it will end one way or another, and so I can't – I don't like to talk of it. So don't reproach me, don't judge me. With your pure heart you can't understand what I suffer.'

She came and sat down beside Dolly, and, peering into her face with a guilty look, took her hand.

'What are you thinking? What do you think of me? Don't despise me! I don't deserve that. I'm simply unhappy. If there is an unhappy creature in this world, it is I.' She turned away and began to weep.

When Dolly was left alone, she said her prayers and got into bed. She had pitied Anna from the bottom of her heart while they were talking together, but now she could not bring herself to think about her. The thought of her own home and children rose in her imagination with a new and peculiar charm. So sweet and precious did her little world now seem that she would not on any account spend another day away from it, and she made up her mind to go back next day without fail.

Anna meantime returned to her boudoir, took a wine-glass and poured into it several drops of a mixture largely composed of morphine. After drinking it and sitting still for a little while, she went into her bedroom in a calm and more cheerful frame of mind.

Vronsky looked at her closely as she entered. He was searching for some indication in her face of the conversation which he knew she must have had with Dolly, since she had stayed so long in the latter's room. But in her expression of restrained excitement, and a sort of reserve, he could find nothing but the beauty that always bewitched him afresh, though he was used to it, and her consciousness of this beauty, and desire that it should affect him. He did not want to ask what they had been talking about but hoped that she would tell him something of her own accord. However she only said:

'I am so glad you like Dolly. You do, don't you?'

'Oh, I've known her a long while, you know. She's good-hearted, I suppose, *mais excessivement terre-à-terre*. Still, I'm very glad to see her.'

He took Anna's hand and looked inquiringly into her eyes.

Misinterpreting the look, she smiled at him.

Next morning, in spite of her hosts' entreaties, Dolly prepared for her homeward journey. Levin's coachman, in a coat by no means new and a shabby hat, with gloomy determination drove the ill-matched horses and the old carriage with its mended splash-boards to the covered, sand-strewn portico.

Dolly took a cold farewell of the Princess Varvara and the gentlemen of the party. The day they had spent together made both Dolly and her hosts distinctly aware that they had no interests in common, and that they were better apart. Only Anna was sad. She knew that with Dolly's departure the feelings the visit had roused in her would never be stirred again. To have those feelings awakened was painful but yet she knew that they belonged to the better part of herself, which was fast becoming smothered by the life she was leading.

Dolly experienced a delightful sense of relief when they reached the open country and she felt tempted to ask the two men how they had liked being at Vronsky's, when suddenly the coachman, Philip, expressed himself unasked.

'Rolling in wealth they may be, but our horses only got three bushels of oats all told! All gone by cock-crow, down to the last grain! What are three bushels? A mere mouthful! And oats nowadays only forty-five kopecks at an inn. That ain't our way. When we have visitors we give their horses as much as they'll eat.'

'The master's a screw,' put in the clerk from the estate office.

'But you liked their horses, didn't you?' asked Dolly.

'The horses weren't amiss. And the food was good too. But I didn't care about it there, Darya Alexandrovna. I don't know how you felt?' he said, turning his handsome, kindly face to her.

'I felt the same. Well, shall we be home by evening?'

'Ay, we must!'

Home again and finding everyone happy and particularly genial, Dolly began a very animated account of her visit, and described how warmly she had been received, and the luxury and good taste at the Vronskys', and their recreations; and would not hear a word against them.

'You have to know Anna and Vronsky – I have got to know him better now – to see how nice they are, and how touching,' she said, speaking now with perfect sincerity, forgetting the indefinable feeling of dissatisfaction and awkwardness she had endured there.

25

VRONSKY and Anna went on living in the same way in the country all that summer and part of the autumn, still taking no steps to get a divorce. It was agreed between them that they should not go away anywhere; but both felt the longer they lived alone, especially in the autumn when their guests had all departed, that they would not be able to stand this existence and a change would have to be made.

One would have said their life could not have been improved upon: they had ample means, good health, a child, and plenty to occupy them both. Anna devoted just as much care to her appearance when they had no visitors, and she spent a great deal of her time reading, both novels and such serious literature as was in fashion. She ordered all the books favourably reviewed in the foreign papers and magazines she took in, and applied herself to them with a concentration possible only in seclusion. She also made a special study, from books and technical journals, of every subject of interest to Vronsky, so that he frequently went straight to her with problems relating to agriculture or architecture, and sometimes even horse-breeding or sport. He was amazed at her knowledge and her memory, and was at first incredulous and inclined to ask for confirmation of her facts. She would then find what he asked for in some book, and show it him.

The hospital, too, interested her. There she not only assisted, but even arranged and thought of many things herself. Nevertheless, her chief preoccupation was still herself – how far she was dear to Vronsky, how far she could compensate to him for all he had given up. Vronsky appreciated this desire not only to please but to serve him, which had become the sole aim of her existence, but at the same time he chafed at the loving snares in which she tried to hold him fast. As time went on, and he saw himself further and further caught in these meshes, the more he longed not so much to escape from them as to try whether they interfered with his freedom. Had it not been for this ever-increasing desire to be free, not to have a scene every time he had to absent himself from home for the sessions or the races, Vronsky would have been quite content with his life. The role he had chosen for himself – the role of a wealthy landowner, whose like should constitute the kernel of the Russian aristocracy – was not only entirely to his taste but now that he had lived it for a good six months afforded him a growing sense of satisfaction. And his management of his estate, which occupied and absorbed him more and more, was most successful. In spite of the huge sums he spent on the hospital, machinery, cows imported from Switzerland, and many other things, he was convinced that he was not wasting his substance but adding to it. Where it was a question of returns – the sale of timber, of grain, of wool, or the leasing of land – Vronsky was as hard as flint, and knew how to hold out for his price. In farming, both on this and on his other estates, he stuck to the simplest methods involving no risk, and in trifling details was calculating and economical in the extreme. In spite of all the cunning and ingenuity of the German steward, who would try to tempt him into purchases by making his original estimate far larger than necessary and then representing to Vronsky that he might get the thing done more cheaply, and so make an immediate profit, Vronsky did not allow himself to be carried away. He would listen to what the steward had to say, put questions to him, and give his consent only when the machinery to be constructed or the implement to be ordered was the very latest thing, hitherto unknown in Russia and likely to excite wonder. Apart from such exceptions, he would agree to a big outlay only when he had capital to spare, and would then go into every detail and insist on getting the very best for his money. Thus from the way he managed his affairs it was clear that he was not wasting but increasing his assets.

In October there were the nobility elections in the Kashin province, where Vronsky's, Sviazhsky's, Koznyshev's, and Oblonsky's estates were, as well as a small area of Levin's.

These elections were attracting public attention on account of the personages taking part in them, and various other circumstances. They were much discussed, and great preparations were being made for them. People who never attended the elections were coming from Moscow, from Petersburg and from abroad.

Vronsky had long ago promised Sviazhsky to be present, and just before the elections Sviazhsky, who often visited Vozdvizhenskoe, drove over to fetch him.

On the day before, Vronsky and Anna had almost had a quarrel about the proposed expedition. It was the very dullest autumn weather, which is so dreary in the country, and Vronsky, bracing himself for a scene, informed Anna of his intention to go, in a sterner, colder tone than he had ever used to her before. But to his surprise

Anna took the news quite calmly, and merely asked when he would be returning. He looked at her closely, at a loss to understand the meaning of her composure. She smiled back at him. He was familiar with that way she had of withdrawing into herself, and knew that it only happened when she had determined in her own mind on some plan that she would not communicate to him. He was alarmed, but so anxious was he to avoid a scene that he fell in with her manner, and half sincerely believed in what he longed to believe in – her good sense.

'I hope you won't be dull?'

'I hope not,' said Anna. 'A box of books came from Gautier's yesterday. No, I shan't be dull.'

'If she wants to adopt that tone, so much the better,' he thought. 'Otherwise, it would be the usual scene all over again.'

And so, without challenging her to a frank explanation, he left for the elections. It was the first time since the beginning of their intimacy that he had parted from her without having come to a full understanding. In one way it troubled him, in another he felt that it was better so. 'At first there will be a sort of vague, dark reserve, as there was to-day, and then she will get used to it. At all events, I don't mind giving up everything else for her, but not my independence,' he reflected.

26

In September Levin moved to Moscow for Kitty's confinement. He had already spent a whole month there with nothing to do, when Koznyshev, who had property in the Kashin province and was actively concerned with the forthcoming elections, invited his brother, who had a vote in the Seleznev district, to accompany him. Moreover, Levin had some extremely important business to see to in Kashin in connexion with a trusteeship and some money due from a mortgage for his sister who lived abroad.

Levin still hesitated, until Kitty, who could see that he was getting tired of Moscow, urged him to go and, without saying anything, ordered the uniform he would need for the occasion, costing eighty roubles. It was these eighty roubles paid for the uniform that mainly decided him in the end, and he left for Kashin.

Levin had now been nearly six days in Kashin, attending the assembly daily and trying to get his sister's affairs settled satisfactorily. All the marshals of nobility were occupied with the elections, and it was very hard to get anything done, even in so simple a matter as the trusteeship. The other matter – about the mortgage money – presented similar complications. After long negotiations over the legal details, the money was at last ready to be paid; but the notary, a most obliging person, could not hand over the order for payment because it needed the president's signature, and the president, who had not appointed a deputy, was attending the sessions. All this worry and bother, the perpetual going to and fro, the endless conversations with well-disposed, excellent people, who fully sympathized with the unpleasantness of the petitioner's position but were powerless to assist him – all his fruitless efforts produced a feeling of affliction in Levin akin to the stricken helplessness one experiences in dreams when one tries to use physical force. He felt this frequently when talking to his most good-natured solicitor. The poor man seemed to be doing his best, straining every nerve to get Levin out of his difficulties. 'I tell you what you might try,' he said more than once. 'Go to So-and-so, and to So-and-so,' and he would draw up an elaborate plan for circumventing the fatal obstacle at the root of all the trouble. But then he would immediately add, 'All the same, they'll put you off. However, have a try!' And Levin would act upon his suggestions, and walk and drive from place to place. Everyone was kind and affable, but the obstacle he was trying to get round seemed to turn up afresh somewhere else and bar his way once more. It particularly annoyed Levin that he could not make out whom he was up against, to whose interest it was that his business should be delayed. No one knew this, apparently; the solicitor certainly did not. If Levin could have understood why, just as he saw why people had to approach the booking-office at a railway station in single file, he would not have felt so injured and annoyed; but no one could explain to him the reason for the hindrances he encountered in the course of the transaction.

However, Levin had changed considerably since his marriage: he was more patient, and if he could not understand why things were arranged thus he told himself that he could not judge without knowing all the facts, and that probably it had to be that way. And he tried not to become exasperated.

Similarly, in attending the elections and taking part in them, he tried not to criticize, not to condemn or argue, but to do his best to understand what it was all these good, honest men, whom he respected, were so earnest and enthusiastic about. Since his marriage so many new and serious aspects of life had been revealed to him which, owing to his superficial attitude to them, had previously appeared of no importance, that he looked for some serious significance in this question of the elections also.

Koznyshev explained to him the meaning and object of the proposed revolution at the elections. The marshal of the province – in whose hands the law placed the control of so many important public functions, like trusteeships (the very department which was giving Levin so much trouble just now), the disposal of enormous sums of money subscribed by the nobility of the province, grammar schools for boys and girls, military academies, public education along the new lines, and finally the *Zemstvo* – this marshal of the province, Snetkov, was a nobleman of the old type. He had run through an immense fortune and, though a good-hearted man and honest after his own fashion, was utterly without any comprehension of modern-day requirements. He took the side of the gentry in everything, was openly opposed to the spread of popular education, and succeeded in giving a purely party character to the *Zemstvo* which ought by rights to be of colossal importance. It was necessary to put in his place a fresh, up-to-date, practical man of the times, and to conduct matters so as to extract from the rights conferred upon the nobles (not as the nobility but as an element of the *Zemstvo*) all the powers of self-government that could possibly be derived from them. Such a preponderance of forces was now gathered in the wealthy province of Kashin, always in the vanguard of progress, that this policy, once carried through properly here, might serve as a m. del for other provinces throughout Russia. The elections, therefore were of the very greatest importance. It was proposed to elect Sviazhsky as marshal in the place of Snetkov – or, better still, Nevyedovsky, a former university professor, a man of remarkable intelligence and a great friend of Koznyshev's.

The assembly was opened by the governor, who made a speech urging the nobles not to be respecters of persons when they voted but to elect candidates according to merit, and with the welfare of the country in mind. He hoped the honourable nobility of Kashin would be scrupulous in the performance of their duty, as they had been in previous elections, and justify the exalted confidence of the monarch.

When he had finished his speech, the governor walked out of the hall, followed noisily and eagerly – in some cases even rapturously – by the nobles, who thronged round him while he put on his fur coat and conversed amicably with the marshal of the province. Levin, who was standing in the crowd anxious to enter into it all and not miss anything, overheard him say: 'Please tell Maria Ivanovna my wife is very sorry she has got to go to the Home.' And thereupon the noblemen in high good humour sorted out their fur coats and drove in a body to the cathedral.

In the cathedral, Levin, lifting his hand like the rest and repeating the words of the archdeacon, swore by the most mighty oaths to perform everything the governor expected of them. Church services always affected Levin and when he pronounced the words 'I kiss the cross', and glanced round at the crowd of men, young and old, repeating the same words, he was moved.

The next day and the day after were spent dealing with business relating to the finances of the nobility and the high school for girls – of no importance whatever, as Koznyshev explained – and Levin, busy seeing after his own affairs, did not trouble to attend. On the fourth day the audit of the provincial funds took place at the high table of the marshal of the province, and the first skirmish between the new party and the old occurred. The committee entrusted with the auditing reported to the assembly that all was in order. The marshal of the province rose and with tears in his eyes thanked the nobility for their confidence. There was loud applause and the nobles pressed his hand. But at that instant an adherent of Koznyshev's party got up and said it had come to his knowledge that the committee had not audited the accounts, considering that a verification would be a reflection on the marshal. A member of the committee incautiously confirmed this. Then a small, very young but very venomous-looking gentleman began to speak, saying that no doubt the marshal would be pleased to give an account of his expenditure of the public moneys, and that the excessive delicacy of the members of the committee was depriving him of this moral satisfaction. Thereupon the members of the committee withdrew their report, and Koznyshev began pointing out in logical terms that the accounts had to be regarded either as audited or as not audited, and went over the vexed point in detail. A windbag from the opposite party replied to him. Then Sviazhsky spoke, and after him the venomous young man again. The debate continued a long time and no conclusion was reached. Levin was surprised that they should dispute the matter so long, especially as when he asked Koznyshev if he thought that money had been misappropriated, the latter answered:

'Oh no! He's an honest fellow. But this antiquated, patriarchal way of managing the affairs of the nobility must be put a stop to.'

On the fifth day came the elections of the district marshals. It was rather a stormy day in several districts. In the Selezensk district Sviazhsky was elected unanimously without a ballot, and he gave a dinner-party at his house that evening.

27

THE sixth day was fixed for the election of the marshal of the province. The halls, large and small, were full of noblemen in all sorts of uniforms. Many had come for that day only. Men who had not seen each other for years, some from the Crimea, some from Petersburg, some from abroad, met at the assembly. At the governor's table beneath the portrait of the Emperor the debate was in full swing.

Both in the large and small halls the noblemen grouped themselves according to party, and from their hostile, suspicious glances and the way they fell silent when a stranger approached, and the fact that some of them even retreated whispering together into the far corridor, it could be seen that each side had secrets it kept from the other. In appearance the nobles were sharply divided into two classes: the old and the new. The former for the most part wore either the old-fashioned uniforms of the nobility, buttoned up closely, and carried swords and hats, or the naval, cavalry, or infantry uniform to which each was individually entitled. The uniforms of the older men were cut in the old-fashioned way, with pleated shoulders: they looked small and too tight and short-waisted, as though their wearers had grown out of them. The younger men wore unbuttoned, long-waisted uniforms, broad across the shoulders, over white waistcoats, or else uniforms with black collars embroidered with laurel leaves – the emblem of the Ministry of Justice. To the younger generation belonged the Court uniforms which here and there brightened the crowd.

But this division into young and old did not correspond with the separation into parties. Some of the young ones, as Levin observed, belonged to the old party, while some very aged noblemen, on the contrary, conversed in whispers with Sviazhsky and were evidently warm supporters of the new party.

Levin stood with his own group in the small hall, where they were smoking or taking light refreshments. He listened intently to what was being said, vainly exerting all his intelligence in an effort to understand. Koznyshev was the centre of the group. He was listening at that moment to Sviazhsky and Hliustov, the marshal of another district, who belonged to their party. Hliustov would not agree to go with his district to invite Snetkov to stand, while Sviazhsky, with Koznyshev's approval, was trying to persuade him to adopt this tactic. Levin could not understand the desire on their part for a man of the opposite camp to stand, when all the time they intended voting against him.

Oblonsky, who had just had something to eat and drink, came towards them in his uniform of a gentleman of the bedchamber, wiping his mouth with his scented and bordered lawn handkerchief.

'We are holding our position, Sergei Ivanich,' he said, smoothing back his whiskers. And after he had given an ear to the conversation, he supported Sviazhsky's contention.

'One district is enough, and Sviazhsky has already come out in opposition,' he said, words which everyone but Levin found comprehensible.

'Why, Kostya, you getting a taste for it too!' he added, turning to Levin and taking his arm.

Levin would have been glad to get a taste for it but he could not make out what the point was and, retreating a few steps from the group, he expressed his perplexity to Oblonsky – why was the marshal of the province being asked to stand?

'O sancta simplicitas!' exclaimed Oblonsky, and briefly and clearly he explained to Levin. If, as at previous elections, all the districts nominated the marshal of the province, he would be elected without a ballot. This must not be. Now eight districts had agreed to invite him to stand: if two refused to do so, Snetkov might decline to stand at all. In that case the old party might put up someone else, which would upset all their calculations. But if only one district, Sviazhsky's, did not call upon him, Snetkov would let himself be balloted for. They were even, some of them, going to vote for him and let him get a good number of votes, to throw the opposition off scent, 'so when a candidate of ours is put forward they will give him some votes.'

Levin understood, but not entirely, and was about to ask some further questions when suddenly there was a general stir and bustle and everyone began moving into the large hall.

'What is it? Eh? Who?' 'A warrant? For whom? What?' 'They won't pass him?' 'No guarantee?' 'Flerov not admitted?' 'Because of that charge against him?' 'At that rate, they could keep anyone out! It's a disgrace!' 'The law!' Levin heard shouted on all sides, and with the rest, who were pressing forward anxious not to miss anything, he hastened into the large hall. Hemmed in by the crowd of noblemen, he drew near the high table where the marshal of the province, Sviazhsky, and other party dignitaries were in heated argument.

28

LEVIN was standing rather far off. The heavy, stertorous breathing of a nobleman at his side, and the creaking of another's thick-soled shoes, prevented him from hearing distinctly. From where he was he could just distinguish the quiet voice of the marshal, then the shrill tones of the venomous-looking gentleman, and finally Sviazhsky's voice. As far as he could make out, they were disputing as to the interpretation to be put on a legal point and the exact meaning of the words 'against whom legal proceedings are pending'.

The crowd parted to make way for Koznyshev approaching the table. Waiting for the venomous gentleman to finish speaking, Koznyshev suggested that the proper course would be to consult the wording of the Act, and he requested a secretary to look it up. The Act provided that in case of difference of opinion there must be a ballot.

Koznyshev read the Act aloud and began to expound its meaning, but a tall, stout landowner with stooping shoulders and dyed whiskers, wearing a tight uniform that cut the back of his neck, interrupted him. Advancing to the table and striking it with the ring on his finger, he shouted loudly:

'A ballot! Put it to the vote! It's no use talking! Put it to the vote!'

Then several voices began speaking all at once, and the tall nobleman with the ring shouted more and more loudly, every minute becoming further incensed. But it was impossible to make out what he said.

He was demanding the very course Koznyshev had proposed; but it was evident that he hated Koznyshev and all his party, and this hatred communicated itself to all those on his side and in turn evoked a similar, though more decently expressed vindictiveness from the opposing party. There was shouting on all sides and for a moment everything was in such confusion that the marshal of the province had to call for order.

'A ballot! A ballot! Every nobleman will understand! We shed our blood … the Emperor's confidence. … No auditing the accounts of the marshal, he's not a shop assistant! … But that's not the point. … Votes, please! Abominable! …' shouted enraged, frenzied voices on all sides. The looks and expressions on the faces were even more enraged and frenzied than the voices. There was implacable hate everywhere. Levin could not at all make out what was the matter, and marvelled at the passion displayed over whether Flerov's case should be put to the vote or not. He forgot, as Koznyshev explained to him afterwards, the syllogism that for the public good it was necessary to get rid of the marshal of the province; that to get rid of the marshal it was necessary to have a majority of votes; that to obtain that majority it was necessary to secure Flerov's right to vote; and that to secure Flerov's right to vote they must elucidate the meaning of the Act.

'A single vote may turn the balance,' Koznyshev concluded, 'and one must be in earnest and consistent if one wants to be of use in public life.'

But Levin had overlooked that, and it was painful to him to see these good men, for whom he had a respect, in such a disagreeable ill-natured state of excitement. To escape from this oppressive sensation he did not wait for the end of the debate but went into the other room, where there was no one except the waiters at the buffet. When he saw the waiters busily wiping crockery and arranging plates and wine-glasses, and looked at their quiet, eager faces, he felt an unexpected sense of relief, as though he had come out of a stuffy room into the fresh air. He began walking up and down, looking at the waiters with pleasure. He particularly liked the way one with grey whiskers was scornfully teaching the younger ones, while they made fun of him, how to fold napkins. Levin was just about to engage the old waiter in conversation when the secretary of the court of trusteeship, a little old man whose speciality it was to know all the nobles of the province by their full names, drew him away.

'If you please, Constantine Dmitrich!' he said. 'Your brother is looking for you. They are voting on the legal point.'

Levin went into the large hall, was given a white ball, and followed his brother, Sergei Ivanich, to the table where Sviazhsky was standing with a grim, ironical expression on his face, gathering his beard in his fist and sniffing at it. Koznyshev inserted his hand into the ballot-box, placed his ball somewhere, and stood aside for Levin. Levin came up but, having entirely forgotten what he had to do, was disconcerted and turned to Koznyshev with the query, 'Where do I put it?' He spoke softly, hoping that in the hum of conversation nearby his question would not be overheard. But the speakers fell silent, and heard what he should not have said. Koznyshev frowned.

'That is a matter of personal conviction,' he said severely.

A few of the bystanders smiled. Levin flushed, hurriedly thrust his hand under the cloth and, as the ball was in his right hand, dropped it in on the right. Having put it in, he suddenly remembered he ought to have put his left hand in also, and thrust it in, but too late; and still more overcome with confusion he beat a hasty retreat into the background.

'One hund'ed and twenty-six fo'! Ninety-eight against!' sang out the voice of the secretary, who could not pronounce his r's. Laughter followed: a button and two nuts had been found in the ballot-box. Fierov was allowed the right to vote, and the new party scored.

The old party did not consider itself defeated, however. Levin heard Snetkov being asked to stand, and he saw a crowd of nobles surrounding the marshal, who was addressing them. Levin went nearer. Replying to the nobles, Snetkov spoke of the confidence and affection they had shown him, which he did not deserve, his only merit being his attachment to the nobility, to whom he had devoted twelve years of service. Several times he repeated the words 'I have served to the best of my ability, faithfully and truly, I appreciate and thank ...' but could not go on for the tears that choked him, and hurried from the room. Whether these tears were due to a sense of the injustice being done him, to his love for the nobility or to the strain of the position he was placed in, feeling himself surrounded by enemies, was difficult to say. At any rate, his emotion communicated itself to the assembly. The majority of those present were touched, and Levin was seized with tenderness for Snetkov.

In the doorway the marshal of the province collided with Levin.

'My fault! I beg your pardon,' he said, as if speaking to a stranger, but, recognizing Levin, he smiled timidly.

Levin had the impression that Snetkov wanted to say something but could not speak for agitation. The expression of his face and his whole figure in his uniform with the crosses and white breeches trimmed with gold lace, as he moved hurriedly along, reminded Levin of some hunted animal who sees that his doom is sealed. This expression on the marshal's face went to Levin's heart, for only the day before he had been at the marshal's house over the matter of the trusteeship, and had seen him in all his grandeur, a kindly family man. The big house with the old family furniture, the respectful old footmen, far from smart and rather shabby – unmistakably former house-serfs who had stuck to their master – his stout, good-natured wife in a lace cap and Turkish shawl, who sat petting a pretty little grandchild (her daughter's daughter), his fine young son in the sixth form at the high school, who had just come home and who kissed his father's large hand in greeting, the imposing, cordial words and gestures of the old man had all aroused an instinctive feeling of respect and sympathy in Levin the day before. Now the old man was a touching and pathetic figure to Levin, and he longed to say something pleasant to him.

'So you are to be our marshal again,' he remarked.

'I doubt it,' replied the marshal, looking round nervously. 'I'm old and worn out. There are younger and better men than I. Let them have a turn.'

And the marshal disappeared through a side-door.

The most solemn moment was at hand. The voting was about to begin. The leaders of both parties were reckoning on their fingers the white and black balls they would probably get.

The debate about Flerov had gained the new party not only his vote but also time in which to rally three more supporters who, by the wiles of the other party, were to have been prevented from attending the elections. Two of these noblemen had a weakness for wine and had been made drunk by Snetkov's henchmen, and the third had been robbed of his uniform.

Learning of this, the new party had managed, while Flerov's case was being discussed, to send some of their men in a sledge with a uniform and also fetch one of the tipsy pair to the assembly.

'I've brought one of them,' the landowner who had gone on this errand whispered to Sviazhsky. 'Had to pour cold water over him, but he'll do.'

'He's not too drunk – he won't fall down?' asked Sviazhsky, shaking his head.

'No, he's all right. If only they don't give him any more here. ... I've told the man at the bar on no account to serve him.'

29

THE narrow room in which they were smoking and taking refreshments was full of noblemen. Excitement was growing and every face betrayed some anxiety. Most agitated of all were the party chiefs, who knew every detail and kept count of all the votes. They were the commanders in the coming contest. The rest, like the rank and file before an engagement, though preparing for the fray, meanwhile sought other distractions. Some of them were eating, standing at the bar or sitting at the table; others walked up and down the long room, smoking cigarettes and chatting with friends they had not seen for a long while.

Levin did not feel like eating, and he was not smoking. He had no wish to join his own set – Koznyshev, Oblonsky, Sviazhsky, and the others – because Vronsky, wearing the uniform of an equerry, stood with them engaged in animated conversation. Levin had noticed him at the previous day's elections, and had carefully avoided an encounter. He went to the window and sat down, scanning the various groups and listening to what was being said around him. He felt depressed, especially as he saw that everyone else was eager, absorbed and astir, with the sole exception of himself and one ancient, mumbling, toothless old man in naval uniform, who had sat down beside him.

'He's such a blackguard! I told him not to! Of course he couldn't collect it in three years!' a short, round-shouldered country gentleman with pomaded hair hanging over the embroidered collar of his uniform was saying emphatically, energetically tapping with the heels of the new boots he had obviously put on for the occasion. He cast an angry look at Levin and sharply turned his back.

'Yes, it's a dirty business, there's no denying,' remarked a little man in a high voice.

Immediately after these two a whole crowd of landowners surrounding a portly general hastily moved in Levin's direction, apparently looking for a place where they could talk without being overheard.

'How dare he say I had his breeches stolen! He probably popped them and spent the proceeds on drink. Damn the fellow and his princely title! Let him dare open his mouth, the swine!'

'My dear fellow, they will fall back on the article of the law,' someone was saying in another group. 'The wife has to be registered as belonging to the nobility.'

'To the devil with your articles of the law! What I say is perfectly true. We're all gentlemen, aren't we? Above suspicion.'

'Come, your excellency. *Fine champagne?*'

Another group followed close on the heels of a nobleman who was shouting in a loud voice: it was one of the three that had been given too much to drink.

'I've always advised Maria Semeonovna to let her estate; she will never make it pay,' said a pleasant voice. The speaker was a country gentleman with grey whiskers, wearing the regimental uniform of an old general staff officer. It was the same landowner Levin had met at Sviazhsky's. He recognized him at once. The landowner took a second look at Levin, and they shook hands.

'Very glad to see you! Why, of course I remember you well. We met last year at Sviazhsky's.'

'Well, and how goes your estate?' inquired Levin.

'Oh, still just the same, working at a loss,' replied the old man as he stopped beside Levin, with a resigned smile that was somewhat belied by his air of calm conviction that it could not be otherwise. 'And how do you come to be in our province?' he asked. 'Come to take part in our *coup d'état?*' He pronounced the French words confidently with a bad accent. 'All Russia's congregated here: we have gentlemen of the bedchamber, everything short of ministers.' He pointed to the imposing figure of Oblonsky in the white trousers and uniform of a gentleman of the bedchamber, walking by with a general.

'I must confess I understand very little about these provincial elections,' said Levin.

The landowner looked at him.

'Why, what is there to understand? The whole thing has lost all meaning. It's a decaying institution that goes on running only by the force of inertia. Look at the uniforms! They tell the tale: this is an assembly of justices of the peace, permanent officials and so on, but not of the nobility.'

'Then why do you attend?' asked Levin.

'Habit, for one thing. Then one must keep up one's connexions. It's a moral obligation of a sort. And then, to tell you the truth, there's one's own interests. My son-in-law wants to stand as a permanent member: they're not well off, and I must give him a push. But why do such people as that come?' he went on, indicating the venomous-looking gentleman, who stood talking at the high table.

'That is the new generation of nobility.'

'New if you like, but there's no nobility. They may own some land but we are the country squires. As noblemen they are cutting their own throats.'

'But you say yourself it's an institution that has served its time.'

'That may be; but still it ought to be treated with a little more respect. Snetkov, now. ... We may not be of much use, but we're the growth of a thousand years. Supposing you wanted to lay out a garden in front of your house, and on the very spot there was a tree that's stood there for centuries. However old and gnarled, you would not cut it down to make room for flower-beds, would you? You would plan your flower-beds round the old tree. You couldn't grow a tree like that again in a year,' he remarked guardedly, and immediately changed the subject. 'Well, and how is your husbandry getting on?'

'Not very well. Yields about five per cent.'

'Yes, but you don't reckon your own work. Aren't you worth something too? Now, look at me. Before I took up farming I was getting three thousand from the service. I work harder now than I did then, and like yourself I clear about five per cent, and that only with luck. But my own labour is thrown in for nothing.'

'Then why do you do it, if it's a clear loss?'

'For the sake of doing it, I suppose. What do you think? Habit. And one knows it's as it should be. I will tell you something more,' he continued, leaning his elbows on the window and warming to his theme; 'farming holds no attractions at all for my son. He is plainly going to be a scholar or a scientist, so there will be no one to carry on after me. Yet I keep on. Here I planted an orchard this year.'

'Yes, yes, that is true enough,' said Levin. 'I always feel I'm making no real profit out of my work on the land, and yet I go on. ... One seems to owe a sort of duty to the land.'

'Another thing,' the landowner pursued. 'A neighbour of mine, a merchant, came to see me one day and I took him over the farm and garden. "No," he said, "everything's all right, but your garden is neglected." (As a matter of fact, my garden is well kept up.) "If I were you, I'd cut down that lime-tree. Only it must be done when the sap is rising. You must have at least a thousand limes here, and each one would yield a fair amount of bark, which fetches a good price nowadays. I'd have the lot down."'

'Yes, and with the money he'd buy up cattle or a bit of ground for a mere song, and let it out in lots to the peasants,' Levin finished for him with a smile, having evidently come across that sort of reasoning before. 'And he will make a fortune, while you and I must be thankful if we can hold on to what we've got and leave it to our children.'

'You are married, I hear?' remarked the old man.

'Yes,' Levin replied with proud satisfaction. 'Yes, it is curious,' he continued. 'We work without making anything, as though we were ordained, like the vestals of old, to keep some sacred fire burning.'

The landowner chuckled under his white moustache.

'There are some among us, too – like our friend Sviazhsky, for example, or Vronsky, who has now settled here – who want to turn agriculture into an industry; but so far they have only succeeded in eating into their capital.'

'But why is it we don't do like the merchants? Cut down our parks for timber?' said Levin, returning to a thought that had struck him.

'Because, as you said, we have to guard the sacred flame. The other way is not for the nobility. Nor is our work done here at the elections, but in our own homesteads. There's a class instinct, too, that tells us what is fitting. I see it often with the peasants. It is the same with them. A good peasant will get hold of as much land as he can, and no matter how poor it may be, he will persist in tilling it. Without a return too. At a dead loss.'

'Just like us,' said Levin. 'Very glad indeed to have seen you again,' he added, seeing Sviazhsky approaching.

'We two have just met for the first time since we were at your place,' said the landowner to Sviazhsky. 'And we've had a good chat.'

'And been abusing the new order?' said Sviazhsky with a smile.

'Of course.'

'We've been letting off steam!'

30

SVIAZHSKY took Levin's arm and led him back to their own group.

This time there was no avoiding Vronsky. He was standing with Oblonsky and Koznyshev, and looking straight at Levin as he drew near.

'Delighted! I believe I've had the pleasure of meeting you ... at the Princess Shcherbatsky's,' he said, extending his hand to Levin.

'Yes, I remember our meeting very well,' said Levin, flushing scarlet and immediately turning away to talk to his brother.

Vronsky smiled slightly and resumed his discussion with Sviazhsky, obviously not having the smallest desire to enter into conversation with Levin. But Levin, as he talked to his brother, kept looking round at Vronsky, trying to think of something to say to him to repair his rudeness.

'What are we waiting for now?' asked Levin, glancing at Sviazhsky and Vronsky.

'For Snetkov. He must either decline or consent to stand,' answered Sviazhsky.

'Well, and what has he done – agreed or not?'

'That's just it – he's done neither,' said Vronsky.

'And if he refuses, who will stand then?' Levin asked, looking at Vronsky.

'Whoever chooses to,' said Sviazhsky.

'Will you?' asked Levin.

'Certainly not,' said Sviazhsky in confusion, casting a nervous look at the venomous gentleman, who was standing beside Koznyshev.

'Who then? Nevyedovsky?' said Levin, feeling that he had put his foot in it somehow.

This was worse still. Nevyedovsky and Sviazhsky were the two prospective candidates.

'I? Not in any circumstances,' answered the venomous-looking gentleman.

It was Nevyedovsky himself. Sviazhsky introduced Levin.

'Well, has it got you too?' said Oblonsky, with a wink at Vronsky. 'It's like the races. One might bet on the results.'

'Yes, it is awfully exciting,' said Vronsky. 'And once having taken the thing up, one's eager to see it through. It's a fight!' he said, scowling and setting his heavy jaws.

'What a capable fellow Sviazhsky is! So business-like.'

'Oh yes,' Vronsky assented indifferently.

There was a pause during which Vronsky, since he had to look at something, looked at Levin: at his feet, his uniform and then his face, and, noticing the gloomy eyes fixed on him, remarked, for the sake of saying something:

'And how is it that you are not a justice of the peace, since you always live in the country? I see you are not wearing the uniform of a justice.'

'Because I consider it an idiotic institution,' morosely replied Levin, who had all the time been waiting for an opportunity to speak to Vronsky in order to atone for his rudeness at their first encounter.

'I don't agree with you; on the contrary,' began Vronsky in quiet surprise.

'It's a farce,' Levin interrupted him. 'We don't need any justices of the peace. I haven't brought a single case during eight years. And when I did, the decision was wrong. The justice of the peace is nearly thirty miles from my place. To settle a matter of a couple of roubles I have to send an attorney, who costs me fifteen.'

And he related how a peasant had stolen some flour from the miller, and when the miller spoke to him about it, the peasant sued him for slander. All this was beside the point and foolish, and Levin himself was conscious of it even as he said it.

'Oh, this fellow's a character!' said Oblonsky, with his most soothing, almond-oil smile. 'We had better go, though. I think they are voting ...'

And they separated.

'I can't make out,' said Koznyshev, who had not missed his brother's awkward sally, 'I can't make out how anyone can be so entirely devoid of political tact. We Russians are hopeless in that respect. The marshal of the province is our opponent, and you are *ami cochon* with him and beg him to stand. Count Vronsky, now. ... I should not choose him for a friend: he's asked me to dinner, and I'm not going. ... Still, he is on our side, so why make an enemy of him? And on top of all that you go and ask Nevyedovsky if he's going to stand! That sort of thing is not done.'

'Well, I don't understand anything about it. And it's all rubbish,' replied Levin gloomily.

'You say it's all rubbish, yet as soon as you have anything to do with it you make a mess of things.'

Levin did not answer, and they walked together into the large hall.

The marshal of the province, though he felt treason in the air and though he had not been unanimously asked to stand, nevertheless offered himself as candidate. All was silence. The secretary announced in stentorian tones that Captain of the Horse Guards, Mihail Stepanich Snetkov, was nominated for the post of provincial marshal and would now be balloted for.

The district marshals, carrying little plates on which were the ballot balls, moved from their tables to the high table, and the balloting began.

'Put it in on the right,' Oblonsky whispered to Levin, as with his brother Levin followed the marshal of his district to the table. But Levin had forgotten by now the plan which had been explained to him, and was afraid Oblonsky must have made a mistake in saying 'on the right'. Surely Snetkov was the enemy. He held the ball in his right hand as he approached the box but, thinking there was a mistake, he shifted it to his left hand at the box, and definitely deposited it on that side. An expert standing beside the box, who could tell by the mere action of the elbow where a ball had been placed, made a wry face. There was nothing for him to exercise his sagacity on this time.

Everything was still, and the counting of the ballot-balls could be heard. Then a solitary voice announced the numbers for and against.

The marshal had received a considerable majority. A hubbub arose, and there was a headlong rush towards the door. Snetkov came in, and the nobles pressed round him with congratulations.

'Well, now is it over?' Levin asked his brother.

'It's only just beginning,' Sviazhsky answered for Koznyshev with a smile. 'Some other candidate may get more votes.'

Levin had again quite forgotten. He had a vague recollection that there was some subtle point in all this, but he was too bored to think what it was exactly. He felt overcome with melancholy, and longed to get away from the crowd.

As no one was paying any attention to him, and no one apparently needed him, he quietly made his way into the little room where the refreshments were, and again felt a sense of relief at the sight of the waiters. The little old waiter pressed him to have something, and Levin agreed. He chatted to the old man about his former masters as he ate a cutlet with beans, and then, not wishing to return to the large hall, where it was all so distasteful to him, proceeded to the gallery.

The gallery was full of fashionably dressed ladies, leaning over the balustrade and trying not to lose a single word of what was being said below. Smart lawyers, spectacled high-school teachers, and officers in uniform sat or stood beside the ladies. Everyone was talking about the elections and saying how harassed the marshal looked and how interesting the debates had been. In one group Levin overheard them praising his brother.

'I am so glad I heard Koznyshev!' a lady was saying to a lawyer. 'It was worth going without dinner. He's fascinating! So clear and distinct! There's not one of you in the law-courts that can speak like that – except perhaps Meidel, and he's far from being an orator!'

Finding a vacant place at the balustrade, Levin leaned over and began looking and listening.

All the noblemen were sitting railed off behind small partitions according to their respective districts. In the middle of the hall stood a man in a uniform, announcing in a loud shrill voice:

'Staff-captain Yevgeny Ivanich Apuhtin is invited to stand for the post of marshal of the province!'

There was dead silence, and then a feeble old man's voice was heard: 'Declined!'

'Privy councillor Peter Petrovich Bohl is called upon!' the voice began again.

'Declined!' cried a youthful squeaky voice.

A third announcement was made, and again followed by 'Declined'. So it went on for about an hour. Levin, with his elbows on the balustrade, looked on and listened. At first he was bewildered and tried to make out what it all meant; but later, when he realized that he could not understand, he began to weary. Then, when he thought of all the agitation and vindictiveness he had seen on every face, he felt depressed and went downstairs, intending to leave. Passing through the lobby behind the gallery, he met a dejected high-school student with bloodshot eyes pacing up and down. On the stairs he came across a couple – a lady running up as fast as she could on her high heels and the jaunty deputy prosecutor.

'I told you you would be in time,' the deputy prosecutor was saying just as Levin stepped aside to let the lady pass.

Levin was already on the staircase leading down to the door and was just feeling in his waistcoat pocket for the cloakroom ticket for his overcoat, when the secretary overtook him. 'Constantine Dmitrich, do come, please! They are voting.'

The candidate who was being balloted for was Nevyedovsky, who had so emphatically denied all idea of standing.

Levin went up to the door of the large hall; it was locked. The secretary knocked, the door opened and two red-faced gentlemen dived out past Levin.

'I can't stand any more of it,' one of them cried.

Then the marshal of the province thrust his head out. The look of dismay and exhaustion on his face was dreadful to behold.

'I told you not to let anyone out!' he cried to the doorkeeper.

'I was letting someone in, your excellency!'

'Oh Lord!' and with a heavy sigh the marshal of the province, head bent, dragged his weary legs in their white trousers down the middle of the hall to the high table.

Nevyedovsky was elected by a majority, as had been expected, and he was the new marshal of the province. There were many who were amused, many pleased and happy, many were in ecstasies, and many disgusted and miserable. The old marshal of the province could not conceal his despair. When Nevyedovsky left the hall he was surrounded and followed by an enthusiastic crowd, just as the governor had been when he opened the elections, and Snetkov the day he had been elected.

31

THE newly-elected marshal and many adherents of the victorious new party dined that evening with Vronsky.

Vronsky had come to the elections partly because he felt bored in the country and wanted to assert his independence before Anna, partly to repay Sviazhsky, by supporting him at these elections, for all the trouble he had taken to get him, Vronsky, elected a member of the *Zemstvo*, but above all because he was anxious strictly to perform all the duties attached to the role of nobleman and landowner that he had adopted for himself. But he had never expected that the elections would interest him so much and rouse him to such enthusiasm, or that he would be so good at this kind of thing. He was an absolute newcomer to the nobility of the province, but his success was unmistakable and he was not wrong in supposing that he had already gained some influence with the local nobility. This influence was favoured by his wealth and distinction, the splendid quarters in the town lent him by his old friend Shirkov, a financier who had founded a flourishing bank in Kashin; by the excellent chef whom he had brought with him from the country, by his friendship with the governor, who had been a schoolfellow and even a protégé of his; but most of all by his simple, equable manner with everyone, which very quickly compelled the majority of the noblemen to change their opinion about his supposed haughtiness. He himself felt that, apart from that crack-brained fellow married to Kitty Shcherbatsky, who had without rhyme or reason poured out a stream of pointless rubbish with such rabid animosity, every nobleman whose acquaintance he had made had become his adherent. It was clear to him, and other people recognized it too, that he had contributed a great deal to Nevyedovsky's success. And now at his own table, celebrating Nevyedovsky's election, he had an agreeable sense of triumph over the success of his candidate. The elections themselves had so fascinated him that he began to think of himself standing in three years' time, if he and Anna were married by then – much as after his jockey had won him a race he was always seized by a desire to race himself.

To-day he was celebrating the success of his jockey. Vronsky sat at the head of the table. On his right was the young governor, a general in the Emperor's suite. To the others the general was the head of the province, who had solemnly opened the elections with his speech and, as Vronsky had remarked, aroused respect and even obsequiousness in many of those present; but to Vronsky he was little Katka Maslov – that had been his nickname in the Corps of Pages – whom he felt to be shy and tried to *mettre à son aise*. On Vronsky's left sat Nevyedovsky, with his youthful, dogged, venomous face. With him Vronsky was simple and deferential.

Sviazhsky bore his defeat cheerfully. Indeed, it was no defeat, as he said himself, turning, glass in hand, to Nevyedovsky; they could not have found a better representative of the new course which the nobility ought to follow. And therefore every honest person, as he remarked, was on the side of to-day's success and was rejoicing over it.

Oblonsky was happy, too, because he was enjoying himself and everyone was pleased. Over an excellent dinner they discussed various incidents of the election. Sviazhsky gave a comic imitation of the old marshal's tearful discourse, and observed, addressing Nevyedovsky, that his excellency would have to select another more ingenious method of auditing the accounts than tears. Another wit recounted how footmen in knee-breeches and stockings had been ordered for the marshal's ball, and that they would now have to be sent back unless the new marshal would give a ball with footmen in knee-breeches.

At dinner Nevyedovsky was continually referred to as 'our marshal' and addressed as 'your excellency', much in the same way and with the same pleasure as a bride is called 'Madame' and addressed by her married name. Nevyedovsky affected to be not merely indifferent but scornful of this designation; but it was obvious that he was highly delighted and having to exercise self-control in order not to betray triumph ill-suited to the new liberal *milieu* in which they all found themselves.

Several telegrams were despatched after dinner to people interested in the result of the elections. And Oblonsky, who was in high good humour, sent one to Dolly as follows: 'Nevyedovsky elected by majority of twenty. Spread the good news.' He dictated it aloud, saying: 'We must let them share our rejoicing.' But when Dolly got the telegram she merely sighed over the rouble wasted on it, and knew that her husband had been dining well. She was familiar with Stiva's weakness for setting the telegraph wires going after a good dinner.

Everything, including the excellent dinner and the wines (not from Russian merchants but imported direct from abroad), was very distinguished, simple, and enjoyable. Sviazhsky had selected the party of twenty from among the more active new liberals, all of the same way of thinking, who possessed both intellect and breeding. Toasts were drunk, also half in jest, to the new marshal of the province, the governor, the bank director, and 'our amiable host'.

Vronsky felt content. He had never expected to find such pleasant form in the provinces.

After dinner things became gayer still. The governor invited Vronsky to a concert in aid of 'our Serbian brothers' which was being organized by his wife, who wished to make Vronsky's acquaintance.

'There is to be a ball afterwards, and you'll see our local beauty. She's really quite remarkable!'

'Not in my line,' answered Vronsky, who was fond of the English expression. But he smiled and promised to come.

They had all begun smoking and were about to rise from table when Vronsky's valet approached him bearing a letter on a salver.

'From Vozdvizhenskoe by special messenger,' he said with a significant expression.

'Extraordinary how like the deputy prosecutor Sventitsky he is!' said one of the guests in French, referring to the valet, while Vronsky, frowning, read the letter.

It was from Anna. Even before he opened it, he knew its contents. Thinking that the elections would not take longer than five days, he had promised to be back on Friday. It was now Saturday, and he knew that the letter was full of reproaches that he had not returned to time. The note he had sent off the previous evening had probably not reached her yet.

The letter was what he had expected, but the form of it was unexpected and particularly disagreeable to him. 'Ani is very ill. The doctor says it may be pneumonia. I get frantic all alone. The Princess Varvara is more of a hindrance than a help. I expected you the day before yesterday, and yesterday, and now I am sending to find out where you are and what you are doing. I wanted to come myself, but thought better of it, knowing you would not like it. Send me some sort of answer, that I may know what to do.'

The child ill, yet she had thought of coming herself! Their daughter ill, and this hostile tone!

Vronsky was struck by the contrast between the innocent festivities over the election and the sombre, burdensome love to which he must return. But he would have to go, and by the first train that night he set off for home.

32

REALIZING that the scenes they had every time he went away could only estrange him instead of binding him more closely to her, Anna determined, before Vronsky left for the elections, to make every possible effort to bear the parting with composure. But the cold, stern look on his face when he came to tell her he was going had wounded her, and her peace of mind was destroyed even before his departure.

Later, meditating in solitude that look which had expressed his right to his personal freedom, she arrived, as usual, at the same point – the sense of her own humiliation. 'He has the right to go when and where he chooses. Not simply to go away, but to leave me. He has all the rights, while I have none. But knowing that, he ought not to have done it. But what did he do, though? Looked at me coldly, severely. Of course, there was nothing definite, nothing one could get hold of – but it wasn't like that before, and it means a great deal,' she reflected. 'That look shows that his love is beginning to cool.'

And though she felt convinced that his affection for her was beginning to cool, there was nothing she could do – she could not in any way alter her relations to him. Just as before, only her love and charm could hold him. And so, just as before, it was only by keeping herself occupied during the day and taking morphine at night that she could stifle the terrible thought of what would happen if he ceased to love her. True, there was one means left: not to hold him – she wanted nothing else but his love to do that – but to become so bound up with him, to be in such a position that he could not abandon her. That means was divorce and marriage. And she began to long for it, and made up her mind to agree the first time he or Stiva approached her on the subject.

Absorbed in such thoughts, she passed five days – the five days he was to be at the elections.

She filled her time with walks, talking to the Princess Varvara, visits to the hospital, and, most of all, reading. She read one book after another. But on the sixth day, when the coachman returned without him, she felt unable any longer to stifle the thought of him and of what he was doing away from her. It was at this point that the little girl fell ill. Anna took it upon herself to nurse the baby, but even that did not divert her thoughts, especially as the illness was not serious. However hard she tried, she could not make herself love her daughter, and to feign love was beyond her power. Towards the evening of that day, still alone, Anna was seized with such panic that she decided to start for the town, but on second thoughts wrote the contradictory letter that Vronsky received, and, without reading it over, despatched it by special messenger. The next morning she got his letter and regretted her own. She dreaded a repetition of that stern look he had thrown her when leaving – especially when he should discover that the baby was not dangerously ill. Still, she was glad she had written.

Though she was now actually admitting to herself that he was getting tired of her and would regret relinquishing his freedom to return, in spite of it she rejoiced that he was coming. What did it matter if he were weary of her, so long as he were with her, so long as she could see him and know his every movement?

She was sitting by a lamp in the drawing-room with a new volume of Taine, reading and listening to the wind moaning outside, and every minute expecting the carriage to arrive. Several times she fancied she heard the sound of wheels, but was mistaken. At last she heard not only the rumble of wheels but also the coachman's shout and the muffled noise of the carriage in the covered portico. Even the Princess Varvara, playing patience, confirmed this, and Anna, flushing scarlet, got up; but instead of going downstairs, as she had done twice before that evening, she stood where she was. She suddenly felt ashamed of having misled him, and still more afraid of how he would greet her. All feeling of injury had passed now: she only feared the expression of his displeasure. She remembered that the child had been perfectly well since the day before. She was even vexed with her for getting better the moment the letter had been sent. Then she thought of him, that he was here, his whole self, his hands, his eyes. She heard his voice, and forgetting everything ran joyfully to meet him.

'Well, how is Ani?' he asked in a constrained voice, looking up to Anna as she ran downstairs to him.

He was sitting on a chair, and a footman was pulling off his warm over-boots.

'Oh, it's nothing! She's better.'

'And you?' he said, giving himself a shake.

She took his hand in both her own, and drew it to her waist, not taking her eyes off him.

'Well, I'm very glad,' he said, coldly surveying her, her hair and the dress which he knew she had put on for him. He liked and admired it all, but he had admired her so often! And the stern, stony expression which she so dreaded settled on his face.

'Well, I'm very glad,' he repeated. 'And how are you yourself?' he asked, wiping his damp beard with his handkerchief and kissing her hand.

'It doesn't matter,' she thought, 'so long as he is here. When he is here he cannot, he dare not, cease to love me.'

The evening passed happily and gaily in the presence of the Princess Varvara, who complained to him that Anna had been taking morphine while he was away.

'What am I to do? I couldn't sleep. ... My thoughts kept me awake. I never take it when he is here – or hardly ever.'

He told them about the elections, and with adroit questions Anna led him on to talk of what pleased him most – his own success. In her turn she told him of everything of interest that had happened at home; and all her news was of the most cheerful description.

But late at night, when they were alone, Anna, seeing that she had regained possession of him, was seized by a desire to erase the painful impression left by the look he had given her over her letter.

'Confess that you were vexed at getting my letter, and didn't believe me?' she said.

The words were hardly out of her mouth before she realized that, no matter how lovingly disposed he might be towards her, he had not forgiven her that.

'Yes,' he said, 'it was such a strange letter. First Ani ill, then you thought of coming yourself.'

'That was all true.'

'Oh, I don't doubt it.'

'Yes, you do! I can see that you are vexed.'

'Not for one moment. Or if I am, it is only because you somehow refuse to realize that there are duties ...'

'The duty of going to a concert. ...'

'Don't let us talk about it,' he said.

'Why not talk about it?'

'I only meant to say that unavoidable business may turn up. Now, for instance, I shall have to go to Moscow about the house. ... Oh, Anna, why are you so irritable? Don't you know that I can't live without you?'

'If so,' said Anna, suddenly in a different tone of voice, 'it must mean that you are sick of this life. ... Yes, you will come home for a day and then go off again, the way all men do. ...'

'Anna, that is cruel. I am ready to give up my whole life ...'

But she did not hear him.

'If you go to Moscow, I shall come too. I will not stay here. Either we must separate or else live together all the time.'

'You know quite well that's my one desire. But for that ...'

'I must get a divorce? I will write to him. I see I cannot go on like this. ... But I shall come with you to Moscow.'

'You make it sound like a threat. But there is nothing I wish for more than never to be parted from you,' said Vronsky, smiling.

But the look that flashed in his eyes as he spoke the tender words was not merely cold – it was the vindictive look of a man persecuted and lashed to fury.

'If that is your way, it means catastrophe!' his glance told her. It was only a momentary impression, but she never forgot it.

Anna wrote to her husband asking him about a divorce, and towards the end of November she said good-bye to the Princess Varvara, who wanted to go to Petersburg, and moved with Vronsky to Moscow. Expecting every day a reply from Karenin, and after that the divorce, they now set up house together like a married couple.

PART SEVEN

I

THE Levins had been over two months in Moscow. The date had long passed on which, according to the most trustworthy calculations of those who knew something about such matters, Kitty should have been confined. But she had not yet been delivered, nor was there any sign that she was nearer her time than she had been two months before. The doctor, the midwife, Dolly, her mother, and, most of all, Levin, who could not think of the approaching event without terror, were beginning to get impatient and anxious. Kitty was the only one who felt perfectly calm and happy.

She was distinctly conscious now of the birth of a new feeling of love for the coming child – the child which to some extent existed for her already – and she abandoned herself to it blissfully. The child was no longer only a part of her body but sometimes lived his own independent life. Often this was the cause of suffering but at the same time her strange new joy made her want to laugh aloud.

She was surrounded by all the people she loved, and they were all so good to her and took such care of her, trying to make everything pleasant, that if she had not known and been aware that this period must soon come to an end, she could not have desired a better or pleasanter life. The only thing that marred the charm of this life was that her husband was not as she loved him best, not as he was in the country.

She loved his quiet, friendly, hospitable manner at home. In town he always seemed restless and on his guard, as though afraid someone might cause him offence or, worse still, offend her. There in the country, feeling himself in his right place, he was never in a hurry to be off elsewhere, yet never without occupation. Here in town he was constantly fidgeting, as though afraid of missing something, and yet he had nothing to do. And she felt sorry for him. To others, she knew, he did not appear at all in need of pity. On the contrary, when Kitty looked at him in society, as one sometimes looks at a person one loves, trying to see him as if he were a stranger, so as to get at the impression he must make on others, she saw, with jealous fear even, that far from being an object of pity he was very attractive with his good breeding, his rather old-fashioned, reserved courtesy to women, his powerful figure, and his uncommonly, as she thought, expressive face. But she saw him from within rather than from without; she saw that in town he was not himself – she could find no other words to define his state. Sometimes she reproached him in her heart for not being able to make himself happier in town; at others she admitted that it really was difficult for him to order his life here so that he could get any satisfaction out of it.

After all, what could he find to do? He did not care for cards. He did not go to a club. As for going out with bright young men of Oblonsky's type – she knew now what that meant ... it meant drinking and then afterwards driving. ... She shuddered to think where men drove to after a drinking party. Was he to go into society? But she knew that to enjoy this he would have to enjoy the company of young women, which she could hardly wish for. He could stay at home with her and her mother and sisters. But agreeable and amusing as the eternal conversations between the sisters might be to her – the talks about the Alines and the Nadines, as the old prince called them – she knew they must be tedious for him. Then what was there left for him to do? Go on working at his book? He did make an effort to do so, and had begun by going to the library to take notes and look up references he needed; but, as he explained to her, the more he did nothing, the less time he seemed to have. Besides, he complained, he had talked too much about his book here, so that all his ideas had become confused and he had lost interest in them.

There was one blessing about this town life – they never quarrelled. Whether it was the living conditions in Moscow, or that they had both grown more careful and sensible, the fact remained that they had none of those scenes of jealousy which they had so dreaded when they moved from the country.

In this respect, an event of great importance to them both occurred. Kitty met Vronsky.

The old Princess Maria Borisovna, Kitty's godmother, who had always been very fond of her, had insisted on seeing her. Kitty was not going out anywhere now because of her condition, but she went with her father to see the venerable old lady, and there met Vronsky.

The only thing Kitty could reproach herself with over this meeting was that for an instant when she recognized Vronsky's once-so-familiar figure in his civilian clothes she caught her breath, the blood rushed to her heart and she could feel the bright colour flooding her face. But this lasted only a few seconds. Her father, who purposely began talking to Vronsky in a loud tone of voice, had barely finished what he was saying before she was quite ready to face Vronsky and, if need be, to converse with him as naturally as she did with the Princess Maria Borisovna; and, what was more, to do so in a way that would gain for her lightest intonation and smile the approval of her husband, whose unseen presence she seemed to feel about her at that moment.

She exchanged a few words with him, and even smiled at a joke he made about the elections, which he called 'our parliament'. (She had to smile to show she saw the joke.) But she immediately turned away to the Princess Maria Borisovna, and did not glance round at him again until he got up to go. She looked at him then, but plainly only because it would be rude not to look at a man when he is saying good-bye to you.

She was grateful to her father for not referring to this encounter with Vronsky, but she could tell by his special tenderness after the visit, when they were taking their usual walk, that he was pleased with her. She was pleased with herself. She had not at all expected to find the strength to shut down somewhere deep in her heart all memories of her former feeling for Vronsky, and not merely appear quite calm and indifferent in his presence but actually be so.

Levin flushed a great deal more than she had done when she told him she had met Vronsky at the Princess Maria Borisovna's. It was very hard for her to tell him this, but still harder to go on and tell him all the details of the meeting, as he did not ask any questions but simply gazed at her frowning.

'I am very sorry you were not there,' she said. 'I don't mean in the same room ... I couldn't have been so natural with you there. ... I am blushing much more now, ever so much more,' she said, blushing till the tears stung her eyes. 'But I wish you could have watched through a crack.'

Her truthful eyes told Levin that she was satisfied with herself, and though she blushed he felt reassured at once and began questioning her, which was all she wanted. When he had heard the whole story, even to the detail that it was only for the first second she could not help flushing but afterwards was as natural and as much at her ease as with any chance acquaintance, Levin cheered up altogether and declared he was very glad it had happened, and in future he would not behave so stupidly as he had done at the elections, but would try at the very next opportunity to be as friendly to Vronsky as possible.

'It is so wretched to think of having anyone who is almost an enemy, whom one dreads meeting,' said Levin. 'I am really very glad indeed.'

2

'YOU will go and call on the Bohls, won't you, please?' Kitty said to her husband, when he came into her room at eleven o'clock one morning before going out. 'I know you are dining at the club: Papa put your name down. But what are you going to do this morning?'

'Only look in at Katavasov's,' answered Levin.

'Why so early?'

'He promised to introduce me to Metrov. I want to have a talk with him about my work. He's a distinguished Petersburg scholar.'

'Oh yes, wasn't it an article of his you were praising so? And what will you do after that?' Kitty asked.

'I may go round to the law-courts to see about my sister's business.'

'And the concert?' she queried.

'What's the good of going alone!'

'Oh yes, do go! They are doing those new things. ... You used to be so interested. I should most certainly go if I were you.'

'Well, in any case, I shall come home for a few minutes before dinner,' he said, glancing at his watch.

'But put on your frock-coat, so that you can call on Countess Bohl on the way.'

'Why, is it absolutely necessary then?'

'Yes, absolutely! He called on us. What difference does it make to you? You drop in, sit down, talk about the weather for five minutes, and then get up and leave.'

'But you can't think how out of practice I have got with that sort of thing – it makes me feel positively ashamed. What happens? A perfect stranger appears, sits down, stays on for no reason whatever, wastes their time and upsets himself, and goes away again!'

Kitty laughed.

'But you used to pay calls before we were married.'

'I know I did, but I always felt uncomfortable, and now I'm so out of the way of it that, by jingo, I'd rather go without my dinner two days running than pay this call! It's so embarrassing! I feel the whole time that they will be irritated and say to themselves, "What has he come for?"'

'No, they won't! I promise you that,' said Kitty, looking laughingly into his face. She took his hand. 'Good-bye now. ... Do call on them, please!'

He kissed his wife's hand and was about to leave when she stopped him.

'Kostya, do you know, I've only fifty roubles left.'

'All right, I'll go and draw some money from the bank. How much?' he said, with a look of dissatisfaction familiar to her.

'No, wait.' She held on to his hand. 'Let's talk it over; it worries me. I don't think I buy anything unnecessary, and yet the money melts away. We must be managing badly somehow.'

'Not at all,' he said, giving a little cough and looking at her from under his brows.

She knew that cough. It was a sign of intense dissatisfaction, not with her but with himself. He certainly was displeased not at so much money being spent but at being reminded of what he wanted to forget, knowing as he did that something was wrong.

'I have told Sokolov to sell the wheat, and to borrow an advance on the mill. We shall not run short in any case.'

'Yes, but I am afraid that altogether we are spending too much ...'

'Not at all, not at all,' he repeated. 'Well, good-bye, my love.'

'Sometimes I'm really sorry I listened to mama. How nice it would have been in the country! As it is, I'm worrying you all, and the money goes like water ...'

'Not at all, not at all. Never once since our marriage have I said to myself that things could have been better than they are ...'

'Truly?' she said, looking into his eyes.

He had said it without thinking, simply to comfort her. But when he looked and saw those sweet, candid eyes fixed inquiringly on him, he repeated what he had said with his whole heart. 'I don't think of her half enough,' he reflected. And he suddenly remembered what awaited them both in the near future.

'Will it be soon? How do you feel?' he whispered, taking her two hands in his.

'I have so often thought so, that now I have given up thinking or knowing.'

'And you're not frightened?'

She smiled scornfully.

'Not an atom!' she answered.

'Well, if anything happens, I shall be at Katavasov's.'

'Nothing will happen, and don't think about it. I shall go for a walk along the boulevard with papa. We shall call and see Dolly. I shall expect you before dinner. Oh yes! Do you know that Dolly's position is becoming utterly impossible? She is in debt all round: she hasn't a penny. Mama and I were talking about it yesterday with Arseny' (this was her sister's husband, Lvov), 'and we decided that you and he should attack Stiva. It's really unbearable. We can't mention it to papa. ... But if you and Arseny ...'

'Why, what can we do?' said Levin.

'You'll be at Arseny's anyway. Have a talk with him, and he will tell you what we decided.'

'Oh, I'm always ready to agree to anything with Arseny. I'll go and see him. By the way, if I do go to the concert, I'll go with Natalie. Well, good-bye.'

On the steps Levin was stopped by his old servant, Kuzma, who had been with him before his marriage and now looked after their household in town.

'Beauty' (the left shaft-horse brought up from the country) 'has been re-shod but still goes lame,' said the old man. 'What shall we do about her?'

When he first came to Moscow, Levin had used his own horses brought from the country. He had tried to arrange this side of their expenses in the best and cheapest way possible; but it turned out that keeping their own horses was more expensive than hiring, and that they had to hire in any case.

'Send for the vet. Maybe it's a bruise.'

'But what will Katerina Alexandrovna do?' asked Kuzma.

It no longer astonished Levin, as it had when he first came to Moscow, that to go a distance of less than a quarter of a mile it was necessary to have two large horses put to a heavy carriage, to take the carriage through the snowy slush and keep it standing there four hours, with five roubles to pay every time. Now he looked upon it as quite natural.

'Hire a pair for our carriage,' he said.

'Yes, sir.'

Having thus, without the least trouble, thanks to the facilities of life in town, solved a difficulty that in the country would have called for much bother and personal attention, Levin went out, called a sledge, seated himself and drove to Nikitsky street. On the way he thought no more of money matters but mused on the introduction that awaited him to the Petersburg savant, whose subject was sociology, and considered what he would say to him about his own book.

It was only during the very first days in Moscow that Levin had been startled by the unproductive but inevitable expenditure, so strange to one accustomed to living in the country, that was demanded of him on every side. But by now he had grown used to it. In this respect the thing happened to him that is said to happen to drunkards – the first glass sticks in the throat, the second flies down like a hawk but after the third they're like wee little birds. When Levin had changed his first hundred-rouble note to pay for livery for his footman and hall-porter, he could not help reflecting that these useless liveries – which, however, must be absolutely indispensable, to judge by the astonishment of the princess and Kitty when he hinted that one could get along without livery – represented the wages of two labourers for a whole summer, that is, about three hundred days of hard work from early morning till late at night, from Easter to Advent. That hundred-rouble note did stick in his throat. But the next, that he changed in order to pay out twenty-eight roubles for provisions for a family dinner, though he could not resist calculating that twenty-eight roubles meant about seventy-two bushels of oats, reaped, bound, threshed, winnowed, sifted and sacked – with sweat and groans. Now, however, the notes he parted with had long ceased to evoke such reflections, and flew away like wee birds. Whether the pleasure afforded by what his money purchased corresponded to the labour expended in acquiring it was a consideration long since lost sight of. In the same way he forgot his business reckonings that certain grain must not be sold below a certain price. After having kept back his rye for a long while, he eventually sold it at fifty kopecks a measure cheaper than it would have fetched a month earlier. Even the consideration that living at the present rate they would not get through the year without running into debt – even that calculation had no force. The one essential was to have money in the bank, without inquiring whence it came, so as to be sure of the wherewithal for tomorrow's meat. Till now he had always observed this condition: he had always had money in the bank. But now the money in the bank was all gone, and he could not quite tell where more was to come from. And it was this that had upset him for a moment when Kitty had mentioned money; but there was no time to go into that now. He drove along, thinking of Katavasov and the meeting with Metrov that was before him.

3

DURING his stay in Moscow, Levin had renewed his intimacy with his old college friend, now Professor Katavasov, whom he had not seen since his marriage. He liked Katavasov on account of his clear and simple conception of life. Levin considered that Katavasov's clarity of outlook resulted from the shallowness of his nature, while Katavasov thought that the inconsistency of Levin's ideas betokened an undisciplined mind; but Levin enjoyed Katavasov's clearness, and Katavasov enjoyed the abundance of Levin's untrained thought, so they liked to meet and argue together.

Levin had read several passages of his book to Katavasov, who had been impressed. Happening to meet Levin the day before at a public lecture, Katavasov had told him that the celebrated Metrov, whose article Levin had been so enthusiastic about, was in Moscow and was much interested by what Katavasov had told him of Levin's book, that he was coming to see him to-morrow at eleven and would be very pleased to make Levin's acquaintance.

'You are decidedly improving, my friend, I'm glad to see,' said Katavasov as he welcomed Levin in the little drawing-room. 'I heard the bell and thought, "It isn't possible he has arrived punctually!" ... Well, what do you say to the Montenegrins? They are born fighters.'

'Why, what's happened?' asked Levin.

In a few words Katavasov gave him the latest news of the war as they proceeded to the study, where he introduced Levin to a short, thick-set man of pleasant appearance. This was Metrov. The conversation touched for a brief space on politics and on how recent events were regarded in the higher spheres in Petersburg. Metrov quoted certain words supposed to have been uttered by the Emperor and one of his ministers, which he had from a reliable source. Katavasov, however, had heard also on excellent authority that the Emperor had said something quite different. Levin tried to imagine circumstances in which both statements might have been made, and the subject was dropped.

'Yes, my friend here has almost finished a book on the natural conditions of the farm labourer in relation to the land,' said Katavasov. 'I'm not a specialist, but as a natural science man I was pleased to see that he did not look upon humanity as something outside biological laws; on the contrary, he recognizes man's dependence on his environment, and in that dependence seeks the laws of his development.'

'That sounds very interesting,' observed Metrov.

'I really began to write a book on agriculture, but in studying the chief instrument of agriculture, the labourer, I found myself arriving at quite unexpected results,' said Levin, reddening.

And, as if feeling his way, Levin began cautiously expounding his views. He knew Metrov had written an article running counter to the generally accepted theory of political economy, but to what extent he could reckon on his sympathy with his own novel views he did not know and could not gather from the calm, clever face of the learned man.

'But in what do you see the special characteristics of the Russian labourer?' asked Metrov. 'In his biological characteristics, so to speak, or in the condition in which he is placed?'

Levin detected in the very question an idea with which he did not agree. But he went on explaining his own theory that that Russian labourer had a special relation to the land, entirely different from that of other people. In proof of this proposition he hastened to add that in his opinion this attitude of the Russian peasant was due to the consciousness of his mission to populate vast uninhabited expanses in the east.

'One may easily be led astray in forming conclusions on the general vocation of a people,' said Metrov, interrupting Levin. 'The condition of the labourer will always depend on his relation to the land and to capital.'

And without giving Levin time to finish, Metrov started explaining to him the special point of his own theory.

In what the point of his theory lay, Levin did not understand, because he did not take the trouble to understand. He saw that Metrov, like all the rest, in spite of his article refuting the teachings of the economists, still looked at the position of the Russian peasant merely from the standpoint of capital, wages, and rent. Though he would indeed have been obliged to admit that in the eastern, and by far the larger, part of Russia there was no such thing as rent, that for nine-tenths of Russia's eighty millions wages meant no more than a bare subsistence, and that capital did not exist except in the form of the most primitive tools, yet he regarded every labourer from that one point of view – though in many points he disagreed with the economists and had his own theory of pay, which he expounded to Levin.

Levin listened reluctantly, and at first made various objections. He would have liked to interrupt Metrov in order to express his own idea, which in his opinion would have rendered all further exposition superfluous. He soon realized, however, that their differences were so wide that they would never be able to reach a common understanding, so he ceased raising objections and simply listened. Though he was no longer in the least interested in what Metrov was saying, he did experience a certain satisfaction in hearing him. It flattered his vanity that such a learned man should explain his ideas to him so eagerly and so painstakingly, and with such confidence in Levin's knowledge of the subject that he sometimes by a mere hint referred him to a whole aspect of the matter. Levin put this down to his own credit, unaware that Metrov had exhausted all his friends with his theory and was delighted to come across a new audience; and moreover that he was ready to talk to anyone on any subject that interested him, even if he were not yet clear about it.

'I am afraid we shall be late,' said Katavasov, consulting his watch the moment Metrov had finished his disquisition.

'Yes, we have a meeting of the Society of Amateurs in honour of Svintich's jubilee,' he went on in answer to Levin's inquiry. 'Metrov and I have arranged to go. I promised to read a paper on his work in zoology. Why not come with us? It will be very interesting.'

'Yes, it is time we were going,' said Metrov. 'Do come with us, and if you like we might go to my place afterwards. I should very much like to hear some of your book.'

'Oh no, it's still in the rough and not finished. But I should like to go to the meeting with you.'

'I say, friends, have you heard? I sent in a separate report,' Katavasov called from the next room, where he was putting on his frock-coat.

And they began to discuss a controversy in the university which had made a great stir in Moscow that winter. Three old professors on the council had not accepted the opinion of the younger professors, and the younger ones had presented a resolution of their own. This resolution was, in the judgement of some people, a monstrous one, while according to others it was quite simple and just. The professors were split into two camps. The one to which Katavasov belonged saw nothing but base treachery and deceit on the other side, which in turn charged them with youthful impudence and lack of respect for the authorities. Though Levin did not belong to the university, he had more than once heard the matter discussed since his arrival in Moscow, and had formed his own opinion on it. He took part in the conversation which continued in the street, as the three of them walked to the buildings of the old university.

The meeting had already begun. Round the cloth-covered table, at which Katavasov and Metrov seated themselves, there were some half-dozen persons, one of whom was reading something aloud, bent close over his manuscript. Levin took one of the vacant chairs at the table, and in a whisper asked a student sitting near what the paper was about.

'The biography,' replied the student, eyeing Levin with disapproval.

Though Levin was not interested in the biography, he could not help listening, and learned some new and interesting facts about the life of the distinguished man of science.

When the reader had finished, the chairman thanked him and read some verses the poet Ment had written in honour of the occasion, adding a few words of thanks to the poet. Then Katavasov, in his loud, strident voice, read his paper on the scientific labours of the man whose jubilee it was.

When Katavasov had finished, Levin looked at his watch, saw it was past one, and reflected that there would be no time to read his manuscript to Metrov before the concert – and besides, he no longer felt any inclination to do so. During the readings he had thought over their conversation. It was now quite clear to him that though there might be something in Metrov's ideas, his own ideas were important too. Only by each of them working separately in his chosen path could their views be formulated and lead to results: nothing would be gained by putting their ideas together. And having made up his mind to decline Metrov's invitation, Levin went up to him at the end of the meeting. Metrov introduced Levin to the chairman, with whom he was discussing the political news. Metrov was telling the chairman what he had already told Levin that morning, and Levin made the same remarks he had made before but for the sake of variety he expressed one new opinion which had only just struck him. After that the university question came up again. As Levin had already heard it all, he made haste to tell Metrov that he was sorry he could not take advantage of his invitation, shook hands and drove off to Lvov's.

4

Lvov, who was married to Kitty's sister, Natalie, had spent all his life in the capitals and abroad, where he had been educated and where he had been in the diplomatic service.

The year before he had left the diplomatic service, not because of any 'unpleasantness' (he never had any 'unpleasantness' with anyone), and had accepted a post in the Palace Department in Moscow, in order to give his two boys the best education possible.

In spite of the acute contrast in their habits and views, and the fact that Lvov was older than Levin, they had seen a good deal of each other that winter and become attached to one another.

Lvov was at home, and Levin went in without being announced.

Wearing an indoor jacket with a belt, and chamois-leather slippers, Lvov was sitting in an arm-chair, pince-nez with tinted glasses on his nose, reading a book supported on a reading-stand, one shapely hand fastidiously holding away from him a half-smoked cigar.

His handsome, sensitive, still youthful-looking face, to which his crisp, glistening silvery hair gave a still more aristocratic air, lighted up with a smile when he saw Levin.

'Splendid! I was just going to send over to you. Well, how's Kitty? Sit here, it's more comfortable ...' He got up and pushed forward a rocking-chair. 'Have you read the last circular in the *Journal de St Pétersbourg*? I think it's excellent,' he said, with a slight French accent.

Levin recounted what he had heard from Katavasov of what was being said in Petersburg and, after talking politics for a while, went on to tell him about Metrov and the meeting they had been to. This interested Lvov very much.

'There now! I envy you for having the entry to these interesting scientific circles,' he said. And once having begun to talk, he changed, as he usually did, into French, the language in which he felt more at ease. 'It's true I have no time to spare – my official duties and the children prevent that. Besides, I'm not ashamed to confess, my education is woefully defective.'

'I don't believe that,' said Levin, with a smile. He was always touched at his brother-in-law's poor opinion of himself, which was absolutely sincere and not in the least put on from a desire to appear or to be modest.

'Yes, really! I feel now how badly educated I am. Even for the boys' lessons I am constantly having to refresh my memory, and indeed learn things for the first time. It is not enough for them to have teachers, you know – there must be someone to keep an eye on them, just as you have to have an overseer as well as labourers on your land. See what I'm reading' – he pointed to Buslaev's *Grammar* on the reading-stand. 'They expect Misha to know this, and it's frightfully difficult. ... Come, I wish you would make it clear to me. ... He says here ...'

Levin tried to explain that the point couldn't be understood but just had to be taught; but Lvov would not agree.

'You're not taking it seriously!'

'On the contrary! You have no idea how looking at you makes me ponder what lies in store for me – the education of my children.'

'Oh come, you've nothing to learn from me!' said Lvov.

'All I know,' said Levin, 'is that I never saw better brought-up children than yours. I only hope my own will be as good.'

Lvov made an obvious effort to repress his delight but his smile was positively radiant.

'If only they turn out better than their father – that's all I desire. You don't know all the difficulties one has to go through with youngsters like mine who have been allowed to run wild abroad.'

'You'll soon put that right. They are such clever children. The chief thing, to my mind, is moral training. That is what I learn when I look at your children.'

'Talk of moral training! You can't imagine how difficult that is! No sooner have you succeeded in combating one tendency than another crops up, and the struggle begins again. Without the support of religion – you remember we talked about that – no father on earth would be able to bring up his children by relying on himself alone.'

This conversation on a topic which always interested Levin was cut short by the entrance of the beautiful Natalie Alexandrovna, dressed to go out.

'Oh, I didn't know you were here,' she said, unmistakably feeling no regret but even being rather pleased at interrupting a conversation she knew so well that she was now weary of it. 'Well, how is Kitty? I am dining with you to-day. I tell you what, Arseny,' she said, turning to her husband, 'you take the carriage …'

And husband and wife began discussing their programme for the day. As Lvov had to go and meet someone on official business, while Natalie was going to the concert and then to some public meeting of a committee on the South-Eastern Question, there was a great deal to consider and arrange. Levin, as one of the family, had to take part in these deliberations. It was settled that he should drive Natalie to the concert and the meeting, and from there they would send the carriage to the office for Arseny, who would then call for his wife and take her on to Kitty's; or if he did not get through with his work he would send the carriage back and Levin would go with her.

'He undermines me, you know,' Lvov said to his wife. 'He assures me that our children are paragons, whereas I know they're full of faults.'

'Arseny goes to extremes, as I always tell him,' said his wife. 'If you look for perfection you will never be satisfied. And it's true what papa says – when we were children they went to one extreme and kept us in the attics, while our parents lived in the best rooms; but now it's the other way round – the lumber-room for the parents, and the first floor for the children. Parents hardly have the right to live nowadays: they must just exist for the children.'

'Why not, if it is more agreeable like that?' Lvov said, with his attractive smile, touching her hand. 'Anyone who didn't know you would think you were a stepmother, instead of a mother.'

'No, extremes are not good in anything,' said Natalie quietly, putting his paper-knife in its proper place on the table.

'Ah, come here, you model children!' said Lvov, turning to two handsome boys just entering the room.

They bowed to Levin and walked over to their father, evidently wishing to ask him about something.

Levin would have liked to talk to them and hear what it was they would say to their father, but Natalie began talking to him, and then a colleague of Lvov's, a man named Mahotin, wearing Court uniform, came in to fetch Lvov to meet someone. There began an endless conversation about Herzegovina, Princess Korzinsky, the Duma, and the sudden death of Madame Apraxin.

Levin had quite forgotten the commission he had been charged with, and only remembered it on his way out into the hall.

'Oh yes, Kitty told me to have a talk with you about Oblonsky,' he said, as Lvov accompanied them to the head of the staircase.

'I know. *Maman* wants us, *les beaux-frères*, to come down on him,' said Lvov, blushing and smiling. 'But I don't see why I should!'

'If you won't, then I will,' said his wife with a smile, as she stood in her white fur-lined cloak, waiting for them to finish. 'Come along now!'

5

Two very interesting works were performed at the matinée concert. One was a fantasia, *King Lear on the Heath*; the other a quartette dedicated to the memory of Bach. Both were new and belonged to the modern school, and Levin was eager to form an opinion about them. After he had escorted his sister-in-law to her stall, he took up his stand by a pillar, resolved to listen as attentively and conscientiously as he could. He tried not to let his thoughts be distracted or his impression of the music marred by watching the conductor in a white tie waving his arms, which always disturbed his enjoyment so much; or by the ladies in their bonnets, the ribbons of which were carefully tied over their ears for the concert, and all these people either thinking of nothing at all or interested in anything in the world but the music. He tried to avoid musical connoisseurs or talkative acquaintances, and stood looking down at the floor in front of him, listening.

But the more he listened to the *King Lear* fantasia, the less did he feel able to form any definite opinion on it. The opening bars seemed perpetually on the point of taking shape for the musical expression of some feeling, and then breaking off into fragments of other themes or even at times into extremely complex but disconnected sounds, according to the whim of the composer. And these fragmentary musical expressions, good as some of them were, did not please the ear because they came quite unexpectedly and were not led up to by anything. Joy and sorrow, despair, tenderness and triumph followed one another like the incoherent thoughts of a lunatic. And they vanished, like the emotions of a lunatic, as suddenly as they had appeared.

Throughout the performance Levin felt like a deaf man watching people dancing. He was in a state of complete bewilderment when the music stopped, and utterly weary from the strain of unrewarded attention. From all sides came loud applause. People began moving from their places, to walk about and talk. Anxious to get some light for his own perplexity by hearing the impression of others, Levin went in search of the experts and was glad to see a well-known music critic in conversation with Pestsov, whom he knew.

'Marvellous!' Pestsov was saying in his deep bass. 'How are you, Constantine Dmitrich? Particularly sculpturesque and plastic, so to speak, and rich in colour is that passage where one feels Cordelia's approach – where woman, *das ewig Weibliche*, enters into conflict with fate. Don't you think so?'

'Why ... what has Cordelia to do with it?' Levin asked timidly, having entirely forgotten that the fantasia was supposed to represent King Lear on the heath.

'Cordelia comes in ... just here!' said Pestsov, tapping his finger on the shiny programme he was holding, and handing it to Levin.

Only then did Levin recall the title of the fantasia, and he hastened to read in the Russian translation the lines from Shakespeare that were printed on the back of the programme.

'You can't follow it without that,' said Pestsov, turning to Levin, as the person he had been speaking to had departed and he had no one to talk to.

In the *entr'acte* Levin and Pestsov fell into an argument on the merits and demerits of the Wagnerian tendency in music. Levin maintained that the mistake of Wagner and his followers lay in trying to make music enter the domain of another art, just as poetry goes wrong when it tries to depict the features of a face, which is the function of painting. As an example of this kind of error he instanced the case of the sculptor who had carved poetic phantasms rising round his marble statue of a poet on a pedestal. 'These phantoms are so far from being phantoms that they even cling to a ladder,' said Levin. The comparison pleased him but he could not remember whether he had not used it before, and to Pestsov, too, and became embarrassed as soon as he had said it.

Pestsov argued that art is one, and attains its highest manifestation only by conjunction of all the various branches of art.

The second part of the concert Levin could not hear. Pestsov, who was standing beside him, kept talking almost the whole time, finding fault with the piece for its mawkish affectation of simplicity, which he compared to the simplicities of the Pre-Raphaelites in painting. On his way out Levin saw a number of acquaintances, with whom he chatted about politics, music, and mutual friends. Among others he met Count Bohl, whom he had quite forgotten to call upon.

'Well, why not go now?' Natalie said, when he told her. 'Perhaps they are not at home, and then you could come for me at the meeting. You have plenty of time.'

6

'PERHAPS they are not "at home"?' said Levin, as he entered the hall of the Countess Bohl's house.

'Yes, they are, sir,' said the hall-porter, resolutely removing Levin's overcoat.

'What a nuisance!' thought Levin with a sigh, pulling off one glove and smoothing his hat. 'What is the good of my going in? And what on earth shall I say to them?'

At the door of the first drawing-room Levin met the Countess Bohl giving some order to a servant, a careworn, severe expression on her face. On seeing Levin she smiled and invited him into the next room, a smaller drawing-room, from which came the sound of voices. In this room, seated in arm-chairs, were the countess's two daughters and a Moscow colonel with whom Levin was acquainted. Levin went up, greeted them and sat down beside the sofa with his hat on his knees.

'How is your wife? Were you at the concert? We couldn't go. Mama had to attend the funeral.'

'Yes, I heard. ... How sudden it was!' said Levin.

The countess came in and, seating herself on the sofa, she, too, asked after his wife and inquired about the concert.

Levin answered and repeated his remark about Madame Apraxin's sudden death.

'She always was delicate, though.'

'Were you at the opera last night?'

'Yes, I was.'

'Wasn't Lucca splendid?'

'Yes, splendid,' he replied, and as it was quite immaterial to him what they thought of him he began repeating what he had heard at least a hundred times about the singer's extraordinary talent. The Countess Bohl pretended to be listening. Directly he had said enough and paused, the colonel, who had so far been silent, also began talking of the opera and the lighting of the opera-house. Finally, after some remark about the proposed *folle journée* at Turin's, the colonel laughed, got up noisily and took his leave. Levin rose, too, but saw by the countess's face that it was not yet time for him to go. He must stay another couple of minutes. He sat down.

As, however, he was thinking all the while how silly it was, he could not find a subject for conversation, and remained silent.

'You are not going to the public meeting? They say it will be very interesting,' began the countess.

'No, but I promised my *belle-sœur* I would call for her there,' said Levin.

Silence again. The mother exchanged a look with one of her daughters.

'It must be time now,' thought Levin, and he got up. The ladies shook hands with him and charged him with *mille choses* for his wife.

Helping him on with his overcoat, the hall-porter asked where he was staying, and at once noted the address in a large, handsomely-bound book.

'Of course, it's all the same to me, but it's so horribly stupid it makes one ashamed,' thought Levin, consoling himself with the reflection that everyone did it; and he went on to the public meeting from which he was to fetch his sister-in-law and take her back with him.

At the meeting he found a great many people and practically the whole of society. He was in time to hear the report, which everyone said was very interesting. When that had been read, people began moving about, and Levin met Sviazhsky, who asked him to be sure and come to a meeting of the Agricultural Society, where an important lecture was to be delivered that evening. Levin also saw Oblonsky, just back from the races, and various other people he knew; and he again heard and expressed various criticisms on the meeting, on the new fantasia, and on some legal case. But, probably because of the mental fatigue he was beginning to feel, he made a mistake in talking of the trial, which he afterwards more than once remembered with vexation. Speculating on the sentence to be passed on a foreigner who was being tried in Russia, and saying how unjust it would be to banish him from the country, Levin repeated what he had heard said the day before by a man he knew.

'It seems to me that to send him out of the country would be like punishing a pike by throwing it into the water,' he said. It was only later that he remembered that this idea, which he had heard from an acquaintance and given out as his own, was a quotation from one of Krilov's fables, and that his acquaintance had got it from a newspaper article.

He took his sister-in-law home and, finding Kitty quite all right and in good spirits, he departed for the club.

7

LEVIN reached the club just at the right time. Members and visitors were driving up as he arrived. Levin had not been there for a very long while – not since the time following his university days, when he had lived in Moscow and frequented society. He remembered the club, the external details of its arrangement, but he had completely forgotten the impression it used to make on him in the old days. But as soon as he drove into the wide semi-circular courtyard, and stepped out of his sledge into the porch, where a hall-porter wearing a shoulder-belt noiselessly opened the door and bowed to him; as soon as he caught sight in the porter's room of the goloshes and coats of members who thought it less trouble to take their goloshes off downstairs than to go up in them; as soon as he heard the mysterious ring that announced his ascent of the shallow, carpeted staircase – there was the statue on the landing – and saw a third porter, a familiar figure grown older, in livery slowly but without loss of time examining each visitor as he opened the door for him – Levin felt the old atmosphere of the club envelop him: an atmosphere of repose, comfort, and propriety.

'Your hat, sir,' the porter requested Levin, who had forgotten the rule that hats must be left in the porter's room. 'It's a long while since you were here! The prince put you down yesterday. Prince Oblonsky has not arrived yet.'

The porter not only knew Levin but knew all his connexions and relatives as well, and immediately mentioned his close friends.

Passing through the outer hall, divided up by screens, and a partitioned room on the right where there was a fruit buffet, Levin overtook an old man walking slowly, and entered the noisy, crowded dining-room.

He continued down the room, walking past tables which were nearly all full, scanning the visitors. He saw all sorts of people he knew – old and young, some mere acquaintances, others intimate friends. There was not a single cross or worried face among them. They all seemed to have left their cares and anxieties with their hats in the porter's room, and were preparing to enjoy the material blessings of life at their leisure. Sviazhsky and Shcherbatsky, Nevyedovsky and the old prince, Vronsky and Koznyshev: all were here.

'Ah! You are late!' said the old prince, with a smile, giving Levin a hand over his shoulder. 'How's Kitty?' he asked, smoothing the table-napkin he had tucked in behind a button of his waistcoat.

'All right, thank you. They are dining at home together, all three of them.'

'Ah, that means plenty of Aline-Nadine gossip! Well, there's no room with us. Be quick and get a place at that table,' said the old prince, turning away and cautiously taking a plate of fish-soup.

'Levin! Here!' a good-natured voice hailed him a little farther on. It was Turovtsin. He was sitting with a young man in military uniform, and two chairs were tilted up against their table.

Levin joined them gladly. He had always had a soft spot for the good-hearted prodigal Turovtsin – with him were associated memories of the evening he had proposed to Kitty – but now, after the strain of all those intellectual conversations, the sight of Turovtsin's simple, jolly face was particularly welcome.

'We kept these for you and Oblonsky. He'll be here directly.'

The young man, holding himself very erect, with merry, laughing eyes, was Gagin, an officer from Petersburg. Turovtsin introduced them to each other.

'Oblonsky's always late.'

'Ah, here he is!'

'Have you only just got here?' asked Oblonsky, hastening up to them. 'How do you do? Had some vodka? Come along, then.'

Levin got up and followed him to a large table spread with vodka and the most varied selection of appetizers. From the score or so of different delicacies on the table it ought not to have been difficult to choose to one's taste, but Oblonsky ordered something special, which one of the liveried waiters brought at once. They drank a glass of vodka each and returned to their table.

They were still at their soup when Gagin was served with a bottle of champagne and told the waiter to fill the four glasses. Levin did not refuse the proffered wine and ordered a second bottle. He was hungry, and ate and drank heartily, and with even greater enjoyment took part in the gay and lively conversation of his companions. Gagin, dropping his voice, began relating the latest good story from Petersburg, which, though improper and silly, was so funny that Levin burst into uproarious laughter, making people turn round to look at him.

'That's like the "That's-just-what-I-can't-bear" story – do you know it?' said Oblonsky. 'It's terribly good! Bring another bottle!' he called to the waiter, and began telling his story.

'With Peter Ilyich Vinovsky's compliments,' interrupted a little old waiter, bringing two slender glasses of sparkling champagne on a tray, and addressing Oblonsky and Levin.

Oblonsky took a glass and, catching the eye of a bald-headed man with a ginger moustache at the other end of the table, nodded to him, smiling.

'Who is that?' asked Levin.

'You met him once at my place, don't you remember? A nice fellow.'

Levin followed Oblonsky's example and took the glass.

Oblonsky's anecdote was amusing, too. Then Levin told his story, which was also appreciated. After that they began to talk about horses, about that day's races and how skilfully Vronsky's Atlas had won the first prize. Levin did not notice how the time passed at dinner.

'Ah, here they are!' said Oblonsky, just as they were finishing dinner, leaning over the back of his chair and holding out his hand to Vronsky, who came up with a tall colonel of the Guards.

Vronsky's face also beamed with the cheerful good humour general in the club. Gaily propping his elbow on Oblonsky's shoulder, he whispered something in his ear, and with the same merry smile held out a hand to Levin.

'Very glad to meet you,' he said. 'I looked for you again at the elections, but I was told you had already gone.'

'Yes, I left the same day. We were just talking of your horse. Congratulations!' said Levin. 'It was very good going!'

'You keep race-horses, too, don't you?'

'No, my father did. But I remember his stable, so I know something about it.'

'Where did you dine?' asked Oblonsky.

'At the second table, behind the pillars.'

'He's been overwhelmed with congratulations,' remarked the tall colonel. 'It's his second Imperial prize! If only I had the luck at cards that he has with horses! ... But why waste the golden moments? I'm off to the "infernal regions",' he added, walking away from the table.

'That's Yashvin,' Vronsky said in response to Turovtsin, and he sat down in the vacated chair beside them. He drank the glass of champagne they offered him, and ordered another bottle. Whether it was the influence of the general atmosphere of the club or the wine he had drunk – at any rate, Levin chatted away to Vronsky about the best breeds of cattle, and was delighted to find that he felt not the least animosity towards this man. He even told him, among other things, that he had heard from his wife that she had met him at the Princess Maria Borisovna's.

'Ah, the Princess Maria Borisovna! There's a woman!' cried Oblonsky, and began a story about her which set them all laughing. Vronsky especially burst into such simple-hearted laughter that Levin felt quite reconciled to him.

'Well, gentlemen, if we have finished, let's go!' said Oblonsky, getting up with a smile.

8

As he left the table and made his way with Gagin through the lofty rooms to the billiard-room, Levin felt his arms swing with unusual ease and rhythm. Crossing the large hall, he encountered his father-in-law.

'Well, and how do you like our temple of idleness?' asked the prince, taking his arm. 'Come along, let us walk round a bit.'

'I was just wanting to take a turn and see the place. I find it all very interesting.'

'Yes, it may be interesting for you. But my interest is of a different character. You look at those little old men now,' he said, indicating a club member with bent back and hanging lower lip, shuffling towards them in his soft boots, 'and you imagine they were born *shlupiks*.'

'*Shlupiks*? What's that?'

'You see, you don't even know the word! It's a club term of ours. You remember the game of egg-rolling? You roll your hard-boiled egg until it's so cracked that it's no good, and it becomes a *shlupik*. It is like that with ourselves: we keep on coming and coming to the club, until we turn into *shlupiks*. Yes, you may laugh! But we are already thinking of the time when we shall be *shlupiks*. Do you know Prince Tchetchensky?' inquired the prince; and Levin saw by his face that he was going to relate something funny.

'No, I don't know him.'

'You don't? What, the famous Prince Tchetchensky? Well, never mind. He's always playing billiards here. Three years ago he was still sprightly and showed a bold front, calling other men *shlupiks*. But one day he looks in at the club and our hall-porter – you know, Vassily, the fat one: he's a great wag. ... Well, Prince Tchetchensky asks him, "I say, Vassily, who's here? Any *shlupiks*?" and Vassily replies, "You make the third, sir." Yes, my boy, that's how it is!'

Talking and exchanging greetings with acquaintances they met, Levin and the prince made the tour of the club, passing through the main room, where the card-tables were already in position and habitual partners were playing for small stakes; the divan-room, where a few members were playing chess, and Koznyshev was engaged in conversation with someone; the billiard-room, where, by a sofa in a recess, a lively party which included Gagin were drinking champagne. They even took a peep into the 'infernal regions', where a number of backers were crowded round a table at which Yashvin had already taken his seat. Careful not to make a noise, they walked into the dim reading-room, where under the shaded lamps a young man with a wrathful countenance sat turning over one journal after another, and a bald old general was buried in a book. From there they passed into what the prince called the 'intellectual' room. Here three gentlemen were arguing about the latest political news.

'We are all ready, Prince,' said one of his partners who had come to look for him, and the prince went off to his card-party.

Levin sat down for a while and listened to the political discussion, but after all the conversations of the kind he had heard that day he suddenly felt fearfully bored. He got up and hurried away to look for Oblonsky and Turovtsin, with whom it was much jollier.

Turovtsin, with a tankard of something to drink, was sitting on the high sofa in the billiard-room, and Oblonsky was talking to Vronsky by the door in the far corner.

'She is not exactly depressed, but the uncertainty, her unsettled position ...' Levin overheard, and tried to turn away, but Oblonsky called to him.

'Levin!' and Levin noticed that though there were not actually tears in Oblonsky's eyes they were moist, as was always the case when he was under the influence of wine or emotion. Just now it was both. 'Levin, don't go,' he said, holding him tightly by the elbow, evidently anxious not on any account to lose him.

'This is a true friend of mine – almost my best friend,' he said to Vronsky. 'You also have become nearer and dearer to me. And I want you both to be friends, and I know you ought to come together because you are both splendid fellows.'

'There seems nothing for it but to kiss and be friends, then,' said Vronsky with good-natured playfulness, holding out his hand.

Levin quickly grasped the outstretched hand and pressed it warmly. 'I am very, very glad,' he said.

'Waiter, a bottle of champagne,' called Oblonsky.

'And I too,' said Vronsky.

But in spite of Oblonsky and their own mutual desire to be friendly, they had nothing to say to one another and both were aware of it.

'What do you think – he has never met Anna,' Oblonsky said to Vronsky. 'I am most eager to take him to see her. Let's go, Levin!'

'Really?' said Vronsky. 'She will be delighted to see you. ... I would go home with you at once, only I'm worried about Yashvin and I want to stay until he gets through.'

'Oh, is he doing badly?'

'He is losing all the time, and I'm the only one who can keep him in check.'

'What do you say to a game of pyramids? Levin, will you play?

That's fine!' said Oblonsky. 'Place the balls for pyramids, please,' he added to the marker.

'Everything is quite ready,' replied the marker, who had long ago set the balls in a triangle and was knocking the red ball about to pass the time.

'Come along, then!'

After the game Vronsky and Levin joined Gagin at his table, and at Oblonsky's suggestion Levin began betting on aces. Vronsky sat by the table surrounded by friends who were continually coming up to him. Every now and then he went to the 'infernal regions' to see how Yashvin was getting on. Levin was enjoying a pleasant feeling of relief after the mental fatigue of the morning. He was glad that the hostility between himself and Vronsky was at an end, and the sense of peace, decorum and comfort never left him.

When they had finished their game, Oblonsky took Levin's arm.

'Well, shall we go and see Anna? At once, eh? She will be at home. I promised her long ago to bring you. Where were you going this evening?'

'Nowhere in particular. I told Sviazhsky I might go to the Agricultural Society's meeting, but I'll come with you if you like,' said Levin.

'Capital! Let's go. Find out if my carriage is here,' Oblonsky said to one of the footmen.

Levin went to the table, paid the forty roubles he had lost, paid his club bill to an old footman who stood by the door and in some miraculous way seemed to know what it came to, and swinging his arms walked through all the rooms to the way out.

9

'Prince Oblonsky's carriage!' shouted the hall-porter in a voice of thunder.

The carriage drove up and both got in. While they were still in the courtyard Levin remained conscious of the peaceful, well-ordered atmosphere of unimpeachable good form about the club; but as soon as they turned out of the gates into the street, and he felt it jolting over the uneven cobbles, heard the angry shout of a sledge-driver coming towards them, saw in the uncertain light the red signboard of a tavern and a small shop, that sense was dissipated and he began to reflect on his actions and to ask himself whether he was right in going to see

Anna. What would Kitty say? he wondered. Oblonsky, however, gave him no time for meditation and, as though divining his doubts, he scattered them.

'I am so glad you are going to make her acquaintance. You know, Dolly has been wanting this for a long time. Lvov, too, calls on her sometimes. Though she is my sister,' Oblonsky went on, 'I don't hesitate to say that she's a remarkable woman. But you'll see for yourself. Her position is a very trying one, especially now.'

'Why especially now?'

'We are negotiating with her husband about a divorce. He is willing, but there are difficulties in regard to the son, and the matter, which ought to have been settled long ago, has been dragging on for the past three months. As soon as she gets a divorce, she will marry Vronsky. How stupid that old ceremony is – walking round and round singing "Rejoice, Isaiah!" No one believes in it, and it stands in the way of people's happiness!' observed Oblonsky. 'When it is all over, their position will be as regular as yours or mine.'

'What is the difficulty?' asked Levin.

'Oh, it's a long, tedious story! The whole business is such an anomaly in this country. But the point is this – here she's been three months in Moscow, where everyone knows her and him, waiting for the divorce. She goes nowhere and doesn't see a single woman except Dolly, because, as you can understand, she does not want people to call on her out of pity. Even that fool Princess Varvara would not stay with her, because she did not think it proper! Any other woman in Anna's position would not have known what to do with herself, but she ... you will see for yourself how she has arranged her life, how quiet and dignified she is. To the left – that little street opposite the church!' shouted Oblonsky, leaning out of the carriage window. 'Phew! How hot it is!' he exclaimed, in spite of twelve degrees of frost, throwing open his unbuttoned overcoat still more.

'She has a daughter, hasn't she, to take up a good deal of her time and attention?' said Levin.

'I believe you look upon every woman as nothing but a female, *une couveuse*, occupied, if she's occupied at all, with children,' said Oblonsky. 'It seems Anna is bringing her daughter up splendidly, but you don't hear about it. She's busy, in the first place, with her writing. I see you smile ironically, but you are wrong! She is writing a children's book – she doesn't talk about it to anyone but she read it to me and

I showed the manuscript to Vorkuyev ... you know, the publisher ... he writes himself, I fancy. He knows what he is talking about and he says it is a remarkable piece of work. But don't imagine she's the typical authoress – not a bit of it. First and foremost, she's a woman with a heart, but you'll see. Just now she has a little English girl with her, and a whole family she's interested in.'

'Why, does she go in for good works?'

'There – you always look at everything in the worst light! It's not good works, but goodness of heart. They had – I mean, Vronsky had – an English trainer, first-rate in his own line, but a drunkard. He drank himself into delirium tremens and left the family destitute. She saw them, helped them, got more and more interested in them, and now has them all on her hands. And she doesn't do it patronizingly, just helping with money – she herself coaches the boys in Russian for the high school, and the girl she has taken into the house. But you'll see for yourself.'

The carriage drove into the courtyard, and Oblonsky gave a loud ring at the front door, before which a sledge was standing.

Without asking the servant who opened the door whether his mistress was at home, Oblonsky walked into the hall. Levin followed, more and more doubtful whether he was doing right in coming.

He saw, as he looked at himself in the glass, that he was very red in the face, but he was sure he had not drunk too much, and went after Oblonsky up the carpeted stairs. At the top a footman bowed to Oblonsky as to a near friend of the house and informed him that Vorkuyev was with Anna.

'Where are they?'

'In the study, sir.'

Passing through a small dining-room with dark-panelled walls, Oblonsky and Levin crossed a thick carpet to the study, dimly lighted by a single lamp with a huge dark shade. A lamp on the wall with a reflector threw its rays on a full-length portrait of a woman, which arrested Levin's attention. It was the portrait of Anna painted in Italy by Mihailov. While Oblonsky went behind the *treillage*, and the man's voice which had been speaking paused, Levin stood gazing at the portrait, which in the brilliant illumination seemed to step out of its frame, unable to tear himself away. He even forgot where he was and did not hear what was being said: he could not take his eyes off the marvellous portrait. It was not a picture but a living, lovely woman with black curling hair, bare shoulders and arms, and a dreamy half-smile on her soft, downy lips: triumphantly and tenderly she looked at him with eyes that disturbed him. The only thing that showed the figure was not alive was that she was more beautiful than a living woman could be.

'I am delighted,' he suddenly heard a voice near him say, evidently addressing him – the voice of the very woman he had been admiring in the portrait. Anna had come out from behind the *treillage* to greet him, and Levin saw in the dim light of the study the woman of the portrait herself, in a dark dress of different shades of blue, not in the same attitude, nor with the same expression, but with the same perfection of beauty which the artist had caught in the picture. She was less dazzling in reality, but, on the other hand, there was something fresh and seductive in the living woman which was not in the portrait.

10

SHE had risen to meet him, not concealing her pleasure at seeing him. In the quiet ease with which she held out her energetic little hand, introduced him to Vorkuyev, and indicated a pretty, red-haired child sitting at her work, whom she called her ward, Levin recognized and admired the manners of a woman of high society, always self-possessed and natural.

'I am delighted, delighted,' she repeated, and on her lips these simple words assumed a special significance for Levin's ears. 'I have known you and liked you a long while, both from your friendship with Stiva and for your wife's sake ... I knew her for a very short time but she left on me the impression of a flower, an exquisite flower. And to think she will soon be a mother!'

She spoke easily and without haste, now and then looking from Levin to her brother, and Levin sensed that the impression he was making was good. He immediately felt comfortable, and as simple and happy with her as if he had known her from childhood.

'We have taken refuge in Alexei's study for that very purpose,' she said, when Oblonsky asked if he might smoke, 'just so as to be able to smoke.' And with a look of inquiry at Levin – instead of asking whether he smoked – she drew towards her a tortoiseshell cigar-case and took out a cigarette.

'How are you feeling to-day?' her brother asked.

'Fairly well. Nerves, as usual!'

'It's wonderfully good, isn't it?' said Oblonsky, noticing that Levin kept looking at the portrait.

'I never saw anything so perfect.'

'And it's a wonderful likeness, don't you think?' said Vorkuyev.

Levin glanced from the portrait to the original. Anna's face lighted up with a peculiar glow as she felt his eyes on her. Levin flushed and, to cover his confusion, was about to ask whether she had seen Dolly lately, but at that moment Anna spoke.

'Ivan Petrovich and I were just talking about Vashchenkov's latest paintings. Have you seen them?'

'Yes, I have,' replied Levin.

'But I am sorry, I interrupted you … you were about to say? …'

Levin asked if she had seen Dolly lately.

'She was here yesterday – highly indignant at the way they treat Grisha at school. The Latin master, it seems, had been unfair to him.'

'Yes, I saw the pictures. I didn't care for them very much,' said Levin, going back to the subject she had started.

Levin no longer spoke now in the matter-of-fact way in which he had been talking all that morning. Every word in his conversation with her had a special significance. It was pleasant to talk to her, and still more pleasant to listen.

Anna talked not merely naturally and cleverly, but cleverly and without pretence, attaching no value to her own ideas and giving great weight to the ideas of the person she was speaking to.

The conversation turned on the new tendency in art, and they began discussing a French artist who had just finished a set of illustrations to the Bible. Vorkuyev attacked the artist for a realism carried to the point of coarseness. Levin said that the French had pushed conventionality in art farther than anyone, and consequently they welcomed a return to realism. They saw poetry in the fact of not lying.

No clever remark uttered by Levin had ever given him so much satisfaction as this one. Anna's face lighted up at once as she took in its point. She laughed.

'I laugh,' she said, 'as one laughs when one sees a very striking likeness. What you just said exactly hits off French art now, literature too, as well as painting – take Zola, Daudet, for example. But perhaps it is always so: an artist begins by forming his conceptions from imaginary, conventional types, and then, when all possible combinations of the imaginary have been made, he tires of the conventional figures and begins to devise something more natural and realistic.'

'That is perfectly true,' observed Vorkuyev.

'So you were at the club?' she said, turning to her brother.

'Yes, what a woman!' thought Levin, quite oblivious of himself and gazing fixedly at her beautiful, mobile face, which at that moment was all at once completely transformed. Levin did not hear what she was saying to her brother as she leaned over to him, but he was struck by the change in her expression. So lovely and tranquil a moment ago, her face suddenly wore a look of strange curiosity, anger, and pride. But this lasted only an instant. She screwed up her eyes, as if trying to remember something.

'Oh well, but that's of no interest to anyone,' she said, and she turned to the little English girl.

'Please order tea in the drawing-room,' she said in English.

The child got up and went out.

'Well, did she pass her examination?' asked Oblonsky.

'Yes, and very well too. She's a very clever child, and has a sweet disposition.'

'You'll end up by being fonder of her than of your own daughter.'

'How like a man! In love there's no such thing as more or less. I love my daughter with one love, and this girl with another.'

'I was just telling Anna Arkadyevna,' said Vorkuyev, 'that if she were to devote to promoting the education of Russian children a hundredth part of the energy she bestows on this English girl she would be doing a great and useful work.'

'Yes, but say what you will, I can't do it. Count Alexei Kirillich' – (as she pronounced Vronsky's name she glanced with appealing timidity at Levin, who unconsciously responded with a deferential reassuring look) – 'Count Alexei Kirillich used to urge me to take an interest in the village school. I did go a few times. The children were very sweet but I could not become attached to the work. You speak of energy. ... Energy is based on love. And love does not come at will: there's no forcing it. But I took to this girl, though I don't myself know why.'

Again she glanced at Levin. And both her smile and her look told him that she was addressing her words exclusively to him, esteeming his good opinion and at the same time sure in advance that they understood one another.

'I quite understand that,' Levin replied. 'One can't put one's heart into a school or an institution of that kind: I believe that is the reason charitable institutions always give such poor results.'

She was silent a moment, and then smiled.

'Yes, yes,' she agreed. 'I never could. *Je n'ai pas le cœur assez large* to love a whole orphanage full of horrid little girls. *Cela ne m'a jamais réussi.* There are so many women who have made a social position for themselves in that way. And now more than ever,' she said with a mournful, confiding expression, ostensibly addressing her brother but unmistakably intending her words only for Levin, 'now, when I do need occupation of some kind, I cannot do it!' And suddenly frowning (Levin saw that she was frowning at herself for talking about herself) she changed the subject. 'They tell me,' she said to Levin, 'that you are not a public-spirited citizen, and I always defend you to the best of my ability.'

'What do you say in my defence?'

'It depends on the attack. But won't you come and have some tea?' She rose and picked up a book bound in morocco.

'Do let me have it, Anna Arkadyevna,' said Vorkuyev, pointing to the book. 'It is well worth taking up.'

'Oh no, it's all so sketchy.'

'I told him about it,' Oblonsky said to his sister, nodding at Levin.

'You shouldn't have. My writing reminds me of those little baskets and carvings which Liza Merkalov used to sell me from the prisons. She was chairman of the prison section of some society,' she added, turning to Levin. 'And the unfortunate wretches achieved miracles of patience.'

And Levin saw a new trait in this woman whom he already found so extraordinarily attractive. In addition to her intelligence, grace, and beauty, she also possessed sincerity. She had no desire to conceal from him the thorns of her position. As she said that she sighed, and her face suddenly assumed a rigid expression, looking as if it were turned to stone. With that expression on her face she was more beautiful than ever; but it was a novel one, quite unlike any of the expressions that radiated and created happiness, which the artist had caught in the portrait. Levin glanced at her portrait again, then back at her, as she took her brother's arm and walked with him through the lofty doors, and a feeling of tenderness and pity came over him, which surprised him.

She asked Levin and Vorkuyev to go into the drawing-room, while she stayed behind to have a few words with her brother. 'About the divorce, about Vronsky, and what he's doing at the club, about me?' Levin wondered; and he was so full of speculations as to the subject of their conversation that he scarcely heard what Vorkuyev was telling him about the merits of the children's story Anna had written.

Over tea they continued the same sort of pleasant interesting talk. They were never at a loss for a topic – on the contrary, each of them felt there was not enough time to say all he wanted to, yet gladly held back to let the other talk. And all that was said, not only by her but by Vorkuyev and Oblonsky, too, was given a special significance, so it seemed to Levin, owing to her attention and the observations she made.

While he followed their interesting conversation Levin was all the time admiring her – her beauty, her intelligence, her cultivated mind, together with her directness and sincerity. He listened and joined in, and all the while he was thinking of her, of her inner life, trying to divine her feelings. And he, who had hitherto judged her so severely, now by some strange chain of reasoning thought only how to exonerate her. At the same time he was sorry for her, and began to fear Vronsky did not fully understand her. Towards eleven, when Oblonsky got up to go (Vorkuyev had left earlier), it seemed to Levin that he had only just come. He rose regretfully.

'Good-bye,' she said, holding his hand and glancing into his face with a look that drew him to her. 'I am so glad *que la glace est rompue*.'

She let go his hand, and screwed up her eyes.

'Tell your wife that I have the same affection for her as before, and that if she cannot forgive me my position, then I hope she may never forgive me; for to forgive, she would have to go through what I have gone through, and may God spare her that!'

'I will tell her by all means ...' said Levin, blushing.

11

'WHAT a wonderful, sweet, pathetic woman!' he was thinking, as he stepped out into the frosty air with Oblonsky.

'Well, what did I tell you?' said Oblonsky, who saw that Levin was completely won over.

'Yes,' answered Levin thoughtfully. 'She is a remarkable woman! It is not just that she is clever – she has such a wonderfully warm heart. I feel dreadfully sorry for her.'

'Please God, everything will soon be settled now. Well, another time don't judge too hastily,' said Oblonsky, opening the carriage door. 'Good-bye! We don't go the same way.'

Still thinking of Anna, of all the talk – simple in the extreme – they had exchanged, and recalling the minutest changes in her expression, entering more and more into her position and feeling sorrier and sorrier for her, Levin reached home.

At home Kuzma informed him that Katerina Alexandrovna was all right, and that her sisters had only just left. He handed him two letters, which Levin read there and then, in the hall, so as not to have his attention taken up by them later on. One was from his bailiff, Sokolov, telling him that it was impossible to sell the wheat just then, as the highest bid he could get was only five and a half roubles a measure, and that there was no other way of raising money. The other letter was from his sister, who reproached him for not having settled her business yet.

'Well, we must sell at five and a half if we can't get more,' Levin decided the first question, which had always before seemed such a weighty one, with the greatest of ease, on the spot. 'It's extraordinary how one's time gets taken up here,' he reflected, thinking of the second letter. He felt a little conscience-stricken that he had not yet done what his sister had asked him. 'Here's another day gone, and I haven't been to the court, but I really had not a moment to spare.' And, resolving that he would attend to the matter in the morning without fail, he proceeded to his wife's room. On the way he briefly ran over in his mind the events of the day. There had been nothing except conversations – conversations to which he had listened or in which he had taken part. All of them had been concerned with matters that would never have held his attention had he been alone in the country, but here they seemed of great interest. They had all been good – there were only two things he was not altogether comfortable about. One was his remark about the pike, and the other – there was something not quite right in his feeling of tender sympathy for Anna.

Levin found his wife sad and depressed. The three sisters had enjoyed their dinner together but afterwards they had waited and wait-

734

ed for him. The evening had seemed long, the other two had departed, and Kitty had been left alone.

'Well, and what have you been doing?' she asked, looking straight into his eyes, which were suspiciously bright. But that she might not prevent his telling her everything, she masked her scrutiny and with an encouraging smile listened to his account of how he had spent the evening.

'I was really very glad to meet Vronsky. I felt quite at ease and natural with him. Of course, I shall avoid him as much as I can, but there won't be the constraint ...' he said, and remembering that by way of trying to 'avoid him' he had immediately gone to call on Anna, he blushed. 'We talk about the peasants drinking, but I really don't know who drinks most – the common people or our own class. The peasants drink at holiday times but ...'

But Kitty was not interested in a dissertation on the drinking habits of the peasants. She had noticed his blush and wanted to know the reason for it.

'Well, and where did you go after that?'

'Stiva absolutely begged me to go and see Anna Arkadyevna.'

Saying this, Levin blushed still more, and his doubts as to whether he had done right in going to call on Anna were finally solved. He knew now that he ought not to have gone.

Kitty's eyes opened wide and flashed at the mention of Anna, but she made an effort to conceal her agitation.

'Oh!' was all she said; and Levin was taken in.

'I'm sure you won't be angry with me for going. Stiva implored me to, and Dolly wished it,' Levin went on.

'Oh no!' she said, but he saw in her eyes a constraint that boded him no good.

'She is very charming, and a nice woman – very, very much to be pitied,' he said, telling her about Anna and her occupations and the message she had sent.

'Yes, of course she is much to be pitied,' Kitty remarked when he had finished. 'Who were your letters from?'

He told her, and misled by her quiet manner went to undress.

Coming back, he found Kitty still sitting in the same arm-chair. When he went up to her, she looked at him and burst into sobs.

'What is it? What is the matter?' he asked, well aware what the matter was.

'You have fallen in love with that hateful woman! She has bewitched you! I saw it in your eyes. Yes, yes! What will be the end of
it? You were drinking and drinking at the club, and gambling, and
then you went ... to her, of all people! No, we must go away ... I
shall go away to-morrow.'

It was long before Levin could pacify his wife. At last he succeeded
in calming her only by acknowledging that the wine he had drunk,
together with his sense of pity, had been too much for him and he had
succumbed to Anna's artful spell; and by promising that in future he
would avoid her. He was sincerest of all when he confessed that living
for so long in Moscow with nothing to do but eat, drink, and gossip
was beginning to demoralize him. They talked till three o'clock in the
morning. Only by three o'clock were they sufficiently reconciled to
be able to go to sleep.

12

AFTER taking leave of her guests, Anna did not sit down but began
pacing the room. Though she had unconsciously been doing her utmost the whole evening to arouse in Levin a feeling of love – as she
had lately fallen into the habit of doing with all the young men she
met – and though she knew she had succeeded in so far as was possible
in one evening with an honourable married man, and though she had
liked him very much (in spite of the striking difference, from the
masculine point of view, between Vronsky and Levin, as a woman she
saw the trait they had in common which had caused Kitty to fall in
love with them both), yet no sooner was he gone than she ceased to
think of him.

One thought, and one only, pursued her in different forms and refused to be shaken off. 'Why, if I have so much effect on others – on
this married man who loves his wife – why is it *he* is so cold and indifferent? No, not cold exactly – I am sure he loves me – but something has come between us. Why does he stay away the whole evening? He sent word by Stiva that he could not leave Yashvin and had to
keep an eye on him while he played. Is Yashvin a child? But admitting
that it's the truth – he never tells lies – there must be something else
behind it. He is glad of an opportunity to show me that he has other
obligations. I know he has, and I submit to it. But why does he have
to keep proving it to me? He wants me to understand that his love

736

for me must not interfere with his freedom. But I don't need to be shown anything: I need love. He ought to realize how wretched my life is here in Moscow – if it can be called life. I don't live – waiting for a solution that never comes is not living. Still no answer! And Stiva says he cannot go and see Alexei Alexandrovich. And I can't write again. I can't do anything, begin anything, change anything. I just have to hold myself in and wait, inventing ways of passing the time – like this English family, my writing, reading – but it's all only to bemuse myself, like taking morphine. He ought to have some sympathy,' she said to herself, feeling tears of self-pity well into her eyes.

She heard Vronsky's impetuous ring at the front door and hastily dried her eyes. She not only wiped away her tears but sat down by the lamp and opened a book, trying to look calm. She must let him see that she was displeased that he had not come home as he had promised – displeased, that should be all: she would on no account show him her misery, still less her self-pity. She might feel sorry for herself, but he must not pity her. She did not want strife, she blamed him for wanting to quarrel, but against her will she assumed a hostile attitude.

'Well, you've not been lonely?' he asked cheerfully, walking briskly up to her. 'Really, gambling is a terrible passion!'

'Oh no, I've long schooled myself against feeling lonely. Stiva and Levin were here.'

'Yes, they told me they were coming to see you. And how did you like Levin?' he asked, sitting down beside her.

'Very much. They only left a short while ago. How did Yashvin get on?'

'He was in luck at first – won seventeen thousand. I very nearly got him to come away then, but he went back, and now he's losing.'

'Then what was the good of your staying?' she asked, suddenly lifting her eyes to him. The expression on her face was cold and hostile. 'You told Stiva you were staying on to bring Yashvin away. And now you abandon him!'

A similar expression of cold readiness for the conflict appeared on his face.

'In the first place, I did not give him any message for you; and secondly, I am not accustomed to tell lies. But the chief point is, I stayed because I wanted to,' he replied, frowning. 'Anna, Anna, why do you do this?' he said after a moment's silence, bending over towards her and putting his hand out, hoping she would lay hers in it.

She was glad of this tender appeal. But some strange spirit of evil held her back, as if the rules of warfare would not permit her to surrender.

'Of course you wanted to stay, and you stayed! You always do what you want to. But why tell me so? Why?' she said, getting more and more excited. 'Does anyone dispute your rights? But you want to be in the right, so in the right you shall be!'

His hand closed, he drew back, and his face became still more set.

'For you it's a matter of obstinacy,' she said, watching him intently and suddenly finding the right word for that look on his face that so exasperated her. 'Sheer obstinacy! For you, it's a question of whether you keep the upper hand, while for me ...' Again the feeling of self-pity overcame her and she almost burst into tears. 'If you only knew what it means for me! When I feel as I do now, that you are hostile – yes, hostile to me – if you only knew what that means for me! If you knew how near disaster I am at such moments, how afraid I am – afraid of myself!' And she turned away to hide her sobs.

'But what is this all about?' he said, alarmed by her expression of despair, and again bending over her he took her hand and kissed it. 'What have I done? Do I seek amusement outside our home? Don't I avoid the society of other women?'

'I should hope so!' she said.

'Well then, tell me what I should do to give you peace of mind? I am ready to do anything to make you happy,' he went on, touched by her despair. 'What wouldn't I do to spare you distress of any sort, such as you are suffering now! Anna!'

'It's nothing, it's nothing!' she said. 'I don't know what makes me like this – whether it's this lonely life, or my nerves. ... But let us say no more about it. What about the race? You haven't told me,' she inquired, trying to conceal her triumph at the victory, which had been hers, after all.

He asked for supper, and began telling her about the races; but his voice and his eyes, which grew colder and colder, showed her that he did not forgive her her victory, and that the obstinacy against which she had fought had settled on him again. He was colder to her than before, as if he repented his surrender. And she, recalling the words which had given her the victory – 'how near disaster I am, how afraid of myself' – realized that this weapon was a dangerous one and must not be used a second time. She felt that side by side with the love that bound them there had grown up some evil spirit of discord, which she could not exorcise from his heart, and still less from her own.

13

THERE are no conditions of life to which a man cannot get accustomed, especially if he sees them accepted by everyone about him. Levin would hardly have believed it possible three months ago that he could have gone quietly to sleep in the circumstances in which he found himself. Here he was leading a stupid, aimless life – and, furthermore, one that was beyond his means. How could he fall quietly asleep after wine-bibbing at the club (was there any other name for it?), after his unsuitable show of friendship to a man with whom his wife had once been in love, and his still more unsuitable call upon someone who could only be called a fallen woman, after becoming fascinated by that woman and grieving his wife? But what with weariness, a late night, and the wine he had drunk, he slept soundly and peacefully.

At five in the morning he was awakened by the creak of a door opening. He sat up quickly and looked round. Kitty was not in bed beside him. But there was a light moving behind the screen, and he heard her steps.

'What is it? ... What is it?' he murmured, half asleep. 'Kitty, what is it?'

'Nothing,' she said, coming, candle in hand, from behind the screen. 'I didn't feel well,' she added, smiling a peculiarly sweet and meaning smile.

'What? Has it begun? Has it begun?' he asked in a frightened voice. 'We must send for ...' and he hurriedly reached for his clothes.

'No, no,' she said, smiling and putting a hand out to stop him. 'I'm sure it's nothing. I just felt a little unwell, that's all. But I am all right again now.'

And getting into bed, she blew out the candle, lay down and was still. Though her quietness, as if she were holding her breath, and especially the peculiar tenderness and excitement with which, coming out from behind the screen, she had said, 'It's nothing,' seemed to him suspicious, he was so drowsy that he at once fell asleep again. Only afterwards he remembered that bated breath and realized what must have been taking place in her dear, sweet soul while she lay motionless by his side, awaiting the greatest event in a woman's life. At seven o'clock he was awakened by the touch of her hand on his shoulder and a gentle whisper. She was torn between regret at waking him and her desire to speak to him.

'Kostya, don't be frightened. It's all right ... but I fancy we had better send for Lizaveta Petrovna.'

She had lighted the candle again and was sitting up in bed, holding some knitting she had been busy with during the last few days.

'Please, you mustn't be frightened. It's all right. I am not a bit afraid,' she said, seeing the look of alarm on his face. She pressed his hand to her bosom and then to her lips.

He jumped out of bed, hardly aware of himself, his eyes fixed on her as he hurried into his dressing-gown. Then he stood still, gazing at her. He must go, yet he could not tear himself away, could not take his eyes off her. He thought he loved her face, knew her every expression, but never had he seen it like this. How he hated himself now when he remembered the distress he had caused her last night. Her flushed face, with the soft little curls escaping from under her nightcap, was radiant with joy and courage.

Little as there was of affectation and conventionality in Kitty's nature, yet Levin was overcome by what was revealed now that every veil was stripped from her and her very soul shone out in her eyes. And in this simplicity, this nakedness of soul, he saw more clearly than ever the woman he loved. She smiled up at him; but suddenly her brow contracted and she lifted her head and going quickly up to him clutched his hand and clung to him, her hot breath burning him. She was in pain and was, as it were, complaining to him of her suffering. For a moment, from force of habit, he felt guilty. But the tenderness in her eyes told him that she was far from reproaching him, that she loved him for her sufferings. 'If not I, then who is to blame?' he thought, involuntarily seeking a scapegoat to punish. But there was no scapegoat. She suffered, complained, triumphed, and rejoiced in her suffering, welcoming it. Something sublime was being accomplished in her soul, but what it was he could not understand. It was beyond his comprehension.

'I have sent to Mama. Now go quickly and fetch Lizaveta Petrovna ... Kostya! ... No, it's nothing. It's passed.'

She moved away from him and rang the bell.

'You go along now. Pasha's coming. I am all right.'

And to Levin's amazement he saw her take up the knitting she had fetched in the night, and begin working on it again.

As Levin was going out of one door he heard the maid enter at the other. He stood at the door and heard Kitty give exact directions for arranging the room, and even start to help her move the bed.

He dressed, and while they were putting in the horses (it was impossible to hire anything at that early hour), he ran back to the bedroom once more, not on tiptoe, it seemed to him, but on wings. Two maids were busy moving something in the bedroom. Kitty was walking up and down with her knitting, the needles flying, and giving orders.

'I'm just off for the doctor. They've already sent for Lizaveta Petrovna but I will call there myself too. Is there anything you want? Oh yes – what about Dolly?'

She looked at him, obviously not hearing what he was saying.

'Yes, yes, all right,' she said quickly, frowning and motioning him away with her hand.

He was already on his way through the drawing-room when suddenly a pitiful moan, that lasted only a second, reached him from the bedroom. He stopped, and for a moment did not understand.

'Yes, it was she,' he said to himself, and clasping his head in his hands he ran downstairs.

'Lord have mercy on us! Pardon us and help us!' he repeated the words that for some reason suddenly sprang to his lips. And he, the unbeliever, went on repeating the words not with his lips only. At that minute neither his doubts nor the fact that his reason stood in the way of faith, as he well knew, hindered him from appealing to God. All that fell away from his soul like dust. To whom was he to turn if not to Him who held in His hands himself, his soul, and his love?

The carriage was not ready yet. Tense in body and mind, anxious not to delay with what he had to do, he started off on foot, telling Kuzma to catch him up.

At the corner of the street he met a night cabman driving hurriedly. In the little sledge sat Lizaveta Petrovna in a velvet cloak with a shawl over her head. 'Thank God! Thank God!' he murmured, overjoyed to recognize her pale little face which wore a particularly serious, even austere expression. Telling the driver not to stop, he ran along beside her.

'Two hours ago, you say? Not more?' she inquired. 'You will find the doctor in but don't hurry him. And get some laudanum at the chemist's.'

'You think it will be all right? Lord have mercy on us and help us!' Levin said, seeing his own horse turn out of the gate. Jumping into the sledge beside Kuzma, he told him to drive to the doctor's.

14

THE doctor was not yet up and his servant said that he had retired late to bed and given orders that he was not to be called. 'But he will be up soon.' The man was cleaning lamp-glasses and appeared quite absorbed in his work. This concentration on lamp-glasses and indifference to what was taking place in Levin at first astonished him, but upon consideration he realized that no one knew or was obliged to know his feelings, and that it was all the more necessary to act calmly, sensibly, and firmly in order to break through this wall of indifference and attain his aim. 'I must not be in a hurry or forget anything,' Levin said to himself, feeling his energy and attention rising more and more to the occasion.

When he learned that the doctor was not up yet, Levin cast about in his mind for the best thing to do and decided on the following: Kuzma should go with a note to another doctor, while he himself went to the chemist's for the laudanum. Should the doctor still be asleep when he returned, he would either bribe the footman or if need be force his way in and wake the doctor at all costs.

At the chemist's a lanky young dispenser was sealing up a packet of powders for a coachman who stood waiting, with the same indifference to Levin's affairs as the latter had noticed in the doctor's footman with his lamp-glasses, and refused to let him have laudanum. Controlling himself with an effort, Levin explained why the laudanum was needed, giving the names of the doctor and the midwife, to try to persuade the dispenser. Whereupon the chemist's assistant called out in German to someone, asking if he should supply the drug, and receiving an affirmative reply from behind the partition reached down a small phial and a funnel, slowly filled it from a larger bottle, stuck on a label, sealed it, in spite of all Levin's entreaties to the contrary, and was about to wrap it up too. This was more than Levin could stand: he firmly snatched the phial from the man's hands and rushed out at the big glass doors. The doctor was still not up, and the footman, now busy putting down a rug, refused to wake him. Levin slowly and deliberately took a ten-rouble note out of his pocket-book and, careful to speak distinctly, though losing no time, handed it to the man, explaining that the doctor (what a great and important personage he seemed to Levin now, this doctor, who had appeared of so little consequence in his eyes before!) had promised to come at any time, and that he would certainly not be angry and must therefore be called at once.

The footman consented, and went upstairs, taking Levin into the waiting-room.

Levin could hear the doctor behind the door, coughing, moving about, washing, and saying something. Three minutes passed: to Levin it seemed like an hour or more. He could wait no longer.

'Peter Dmitrich! Peter Dmitrich!' he cried imploringly through the open door. 'Forgive me for heaven's sake. ... See me as you are. It's over two hours ...'

'Coming, coming!' replied the doctor, and Levin was astounded to hear a smile in his voice.

'For one instant ...'

'Coming!'

Two more minutes passed while the doctor was putting on his boots, and another two while he put on his coat and brushed his hair.

'Peter Dmitrich!' Levin was beginning again in a piteous voice just as the doctor came in dressed and ready. 'These people have no conscience,' thought Levin. 'They can brush their hair while we lie dying!'

'Good morning!' said the doctor, holding out his hand, his composure seeming to mock Levin. 'There's no hurry. How is she?'

Trying to be as accurate as possible, Levin began a long account of his wife's condition, giving every unnecessary detail and interrupting himself continually to urge the doctor to come with him at once.

'Don't be in such a hurry. You're new at this, you see. I don't suppose I shall be needed, but I promised, so if you like I'll come. But there's no hurry. Please sit down. Won't you have a cup of coffee?'

Levin stared with eyes that asked if he was laughing at him. But the doctor had no idea of making fun of him.

743

'I know, I know,' he said with a smile. 'I'm a married man myself. We husbands cut a sorry figure at such times. I have one patient whose husband always takes refuge in the stables on such occasions.'

'But what do you think, Peter Dmitrich? Do you think everything will be all right?'

'I have every reason to believe so.'

'Then you'll come at once?' said Levin, with a spiteful look at the servant bringing in coffee.

'Within the hour.'

'For heaven's sake ...'

'Well, give me time to drink my coffee.'

The doctor started on his coffee. Both were silent.

'It seems the Turks are decidedly getting the worst of it. Did you read yesterday's despatch?' said the doctor, munching a roll.

'No, I can't stand this!' said Levin, jumping up. 'You'll be with us in a quarter of an hour, then?'

'Half an hour.'

'On your honour?'

Levin got home just as the princess arrived, and they went up to the bedroom door together. The princess had tears in her eyes and her hands shook. When she saw Levin, she fell on his neck and began to cry.

'Well, Lizaveta Petrovna, my dear?' she queried, seizing the midwife's hand as the latter came out to meet them with a beaming but preoccupied face.

'Everything is going on all right,' she said. 'But I wish you would persuade her to lie down. It would be easier for her.'

Ever since Levin had waked that morning and understood the situation, he had been bracing himself to endure what was before him, without reflection, without anticipation, tightly suppressing his own thoughts and feelings, resolved not to upset his wife but on the contrary to reassure her and keep up her courage. Without allowing himself to think of what was happening and about to happen, judging by inquiries he had made as to the usual duration of these ordeals, he had steeled himself to endure and keep his heart under control for five hours or so, and it had seemed to him he could do this. But when he came back from the doctor's and again saw Kitty suffering, he fell to repeating more and more frequently, 'Lord have mercy on us, and succour us!', sighing and flinging his head back. He was assailed by

744

terror lest he should not be able to bear the strain and should burst out crying or run away, such agony was it for him. And only one hour had passed.

But after that hour another passed, a second, a third, and the full five hours he had fixed upon as the longest possible term of endurance, and still the situation was unchanged; and he went on enduring because there was nothing else to do but endure, every moment feeling that he had reached the utmost limits of endurance and that his heart would burst with compassion and pain.

But the minutes went by, and the hours, and then more hours, and his misery and terror and strain grew tenser.

All the ordinary conditions of life without which one can form no conception of anything had ceased to exist for Levin. He lost all sense of time. Minutes – those minutes when she called him to her side and he held her moist little fingers now clutching his convulsively, now pushing him away – seemed like hours; and then again hours seemed no more than minutes. He was surprised when Lizaveta Petrovna asked him to light a candle behind the partition, and he found that it was five o'clock in the afternoon. Had he been told it was ten in the morning he would have been equally surprised. He had just as little idea of where he had been all that time. He saw her burning face, sometimes bewildered and full of pain, sometimes smiling and trying to comfort him. He saw the old princess, flushed and overwrought, her grey hair out of curl, biting her lips to keep back her tears. He saw Dolly, and the doctor smoking fat cigarettes, and the calm, resolute, reassuring face of the midwife, and the old prince pacing up and down the ballroom and frowning. But how they came and went, where they were, he did not know. The princess was one moment in the bedroom with the doctor, and the next in the study, where a table laid for a meal suddenly appeared; then it was not the princess, but Dolly. Afterwards Levin remembered that he had been sent somewhere. Once he was asked to move a table and a couch. He did it with alacrity, imagining that it was something for Kitty, and only later discovered that he had been preparing his own bed for the night. Then he was sent to the study to ask the doctor something. The doctor had answered, and then begun talking about the scenes in the Duma. After that he had been sent to fetch an icon with silver-gilt mounts from the princess's bedroom, and he and the princess's old lady's maid had climbed on to a small cabinet to reach it down, and he had broken the little lamp that burned before it, and the old servant had tried to console him about his wife and the lamp. He carried the icon back with him and put it at Kitty's head, carefully tucking it in behind the pillows. But where, at what hour, and why all this happened he did not know. Nor did he understand why the princess took his hand and, looking compassionately at him, entreated him not to worry; nor why Dolly tried to persuade him to eat something and led him out of the room; nor why even the doctor looked at him gravely and with commiseration, offering him some drops.

He only knew and felt that what was happening was similar to what had happened a year ago at the deathbed in a provincial hotel of his brother Nikolai. Only that had been sorrow, and this was joy. But that sorrow and this joy were equally beyond the usual plane of existence: they were like openings through which something sublime became visible. And what was being accomplished now, as in that other moment, was accomplished harshly, painfully; and in contemplation of this sublime something the soul soared to heights it had never attained before, while reason lagged behind, unable to keep up.

'Lord have mercy on us, and succour us!' he repeated incessantly, appealing to God, in spite of his long and, as it seemed, complete alienation from religion, just as trustfully and simply as he had done in the days of his childhood and early youth.

All this time two conflicting moods swayed him. One mood when he was away from her, with the doctor, who smoked one fat cigarette after another, extinguishing them against the rim of the overflowing ash-tray, or with Dolly and the old prince, where there was talk about dinner, about politics, about Maria Petrovna's illness, and so on, and where Levin suddenly forgot for a minute what was happening and felt as if he were waking from a dream; the other was at her bedside, by her pillow, where his heart was ready to burst with pity, and yet did not burst, and he prayed without pause to God. And every time a scream from the bedroom roused him from a moment of oblivion he would fall into the same strange delusion that had possessed him right at the beginning: every time he heard a cry he would start up and run to justify himself, and remember on the way that he was not to blame and that he was only anxious to protect and help her. But when he looked at her he saw once more that he could not help, and was filled with terror and repeated his prayer: 'Lord have mercy on us and help us!' And as time went on both these moods grew more intense:

out of her presence he seemed to forget her and become calmer, so that when he returned the consciousness of her suffering and his own helplessness hurt him the more. He would jump up to run away somewhere and would run to her room.

Sometimes, when she called him again and again, he felt like reproaching her; but seeing her patient smile and hearing her say, 'I am wearing you out,' he wanted to throw the blame on God. But thinking of God at once brought him back to his prayer for forgiveness and mercy.

15

HE did not know whether it was late or early. The candles had all burned low. Dolly had just entered the study and suggested that the doctor should lie down. Levin sat listening to the doctor's stories about some quack who went in for hypnotic healing, and stared at the ash of his cigarette. It was an interval of rest and oblivion. He had quite forgotten what was going on. He heard the doctor's tale and took it in. Suddenly an unearthly scream rang through the house. It was so awful that Levin did not even jump up but holding his breath gazed in petrified inquiry at the doctor. The doctor put his head on one side, listened and smiled approvingly. Everything was so far from the ordinary that nothing any longer surprised Levin. 'It must be all right,' he thought, and sat where he was. But who was it screamed like that? He jumped up and ran on tiptoe to the bedroom, rushing past the midwife and the princess to take up his post at the head of the bed. The screaming had ceased but there was a change: what it was he could not see or understand, and had no wish to see or understand. But he read it in the midwife's face. Lizaveta Petrovna, stern and pale, and as resolute as before though her jaw trembled a little, had her eyes fixed intently on Kitty. Kitty's flushed, agonized face, a lock of hair clinging to her clammy forehead, was turned to him, seeking his eyes. Her raised hands asked for his. Clutching his cold hands in her perspiring ones, she pressed them to her face.

'Don't go, don't go! I'm not afraid, I'm not afraid!' she said rapidly. 'Mama, take off my ear-rings, they're in the way. You're not frightened? Soon, Lizaveta Petrovna, soon now ...'

She spoke fast, and tried to smile, but suddenly her face distorted with pain and she pushed him away.

'Oh, this is terrible! I am dying ... I shall die! Go away, go away!' she cried, and the same unearthly shriek echoed through the house.

Levin clasped his head in his hands and ran out of the room.

'It's nothing, it's nothing, everything is going all right!' Dolly called after him.

But no matter what they said, he knew now that all was over. Leaning his head against the doorpost, he stood in the next room and heard someone shrieking and moaning in a way he had never heard before, and he knew that these sounds came from what had once been Kitty. He had long ceased wishing for the child, and now he hated it. He no longer even prayed for her life – all he longed for was an end of this terrible suffering.

'Doctor, what is it? What does it mean? Oh, my God!' he said, seizing the doctor's hand as the latter entered the room.

'It will soon be over now,' said the doctor. And the doctor's face was so grave as he said it that Levin thought he meant that it would soon be over with Kitty and she was dying.

Beside himself, he rushed into the bedroom again. The first thing he saw was the midwife's face looking more frowning and stern than ever. Kitty's face was not there. In its place was something fearful – fearful in its strained distortion and the sounds that issued from it. He let his head drop on to the wooden rail of the bed, feeling that his heart was breaking. The terrible screams followed each other quickly until they seemed to reach the utmost limit of horror, when they suddenly ceased. Levin could not believe his ears, but there was no doubt about it: the screaming had ceased, and he heard a soft stir, a bustle, and the sound of hurried breathing, and her voice, faltering, vibrant, tender, and blissful as she whispered, 'It's over!'

He lifted his head. With her arms feebly stretched out on the counterpane, she lay gazing silently at him, looking extraordinarily lovely and serene, trying unsuccessfully to smile.

And suddenly Levin felt himself transported in a flash from the mysterious, awful, far-away world in which he had been living for the last twenty-two hours back to his old everyday world, glorified now with such luminous happiness that he could not bear it. The taut strings snapped, and the sobs and tears of joy which he had never foreseen rose within him with such force that they shook his whole body and for a long time prevented him from speaking.

Falling on his knees by the bed, he held his wife's hand to his lips and kissed it, and the hand, with a weak pressure of the fingers, responded to his kiss. Meanwhile, at the foot of the bed, in Lizaveta Petrovna's skilful hands flickered the life of a human being, like the small uncertain flame of a night-light – a human being who had not existed a moment ago but who, with the same rights and importance to itself as the rest of humanity, would live and create others in its own image.

'Alive, alive! And a boy too! Set your mind at rest!' Levin heard the midwife say as she slapped the baby's back with a shaking hand.

'Mama, is it true?' asked Kitty.

The princess's only reply was a sob.

And in the silence there came, in unmistakable answer to the mother's question, a voice quite unlike the subdued voices that had been speaking in the room: a bold, insistent, self-assertive cry of the new human being who had so incomprehensibly appeared from some unknown realm.

Had Levin been told but a short time earlier that Kitty was dead, and that he had died with her, and that their children were angels in heaven, and that God was present before them – he would have been surprised at nothing. But now that he had returned to the world of reality, it took a prodigious effort to realize that she was alive and well, and that the little creature yelling so desperately was his son. Kitty was alive, her agony was over. And he was unutterably happy. That he could understand, and it filled him with joy. But the baby? Whence, wherefore had it come, and who was it? He could not understand at all, nor accustom himself to the idea. It seemed to him too much, a superabundance, to which he was unable to get used for a long time.

16

TOWARDS ten o'clock the old prince, Koznyshev, and Oblonsky were sitting at Levin's. They inquired about the young mother and then began discussing other matters. Levin listened to them, involuntarily recalling the events of the past twenty-four hours up to that morning and remembering himself as he had been the previous day. A hundred years seemed to have elapsed since then. He felt as though he were on some unattainable height, from which he painstakingly lowered himself every now and then, so as not to hurt the feelings of the people he was talking to. He talked, but never ceased thinking of his wife, of how she was at that moment, and of his son – in whose existence he was schooling himself to believe. The significance of a woman's life which had begun to dawn on him after his marriage now rose so high in his estimation that his imagination could not grasp it. As he listened to the others talking of yesterday's dinner at the club he wondered what was happening with her now. Is she asleep? How is she? What is she thinking about? Is he crying, our son Dmitri? And in the middle of the conversation, in the middle of a sentence, he jumped up and went out of the room.

'Find out and let me know if I can see her,' said the old prince.

'All right,' answered Levin, and without stopping to look round he went to her room.

She was not asleep but talking softly with her mother, planning the christening.

Made tidy, her hair brushed, a neat little cap trimmed with blue on her head, her arms out on the counterpane, she was lying on her back, and when she saw him she drew him to her with a look. Her look, already bright, grew brighter still as he approached. There was the same change in her face from earthly to unearthly that is seen on the faces of the dead; but there it means farewell, with Kitty it was a welcome to new life. Agitation gripped his heart again, as it had done at the moment of the child's birth. She took his hand and asked him if he had slept. He could not answer and turned away, aware of his own weakness.

'I have had a nap, Kostya!' she said. 'And now I feel so nice and comfortable.'

She looked at him but suddenly her expression changed.

'Let me have him,' she said, hearing the baby give a wail. 'Let me have him, Lizaveta Petrovna. I want to show him to his papa.'

'To be sure, we'll let papa have a look,' said the midwife, lifting up a strange, red, squirmy little object. 'But wait, we must make him tidy first,' and Lizaveta Petrovna deposited the wriggly little red object on the bed and began unswaddling and swaddling the baby, supporting its tiny body with one finger as she applied the powder-puff.

Gazing at this pitiful little bit of humanity, Levin searched his soul in vain for some trace of paternal feeling. He could feel nothing but aversion. But when it was undressed and he caught a glimpse of wee, wee little tomato-coloured hands and feet with fingers and toes – the big one distinguishable from the others even – and saw Lizaveta

Petrovna bending the sticking-up little arms as if they were soft springs and encasing them in linen garments, such pity for the little creature overwhelmed him, and such fear lest she should hurt it, that he put out a hand to restrain her.

Lizaveta Petrovna laughed.

'Never fear, never fear!'

When the baby had been put to rights and transformed into a firm little doll, Lizaveta Petrovna tossed him up as though proud of her work, and drew back that Levin might see his son in all his glory.

Kitty watched sideways, never taking her eyes off the baby.

'Give him to me, give him to me!' she said, and even made to raise herself in bed.

'What are you thinking of, Katerina Petrovna; you mustn't do that! Wait a moment, you shall have him. But we must show papa what a fine fellow we are!'

And on one hand (the other merely supporting the wobbling little head) Lizaveta Petrovna held out to Levin the strange, wriggling red creature that tried to hide its face in its swaddling clothes. But there was a nose, two squinting eyes, and sucking lips.

'A beautiful baby!' said Lizaveta Petrovna.

Levin sighed bitterly. This beautiful baby only inspired him with a feeling of disgust and pity, which was not in the least what he had anticipated.

He turned away while Lizaveta Petrovna laid the child to the unaccustomed breast.

A sudden laugh made him lift his head. It was Kitty laughing. The baby had taken the breast.

'Come, that's enough, that's enough!' said Lizaveta Petrovna, but Kitty would not part with her son, who fell asleep in her arms.

'Look at him now,' said Kitty, turning the baby so that Levin could see it. The little face, like that of an old man, screwed itself up still more and the baby sneezed.

Smiling, hardly able to keep back his tears, Levin kissed his wife and left the darkened room.

His feelings for this little creature were not at all what he had expected. There was not an atom of pride or joy in them; on the contrary, he was oppressed by a new sense of apprehension – the consciousness of another vulnerable region. And this consciousness was so painful at first, the apprehension lest that helpless being should suffer was so acute, that it drowned the strange thrill of unreasoning joy and even pride which he had felt when the infant sneezed.

17

OBLONSKY'S affairs were in a bad way.

Two of the three instalments of the money for the forest had already been spent down to the last penny, and, by allowing a discount of ten per cent, he had obtained from the merchant almost the whole of the last instalment. But the dealer would not advance any more, especially as Dolly that winter had for the first time in her life asserted her rights to her own property and declined to endorse the contract with a receipt for the final payment. All Oblonsky's salary went on household expenses and small pressing bills, so there was no money whatever.

This was disagreeable and awkward, and Oblonsky felt it should not be allowed to continue. The whole trouble, in his view, was that his salary was too low. The post he filled had certainly been a very good one five years ago, but things had changed since then. There was Petrov, the bank director, getting twelve thousand a year; Sventitsky, a company director, with seventeen thousand; and Mitin, who had founded a bank, had an income of fifty thousand. 'I must have been asleep and got overlooked,' thought Oblonsky. And he began pricking up his ears and casting around, and towards the end of the winter he heard of a very good post and began an attack on it, first from Moscow through uncles, aunts, and friends, and then in the spring, when matters had matured, he himself went to Petersburg. It was one of those snug, lucrative appointments, far more numerous now than they used to be, carrying salaries of from one thousand to fifty thousand roubles a year – the post of secretary to the committee of the consolidated agency of credit balance of the southern railways, and of certain banking houses. Like all such posts, this position required such immense energy and such varied qualifications that could hardly be united in one man. And since there was no hope of finding a man combining all these qualifications, it was thought better to put in an honest rather than a dishonest one. And Oblonsky was not merely an honest man – in the ordinary sense of the word – but he was honest with the emphasis attached to the word in Moscow, where an 'honest' politician, an 'honest' writer, an 'honest' paper, an 'honest' institution, an 'honest' tendency means not simply that the man or the institution is not dishonest, but that they are capable on occasion of taking a firm line with the Government. Oblonsky moved in those circles in Moscow, where the word had come into use, was regarded there as an honest man, and so had a better claim than others to the appointment.

The particular post carried a salary of from seven thousand to ten thousand a year, and Oblonsky could hold it without resigning his government office. The power to confer it lay in the hands of two ministers, a certain lady, and two Jews; and though the way had been paved with all of them it was still necessary for Oblonsky to pay a personal visit to Petersburg to see them. Moreover, he had promised his sister Anna to extract a definite answer from Karenin about the divorce. So, after begging fifty roubles from Dolly, he departed for Petersburg.

Sitting in Karenin's study and listening to his report on the causes of the unsatisfactory state of Russian finance, Oblonsky simply waited for him to finish, so as to put in a word about his own business and about Anna.

'Yes, that's very true,' he said, when Karenin took off the pince-nez without which he could not read now and looked inquiringly at his ex-brother-in-law. 'That's very true in particular cases, but still the principle of our age is freedom.'

'Yes, but I lay down another principle which embraces the principle of freedom,' said Karenin, with emphasis on the word 'embraces', and, putting on his pince-nez again, he re-read the appropriate passage.

He turned over the beautifully written, wide-margined manuscript and read the conclusive passage again.

'I am not advocating protection for the benefit of private interests, but for the public weal – for the lower and upper classes alike,' he said, looking at Oblonsky over his pince-nez. 'But *they* cannot grasp that, *they* are concerned with their personal interests, and are carried away by phrases.'

Oblonsky knew that when Karenin began to talk of what *they* were doing and thinking – *they* being the persons who opposed his projects and were the cause of all the evil in Russia – the end was in sight, and so he willingly relinquished his argument in favour of the principle of freedom, and fully agreed. Karenin paused, thoughtfully turning over the pages of his manuscript.

'Oh, by the way,' Oblonsky began, 'I wanted to ask you, some time when you see Pomorsky, to drop him a hint that I should be very glad to get that vacant post on the committee of the consolidated agency of credit balance of the southern railways.' Oblonsky was by now so familiar with the title of the post he coveted that he could bring it out rapidly without mistake.

Karenin inquired about the functions of this new committee, and became thoughtful. He was considering whether its activity was at all likely to clash with his own projects. But as the functions of the new institution were of a very complex nature and his own projects covered a very wide field, he felt he could not decide this straight away.

'Of course, I could speak to him,' he said, taking off his pince-nez. 'But why exactly do you want the post?'

'The salary is good, rising to nine thousand, and my means ...'

'Nine thousand!' repeated Karenin, and he frowned. This high salary made him reflect that, in this respect, Oblonsky's proposed activity would run counter to the main tendency of his projects, which always leaned towards economy.

'I consider – and I have written a memorandum on the subject – that the enormous salaries of to-day are evidence of the unsound economic policy of our administration.'

'Yes, but what would you do?' said Oblonsky. 'Suppose a bank director gets ten thousand – well, he's worth it; or an engineer twenty thousand. Their jobs are no sinecures, you know!'

'I assume that a salary is a payment for value received, and should conform to the law of supply and demand. If that law be ignored when fixing a salary – as, for instance, when I see two engineers leaving college together, both equally well trained and efficient, and one getting forty thousand while the other is content with two; or when hussars and graduates of the law schools, having no special qualifications, are appointed directors of banking societies with gigantic salaries – I conclude that these salaries are not determined in accordance with the law of supply and demand but simply through personal influence. And this is an abuse of great gravity in itself, and one which has an injurious effect on the Government service. I am inclined to think ...'

Oblonsky hastened to interrupt his brother-in-law.

'Yes,' he said, 'but you must agree that it's a new institution of undoubted utility that is being started – we can call it a vital work! They are particularly keen to have an *honest* man to manage it,' concluded Oblonsky.

But the Moscow significance of the word 'honest' was lost on Karenin.

'Honesty is only a negative quality,' he said.

'Still, you would be doing me a great favour if you put in a word to Pomorsky – just in the way of conversation …'

'But I fancy it rests more with Bolgarinov,' said Karenin.

'Bolgarinov has no objections for his part,' returned Oblonsky, reddening at the mention of Bolgarinov.

He had called on the Jew that morning and had come away with a disagreeable impression. He was firmly convinced that the business he wished to serve was new, vital, and honest; but that morning, when Bolgarinov had, with obvious intention, kept him waiting a couple of hours in the waiting-room with a lot of other petitioners, had suddenly made him feel ill at ease. Whether it was that he, Prince Oblonsky, a descendant of the founder of Russia, found himself sitting for two hours in a Jew's waiting-room, or that for the first time in his life he was departing from the example of his ancestors of serving the state only, and was seeking to enter a new field – at any rate, he felt most uncomfortable. During those two hours in Bolgarinov's waiting-room Oblonsky had walked jauntily about the room, smoothing his whiskers, entering into conversation with the other petitioners, and trying to invent a pun to repeat afterwards – how he had had to *chew* the cud of expectation at the *Jew*'s – carefully concealing his feelings from others and even from himself.

But the whole time he had felt uncomfortable and disgruntled, though he could not have said why. Was it because he could not get the pun right, or was there some other reason? And when Bolgarinov at length received him with exaggerated politeness and unmistakable triumph at his mortification, and practically refused the favour asked of him, Oblonsky had hastened to forget it all as quickly as possible. So now the blood rushed to his face at the mere recollection.

18

'Now there's something else I want to talk about, and you know what it is. It's about Anna,' said Oblonsky, pausing for a brief space and shaking off the disagreeable memory.

755

At the mention of Anna's name, Karenin's face completely altered: all the animation went out of it, to be replaced by a weary, lifeless look.

'What exactly is it you wish of me?' he asked, turning round in his chair and closing his pince-nez with a snap.

'A decision. Some sort of decision, Alexei Alexandrovich! I address myself to you not as ...' ('an injured husband', he was going to say, but fearing thereby to prejudice his case he substituted the word 'statesman' – which sounded rather incongruous) '... as a statesman but simply as a man, a good man, and a Christian. You must have pity on her,' he said.

'How do you mean exactly?' asked Karenin quietly.

'Yes, pity on her. If you had seen her all this winter, as I have, you would take pity on her. Her position is awful, literally awful!'

'I was under the impression that Anna Arkadyevna had everything she desired for herself,' Karenin replied in a more high-pitched, almost shrill tone.

'Oh, Alexei Alexandrovich! For God's sake don't let us indulge in recriminations! What is past is past, and you know what she is waiting and hoping for – a divorce.'

'But I understood Anna Arkadyevna declines a divorce, if I insist on keeping the boy. I replied to her in that sense and presumed the matter closed. I consider it closed,' shrieked Karenin.

'For heaven's sake let us keep calm,' said Oblonsky, laying a finger on his brother-in-law's knee. 'The matter is not closed. If you will allow me to recapitulate, this is how things stood: when you and Anna separated you were great, you were magnanimity itself; you were ready to give her everything – her freedom, even a divorce. She appreciated it. Yes, don't think otherwise: she appreciated it so much that at the first moment, feeling how she had wronged you, she did not consider and could not consider everything. She renounced all. But experience, time, have shown that her situation is agonizing and intolerable.'

'Anna Arkadyevna's life can have no interest for me,' interrupted Karenin, raising his eyebrows.

'Allow me not to believe that,' Oblonsky rejoined gently. 'Her situation is intolerable for her, and it benefits no one. She has deserved it, you may say. She knows that, and does not ask you for anything. She says plainly that she dare not ask you. But I, her relatives, all who love her, beg and implore of you. What is the point of her suffering? Who gains by it?'

'Excuse me, you seem to be putting me in the position of defendant,' Karenin remonstrated.

'Oh no, oh no, not at all! Please understand me,' said Oblonsky, touching Karenin's hand this time, as if he were sure the physical contact would soften his brother-in-law. 'I am only saying that her position is unbearable, and that it lies in your power to alleviate it, and that you will lose nothing by doing so. I will arrange it all for you, so that you'll not notice. You did promise, you remember.'

'That promise was given earlier. And I had supposed the question of my son had settled the matter. Besides, I hoped that Anna Arkadyevna had enough generosity ...' Karenin spoke with difficulty, his lips trembling and his face turning pale.

'She leaves it all to your generosity. She begs, she pleads for one thing only: extricate her from the impossible position she is in! She no longer asks for her son. Alexei Alexandrovich – you are a good man. Put yourself in her place for a moment. The question of divorce for her, in her position, is one of life or death. Had you not promised it once, she might have grown reconciled to her position and gone on living in the country. But you did give your promise, so she wrote to you and moved to Moscow. She has been there for six months now, every day expecting your decision. Each time she meets an acquaintance it is like a knife in her heart. Why, it's like keeping a condemned man for months with the rope round his neck, promising him perhaps death, perhaps a reprieve! Have pity on her, and I will undertake to arrange. ... *Vos scrupules* ...'

'I was not thinking of them ... of my scruples ...' Karenin interrupted him in disgust. 'But it may be I promised what I had no right to promise.'

'Do you mean you go back on your promise?'

'I have never refused to do all that I could, but I must have time to consider how far what I promised is possible.'

'No, Alexei Alexandrovich!' exclaimed Oblonsky, jumping to his feet. 'I won't believe that! She is as wretched as only a woman can be, and you cannot refuse in such ...'

'I will keep my promise in so far as it is possible. *Vous professez d'être libre penseur*. But I, as a believer, cannot go against the teaching of Christianity in a matter of such gravity.'

'But in Christian societies, and in ours, too, as far as I'm aware, divorce is allowed,' said Oblonsky. 'Divorce is sanctioned even by the Church. And we see ...'

'Maybe, but not in a case of this kind.'

'Alexei Alexandrovich, you are not yourself,' said Oblonsky, after a pause. 'Wasn't it you (and didn't we all appreciate it?) who forgave everything, and guided by that same Christian spirit was ready to make any sacrifice? You said yourself, "If any man will take away thy coat, let him have thy cloak also," and now ...'

'I beg you,' began Karenin shrilly, rising suddenly to his feet, pale and with trembling jaw, 'I beg you to drop ... to drop ... this subject!'

'Oh no! Forgive me, then, forgive me if I have caused you pain,' said Oblonsky with an embarrassed smile, holding out his hand. 'I merely came as a messenger, that is all.'

Karenin gave him his hand.

'I must think it over,' he said, after a moment's reflection. 'I must seek guidance. The day after to-morrow you shall have a final answer,' he added, upon consideration.

19

OBLONSKY was just about to leave when Korney came in to announce:

'Sergei Alexeyich!'

'Who is Sergei Alexeyich?' Oblonsky began, but immediately recollected. 'Oh, Seriozha!' he said. 'Sergei Alexeyich! I thought it was the director of a department,' and he remembered that Anna had asked him to see the boy.

He recalled the timid, pathetic look with which Anna had said to him at parting, 'Anyhow, you will see him. Find out all about him: where he is, who looks after him. And Stiva ... if possible. ... It is possible, isn't it?' He knew what that 'If possible' meant – it meant, if possible arrange the divorce so as to let her have her son. ... Though Oblonsky saw now that it was useless to dream of that, still he was glad to see his nephew.

Karenin reminded his brother-in-law that they never mentioned his mother to the boy, and he asked him not to say a word about her.

'He was very ill after that interview with his mother, which we had not foreseen,' remarked Karenin. 'Indeed, we feared for his life. But sensible treatment and sea-bathing this summer have restored his health, and now, on the doctor's advice, I send him to school. And certainly the companionship of his school-fellows has had a good effect on him, and he is perfectly well and making excellent progress with his studies.'

'Hullo! What a fine fellow! True enough, it's not little Seriozha now but a full-grown Sergei Alexeyich!' said Oblonsky smiling, as he looked at the handsome, broad-shouldered lad in a dark-blue jacket and long trousers, who walked in boldly and confidently. The boy looked the picture of health. He bowed to his uncle as to a stranger, but, recognizing him, he blushed and hurriedly turned his head away, as though offended and angry about something. He went up to his father and handed him his school report.

'Well, that's pretty good,' said his father. 'You can go now.'

'He's thinner and taller, and has grown from a child to a regular boy. I like it,' said Oblonsky. 'Do you remember me?'

The boy threw a hasty look at his father.

'Yes, *mon oncle*,' he answered, glancing at his uncle and then lowering his eyes again.

Oblonsky called him nearer and took his hand.

'Well, and how are you getting on?' he asked, wanting to talk but not knowing what to say.

The boy blushed and did not reply but cautiously withdrew his hand from his uncle's grasp. As soon as Oblonsky let go his hand, Seriozha, after an inquiring glance at his father, flew from the room like a bird set free.

A year had passed since Seriozha last saw his mother. Since then her name had never been mentioned. During that year he had been sent to school and had learned to know and like his schoolmates. The dreams and memories he had cherished of his mother, and which had made him ill after he had seen her, no longer filled his mind. If they did come back now and again, he studiously drove them away, regarding them as shameful and fit only for girls, not for a boy who went to school. He knew that there had been a quarrel between his parents which separated them, knew that it was his lot to remain with his father, and did his best to get used to the idea.

The sight of his uncle, so like his mother, was unpleasant, since it awakened those very memories which he was ashamed of. It was the more unpleasant because from certain words he had overheard as he waited at the door of the study, and especially from the expressions on the faces of his father and uncle, he guessed that they had been talking of his mother. And in order not to blame his father, with whom he lived and upon whom he depended, and above all not to give way to the emotion which he considered so degrading, Seriozha tried not to look at this uncle, who had come to upset his peace of mind, and not to think of what he reminded him of.

But when Oblonsky, going out after him, saw him on the stairs, and calling to him asked how he spent his playtime at school, Seriozha, away from his father's presence, became quite communicative.

'We play at railways now,' he said in answer to his uncle's question. 'You see, it's like this: two boys sit on a form – they're the passengers. Another boy stands up on the form, and all the others harness themselves to it with their hands or their belts, and we tear through the rooms – we open the doors beforehand, you see. It's not easy work being the guard!'

'That's the one standing up?' asked Oblonsky with a smile.

'Yes, you have to have pluck for it, and be on the lookout, especially when the train stops all of a sudden, or someone falls down.'

'Yes, that's no joke,' said Oblonsky, looking sadly into the boy's eager eyes, so like his mother's – they had lost their childish look of innocence now. And though he had promised Karenin not to mention Anna, he could not restrain himself.

'Do you remember your mother?' he asked suddenly.

'No, I don't!' answered Seriozha quickly, and, blushing scarlet, hung his head. His uncle could not get another word out of him.

Half an hour later the tutor found his pupil on the stairs, and for a long while could not make out whether he was in a temper or crying.

'What is it? I expect you hurt yourself when you fell down?' said the tutor. 'I told you not to play that dangerous game. I shall have to speak to your headmaster about it.'

'If I had hurt myself I wouldn't let anyone see, that's quite certain.'

'Well, what is it, then?'

'Leave me alone! What business is it of his whether I remember or don't remember? Why should I remember? Leave me alone!' he said, addressing not his tutor now, but the whole world.

20

OBLONSKY, as usual, did not waste his time in Petersburg. On this occasion, in addition to the two matters of business he had to attend to – his sister's divorce and the post for himself – he wanted to shake off some of the Moscow fustiness, as he put it.

Moscow, in spite of its *cafés chantants* and its omnibuses, was still a backwater. Oblonsky always felt this. Life in Moscow, especially in the bosom of his family, caused his spirits to flag. A long time there without a break reduced him to a state where he began to be affected by his wife's ill-humour and reproaches, worry over the health and education of his children, and the petty details of his work; and, an unheard-of thing, even to allow his debts to trouble him. But no sooner did he set foot in Petersburg and settle down in his own circle, where people lived, really lived, instead of vegetating as in Moscow, than his cares immediately vanished, melting away like wax before a flame.

His wife? … Only that day he had been talking to Prince Tchetchensky. Prince Tchetchensky had a wife and a grown family of boys in the Corps of Pages; and in addition he had an illegitimate family. Naturally, the first family was well enough, but somehow Prince Tchetchensky felt happier with the second. He had even introduced his eldest son to them, and told Oblonsky that he considered it good for the boy's education. What would Moscow have said to that?

The children? In Petersburg children did not prevent their fathers from enjoying life. They were sent to school, and there was none of that silly nonsense such as was becoming prevalent in Moscow – Lvov's was a case in point – that the children should have all the luxuries of life and the parents nothing but work and anxiety. Here it was understood that a man should live for himself, as every civilized being should.

The service? Government service, too, was not that hopeless, monotonous treadmill that it was in Moscow. Here there was some interest in belonging to the official world. A chance meeting, a service rendered, a word slipped in at the right moment, a talent for mimicry – and behold, a man's career was made. So it had been with Bryantsev, whom Oblonsky had met the day before, who was now at the top of the bureaucratic ladder. There was some interest in official work of that kind.

But it was the Petersburg attitude to pecuniary matters that had the most soothing effect of all on Oblonsky. Bartnyansky, who must be spending at least fifty thousand a year to judge by the style he lived in, had made a remark worthy of note on that score the previous night.

As they were having a chat before dinner, Oblonsky had said to Bartnyansky:

'You're friendly, I fancy, with Mordvinsky? You might do me a good turn and put in a word for me. There's an appointment I should like to get ... secretary of the agency ...'

'Never mind the name, I shouldn't remember it. ... But why on earth do you want to mix yourself up with railways and Jews? ... Whatever way you look at it, it's an obnoxious business!'

Oblonsky had not stopped to explain that it was a 'vital' thing – Bartnyansky would not have understood.

'I want the money; I've got nothing to live on.'

'But you live, don't you?'

'Yes, but in debt.'

'Really? Is it much?' Bartnyansky had asked sympathetically.

'A good deal: about twenty thousand.'

'Lucky fellow!' Bartnyansky had exclaimed, bursting into a merry laugh. 'My debts run to a million and a half, and I've nothing – still, as you see, I manage to live!'

And Oblonsky saw, not just on hearsay but in actual fact, that this was true. Zhivahov was in debt to the tune of three hundred thousand and hadn't a farthing to bless himself with, yet he lived, and in style too! Then there was Count Krivtsov, considered a hopeless case by everyone, but he still kept two mistresses. Petrovsky had run through five million, continued on just the same, and was even in charge of the Finance Department with a salary of twenty thousand.

Apart from all this, Petersburg had an agreeable effect on Oblonsky physically, making him feel younger. In Moscow he noticed his grey hairs, dozed off after dinner, yawned and stretched himself, took the stairs slowly, breathing heavily, was bored by the society of young women and did not dance at balls. In Petersburg he always felt he had shaken off ten years. Petersburg did for him what being abroad did for the sixty-year-old Prince Peter Oblonsky, who had just returned from Baden.

'We don't know the way to live here,' Peter Oblonsky had said to him the evening before. 'Would you believe it – I spent the summer in Baden and felt quite a young man again. Whenever I saw a pretty woman, my fancy ... A couple of glasses of wine with my dinner and I was strong and ready for anything. I return to Russia to see my wife – in the country, what's more – and in a fortnight I take to living in my dressing-gown and not changing for dinner! Good-bye to the young beauties! I become an old man with nothing left but to think of saving my soul. A trip to Paris now, and I'm as right as rain.'

Oblonsky felt precisely the same as old Prince Peter. In Moscow he let himself go to such an extent that a little longer and he, too, would reach the soul-saving stage. Petersburg, however, made him feel a young man about town again.

Between the Princess Betsy Tverskoy and Oblonsky there existed long-established and very odd relations. Oblonsky always jestingly paid court to her and made the most improper remarks, also in fun, knowing that nothing delighted her so much. The day after his interview with Karenin he went to call on her, and his feeling of rejuvenation carried him to such lengths in this bantering flirtation that he did not know how to extricate himself, for, unfortunately, he was not in the least attracted by the Princess Betsy – on the contrary, he positively disliked her. It had all come about because she found him very attractive. He was consequently considerably relieved when the Princess Myagky was announced to cut short their *tête-à-tête*.

'Ah, so you're here!' she greeted him. 'Well, and what news of your poor sister? You needn't look at me like that,' she went on. 'Ever since everyone started throwing stones at her – and they're all a hundred thousand times worse than she is – I've thought she did a very fine thing. I can't forgive Vronsky for not letting me know when she was in Petersburg. I would have called on her and gone about with her everywhere. Please give her my love. Come, tell me about her.'

'Well, her position is very difficult; she ...' began Oblonsky, in the simplicity of his heart accepting the Princess Myagky's 'Tell me about your sister' for sterling coin. But Princess Myagky interrupted him immediately, as she always did, to talk herself.

'She did what everyone else does, except me – only they hide it. But she wouldn't be deceitful, and she did a fine thing. And she did better still in throwing up that half-witted brother-in-law of yours.

You must excuse me. I always maintained he was a fool, though everyone would insist that he was so clever. Now that he is hand in glove with Lydia Ivanovna and Landau, they all say he is half-witted. I hate to agree with other people, but this time I can't help it.'

'Do explain to me what it means,' said Oblonsky. 'I went to see him yesterday, on my sister's behalf, to ask for a definite decision about the divorce. He told me he must think it over, but this morning, instead of an answer, I receive an invitation from the Countess Lydia Ivanovna for this evening.'

'Yes, that's just what I should expect!' exclaimed Princess Myagky gleefully. 'They're going to consult Landau and see what he says.'

'Why Landau? Why should he be consulted? Who's Landau?'

'What! You don't know Jules Landau, *le fameux Jules Landau, le clairvoyant*? He's another half-wit, but your sister's fate depends on him. See what comes of living in the provinces – you don't know a thing about anything! Landau, let me tell you, was a shop-assistant in Paris. One day he went to see a doctor, and fell asleep in the doctor's waiting-room. In his sleep he began giving advice to the other patients. And wonderful advice it was! Then the wife of Yury Meledinsky – you remember him, he's always been an invalid? – heard of this Landau and had him to see her husband. The man is treating him. I can't say I think he's done him much good, for Meledinsky is just as ill as ever, but they believe in him and hang on to him. They brought him to Russia. Here there's been a general rush to him and he's been treating one and all. He cured Countess Bezzubov, and she took such a fancy to him that she adopted him.'

'Adopted him?'

'Yes, as her son. He's not Landau any more now, but Count Bezzubov. However, that's neither here nor there. But Lydia – I am very fond of her, though her head is not screwed on in the right place – naturally has to be smitten with this Landau, and now neither she nor Karenin can take the smallest decision without consulting him. So your sister's fate is now in the hands of this Landau, *alias* Count Bezzubov.'

21

AFTER an excellent dinner with unlimited cognac at Bartnyansky's, Oblonsky arrived at the Countess Lydia Ivanovna's only a little after the appointed time.

'Who else is with the countess – a Frenchman?' he asked the hall-porter, as he glanced at Karenin's familiar overcoat and a queer, rather absurd-looking garment with clasps.

'Alexei Alexandrovich Karenin and Count Bezzubov,' the hall-porter replied severely.

'The Princess Myagky was right,' thought Oblonsky, as he went upstairs. 'Odd! However, it would be as well to get on friendly terms with her. She has tremendous influence. A word from her to Pomorsky and the thing's in the bag.'

It was still quite light out of doors but in the Countess Lydia Ivanovna's little drawing-room the blinds were drawn and the lamps lit.

At a round table under a lamp sat the countess and Karenin, talking in low tones. A short, thin-bodied man with hips like a woman's, knock-kneed and very pale, was standing at the other end of the room gazing at the portraits on the wall. He had a fine face with beautiful shining eyes and long hair that fell over the collar of his frock-coat. Oblonsky greeted his hostess and Karenin, and then involuntarily turned to have another look at the stranger.

'Monsieur Landau!' called the countess gently and with a circumspection that impressed Oblonsky.

Landau looked round hurriedly, approached with a smile and when the countess introduced them put a moist, flabby hand into Oblonsky's outstretched one, before immediately returning to the portraits. The countess and Karenin exchanged meaning eyes.

'I am very pleased to see you, to-day especially,' said the Countess Lydia Ivanovna, motioning Oblonsky to a seat beside Karenin. 'I introduced him as Landau,' she added, lowering her voice and glancing at the Frenchman and then back to Karenin, 'but he is really Count Bezzubov, as you probably know. Only he does not like the title.'

'Yes, I did hear,' replied Oblonsky. 'They say he completely cured the Countess Bezzubov.'

'She was here to-day, poor thing!' the countess said, turning to Karenin. 'His departure and the parting from him are a terrible blow.'

'Is he really going?' asked Karenin.

'Yes, back to Paris. He heard a voice yesterday,' said the countess, with a look at Oblonsky.

'Ah, a voice!' repeated Oblonsky, feeling that he must be as much

765

on his guard as possible in this company, where such mysterious things occurred or were supposed to occur, to which he as yet lacked a clue.

There was a moment's silence, after which the Countess Lydia Ivanovna turned with a subtle smile to Oblonsky, as though she were about to broach the main topic of conversation.

'We have been acquainted for a long while, and I am very glad to have this opportunity of getting to know you better. *Les amis de nos amis sont nos amis.* But to be a true friend one must try to enter into the spiritual state of one's friend, and I fear you have not done this in the case of Alexei Alexandrovich. You understand my meaning?' she said, lifting her beautiful dreamy eyes.

'Not altogether, Countess. I understand that the position of Alexei Alexandrovich ...' began Oblonsky. He did not quite grasp what she was driving at, and therefore resolved to confine himself to generalities.

'The change has no reference to his external circumstances,' the countess interrupted him severely, while her enamoured eyes followed Karenin, who had risen to join Landau. 'The change is in his heart. He has been vouchsafed a new heart, and I fear you have not sufficiently realized the change that has been accomplished in him.'

'Well, in a general sort of way I can conceive the change. We have always been friendly, and now ...' said Oblonsky, responding to her look with a warm glance while he considered with which of the two ministers she was the more closely connected and which of them he should ask her to influence on his behalf.

'The change that has taken place in him cannot diminish his love for his neighbour: on the contrary, that change can only strengthen love in his heart. But I am afraid you do not understand me. Won't you have some tea?' she asked, indicating with her eyes the footman who was handing tea round on a tray.

'Not altogether, Countess. Of course, his misfortune ...'

'Yes, a misfortune which has proved to be the greatest blessing now that his heart has been made new and is filled with Him,' she said, gazing at Oblonsky with lovesick eyes.

'I dare say she might mention it to both if I asked her,' thought Oblonsky.

'Oh, assuredly, Countess,' he said. 'But I imagine these changes are of such an intimate nature that no one, not even the closest of friends, would care to speak of them.'

'On the contrary! We ought to open our hearts and so help one another.'

'I quite agree, but sometimes people's convictions differ so, and besides ...' and Oblonsky gave an ingratiating smile.

'There can be no differences in matters of Sacred Truth.'

'Oh no, of course not! But ...' Oblonsky stopped in confusion. He realized that she was talking of religion.

'I fancy he will be going to sleep now,' said Karenin in a significant whisper, approaching the countess.

Oblonsky looked round. Landau was sitting by the window, leaning against the arm and back of an easy-chair, his head drooping. Noticing that all eyes were directed on him, he raised his head and smiled a naïve child-like smile.

'Don't pay any attention,' said Lydia Ivanovna, and with an agile movement she moved a chair up for Karenin. 'I have observed ...' she was beginning, when a footman came in with a letter. Lydia Ivanovna quickly ran her eyes over the note and, excusing herself, with extreme rapidity wrote an answer, handed it to the man and came back to the table. 'I have observed,' she resumed, continuing her interrupted sentence, 'that Moscow people, the men especially, are more indifferent to religion than anyone.'

'Oh no, Countess! I always understood Moscow people had the reputation of being staunch believers,' replied Oblonsky.

'But, as far as I can make out, you unfortunately are one of the indifferent?' Karenin remarked, turning to him with a weary smile.

'How can one be indifferent?' exclaimed Lydia Ivanovna.

'It is not so much that I am indifferent but rather that I suspend judgement,' said Oblonsky, with his most appeasing smile. 'I hardly think the time for such questions has come for me yet.'

Karenin and Lydia Ivanovna exchanged glances.

'We can never tell whether the time has come for us or not,' said Karenin severely. 'We ought not to think whether we are ready or not ready. Grace is not influenced by human considerations: sometimes it descends not on those that strive for it, but on the unprepared, as in the case of Saul, for instance.'

'No, I don't believe it will be just yet,' said Lydia Ivanovna, who had been keeping an eye on the Frenchman.

Landau got up and walked over to them.

'May I listen?' he asked.

'Oh yes; I did not want to disturb you,' said Lydia Ivanovna, giving him a tender look. 'Sit here with us.'

'The essential thing is not to close one's eyes to the light,' continued Karenin.

'Ah, if you but knew the happiness we know, feeling His presence ever in our hearts!' cried the Countess Lydia Ivanovna, with a beatific smile.

'But a man may feel himself incapable of rising to such heights,' remarked Oblonsky, conscious that it was not quite honest of him to appear to acknowledge the existence of religious heights, yet not venturing to confess his agnosticism in the presence of one who, by a single word to Pomorsky, might secure him the coveted appointment.

'You mean to say that he may be prevented by sin?' asked Lydia Ivanovna. 'But that is the wrong way to look at it. For him who believes, there is no sin – their sin has already been atoned for … *Pardon!*' she added, glancing at the footman who came in with another note, which she read and answered verbally: 'To-morrow at the Grand Duchess's, tell him,' she said to the footman. 'For a true believer, sin is not,' she went on.

'Yes, but faith without works is dead,' observed Oblonsky, recalling the words of the catechism, and only by a smile maintaining his independence.

'You see – the Epistle of St James!' said Karenin, addressing Lydia Ivanovna with a note of reproach in his voice. Evidently this was a point they had discussed more than once. 'What a lot of harm has been done by the false interpretation of that passage! "I have no works, therefore cannot have faith!" Nothing turns people away so much as that, yet that is not what is said anywhere, but just the opposite.'

'To labour for God with works; to save one's soul by fasting,' said the Countess Lydia Ivanovna, with fastidious disdain, 'those are the crude ideas of our monks. … Yet nowhere do we find that said. It is all far simpler and easier,' she added, giving Oblonsky the same encouraging smile with which she rallied young maids of honour confused by their new surroundings at court.

'We are saved through Christ who suffered for us. We are saved by faith,' Karenin put in, giving her a look to show his approval of her words.

'*Vous comprenez l'anglais?*' asked Lydia Ivanovna, and receiving an affirmative answer she got up and began looking along a shelf of books. 'I want to read him *Safe and Happy, or Under the Wing*,' she said, looking inquiringly at Karenin. And finding the book, and sitting down in her place again, she opened it. 'It is quite short. It describes the way to acquire faith, and the joy, above all earthly bliss, with which faith fills the soul. A man who believes cannot be unhappy, because he is not alone. But you will see.' She was just settling herself to read when the footman appeared again. 'Madame Borozdin? Say to-morrow, at two. ... Yes,' she went on, keeping her finger in the book to mark the place, and sighed, her beautiful dreamy eyes gazing before her, 'let me tell you how true faith acts. You know Maria Sanin? You have heard about her tragedy? She lost her only child. She was in despair. Well, and what happened? She found this Friend, and now she thanks God for the death of her child. Such is the happiness faith can give!'

'Oh yes, that is most ...' began Oblonsky, glad that she was going to read and so give him time to bethink himself. 'No, obviously better not ask her about anything to-day,' he reflected. 'The thing now is to get away without putting my foot in it!'

'This will be dull for you, as you don't know English,' the countess said, turning to Landau. 'But it won't take long.'

'Oh, I shall understand,' Landau replied, with the same smile, and he closed his eyes.

Karenin and Lydia Ivanovna looked at one another, and the reading began.

22

OBLONSKY was completely baffled by the strange, novel language he was listening to. Generally the complexity of Petersburg life had a stimulating effect on him, lifting him out of the stagnation of Moscow. But complexity he liked and understood in spheres congenial and familiar to him. In this strange sphere he was puzzled and nonplussed, and did not know what to make of it all. As he listened to the Countess Lydia Ivanovna and felt Landau's fine, artless – or was it artful, he could not decide which – eyes fixed upon him, Oblonsky began to be conscious of a peculiar heaviness in his head.

The most incongruous thoughts whirled through his brain. 'Marie Sanin is glad her child's dead. ... It would be nice to have a smoke now. ... To be saved, one need only have faith, and the monks don't know the way to salvation but the Countess Lydia Ivanovna does. ... I wonder why my head feels so heavy? Is it the cognac or because all this is so very odd? I think I've behaved all right so far. Still, it wouldn't do to ask any favour of her now. I've heard it said they make one say one's prayers. Supposing they want me to! That would be too absurd! And what twaddle she is reading, but she has a good accent. ... Landau – Bezzubov – what's he Bezzubov for?' All at once Oblonsky felt his lower jaw dropping irresistibly into a yawn. He smoothed his whiskers to hide the yawn, and gave himself a shake. But the next moment he became aware that he was falling asleep and on the point of snoring. He roused himself just as the Countess Lydia Ivanovna said, 'He's asleep.'

Oblonsky came to with a guilty start, feeling that he had been caught out. But he was relieved to see that the words referred to Landau, the Frenchman like himself having fallen asleep. But Oblonsky's being asleep might have offended them (though he was not even sure of this, so queer did everything seem), whereas Landau's slumber afforded them extreme pleasure, the countess especially.

'Mon ami,' said Lydia Ivanovna, carefully holding the folds of her silk gown so as not to rustle, and in her excitement calling Karenin 'mon ami' instead of Alexei Alexandrovich, 'donnez-lui la main. Vous voyez? Sh-h!' she hissed at the footman who came in again. 'I am not at home.'

The Frenchman was asleep, or pretending to be, his head leaning on the back of the chair, and his clammy hand resting on his knee and making feeble gestures as though trying to catch something. Karenin got up cautiously, but not without knocking against the table, and went and put his hand in the Frenchman's. Oblonsky rose, too, and opening his eyes wide to wake himself up in case he were asleep looked first at one and then at the other. It was all quite real. Oblonsky felt his head getting worse and worse.

'Que la personne qui est arrivée la dernière, celle qui demande, qu'elle sorte!' muttered the Frenchman, without opening his eyes.

'Vous m'excuserez, mais vous voyez. ... Revenez vers dix heures, encore mieux demain.'

'Qu'elle sorte!' repeated the Frenchman impatiently.

'C'est moi, n'est-ce pas?' And receiving an answer in the affirmative Oblonsky tiptoed out of the room, forgetting the request he had

770

meant to make of Lydia Ivanovna, forgetting his sister's affairs, impelled only by the desire to get away as quickly as possible. He rushed out into the street as if fleeing from a house with the plague. To recover his spirits he chatted and joked for some while with the cabman who drove him to the French theatre, where he arrived in time for the last act. Afterwards he went on to the Tartar restaurant for some champagne and began to feel more like himself in the congenial atmosphere. But all the same the evening had had a thoroughly upsetting effect on him.

On getting home to Peter Oblonsky's house, where he was staying, he found a note from Betsy, inviting him to come and see her the next day to finish their interrupted conversation. He was just making a grimace over the note when he heard below the ponderous tread of men carrying something heavy.

Oblonsky went out to see what it was. It was the rejuvenated Peter Oblonsky, so drunk that he could not walk upstairs, but when he saw Oblonsky he ordered the men to set him on his feet and, clinging to Stepan, went back to his room with him, and there while relating the events of the evening fell fast asleep.

Oblonsky was in low spirits, which happened rarely with him, and it was a long time before he could get to sleep. Everything he recalled to mind was nauseous, but most nauseating of all was the memory, like something shameful, of the evening at the Countess Lydia Ivanovna's.

Next morning he received from Karenin a flat refusal to divorce Anna, and he realized that this decision was based on what the Frenchman had said in his real or pretended trance the evening before.

23

BEFORE anything can be embarked upon in married life, there must necessarily be either absolute antagonism between husband and wife or loving agreement. When relations are uncertain, neither one thing nor the other, no move can be made.

Many families continue for years in the same old rut, which both parties heartily detest, simply because husband and wife are not sufficiently united to agree upon anything or sufficiently disunited for one of them to take things into his or her own hands.

Both for Vronsky and Anna life in Moscow in the heat and dust, when the spring sunshine was followed by the glare of summer and all the trees on the boulevards had long been in leaf and were already covered with dust, was intolerable. But instead of going back to Vozdvizhenskoe, as they had long ago decided to do, they still stayed on in Moscow, which they had both grown to loathe, because of late there had been no harmony between them.

The irritability which kept them apart had no tangible cause, and all efforts to come to an understanding only made it worse, instead of removing it. It was an inner irritation, grounded in her mind on the conviction of a decline in his love for her; in his, on regret that for her sake he had placed himself in a difficult position which she, instead of trying to ease, made harder still. Neither would give expression to their grievance, but each thought the other in the wrong and seized every opportunity to prove it.

In her eyes Vronsky, with all his habits, ideas, desires – his whole spiritual and physical temperament – could be summed up in one thing – love for women, and this love, which she felt ought to be wholly concentrated on her, was diminishing. Therefore, she reasoned, he must have transferred part of it to other women, or to another woman, and she was jealous. She was jealous not of any particular woman but of his love. Not having as yet an object for her jealousy, she was on the look-out for one. At the slightest provocation she transferred her jealousy from one object to another. Now she was jealous of the low *amours* he might so easily enter into through his bachelor connexions; now it was the society women he might meet; now she was jealous of some imaginary girl whom he might want to marry and for whose sake he would break with her. And this last tortured her most of all, especially since in an expansive moment he had unwarily remarked that his mother understood him so little that she had even tried to persuade him to marry the young Princess Sorokin.

And being jealous made her quarrelsome, and she was constantly seeking grounds for her discontent. She blamed him for everything she had to bear. The agonizing state of suspense in which she lived in Moscow, Karenin's procrastination and indecision, her own loneliness – they were all put down to him. If he had loved her he would have realized the misery of her position and rescued her from it. It was his fault, too, that they were living in Moscow instead of in the country. He could not live buried in the country as she would have liked to. He must have society, and so he had put her in this awful position, the

772

bitterness of which he wilfully shut his eyes to. And it was likewise his fault that she was parted from her son for ever.

Even the rare moments of tenderness that came from time to time did not soothe her: in his tenderness now she saw a shade of complacency, of self-confidence, which had not been there before and which provoked her.

It was already dusk. Anna all alone, awaiting his return from a bachelor dinner-party, paced up and down his study (the room where the noise from the street was least audible), going over in her mind every detail of their quarrel the day before. She recalled the words that had hurt her most cruelly and traced them to the thing that had occasioned them, finally arriving back at the beginning of their conversation. For a long while she could not believe that the dispute could have arisen from such an inoffensive exchange about a matter that was not close to the heart of either. But so in fact it had been. It had all begun by his laughing at high schools for girls, which he considered unnecessary and she defended. He had spoken slightingly of women's education in general, and said that Hannah, Anna's little English *protégée*, did not at all need to know physics.

This irritated Anna. She saw in it a contemptuous allusion to her own occupations, and bethought herself of an answer that should make him pay for the pain he had caused her. 'I don't expect you to understand me or my feelings, as anyone who loved me would, but ordinary delicacy I did expect,' she said.

And he had actually flushed with anger and made some disagreeable retort. She could not recall her reply but remembered that in response he had said, with obvious intent to hurt her too:

'You are right: I can take no interest in your passion for the child because I can see in it nothing but affectation.'

The cruelty with which he shattered the world she had so laboriously created for herself to enable her to endure her difficult life, the injustice of his accusation that she was false and affected, stung her.

'I am very sorry that only the coarse and material things are comprehensible and natural to you,' she flung at him, and walked out of the room.

When he came to her in the evening, they did not refer to the quarrel, but both felt that it was only smoothed over, not settled.

Now he had been away from home the whole day, and she felt so lonely and wretched at being on bad terms with him that she was

773

ready to forget and forgive everything in order to be reconciled with him. She would even take the blame on herself and justify him.

'It is my fault. I am irritable and unreasonably jealous. I will make it up with him, and we'll go back to the country. I shall be more at peace there,' she said to herself.

'Affectation!' She suddenly recalled what had hurt her most of all – not so much the word itself as the intent to wound her with which it had been said. 'I know what he meant: he meant that it is unnatural to love someone else's child and not my own daughter. What does he know of love for children – of my love for Seriozha, whom I gave up for him? And this desire to hurt me! No, he must be in love with another woman: it can't be anything else.'

Suddenly she realized that in her attempt to regain her peace of mind she had only gone the round of the circle completed so often before, and arrived back at her old state of irritation, and she was frightened at herself. 'Is it possible that I can't ... Is it possible that I can't take it on myself?' she wondered, and began again from the beginning. 'He is upright, he is the soul of honour, he loves me. I love him. In a day or two the divorce will come. What more do I want? I must be calm and have more faith in him; and I will take the blame on myself. Yes, now, as soon as he comes home, I will tell him I was wrong, though in fact I was not, and we will go away.'

And to avoid further thought and irritation she rang and asked for her trunks, ready to pack their things for the country.

At ten o'clock Vronsky came in.

24

'Well, did you have a good time?' she asked, going out to meet him with a penitent, meek expression on her face.

'The same as usual,' he replied, perceiving at a glance that she was in one of her good moods. He had become accustomed to these transitions, and to-day especially was glad to see her happier, as he was in the best of spirits himself.

'What do I see? Ah, that's right!' he said, pointing to the trunks in the passage.

'Yes, we must go away. I went out for a drive, and it was so lovely I longed to be in the country. There's nothing to keep you here, is there?'

'My one wish is to get away. I won't be a moment, and we'll talk it over. I must just go and change first. Order tea, will you?'

And he went to his room.

There was something offensive in the way he had said, 'Ah, that's right!' – the sort of thing one says to a child when it stops being naughty – and still more offensive was the contrast between her penitent tone and his self-assurance. For a moment she felt a desire to fight rising up in her, but with an effort she mastered it and met Vronsky with the same good humour as before.

When he came in she told him, partly repeating words she had rehearsed, how she had spent the day, and her plans for their departure.

'You know, it came over me almost like an inspiration,' she began. 'Why should we go on waiting here for the divorce? Won't it do just as well in the country? I can't wait any longer. I don't want to go on hoping – I don't want to hear any more about the divorce. I have made up my mind that it shan't influence my life any more. Do you agree?'

'Oh yes!' he replied, looking uneasily at her excited face.

'What did you do at your dinner-party? Who was there?' she asked, after a pause.

Vronsky mentioned the names of the guests. 'The dinner was first-rate, and the boat-race and all that quite enjoyable, but in Moscow they can't manage without doing something ridiculous. Some lady or other appeared on the scene – the Queen of Sweden's swimming-instructress – and gave a display of her art.'

'What? Do you mean to say she swam?' asked Anna, with a frown.

'Yes, in some sort of red *costume de natation* – a hideous old creature she was too. Well, when are we off?'

'What an absurd idea! Was there anything particular about her swimming?' said Anna, not answering his question.

'Absolutely nothing at all. I told you, it was awfully silly. ... Well, when do you think of going?'

Anna shook her head as though to drive away an unpleasant thought.

'When are we going? Why, the sooner the better! We can't get off to-morrow, I'm afraid, but we could be ready the day after.'

'Yes ... oh no, wait a moment – the day after to-morrow is Sunday and I have to go and see *maman*,' said Vronsky, embarrassed, for no sooner had he mentioned his mother than he felt Anna's eyes fixed on him suspiciously. His embarrassment confirmed her suspicions. She flushed and turned away from him. Now it was no longer the Queen of Sweden's swimming instructress who was uppermost in her mind but the young Princess Sorokin, who lived with the Countess Vronsky in the country outside Moscow.

'You could go there to-morrow,' she said.

'No, I tell you! I am going there on business to do with a power of attorney and the money won't be ready to-morrow,' he replied.

'In that case, then, we won't go at all.'

'Why ever not?'

'I won't go any later! Monday or not at all!'

'But why?' asked Vronsky, as if in surprise. 'There's no sense in that.'

'You see no sense in it because you care nothing for me. You seem unable to understand my position. The one thing I was interested in here was Hannah – you say that is all affectation. You said yesterday that I don't love my own daughter but make out I love this English girl, and that it's unnatural. I should like to know what life could be natural for me here!'

For a moment she recollected herself and was appalled at how she had fallen away from her resolutions. But though she knew it was her own ruin, she could not restrain herself, could not resist pointing out to him how in the wrong he was, could not give way to him.

'I never said anything of the kind. All I said was that I did not sympathize with that sudden show of affection.'

'You might as well speak the truth – you are always boasting of your straightforwardness!'

'I never boast, and I never tell lies,' he said quietly, restraining his rising anger. 'It is a great pity if you can't respect ...'

'Respect was invented to cover up the empty place where love should be. And if you don't love me any more, it would be better and more honest to say so!'

'Oh really! This is becoming unbearable!' exclaimed Vronsky, getting up from his chair. And standing before her he brought out slowly: 'Why do you try my patience?' He looked as if he could have said a great deal more but was holding himself in. 'It has its limits.'

'What do you mean by that?' she cried, looking with terror at the undisguised hatred on his whole face, and especially in the cruel, menacing eyes.

'I mean ...' he began, but checked himself. 'I must ask what it is you want of me.'

'What can I want? All I want is that you should not desert me as you are thinking of doing,' she said, understanding all that he had left unsaid. 'No, I don't want that ... that is of secondary importance. I want your love, and it has gone. So it is all over.'

She turned towards the door.

'Wait! Wa-i-t!' said Vronsky, his brow still knit but holding her back by the hand. 'What is it all about? I said we must put off our departure for a matter of three days, and you answer by accusing me of lying and being dishonourable.'

'Yes, and I repeat that a man who reproaches me because he has given up everything for me,' she said, recalling the words of an earlier quarrel, 'is worse than dishonourable – he is heartless!'

'No, there are limits to one's endurance!' he exclaimed, and quickly let go her hand.

'He hates me, that is clear,' she thought, and in silence, without looking round, she walked with faltering step out of the room. 'He is in love with another woman; that is clearer still,' she said to herself, going into her own room. 'I want love, but that is gone. So it is all over,' she repeated the words she had said, 'and I must end it.'

'But how?' she asked herself, and sat down in a low chair before the looking-glass.

Thoughts of where she would go now – to the aunt who had brought her up, to Dolly, or simply abroad by herself? – of what *he* was doing alone in the study; of whether this was the final quarrel, or whether reconciliation were still possible; of what all her old Petersburg acquaintances would say about her now; how Karenin would regard it; and many other speculations as to what would happen now after the rupture, passed through her mind; but there was something else. A dim thought was lurking somewhere at the back of her brain, which was the only one that mattered but which she could not get hold of. Thinking of Karenin again, she recalled the time of her illness, after her confinement, and the feeling that had never left her at that time. 'Why didn't I die?' – she remembered the words she had uttered then and how she had felt. And all at once she knew what was at the back of her mind. 'Yes, death!' – that would solve everything.

'The shame and disgrace I have brought on Alexei Alexandrovich, and on Seriozha, and my own awful shame – would all be wiped out by my death. If I die *he*, too, will be sorry. He will pity me and love me and suffer on my account.' A smile of self-pity settled on her lips as she sat in the chair, pulling off and on the rings on her left hand, imagining to herself all his different feelings after she was dead.

The sound of approaching footsteps – his steps – roused her. Pretending to be busy putting away her rings, she did not turn round. He came up close to her and took her hand.

'Anna, we'll go the day after to-morrow if you like,' he said gently. 'I agree to anything.'

She was silent.

'What is it?' he asked.

'You know yourself!' she said, and at the same instant, unable to control herself any longer, she burst into sobs.

'Abandon me, abandon me!' she murmured between her sobs. 'I'll go away to-morrow. I will do more. What am I? A wanton! A millstone round your neck. I won't torment you any longer. I'll set you free. You don't love me; you love someone else!'

Vronsky implored her to be calm and assured her that there was not the slightest foundation for her jealousy, that he had never ceased loving her and never would, and that he loved her more than ever.

'Anna, why will you torture yourself and me like this?' he said, kissing her hands. There was a look of tenderness in his face now, and she fancied she detected the sound of tears in his voice and felt them wet on her hand. And instantly her despairing jealousy changed to desperate, passionate tenderness. She threw her arms round him and covered his head and neck and hands with kisses.

25

THE next morning, feeling that the reconciliation was complete, Anna began making eager preparations for their move. Though it was not settled whether they should go on the Monday or the Tuesday, as the night before each had been anxious to give way to the other, Anna packed busily, feeling quite indifferent now over a day more or less. She was standing in her room before an open trunk, sorting clothes, when he came in earlier than usual, dressed to go out.

'I am just off to *maman*. She can send me the money by Yegorov, and I shall be ready to leave to-morrow,' he said.

Good as her mood might be, the mention of going to see his mother lashed her.

'No, I shan't be ready myself,' she said; and at once reflected, 'So it was possible to arrange to go when I wanted to, after all!'

'No, do as you were going to. And now go to the dining-room. I will come as soon as I have sorted out these things that are not wanted,' she added, piling more old clothes into Annushka's already full arms.

Vronsky was eating his beefsteak when she entered the dining-room.

'You can't imagine how I have come to loathe these rooms,' she remarked, sitting down beside him to her coffee. 'There's nothing more awful than these *chambres garnies*! They have no individuality, no soul. This clock, the curtains, and, worst of all, the wall-papers – they're a nightmare! Vozdvizhenskoe seems like the Promised Land! You are not sending the horses off yet?'

'No, they will come on after us. Were you thinking of going out?'

'I wanted to go to Mrs Wilson's to take her some dresses. So it is decided that we go to-morrow?' she asked in a cheerful voice; but suddenly her face changed as Vronsky's valet came in to fetch a receipt for a telegram from Petersburg. There was nothing extraordinary in Vronky's getting a telegram, but the way he told the man that the receipt was in the study and then hastily turned to her, saying, 'I shall certainly have everything settled by to-morrow,' made her think that he had something to conceal from her.

'Who was your telegram from?' she asked, taking no notice of what he had said.

'From Stiva,' he replied reluctantly.

'Why didn't you show it to me? What secrets can Stiva have from me?'

Vronsky called the valet back and told him to bring the telegram.

'I didn't want to show it to you because Stiva has a passion for wiring. Why telegraph when nothing is settled?'

'About the divorce?'

'Yes, but he wires: "Could get nothing out of him. Promises definite answer soon." But read it for yourself.'

Anna took the telegram with shaking fingers and saw exactly what Vronsky had said. But at the end were added the words: 'Little hope but will do everything possible and impossible.'

'I said yesterday that it is all the same to me when I get the divorce

779

or whether I never get it,' she said, flushing crimson. 'There was not the slightest necessity to hide it from me.'

'If he conceals this, he can also conceal his correspondence with women, and probably does,' she thought.

'Oh, Yashvin meant to call this morning with Voitov,' said Vronsky. 'It seems he's won from Pevtsov all and more than Pevtsov can pay – about sixty thousand.'

'But why do you imagine,' she said, irritated because his sudden change of subject showed so obviously that he saw she was angry, 'that this news interests me so much that you must needs conceal it from me? I told you I don't want to think about it, and I wish you gave it as little thought as I do.'

'I am interested because I like things to be definite,' he replied.

'It's love, not the outward form that counts,' she said, more and more irritated, not by his words but at the tone of cool composure in which he spoke. 'Why should you want it?'

'Oh Lord, love again?' he thought, with a grimace. 'You know very well why – for your sake and that of the children we may have,' he said.

'We shan't have any.'

'That's a great pity,' he said.

'You want it for the sake of the children but you don't think of me, do you?' she pursued, quite forgetting or not having heard that he had said, 'for *your* sake and that of the children.'

The question of having children had long been a thorny subject of dispute. His desire to have children she interpreted as a proof of his indifference to her beauty.

'Oh, I said *for your sake*! Most of all for your sake,' he repeated, his face contorted as though in pain, 'because I am sure that a great deal of your irritability is due to the uncertainty of your position.'

'Ah, here it is – now he has thrown off the mask and I can see all his cold hate for me,' she thought, paying no heed to his words but watching with terror the cold, cruel judge who looked mockingly at her out of his eyes.

'That is not the reason,' she said, 'and, indeed, I don't see how my irritability, as you call it, can be due to that. I am entirely in your power – what uncertainty of position is there about that? Quite the contrary!'

'I am very sorry that you don't want to understand me,' he interrupted, stubbornly bent on expressing his thought. 'The indefiniteness consists in your imagining that I am free.'

'As far as that goes, you can set your mind at rest,' she said, and, turning away from him, began drinking her coffee.

She lifted her cup, sticking out her little finger, and put it to her lips. After a few sips she glanced at him. The expression on his face told her clearly that he found her hand, her gesture, and the sound made by her lips repulsive.

'It is a matter of complete indifference to me what your mother thinks and whom she wants to marry you to,' she went on, putting down her cup with trembling hand.

'But we are not talking about that.'

'Precisely about that. And let me tell you, a heartless woman, be she old or not old, your mother or anyone else, is of no consequence to me, and I do not want to have anything to do with her.'

'Anna, I beg you not to speak disrespectfully of my mother.'

'A woman whose heart does not tell her where her son's happiness and honour lie has no heart.'

'I repeat my request that you should not speak disrespectfully of my mother, whom I respect,' he said, raising his voice and regarding her sternly.

She did not answer. Looking fixedly at him, at his face, his hands, she recalled in every detail the scene of their reconciliation the evening before, and his passionate kisses and caresses. 'Just such caresses he has lavished, and longs to lavish on other women,' she thought.

'You don't love your mother! That's all talk, talk, talk!' she said, looking at him with hate in her eyes.

'If that's so, we must ...'

'Make up our minds, and I have already made up mine,' she said, and was preparing to leave the room when Yashvin walked in. Anna greeted him and stopped.

Why, when a storm was raging in her heart and she felt she was at a turning-point in her life, which might have fearful consequences – why at this very moment she had to keep up appearances before an outsider who sooner or later would know all, she could not tell. But immediately quelling the tumult within her she sat down and began talking to their visitor.

'Well, how are you getting on? Has the money been paid?' she asked Yashvin.

'Oh, pretty fair. I fancy I shan't get it all, but I shall get a good half. And when are you off?' asked Yashvin, looking at Vronsky with a frown and evidently guessing that they had been quarrelling.

'The day after to-morrow, I believe,' said Vronsky.

'You've been meaning to go, I know, for a long time.'

'But now it is all decided,' said Anna, looking Vronsky straight in the face with a look which warned him not to dream of a reconciliation.

'Don't you feel sorry for that unfortunate Pevtsov?' she went on, talking to Yashvin.

'That's a question I have never asked myself, Anna Arkadyevna. You see, all my fortune's here' – he touched his breast-pocket – 'and just now I'm a rich man. But I'm going to the club to-night, and I may come out a beggar. You see, whoever sits down to play with me would gladly leave me without a shirt to my back, and I him. And so we fight it out, and that's where the enjoyment lies.'

'Well, but suppose you were married?' said Anna. 'How would your wife feel about it?'

Yashvin laughed.

'I expect that's why I never married, and never mean to.'

'What about Helsingfors?' said Vronsky, joining in the conversation and glancing at Anna, who had smiled. Meeting his eyes, Anna's face instantly assumed a coldly severe expression as if to say: 'I have not forgotten. Everything is still the same.'

'Have you really never been in love?' she asked Yashvin.

'Oh Lord, dozens of times! But you see, some men can sit down to cards and always be able to leave when the hour comes for a *rendez-vous*. But when I play the love-game I manage it so as not to be late for cards in the evening. That's my way!'

'No, I didn't mean that – I was asking about the real thing.' She was going to say *Helsingfors*, but did not want to repeat the word used by Vronsky.

Voitov, who was buying a horse from Vronsky, arrived, and Anna rose and went out of the room.

Before leaving the house, Vronsky came to her room. She would have pretended to be looking for something on the table but ashamed of making a pretence she looked him straight in the face with cold eyes.

'What do you want?' she asked in French.

'Gambetta's pedigree. I've sold him,' he replied, in a tone which said more clearly than words, 'I have no time for discussing things, and it would lead to nothing.'

'I'm not to blame in any way,' he thought. 'If she will punish herself, *tant pis pour elle*!' But as he was going out he thought he heard her say something and his heart suddenly ached with pity for her.

'What, Anna?' he queried.

'Nothing,' she answered in the same cold, quiet voice.

'If it's nothing, then *tant pis*,' he thought, chilled again.

He turned to go and on his way out caught a glimpse of her face, white and with trembling lips, in the looking-glass. He wanted to stop then and give her a word of comfort but his legs carried him out of the room before he could think of anything to say. He was away all day and when he returned late at night the maid told him that Anna Arkadyevna had a headache and asked him not to go in to her.

26

NEVER before had a whole day gone by without bringing a reconciliation. To-day was the first time. And this was not a quarrel. It was an obvious admission of complete estrangement. How could he look at her as he had done when he came into the room for the pedigree? Look at her, see that her heart was torn with despair, and then walk out without a word, with that face of callous indifference? Not only had he cooled towards her – he hated her because he loved another woman: that was clear.

And remembering all the cruel words he had uttered, Anna supplied others he had unmistakably wanted to say and might have said to her, and she grew more and more exacerbated.

'I am not holding you,' he might have said. 'You are at liberty to go where you please. You probably did not want to be divorced from your husband so that you could return to him. Return then! If you need money, I'll give it you. How much do you want?'

All the cruellest things that a brutal man could say, in her imagination he said to her, and she could not forgive him for them any more than if he had actually said them.

'But wasn't it only last night that he, a truthful and sincere man, swore that he loved me? Have I not often before despaired for nothing?' she said to herself a moment later.

All that day, except for the couple of hours she took going to Mrs Wilson, Anna spent wondering whether everything were over or if there were still hope of a reconciliation, whether she should go away now or see him once more. She waited for him the entire day, and in the evening when she retired to her room, having left word for him that she had a headache, she said to herself, 'If he comes in spite of the maid's message, it means that he loves me still. If he doesn't, it means that all is over, and then I shall have to decide what to do ...'

In the evening she heard his carriage stop, heard him ring, heard his steps and his voice talking to the maid. He had taken the maid's word, did not care to find out more, and went to his room. So all was over!

And the idea of death presented itself clearly and vividly as the sole means of reviving his love for her, of punishing him and of gaining the victory in the contest which the evil spirit in her heart was waging against him.

Nothing mattered to her now – whether they went to Vozdvizhenskoe or not, whether she got a divorce or not: it was all useless. The one thing that mattered was to punish him.

When she poured out her usual dose of opium and thought that she had only to swallow the whole bottleful to die, it seemed to her so simple and easy that she again knew real enjoyment in imagining how he would suffer, repent, and cherish her memory when it was too late. She lay in bed with wide-open eyes staring in the light of a single burned-down candle at the moulded cornice of the ceiling, and the shadow the screen cast on it, while she vividly pictured to herself what he would feel when she was no more, when she was nothing but a memory for him. 'How could I have said those cruel things to her?' he would think. 'How could I have left the room without a word? But now she is no more. She has gone from us for ever. She is there ...' Suddenly the shadow of the screen wavered, pounced on the whole cornice, the whole ceiling. Shadows from the other side darted across to meet it. For an instant they rushed back, then moved up with fresh swiftness, flickered, blended, and all was darkness. 'Death!' she thought. And such horror fell upon her that for a long while she could not make out where she was, and her trembling hands could not find a match with which to light another candle in the place of the one that had burned low and gone out.

'No, anything – only to live! Why, I love him! And he loves me! All this was in the past and will go,' she said, feeling tears of joy at her return to life trickling down her cheeks. And to escape from her panic she hurried down to his room.

He was sound asleep. She went up to him and holding the candle above his face stood a long while gazing at him. Now, when he slept, she loved him so that she could not restrain tears of tenderness at the sight of him. But she knew that if he were to wake he would look at her coldly, conscious of his own righteousness, and that before she could tell him of her love she would have to prove to him how wrong he had been to her. She went back to her room without waking him, and after a second dose of opium towards morning fell into a heavy, troubled sleep, during which she never quite lost consciousness.

At dawn a horrible nightmare, which she had had several times even before her connexion with Vronsky, repeated itself and woke her. A little old man with unkempt beard was leaning over a bar of iron, doing something and muttering meaningless words in French, and – this was what always made the nightmare so horrible – she felt that though this peasant seemed to be paying no attention to her he was doing something dreadful to her with the iron. She awoke in cold perspiration.

When she got up, the events of the previous day came back to her as in a fog.

'There had been a quarrel. It had happened several times before. I said I had a headache and he did not come in to see me. To-morrow we go. I must see him and get ready for the journey,' she said to herself. And learning that he was in the study, she started off to him.

As she passed through the drawing-room she heard a carriage stop at the front door, and looking out of the window she saw a young girl in a lilac hat leaning out of the carriage window and giving some directions to a footman who was ringing the bell. After a colloquy in the hall, someone came upstairs, and Anna heard Vronsky's steps outside the drawing-room. He ran swiftly down. Anna went to the window again. There he was on the steps, hatless, going down to the carriage. The young girl in the lilac hat handed him a packet. Vronsky said something to her and smiled. The carriage drove off; he ran quickly upstairs again.

The mist that had shrouded everything suddenly lifted from Anna's soul. The feelings of yesterday returned to pierce her aching heart with fresh pain. She could not understand now how she could have humiliated herself to remain a whole day with him under his roof. She went to his study to inform him of her decision.

'That was Princess Sorokin and her daughter. They came with the money and documents from *maman*. I couldn't get them yesterday. How is your head – better?' he said quietly, taking no notice of the sombre, tragic look on her face.

In silence she stood in the middle of the room, gazing intently at him. He glanced at her, frowned for an instant, and continued reading his letter. She turned and slowly moved towards the door. He could still call her back but she reached the door and he remained silent; the only sound was the rustle of the sheet of paper as he turned it over.

'Oh, by the way,' he said when she was already in the doorway, 'we are definitely going to-morrow, aren't we?'

'You are, but not I,' she said, turning round to him.

'Anna, we can't go on like this …'

'You are, but not I,' she repeated.

'This is becoming intolerable!'

'You … you will be sorry for this,' she said, and went out.

Alarmed by the despairing look with which she had spoken these words, he jumped up, meaning to run after her, but on second thoughts he sat down again, firmly setting his teeth and frowning. Her vague threat, which he considered vulgar, exasperated him. 'I've tried everything,' he thought; 'the only thing left now is to take no notice,' and he began getting ready to drive into town, and then to his mother's again, to get her signature to the power of attorney.

She heard his steps in the study, then in the dining-room. He paused at the drawing-room door but did not come in to her, merely giving orders to let Voitov have the horse if he came while he was away. Then she heard the sound of the carriage, and the door open, and he went out again. But now he was back in the hall, and someone ran upstairs. It was his valet who had run back for the gloves his master had forgotten. She went to the window and saw him take the gloves without looking up, tap the coachman on the back and say something to him. Then, without a glance at the window, he settled himself in the carriage, crossing one leg over the other in his usual fashion, and, pulling on a glove, disappeared round the corner.

27

'HE's gone! It is all over!' Anna said to herself, standing at the window; and in response to the question the same icy horror which she had felt in the night when the candle had flickered out, leaving her to darkness and nightmare, seized her heart.

'No, it cannot be!' she exclaimed, and crossing the room she rang loudly. She was so terrified of being alone that she did not wait for the servant but went out to meet him.

'Find out where the count has gone,' she said.

The man replied that the count had gone to the stables. 'The count left word that the carriage will return directly, in case Madame should wish to go out.'

'Very well. Wait a moment. I'll write a note at once. Send Mihail with it to the stables. Make haste.'

She sat down and wrote:

'It is all my fault. Come back home. We must talk things over. For God's sake come! I am frightened.'

She sealed the note and gave it to the servant.

Afraid of being left alone now, she followed him out of the room and went to the nursery.

'How is this? This is not right – this is not he! Where are his blue eyes, his sweet, shy smile?' was her first thought on seeing her chubby, rosy-cheeked little girl with her black curly hair instead of Seriozha, whom in the confusion of her thoughts she had expected to find in the nursery. The baby, sitting at the table and noisily pounding it with the stopper of a bottle, gazed blankly at its mother with two black little eyes like currants. In reply to the English nurse, Anna said that she was quite well and that they were going to the country next day. Then she sat down beside the little girl and began twirling the stopper round in front of her. But the child's loud, ringing laugh and a movement of her eyebrows reminded Anna so vividly of Vronsky that, choking down her sobs, she rose and hurried from the room. 'Is it really all over? No, it cannot be!' she thought. 'He will come back. But how can he explain away that smile, his animation after he had spoken to her? But even if he fails to explain it, I shall believe him all the same. If I don't believe him, there's only one thing left for me … and I don't want that.'

She looked at the clock. Twelve minutes had passed. 'Now he must have received my note and be on his way back. It won't be long now – another ten minutes. ... But supposing he doesn't come? No, that is impossible! But I mustn't let him see that I've been crying. I'll go and bathe my eyes. And what about my hair – have I done it or not?' she wondered, but could not remember. She put her hand to her head. 'Yes, I did my hair, but I don't in the least remember when.' She did not even trust the evidence of her hand and went up to the pier-glass to see whether she really had done her hair or not. She had, but she could not remember doing it. 'Who's that?' she thought, gazing in the mirror at the feverish, scared face with the strangely glittering eyes looking out at her. 'Why, it's I!' she realized all at once, and looking at herself full length she suddenly seemed to feel his kisses on her, gave a shiver and moved her shoulders. Then she lifted her hand to her lips and kissed it.

'I must be going out of my mind!' she said to herself, and went to her bedroom, where Annushka was tidying up.

'Annushka!' she said, stopping before the maid and staring at her, not knowing what to say.

'You were going to see the Princess Oblonsky,' said the girl, apparently understanding what it was Anna had meant to ask.

'Princess Oblonsky? Yes, of course.'

'Fifteen minutes there and fifteen back. He is already on the way. He will be here any moment.' She took out her watch and consulted it. 'But how could he go away leaving me in such a state? How can he live, without having made it up with me?' She went to the window and looked out into the street. He had had time to get back by now. But her calculations might have been wrong, and she began reckoning up the minutes again from the time he had left the house.

Just as she was walking over to the clock to verify her watch a carriage drove up to the door. Glancing out of the window she saw it was his carriage. But no one came upstairs, and she heard voices below. It was her messenger who had come back in the carriage. She went down to him.

'I didn't catch the count. He had gone to Nizhny station.'

'What did you say? What? ...' she said to the jolly, rosy-faced Mihail, as he handed her back the note.

'Oh, of course, he did not get it,' she realized.

'Go with this note to the Countess Vronsky's country-house, do you know it? And bring back an answer at once,' she told the man.

'But what shall I do with myself meanwhile?' she thought. 'Yes, I'll drive to Dolly's, of course. Otherwise I shall go out of my mind. Ah, and I could telegraph as well.' And she wrote out a telegram.

I absolutely must talk to you; come at once.

Having sent off the telegram, she went upstairs to dress. Ready and with her bonnet on, she glanced again at the plump, placid Annushka, whose kindly little grey eyes were full of sympathy.

'Annushka, dear, what am I to do?' murmured Anna, sobbing and sinking helplessly into a chair.

'Why take it to heart so, Anna Arkadyevna? These things will happen. Go out: a change will do you good,' advised the maid.

'Yes, I will go out,' said Anna, recovering and getting up. 'And if a telegram comes while I'm away, send it on to Darya Alexandrovna's ... but no, I'll come back myself.

'Yes, I mustn't think, I must do something, go out, get away from this house at any rate,' she said, listening in terror to the dreadful beating of her heart, and she hurriedly went down and got into the carriage.

'Where to, ma'am?' asked Peter before climbing to the box.

'Znamenka street, the Oblonskys'.'

28

THE weather was bright. A fine drizzling rain had fallen all the morning but now it had lately cleared up. The iron roofs, the flag-stones of the pavements, the cobbled roadway, the wheels, the leather, brass, and metal-work of the carriages – all glistened brightly in the May sunshine. It was three o'clock in the afternoon and the streets were full of people.

Sitting in the corner of the comfortable carriage that swayed lightly on its elastic springs with the swift trot of the pair of greys, Anna, to the accompaniment of the rumble of wheels and the rapidly changing impressions in the open air, once more went over the events of the last few days, and saw her position in an entirely different light from how it had appeared to her at home. Now the idea of death no longer seemed so terrible and distinct, and death itself no longer so inevitable. She rebuked herself now for having sunk so low. 'I implore him to forgive me! I gave in to him, confessed myself in the wrong. What for? Surely I can live without him?' And leaving the question un-answered she fell to reading the signboards. 'Office and warehouse. ... Dental surgeon. ... Yes, I will tell Dolly everything. She doesn't like Vronsky. It will be painful and humiliating, but I'll tell her all about everything. She is fond of me and I will follow her advice. I won't give in to him. I won't allow him to teach me. ... Filippov, pastry cook – I've heard he sends his pastry to Petersburg. The Moscow water is so good. Ah, the springs at Mitishchen, and the pancakes! ...' And she remembered how long, long ago, when she was a girl of seventeen, she had gone with her aunt to visit the Troitsa Monastery. 'There were no railways in those days. Was that really me, that girl with the red hands? How many of the things I used to think so beau-tiful and unattainable have become insignificant since then; and the things I had then are now for ever beyond reach! Could I have be-lieved then that I could fall so low? How proud and self-satisfied he will feel when he gets my note! But I will show him ... How nasty that paint smells! Why is it they're always painting and building? *Dressmaking and millinery*,' she read. A man bowed to her. It was Annushka's husband. 'Our parasites,' she remembered the words Vronsky had used. 'Our? Why our? What's so dreadful is that one can't tear up the past by its roots. Yes, but I can try not to think of it. I must do that.' She suddenly remembered her past with Karenin and how she had blotted that from her memory. 'Dolly will think I am leaving a second husband and so I certainly must be in the wrong. As if I cared about being in the right! I can't help it!' She was almost on the point of tears. Two girls passed, laughing. 'I wonder what they can be smiling at!' she thought. 'Love, most likely. They don't know how dreary it is, how wretched. ... The boulevard and the children. Three boys running about playing at horses. Seriozha! And I shall lose everything and never get him back. Yes, everything will be lost if he doesn't return. Perhaps he missed the train and is back by now. Want-ing to humiliate yourself again!' she said to herself. 'No, I shall go to Dolly and tell her straight out: "I'm unhappy, I deserve it and it's my fault, but all the same I'm unhappy. Help me." These horses, this car-riage – how I despise myself for being in this carriage! They are all his; but I will never see them again.'

Going over in her mind what she would say to Dolly, and deliber-ately lacerating her own heart, Anna went up the steps.

'Is anyone with her?' she asked in the hall.

'Katerina Alexandrovna Levin,' answered the footman.

'Kitty? That same Kitty with whom Vronsky had once been in love!' thought Anna. 'The girl he thinks of with affection, sorry he did not marry her. But me he thinks of with hate, sorry he ever met me!'

When Anna called, the two sisters were having a consultation about nursing the baby. Dolly went out alone to meet the visitor who had come and interrupted their talk.

'Oh, you have not gone yet? I meant to come and see you,' said Dolly. 'I had a letter from Stiva to-day.'

'We had a wire from him too,' Anna replied, looking round for Kitty.

'He writes that he can't make out what it is that Alexei Alexandrovich really wants, but that he won't leave without getting some definite answer.'

'I thought you had someone with you. May I see the letter?'

'Yes, Kitty's here,' said Dolly, embarrassed. 'She is in the nursery. You know she has been very ill.'

'So I heard. May I see the letter?'

'I'll fetch it at once. But he has not refused: on the contrary, Stiva has hopes ...' said Dolly, pausing at the door.

'I haven't, and indeed I don't want anything,' said Anna.

'What, does Kitty think it beneath her dignity to meet me?' Anna asked herself when she was alone. 'Perhaps she is right, too. But it's not for her, the girl who was in love with Vronsky – it's not for her to let me see it, even if it is true. I know that in my position I can't be received by any respectable woman. I knew that from the first moment I sacrificed everything to him. And this is my reward! Oh, how I hate him! And what did I come here for? It's worse here – I am more wretched here than at home.' She heard the voices of the two sisters conferring in the next room. 'And what am I going to say to Dolly now? Shall I give Kitty the satisfaction of seeing that I am unhappy, and let her patronize me? No; and even Dolly wouldn't understand. It is no use my telling her. It would have been interesting, though, just to see Kitty and show her how I despise everybody and everything, how nothing matters to me now.'

Dolly came in with the letter. Anna read it and handed it back without a word.

'I knew all that,' she said, 'and it doesn't interest me in the least.'

'But why not? I, on the contrary, am hopeful,' said Dolly, looking at Anna intently. She had never seen her in such a strange and irritable mood. 'When are you leaving?' she asked.

Anna, screwing up her eyes, gazed straight before her and did not answer.

'Is Kitty hiding from me, then?' she said, looking at the door and flushing.

'Oh, what nonsense! She's nursing the baby and having trouble, and I was advising her ... She will be delighted to see you. She'll be here directly,' said Dolly awkwardly, not clever at lying. 'Here she is now.'

When Kitty heard that Anna had called, she had not wanted to appear but Dolly had persuaded her. Nerving herself, Kitty came in and, blushing, went up to Anna and held out her hand.

'I am so glad to see you,' she began in a trembling voice.

Kitty was torn between her hostility to this bad woman and a desire to make allowances for her; but the moment she saw Anna's dear, lovely face all her hostility vanished.

'I should not have been surprised if you had not cared to meet me. I am used to all that. You have been ill? Yes, you have changed,' said Anna.

Kitty felt that Anna was looking at her with animosity but put this down to the awkward position Anna, who had once befriended her, now felt herself to be in, and she was sorry for her.

They talked about Kitty's illness, about the baby, about Stiva, but it was evident that nothing interested Anna.

'I came to say good-bye,' she said, rising.

'When is it you are going?'

But again Anna did not reply, and turned to Kitty.

'Yes, I am very glad to have seen you,' she said with a smile. 'I have heard so much about you from all sides, even from your husband. He came to see me and I liked him very much,' she added, with obvious ill intent. 'Where is he?'

'He has gone to the country,' Kitty replied, blushing.

'Remember me to him – be sure you do!'

'I will be sure to,' repeated Kitty naïvely, looking compassionately into her eyes.

'Well, good-bye, Dolly!' And kissing Dolly and pressing Kitty's hand, Anna hurried away.

'She's just the same, and as attractive as ever. How beautiful she is!' Kitty said when Anna had gone. 'But there is something pitiful about her, terribly pitiful!'

'Yes, there's something peculiar about her to-day,' said Dolly. 'When I was seeing her out, I fancied she was almost crying.'

29

ANNA reseated herself in the carriage, feeling even worse than when she left home. To her previous tortures was now added a consciousness of having been affronted and rejected, of which she had been so clearly sensible during the meeting with Kitty.

'Where to, ma'am? Home?' asked Peter.

'Yes, home,' she said, not even thinking now where she was going.

'How they looked at me – as if they were seeing something dreadful and strange and incomprehensible! What can that man be telling the other with such ardour?' she thought, glancing at two passers-by. 'Can one ever tell anyone what one is feeling? I wanted to tell Dolly, but it's a good thing I didn't. How pleased she would have been at my misery! She would have concealed it but in her heart she would have been delighted at my being punished for the happiness she envied me. Kitty, she would have been still more pleased. I can read her like a book. She knows I was more than usually cordial to her husband. She's jealous of me and hates me. And she despises me too. In her eyes I'm an immoral woman. If I were an immoral woman I could have made her husband fall in love with me ... if I'd cared to. And, indeed, so I did. There goes someone satisfied with himself!' she thought, seeing a portly, red-faced gentleman driving past in the opposite direction. He mistook her for an acquaintance and raised his shiny hat from his bald, shiny head, and then perceived his mistake. 'He thought he knew me. Well, he knows me as little as does anyone else in the world. I don't know myself. I only know my appetites, as the French say. Those two boys want some of that filthy ice-cream. They know that for a certainty,' she thought, noticing two boys stop an ice-cream vendor, who lifted his tub down from his head and wiped his perspiring face with the end of the cloth. 'We all want what is sweet, what is nice. If we can't have bon-bons, then dirty ice-cream! And Kitty's just the same: she couldn't get Vronsky, so she took Levin. And she envies and hates me. And we all hate each other – I Kitty, and she

793

me. Yes, that is the truth. *"Tuttikin, coiffeur." Je me fais coiffer par Tuttikin* ... I'll tell him that when he comes home,' she thought and smiled. But then she remembered that she had no one now to tell funny things to. 'Besides, there is nothing funny, nothing amusing, really. Everything's hateful. They are ringing the bell for vespers – how carefully that shopkeeper crosses himself, as if he were afraid of dropping something! Why these churches, the bells and the humbug? Just to hide the fact that we all hate each other, like those cabdrivers so angrily abusing one another over there. Yashvin was quite right when he said, "He is after my shirt and I'm after his!" '

She was so occupied by these thoughts that she even forgot her troubles until they drew up at the porch of the house. It was only when she saw the hall-porter coming out to meet her that she remembered the note and the telegram she had sent.

'Is there any answer?' she inquired.

'I will go and see,' the porter replied, and glancing at his desk he took up and handed her the thin square envelope of a telegram.

'*I cannot return before ten – Vronsky,*' she read.

'And isn't the messenger back yet?'

'Not yet,' replied the hall-porter.

'If that is so, then I know what I must do,' she said to herself, and feeling a vague fury and craving for vengeance rising within her she ran upstairs. 'I shall go to him myself. Before leaving him for good, I'll tell him all I think. Never have I hated anyone as I hate that man!' she thought. Catching sight of his hat on the hat-rail she shuddered with aversion. She did not consider that his telegram had been in reply to hers and that he had not yet received her note. She pictured him calmly chatting with his mother and the Princess Sorokin, and rejoicing at her sufferings. 'Yes, I must go at once,' she thought, not yet sure where to go. She wanted to get away as quickly as possible from the sensations she experienced in that awful house. The servants, the walls, the things in the house – they all filled her with loathing and malice, and oppressed her like a weight.

'Yes, I must go to the railway station, and if I don't find him there I must go to the house and catch him.' Anna looked at the time-table in the daily paper. There was an evening train at two minutes past eight. 'Yes, I shall be in time.' She gave orders for the other horses to be put in the carriage, and busied herself packing a travelling-bag with the things she might need for a few days. She knew she would never return. She vaguely resolved on one of the plans that passed through her mind: after what would happen at the railway station or at the countess's house, she would go on by the Nizhny line and stop at the first town she came to.

Dinner was on the table. She entered the room but the smell of the bread and the cheese – the whole idea of food revolted her. She ordered the carriage and went out. The house already threw a shadow right across the street; it was a bright evening and still warm in the sun. Annushka, who came out with Anna's things, and Peter, who put them in the carriage, and the coachman, evidently disgruntled, were all objectionable to her, and irritated her by their words and movements.

'I shan't need you, Peter.'

'But how about your ticket?'

'Well, as you like, it doesn't matter,' she said pettishly.

Peter jumped up on the box and arms akimbo told the coachman to drive to the station.

30

'THERE, it is that girl again! Again I see it all!' said Anna to herself as soon as the carriage started and, rocking slightly, rumbled over the little cobbles of the roadway. Once more the impressions succeeded one another in her brain.

'Now, what was the last thing I thought of that was so good?' she tried to remember. '*Tuttikin, coiffeur?* No, not that. I know – what Yashvin said: the struggle for existence and hate are the only things that hold men together. No, it's a useless journey you're making,' she mentally addressed a party of people in a coach and four who were evidently going on an excursion into the country. 'And the dog you are taking with you won't help either. You can't get away from yourselves.' Glancing in the direction in which Peter was looking, she saw a workman, almost dead-drunk, his head swaying, being led off by a policeman. 'He's found a quicker way,' she thought. 'Count Vronsky and I did not find our happiness either, though we expected so much.' And now for the first time Anna turned the glaring light in which she was seeing everything upon her relations with him, which she had hitherto avoided thinking about. 'What did he look for in me? Not love so much as the gratification of his vanity.' She remembered his words, the expression of his face, like a faithful setter's, in the early days of their liaison. And everything now confirmed that. 'Yes, in him there was triumph over a success for his vanity. Of course there was love too, but the chief element was pride of success. He gloried in me. Now that is past. There is nothing to be proud of – nothing to be proud of, only ashamed. He has taken from me everything he could, and now I am no more use to him. He is tired of me and is trying not to act dishonourably towards me. Only yesterday he blurted out that he wants divorce and marriage so as to burn his boats. He loves me, but how? *The zest is gone,*' she said to herself in English. 'That fellow wants everyone to admire him, and is very well pleased with himself,' she thought, looking at a ruddy-cheeked clerk riding by on a hired horse. 'No, there's not the same flavour about me for him now. If I leave him, at the bottom of his heart he will be glad.'

This was not surmise – she saw it distinctly in the piercing light which revealed to her now the meaning of life and human relations.

'My love grows more and more passionate and selfish, while his is dying, and that is why we are drifting apart,' she went on musing. 'And there's no help for it. He is all in all to me, and I demand that he should give himself more and more entirely up to me. And he wants to get farther and farther away from me. Up to the time of our union we were irresistibly drawn together, and now we are irresistibly drawn apart. And nothing can be done to alter it. He says I am insanely jealous and I have kept on telling myself that I am insanely jealous; but it is not true. I am not jealous, but unsatisfied. But ...' Her mouth dropped open and she was so agitated by the sudden thought that came to her that she changed her place in the carriage. 'If I could be anything but his mistress, passionately caring for nothing but his caresses – but I can't, and I don't want to be anything else. And my desire arouses his disgust, and that excites resentment in me, and it cannot be otherwise. Don't I know that he wouldn't deceive me, that he has no thought of wanting to marry the Princess Sorokin, that he is not in love with Kitty, that he won't be unfaithful to me? I know all that, but it doesn't make it any the easier for me. If he does not love me, but treats me kindly and gently out of a sense of *duty*, and what I want is not there – that would be a thousand times worse than having him hate me. It would be hell! And that is just how it is. He has long ceased to love me. And where love ends, hate begins. I don't know these streets at all. How hilly it is – and houses and houses everywhere. ... And in

796

the houses people, and more people. ... No end to them, and all hating each other. Suppose I think to myself what it is I want to make me happy. Well? I get a divorce, and Alexei Alexandrovich lets me have Seriozha, and I marry Vronsky.' Thinking of Karenin she immediately saw him before her with extraordinary vividness – the mild, lifeless, faded eyes, the blue veins in his white hands – heard his intonations and the cracking of his finger joints, and remembering the feeling that had once existed between them, and which had also been called love, she shuddered with revulsion. 'Well, I get divorced, and become Vronsky's wife. What then? Will Kitty cease looking at me as she looked at me to-day? No. And will Seriozha leave off asking and wondering about my two husbands? And is there any new feeling I can imagine between Vronsky and me? Could there be if not happiness, just absence of torment? No, and no again!' she answered herself now without the smallest hesitation. 'Impossible! Life is sundering us, and I am the cause of his unhappiness and he of mine, and there's no altering him or me. Every attempt has been made but the screw has been twisted tight. ... A beggar-woman with a baby. She thinks she inspires pity. Are we not all flung into the world for no other purpose than to hate each other, and so to torture ourselves and one another? There go some schoolboys, laughing. Seriozha?' she remembered. 'I thought, too, that I loved him, and used to be moved by my own tenderness for him. Yet here I have lived without him. I exchanged him for another love, and did not complain so long as the other love satisfied me.' And she thought with disgust of what she called the 'other love'. The clearness with which she saw her own life now, and everyone else's, gave her a sense of pleasure. 'So it is with me, and Peter, and Fiodor the coachman, and that tradesman, and all those people who live by the Volga where those advertisements there invite us to go. It is the same everywhere and always,' she thought as they drove up to the low building of Nizhny station, and the porters ran to meet her.

'Shall I take a ticket to Obiralovka?' asked Peter.

She had completely forgotten where she was going, and why, and only by a great effort could she understand his question.

'Yes,' she said, handing him her purse; and, hanging her little red bag on her arm, she got out of the carriage.

As she made her way through the crowd to the first-class waiting-room she gradually recalled all the details of her situation and the plans between which she was wavering. And again hope and despair in turn, chafing the old sores, lacerated the wounds of her tortured, cruelly throbbing heart. Sitting on the star-shaped couch waiting for her train, she looked with aversion at the people coming in and out. They were all objectionable to her. She thought of how she would arrive at the station and send him a note, of what she would write, and of how he was at this moment complaining to his mother (not understanding her sufferings) of his position, and of how she would enter the room and what she would say to him. Then she thought of how life might still be happy, and how wretchedly she loved and hated him, and how dreadfully her heart was beating.

31

THE bell rang, and some ugly, insolent young men passed by, hurriedly yet mindful of the impression they were creating. Then Peter, in his livery and gaiters, with his dull, animal face also crossed the room to come and see her into the train. The noisy young men fell silent as she passed them on the platform, and one of them whispered some remark about her to his neighbour – something vile, no doubt. Anna climbed the high step of the railway carriage and sat down in an empty compartment on the once white but now dirty seat. Her bag gave a bounce on the cushion and then was still. With a foolish smile Peter raised his gold-braided hat at the window to take leave of her, and an impudent guard slammed the door and pulled down the catch. A misshapen lady wearing a bustle (Anna mentally undressed the woman and was appalled at her hideousness), followed by a girl laughing affectedly, ran past outside the carriage window.

'Katerina Andreevna has everything, *ma tante*!' cried the little girl.

'Even the girl is grotesque and affected,' thought Anna. To avoid seeing people she got up quickly and seated herself at the opposite window of the empty compartment. A grimy, deformed-looking peasant in a cap from beneath which tufts of his matted hair stuck out, passed by this window, stooping down to the carriage wheels. 'There's something familiar about that deformed peasant,' thought Anna. And remembering her dream she walked over to the opposite door, trembling with fright. The guard opened the door to let in a man and his wife.

'Are you getting out?'

Anna made no reply. Neither the guard nor the passengers getting in noticed, under her veil, the terror on her face. She went back to her corner and sat down. The couple took their seats opposite her and cast stealthy curious glances at her dress. Anna found both husband and wife repellent. The husband asked her if she would object if he smoked, evidently not because he wanted to smoke but in order to get into conversation with her. Receiving her permission, he then began speaking to his wife in French of things he wanted to talk about still less than he wanted to smoke. They made inane remarks to one another, entirely for her benefit. Anna saw clearly that they were bored with one another and hated each other. Nor could such miserable creatures be anything else but hated.

The second bell rang, and was followed by the shifting of luggage, noise, shouting and laughter. It was so clear to Anna that nobody had any cause for joy that this laughter grated on her painfully, and she longed to stop her ears and shut it out. At last the third bell went, the engine whistled and screeched, the coupling chains gave a jerk, and the husband crossed himself.

'It would be interesting to ask him what meaning he attaches to that,' thought Anna, regarding him spitefully. She looked past the lady out of the window at the people standing on the platform who had been seeing the train off and who looked as though they were gliding backwards. With rhythmic jerks over the joints of the rails, the carriage in which Anna sat rattled past the platform, past a brick wall, past the signals and some other carriages. The wheels slid more smoothly and evenly along the rails, making a slight ringing sound. The bright rays of the evening sun shone through the window, and a little breeze played against the blind. Anna forgot her fellow-passengers. Rocked gently by the motion of the train, she inhaled the fresh air and continued the current of her thoughts.

'Where was it I left off? On the reflection that I couldn't conceive a situation in which life would not be a misery, that we were all created in order to suffer, and that we all know this and all try to invent means for deceiving ourselves. But when you see the truth, what are you to do?'

'Reason has been given to man to enable him to escape from his troubles,' said the lady in French, obviously pleased with her phrase and mouthing it.

The words fitted in with Anna's thoughts.

'To escape from his troubles,' Anna repeated to herself. She glanced at the red-cheeked husband and his thin wife, and saw that the sickly woman considered herself misunderstood, and that the husband was unfaithful to her and encouraged her in that idea of herself. Directing her searchlight upon them, Anna as it were read their history and all the hidden crannies of their souls. But there was nothing of interest, and she resumed her reflections.

'Yes, I am very troubled, and reason was given man that he might escape his troubles. Therefore I must escape. Why not put out the candle when there's nothing more to see, when everything looks obnoxious? But how? Why did that guard run along the footboard? Why do those young men in the next carriage make such a noise? Why do they talk and laugh? Everything is false and evil – all lies and deceit!'

When the train stopped at the station, Anna got out with a crowd of other passengers and shunning them as if they were lepers she stood still on the platform trying to remember why she had come and what it was she had intended doing. Everything that had seemed possible before was now so difficult to grasp, especially in this noisy crowd of ugly people who would not leave her in peace. Porters rushed up, offering their services. Young men stamped their heels on the planks of the platform, talking in loud voices and staring at her. The people that tried to get out of her way always dodged to the wrong side. Recollecting that she had meant to go on in the train should there be no answer, she stopped a porter and asked him if there was not a coachman anywhere with a note from Count Vronsky.

'Count Vronsky? Someone from there was here just now, to meet Princess Sorokin and her daughter. What is the coachman like?'

As she was talking to the porter, Mihail the coachman, rosy-faced and cheerful, came up in his smart blue coat with a watch-chain, and handed her a note, evidently proud that he had carried out his errand so well. She tore open the note, and her heart contracted even before she had read it.

'Very sorry your note did not catch me. I shall be back at ten,' Vronsky had written in a careless hand.

'Yes, that is what I expected!' she said to herself with a malicious smile.

'All right, you may go home,' she said quietly to Mihail. She spoke softly because the rapid beating of her heart interfered with her breathing. 'No, I won't let you torture me,' she thought, addressing her warning not to him, not to herself, but to the power that made her suffer, and she walked along the platform past the station buildings.

Two servant-girls strolling up and down the platform turned their heads to stare at her and made some audible remarks about her dress. 'Real,' they said, referring to the lace she was wearing. The young men would not leave her in peace. They passed by again, peering into her face and talking and laughing in loud, unnatural voices. The station-master as he walked by asked her if she was going on in the train. A boy selling kvas never took his eyes off her. 'Oh God, where am I to go?' she thought, continuing farther and farther along the platform. At the end she stopped. Some ladies and children, who had come to meet a gentleman in spectacles and who were laughing and talking noisily, fell silent and scanned her as she drew even with them. She hastened her step and walked away to the edge of the platform. A goods train was approaching. The platform began to shake, and she fancied she was in the train again.

In a flash she remembered the man who had been run down by the train the day she first met Vronsky, and knew what she had to do. Quickly and lightly she descended the steps that led from the water-tank to the rails, and stopped close to the passing train. She looked at the lower part of the trucks, at the bolts and chains and the tall iron wheels of the first truck slowly moving up, and tried to measure the point midway between the front and back wheels, and the exact moment when it would be opposite her.

'There,' she said to herself, looking in the shadow of the truck at the mixture of sand and coal dust which covered the sleepers. 'There, in the very middle, and I shall punish him and escape from them all and from myself.'

She wanted to fall half-way between the wheels of the front truck which was drawing level with her. But the red bag which she began to pull from her arm delayed her, and it was too late: the truck had passed. She must wait for the next. A sensation similar to the feeling she always had when bathing, before she took the first plunge, seized her and she crossed herself. The familiar gesture brought back a whole series of memories of when she was a girl, and of her childhood, and suddenly the darkness that had enveloped everything for her lifted, and for an instant life glowed before her with all its past joys. But she did not take her eyes off the wheels of the approaching second truck.

And exactly at the moment when the space between the wheels drew level with her she threw aside the red bag and drawing her head down between her shoulders dropped on her hands under the truck, and with a light movement, as though she would rise again at once, sank on to her knees. At that same instant she became horror-struck at what she was doing. 'Where am I? What am I doing? Why?' She tried to get up, to throw herself back; but something huge and relentless struck her on the head and dragged her down on her back. 'God forgive me everything!' she murmured, feeling the impossibility of struggling. A little peasant muttering something was working at the rails. And the candle by which she had been reading the book filled with trouble and deceit, sorrow and evil, flared up with a brighter light, illuminating for her everything that before had been enshrouded in darkness, flickered, grew dim and went out for ever.

PART EIGHT

I

NEARLY two months had passed. The hot summer was half over, but Koznyshev was only now preparing to leave Moscow.

Koznyshev's life had not been uneventful during this time. His book, the fruit of six years' labour – *Sketch of a Survey of the Principles and Forms of Government in Europe and Russia* – had been finished about a year ago. Several sections of this book, and the introduction, had appeared in periodicals, and other parts had been read by Koznyshev to persons of his circle, so that the leading ideas of the work could not be very new to the public. But still Koznyshev had expected that on its publication his book would be sure to make a serious impression on society, and if it did not cause a revolution in social science it would, at any rate, make a great stir in the scientific world.

After the most conscientious revision the book had been issued last year and sent out to the booksellers.

Never asking anyone about it, reluctantly and with feigned in-difference answering his friends' inquiries as to how it was going, never even inquiring of the booksellers how it was selling, Koznyshev watched eagerly, with strained attention, for the first signs of the book's effect on the public and on literature in general.

But a week passed, a second, a third, without the least ripple being apparent. His friends, the specialists and savants, occasionally, out of a sense of politeness, alluded to it. The rest of his acquaintances, not in-terested in learned works, did not talk of it at all. And in society, just now particularly taken up with other things, complete indifference reigned. In the press, too, for a whole month, there was not a word about his book.

Koznyshev had calculated to a nicety the time necessary for a re-view to appear; but a month went by, then another, and still there was silence.

Only in the *Northern Beetle*, in a humorous *feuilleton* on the singer

Drabanti, who had lost his voice, was a remark slipped in about Koznyshev's book, suggesting in a few contemptuous words that it had long ago been seen through by everybody and consigned to general ridicule.

At last, in the third month, a critical article appeared in a serious review. Konyshev knew the author of the article. He had met him once at Golubtsov's.

The writer was a very young journalist, an invalid, bold enough in print but a man of very little culture and socially unsure of himself.

In spite of his absolute contempt for the writer, Koznyshev prepared to read his review with the greatest respect. The article was abominable.

The critic had undoubtedly put an interpretation upon the book which could not possibly be put on it. But he had so skilfully selected his quotations that to those who had not read the book (and obviously scarcely anyone had read it) it was made to appear simply a conglomeration of high-sounding words, and these not always appropriate – as frequent interrogation marks testified – and its author a totally ignorant individual. And all this was so wittily done that Koznyshev himself would not have been averse to putting his name to it. But that was just what was so awful.

In spite of the scrupulously conscientious way Koznyshev examined the accuracy of the critic's arguments, he did not for a minute stop to ponder over the deficiencies and errors which were ridiculed – it was too evident that they had been picked out deliberately – but at once found himself recalling down to the last detail his meeting and conversation with the author of the review.

'Did I not offend him somehow?' Koznyshev wondered.

And remembering that when they had met he had corrected the young man in some word he had used that betrayed ignorance, Koznyshev hit upon what was behind the article.

Dead silence, both in print and conversation, followed that review, and Koznyshev saw that the labour of six years into which he had put so much love and care had gone, leaving no trace.

His position was the more painful because, having finished his book, he no longer had any literary work to do, such as had hitherto occupied the greater part of his time.

Koznyshev was clever, cultivated, healthy and active, and he did not know how to make use of his energy. Drawing-room discussions, debates at meetings, assemblies and in committees – and anywhere where talk was possible – took up part of his time. But being used for years to town life, he did not allow himself to be entirely absorbed in talk, as his less experienced brother did when he was in Moscow, so he had a good deal of leisure and mental energy to spare.

Fortunately for him, at this most trying time after the failure of his book, topics of conversation like the dissenting sects, our American friends, the Samara famine, the exhibitions, and spiritualism were pushed into the background by the Slavonic question, which had previously only smouldered in society – and Koznyshev, who had been one of the first to raise the subject, threw himself into it heart and soul.

In the circle to which he belonged nothing else was written or talked about at that time except the Slavonic question and the Serbian war. Everything the idle crowd usually does to kill time, it now did for the benefit of the Slavs. Balls, concerts, dinners, speeches, fashions, beer, restaurants – all bore witness to public sympathy with the Slavs.

With much that was said and written on the subject, Koznyshev did not agree in detail. He saw that the Slav question had become one of those fashionable distractions which follow one another in quick succession as an occupation for society; he saw also that too many people were taking up the question from motives of self-interest and self-advertisement. He recognized that the newspapers printed much that was unnecessary and exaggerated for the sole purpose of attracting attention and outcrying their rivals. He noticed that the people who leaped to the front and shouted loudest in this general surge of enthusiasm were the failures and those who were smarting under a sense of injury – generals without armies, ministers without portfolios, journalists without papers, and party leaders without followers. He saw much that was frivolous and absurd. But he also saw and admitted an unmistakable, ever-growing enthusiasm, uniting all classes, with which it was impossible not to sympathize. The massacre of Slavs who were co-religionists and brothers excited sympathy for the sufferers and indignation against their oppressors. And the heroism of the Serbians and Montenegrins, fighting for a great cause, begot in the whole nation a longing to help brothers not only in word but in deed.

At the same time another phenomenon rejoiced Koznyshev's heart. It was the manifestation of public opinion. The public had definitely expressed its wishes. 'The soul of the nation had become articulate,' as Koznyshev put it. The more he studied the movement the more incontestable it seemed to him that it was a cause destined to assume vast dimensions and mark an epoch in the history of Russia.

He threw himself heart and soul into the service of this great cause, and forgot to think about his book.

His whole time was now so taken up that he was unable to answer all the letters and appeals addressed to him.

Having worked all through the spring and part of the summer, it was not until July that he got ready to go to his brother's in the country.

He looked forward both to a fortnight's rest and the pleasure of seeing – at the sacred heart of the nation, the deep depths of the country – that uprising of the national spirit of which he and all the inhabitants of the capital and the large cities were so fully convinced. Katavasov, who had long promised to pay Levin a visit and had long been meaning to keep that promise, went with him.

2

KOZNYSHEV and Katavasov had barely reached the station of the Kursk line, unusually animated that day, got out of their carriage and looked round for the footman who was following with their luggage, before a party of volunteers drove up in four cabs. The volunteers were met by ladies, who brought them nosegays and accompanied them into the station, the crowd surging after.

One of the ladies who had met the volunteers, emerging from the waiting-room, spoke to Koznyshev.

'Have you come to see them off too?' she asked in French.

'No, Princess, I'm going down to my brother's place for a rest. And do you always come to see them off?' he asked with a slight smile.

'That would hardly be possible!' replied the princess. 'Is it true that we have already sent eight hundred? Malvinsky wouldn't believe me.'

'More than eight hundred. Counting those who did not go from Moscow direct, there must be over a thousand,' said Koznyshev.

'There now! I said so!' exclaimed the lady joyfully. 'And isn't it true, too, that some million roubles have been subscribed?'

'More, Princess.'

'What do you think of to-day's despatch? The Turks beaten again!'

'Yes, so I saw,' replied Koznyshev.

They were speaking of the latest telegram confirming the report that for three days in succession the Turks had been beaten on all fronts and were in flight, and that a decisive engagement was expected on the morrow.

'Oh, by the way, such a nice young man wants to go. I don't know why they are making difficulties. I meant to ask you – I know him – could you write a note for him? He's being sent by the Countess Lydia Ivanovna.'

Having obtained such particulars as the princess could give about the would-be volunteer, Koznyshev went into the first-class waiting-room and wrote a note to the right authority and handed it to the princess.

'You know, the famous Count Vronsky is going by this train?' remarked the princess with an exultant, meaning smile, when Koznyshev had found her again and given her the note.

'I heard he was going but did not know when. On this train, you say?'

'I have seen him. He is here. His mother is the only person seeing him off. In the circumstances, it's the best thing he could do.'

'Quite so!'

While they were talking the crowd rushed past them towards the refreshment-room. They, too, moved on and heard the loud voice of a gentleman who, glass in hand, was making a speech to the volunteers. 'In the service of faith, humanity, and our brothers!' he was saying, raising his voice more and more. 'To this great cause Mother Moscow dedicates you with her blessing. *Zhivio!*' (this was the Serbian word for *Hurrah*), he concluded, loudly and tearfully.

Everyone shouted *Zhivio!* and a fresh crowd surged into the refreshment-room, nearly knocking the princess off her feet.

'Ah, Princess! That was something like!' said Oblonsky, suddenly appearing in the midst of the crowd and beaming happily. 'Didn't he speak well, and with such warmth! Bravo! And Koznyshev here, too! Why, you ought to say something – just a few words of encouragement, you know. You do it so well,' he added with a soft, respectful, discreet smile, gently pushing Koznyshev forward by the arm.

'No, I'm just off myself.'

'Where to?'

'Down to my brother's in the country,' replied Koznyshev.

'Then you'll see my wife. I've written to her but you'll see her before she gets the letter. Do please tell her you've seen me and that it's "all right", as the English say. She will understand. Oh, and tell her, if you will be so kind, that I am appointed secretary of the committee of the consolidated. ... But she'll understand! You know, *les petites misères de la vie humaine*,' he said, as it were apologizing to the princess. 'And Princess Myagky, not Liza, but Bibish, is really sending a thousand rifles and twelve nurses! Did I tell you?'

'Yes, I heard so,' replied Koznyshev grudgingly.

'What a pity you are going away,' said Oblonsky. 'To-morrow we're giving a dinner to two who are setting off – Dimer-Bartnyansky from Petersburg and our Veslovsky, Grisha. They're both going. Veslovsky married recently. There's a fine fellow for you! Isn't he, Princess?' he added, turning to the lady.

The princess looked at Koznyshev without replying. But the fact that Koznyshev and the princess seemed anxious to get rid of him did not abash Oblonsky in the least. Smiling, he stared at the feather on the princess's hat, then about him, as if trying to remember something. Seeing a lady with a collecting-box, he beckoned to her and put in a five-rouble note.

'I can never see those collecting-boxes unmoved while I've money in my pocket,' he said. 'And what a despatch that was to-day! Splendid fellows, those Montenegrins!'

'You don't say so!' he exclaimed, when the princess told him that Vronsky was going by that train. A look of grief passed over his face, but a moment later when, with a slight spring in his step and smoothing his whiskers, he entered the waiting-room where Vronsky was, he had quite forgotten his own heartbroken sobs over his sister's dead body, and saw in Vronsky only a hero and an old friend.

'With all his faults, one must do him justice,' the princess remarked to Koznyshev as soon as Oblonsky had left them. 'He has the true Russian, Slav nature! Only I'm afraid it will be painful for Vronsky to see him. Say what you will, I am moved by the fate of that man. Try to talk to him a little on the journey,' said the princess.

'Yes, I might if opportunity offers.'

'I never liked him. But this atones for much. He's not only going himself, he's taking a whole squadron at his own expense.'

'So I heard.'

A bell was rung. Everybody crowded towards the door.

'There he is!' said the princess, pointing to Vronsky in a long over-coat and broad-brimmed black hat walking by with his mother on his arm. Oblonsky talked vivaciously at his side.

Vronsky was frowning and looking straight before him, as though he did not hear what Oblonsky was saying.

Probably at Oblonsky's indication he looked round to where the princess and Koznyshev were standing, and without speaking raised his hat. His face, aged and full of suffering, looked like stone.

Coming up to the train, Vronsky let his mother pass before him and silently disappeared into one of the compartments.

'God save the Tsar,' was struck up on the platform, followed by shouts of 'Hurrah!' and 'Zhivio!' One of the volunteers, tall, flat-chested, and very young, was bowing in an exaggerated fashion and waving his felt hat and a bouquet over his head. From behind him two officers, and an elderly man with a large beard and a greasy cap, thrust their heads out and also bowed.

3

TAKING leave of the princess, Koznyshev, followed by Katavasov, who had joined him, got into the packed carriage, and the train started.

At Tsaritsyno station the train was met by a melodious choir of young men singing a patriotic song. Again the volunteers bowed and poked their heads out of the carriage windows, but Koznyshev paid no attention to them. He had had so much to do with volunteers that the type was familiar and did not interest him. Katavasov, on the other hand, whose scientific work had offered him no opportunities of studying them, was very much interested, and cross-questioned Ko-znyshev about them.

Koznyshev advised him to go along to the second-class and talk to some of them himself. At the next station Katavasov acted on this suggestion. As soon as the train stopped he changed into a second-class carriage and made acquaintance with the volunteers. They were sit-ting in a corner of the compartment, talking loudly, obviously aware that the attention of the other passengers, as well as that of Katavasov, who had just entered, was directed upon them. The tall, hollow-chested young man spoke the loudest of all. He was unmistakably drunk, and was telling the story of something that had happened at his school. Facing him sat a middle-aged officer, wearing the military jacket of the Austrian Guards. He was listening to the youth with a smile and trying to stop him. A third volunteer, in an artillery uniform, sat beside them on a trunk. A fourth was fast asleep.

Getting into conversation with the young man, Katavasov learned that he was a wealthy Moscow merchant who had run through a large fortune before he was two-and-twenty. Katavasov did not like him because he was effeminate, spoilt, and delicate. He was evidently convinced, especially now that he had been drinking, that he was doing something very heroic, and he bragged in the most unpleasing manner.

The second, the retired officer, also made a disagreeable impression upon Katavasov. He was a man who seemed to have tried everything. He had had a post to do with the railways, had been a steward on an estate, and had started factories. And he talked about it all without the slightest necessity, using inappropriate technical terms.

The artilleryman, however – the third of the volunteers – Katavasov liked very much. He was a modest, quiet fellow, evidently impressed by the knowledge of the ex-guardsman and the heroic self-sacrifice of the merchant, and saying nothing about himself. When Katavasov asked him what prompted him to go to Serbia, he replied modestly:

'Well, everybody's going. The Serbians want help too. I'm sorry for them.'

'Yes, they are particularly short of you artillery-men.'

'Oh, I wasn't long in the artillery. Perhaps they'll put me in the infantry or the cavalry.'

'Why into the infantry when they need artillery-men most of all?' asked Katavasov, concluding from the man's age that he must have reached fairly high rank.

'I wasn't long in the artillery. I'm a retired cadet,' he said, and began to explain why he had not taken the examination for a commission.

The general impression produced on Katavasov by all this was not favourable, and when the volunteers got out at the next station for a drink he felt he must talk to someone and compare views. There was an old man in the carriage, wearing a military overcoat, who had been listening all the while to Katavasov's conversation with the volunteers. When they were left alone, Katavasov addressed him.

'What a difference there is in the positions of these volunteers,' he observed vaguely, wishing to express his own opinion and at the same time to draw the old man.

The old soldier had fought two campaigns. He knew what makes a soldier, and judging by the appearance and talk of the volunteers, and the swagger with which they applied themselves to the bottle, he had formed a poor opinion of them. Moreover, he lived in a provincial town, and he was longing to tell someone about a discharged soldier who had volunteered from his town, a drunkard and a thief whom no one would employ. But, knowing by experience that in the present temper of the public it was dangerous to express an opinion contrary to the prevailing one, and especially dangerous to criticize the volunteers unfavourably, he was wary with Katavasov.

'Well, men are wanted there,' he said, with a twinkle in his eye. And they fell to discussing the latest war news, each concealing from the other his perplexity as to whom to-morrow's battle was to be fought with, since the Turks, according to the most recent intelligence, had been beaten at all points. And so they parted without either of them having expressed his opinion.

Katavasov returned to his own carriage and reluctantly prevaricated: the account he gave Koznyshev let it appear that the volunteers were excellent fellows.

At the next big station the volunteers were again greeted with songs and cheers. Here, too, there were men and women with collecting-boxes, and the provincial ladies presented the volunteers with nosegays, and followed them to the refreshment-room; but it was all on a much smaller and feebler scale than in Moscow.

4

WHEN the train stopped at the principal town of the province, Katavasov did not proceed to the refreshment-room but walked up and down the platform.

The first time he passed Vronsky's compartment he noticed that the blind was down. But the next time he walked by the old countess was at the window. She beckoned to Koznyshev.

'You see, I am going as far as Kursk with him,' she said.

'Yes, so I heard,' replied Koznyshev, stopping by her window and glancing inside. 'What a fine thing he's doing!' he added, seeing that Vronsky was not in the compartment.

'Yes, after his misfortune, what else was there for him to do?'

'What a dreadful thing it was!' said Koznyshev.

'You can't think what I have gone through! But won't you come in? ... You can't think what I have gone through!' she repeated, when Koznyshev had got in and taken a seat beside her. 'You can't conceive it! For six weeks he never said a word to anyone, and would not touch food except when I implored him. And we dared not leave him alone for a single minute. We took away everything he could have used against himself. We lived on the ground floor, but one could not tell what he might do. You know he shot himself once before on her account,' she said, and the old brows knit at the recollection. 'Yes, she ended as such a woman deserved to end. Even the death she chose was low and vulgar.'

'It is not for us to judge, Countess,' Koznyshev ventured with a sigh. 'But I can quite understand how distressing it was for you.'

'Oh, don't speak of it! I was living at my country-place at the time, and he was with me. A note was brought. He wrote an answer and sent it off. We had no idea that she was there at the station. In the evening I had only just retired to my room when my Mary told me that a lady had thrown herself under the train. I felt as if I had received a blow. I knew it was she. My first words were: "Don't tell him!" but he had already heard. His coachman was there and saw it all. When I ran to his room he was already beside himself – it was terrible to see him. Without saying a word he tore to the station. I don't know to this day what happened there, but they brought him back like one dead. I shouldn't have recognized him. *Prostration complète*, the doctor said. Then he went raving mad, almost! ... Ah, one can't speak of it!' exclaimed the countess with a movement of her hand. 'It was a terrible time. No, whatever you say, she was a bad woman. Can you understand these desperate passions? All for the sake of being original. Well, she was that all right! She brought ruin to herself and two fine men – her husband and my unfortunate son.'

'And how about her husband?' asked Koznyshev.

'He took the little girl. Alexei was ready to agree to anything at first. But now he is dreadfully distressed at having given up his own daughter to another man. He can't go back on his word, though. Karenin came to the funeral. But we did all we could to prevent his meeting Alexei. For him, for her husband, it is easier, all the same. She had set him free. But my poor son was utterly given up to her. He had sacrificed everything – his career, me – and even then she had no mercy on him but deliberately dealt him a mortal blow. No, whatever you say, her very death was the death of a bad woman, a woman without religion. God forgive me, but I can't help hating her memory when I look at the ruin of my son!'

'But how is he now?'

'This Serbian war is a blessing from Providence for us. I am an old woman, and I don't understand the rights and wrongs of it, but for him it is a godsend. Of course, as his mother, I feel dreadful; and, what's worse, I hear *ce n'est pas très bien vu à Petersbourg*. But it can't be helped. It was the only thing that could rouse him. Yashvin – a friend of his – had gambled away all he possessed, and he volunteered. He came to see him and persuaded him to go to Serbia with him. Now it's an interest for him. Do please go and have a talk with him: I am so anxious to distract his mind. He is so miserable. And added to his other miseries he has toothache. But he will be very glad to see you. Please go and talk to him. He's walking up and down on the other side of the platform.'

Koznyshev said he would be delighted to, and crossed over to the other side of the train.

5

IN the slanting shadow of a pile of sacks heaped up on the platform, Vronsky, in a long overcoat, his hat pulled down low and his hands in his pockets, was striding up and down like an animal in a cage, turning about sharply after a score of steps in each direction. Koznyshev fancied, approaching him, that Vronsky saw but pretended not to see him, but he did not mind. His relations with Vronsky were beyond all personal considerations. In his eyes at that moment Vronsky was an important factor in a great cause, and Koznyshev considered it his duty to encourage and acclaim him. He went up to him.

Vronsky stopped short, looked intently at Koznyshev, recognized him and, advancing a few steps to meet him, pressed his hand hard.

'Perhaps you would rather not have seen me,' began Koznyshev, 'but I thought I might be of use to you.'

'There is no one I should dislike seeing less than you,' Vronsky replied. 'Forgive me. There is nothing in life for me to like.'

'I understand, and I merely meant to offer you my services,' said Koznyshev, scanning Vronsky's face which bore unmistakable signs of suffering. 'Wouldn't a letter to Ristitch – or to Milan – be of use to you?'

'Oh no!' Vronsky said, as though it cost him an effort to understand. 'If you don't mind, let us walk on. It's so stuffy in the carriages. A letter? No, thank you. One needs no letters of introduction to meet death. Unless it be to the Turks …' he added, smiling with his lips only. His eyes retained their look of bitter suffering.

'Yes; but you might find it easier to establish connexions, which are after all essential, if you have been introduced. However, as you please. I was very glad to hear of your decision. The volunteers have been widely attacked, so that a man like you raises them in public estimation.'

'As a man I have the merit that my life is of no value to me. And I've physical energy enough to hack my way into the fray and slay or fall – I know that. I am glad there is something for which I can lay down the life which is not simply useless but loathsome to me. Anyone's welcome to it,' and he moved his jaw impatiently because of the incessant gnawing ache in his tooth which prevented him from even speaking with the expression he desired.

'You will come back another man, I predict,' said Koznyshev, feeling touched. 'To deliver one's brother-men from oppression is an aim worth dying and living for too. God grant you success – and inward peace,' he added, holding out his hand.

Vronsky pressed it warmly.

'Yes, as a weapon I may be of some use. But as a man I'm a wreck,' he jerked out.

He could hardly speak for the agonizing pain in the big tooth, which filled his mouth with saliva. He was silent, gazing at the wheels of the approaching tender gliding slowly and smoothly along the rails.

And all at once a different feeling, not an ache but a tormenting inner discomfort, made him for an instant forget his toothache. At the sight of the tender and the rails, and under the influence of the conversation with someone he had not met since the catastrophe, he suddenly recalled *her* – as much as was left of her when he had rushed like one distraught into the railway shed and seen her mangled body, still warm with recent life, stretched out on a table shamelessly exposed to the gaze of all. The head, which had escaped hurt, with its heavy plaits and the curls about the temples, was thrown back, and the lovely face with its half-open red lips had frozen into a strange expression – pitiful on the lips and horrible in the fixed open eyes – as though she were repeating that fearful threat – that he would be sorry for it – that she had uttered during their last quarrel.

And he tried to remember her as she was when he met her the first time – also at a railway station – mysterious, exquisite, loving, seeking and bestowing happiness, and not cruel and vindictive, as he remembered her at the last. He tried to recall his best moments with her but those moments were poisoned for ever. He could only think of her as triumphant in having carried out her threat to inflict on him futile but ineffaceable remorse. He ceased to feel the pain in his tooth, and sobs distorted his face.

He walked up and down twice past the sacks, mastered himself and turned calmly to Koznyshev.

'You have not seen any despatch since yesterday's? They've been driven back for the third time, but a decisive engagement is expected for to-morrow.'

And after a few words about the proclamation of Milan as king, and the immense effect this might have, they returned to their respective carriages at the ringing of the second bell.

6

UNCERTAIN when he would be able to leave Moscow, Koznyshev had not telegraphed to his brother to send to meet him. Levin was not at home when Katavasov and Koznyshev, black as Negroes from the dust, drove up to the steps of the Pokrovskoe house at about noon in the station fly. Kitty, sitting on the balcony with her father and sister, recognized her brother-in-law and ran down to meet him.

'What a shame of you not to have let us know,' she said, holding out her hand to Koznyshev and putting her forehead up for him to kiss.

'We got here splendidly, without putting you out,' replied Koznyshev. 'I'm so dusty, I daren't touch you. I was so busy, I didn't know when I should be able to tear myself away. And you, as usual,' he said, smiling, 'are enjoying your tranquil happiness in your quiet backwater beyond the reach of the current. And here is our friend Fiodor Vasilyich come to see you at last.'

'But I am not a Negro! A wash and I shall look like a human being!' said Katavasov in his jesting fashion, holding out his hand with a smile, his teeth flashing white in his black face.

'Kostya will be so pleased. He has gone over to the farm. He should be back any moment now.'

'Still busy with his farming! "Backwater" is the right word,' remarked Katavasov. 'And we in town have ears for nothing but the Serbian war. Well, and what does our friend think of it? Surely not the same as other folk?'

'Oh, nothing in particular – the same as everyone else,' Kitty replied, a little embarrassed, looking round at Koznyshev. 'Well, I'll send for him. Papa's staying with us. He's not long returned from abroad.'

And having despatched someone to fetch Levin and arranged for the dusty visitors to be shown where to wash – one of them in Levin's study and the other in Dolly's big room – and seen about lunch for them, Kitty, exercising the freedom of rapid movement which had been denied her during the months of her pregnancy, ran out on to the balcony.

'It's Sergei Ivanich and Professor Katavasov,' she said.

'Oh, how trying in this heat!' said the prince.

'No, Papa, he's very nice, and Kostya's very fond of him,' Kitty said with a smile of entreaty, noticing the quizzical look on her father's face.

'Oh, I didn't say anything.'

'Do go and look after them, dearest,' Kitty said to her sister. 'They saw Stiva at the station; he was quite well. I must run to Mitya. I haven't had a chance to feed him since breakfast. He will be awake by now and is sure to be screaming.' And feeling the flow of milk she hurried to the nursery.

Indeed, it was not a mere guess – the bond between herself and the baby was still so close – she knew for certain by the flow of her milk that he was in need of food.

She knew he was screaming before she reached the nursery. And so he was. She heard him and hurried. But the faster she went the louder he screamed. It was a fine healthy cry, hungry and impatient.

'Has he been awake long, nurse? Very long?' Kitty asked, hastily seating herself on a chair and undoing the bodice of her dress. 'Be quick and give him to me. Oh, nurse, how tiresome you are! You can tie his bonnet afterwards!'

The baby was convulsed with hungry yells.

'But that wouldn't do at all, ma'am,' said Agatha Mihalovna, who could not keep out of the nursery. 'He must be put straight. Goo, goo!' she cooed to the baby, paying no attention to the mother.

The nurse carried the baby over to his mother. Agatha Mihalovna followed behind, her face aglow with tenderness.

'He knows me, he does! As God is my witness, Katerina Alexandrovna, ma'am, he knew me!' cried Agatha Mihalovna, raising her voice above the baby's screams.

But Kitty was not listening. Her impatience was increasing with the baby's.

Their impatience hindered things for a while. The baby had difficulty in taking the breast and grew angry. At last, after desperate screaming and choking, and vain sucking, matters were settled satisfactorily, and mother and child breathed a sigh of content, and both subsided into calm.

'But he, too, poor mite, is all in a perspiration,' whispered Kitty, feeling him with her hand. 'What makes you think he knows you?' she added, putting her head on one side to see the baby's eyes, which seemed to her to peep roguishly from under his cap, which had slipped forward, and watching the rhythmic sucking in and out of the little cheeks and the circular movement of the baby hand with its rosy palm.

'It's impossible! If he knew anyone, it would be me,' Kitty said in response to Agatha Mihalovna's statement, and she smiled.

She smiled because, though she said he could not know her, in her heart she was sure that he knew not only Agatha Mihalovna, but that he knew everything and understood a whole lot of things that no one else knew, and which she, his mother, was only just beginning to find out and understand thanks to him. To Agatha Mihalovna, to the nurse, to his grandfather, to his father even, Mitya was just a little human being requiring only material care; but for his mother he had long been a personage endowed with moral faculties with whom she already had a whole history of spiritual relations.

'Well, wait till he wakes up and you will see for yourself. When I do like this he beams, the darling! Brightens like a sunny morning,' said Agatha Mihalovna.

'Very well, very well, we shall see,' Kitty whispered. 'But go away now, he's going to sleep.'

7

AGATHA MIHALOVNA went out on tiptoe. The nurse pulled down the blind, chased the flies from under the muslin canopy of the cot and a bumble-bee buzzing against the window-pane, and sat down, waving a withered birch branch over mother and child.

'How hot it is! If the Lord would only send a drop of rain,' she said.

'Yes, yes, sh..sh..sh!' was all Kitty answered, rocking to and fro and tenderly squeezing the plump little arm, which looked as if a piece of thread had been tied tightly round the wrist, and which Mitya still waved feebly as he opened and shut his eyes. This little arm agitated Kitty: she longed to kiss the little hand but was afraid to, for fear of waking the baby. At last the arm ceased waving and the eyes closed. Only from time to time, as he went on sucking, the baby lifted long curly lashes and gazed at its mother with dewy eyes that looked black in the dim light. The nurse stopped fanning them and began to doze off. From upstairs came the peal of the old prince's voice and Katavasov's boisterous laughter.

'They seem all right without me,' thought Kitty. 'But all the same it is provoking that Kostya's not back yet. He must have gone to the apiary again. Though it's a pity he's there so often, still I'm glad. It distracts his mind. He's altogether happier and better now than he was in the spring. He used to be so gloomy and worried that I felt alarmed about him. What a funny man he is!' she whispered, smiling.

She knew what was tormenting her husband. It was his want of faith. Although, if she had been asked whether she thought there could be no salvation for him in the future life unless he were a believer, she would have been compelled to agree, yet his unbelief did not make her unhappy; and she, who accepted the doctrine that there could be no salvation for an unbeliever, and to whom her husband's soul was dearer than anything in the world, smiled when she thought of his scepticism and called him funny.

'Why does he keep on reading those philosophy books of his all the year round?' she wondered. 'If it's all written in those books, he can understand them. If what they say is all wrong, why read them? He says himself that he would like to believe. Then why doesn't he? It must be because he thinks too much. And he thinks too much because of being solitary. He's always alone, always. He can't talk about it all to us. He will be glad of these visitors, I think, especially Katavasov. He likes arguing with him,' she reflected, and immediately turned her mind to the problem of where to put Katavasov – should he have a separate room or share with Koznyshev? And here a thought suddenly struck her that made her start with agitation and even disturb Mitya, who gave her a severe look in consequence. 'I don't believe the laundry-woman has brought the washing back yet, and all the best sheets are in use. If I don't see to it, Agatha Mihalovna will give Sergei Ivanich the wrong sheets!' and the very idea of this sent the blood rushing to Kitty's face.

'Yes, I must see about it,' she decided, and, returning to her former train of thought, she remembered that there was something important, some spiritual question, that she had not yet got to the bottom of, and tried to recollect what it was. 'Oh yes, Kostya, an unbeliever,' she remembered again with a smile.

'Well, and if he is? I would rather have him that than see him like Madame Stahl, or as I wanted to be in those days abroad. No, he would never sham anything.'

And a recent instance of his goodness came vividly to her mind. A fortnight ago Dolly had received a penitent letter from her husband, imploring her to save his honour by selling her estate to pay his debts. Dolly had been in despair: she detested her husband, despised him, was sorry for him, made up her mind to refuse and to divorce him, but ended by agreeing to dispose of part of the estate. Here Kitty, with an involuntary smile of tenderness, recalled the shamefaced way her own husband had gone about his repeated awkward attempts to approach the subject, and how at length, having thought of the one means of helping Dolly without wounding her pride, he had suggested to Kitty that she should make over to her sister the portion of the estate that belonged to her – a device that had never occurred to Kitty.

'He an unbeliever indeed! With his heart, his dread of hurting anyone's feelings, even a child's! With him it's everything for others, nothing for himself. Sergei Ivanich quite seems to think it's Kostya's duty to be his steward. And it's the same with his sister. Now he has Dolly and her children on his hands as well. And then there are all these peasants who come to him every day, as if it were his business to be at their service. Yes, you cannot do better than try to be like your father,' she murmured, handing Mitya over to the nurse and touching his little cheek with her lips.

8

EVER since, by his beloved brother's deathbed, Levin had for the first time looked at the questions of life and death in the light of his new convictions, as he called them, which between the ages of twenty and thirty-four had imperceptibly replaced the beliefs of his childhood and youth, he had been stricken with horror, not so much at death, as at life, without the least conception of its origin, its purpose, its reason, its nature. The organism, its decay, the indestructibility of matter, the law of the conservation of energy, evolution, were the terms that had superseded those of his early faith. These terms and the theories associated with them were very useful for intellectual purposes. But they gave no guidance for life, and Levin suddenly felt like a person who has exchanged his warm fur coat for a muslin garment, and out in the frost for the first time is immediately convinced, not by arguments but with his whole being that he is as good as naked and must inevitably perish miserably.

From that time, though he did not realize it and continued to live as before, Levin had never lost this sense of terror at his lack of knowledge.

He was vaguely conscious, too, that what he called his new convictions were not merely ignorance but that they were part of a whole order of ideas which actually stood in the way of the knowledge he needed.

In the early days of his marriage his new joys and responsibilities had completely stifled these thoughts; but latterly, while he was staying in Moscow after his wife's confinement, with nothing to do, the question that clamoured for solution had more and more often, more and more insistently, haunted Levin's mind.

For him the problem was this: 'If I do not accept the answers Christianity gives to the questions of my life, what answers do I accept?' And in the whole arsenal of his convictions he failed to find not only any kind of answer but anything resembling an answer. He was in the position of a man seeking food in a toyshop or at a gunsmith's.

Instinctively, unconsciously, in every book he read, in every conversation, in every person he met, he was on the look-out for their connexion with the questions that absorbed him and for a solution of these questions.

What astounded and upset him most was that the majority of men of his circle and age who had, like himself, substituted science for religion, saw nothing to be distressed about and were perfectly content and happy. So that, apart from the principal problem, Levin was tormented by other questions too. Were these people sincere? he asked himself. Were they not counterfeiting? Or was it that they got from science some different, clearer answer than he did to the problems he was concerned with? And he took to studying diligently both the opinions of those people and the books which treated of these scientific explanations.

One thing he had discovered since these questions had begun to occupy his mind – namely, that he had been mistaken in supposing with his contemporaries at the university that religion had outlived its day and was now practically non-existent. The best people he knew were all believers: the old prince, Lvov, whom he liked so much, his brother Koznyshev, and all the women. His wife had a childlike faith just like his as a small boy, and ninety-nine out of a hundred of the Russian people, all the working-people whose lives inspired him with the greatest respect, believed.

Another thing was that, after reading a great many scientific books, he became convinced that the men who shared his views got no more out of their convictions than he did. Far from explaining the problems without a solution to which he felt he could not live, they set them aside and took up others of no interest to him, such as, for instance, the evolution of organisms, a mechanical explanation of the soul, and so forth.

Moreover, at the time of his wife's confinement an extraordinary thing had happened to him. He, an unbeliever, had prayed, and prayed with sincere faith. But that moment had passed, and he could not allot any place in his life to the state of mind he had been in then.

He could not admit that at that moment he had known the truth, and was now in error, for as soon as he began to reflect on it calmly it all fell to pieces. Nor could he admit that he had been mistaken then, for he valued his spiritual condition then and to attribute it to weakness would be to defile those moments. He was wretchedly divided against himself, and strained all his mental powers to put himself right.

9

THERE were days when these doubts fretted and harassed him more than others, but they never left him entirely. He read and thought, and the more he read and the more he thought the farther he felt from the goal he was pursuing.

During the latter part of his stay in Moscow, and after his return to the country, he became convinced that he would get no answer from the materialists, and so he went back to Plato, Spinoza, Kant, Schelling, Hegel, and Schopenhauer, the philosophers who gave a non-materialistic explanation of life.

Their ideas seemed to him fruitful while he was reading or was himself devising arguments to refute other theories, especially those of the materialists; but directly he began to read or himself devise solutions to life's problems, the same thing occurred every time. As long as he followed the fixed definitions given to such vague terms as *spirit*, *will*, *freedom*, *substance*, deliberately entering the verbal trap set for him by the philosophers, or by himself, he seemed to comprehend something. But he had only to forget the artificial train of reasoning, and to turn from real life to what had satisfied him so long as he kept to the given chain of argument, for the whole artificial edifice to tumble down like a house of cards, and it became evident that the edifice had been constructed of those same words transposed and regardless of something in life more important than reason.

When reading Schopenhauer one day he substituted the word *love* for the word *will*, and for a day or two this new philosophy cheered him, so long as he did not wander from it; but it, too, collapsed when he reviewed it in relation to real life, and proved to be a muslin garment with no warmth in it.

His brother Koznyshev advised him to read the theological works of Khomyakov. Levin read the second volume of Khomyakov's works and, in spite of the polemical, elegant, brilliant style which at first repelled him, he was impressed by its teaching about the church. He was struck in the beginning by the idea that apprehension of divine truth is not given to man in isolation but to the totality of men united by love – the Church. The thought rejoiced him of how much easier it was to believe in an existing, living Church embracing all the beliefs of men and having God at its head – a Church therefore holy and infallible – and from it to accept belief in God, the Creation, the Fall and Redemption, than to begin with some distant, mysterious God, the Creation, and so on. But afterwards, when he read a history of the Church by a Catholic writer, and another by a Greek Orthodox writer, and saw that the two Churches, in their very conception infallible, each repudiated the other, he became disenchanted with Khomyakov's doctrine of the Church, and this structure fell to pieces just as the philosophers' edifices had done.

All that spring he was not himself, and experienced some terrible moments.

'I cannot live without knowing what I am and why I am here. And that I can't know, so therefore I can't live,' Levin would say to himself.

'In infinite time, in infinite matter, in infinite space an organic cell stands out, will hold together awhile and then burst, and that cell is Me.'

This was an agonizing fallacy, but it was the sole, the supreme result of centuries of human thought in that direction.

It was the ultimate belief on which all the systems of thought elaborated by the human mind in almost all their ramifications were based. It was the dominant conviction, and of all other explanations Levin had unconsciously chosen it, without knowing when or how, as being at any rate the clearest, and made it his own.

But it was not only a fallacy, it was the cruel jest of some evil power, some evil, inimical power, to which one could not submit.

He must escape from this power. And each man held the means of escape in his own hands. An end must be put to this dependence on evil. And there was one means – death.

And Levin, a happy father and husband, in perfect health, was several times so near suicide that he had to hide a rope lest he be tempted to hang himself, and would not go out with a gun for fear of shooting himself.

But Levin did not shoot himself, and did not hang himself: and he went on living.

10

WHEN Levin puzzled over what he was and what he was living for, he could find no answer and fell into despair; but when he left off worrying about the problem of his existence he seemed to know both what he was and for what he was living, for he acted and lived resolutely and unfalteringly. Indeed, latterly he was far more decided and unfaltering than ever before.

On his return to the country at the beginning of June, he returned also to his customary pursuits. The management of the estate, his relations with the peasants and the neighbouring gentry, the care of his household, and looking after his sister's and brother's affairs, of which he had the direction, his relations with his wife and her relatives, solicitude for the baby, and the new hobby of beekeeping which he had taken up with enthusiasm that spring, absorbed all his time.

These things occupied him now, not because he justified them to himself by any sort of general principles, as he had done in former days; on the contrary, disenchanted as he was on the one hand by the failure of his earlier efforts for the general welfare, and too much occupied on the other with his own thoughts and the mass of business with which he was burdened from all sides, he had completely abandoned all considerations of public weal and busied himself with all this work for no other reason than because it seemed to him that he must do what he was doing – that he could not do otherwise.

Formerly (and this had been so almost from childhood, increasing as he reached full maturity), whenever he had tried to do anything for the general good, for the good of humanity, for Russia, for the village as a whole, he had observed that the idea of it had been pleasant but the activity it entailed had always been incoherent. There had never been full conviction of its absolute necessity, and the work itself, from at first appearing so great, had grown less and less, till it vanished into nothing. But now, since his marriage, when he had begun to confine himself more and more to living for himself, though he no longer found any delight at the thought of the work he was doing, he felt confident of its usefulness, saw that it succeeded far better than in the old days, and that it was always growing instead of getting smaller.

Now, involuntarily as it were, he cut deeper and deeper into the soil, so that like a ploughshare he could not be drawn out without turning up the furrow.

For his family to live as his father and forefathers had been accustomed to live – that is, at the same cultural level – and so to bring up his children, was an undoubted necessity. It was just as necessary as eating when one was hungry. And for that, just as a meal has to be cooked, so Pokrovskoe must be farmed in such a manner as to yield an income. As surely as one must pay one's debts, so surely was it necessary to keep the patrimony in such a condition that when his son inherited it he would thank his father, as Levin had thanked his grandfather for all he had built and planted. And to do this he must not lease out the land but must farm it himself, must breed cattle, manure the fields, and plant woods.

It was as impossible not to look after the interests of his brother and sister, and of all the peasants who came to him for advice and were accustomed to do so, as it is impossible to fling down a child one is carrying in one's arms. Then he had to see to the comforts of his sister-in-law and her children, whom he had invited to stay with them, and of his wife and baby, and it was impossible not to spend at least a small portion of each day with them.

And all this, together with shooting and his new hobby of beekeeping, filled up that life of his which seemed to have no meaning at all when he began to think about it.

But besides knowing thoroughly *what* it was he had to do, Levin knew in just the same way *how* he had to do it all, and which of any two matters was the more important.

He knew he must hire labourers as cheaply as possible; but to take men in bond for less than they were worth by advancing them money, he must not do, though this would be very profitable. There was no harm in selling peasants straw in times of shortage, even though he felt sorry for them; but the inn and the tavern must be abolished, even though they were a source of income. The stealing of timber must be punished as severely as possible, but he would exact no fines if the peasants drove their cattle on to his fields, and though it riled the watchmen and made the peasants not afraid to graze their cattle on his land, the strayed cattle must not be impounded.

He must make a loan to Piotr to get him out of the claws of a moneylender who was charging him ten per cent a month; but he could not let off peasants who did not pay their rent, nor let them fall into arrears. The bailiff was not to be excused for failing to have the small meadow mown and wasting the grass; but the two hundred acres which had been planted with young trees must not be mown at all. No mercy must be shown a labourer who went home in a busy season because his father had died – sorry as Levin might be for the man: part of his pay must be deducted for those costly months of idleness; but old house-servants who were of no use for anything must have their monthly allowance.

Levin knew, too, that when he got home he must first of all go to his wife, who was unwell, and that the peasants who had been waiting three hours to see him could wait a little longer; yet he knew that he must forgo the pleasure of hiving a swarm and let the old beekeeper do it without him, while he went to talk to the peasants who had come after him to the apiary.

Whether he was acting rightly or wrongly he did not know – indeed, far from laying down the law, he now avoided talking or thinking about it.

Deliberation led to doubts and prevented him from seeing what he ought and ought not to do. But when he did not think, but just lived, he never ceased to be aware of the presence in his soul of an infallible judge who decided which of two possible courses of action was the better and which the worse, and instantly let him know if he did what he should not.

So he lived, not knowing and not seeing any chance of knowing what he was and for what purpose he had been placed in the world. He was tormented by this ignorance to the extent of fearing suicide, yet at the same time he was resolutely cutting his own individual and definite path through life.

II

THE day Koznyshev arrived at Pokrovskoe was one of Levin's most wretched days.

It was the most pressingly busy season of the year, when an extraordinary tension of self-sacrificing labour manifests itself among the whole peasantry, quite unknown in any other conditions of life, and which would be highly esteemed if the people who exhibited this quality prized it themselves, and if it were not repeated every year, and if it did not produce such very simple results.

Reaping or binding the rye and oats, carting them, mowing the meadows, repl)oughing the fallow land, threshing the seed, and sowing the winter corn – all labours that seem simple and commonplace enough; but to get it all done, everyone, from the oldest to the youngest, for those three or four weeks must toil incessantly, three times as hard as usual, living on rye-beer, onions, and black bread, threshing and carting the sheaves at night, and not giving more than two or three hours in the twenty-four to sleep. And every year this is done all over Russia.

Having lived the greater part of his life in the country and in close contact with the peasants, Levin always felt infected by this general quickening of energy at this busy time.

In the early morning he rode out to where the first rye was being sown, then to see the oats carted and stacked, and returning home when his wife and sister-in-law were getting up he drank his coffee with them, and afterwards departed on foot to the out-farm, where the new threshing-machine was to be started to thresh the seed-corn.

All that day, while talking to the bailiff and the peasants, at home with his wife, with Dolly, her children, and his father-in-law, Levin's thoughts were busy with the one and only subject, outside his farming, that interested him at this time, and in everything he sought a bearing on his questions: 'What am I? Where am I? And why am I here?'

Standing in the cool of the newly-thatched barn, with its wattled walls of hazel which had not yet shed its fragrant leaves pressed against the freshly stripped aspens of the joists under the thatch, he gazed now through the open doorway in which the dry, bitter chaff-dust rushed and whirled at the grass round the threshing-floor in the hot sunshine and at the fresh straw that had just been brought in from the shed, now at the parti-coloured heads of the white-breasted swallows that flew chirping in under the roof and, fluttering their wings, paused in the doorway, now at the peasants bustling about in the dark and dusty interior; and strange thoughts came into his head.

'What is all this being done for?' he wondered. 'Why am I standing here, making them work? Why are they all bustling about, trying so hard to show me their zeal? Why is my old friend Matriona toiling so? (I remember being her doctor when the beam fell on her in the fire),' he thought, looking at a haggard old woman who was raking up the grain, stepping painfully with her bare, sun-blackened feet over the rough, uneven barn-floor. 'She recovered then, but to-day or to-morrow, or in ten years' time, she will be dead and buried and nothing will be left of her, or of that pretty girl in the red skirt, husking corn with such nimble, dexterous grace. They'll bury her, and this piebald gelding, and very soon too,' he reflected, gazing at the horse breathing heavily through dilated nostrils, its belly rising and falling, as it trod the slanting wheel that turned under it. 'They will carry it off, and Fiodr, who is feeding the machine, his curly beard full of chaff and his shirt torn on his white shoulder. But now he loosens the sheaves and gives directions, shouts at the women, and with a swift movement puts the strap right on the fly-wheel. And what's more, not only they but I, too, shall be buried, and nothing will be left. What is it all for?'

He thought this, and at the same time looked at his watch to reckon how much they could thresh in an hour. He had to know that so as to set them their day's task accordingly.

'They've been at it nearly an hour, and only just started on the third rick,' he thought. He walked over to the man who was feeding the machine, and, shouting above the din, told him to feed it more evenly. 'You put in too much at a time, Fiodr! It gets jammed, you see, and doesn't go well. Feed it in evenly!'

Fiodr, black with the dust that stuck to his perspiring face, shouted something in reply but still did not do as Levin wanted him to.

Levin went up to the drum, motioned Fiodr aside and himself began feeding the machine.

He worked on until the peasants' dinner-hour, which was not long in coming, and then, in company with Fiodr, left the barn and began chatting, stopping beside a neat yellow stack of rye laid on the threshing-floor for seed.

Fiodr came from a distant village, the very one where Levin had once let land to be worked co-operatively. At present a former house-porter had it.

Levin got talking with Fiodr about this land and asked if Platon, a well-to-do and worthy peasant belonging to the same village, might not take it for the coming year.

'It's a high rent. It wouldn't pay Platon, Constantine Dmitrich,' answered the peasant, picking the ears of rye off the front of his damp shirt.

'Then how does Kirilov make it pay?'

'Oh, Mityuka' (as he contemptuously called the house-porter), 'he could make anything pay! He'll squeeze a fellow until he gets what he wants. He won't spare a Christian. But Uncle Fokanich' (so he called the old peasant Platon), 'do you suppose he'd flay the skin off a man? He'll give credit, and sometimes he'll let a man off. And go short himself, too. He's that sort of person.'

'But why should he let anyone off?'

'Oh well, of course, folks are different. One man lives for his own wants and nothing else – take Mityuka, who only thinks of stuffing his belly – but Fokanich is an upright old man. He thinks of his soul. He does not forget God.'

'Not forget God? And how does he live for his soul?' Levin almost shouted.

'Why, that's plain enough: it's living rightly, in God's way. Folks are all different, you see. Take yourself, now, you wouldn't wrong a man either ...'

'Yes, yes, good-bye!' stammered Levin, deeply agitated, and, turning away, he took his stick and walked rapidly towards the house. At the peasant's words about Platon living for his soul, rightly, in God's way, dim but important thoughts crowded into his mind, as if they had broken loose from some place where they had been locked up, and all rushing forward towards one goal, whirled in his head, blinding him with their light.

12

LEVIN strode along the highroad, attending not so much to his thoughts (he could not yet disentangle them) as to a mental condition he had never known before.

The peasant's words had the effect of an electric spark, suddenly transforming and welding into one a whole series of disjointed, impotent, separate ideas that had never ceased to occupy his mind. They had been in his mind, though he had been unaware of it, even while he was talking to Fiodr about letting the land.

He felt something new in his soul and took a delight in probing it, not yet knowing what this new something was.

'Not to live for one's own needs, but for God! For what God? And could anything be more senseless than what he said? He said we must not live for our own wants – that is, we must not live for what

829

we understand, what we are attracted by, what we desire, but must live for something incomprehensible, for God, whom no one can know or define. Well? Didn't I understand those senseless words of Fiodr's? And understanding them, did I doubt the truth of them? Did I think them stupid, obscure, unsound?

'No, I understood them just as he understands them: understood fully and more clearly than I understand anything in life; and never in my life have I doubted them, nor could doubt them. And not only I but everyone – the whole world – understands nothing but this one thing fully: about this alone men have no doubt and are always agreed.

'Fiodr says that Kirilov lives for his belly. That is intelligible and rational. All of us as rational beings can't do anything else but live for our bellies. And all of a sudden this same Fiodr declares that it is wrong to live for one's belly; we must live for truth, for God, and a hint is enough to make me understand what he means! And I and millions of men, men who lived centuries ago and men living now – peasants, the poor in spirit and the sages, those who have thought and written about it, in their obscure words saying the same thing – we are all agreed on this one point: what it is we should live for and what is good. The only knowledge I and all men possess that is firm, incontestable, and clear is here, and it cannot be explained by reason – this knowledge is outside the sphere of reason: it has no causes and can have no effects.

'If goodness has a cause, it is no longer goodness; if it has consequences – a reward – it is not goodness either. So goodness is outside the chain of cause and effect.

'It is just this that I know, and that we all know.

'And I sought for miracles – complained that I did not see a miracle which would convince me. But here is a miracle, the one possible, everlasting miracle, surrounding me on all sides, and I never noticed it!

'What could be a greater miracle than that?

'Can I have found the solution to everything? Are my sufferings really at an end?' thought Levin, striding along the dusty road, oblivious of heat and fatigue, filled with a feeling of relief after his long travail. The sensation was so joyous that it seemed almost incredible. He was breathless with emotion and, incapable of going farther, left the road and turned into the forest to sit down on the uncut grass in the shade of the aspens. Taking off his hat from his perspiring head, he stretched himself out, leaning on his elbow in the lush, feathery, woodland grass.

'Yes, I must bethink myself and consider it carefully,' he thought, gazing intently at the untrodden grass before him, and following the movements of a little green beetle crawling up a stalk of couch-grass and hindered in its ascent by a leaf of goutwort. 'Let me go back to the beginning,' he said to himself, bending the leaf out of the beetle's way and twisting another blade of grass for it to cross over on to. 'What makes me so happy? What have I discovered?

'I used to say that in my body, that in the body of this grass and of this beetle (there, it didn't want to go on to the other blade of grass – it has spread its wings and flown away) a transformation of matter takes place in conformity with certain physical, chemical, and physiological laws. And in all of us, including these aspens and the clouds and the misty patches in the sky, evolution is proceeding. Evolution from what? Into what? An unending evolution and struggle? ... As if there could be any sort of tendency and struggle in the infinite! And I was surprised that in spite of the utmost efforts of my reason in that direction I could not discover the meaning of life, the meaning of my own impulses and yearnings. But the meaning of my impulses is so clear that they form the very foundation of my existence, and I marvelled and rejoiced when the peasant put it into words for me: to live for God, for my soul.

'I have discovered nothing. I have simply opened my eyes to what I knew. I have come to the recognition of that Power that not only in the past gave me life but now too gives me life. I have been set free from fallacy, I have found the Master.'

And he briefly went over the whole progress of his thoughts during the last two years, beginning with the plain confronting of death at the sight of his beloved brother lying hopelessly ill.

Then, for the first time, realizing that for every man, and himself too, there was nothing ahead but suffering, death, eternal oblivion, he had decided that to live under such conditions was impossible – he must either find an explanation to the problem of existence which would make life seem something other than the cruel irony of a malevolent spirit, or he must shoot himself.

But he had done neither the one nor the other: he had gone on living, thinking and feeling, had even at that very time married, had experienced many joys and been happy whenever he was not pondering on the meaning of his life.

What did that show? It showed that he had been living rightly, but thinking wrongly.

He had been living (without being aware of it) on those spiritual truths that he had imbibed with his mother's milk, yet in thinking he had not only refused to acknowledge these truths but had studiously ignored them.

Now it was clear to him that he could only live by virtue of the beliefs in which he had been brought up.

'What should I have been, and how should I have spent my life had it not been for those beliefs, had I not known that one must live for God and not for one's own needs? I should have robbed, lied, murdered. Nothing of what makes the chief happiness of my life would ever have existed for me.' And try as he would he was unable to picture to himself the brutal creature he would have been if he had not known what he was living for.

'I was in search of an answer to my question. But reason could not give an answer to my question – reason is incommensurable with the problem. The answer has been given me by life itself, through my knowledge of what is right and what is wrong. And this knowledge I did not acquire in any way: it was given to me as it is to everybody – *given*, because I could not have got it from anywhere.

'Where did I get it from? Would reason ever have proved to me that I must love my neighbour instead of strangling him? I was told that in my childhood, and I believed it gladly, for they told me what was already in my soul. But who discovered it? Not reason. Reason discovered the struggle for existence, and the law demanding that I should strangle all who hinder the satisfaction of my desires. That is the deduction of reason. But loving one's neighbour reason could never discover, because it's unreasonable.

'Yes, pride,' he said to himself, rolling over on his stomach and beginning to tie blades of grass into knots, trying not to break them.

'And not merely pride of intellect, but folly of intellect! And most of all – dishonesty of mind, sheer dishonesty. Sheer intellectual fraud,' he repeated.

13

AND Levin remembered a recent scene between Dolly and her children. The children, left to themselves, had started making raspberry jam over lighted candles, and pouring jets of milk into each other's mouths. Their mother catching them at these antics had tried in front of Levin to impress on them that they were wasting what had cost their elders a large amount of labour, undertaken for their sakes, that if they broke the cups they would have nothing to drink their tea out of, and that if they spilt the milk they would have nothing to eat, and die of hunger.

And Levin had been struck by the passive, weary scepticism with which the children listened to these remarks from their mother. They were only sorry to have their interesting game interrupted, and did not believe a word of what their mother was saying. They could not believe it indeed, because they could not take in the magnitude of all they habitually enjoyed, and so could not conceive that what they were destroying was the very thing they lived by.

'That all happens by itself,' they thought. 'And there's nothing interesting or important about it, because those things always have been and always will be. And it's always the same. We don't need to worry, it's all done for us. We want to invent something new of our own. It was quite a good idea to put raspberries in a cup and cook them over a candle, and squirt milk into each other's mouths like fountains. That was fun, and something new, and not a bit worse than drinking out of cups.'

'Don't we – didn't I? – do just the same, searching by the aid of reason to discover the significance of the forces of nature and the purpose of human life?' he thought.

'And don't all the theories of philosophy do the same, trying by the path of thought, which is strange and not natural to man, to bring him to a knowledge of what he has known long ago, and knows so surely that without it he could not live? Is it not plainly evident in the development of every philosopher's theory that he knows beforehand, just as positively as the peasant Fiodr and not a whit more clearly than he, the real meaning of life, and is simply trying by a dubious intellectual process to come back to what everyone knows?

'Supposing now that the children were left to get things for themselves, make the cups, milk the cows, and so on – would they play pranks? No, they would starve to death! Well then, give us over to our passions and thoughts, without any idea of the one God, of the Creator, or without any idea of what is right, any explanation of moral evil!

'Just try to build up anything without those conceptions!

'We destroy because we have had our fill spiritually. Exactly like the children!

'Whence comes the joyful knowledge I have in common with the peasant, that alone gives me peace of mind? Where did I get it?

'Here am I, a Christian, brought up in the knowledge of God, brimful of the spiritual blessings Christianity has given me, overflowing with them and living on these blessings, and like the children I don't understand, and destroy – or rather, try to destroy that by which I live. But directly an important moment in life comes, like for children when they are cold and hungry, I run to Him, and even less than the children when their mother scolds them for their childish mischief do I feel that my childish essays at wanton madness should be reckoned against me.

'Yes, what I know, I know not by my reason but because it has been given to me, revealed to me, and I know it with my heart, by my faith in the chief things which the Church proclaims.

'The Church? The Church!' repeated Levin. He rolled over on his other side and, leaning on his elbow, fell to gazing into the distance at a herd of cattle going down to the farther bank of the river.

'But can I believe in all the Church professes?' he asked in order to test himself and bring up everything that could destroy his present sense of security. He purposely made himself think of those teachings of the Church which had always seemed to him strange and had most alienated him. 'The Creation? Yes, but how did I explain existence? By existence? By nothing? ... The devil and sin? And how do I explain evil? ... The Atonement? ...

'But I know nothing, nothing, and cannot know other than what I have been told with the rest.'

And it seemed to him now that there was not a single article of faith which could disturb the main thing – belief in God, in goodness, as the one goal of man's destiny.

At the back of every article of faith of the Church could be put belief in serving truth rather than one's personal needs. And each of these dogmas not only did not violate that creed but was essential for the fulfilment of the greatest of miracles, continually manifest upon earth – the miracle that made it possible for the world with its millions of individual human beings, sages and simpletons, children and old men, everyone, peasants, Lvov, Kitty, beggars and kings, to comprehend with certainty one and the same truth and live that life of the spirit, the only life that is worth living and which alone we prize.

Lying on his back, he was now gazing high up into the cloudless sky. 'Do I not know that that is infinite space, and not a rounded vault? But however much I screw up my eyes and strain my sight I cannot see it except as round and circumscribed, and in spite of my knowing about infinite space I am incontestably right when I see a firm blue vault, far more right than when I strain my eyes to see beyond it.'

Levin ceased thinking and, as it were, only hearkened to mystic voices that seemed to be joyfully and earnestly conferring among themselves.

'Can this be faith?' he wondered, afraid to believe in his happiness. 'My God, I thank Thee!' he breathed, gulping down the sobs that rose within him and with both hands brushing away the tears that filled his eyes.

14

LEVIN looked before him and saw a herd of cattle, then he caught sight of his trap with Raven in the shafts, and the coachman, who drove up to the herd and spoke to the herdsman. After that, close by, he heard the sound of wheels and the snorting of the sleek horse; but he was so engrossed in his thoughts that he did not even wonder why the coachman was coming towards him, until the latter had driven up quite near and called:

'The mistress sent me! Your brother has come, and another gentleman with him!'

Levin got into the trap and took the reins.

He felt as though he had just awakened from a deep sleep and it took him a long while to collect his faculties. He stared at the sleek horse, flecked with lather between its haunches and on its neck where the harness rubbed, stared at Ivan the coachman sitting beside him, and remembered that he had been expecting his brother and that his wife was probably worried at his long absence, and tried to guess who the visitor could be who had come with his brother. And his brother, his wife, and the unknown visitor appeared to him in a different light now. He fancied now that his relations with all men would be different.

'With my brother there will be none of that aloofness there always used to be between us – there will be no more disputes; with Kitty no more quarrels; to the visitor, whoever he may be, I shall be friendly and nice; and with the servants, with Ivan, it will all be different.'

Tightly holding in the good horse, which was snorting impatiently and pulling at the reins, Levin looked round at Ivan sitting beside him not knowing what to do with his idle hands and continually pushing down his shirt as the wind puffed it out. Levin tried to think of something to say to start a conversation with him. He was about to remark that Ivan had pulled the saddle-girth too high, but that would have sounded like a reproof, and Levin longed for a warm, friendly exchange.

'Bear to the right, sir, there's a stump there,' said the coachman, pulling the rein Levin held.

'Have the goodness to leave it alone, and don't give me lessons!' said Levin, annoyed at the coachman's interference. Interference always made him angry, and as he spoke he could not help thinking sorrowfully how mistaken had been his conclusion that his new spiritual condition could all of a sudden alter his character once in contact with reality.

When they were still a quarter of a mile from the house Levin saw Grisha and Tanya running to meet him.

'Uncle Kostya! Mama's coming, and grandpapa, and Sergei Ivanich, and another man!' they cried, clambering into the trap.

'Who is it?'

'An awfully dreadful man! And he goes like this with his arms,' said Tanya, standing up in the trap and imitating Katavasov.

'Is he old or young?' asked Levin laughing, as Tanya's performance reminded him of someone, he did not know whom. 'I hope it's not some tiresome person!' he thought.

As soon as they were round the bend in the road and saw the little party coming towards them, Levin recognized Katavasov in a straw hat, walking along swinging his arms just as Tanya had shown him.

Katavasov was very fond of discussing metaphysics, his notions of which were acquired from natural science writers who had never studied philosophy, and during his last stay in Moscow Levin had had many arguments with him.

The first thing Levin recalled as he saw him was one occasion when Katavasov had obviously considered that he came off victorious.

'But this time I will on no account argue or lightly express my opinions,' he thought.

Getting out of the trap, he exchanged greetings with his brother and Katavasov, and asked where Kitty was.

'She has taken Mitya to the woods, to sleep there, because it is so hot in the house,' said Dolly.

Levin had always advised his wife against taking the baby into the woods, thinking it unsafe, and he was not pleased to hear this news.

'She carries that son of hers about from pillar to post,' said the old prince, with a smile. 'I told her to try putting him in the ice-cellar.'

'She meant to come to the apiary. She thought you were there. That's where we're going,' said Dolly.

'Well, and what are you doing?' said Koznyshev, falling behind the rest and walking beside his brother.

'Oh, nothing in particular. Busy as usual with the farm,' Levin replied. 'You've come for a good stay, I hope? We have been expecting you for such a long time.'

'Only for about a couple of weeks. There is so much to do in Moscow.'

At these words the brothers' eyes met, and Levin, in spite of the desire he always felt, and now more than ever, to be on affectionate and especially free-and-easy terms with his brother, felt awkward when he looked at him. He dropped his eyes and did not know what to say.

Running over in his mind the subjects that might be agreeable to Koznyshev and keep him off the Serbian war and the Slavonic question, at which he had hinted by alluding to all he had to do in Moscow, Levin began about Koznyshev's book.

'Well, have there been reviews of your book?' he asked.

Koznyshev smiled at the premeditation of the question.

'No one is interested in that now, and I least of all,' he replied.

'Look over there, Darya Alexandrovna! We shall have a shower,' he added, pointing with his umbrella to some white clouds that had made their appearance above the aspens.

And these words were enough to re-establish the old relationship – if not unfriendly, at least cool – between the brothers, which Levin had so much wanted to get away from.

Levin joined Katavasov.

'It was nice of you to make up your mind to come,' he said.

'I've been meaning to for a long while. Now we'll have some talks, and we'll see! Have you read Spencer?'

'I haven't finished him yet,' replied Levin. 'However, I don't think I need him now.'

'How's that? That sounds interesting! Why not?'

'I mean I've finally come to the conclusion that in him and his like I shall never find the solution to the problems that interest me. Now ...'

But he was suddenly struck by the serene expression of Katavasov's jolly face, and felt so anxious not to spoil his own exalted mood to which the conversation was obviously damaging that, recollecting his resolution, he broke off. 'But we can talk about that by and by,' he added. 'If we're going to the apiary, it's this way – along this little path,' he said, addressing the others too.

Going along the narrow footpath to a little uncut glade bright all down one side with thick clusters of wild pansies with tall dark green tufts of hellebore between them, Levin settled his guests in the deep cool shade of the young aspens, on a bench and some tree stumps specially put there for visitors to the apiary who might be afraid of the bees, while he himself went to the hut to fetch bread, cucumbers, and fresh honey for the whole party.

Trying to move as gently as possible and listening to the bees that hummed past him more and more frequently, he walked along the little path to the hut. As he reached the door a bee got caught in his beard and started buzzing angrily, but he extricated it carefully. Going into the shady passage of the hut, he took down his veil, which hung on a peg on the wall, put it on and, thrusting his hands in his pockets, went into the fenced-in apiary where – ranged in rows and tied with bast to stakes – in the middle of a space where the grass had been mown, stood all the hives he knew so well, the old stocks each with its own history, while along the wattle fence stood the new swarms hived that year. Bees and drones jostled in front of the hives, dancing before his eyes, whirling over the same spot. Between them flew the working bees, making straight for the wood and the flowering lime-trees or returning laden to the hives.

His ears rang with many different sounds – a busy working bee flying swiftly past, a buzzing idle drone, excited sentinel bees guarding their treasure from an enemy and ready to sting. On the farther side of the fence an old man was planing a hoop for a cask, not noticing Levin, who stood still in the middle of the apiary and did not call him.

He was glad of this chance to be alone, to recover from the reality which had already brought low his mood of spiritual elation. He remembered that in quite a short space of time he had lost his temper with Ivan, shown coolness to his brother, and talked thoughtlessly with Katavasov.

'Can it have been only a transitory mood, and will it pass and leave no trace?' he wondered.

But at that very moment, returning to his mood, he felt with joy that something new and important had happened to him. The spiritual peace he had found was still unharmed, though everyday life had shrouded it for a time.

Just as the bees, now circling round him, threatened him and distracted his attention, robbing him of complete physical calm and compelling him to shrink to avoid them, so had the petty cares that had beset him from the moment he took his seat in the trap restricted his spiritual freedom; but that lasted only so long as he was in the midst of them. Just as his physical powers remained intact, in spite of the bees, so his newly realized spiritual powers were intact also.

15

'KOSTYA, do you know whom Sergei Ivanich came across in the train?' said Dolly, after she had distributed cucumbers and honey among the children. 'Vronsky! He's going to Serbia.'

'Yes, and not alone either. He's taking a whole squadron with him at his own expense,' Katavasov put in.

'That is like him,' said Levin. 'Are volunteers still going out then?' he added, glancing at Koznyshev.

Koznyshev did not answer. With the blunt side of a knife he was carefully trying to extricate from a bowl in which lay a wedge of white honeycomb a live bee that had got stuck in the running honey.

'I should say so! You ought to have seen what went on at the station yesterday!' said Katavasov, crunching off a chunk of cucumber.

'What on earth is it all about? For heaven's sake, do explain to me, Sergei Ivanich, where all these volunteers are going and whom they are fighting,' said the old prince, evidently continuing a conversation that had been started in Levin's absence.

'The Turks, of course,' Koznyshev replied with a quiet smile, rescuing the bee, dark with honey and helplessly kicking, and shifting it from the knife to a stout aspen leaf.

'But who has declared war on the Turks? Ivan Ivanich Ragozov and the Countess Lydia Ivanovna, in collaboration with Madame Stahl?'

'No one has declared war, but people sympathize with their suffering brethren and are eager to help them,' said Koznyshev.

'But the prince is not talking of help but of war,' Levin put in, coming to the assistance of his father-in-law. 'The prince means that private individuals cannot take part in war without the sanction of the government.'

'Kostya, mind! There's a bee – I'm afraid we shall get stung,' said Dolly, warding off a wasp.

'That's not a bee, it's a wasp,' said Levin.

'Well, come along, give us your theory,' Katavasov said to Levin with a smile, evidently wanting to challenge him to a discussion. 'Why have private individuals no right to go to war?'

'Oh, my theory's this: on the one hand war is such a bestial, cruel, dreadful affair that no man – to say nothing of a Christian – can take upon himself personally the responsibility of beginning a war: that can only be done by a government, whose business it is to look to these things when they become inevitable. On the other hand, both political science and common sense teach us that in matters of state, especially in the matter of war, private citizens must renounce their personal individual will.'

Koznyshev and Katavasov, both ready with their rejoinders, began speaking together.

'But the point is, my dear fellow, that there may be cases when the

Government does not carry out the will of the people and then the public asserts its will,' said Katavasov.

But Koznyshev evidently did not approve of this reply. He frowned at Katavasov's words and began differently:

'It is a pity you put the question that way. There is no declaration of war in this case but simply an expression of humane Christian feeling. Our brothers, men of the same blood, the same faith, are being massacred. Even supposing they were not our brothers, our co-religionists, but merely children, women, and old people, feeling is aroused and Russians fly to help check these atrocities. Imagine you were walking along the street and saw some drunken men beating a woman or a child – I don't think you would stop to inquire whether war had been declared on the men: you would rush at them and defend the victim.'

'Yes, but I should not kill them,' said Levin.

'You might.'

'I don't know. If I saw such a sight, I might yield to my immediate impulse; but I can't say beforehand. But there is no immediate impulse in the case of the oppression of the Slavonic people, nor can there be.'

'Possibly not for you; but there is with others,' said Koznyshev, frowning with displeasure. 'There is still a racial memory among the people of Orthodox Christians groaning under the yoke of the "infidel Musulman". The people have heard of the sufferings of their brethren and have spoken.'

'That may be,' said Levin evasively, 'only I don't see it. I'm one of the people myself, and I don't feel it.'

'Nor do I,' said the prince. 'I was staying abroad and reading the papers, and I confess, up to the time of the Bulgarian atrocities, I couldn't make out why all Russia suddenly grew so fond of our Slavonic brethren, when I felt not the slightest affection for them. I was very much upset – I thought I must be a monster, or that the waters of Karlsbad were having that effect on me. But since I came home my mind's been set at rest. I see that there are other people besides myself who are only interested in Russia, and not in their brother-Slavs. Kostya, for example.'

'Personal opinions don't count in this matter,' said Koznyshev. 'There is no room for personal opinions when all Russia – the whole nation – has expressed its will.'

'But, excuse me, I don't see that. The people don't know a thing about it,' said the old prince.

'Oh, Papa! ... how can you say that? What about in church last Sunday?' remarked Dolly, who was following the conversation. 'Get me a cloth, please,' she said to the old bee-keeper who was smiling at the children. 'It can't be that all ...'

'But what was there in church on Sunday? The priest had been told to read that. He read it. The people didn't understand a word of it and sighed, just as they do at any sermon,' went on the prince. 'Then they were told that there was to be a collection for some salutary object, so they each produce their kopeck, but what for – they have no idea!'

'The people cannot help knowing. A consciousness of their destiny always exists in the people, and at moments like the present that consciousness finds utterance,' maintained Koznyshev, glancing at the old bee-keeper.

The handsome old man, with his black beard in which the grey was beginning to show and his thick silvery hair, stood there motionless, a bowl of honey in his hand, looking down from his great height at the gentlefolk with a mild, placid air, clearly neither understanding nor caring to understand what they were talking about.

'That is so, no doubt,' he said with a significant shake of his head at Koznyshev's words.

'Here, ask him about it. He knows nothing and has no ideas,' said Levin. 'Have you heard about the war, Mihalich?' he asked, addressing the old man. 'What they read in church? What do you think now? Ought we to fight for the Christians?'

'Why should we bother our heads? Alexander Nikolayevich our Emperor has thought about it for us, as he always does. He knows best. ... Shall I bring a bit more bread? Give the wee lad some more?' he asked Dolly, pointing to Grisha, who was finishing his crust.

'I don't need to ask,' said Koznyshev. 'We have seen and still see hundreds upon hundreds of men throwing up everything to serve the righteous cause – men from every corner of Russia, openly and clearly declaring their thought and aim. They bring their halfpence or enlist themselves, and say straight out what for. What does that mean?'

'It means, to my mind,' said Levin, beginning to get excited, 'that in a nation of eighty millions there will always be found, not hundreds, as now, but tens of thousands of men who have lost caste, a restless crew ready for anything – to join Pugachev's robber band, to go to Khiva, or to Serbia … anywhere.'

'I tell you it's not a case of hundreds, and they are not a "restless crew" but the best representatives of the people!' said Koznyshev, as heatedly as if he were defending the last penny of his fortune. 'And what about the donations? There at any rate is the whole people directly expressing its will.'

'That word "people" is so vague,' said Levin. 'Parish clerks, teachers, and perhaps one in a thousand of the peasantry may know what it's all about. The rest of our eighty million, like Mihalich here, far from expressing their will, haven't the faintest idea what there is for them to express their will about! What right then have we to say that this is the people's will?'

16

KOZNYSHEV, being an experienced dialectician, made no rejoinder but at once turned the conversation to another aspect of the subject.

'Oh, if you want to gauge the national spirit arithmetically, of course, it will be very difficult. Voting has not been introduced into our country, and cannot be, for it does not express the will of the people; but there are other means. It is felt in the air; the heart feels it. I won't speak of those deep undercurrents which have stirred the stagnant mass of the nation – currents evident to every unprejudiced person. Let us look at society in the narrow sense. All the most diverse sections of the intellectual world, hostile before, have combined on this point. All differences are at an end, all the organs of society say the same thing over and over again, all have become aware of an elemental force that has seized them and is carrying them, one and all, in one direction.'

'Yes, the papers all say the same thing,' said the prince. 'That's true. So much the same that they are just like frogs before a storm! You can't hear anything else for their croaking!'

'Frogs or no frogs – I am not a newspaper editor and I don't want to defend them: I am speaking of the unanimity of opinion in the intellectual world,' said Koznyshev, turning to his brother.

Levin was about to reply but the old prince forestalled him.

'As to that unanimity, there's something else to be said on that score,' he observed. 'There's my son-in-law, Stepan Arkadyevich;

you know him. He's got a place now on the committee of a commission of something or other – I don't remember what. All I know is that there's no work to do – why, Dolly, it's no secret! – and a salary of eight thousand. Try asking him if his office is of use, and he'll prove to you that it's indispensable. And he is a truthful man too, but there's no refusing to believe in the usefulness of eight thousand roubles.'

'Yes, he asked me to tell Darya Alexandrovna that he has got the post,' said Koznyshev, ill-pleased at what he considered irrelevance on the part of the prince.

'So it is with the unanimity of the Press. It's been explained to me: as soon as there is a war their circulation is doubled. How can they help considering that the fate of the people and the Slavonic races … and all the rest of it?'

'Many of the papers I don't care for, but that is unjust,' said Koznyshev.

'I would make just one stipulation,' pursued the old prince. 'Alphonse Karr put it very well before the war with Prussia, when he wrote: "You say this war is absolutely necessary? Very well! He who advocates war – off with him in a special advance legion to lead the first onslaught, the first attack!"'

'What fine figures the newspaper editors would cut!' remarked Katavasov with a loud laugh, picturing the editors of his acquaintance in this picked legion.

'Oh, but they'd run,' said Dolly; 'they'd only be in the way.'

'If they run, fire grapeshot into their backsides, or send Cossacks after them with horsewhips,' said the prince.

'But that was only meant as a joke, and it's not a very good one, if you'll excuse my saying so, Prince,' said Koznyshev.

'I don't see that it was a joke; it …' Levin began, but Koznyshev interrupted him.

'Every member of society is called upon to do his proper task,' he said, 'and intellectuals perform theirs by expressing public opinion. The unanimous and full expression of public opinion is the service of the Press and a phenomenon to rejoice us at the same time. Twenty years ago we should have been silent, but to-day the voice of the Russian people is heard, ready to rise as one man and sacrifice themselves for their oppressed brethren. That is a great step forward and a token of strength.'

'But it's not a question of sacrificing themselves only, but of killing

Turks,' observed Levin timidly. 'The people sacrifice themselves and are prepared to go on doing so for the good of their souls, but not for the purpose of murder,' he added, involuntarily connecting the conversation with the ideas that so engrossed his mind.

'What do you mean by soul? That is a puzzling term for a natural scientist, you know. What is a soul?' Katavasov inquired with a smile.

'You know quite well!'

'Upon my word, I haven't the faintest idea,' said Katavasov, laughing loudly.

'Said Christ, "I came not to send peace, but a sword," ' remarked Koznyshev for his part, quoting quite simply, as if it were the easiest thing in the world to understand, the very passage from the Scriptures that had always perplexed Levin more than any other.

'That's so, no doubt,' repeated the old beekeeper, who was standing near them, in response to a chance look turned in his direction.

'No, my dear friend, you're worsted, completely worsted!' cried Katavasov merrily.

Levin flushed with annoyance, not at being worsted but because he had let himself be drawn into argument, and not contained himself.

'No, I can't argue with them,' he thought. 'They wear impenetrable armour, while I'm naked.'

He saw that it was impossible to convince his brother and Katavasov, and still less did he see any possibility of agreeing with them himself. What they were advocating was the very pride of intellect that had almost been his ruin. He could not admit that it was right for a handful of men, among them his brother, to assert, on the strength of what they were told by a few hundred volunteers with the gift of the gab swarming to the city, that they and the newspapers were expressing the will and feeling of the people – especially when that feeling found its expression in bloodshed and murder. He could not admit this, because he saw no confirmation of such feelings in the masses among whom he was living, nor did he find any such thoughts in himself (and he could not consider himself as other than one of the people making up the Russian nation). Above all, he could not agree because he, in common with the people, did not know and could not know wherein lay the general welfare, though he knew beyond a doubt that this welfare could only be achieved by strict observance of that law of right and wrong which has been revealed to every man, and therefore he could not wish for war or advocate war for any public advantage. He upheld Mihalich, and the people who had expressed their feeling in the legend of the invitation to the Varangians:* 'Come and rule over us. Gladly we swear complete submission. All the toil, all humiliations, all sacrifice shall be ours; but we do not wish to have to judge and make decisions.' Now, however, according to his brother, the people were forgoing the right they had purchased so dearly.

He wanted to ask, too, why, if public opinion were an infallible guide, a revolution, a commune were not as legitimate as the movement in favour of the Slavonic peoples. But these were all thoughts that could lead nowhere. One thing stood out clearly, and that was that at the actual moment the altercation was irritating his brother, and so it was wrong to continue it. And Levin held his peace, and drew the attention of his guests to the clouds that were gathering, and suggested a speedy return to the house before it rained.

17

THE prince and Koznyshev got into the trap and drove off. The rest of the party, hastening their steps, started home on foot.

But the clouds, turning white and then black, gathered so rapidly that they had to quicken their pace still more if they were to reach home before the rain. The leading clouds, lowering and black as soot-laden smoke, drove with extraordinary swiftness across the sky. The party was still some two hundred paces from the house when the wind rose and the downpour was to be expected at any moment.

The children ran on ahead shrieking with fear and delight. Dolly, struggling with the skirts that clung round her legs, was not walking but running, her eyes fixed on the children. The men hurried along, holding on to their hats and taking long strides. They just got to the steps when a large rain-drop splashed on the edge of the iron guttering. The children and their elders after them ran under the roof for shelter, talking merrily.

'And Katerina Alexandrovna?' Levin asked Agatha Mihalovna, who met them in the hall with shawls and rugs.

'We thought she was with you.'

'And Mitya?'

---

* The Norse chiefs who, at the dawn of Russian history, were invited by the Slav tribes of Russia to come and rule over them and establish order. *Tr.*

'He must be in the woods, and nurse is with them.'

Levin snatched up the rugs and rushed to the woods.

In that brief interval of time the heart of the storm-cloud had already so blotted out the sun that it was as dark as during an eclipse. The wind pushed Levin back stubbornly, as though insisting on its own, tearing the leaves and blossoms off the lime-trees, stripping the white birch branches into strange unseemly nakedness, and twisting everything, acacias, flowers, burdocks, grass, and tree-tops all in one direction. The peasant girls who had been working in the garden ran screeching to shelter in the servants' quarters. A driving white curtain of rain was already descending over the distant forest and half the field next to it, and was advancing rapidly towards the woods. The air was filled with the moisture of the rain, shattered into tiny drops.

Lowering his head and struggling with the wind that strove to tear the wraps out of his hands, Levin had almost reached the copse and could see something white gleaming behind an oak-tree, when suddenly there was a glare of light, the whole earth seemed on fire, and the vault of heaven cracked overhead. Opening his blinded eyes, to his horror the first thing Levin saw through the thick curtain of rain between him and the woods was the uncannily altered position of the green crest of a familiar oak in the middle of the copse. 'Can it have been struck?' The thought had barely time to cross his mind when, gathering speed, the oak disappeared behind the other trees and he heard the crash of the great tree falling on to the others.

The flash of lightning, the peal of thunder, and the instantaneous chill that ran through his body all merged for Levin into a single sensation of terror.

'Oh God! Oh God! Not on them!' he breathed.

And though he thought at once how senseless was his prayer that they should not have been killed by the oak which had fallen now, he repeated it, knowing that he could do nothing better than utter this senseless entreaty.

Running to the spot where they generally went, he did not find them there.

They were at the other end of the copse under an old lime-tree, and were calling to him. Two figures in dark dresses (they had been light summer frocks before they got drenched) were crouching over something. It was Kitty and the nurse. The rain was already leaving off, and it was growing lighter when Levin came running up to them.

847

The lower part of the nurse's dress was dry but Kitty was wet through and her clothes clung to her body. Though it had stopped raining, they still stood in the same postures they had adopted when the storm broke: both stood bending over a baby-carriage with a green hood.

'Alive? Safe? Thank God!' he muttered, splashing up to them through the puddles, one shoe half off and full of water.

Kitty's wet rosy face was turned to him and she smiled timidly beneath her bedraggled hat.

'Well, you ought to be ashamed of yourself! I can't think how you can be so reckless!' said Levin, falling on his wife in vexation.

'It wasn't my fault, really. We were just going home when there was an accident and we had to change him. We had hardly …' Kitty began defending herself.

Mitya was unharmed and dry, and still fast asleep.

'Well, thank God! I don't know what I'm saying!'

They gathered up the wet napkins; the nurse picked up the baby in her arms and carried him. Levin walked beside his wife, conscience-stricken at having been angry, and stealthily, when the nurse was not looking, squeezed Kitty's hand.

18

For the whole of the rest of the day, in the most diverse conversations in which he took part only as it were with the top layer of his mind, Levin did not cease to be joyfully conscious of the fulness of his heart, in spite of his disappointment at not finding the change he expected in himself.

After the rain it was too wet to go for a walk; besides, the storm-clouds still hung about the horizon and gathered here and there, black and thundery, on the rim of the sky. So the whole company spent the rest of the day in the house.

No more disputes sprang up – on the contrary, after dinner everyone was in the most amiable frame of mind.

To begin with, Katavasov amused the ladies with his funny jokes, which always pleased people on their first acquaintance with him. Then Koznyshev induced him to tell them of the extremely interesting observations he had made on the difference in character, and even in physiognomy, between the male and female house-flies, and on their habits. Koznyshev, too, was in good spirits, and at tea, led on by his brother, expounded his views on the future of the Eastern question, and talked so simply and so well that everyone listened eagerly.

Kitty was the only one who did not hear it all – she was called away to give Mitya his bath.

A few minutes after Kitty had left the room a message was brought to Levin that she wanted to see him in the nursery.

Leaving his tea, and regretfully interrupting such an interesting conversation, Levin went to the nursery, uneasily wondering why he had been thus summoned, as this only happened on important occasions.

Though Koznyshev's theory, which Levin had not heard to the end – of how an emancipated world of forty million men of Slavonic race, acting with Russia, would create a new epoch in history – interested him very much as something quite new to him, and though he was disturbed by uneasy wonder as to why he was being sent for, yet as soon as he left the drawing-room and found himself alone his mind reverted at once to the thoughts of the morning. All those speculations about the significance of the Slav element in world history seemed to him so trivial compared with what was going on in his own soul that he there and then forgot it all and dropped back into the frame of mind he had been in that morning.

He did not now go over, as he had done at other times, the whole sequence of his thoughts (he had no need to). He returned straight to the feeling that governed him, which was connected with those thoughts, and found that feeling in his soul still stronger and clearer than it had been that morning. Before when he had devised a comforting argument for himself he had been obliged to recapitulate the whole chain of ideas in order to arrive back at the feeling; but it was not like that now. On the contrary, this time the feeling of joy and tranquillity was more vivid than before, and thought could not keep pace with feeling.

He walked across the terrace and looked at two stars that had appeared in the already darkening sky, and suddenly he remembered. 'Yes,' he said to himself, 'as I looked at the heavens I thought that the vault that I see is not a deception – but there was something I only half thought out, something I shut my eyes to. But whatever it was, it cannot have been a refutation. I need only think it over and all will become clear.'

Just as he was entering the nursery he remembered what it was he had shut his eyes to. It was this – that if the chief proof of the existence of a Deity lies in His revelation of what is right, why is that revelation confined to the Christian Church alone? How about the Buddhist, the Mohammedan faiths which also preach and do good?

It seemed to him that he had the answer to that question; but he had no time to formulate it to himself before entering the nursery.

Kitty, with her sleeves tucked up, was bending over the bath in which the baby was splashing about. Hearing her husband's step she turned her face towards him and beckoned him with a smile. With one hand she was supporting the head of the fat, kicking baby which lay floating on its back, while with the other she squeezed the sponge over him, the muscles in her arm straining rhythmically each time.

'Oh, look, look!' she said when her husband came up. 'Agatha Mihalovna was right. He does know us!'

The fact was that Mitya had that day begun to show unmistakable, incontestable signs of recognizing his nearest and dearest.

Directly Levin approached the bath, an experiment was tried, and it was completely successful. The cook, summoned with this object, bent over the baby. The baby frowned and moved his head from side to side in protest. Kitty leant over him – his face lit up with a smile. He pushed his little hands against the sponge and bubbled with his lips, making such a queer little contented sound that Kitty and the nurse were not alone in their raptures. Levin, too, was surprised and delighted.

The nurse lifted the baby out of the bath, rested him on one hand and poured fresh water over him. Then he was wrapped up in a bath-sheet and dried and, after a penetrating yell, turned over to his mother.

'Well, I am glad you are beginning to grow fond of him,' said Kitty to her husband, when she had settled herself comfortably in her usual place with the child at her breast. 'I am so glad. You said you had no feeling for him, and it was beginning to worry me.'

'No, did I really say that? I only meant that I was disappointed.'

'What? Disappointed in him?'

'Not exactly in him, but in my own feeling for him. I had expected more. I had expected some novel pleasant emotion to awaken in me, like a surprise, and instead there was only a sensation of disgust, pity ...'

She listened attentively, looking at him over the baby, while she replaced on her slender fingers the rings she had taken off before bathing Mitya.

'And above all, at there being far more anxiety and pity than satisfaction. I never knew until to-day, after that fright during the storm, how I loved him.'

Kitty's smile was radiant.

'Were you very frightened?' she asked. 'I was too, but it feels more dreadful now that it is past. I must go and look at that oak. What a dear Katavasov is! And taken all round what a happy day we've had! And you are so nice with your brother when you like. ... You had better go back to them now. It's always hot and steamy in here after the bath.'

19

WHEN he left the nursery and was alone again, Levin immediately remembered the thought that had not been very clear to him.

Instead of going back to the drawing-room, where he heard the sound of voices, he stopped on the terrace and, leaning his elbows on the balustrade, gazed up at the sky.

It had grown quite dark, and to the south, where he was looking, the sky was clear. The clouds had drifted over in the opposite direction, where lightning flashed and there was a distant rumble of thunder. Levin listened to the raindrops monotonously dripping from the lime-trees in the garden and looked up at a familiar triangle of stars and at the ramifications of the Milky Way intersecting it. At each flash not only the Milky Way but even the brightest of stars vanished, but immediately afterwards they would reappear in their places as if thrown there by some unerring hand.

'Well, what is it that troubles me?' Levin asked himself, feeling in advance that the solution of his doubts was ready in his soul, though he did not know it yet. 'Yes, the one obvious, unmistakable manifestation of the Deity is the law of good and evil disclosed to men by revelation, which I feel in myself and in the recognition of which I do not so much as unite myself as am united, whether I will or no, with other men into one body of believers which is called the Church. But the Jews, the Mohammedans, the Confucians, the Buddhists – what of them?' he put to himself the dilemma that had threatened him before. 'Can those hundreds of millions of human beings be deprived of that greatest of blessings without which life has no meaning?' he pondered, but immediately pulled himself up. 'But what is it that I want to know?' he said to himself. 'I am asking about the relation to the Deity of all the different religions of mankind. I am seeking to fathom the general manifestation of God to the universe with all its stars and planets. What am I about? Knowledge, sure, unattainable by reason, has been revealed to me, to my heart, and here am I obstinately trying to express that knowledge in words and by means of reason.

'Do I not know that it is not the stars that are moving?' he asked himself, looking at a bright planet that had already shifted its position to the top branch of a birch-tree. 'But seeing the stars change place and not being able to picture to myself the revolution of the earth, I am right in saying that the stars move.

'And the astronomers – could they have understood and calculated anything if they had taken into account all the complicated and varied motions of the earth? All the marvellous conclusions they have reached about the distances, weight, movements, and disturbances of the celestial bodies are based on the apparent movement of the stars round a stationary earth – on the very movement I am witnessing now, that millions of men have witnessed during long ages, that has been and always will be the same, and that can always be trusted. And just as the conclusions of the astronomers would have been idle and precarious had they not been founded on observations of the visible heavens in relation to a single meridian and a single horizon, so all my conclusions would be idle and precarious if not founded on that understanding of good and evil which was and always will be alike for all men, which has been revealed to me by Christianity and which can always be trusted in my own soul. I have no right to try to decide the question of other religions and their relations to the Deity; that must remain unfathomable for me.'

'Oh, you haven't gone in yet?' he suddenly heard Kitty's voice, as she passed that way to the drawing-room. 'You're not upset about anything, are you?' she inquired, peering intently into his face in the starlight.

But she would not have been able to make out its expression had not a flash of lightning that blotted out the stars illuminated it for her. The lightning showed her his face distinctly, and seeing that he was calm and happy she smiled at him.

'She understands,' he thought. 'She knows what I am thinking about. Shall I tell her or not? Yes, I will ...' But just as he opened his mouth to speak she turned to him first.

'Oh, Kostya, be nice and go and see if Sergei Ivanich will be comfortable in the corner room. I can't very well go myself. See if they've put the new washstand in.'

'Very well, I'll go directly,' said Levin, straightening up and kissing her.

'No, I had better not speak of it,' he thought, as she passed in before him. 'It is a secret for me alone, of vital importance for me, and not to be put into words.

'This new feeling has not changed me, has not made me happy and enlightened all of a sudden, as I dreamed it would. It is like the way it was with my feeling for my son. There was no surprise about this either. But be it faith or not – I don't know what it is – through suffering this feeling has crept just as imperceptibly into my heart and has lodged itself firmly there.

'I shall still lose my temper with Ivan the coachman, I shall still embark on useless discussions and express my opinions inopportunely; there will still be the same wall between the sanctuary of my inmost soul and other people, even my wife; I shall probably go on scolding her in my anxiety and repenting of it afterwards; I shall still be as unable to understand with my reason why I pray, and I shall still go on praying – but my life now, my whole life, independently of anything that can happen to me, every minute of it is no longer meaningless as it was before, but has a positive meaning of goodness with which I have the power to invest it.'

MORE ABOUT PENGUINS
AND PELICANS

Penguinews, which appears every month, contains details of all the new books issued by Penguin as they are published. From time to time it is supplemented by *Penguins in Print*, which is our complete list of almost 5,000 titles.

A specimen copy of *Penguinews* will be sent to you free on request. Please write to Dept. EP, Penguin Books Ltd, Harmondsworth, Middlesex, for your copy.

In the U.S.A.: For a complete list of books available from Penguins in the United States write to Dept CS, Penguin Books, 625 Madison Avenue, New York, New York 10022.

In Canada: For a complete list of books available from Penguins in Canada write to Penguin Books Canada Ltd, 2801 John Street, Markham, Ontario L3R 1B4.

Mikhail Sholokhov

AND QUIET FLOWS THE DON

Mikhail Sholokhov's story of the years in which the Russia of today was created has, with justice, been compared with Tolstoy's *War and Peace*. Here are the Cossacks in peace, and war, and revolution. Here are the peasants of the Don steppes, barbarous, compassionate, unpredictable, portrayed with astounding vitality and eloquence.

THE DON FLOWS HOME TO THE SEA

Citation, Nobel Prize for Literature 1965:

'. . . the artistic power and integrity with which, in his epic of the Don, he has given creative expression to a historic phase in the history of the Russian people.'

With panoramic sweep, characterization, energy and truth, the international best-selling sequel to *And Quiet Flows the Don* portrays, without dogma, the tragic clash between the primitive Don Cossacks and the dialectical concept of history at the time of the Russian Revolution.

Alexander Solzhenitsyn

ONE DAY IN THE LIFE OF
IVAN DENISOVICH

His masterpiece on life in a Stalinist labour camp which shook Russia and shocked the world.

A crisp, shattering glimpse of the fate of millions of Russians under Stalin.

Khrushchev himself, during the Russian thaw, is said to have authorized the publication of this spare, stark description of life in a Siberian labour camp.

'A masterpiece in the great Russian tradition' – *New Statesman*

'Like Dostoyevsky's work, Solzhenitsyn's story is also a major artistic accomplishment' – *The Times*

'It is a blow struck for human freedom all over the world . . . And it is gloriously readable' – Cyril Connolly in the *Sunday Times*

Also published in Penguins:

A CANDLE IN THE WIND
THE LOVE-GIRL AND THE INNOCENT
MATRYONA'S HOUSE AND OTHER STORIES

Alexander Solzhenitsyn

AUGUST 1914

Solzhenitsyn is Russia's greatest living writer, a man whose spirit stands in solitary splendour against tyranny and oppression. *August 1914* is his greatest book, a vast, panoramic epic of war, its heroism and its tragic bearing on the destiny of a nation. Of it he has said, 'it is the main task of my life'.

CANCER WARD
(Parts I and II)

Solzhenitsyn, like Oleg Kostoglotov the central character of this novel, went in the mid-1950s from concentration camp to cancer ward and later recovered. The British publication of *Cancer Ward* in 1968 confirmed him as Russia's greatest living novelist, although it has never been openly published in the Soviet Union.

Part I assembles a fascinating cross-section of Soviet society in the cancer ward of a provincial hospital: Rusanov, the Stalinist secret policeman; Yefrem, a womanizing contractor struck down in his prime; Dyoma and Proskha, students doomed by more than disease . . .

Part II completes the story of Kostoglotov's fight for existence. Emotionally torn between Vega and Zoya, his doctor and nurse, Kostoglotov is at the centre of stormy debates about the grassroots of Soviet socialism. Heckling Rusanov the secret policeman. Gently chided by Shulubin, a Bolshevik scholar ashamed of the compromises represented by his survival . . . all of them, medical staff included, threatened by cancer literally and metaphorically; within and without the ward.

UNDER THE VOLCANO

Malcolm Lowry

It is the Day of Death, and a fiesta is in full swing. In the shadow of Popocatepetl ragged children beg coins to buy skulls made of chocolate . . . and the ugly pariah dogs roam the streets. Geoffrey Firmin, H.M. ex-consul, is drowning himself in liquor and mescal, while his ex-wife and half-brother look on, powerless to help him. As the day wears on, it becomes apparent that Geoffrey must die. It is his only escape from a world he cannot understand.

'If there is morbidity here, it is akin to that of Elizabethan tragedy . . . he has created a character in whose individual struggle is reflected something of the larger agony of the human spirit' – *The Times Literary Supplement*

'Mr Lowry . . . has written a genuinely tragic novel of great concentration and power' – *New Statesman*

Like most of the work of Lowry, who died in 1957 and has since become a literary legend, this book is in the main autobiographical.

Two classic historical novels
by Robert Graves

I, CLAUDIUS

Robert Graves's magnificent reconstruction of the grandeur and folly
and vileness of early Imperial Rome is one of the most distinguished
historical novels of this generation. Its setting varies from a Roman
palace to a desert in Tripoli, a dark German forest, a garden at
Pompeii, a camp in the Balkans, the Sibyl's cavern at Cumae, and
a cliff-top on the island of Rhodes. The action is strange, tragic,
and ludicrous, for Rome knows herself under a long-standing
curse – the curse of the gods with whom she broke faith when she
destroyed Carthage – and has lost all moral self-control. Treachery,
incest, black magic, and unnatural vice flourish. Insane cruelties
are committed. And through it all moves the strange, lovable figure
of Claudius himself, despised, neglected, and apparently ineffective,
but destined in the end to become Emperor against his will.

CLAUDIUS THE GOD

The hairy fifth to enslave the State,
Shall be that idiot whom all despised.
He shall have hair in his generous mop,
He shall give Rome water and winter bread,
And die at the hand of his wife, no wife,
To the gain of his son, no son.

So ran the Sibylline prophecy which Claudius found among the
private papers of Augustus, and he could not fail to recognize in this
description of the last great Caesar but one, himself, the paralytic
idiot 'Clau-Clau-Claudius', as he was derisively nicknamed. In this
book he continues his historical memoirs, bringing the story from
his own acclamation as Emperor at the death of his terrible nephew,
Caligula, to his assassination in the year 54. Like its forerunner,
Claudius the God presents an astonishing picture of the grandeur and
degeneracy of first-century Rome. But Claudius himself, quite as
much as his age, comes to life in these pages – Claudius, who survived the violent reigns of four earlier Caesars, who remained
Emperor for fourteen years, and who yet was thought by his contemporaries to be a fool.

SAUL BELLOW

Winner of the 1976 Nobel Prize for Literature

HUMBOLDT'S GIFT

'The writing in *Humboldt's Gift* is of a very high order indeed. Sharp, erudite, beautifully measured . . . he is one of the most gifted chroniclers of the Western world alive today' – Jacky Gillot in *The Times*

THE ADVENTURES OF AUGIE MARCH

Spawned in Chicago, torpedoed from the Merchant Marine apprenticed to the 'International Set', ex-poker-player *extraordinaire*, Augie March is the all-time once-met-never-forgotten American hero.

HENDERSON THE RAIN KING

How Henderson drank. How he walked out of his marriage to 'darkest Africa'. How he rose to be rain-maker and right-hand-man to the chief of a primitive tribe. This is Saul Bellow at his bullroaring best.

MR SAMMLER'S PLANET

Mr Sammler is assured by Dr Lal that a perfect society *is* attainable – on the moon. But on Mr Sammler's Planet, so recognizably our own, there seems to be little chance of getting it. Unless we all learn to be like Mr Sammler.

HERZOG

'A well-nigh faultless novel' – *New Yorker*
'Clearly a major work of our time' – *Guardian*

Also published in Penguins:

SEIZE THE DAY
MOSBY'S MEMOIRS AND OTHER STORIES
DANGLING MAN
THE VICTIM

ISAAC BASHEVIS SINGER

THE MANOR

In *The Manor* Isaac Bashevis Singer portrays the difficulties encountered by traditionalist Jews coming to terms with the convulsive social changes that rocked Poland in the late nineteenth century.
Calman Jacoby stands between the old and the new, unable to em-
brace either wholeheartedly. A pious and conservative Jew, he is
upset when he finds that his daughter has married a sceptic; and yet
his own business methods are the most modern in Poland.

THE ESTATE

The Estate concludes this epic work in which Singer depicts, through
the history of one family, the evolution of Europe and its Jewish
community from feudal traditions into the modern world. It is
loose-living Clara, Calman Jacoby's second wife, who figures so
largely in this sequel.

THE SÉANCE

Isaac Bashevis Singer is a master story-teller of our time. *The Séance*,
one of his finest collections, is set in the terrain of the imagination, a
world of shadows inhabited by saints and sinners, the quick and the
dead, angels and demons.

THE SLAVE

The Slave is a powerful love story set against the exotic background
of seventeenth-century Poland with all its superstitions, witchcraft
and witch-hunts, abundant life and appalling prejudices.

Also published in Penguins:

A FRIEND OF KAFKA AND OTHER STORIES
ENEMIES: A LOVE STORY
A CROWN OF FEATHERS AND OTHER STORIES

TOLSTOY IN PENGUINS

WAR AND PEACE (Two volumes)

Few would dispute the claim of *War and Peace* to be regarded as the greatest novel in any language. This massive chronicle, to which Tolstoy devoted several years shortly after his marriage, portrays Russian family life during and after the Napoleonic war.

CHILDHOOD, BOYHOOD, YOUTH

These semi-autobiographical sketches, published in Tolstoy's early twenties, provide an expressive self-portrait in which one may discern the man and the writer he was to become.

THE COSSACKS

The three stories in this volume illustrate different aspects of Tolstoy's knowledge of human nature.

RESURRECTION

Tolstoy's last novel reveals the teeming underworld of Russian society; the rotten heart of his country.

PENGUIN BOOKS

ANNA KARENIN

COUNT LEO NIKOLAYEVICH TOLSTOY was born in 1828 at
Yasnaya Polyana in the Tula province, and educated privately.
He studied Oriental languages and law at the University of
Kazan then led a life of pleasure until 1851 when he joined an
artillery regiment in the Caucasus. He took part in the Crimean
war and after the defence of Sevastopol he wrote *The Sevastopol
Stories*, which established his reputation. After a period in St
Petersburg and abroad, where he studied educational methods
for use in his school for peasant children in Yasnaya, he married
Sophie Andreyevna Behrs in 1862. The next fifteen years was a
period of great happiness; they had thirteen children, and Tolstoy
managed his vast estates in the Volga Steppes, continued his
educational projects, cared for his peasants and wrote *War and
Peace* (1865–68) and *Anna Karenin* (1874–76). *A Confession* (1879–
82) marked an outward change in his life and works; he became
an extreme rationalist and moralist, and in a series of pamphlets
after 1880 he expressed theories such as rejection of the state
and church, indictment of the demands of the flesh, and denun-
ciation of private property. His teaching earned him numerous
followers in Russia and abroad, but also much opposition and
in 1901 he was excommunicated by the Russian holy synod.
He died in 1910, in the course of a dramatic flight from home,
at the small railway station of Astapovo.

L · N · TOLSTOY

ANNA
KARENIN

TRANSLATED AND
WITH AN INTRODUCTION
BY
ROSEMARY EDMONDS

PENGUIN BOOKS

Penguin Books Ltd, Harmondsworth, Middlesex, England
Penguin Books, 625 Madison Avenue, New York, New York 10022, U.S.A.
Penguin Books Australia Ltd, Ringwood, Victoria, Australia
Penguin Books Canada Ltd, 2801 John Street, Markham, Ontario, Canada L3R 1B4
Penguin Books (N.Z.) Ltd, 182–190 Wairau Road, Auckland 10, New Zealand

—

This translation first published in Penguin Classics 1954
Reprinted 1956, 1960, 1962, 1964, 1965, 1967, 1968, 1969, 1971, 1972
1973, 1974, 1975 (twice), 1976
Reprinted in this edition 1977
Reprinted 1977

—

—

Made and printed in Great Britain
by Richard Clay (The Chaucer Press) Ltd,
Bungay, Suffolk
Set in Monotype Bembo